With tears choking her, she inched out the tip of the gun barrel. Her legs stopped shaking and her hand was steady as she waited until he was a bare twenty yards away before she fired. And though the recoil of the rifle almost broke her shoulder, she stood stubbornly, determined not to fall back until she saw him fall first. And he did, headlong, like a tree that had been axed through . . . and never moved a muscle.

OH, KENTUCKY!

Betty Layman Receveur

Copyright © 1990 by Betty Layman Receveur
Maps copyright © 1990 by Anita Karl and James Kemp

All rights reserved under International and Pan-American Copyright Conventions. Published in the United States of America by Ballantine Books, a division of Random House, Inc., New York, and simultaneously in Canada by Random House of Canada Limited, Toronto.

Library of Congress Catalog Card Number: 89-92607

ISBN: 0-345-31717-3

Manufactured in the United States of America

First Trade Edition: October 1990
First Mass Market Edition: July 1992

This book could be only for my grandparents
Frank Fuller and Addie Shelton Layman

They were true Kentuckians
All that I am of worth or note, I owe to them

The author wishes to express gratitude for the careful work of historians and researchers, both living and dead, who contributed to this work. My thanks to the Filson Club at Louisville, Ky., and to the Kentucky Historical Society, Frankfort, Ky. Also to the Kentucky Section of the Louisville Free Public Library.

A very special thanks must go to Bobbie L. Callaway of Monett, Missouri, Historian of the Callaway Family Association, Inc. Miss Callaway provided me with invaluable material.

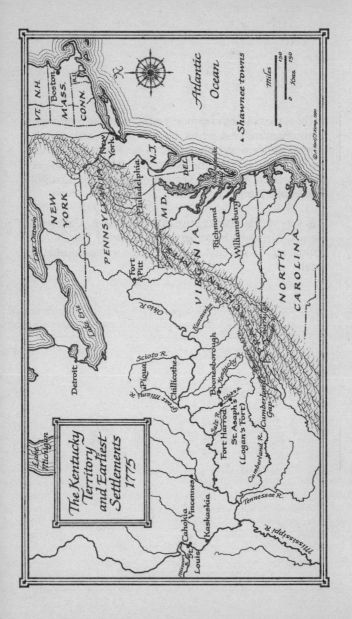

The Kentucky
Territory
and Earliest
Settlements
1775

NEW YORK

PENNSYLVANIA

VIRGINIA

NORTH CAROLINA

N.J.

DEL.

MD.

VT. N.H.

MASS.

CONN. R.I.

Boston

New York

Philadelphia

Richmond

Williamsburg

Atlantic
Ocean

Lake Michigan

Lake Erie

Lake Ontario

Detroit

Fort Pitt

Ohio R.

Kanawha R.

Scioto R.

Great Miami R.

Piqua

Chillicothe

Boonesborough

Salt R.

Fort Harrod

St. Asaph's
(Logan's Fort)

Dick's R.

Kentucky R.

Cumberland R.

Cumberland Gap

Tennessee R.

Mississippi R.

Missouri R.

Cahokia

St. Louis

Vincennes

Kaskaskia

▲ Shawnee towns

miles
0   150
0   150
Kms.

© A. Karl / J. Kemp 1990

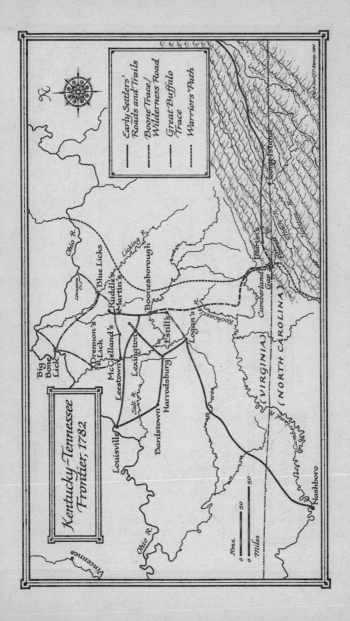

Kentucky-Tennessee Frontier, 1782

Early Settlers' Roads and Trails
Boone Trace/ Wilderness Road
Great Buffalo Trace
Warriors' Path

Vincennes

Ohio R.

Big Bone Lick

D'remon's Lick

McClelland's
Leestown

Louisville

Salt R.

Lexington

Bardstown

Harrodsburg

Estill's

Logan's

Ohio R.

Limestone Cr.

Blue Licks

Ruddle's
Martin's

Boonesborough

Licking R.

Rockcastle R.

Cumberland Gap

Martin's

(VIRGINIA)

(NORTH CAROLINA)

Powell R.

Clinch R.

Holston R.

Long Island

Cumb'd R.

Nashboro

Kms. 0   50

Miles 0   50

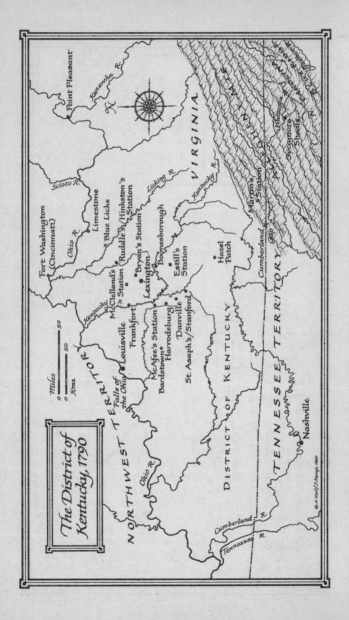

The District of Kentucky, 1790

Point Pleasant
Kanawha R.

NORTH CAROLINA

VIRGINIA

Scioto R.
Fort Washington (Cincinnati)
Ohio R.
Limestone
× Blue Licks
Licking R.
Ruddle's/Hinkston's Station
Bryan's Station
Lexington
Boonesborough
Estill's Station
Hazel Patch
Kentucky R.
McClelland's Station
Frankfort
Louisville
Falls of the Ohio
McAfee's Station
Bardstown
Harrodsburg
Danville
St. Asaph's/Stanford
Martin's Station
Sycamore Shoals
Cumberland Gap

NORTHWEST TERRITORY

Ohio R.

DISTRICT OF KENTUCKY

TENNESSEE TERRITORY

Cumberland R.
Tennessee R.
Nashville

Miles
0   50
Kms
0   50

© A. Karl/J. Kemp, 1990

✤ PROLOGUE ✤

March 1775

ROMAN GENTRY SHIFTED HIS LEAN FRAME TO A MORE COMfortable position against the smooth trunk of a sycamore. His piercing blue eyes swept the hundreds of wigwams, built of poles and skins, that dotted the foothills of Yellow Mountain and the flat, greening banks of the Watauga River. The sun was dipping toward the mountains to the west, and the acrid smell of smoke from countless campfires mingled pleasantly with the aroma of roasting venison, rabbit, and pork. Smoke curled, too, from the chimneys of the sprawling line of cabins that made up the small settlement of Sycamore Shoals. Despite the week-long presence of the strangers from across the "Ridge"—as the local people called the Blue Ridge Mountains to the east—and the hordes of Indians up from their haunts to the south, the women of the settlement went about their supper preparations as usual. But the bargaining that had been going on for days, there beneath an aged oak tree whose branches spread almost to the riverbank, continued still. Later than usual.

The great chiefs of the Cherokee sat on one side of the table, suffering with a wry amusement the chairs that the white men favored. Braves hunkered down around their leaders, their dark, heavy hair befeathered, silver bracelets gleaming here and there on muscular arms. On the opposite side of the table the negotiators for the newly formed Transylvania Company looked stiffly out of place in their woolen coats and ruffled stocks. Among them was Richard Henderson, a former Associate Justice of the Colony of North Carolina and founder of the company.

Twenty paces away, Roman Gentry had been observing it all with a patient detachment when, suddenly, his attention shifted to a lad of nine or ten who had sidled up to him, faded blue shirttail escaping the confines of stout homespun breeches. The boy squinted to look Roman up and down leisurely, taking in the fringed hunting shirt and deerskin leggings, his gaze traveling upward to the hawklike face which was all planes and angles, then to the shock of flaming red hair. Finally his eyes came to rest on the long rifle that lay so easily in the crook of the young scout's arm.

"You ever been to Kaintuck?" The boy jerked his thumb in the direction of the western mountains and the great wilderness that everyone knew lay beyond.

At Roman's nod the boy's eyes narrowed thoughtfully.

"You aimin' to go back, are ye? Oncet they're through with all their palaverin'?"

Roman looked toward the Indian chiefs. At the aged Ocanostota and Attacullaculla, at Dragging Canoe and Savanooko, who even now was speaking earnestly, a translator relaying his words to Judge Henderson and the others.

"Aye," said Roman. "And it's not Kaintuck, boy. It's Kentucke. *Ken-tuc-kee*," he repeated.

A skinny slip of a girl ran up, hair flying in the breeze. "Ma's been a-callin' and a-callin' you, Henry. It'll be your hide for it if you don't get some wood chopped, and right quick!" The boy grimaced but allowed himself to be tugged away.

Roman watched them go, a slow, half smile coming to soften his face. Kaintuck. Kentucke. The Iroquois called it Kentake, which meant Great Meadow. In the language of the Wyandot it was Kahten-tah-teh, which meant Land of Tomorrow. But whatever it was called, he thought, the rich land out there beyond the mountains, so fiercely claimed by the Cherokee and Shawnee as their hunting ground, had beckoned to white men for years. Tantalizing some almost beyond endurance.

The French had tried to keep claim to it but were defeated by the British. The land would have been settled long ago were it not for the English king's edict at the end of the war that forbade any settlement west of the Alleghenies. That had not gone down well with colonists who'd been promised land there as payment for their services during the conflict. It was muttered bitterly that England had not wanted to endanger its profitable fur trade with the Indians. But even now, twelve years after the end of the French and Indian War, Kentucke had seen little of the white man, but for a few hunters and surveyors.

Roman's friend Daniel had attempted to lead a party of settlers through the Cumberland Gap the year before last, but that ill-fated effort had cost him his oldest son, James. The Indians had tortured the boy before they'd finally killed him. Roman hadn't been there, but it was a bitter thing to think of.

In spite of what happened, Daniel had wanted to press on, but the rest of the party, fearful for their lives, had hurried back to safety. Big Jim Harrod, a seasoned woodsman and surveyor, had gone in with a handful of men and built a few cabins not far from Salt River last year, but Indians had driven them out soon after— Roman had gone with Daniel to warn them that Cornstalk and his Shawnee braves had taken to the warpath.

Still, none of that, Roman mused, would change things in the end. There were those who were bound and be damned to go to that beautiful, fertile land across the mountains, and the time had come when nothing, neither an English king nor savage Indians, could stop them. The word was that Harrod was already rebuilding his small settlement.

The peaks of the western mountains were bathed in red and purple now, and the Cherokee chiefs and the company men had left the bargaining table and were going their separate ways until the morning, taking their leave of one another as courteously as the diplomats of two great nations might. A yellow dog ran about, barking and wagging its tail as the white men gathered in small clusters to recount the day's progress and the Indians walked with solemn dignity toward their campfires, where stewpots and roasting spits heavy with dripping meat awaited them.

Judge Henderson—a man of about forty—came toward Roman, the flawlessly curled and powdered wig more in keeping with his duties on the bench a few years past than his activities here on the banks of the Watauga. There was a spring to his step and a look of excitement about his eyes.

"By God, but I believe it is nearly done, Mr. Gentry! I believe they are near to signing a treaty. If not tomorrow, surely the next day. We have raised our offer to £10,000 in goods. Will you be ready to carry the news to Captain Boone at once if they accept?"

"I'll be ready," Roman said.

Daniel waited a few miles away on Long Island in the Holston River. With him were the men he had handpicked to lead the way over the mountains and on to the spot on the banks of the Kentucke River that had been chosen for the site of the proposed settlement. Among the group, about thirty in all, were Daniel's brother, Squire, and the stalwart old colonel Richard Callaway. Once Roman brought the news that the bargain had been struck, they would set out at once to blaze a trail in for others to follow.

"Splendid!" Henderson beamed. "As soon as your group is well started, I shall come along directly with additional men and supplies." He took a small silver snuff box from his pocket and, opening the lid, offered it to Roman.

Roman shook his head.

Henderson moaned. "Damned lucky if you never picked up the habit." He took a pinch of the powdery tobacco between his thumb and forefinger and delicately sniffed a bit of it up each nostril. Then he sneezed violently, retrieving a lace handkerchief from an inside pocket to dab at a reddening nose. "I received word today that Lord Dunmore, His Majesty's Royal Governor of the Colony of Virginia, has joined our own Governor Martin here in North Carolina in denouncing our endeavor. I believe it was said he used the word 'outlaws.' " Henderson chuckled. "It seemed ever so much more grandiose when Martin threatened us with the 'pain of His Majesty's displeasure and the most rigorous penalties of the law!' " He snorted, dabbing again at his nose. "Let them issue their proclamations against us. 'Tis like trying to stop the tide now that it has begun."

Roman was silent. The company Henderson headed stood to make a good deal of money if the venture were successful. The Transylvania Company intended to set up a proprietary government, not only charging for the land initially, but requiring quitrents annually thereafter. Still, perhaps they shouldn't be begrudged that. Henderson and the other shareholders were risking a lot themselves.

"I understand," Henderson went on, "that you are a young man of education and background, Mr. Gentry. That in addition to being an excellent scout—that from Daniel Boone himself—you were educated at William and Mary and read law under Thomas Jefferson of Albemarle County in your native Virginia."

Roman nodded.

"I would venture a hope that you intend to take up land and settle in Kentucke once we are there."

"I expect to stay awhile, sir," Roman said.

"Good. Good. We shall need men like you." A chilly wind gusted off the river and Henderson shivered. "Well then, I shall bid you a good evening. 'Twill soon be dark, and a warm hearth and hearty meal will be most welcome, eh?" He went his way, dabbing at his nose still and stifling another sneeze.

Roman stood, watching the retreating figure. He did not himself have any direct connection to the company. He was there only because of Daniel, who'd been taken on as chief scout and agent, undoubtedly because he knew as much about the land out there as any white man alive.

It was Daniel who'd been able to persuade the Cherokee to come here for this meeting. And Roman had decided that if Daniel wanted to throw in his lot with the company, then he would go along, too. For a while. Though he was struck with a wry amusement when he pondered the fact that the Cherokee appeared on the verge of selling millions of acres of land to which they had no more right than the Iroquois, the Miami, the Wyandot, or the Shawnee—and to a purchaser who had no lawful right to buy it. And to complicate matters further, both Virginia and North Carolina, by virtue of their charters, could lay valid claims to large areas out there. And further still, none of that touched on the issue of the soldiers' claims, promised them during the war.

The Colonies grew ever more restive under British rule. There were more and more citizens who not only chafed under the laws and edicts of an English king who sat on his throne so far across the sea, but were increasingly ready to defy them. The pot was boiling, and Roman wondered how long it would take for it to bubble over.

Wasn't this meeting proof of it? The Transylvania Company had been formed with the objective of taking settlers into Kentucke in direct defiance of the royal edict. But in order to achieve its ends, the company had to consider the Indian peril.

The warlike Shawnee, to the north of the Ohio, had been defeated only last fall at the Battle of Point Pleasant, and had signed a treaty that they would stay north of the river and no longer hunt down into Kentucke. If the Cherokee now agreed to sell their claim on the land to the company, that would seem to take care of the Indian menace . . . though Roman wondered wryly if the Indians had any real concept of selling or buying land. And he knew the Shawnee too well to think that they would abide by their treaty. Henderson was a pleasant enough fellow, clearly determined to found a new colony out in the wilderness, but it was doubtful that he had any idea of what he was getting into.

Roman's stomach tightened, as if to remind him that it was time he, too, thought about supper. He had been offered the hospitality of more than one of the cabins in Sycamore Shoals but had declined with thanks. He had some beef jerk and a bag of parched corn, and each night, after he filled his stomach, he would roll up in his blankets and sleep under a sky filled with stars. Now, however, with the smell of roasting meat heavy in the air, it occurred to him that a rabbit cooked to a turn might taste good this chilly night. It would not take long to flush one out, especially if he rode down away from the settlement a piece.

He had turned to get his horse when suddenly the old chief Attacullaculla was beside him, coming with the barest whisper of sound, as faint as the rustling of a leaf. The withered, mahogany-colored face was scored with two ceremonial scars that ran down each cheek. Pierced ears held heavy silver ornaments that hung nearly to his shoulders.

Roman inclined his head respectfully to the "Little Carpenter," as the white men called him. One of the most powerful of the Cherokee chiefs, he had in his younger days been taken to England and received by the king. He spoke English well, the voice still vigorous from that ancient body.

"How do you this day, Firehair?" he said, using part of the name the Cherokee had given to Roman Gentry. In their language, the entire name was almost unpronounceable and meant "Man with Firehair Who Does Not Let His Tongue Run Like a Woman's." The old chief had long ago shortened it.

"Well, Attacullaculla," Roman replied gravely. "And you?"

"Well." The old man nodded his head, the silver earrings swaying. The ridges across his forehead deepened. "I have thought on why you do not sit at the table. I would have you there."

The half smile came to Roman's face. "It is not my place to be there. I do not speak for Henderson or the others. I am not with the company."

"You are with Boone."

"Yes."

"And Boone speaks for the company."

"In a way. Yes."

Attacullaculla shrugged, looking out toward the campfires that winked in the dusk. "Is it a good thing that this Henderson wishes, Firehair?"

It took a long moment for Roman to reply. "Attacullaculla must decide for himself. But," he added slowly, "no matter what happens here, the white man will go into Kentucke." He turned toward the west, suddenly filled with the memory of Rebecca Boone's face whenever she spoke of her firstborn, his mutilated body lying in a grave out there not far from the gap. "It is my hope," he went on after a moment, "that when they go, it can be in peace."

"I will think on it." Attacullaculla turned away, but after a few paces he stopped and looked back. "Dragging Canoe says he sees a dark cloud over the land beyond the mountains. I fear he is right. We can give the word of the Cherokee, but there are others to the north . . ." He left the rest unsaid, and out among the winking fires a slow and measured tribal chant began, echoing through the foothills and along the river.

"Will you share my campfire this night, Firehair?" Attacullaculla asked. "My women will have much food prepared."

"I would be honored, Attacullaculla," Roman answered.

And slowly, the tall lean scout and the aged chief of the Cherokee walked side by side into the deepening twilight.

PART ONE

❋

Summer 1775

❄ 1 ❄

MOONLIGHT WASHED THE DARKENED CABINS THAT MADE up the small settlement of Old Fields, nestled in the valley that stretched between the mountain ranges to the east and west. A warm night air stirred the green leaves of sycamore and beech, rustling gently through the long grasses that grew close to the river. At the Gentry place, Lady, a spotted hound of some hunting renown, lifted her liver-colored nose to sniff and a moment later bounded from her resting place on the porch, her baying a raucous cry in the night.

Inside the cabin, in the room upstairs that she shared with her little sister, Priscilla, Kitty Gentry raised her head from the pillow to listen to the dog's frantic barking until it began to grow fainter in the distance. Then she sighed and sank back on the narrow bed. Though it was well past midnight, she was awake still, thoughts of the morning and what it would bring an excited clamor within her. If what everyone said was true, Lady would have more than her share of raccoons to tree in Kentucke.

Most of the worldly possessions of the Gentrys had been packed. The pots and pans they would need for cooking. The big old wash boiler. The bed linens and clothing. Pa's tools—he was a joiner by trade—and Ma's sewing supplies and enough stout homespun to last them for a while. Ma had been careful to pack the blue Delft cups in that so they wouldn't get broken. A person would never dream how many things they accumulated unless they moved often, the way the Gentrys did, Kitty thought. Her mother always said, "Pity the woman who's got a man with an itchy foot." But Amelia Gentry usually smiled when she said it.

They had moved three times in the last ten years. Kitty had been six when they'd sold the family place and left their native

Culpeper County in Virginia to begin the series of moves that would bring them here to North Carolina and the Old Fields settlement along the Watauga and finally to tomorrow.

Along the way, the two oldest Gentry girls had found husbands of their choosing and stayed behind to start their own families. A third sister, Faith, had married right in Old Fields last year. Faith was eighteen, two years older than Kitty.

As long as Kitty could remember, it had been her father's heart's desire to settle in Kentucke. Usaph Gentry had talked and dreamed of it endlessly, cornering any who would listen to regale them with glowing accounts of that virgin land and the unparalleled opportunities it offered to those who were bold enough. It was true, Usaph admitted, that he hadn't ever actually been across the mountains and seen it for himself, but he'd talked with those who had. More than one of them. And hadn't his own kinsman, a Gentry, been there with no less than Daniel Boone himself? A cousin of his, he always added in a tone just short of boasting, who'd lived with the Boones for several years off and on.

Usaph Gentry had been ready and waiting when Judge Richard Henderson, late of the North Carolina bench, advertised for hardy people interested in joining his venture to found a settlement out in the wilderness that lay beyond the mountains. He had been one of the first to sign up with the Transylvania Company.

"Damnation, but I'll bend no knee to an English king!" he'd sputtered when Amelia had expressed some trepidation about breaking the edict against settling in the Indian country. But in the wake of Lexington and Bunker Hill, even Kitty's mother had come to admit that the British now had more on their minds than a handful of settlers going across the mountains. Governor Martin of North Carolina, and Lord Dunmore of Virginia, both of whom had denounced the Transylvania venture so vehemently, had already fled their respective colonies, and the newly formed Continental Congress had named George Washington commander-in-chief of the Colonial army. The Revolution had begun.

"I guess," Amelia had conceded with a sigh, "if you're bound for us to go, Usaph Gentry, that now is the time."

Kitty shivered despite the warm night air that wafted through the one window of the small room. It was actually going to happen. After all the talking and the planning, they would really begin that journey tomorrow morning. And the man who would guide them across the mountains and take them into the wilderness to their destination was even now sleeping on his blanket under the apple trees out in the orchard. To everyone's surprise, Pa's legendary cousin, a tall, red-haired man in buckskins, had shown up less than a week past and told them to get their things ready because he'd come to take them to Boonesborough, the tiny fort built out in the heart of that vast land.

Roman Gentry. Kitty thought now of the clean, sharp lines of her unexpected kinsman's face, the intense blue eyes. She had surely never dreamed that the cousin Pa had talked so much about would be such a young man. No more than twenty-three or -four, if she guessed rightly. And though he was related, she knew little about him. The Gentry clan was large back in Virginia, and she had been young when her family had moved away. Besides, Roman's father was only a second cousin to Pa, and she wasn't sure what that made Roman to her. Second cousins once removed, maybe. She did know that the young scout newly back from Boonesborough was rather grave of manner and slow to speak . . . but not shy. Somehow, she was sure of that.

She got out of bed carefully so as not to wake Priscilla and moved to the window, where the moonlight outlined the petite but lissome body beneath a thin linen nightgown, emphasizing the delicate lines of a heart-shaped face with a small straight nose and perfect mouth. She lifted the wealth of black hair and held it high for a moment, letting the breeze cool her neck as she looked out on the side yard.

There was the familiar woodpile—Pa's ax still sunk in an upturned chunk of wood—and the vegetable patch, and beyond that the fruit trees, all silver under the night sky. Lady's baying had long since faded away, but the crickets had set up a lively chorus.

"Bet you're lookin' out there thinkin' you might catch sight of Roman." Priscilla's teasing voice caused Kitty to jump.

"Priscilla Gentry, I thought you were sound asleep," she said, flustered.

Her eight-year-old sister rubbed a fist across her snubbed nose and then began to tug at one of the long wheat-colored braids. "I couldn't," she said.

"And I don't know what you mean, thinking that I'd take the trouble to come look out this window just to see Pa's cousin out there someplace."

Priscilla shrugged. "Seems to me you kind of like him. And

seein' as how you ain't favored a one of the boys around here—''

"Haven't favored," Kitty corrected her. Their mother had been a schoolmistress before she married, and had always tried to see that her girls spoke properly.

"Seein' as how you *haven't* favored a one of them," Priscilla went on unperturbed, "I was thinkin' that you and Roman just might get married.''

"Married?" said Kitty, dumbfounded.

"Faith said it was about time you started to think on it.''

Kitty made a face. "Just because Faith got herself wed doesn't mean that I have to.''

Priscilla drew closer to her sister, and together they looked out the window, squeezing in a little so they could both lean on the sill.

"I think it would be kind of nice," Priscilla said after a moment. "You wouldn't even have to change your name.''

"Prissy!" Kitty laughed softly. "Roman hasn't paid the slightest attention to me. Nor I to him, for that matter. Except that he's a kinsman.''

Priscilla sighed, and they continued to look out the window, the crickets' constant song joined by the sound of a bullfrog's deep voice from down on the river. After a minute Priscilla snuggled in even closer, and Kitty put an arm around her.

"I wish we didn't have to move away from here," the little girl said. "I'll never see Annie again.'' Annie Franklin, who lived in Old Fields, was Priscilla's best friend, and now a tear trembled on the edge of her thick, wheat-colored lashes and slipped down the rounded cheek.

"Maybe you will." Kitty tried to comfort her. "Maybe we can even come back for a visit sometime.''

A floorboard creaked, and the two girls turned to see their mother standing in the bedroom doorway, the candle she held throwing a soft light before her. "That's not likely," Amelia Gentry said, honest as always. She prided herself on never lying to her daughters, no matter how unpalatable the truth might be. But if at times she was blunt, she always followed with quick comfort. "We'll make new friends in Kentucke. You'll see.'' Her voice carried the bright determination of a woman who had learned to make accommodations.

"But it won't be the same," Priscilla protested.

"That's true." Amelia came across the room, setting the candlestick down on the bedside table. She was small, and her long white gown made her seem almost girlish despite the fine lines about her eyes and mouth. Her black hair hung unbound beneath her nightcap almost to her hips. "It won't be exactly the same. You couldn't expect that. But it'll be just as good in its own way." She gave her youngest daughter a quick hug. "And what in the world are you girls doing up at this time of night?" she demanded.

"We couldn't sleep," Kitty said. "I hope we didn't wake you."

Amelia smiled and shook her head. "Guess I couldn't sleep, either."

The three of them sat on Kitty's bed, where Amelia gave the plump feather mattress a few pats with her hand and sighed. "In the morning you two strip the beds and take the mattresses out in the yard and empty out the feathers. Your pa says there's no room for them the way they are. But we can fold the ticks flat and we'll find something to stuff them with when we get to the fort. While you're doing that, I'll have Roman and your pa take these beds apart and load them on the wagon with the other things."

"Roman says we ought not take the wagon," Priscilla piped up. "He says there's places we can't get it through."

"I don't care what he says." Amelia set a mouth that was much like Kitty's into a straight line. "I don't intend to go into that wilderness without my furniture. Why, the chest in my and your pa's room belonged to my mother. I'm not going to leave that. Nor any of the rest of it," she added firmly.

"Yes'm," the girls said dutifully. In her own way, their mother was as strong-minded as Pa, and everyone in the family knew it.

"And mind you empty out the chamber pots and clean them. Scour them out good, then pack them as well." She smiled ruefully. "It'll likely be the last time we see them until we get a roof above our heads again. Meanwhile, we'll have to squat behind a bush like any heathen savage."

Priscilla made a face and giggled.

"I'm glad Faith and Ben decided to come, too," Kitty said.

Amelia nodded. "So am I. I only wish . . . ." Her voice trailed off, and Kitty guessed that she was thinking about her daughters left back in Virginia.

"Did you remember to pack your flower seeds, Ma?" Kitty asked quickly.

"And everything else as well, 'twould seem!" Usaph Gentry

thundered as he strode across the hallway. "She'll have the horses broke down before we're halfway there." He loomed up in the doorway, a certain twinkle in his eyes belying the bombastic tone. He was a great tall man with a broad chest and thick shoulders. His hair, once sandy-colored, now mostly gray, hung about his ears instead of in its usual queue, and as he crossed the room, his long nightshirt flapped about bare ankles.

"I'm not taking a thing that we won't have need of, Usaph," Amelia said, clearly undaunted by her big husband.

He settled heavily onto Priscilla's bed, the frame squeaking beneath his weight. "Can you tell me what in damnation you're doin' up talking about *flower seeds* this time of night?" he demanded.

They looked at him blankly and he stared back, waiting for his answer. A giggle escaped Priscilla, and soon Kitty and her mother joined in, the three of them laughing almost uncontrollably, releasing some of the tension they all felt.

He shook his head. "Heaven help me! Here I am, fifty-one years old, and fate has decreed that I shall go into the wilderness with three giggling females. I should have had sons! But instead God saw fit to send me a houseful of girls, and I suppose I'll just have to bear it." They had heard it many times and knew that he didn't mean a word of it, so they only laughed harder. The corners of his wide mouth spread, and soon the room was echoing with his own loud guffaws.

"Do you suppose there'll be any girls my age when we meet up with the others, Pa?" Priscilla inquired once her hiccuping laughter had subsided. Roman had arranged for them to rendezvous with the Callaways and two other families before they went through the gap into Kentucke.

"It's possible, Priss. There may well be others as afflicted as I," Usaph teased. He winked at her, and scooping her up in his arms, kissed her soundly before depositing her on her bed. "To sleep with you now! We have hard weeks ahead of us. You'll need all your rest this night."

As Kitty settled down in her bed, her father reached a big-knuckled hand to rest it a moment atop her head; then he beckoned to his wife, who took up the candlestick, still wiping tears of laughter from her eyes.

"Not a peep out of any of you before daylight." He turned back at the doorway to caution them. "I'll wager you'll be snorin' away and I'll have to turn the lot of you out of your beds come morning."

* * *

The hot August sun bore down, and though Kitty was a passable rider, she was stiff and sore after two weeks of bone-wearing days astride the stumpy little black horse. Perspiration formed a fine film across her upper lip, and she could feel a trickle of moisture between her breasts, feel the dampness of her stock-inged legs clamped against the warm hide of the animal.

Just ahead of her the wagon jolted, creaking under its burden of furniture, her father calling out to the pair of grays as he skillfully maneuvered them around a deep rut and pulled to higher ground. Ma was with him on the wagon seat, and Priscilla sat between them, her head resting against her mother's shoulder. Prissy's horse followed, hitched to one of the iron rings at the back of the wagon while its young rider rested. And up ahead, Kitty could catch glimpses of Roman Gentry's sorrel gelding, its white mane glinting in the sunlight.

To the left wound a creek, edged by water maples and willows and red oaks. They'd stopped to water the horses earlier, but that seemed a long time past now. Remembering the relief of the shade, Kitty spurred her horse up abreast of the wagon.

"I think I'll walk awhile," she called.

Priscilla didn't stir, but Amelia nodded and smiled as she tightened her hold on the dozing girl.

"Mind you don't fall too far behind," Usaph directed, elbows well out from his thick body, big-knuckled hands holding the reins firmly.

"I won't," said Kitty. She swung to the ground and brought her mount around to hitch it to the rear of the moving wagon, where it fell into step beside her sister's horse.

She stretched her aching back and shoulders, glad to be down on her own two legs and quit for the moment of the chafing saddle. Standing aside, she watched as the cattle—two grown milch cows and a bull calf—meandered by, followed by a pair of pigs, all herded along by Lady, who bounded back and forth nipping at their heels when they showed signs of lagging.

Faith, a tall, fair-haired girl in a yellow sunbonnet, rode next, leading the line of packhorses—Usaph had bought them all from the Transylvania Company and expected to sell them back once they reached Boonesborough. Deep hickory baskets had been fastened across the pack saddles to swing on either side of the animals, each basket packed full with the worldly possessions of the Gentrys and the Tylers. Ben Tyler, Faith's husband, brought up the rear.

Faith edged up in her saddle to flash a grin and wave at Kitty. She rode sidesaddle because Ben didn't approve of her riding astride the way the other Gentry females did.

"I'll catch up in a minute and spell you," Kitty called out, and Faith nodded.

From his place, Ben had taken note and raised his hand in a spare gesture. Though she was too far away to see his face clearly, Kitty was familiar with the slight raising of the colorless eyebrows and the thin smile of her brother-in-law. Sometimes she wondered how Faith had come to choose such a joyless man, who only seemed alive when he was down on his knees at the Sunday meeting. But Ma said there was no accounting for love, and Kitty guessed it must be so.

Gaining the shade of the trees, she sighed with relief at the sudden coolness, unfastening the linen sunbonnet and shaking her head to let her black tresses swing freely about her shoulders. She could take a few minutes here to herself, she decided. The wagon was creaky and slow, since Pa was taking care to avoid the rocks lest they break an axle. And the cows moved at their own pace no matter how much Lady might try to hurry them. She would have no trouble catching up.

Until today the terrain had not been too bad. Roman had kept them along an old trail that crossed the parallel ranges and valleys in easy zigzag stages past Clinch Mountain. They had forded the Clinch River easily enough; the water was low. But today the going was rougher, with outcroppings of rock studding the sloping ground and sudden deep ruts, filled deceptively with tall and prickly grasses.

Last night, as the women had cleared the wooden supper plates and the men sat contentedly smoking their pipes, Kitty heard Roman say that he was pleased with their time. They still had the Powell River to cross and perhaps the hardest stretch this side of the Cumberland Gap, the steep four-mile climb to Kane's Gap in Powell Mountain. Once there, he said, they'd be able to see the Cumberlands, ten or twelve miles distant. Their last stop before heading for the gap would be in Powell Valley at Martin's station. It was there that they would rendezvous with Colonel Callaway and his group.

Once through the mountains, it was doubtful that they would set eyes on another human besides those in the party until they reached Boonesborough—that is, if they were lucky, Roman had added, clearly referring to the Indian attack the Boone party had suffered on their way in last April. Three men had been killed and one badly wounded.

"Any savage that thinks to give trouble to me or mine will feel the sting of this!" Usaph had declared, patting the well-oiled stock of his rifle.

Now, Kitty turned to watch him sitting broad-backed beside her mother and Priscilla on the wagon seat, leaning up to coax Old Moll and Nell along. She had always thought him the strongest man in the world.

Searching out a dense shield of bushes, she relieved herself so she wouldn't have to stop again soon. Some days it did seem that she sweat more than she peed, she thought. Birds chattered in the branches above, and the soft mud of the creekbank was stippled here and there with the prints of small animals. The water rippled invitingly over a white-pebbled bottom, and she longed to strip down and bathe.

For an instant she considered taking off her stout leather shoes and long stockings to wade, then reluctantly decided against it. She mustn't let the others get too far ahead.

She contented herself with finding a firm spot along the bank and, kneeling, splashing her face and throat again and again. She ran her wet hands down the low top of the loose-fitting linen smock she wore tied in at the waist, looking down to catch a glimpse of the small, pink, crescent-shaped birthmark deep within the cleft of her breasts. She scooped up more water to splash her bare forearms, shivering in delight.

At last she stopped, still leaning forward to look down into the water that eddied up between the rocks and reflected her image . . . showing the delicately arched brows, the graceful curve of her neck, the violet eyes.

She was the only one of the Gentry girls with those eyes. Amelia said they had come from her own grandmother, who'd been the daughter of the second son of an earl and had come from England to the Colonies with her husband in search of a fortune.

Cupping her hands, she drank her fill of the sweet water, droplets falling from her chin. Spying a clump of harebell growing between the rocks nearby, she plucked a sprig of it and, laughing, tucked the cluster of small, bell-shaped lavender flowers above her left ear.

She lay back in the tall grasses behind her, edging her skirt up to her knees and spreading her legs to let the breeze cool her chafed thighs. Constant contact with a sweaty saddle was not exactly good for one's nether parts, she thought ruefully. But then maybe she would toughen up there as well as other places.

Probably the most bothersome thing about the trip had been the utter lack of privacy. The first evening out, she had come inadvertently upon her brother-in-law, hunkered down, his white and skinny hind end shining in the moonlight. Fortunately she'd been able to back away without Ben's knowing she'd been there. But now she was growing accustomed to having Faith's husband and Roman Gentry share virtually every minute of the day with them.

Her tall and taciturn cousin had proven easy to get along with. Though he was clearly in charge, his instructions were delivered with such quiet courtesy that they seemed requests as much as orders, and Kitty had not seen him press an issue. The wagonload of furniture was proof of that.

Clearly he had become a favorite of her mother's. Amelia had declared almost immediately that she intended to "fatten him up." But though he cleaned the ample plates she dished up for him at mealtime, his lean frame had thus far changed not a whit. In some ways he seemed a paradox. Pa said that he'd studied law. Why, then, Kitty wondered, was he not back east in some polished office filled with leather books instead of on his way into the wilderness?

Sighing, she closed her eyes, allowing herself one more minute, reminding herself that she must not linger much longer. Faith would need spelling soon.

A small, soft rustling in the brush nearby caught her ear, and she rolled over, expecting to see a fleeing rabbit or chipmunk. Instead she found herself staring full up into the face of Roman Gentry, who stood looking down at her from his impressive height, bridle in hand, his horse behind him.

A small "Oh!" escaped her as she scrambled to her feet.

"I didn't mean to startle you," he said quickly.

"It's all right . . . I should have heard you." She laughed, more than a little embarrassed at the position in which he had caught her and unaccountably conscious of the dark tresses that tumbled wildly over her shoulders. She saw his eyes linger for an instant at a point above her left ear, and to her horror, remembered the sprig of harebell tucked there. Coloring, she hastily raised a slender hand to retrieve it and let it fall to the ground. He must think her a silly young woman indeed.

His tow linen hunting shirt fit across the broad chest smoothly, sleeves cut away almost to the shoulders to reveal the deeply tanned skin of well-muscled arms. His hawklike features were accented in the play of light and shade, the mane of red hair tied back with a whang—a thin strip of supple leather.

"I should have called out to you," he said, sober in the way he was sometimes. "My apologies. But I would ask you to stay closer to the others. Remember that I am not the only man who can move silently when it pleases him."

"Of course. I hadn't thought . . . I was tired of riding and decided to walk for a while. And the creek seemed so inviting."

He nodded.

She looked through the trees toward the small procession, surprised to see that they were farther away than she had expected. The wagon was just clearing the top of a steep ridge, and in the next instant had disappeared down the opposite side. "Well," she said, smoothing the tangle of black hair away from her face and retrieving her sunbonnet, "I'd best catch up."

With a nod to him she set out after the others, but after a few paces was surprised when he fell in beside her, his long legs taking one step to her two, the big sorrel following along after them. He seemed quite comfortable with the silence between them, but after a time she ventured a question.

"Are we in danger from Indians? Even here? Before we cross over the mountains?"

He took his time answering. "It doesn't hurt to be prudent," he said finally.

"No. I suppose not."

As they continued to walk, she noticed that though he seemed so quiet, so drawn within himself, he was really missing nothing. His eyes swept the line of trees along the creek, moving ahead to the ridges and ravines. She had the feeling that there wasn't a sound he failed to hear, no matter how slight.

He was, she thought, greatly different from the young men who had crowded onto the Gentry porch most Saturday evenings, vying for a sign of approval from her. They were vocal and brash, awkward as half-grown puppies in their eagerness to please. Of course, they had been bent on courting her, and she certainly meant to make no comparisons between Roman and them in that respect . . .

She realized that he was walking rather slowly because of her, and she quickened her pace as they cleared a ridge and the wagon came into full view ahead.

"I believe I heard you say that from Captain Martin's cabin it's only twenty miles or so to the gap." Her attempt to spark a conversation elicited no more than a nod, and they covered the rest of the way in silence.

As they approached the rear of the procession, the spotted hound ran back to greet them, executing wide circles and wagging her tail vigorously. When she darted in, Kitty gave her an affectionate pat.

"I won't lag behind again," she said to Roman, giving him a quick smile. "I promise." And with Lady trotting beside her, she started forward, bent on retrieving her mount.

"Kitty Gentry . . ."

Surprised, she turned back to see him holding something out to her. A half smile—a little crooked, really—marked that strong face, softened the fierce blue eyes. And there in the palm of his hand, where it had been hidden all the time, was the sprig of harebell.

"You shouldn't have thrown it away," he said. "It looked . . . fine." One stride brought him up to her, and she felt the rush of blood to her cheeks as she took it from him.

"I thank you," she said, formal suddenly, and his nod was gravely courteous as he swung up into the saddle and wheeled the big, rangy horse away.

＊ 2 ＊

WITH THE LONG, BLUE-GRAY LINE OF THE CUMBER-land mountains looming in the sky to the northwest, the Gentry party finally arrived at Martin's station. Captain Martin, a lean and loose-jointed woodsman, inquired as to the welfare of all, and Colonel Richard Callaway came striding out of one of the small rough cabins to seize Roman's hand.

"Roman . . . 'tis good to see you, lad." His smile was broad, displaying teeth that were still strong and white. "We've been here nearly a week, and growing fearful something had happened.''

''The wagon slowed us down,'' Roman told him.

Callaway eyed the load of furniture and shook his head. Upward of ten years older than Usaph Gentry, he was still a fine-looking man, standing straight as a rifle barrel in his buckskins, silver-gray hair falling unbound to his shoulders. A man of some repute, Callaway had seen action in the French and Indian War, then, on leaving Virginia for North Carolina, had earned his colonelcy in the Bedford County militia.

Like Roman, he had gone in with Boone to establish the new fort on the banks of the Kentucke River and now had come east to fetch his family back. Eight of his children were with him, ranging in age from fifteen-year-old Betsey down to the baby boy, only a few weeks old, at Elizabeth Callaway's breast. And his nephew Flanders was along as well.

Usaph and the Old Colonel, as everyone called Callaway, hit it off at once. ''Damnation, eight with him and more back in Virginia,'' he told Amelia the first chance he got, a gleam of admiration in his eye. ''Got grandchildren older'n some of the young ones.''

Two other families were making the trip into Kentucke: the Porters, plump and affable, with three nearly grown boys and a girl, Lureen; and the Sherrills, a young couple with a baby five or six months old.

Captain Martin turned one cabin over to the women and girls, and Amelia seized the opportunity to heat water for baths and hair washing—an action that caused the other women to look at her a little askance.

''Ain't you afraid you'll get sick?'' Elvie Porter asked as Amelia, aided by Kitty and Faith, carried enough hot water for the first bath into the cabin. Elvie looked to be in her thirties, with light hair and a face as round as a pumpkin.

''Mercy, no,'' said Amelia. ''I believe in a strip-down bath once a week in the winter, and oftener in the summer. It's never hurt a one of us.''

The other women exchanged doubtful looks, but as the bathing proceeded, Elizabeth Callaway, who'd gotten her infant to sleep finally, said maybe it wouldn't be such a bad idea. After all, it was a long way to Boonesborough yet, and it was still good and hot. Then young Callie Sherrill said that maybe she would wash her hair if some of the girls wouldn't mind seeing to her baby for a few minutes. Kitty, finished with her own bath, volunteered.

As the cabin grew dim and steamy from fresh-washed bodies, the women began to exchange quick and tentative confidences, as if they must explain why they were there.

"My Robert," Callie Sherrill volunteered, "could work somebody else's land till he died and never have a thing, like his pappy afore him. We're aimin' for better."

"Oh, we had a piece of land," Elvie Porter chimed in. "Dirt wore out from tobacco. Wouldn't grow peas for the hogs!"

Amelia finished braiding Priscilla's shining blond tresses. "Usaph wouldn't have died happy if we didn't go," she said, deftly twisting a wisp of hair about the end of each plait. The moment Priscilla was free, she ran outside with the Porter girl and Keziah Callaway, both of whom were near her age.

The two older Callaway girls, Betsey and Fanny, sat on the floor with Kitty, the three of them taking turns playing patty-cake with the Sherrill baby, who laughed and hiccuped, the barest edge of one tiny tooth showing in the little pink gums.

"I declare," Callie Sherrill said, smiling at her son and the girls, "it's a pure pleasure to see him in such good humor. He's been frettin' hisself for a while now. Tryin' to cut that tooth stickin' through there and deviled by chigger bites."

"We'll find some squaw mint," Elizabeth Callaway volunteered. "The juices boiled down work tolerably well for keeping away mosquitoes and chiggers and the like." She was a tall and bony woman with an aristocratic bearing and iron-gray hair that peeped from beneath a white mobcap.

"Bless the little thing," Amelia said, smiling. "It's hard traveling with one."

"It is indeed," Elizabeth Callaway said, looking over at her own infant, who was still sleeping peacefully on the pallet she'd spread for him in the corner.

"The worst is tryin' to keep in dry didies." Callie Sherrill's grin was broad enough to show that she had lost a jaw tooth.

"Lord help me, I'm glad I don't have any little ones now," Elvie Porter said, "cute as they are."

"It's not easy after you get older," said Elizabeth with a touch of weariness. "At forty-two, I'd just as soon this last one would be all." She sighed. "Rebecca Boone was expecting another, you know. I expect she's had it by now. Richard said that Daniel was going back to fetch her and the children to the fort as soon as she was able to travel."

"The poor woman"—Amelia was forthright, as usual—" 'tis said that Captain Boone's only home long enough to get her caught with another before he's off again to some wild place, and her left behind to see to the crops and the children."

"That's been the way of it," Elizabeth Callaway admitted. "But now that Daniel has finally got to Kentucke . . ." She left the rest unsaid.

Faith finished pinning up her braid and came to sit beside Kitty on the floor to smile at the baby with his fuzz of dark hair and dimpled hands. But the infant had tired of playing and screwed his face up and begun to whimper. His mother reached for him and opened the top of her dress to put him to a full, blue-veined breast.

"Is it true," she asked, the slightest quaver in her voice, "that Indians killed the oldest Boone boy when they tried to go in before?"

There were a few nods, and a sudden silence fell over the room but for the Sherrill baby's loud sucking as he pulled and tugged at his mother's nipple, his fingers digging greedily at the soft flesh.

Amelia's chin came up. "That was two years ago." She began taking down the blanket they'd hung from the smoky rafters to give the bathers privacy. "Things are different now."

"They are," Elizabeth said. "Not only are there treaties with the Indians now, but my husband and Roman, not to mention the other good men along, will see that we get safely to the fort. Don't worry yourself, child."

As Elvie Porter began to talk about the quilt patterns she had brought along, Fanny Callaway edged closer to Kitty. "I wouldn't mind a bit if Roman Gentry protected *me* from the Indians," she whispered, blushing. Her sister Betsey giggled softly. They were pretty girls, as handsome as the rest of the Callaways.

Kitty smiled.

In a little, she stood to stretch her legs, turning so that she could see out the window—nothing more than a square opening that could be covered over by a hinged wooden door—out to where Roman and her father and Colonel Callaway stood. As she watched, Roman said something to the other men and gestured with a broad sweep of his arm toward the mountains. Maybe, she thought, Ma was right when she said that there was a strong streak of wanderlust in the Gentry blood. As courteous and quiet as he was, there were times when she felt something

wild within Roman, something that could not be caged any more
than a catamount could.

The men had killed and cleaned a deer, and the women went
to cook thick steaks from it, salting down as much of the remaining meat as they could carry with them when they went.
The rest they left for Captain Martin, who broke out a cask of
ale.

"Best get to bed early," Usaph cautioned Amelia, "you and
the girls. Roman's decided we should leave at first light."

They did, and it was apparent from the first that more precautions would be taken now that they were so close to crossing
into Kentucke. The men and older boys took up the front and
rear positions, with the women and children and livestock in the
middle. In addition to the extra packhorses, three more cows
and a pair of pigs were added. Lady adopted the new charges at
once. With Usaph in the rear, Amelia drove the wagon, which
she still insisted must go with them, though Colonel Callaway
and Roman had both advised that it couldn't be gotten through.

They followed the path along Indian Creek, going easily. The
skyline of peaks was magnificent, reaching into the brilliant
blue, green-topped with pine and cedar. Small animals darted
through the underbrush as they passed, and once that morning
Kitty caught sight of a bear, lumbering away through the trees.
But within a couple of hours the trace had narrowed and the
thick matted growth at either side squeezed in upon the wagon
to slow it down and finally bring it to a halt.

The willing horses dug at the rocky earth with their hooves,
haunches set and straining, until Amelia could see that it did no
good and reined them in. She gave her head a shake and climbed
down to assess the predicament.

"All it will take is just a stroke or two," she declared to Faith
and Kitty, who had come to stand beside her. Her mouth was
set into its firmest line.

Roman, up in front, called out a long "Hold . . ." as he
realized what had happened. He turned his horse back as Usaph
came up from the rear, and the two of them set to work with
hatchets and axes, some of the other men and boys pitching in
to clear the way.

It took a few minutes, but soon the party was able to proceed.
"You see"—Amelia brought the reins down smartly, a gleam
of triumph in her eye as she leaned toward Priscilla on the seat
beside her—"it *can* be done."

But by the middle of the afternoon they had had to stop four more times in less than that many miles to make way for the bulky conveyance, and now the procession had been brought to a halt again, with Amelia sitting rigidly on the wagon seat. This time the trace narrowed still more ahead of them, through a stand of mature trees and young saplings that made it apparent at once that making way for the furniture-laden wagon would take a prodigious amount of labor. The timber stretched ahead as far as they could see.

The travelers gathered, all eyes turned toward Amelia, except for Usaph and Roman, who had taken up their axes. Flanders started to say something, but his uncle silenced him with a look.

The solid *whump* of Usaph's and Roman's axes had started to echo, and Kitty, standing beside her mother, could see how pale and drawn Amelia's face had grown. She put out a tentative hand to clasp her mother's fingers, but Amelia just gave her a stiff smile and pulled away.

She looked off up ahead for a long minute, at the narrow trace, then straightened her shoulders and climbed up in the wagon to retrieve the carved mahogany Bible box and her small bundle of books. Flanders and the oldest Porter boy jumped to help her down.

"Unhitch the horses," she called to Usaph and Roman, her voice dry as ashes. Then she started along the trail, carrying her things in her arms, her head high.

Through tears, Kitty saw Colonel Callaway's quick gesture, and some of the young men sprang forward to see to the pair of grays, while Roman and Usaph put aside their axes and went after the lone figure. Kitty spied the small bundle of apple-tree seedlings that her mother had watered so faithfully, and she climbed up and got them.

Up ahead, Roman had come abreast of Amelia and gently took the things from her arms, then walked back to tuck them into one of the panniers atop a packhorse. But Usaph, looking very large beside his diminutive wife, fell into step beside her, his big arm around her loosely. And Amelia Gentry kept facing straight ahead, never looking back as the wagon with its heavy furniture was rolled backward to a clear place and abandoned.

Kitty had never seen anything as breathtaking as the Cumberland Gap, a wide, saddle-shaped opening in the otherwise impenetrable ridges, with a barren but beautiful white limestone cliff towering hundreds of feet on its northern side and a somewhat lower peak to the south. The narrow way stretched for five or six miles between mountainsides that rose above her a thousand feet or more, seedling trees struggling for rootholds on the sheer cliffs and trickling water leaving green patches of stubborn mosses in its wake. The voices of the travelers echoed loudly, and Priscilla and her new friends sang all the songs they knew just to hear the strains bounce back to them as they moved along.

But when the party finally emerged on the far side and caught sight of that stretch of sun-drenched peaks and green valleys, shrouded still in morning mist, they all fell silent. No one moved or said a word. There was only the sound of a horse stamping, and high up in the distance a pair of eagles circled, powerful wings spread to catch the air currents.

Kitty could see that Roman was down from his horse ahead of her, standing tall and motionless, the bronzed features so sharp, so clean, they could have been carved right out of the rocks around them. His eyes were fixed out there, as if he could see past the mountains and the knob country beyond them, could see the rivers and the gently rolling hills and meadows they'd all heard so much about.

The moment stretched, seemed encapsulated, then Usaph Gentry's shrill whoop cracked the air. "Damnation!" he thundered. "There it is! We've made it, m'girl!" And with that, he scooped Amelia from atop of Old Moll and swung her around as the others climbed down from their horses to clap one another on the back, kissing and hugging.

"Miss Gentry!" Flanders Callaway stood there grinning down at Kitty, his handsome features flushed. "What do you think of your first glimpse of Kentucke, then?"

She laughed with excitement. "It's grand, Mr. Callaway! Grand!" she replied, all the while aware that the pretty Callaway girls had sidled up to Roman and were turning dimpled faces up to him and chattering away. She saw him respond with that half smile she had come to know.

"We must give thanks," Ben Tyler said, and to nods of agreement, he snatched off the stained slouch hat and dropped to his knees, bowing his head. As the others gathered close, he offered their gratitude to God for bringing them this far, beseeching the Almighty to see them safely through the miles ahead, his thin frame rocking slightly with each word.

"Amen," came the heartfelt chorus once he'd finished.

They milled about now, elated. If they had not yet reached their destination, they were at least, and at last, in Kentucke. Colonel Callaway and Elizabeth stood side by side, the tiny baby in her arms. The younger children ran about shouting raucously. The cattle and pigs had wandered off the trail to graze in the thick clumps of grass that studded the rocky soil, and Lady raced back and forth barking.

But after a few minutes Roman called a halt to the unscheduled stop. "We'd best get on," he said. "The day is early, the weather fine. But it may not stay that way," he added cryptically.

As if in answer, by late afternoon the wind had risen noticeably and swollen dark clouds swept in to blot out the sunlight. The rain began, settling into a steady, leaden downpour that made the cows switch their tails and the horses' hides ripple.

At first Kitty welcomed the coolness of it, but after nearly an hour she was soaked through and chilled. Up ahead of her the Sherrill baby whined thinly, and Callie leaned far forward atop her mount to shelter the child with her body.

"Can I help you with him?" Kitty called to her, knowing she must be worn out.

Callie looked back over her shoulder to give Kitty a harried smile, sodden sunbonnet hanging limply about her cheeks. "I thank you kindly, but he's cross as two sticks. Still tryin' to get the teeth through. Likely he'd squall all the louder."

Darkness was no more than an hour or so away now, and the cold rain showed no sign of stopping. Flanders Callaway came riding back down the line to tell each of them that Roman knew a large cave not too far away. It would take them out of their way a little but would provide shelter for the night and a dry place to build a fire and cook their supper.

"He says the going will get a little steep," Flanders warned Kitty as he reined his horse close to hers, raising his voice to be heard. Kitty nodded, and he moved on past her to her mother and Priscilla.

The party veered off to the left, and Kitty soon saw that the warning had been justified. The way rose sharply, dripping branches swiping at her until she huddled forward, whispering encouragement to the horse beneath her.

After a few minutes of such hard going, the path leveled out and widened a little, and she was glad to hear the call to hold passed back, thinking that they must have reached the cave. But once they were down from their horses and gathered, she saw that the way ahead lay past a steep cliff; the rocky ledge that they must travel measured about seven or eight feet wide, the drop-off forty feet down to the tops of thick pine trees and jutting boulders.

"There's plenty of room," Roman said in that calm way he had. "We'll lead the horses one by one. Just stay close to the rock wall side."

"Mistress Callaway and I shall go first," the Old Colonel said. As she sheltered her baby inside of her cloak, he helped her back up onto her horse, then grasped the bridle and walked her around the path to where the ledge widened out comfortably and began a gradual descent to the bottom below. Ben took Faith across next, and they were followed by the Sherrills.

The cattle and pigs meandered across unconcernedly, the dog trotting behind them, and Colonel Callaway and Ben came back to help with the packhorses.

" 'Melia?" Usaph looked at his wife inquiringly.

"Merciful heaven, I don't need any help," she declared. "Just see to the girls, Usaph." She went ahead, walking sure-footedly, her horse following behind her.

Usaph took Priscilla's bridle and started across. Kitty stood beside her little black mount to watch for a moment, and suddenly Flanders Callaway was at her side, his dark hair plastered to his ears beneath his hat and dripping down his collar.

"Miss Gentry . . . allow me."

"That's kind of you Mr. Callaway, but no," she declined, laughing. "I've ridden more dangerous places back home."

"Let him take you." She heard Roman's voice and turned to find him behind her.

She was tired and cold, and hungry, and somehow put out with the order. "I can take myself perfectly well," she said crisply.

"Then walk your horse. Don't ride," he replied in that exasperatingly calm voice.

She grasped the black gelding's bridle and started confidently ahead on the path. Did he think she was one of the children to be ordered about? she fumed. If her mother could go alone, so could she.

To her left the limestone rock that stretched upward was marked with pockets of prickly bushes and tangled trumpet vines. And when she allowed herself to look over the cliff on the right, far down to the bottom, the tops of the pine trees seemed so far away that it made her dizzy. She shifted her gaze at once.

The path was slippery underfoot, with numerous small and

not-so-small rocks that had dislodged and fallen from above. Her horse blew through his nostrils, jerking his head skittishly, but she held on firmly and pulled him back into a steady walk, thinking how much farther it seemed across than it had back on the other side. But at least the rain was slowing down to a drizzle, she noted.

Veering closer to the safe side, she had taken a few more steps when the black's hoof dislodged a small pile of rocks to send them rolling. Suddenly Kitty stiffened as she caught a glimpse of the gleaming, slithery dark ribbon, heard the ominous rattle. The horse whinnied shrilly, rearing as the snake struck; but Kitty held on grimly, her feet leaving the ground. As the animal came down hard and turned, she lost her grasp, and as he lunged she was caught by the weight of his flank and thrown sideways toward the edge.

She flung out her arms as she went sprawling, trying to hold to the gravelly shelf, digging her fingernails in to claw at the earth; but to her horror she felt herself slipping . . . slipping . . . There was a terrible roaring in her ears, a steady pulsing behind her eyes as she fell, the uneven surface tearing at her.

It seemed forever, and then, miraculously, she felt her feet hit something solid. Instinctively she clung to the almost perpendicular side, snatching at the clumps of wiry grass and wet, irregular surfaces that offered a slim hold.

She hung there precariously, not daring even to breathe for a moment, the steady pounding roar still in her ears. And then sounds from above intruded. She heard male voices shouting and a woman's scream. It sounded like her mother. She had never heard her mother scream. She'd never seen her cry, not even when the baby three years ago had been stillborn. It was that, her mother's scream, that frightened her as much as anything.

"Kitty . . . Kitty, m'dear!" She heard her father's frantic call, but when she tried to open her mouth to answer, only a hoarse whisper came out at first. Then she took another breath and called back.

"Pa . . ." But it was all that she could get out, for with the effort of speaking she could feel herself slip a little. She moaned softly, her face close against the wet rock, not daring to look up.

She heard voices again but couldn't make out what they were saying until her father called out again: "Hold still now, girl! We'll get you!"

In a moment she heard scratching noises, sounds that seemed to come right through the rock. Her heart gave a sudden flutter as she realized that someone was climbing down. Pa, she thought joyfully, Pa was coming after her.

The sound grew louder, and she heard the squeaky noise that a stout hemp rope made when stretched. She realized that he was just above her and coming fast. She turned her head to try to see him, but the action started her slipping again.

Terrified, she felt the ledge begin to crumble away beneath her feet, and she closed her eyes, sure that she was gone. But in that last fearful second, she felt a strong arm grab her about the waist and swing her in to a hard, muscular side.

As she had clung to her precarious perch, she now clung to this warm, living body. Aware in an instant that it wasn't her father, she let out her breath and opened her eyes to see Roman Gentry's chiseled features.

"Be easy," he said, tightening his hold on her until she was pressed against the length of his side from chest to thigh. One of her arms was laced through his and around to his back, while the other hand held fiercely to the fistful of hunting shirt she'd been able to grab. "Put your arms up around my neck," he commanded, "one at a time."

"Roman . . ." she breathed, too terrified still to move, conscious that her feet dangled uselessly and that the only thing holding her up was his arm.

"Go ahead," he said. And that deep, quiet calm had its effect on her; taking a shaky breath, she slowly did as he'd said.

"Good . . . good. Now, hold on," he instructed as he re-braced his feet against the rock, and she realized that they were both being supported by the rope that was tied about his waist.

"God, you're a little mite of a thing," he said, so softly that she wasn't sure she'd heard him correctly. Then in the next instant he was shouting up to the others. "I have her. Haul away!"

She could feel his muscles tense as they inched upward, and he rebraced his feet with every movement, as if he were walking her up the cliff to safety. "Easy," he called out once as he struggled with the slippery surface.

Kitty could hear the voices from above, the excited cries as they edged their way upward, but she didn't dare look. Her head was tucked under Roman's chin, her face pressed close in to the damp hollow of his neck. She could feel a warm pulse there, could smell the decidedly male odor of him, not at all unpleasant—in fact, strangely heady. And in that moment she trusted her safety to him completely, closing her eyes and listening to her own heartbeat as it seemed to set itself to the pulsing in his throat.

"We're almost there," he murmured encouragingly, that deep voice rumbling from within his chest.

A minute more and she heard her father's shout, drowning out the others. "Thank God Almighty! Kitty! My Kitty, girl!"

She was suddenly caught up in her father's arms like a baby, and everything seemed to happen at once. Ma was smoothing at her hair, searching her face anxiously. "Are you hurt, child? Tell me . . ." she was saying, and the others were pressing 'round. Faith and Priscilla were crying.

"I'm all right," she insisted, though she had begun to tremble violently now that it was over.

The rain had stopped, but there was still the sound of water dripping from the bushes, trickling from the rocks above.

"Let's all get off this confounded ledge," Ben Tyler shouted. "There could well be a nest of vipers amongst them other rocks."

There was a general agreement, and a few minutes later Kitty was in the cave that Roman had spoken of earlier. It was roomy and dry, and down toward the mouth of it a fire burned brightly.

The males had withdrawn discreetly so that the womenfolk could see to her, but a close inspection had turned up nothing worse than a few bruises and some skinned places on her arms and legs and hands. Her stockings were torn and a sleeve of her blouse ripped. Once satisfied that her daughter was all right, Amelia had gone to tell Usaph, and now Kitty lay stretched out on a blanket, Faith and Priscilla sitting beside her.

"You gave us a scare," Faith said.

"Flanders Callaway wanted to come down for you," Priscilla chattered, "but Roman said *he* was going to."

For some strange reason, Kitty found herself blushing, and Elizabeth Callaway, who sat nearby nursing her baby, smiled.

The sudden crack of a rifle brought Kitty bolt upright. Elvie Porter, who'd been stirring at the fire, turned back to quiet her. "That timber rattler bit your horse, honey. The poison must've got right into his blood, 'cause he got down out there and couldn't get up. Nothin' for it but to shoot him." She shook her head. "Lord o' mercy, but I do hate to see good horseflesh put down."

With Kitty painfully stiff and sore after her ordeal, the small group pressed on, fording the clear green waters of the Cumberland River without mishap. But a few days later one of the packhorses came up lame, and after unloading it, the men turned it loose.

"She'll be all right," said Callie's husband. Not a handsome man, with ears too big and crooked teeth, Robert Sherrill was nonetheless a stout fellow of solid bone and body, and always willing to extend a ready hand. "That leg'll heal up if it don't have strain on it. Horses are smart enough to fend for theirselves. That old mare'll likely end up back in Caroline."

The country was still rugged, with steep bluffs and deep valleys. Two horses short now, the men and older boys took turns walking, except for Roman, who needed his horse to scout ahead and back. He would take no chances on a surprise attack. Luckily, his careful attention turned up no Indian sign, no indication that any man, red or white, was in their immediate vicinity.

Flanders Callaway was openly interested in Kitty, but she showed him no more favor than she had the suitors back home in Old Fields. Still, she did like the tall, good-natured young man well enough. In fact, over the weeks they had spent together, the whole party had come to seem like a family of sorts.

Colonel Callaway and Usaph sat around the fire of a night, smoking their pipes and exchanging stories . . . one who had lived his dreams to the fullest, the other just beginning to realize his. And if Amelia ever admitted to anyone what it had cost her to leave her furniture on the other side of the gap, it was to Elizabeth Callaway and Elvie Porter. Elizabeth had revealed early on that she was the Old Colonel's second wife. The five older children, from Betsey down to Theodosia, who was nine, were her stepchildren, but she'd come to love them almost as much as her own three, she said. Still, it wasn't easy, she admitted, coming that late to being a mother. She'd been thirty-five when Keziah was born.

The Callaway and Sherrill babies were passed around and made much of, though Callie's boy was still fretful and seemed thinner than he had been when they'd started out from Martin's Station. But it was the friendship that allowed them to endure the grinding physical fatigue, the insect bites, the moldy shoes when it rained three days straight, the glaring heat of the sun when it was dry.

They passed the Rockcastle River, which Colonel Callaway said was really a tributary of the Cumberland, many days behind them, and after twenty miles or so of thick brush, they came into a stretch of canebreaks that stretched ahead for as far as they could see. Kitty was sure that she had never been so miserable; the cane hung like a thick curtain from above their heads and cut out any breath of air. The Sherrill baby cried incessantly. Insects plagued them all unmercifully, and because of the constant dampness underfoot, Roman made them wash their feet and dry them carefully each night to guard against the painful "scaldfoot," which was the bane of hunters when they were out in the wet too long.

But once beyond the cane country, they emerged into the promised heart of Kentucke, where the hills rolled gently and the forests were thick and lush and green . . . trees six feet across and rising a hundred feet into the sky.

"Will ye just look at it!" Usaph whispered as they beheld the first natural meadow, knee-deep in clover. Robert Sherrill, who'd come to Kentucke with an all-abiding hunger for his own land, hunkered down in the rich, sweet-smelling grass, digging into the fecund earth with his fingers and not ashamed of the tears in his eyes.

In those next two days, Kitty thought that she had never seen anything as beautiful as the country they traveled. The line of it rose and fell as gently as a woman's body curved, luxuriant grass giving way to deep groves of hickory and maple, cherry and ash. The dark green of cedars studded the hillsides, and everywhere she saw goldenrod in full bloom, and hawthorn, and wild flax. She had heard often enough that the Indians used this place freely for their hunting grounds, yet it seemed so perfect, so untouched, it was hard to imagine that any person had been here before.

Game was so plentiful that they could almost decide what they wanted for supper. The woods were replete with deer and bear, opossum and rabbit, as well as turkey and small coveys of quail, which when disturbed would fly up with a great whirring of wings. Occasionally glimpses were caught of huge, hairy buffalo, grazing unafraid, calves gamboling at their sides.

Toward the middle of the afternoon of that second day, they came upon a spring bubbling up out of the hillside to form a clear creek, and the travelers prevailed upon Roman to stop and make camp. The men went off to the nearby woods to hunt, while the women washed clothing long in need of it. They feasted that night on roasted turkeys stuffed with wild onions and the last of the potatoes they had brought from home. Roman seemed mellow, almost talkative. If they made good time, he said, they should reach Boonesborough within the week.

That night Kitty was awakened by the persistent crying of the Sherrill baby and the quiet comings and goings of the older women. Between spells of crying, the infant lay listless, the normally bright eyes dulled with fever.

As soon as it was good daylight, Amelia sent Kitty and Faith out to look for something that might help the child.

"Might be some purple boneset growing out there, or some wild raspberry bushes," she said. "Bring me the leaves if you find some. And mind you don't go too far," she called after them.

Both Kitty and her sister had helped their mother gather medicinal herbs many times before, and they searched diligently now for something that looked familiar. Once, Kitty caught a glimpse of Roman through the trees and realized that he was keeping a watchful eye on them. But finally, after failing to come upon anything they knew to be safe, they returned to camp empty-handed.

They found the Sherrill baby still crying weakly, despite all his mother could do to comfort him. But Elvie Porter was making a tea with some dried yellowroot she'd found in her things.

"Let me spell you for a while." Amelia put her hand on Callie's shoulder, but the worried mother just shook her head. She would hardly take her eyes from the child.

Robert came once to look at his son helplessly and then walked back to the men, who sat a distance away under the trees, looking useless and self-conscious. Sickness, they agreed tacitly, was something the womenfolk were best at.

"It's probably the summer grippe," Amelia soothed. "My oldest girl, Abigail, had it when she wasn't much bigger than he is. I don't know anything better for it than yellowroot tea."

"Make it strong," Elizabeth Callaway agreed.

The tea made, they spooned small amounts of it between the baby's lips now and again and tried to cool the little body with cloths they'd wet in the creek. He fell into a restless sleep, and the older women tried to get Callie to lie down and get what rest she could; but she said she couldn't.

The night before, what was left of the turkey and potatoes had all been put into an iron pot along with some water and allowed to simmer through the night to make a thick stew. The Callaway girls had passed plates of it for breakfast while Kitty and Faith were out searching for herbs, but the pot still gave off a delicious aroma of onion and well-cooked meat, and the Gentry girls helped themselves.

Catching sight of Roman sitting apart from the other men, and realizing that he hadn't eaten yet, Kitty impulsively spooned up a wooden plateful, added a thick wedge of cornbread, and poured a tin cup of scalding coffee for him.

He looked up in surprise at her approach, his back against a huge old oak, which allowed him an excellent view of the entire sweep of open country that bordered the grove of trees where they camped.

"I thank you, Kitty Gentry," he said as he took the trencher of food and set to eating with relish.

She lingered. "Why do you call me that?"

He swallowed. "What?"

She laughed. "Kitty Gentry. Surely a kinsman need not be so formal. Kitty will do well."

The half smile marked his face. "Very well. Kitty it shall be."

"May I sit?" She felt herself blush at her boldness.

"Please," he said quickly, and she found a soft spot in the grass nearby.

She was aware that her hair was clean for the first time in two weeks—she had washed it in the creek. And though her dress was faded, it, too, was clean and fit her figure well, cupping under her small breasts and snugging to her waist, baring her arms to well above the elbows.

"I don't believe I have thanked you properly for saving me that day," she said, a certain shyness seizing her now that she was here. She was reminded of how closely she had been pressed to his side and the damp, warm smell of his neck as she'd held to him. "I do now."

He acknowledged what she'd said with a brief nod and continued to eat.

"Prissy said that Flanders wanted to come down for me," she said, unaccountably annoyed with him.

There was the slightest response in those blue eyes. "It wasn't Flanders's job to do it," he said. "It was mine."

"Of course," she said, feeling somehow foolish.

They were silent for a moment while Roman applied himself to the food with his usual good appetite.

"I confess," Kitty ventured finally, "that I don't remember you at all from back in Virginia. I think I do recall your father." She had a dim memory of a tall man with hair as red as Roman's.

"I remember you," said Roman.

"You do?"

He nodded slowly. "You were a little mite of a thing even then. With . . ."

Kitty waited.

"With eyes the color of wood violets." He seemed a little flustered for a moment but assumed his usual placid exterior almost at once. "You were still very young when you left Culpeper County, weren't you?"

"Six . . . only six," she stammered, still thinking of what he'd said about her eyes.

He took a drink of the steaming coffee. "I had gone to stay with Daniel and Rebecca by then."

"Why did you go?" she asked, recovering a little, and interested.

He ran a finger over the rim of the cup. "I had a yearning for the wilds, I guess. Papa said I reminded him of Daniel. They'd met years earlier in the war with the French. My father had been with the Virginia militia. Daniel, not more than twenty years old then, was a wagoneer for the troops."

"They became friends?"

Roman nodded. "When I was twelve, Papa agreed to let me go stay with the Boones at their place on the Yadkin River. I believe he hoped I'd get it out of my system."

"But you didn't."

"I guess not," he said, his expression unreadable. "But I did go back when I was sixteen. I did what my father wanted me to do . . . for a time."

"I know. Pa told me."

"Then you must know the rest. That my father is disappointed in an only son who would not follow the path laid out for him."

"Perhaps *could* not," Kitty said, her voice soft. "Ma says there are times when only we can know what we have to do."

Roman looked at her long and thoughtfully and had opened his mouth to speak when Callie Sherrill's agonized cry brought them both to their feet.

They hurried back to find that the baby was convulsing, his small head drawn back, eyelids swollen and faintly blue. Bending over him, lips pulled back from her teeth, Callie began a low keening, a sound that made Kitty's skin prickle.

"Get him to the creek," Elvie said, but Callie just stared, white-faced, as if she couldn't move, that same godawful sound still coming from her.

Amelia snatched up the baby, and she and the older woman ran the few yards to the water—Elizabeth Callaway had handed her little one over to Betsey and hurried to help. Callie managed, somehow, to get to her feet and follow—her arms and legs jerking like somebody with St. Vitus' dance, Kitty thought, watching.

Her arms crossed, hugging herself, Callie stood looking on as the women worked with the baby, bathing him in the cool water to try to lower the fever enough to bring him out of the convulsion. The others gathered to watch, helplessly. Priscilla had flown into Faith's arms. Fanny Callaway stood beside Kitty anxiously. Ben had knelt down and was praying quietly. And Robert Sherrill stood apart, beads of sweat standing out along his upper lip.

It seemed forever, and then there was a sorrowing "Oh, Lord!" from Elvie. And Kitty saw her mother lean her face down and begin to blow breath into the infant's mouth. After a little, when there was no response, she stopped, sagging wearily, and the three women, hunched yet over the still, wet little thing, turned to look at Callie, pity and grief in their eyes.

Callie was silent now, and for an instant could have been made of stone; then she held out her arms, and they passed the baby to her. She hugged him to her breast, as if by some miracle he might suckle once more, and then she turned, her eyes seeking out her husband.

He came to her, his face red and pinched, and together they walked into the copse of trees, back into the shady depths of pine needles and bunchberry.

"Shouldn't you take the baby, Ma?" Faith was pale. "Wouldn't it be better?"

Amelia shook her head. "They have to say good-bye. You can't short them that."

The child was buried there in the open meadow, a flat stone marking the spot. Into it was painstakingly scratched: ROBERT MORGAN SHERRILL AGED 6 MONTHS, ONE WEEK, THREE DAYS.

❋ 3 ❋

"LORD O' MERCY, THERE IT IS!" BEN TYLER SANG OUT. And there were cries of joy around, not unmixed with relief. On a hot and humid day, nearly two months after they had begun the hard journey, their destination was in full sight ahead—a rectangle of rude cabins on a high bank of the Kentucke River, which ran deep and beautiful between the rugged, steep shores of its southern side and the rising wooded hills of the far shore.

Roman called out a long "Helloooo," his deep voice reverberating. At an answering call from the fort, he lifted his hand and led the way past the corn patch and the small vegetable plot. The others followed, looking ahead, smiling and calling out to one another. The older boys urged the packhorses along, and Lady nipped at the heels of one old cow that was reluctant to budge from the lush green grass near to the river.

"What do you think, 'Melia?" Usaph grinned over at his wife.

She laughed. "It'll be good to get a bath . . . and sleep under a roof tonight."

"You and your baths, woman . . . It's a wonder they haven't killed me in twenty-five years of marriage." He shook his head good-naturedly.

It struck Kitty suddenly that, after nearly two months, she would not wake in the morning to climb back into the saddle and press on, sweating and slapping at the ever-present mosquitoes. She would not have to hurriedly wash out the strips of linen she needed to use during her monthlies and spread them over the top of one of the panniers for all to see as they dried. She would be able to boil them white again, and her petticoats and drawers as well. And wash her hair as often as she wanted. Pleasant thoughts, all.

They approached the hollow just below the fort, and Kitty could see that several men had emerged from the center gap between cabins spaced on either side at the front. They waved and called to Roman.

"I thought there'd be a gate," said Amelia, who rode just ahead of Kitty.

The fort did look unfinished, Kitty noted. There were no upright logs to form palisades between the cabins along the sides and the blockhouses at the four corners. Still, it was a welcome sight. In the hollow, two springs bubbled out of the ground, and not far away stood three tiny cabins, apart from the others up ahead. There were some sycamores of uncommon size and a huge old elm tree. Out to the right there was a sweep of cleared land, raggedy stumps here and there, a low-lying horizontal ridge in the distance.

As they made their way up the gentle incline to the fort itself, fully a dozen dogs raced toward them, yelping excitedly. Lady abandoned the livestock to advance cautiously, setting her legs stiffly, tail giving a tentative wag.

"By God, come on in here, Roman Gentry, and bring those good folk with you," a male voice sang out.

It seemed to Kitty, as she climbed down from her horse, that the whole fort had turned out to greet them—great, raucous men in greasy homespun and buckskins. But what they lacked in appearance, they made up for in the warm exuberance of their welcome. A crusty and bewhiskered fellow, whose name they would later learn was Ezekial Turner, caught up his fiddle and sawed a lively tune, jigging a little as he played.

"Whooee! If you girls ain't a sight fer sore eyes," whooped one young fellow, and the others around him shushed and jostled him, all of them grinning and elbowing one another for a better look.

"He begs y'r pardon, miss," another called out. "He's forgot his manners."

There was more good-natured jostling.

"Will ye leave off, 'Zekial?" a huge fellow, sleeves rolled up to show his heavy forearms, grumbled at the bearded fiddler. "Here comes Dan'l, and you makin' so much racket he won't be able to hear hisself fart, let alone talk."

Kitty looked at Usaph, but he just winked at her.

A middle-aged man with prominent cheekbones and sandy-brown hair pushed through the gathering, an already wide mouth stretching into a grin as he caught sight of Roman. "Well, it's about time I had the services of my best scout again." He clapped Roman on the back.

Roman smiled. "Daniel . . ."

"And you, Richard"—Boone turned to his old friend Callaway—"are a welcome sight. I confess I had begun to worry, since I have been here a full three weeks with Rebecca and the children. Any trouble?" He eyed the two men.

Roman shook his head. "No sign, even."

"Good."

Boone gave his head a nod and began to move among the new settlers, shaking men's hands and smiling a welcome to the women. Kitty watched, surprised at the thinning hair and sagging chin. Neither did she miss the beginnings of a paunch beneath the roomy hunting shirt. For most of her life she had heard about the exploits and adventures of the great scout and hunter, but to see the hero now in the flesh was more than a little disappointing. She had expected someone tall and lean and handsome, someone like . . . *Roman*. The thought occurred to her without warning, her eyes seeking the hard-etched line of his brow and nose and chin, turned away from her now in profile. She was thankful that the flush that rose to her cheeks seemed natural in light of all the hullabaloo.

"I know that Rebecca will be pleased to have you here," Boone was saying to Amelia Gentry and Elvie Porter. "She's been the only woman at Boonesborough thus far, except for my daughter, Jemima."

Kitty heard a giggle and turned to see a pretty, fair-haired girl who looked to be thirteen or fourteen amidst the Boone family edging through the group of men. There were five other children in evidence. The oldest—Israel, someone called him—was a pimply-faced lad of about sixteen, who stood by smiling quietly, while the littlest, a two-year-old, tugged at his mother's skirt until Jemima snatched him up. "Don't be botherin' Ma now, Jesse."

Rebecca Boone, a slender, dark-haired woman whose strength showed in her eyes, came forward to hug Elizabeth Callaway and make a fuss over the baby, which Fanny was holding. Saying hello all around, she rescued the women and older girls from the curious stares of the men, taking them inside the fort to show them to the cabin each family had been assigned.

"They don't mean any harm," she said of the men out front,

smiling. "They just need to look a little. Hadn't laid eyes on a female since last spring, I guess, until Jemima and me came in three weeks ago. They're all right, though."

The men present, she said, were only about half the actual number who'd come to Boonesborough. Some had gone back. Others had taken up land already and had built their cabins and planted a little corn to validate their claims. They only came in to socialize or to trade at the company store, which she admitted had little to offer, given the difficulty of getting merchandise in.

"Has there been any trouble from the savages since you've been here?" Elizabeth Callaway asked her.

"No." Rebecca Boone's finely freckled skin stretched across pleasing face bones, her eyes wide-set beneath a broad forehead. "Coming in, we saw a couple of Cherokee, but they were friendly."

Rebecca opened cabin doors as they went, all of them facing inward to the fort yard. Each was a small, one-room log structure with a fireplace of river stone and a cramped loft space above. There was one window in the front and, spaced along the back wall, two elongated loopholes just big enough to slide a rifle barrel through.

"Jemima and me tried to tidy up as many as we could for you," Rebecca said, "but the ones we haven't got to are a sight. You know well enough, I guess, how men are when they get off to theirselves. They hadn't even bothered to put up a necessary house when we got here. There's one now. Far end of the yard down there."

In the large, grassy center of the stockade, Kitty noticed several big iron pots hanging from cranes. A blacksmith's forge was set up, coals still glowing. The smithy, undoubtedly off with the rest of the men, had left his leather apron draped over a stump.

"I warned you." Rebecca Boone laughed ruefully as she opened a cabin meant for the Porters and the women beheld a rough, mud-spattered floor and a blackened hearth strewn with well-picked meat bones and moldy pieces of cornbread.

"We'll make short work of it," said Elvie.

"Jemima and I will help," Rebecca volunteered.

"We'll all help," said Amelia.

They left Elvie, who had already rolled up her sleeves, to walk ahead to the next cabin. Amelia lagged behind a minute to speak to Priscilla, and Callie Sherrill was already looking over her small place.

"How are you feeling, Rebecca?" Elizabeth asked her old neighbor. "And what of the baby?"

"Well enough myself, but the babe was stillborn."

"Oh, Lord . . ." Elizabeth clucked her tongue. "I'm sorry."

Rebecca nodded. "You'd think as many as I've had, it'd get easier to lose one, but it doesn't."

"I know." Elizabeth sighed. "That girl down there . . . Callie . . . We just buried her first out there a week ago." She shook her head. "He was a cute little thing. Six months."

Rebecca turned to look down the path to where Callie Sherrill stood, sunbonnet off, the breeze blowing curly brown hair back to reveal her set, pale face. "Poor child . . . I must speak to her later." After a moment she put a hand out to draw Kitty toward her. "And who is this pretty young woman?"

"Kitty Gentry, Mistress Boone," Kitty answered dutifully.

"So you're one of Roman's kin. I should never have thought it," Rebecca teased. "I thought all the Gentrys would have flaming red hair and be tall as sourwood trees."

Kitty laughed.

"You look like your mother. Such a little thing. But those eyes are different."

"Yes'm. Ma says they came from my great-grandmother." Kitty blushed, and Rebecca Boone smiled.

"Plain to see you'll have your pick of any of the young men out here. Mind you, choose well."

"Yes, Mistress Boone," said Kitty.

The older woman's hand quickened on hers. "You must call me Rebecca," she said. "It would please me."

While the women and girls pitched in to make the cabins livable, the young men of the settlement vied to unload pack-horses and carry in the household necessities, particularly for the Gentry and the Callaway cabins, which between them would house three pretty and eligible young girls. Meanwhile, Daniel Boone and some of the men closeted themselves in one of the blockhouses, which were roomy, two-story structures carefully built to withstand an attack.

Squire Boone, who was several years younger than his better-known brother and resembled him somewhat, manned a jug of corn liquor, one of several that Daniel's party had brought in three weeks before. The potent liquid was sloshed into tin cups and passed around the long puncheon table. Usaph and his son-in-law Ben, Henry Porter, and Robert Sherrill sat along one side, while Colonel Callaway, Roman, and the Boone brothers sat opposite.

"To your good fortune in Kentucke. . . ." Daniel lifted his cup.

"Hear, hear!" said Richard Callaway.

"Not bad a-tall," said Usaph, drawing the back of his hand across his mouth once he'd swallowed. The others nodded in agreement.

"Best enjoy it," Daniel said. "Once it's gone there'll be a long dry spell. What corn we've got will have to go for food. As you no doubt saw, we've also raised a sizable crop of potatoes and turnips and such outside the fort here. We'll be glad to share what we have to see you through the winter. We ask in return that you share your skills or labor with us."

There were nods of agreement all around.

"I expected that the palisades and the gates would be up by now," Roman said in his quiet way.

Daniel shrugged, an easy grin marking his high-cheekboned face. "We'll get to them when we can. I brought a goodly supply of salt with me, and we must commence to put away as much meat as we can before cold weather sets in. We don't want to starve over winter. The Indians won't move after first snow flies, and before that, it appears to me that they'd be reluctant to take on this many rifles.

"Since it is the last of September," he went on, "some of you may want to lay out your claims and then stay here at the fort through the winter . . . wait until spring to build your cabin. You're welcome."

Usaph shook his head. "I thank you, but I figure there's plenty of time before hard winter, and I plan to get my family settled as quick as I can."

"In the other stations"—Squire spoke up—"Fort Harrod and the like, the womenfolk and young'uns are stayin' within the fort for safety. You might want to think on that."

"My wife and me trust in the Lord to watch over us," said Ben.

Usaph scratched his chin. "If I know Amelia Gentry, she'll not take to stayin' any place but our own."

"Well, it's up to you," Daniel told them. "The offer to spend the winter here still stands if you should change your minds, or cold weather sets in too soon."

"I aim to do my best for it. I'm not as young as these"—

Usaph waved his hand at the younger men—"but I've a strong back and can still work beside any man step for step."

Daniel eyed the thick shoulders, the big chest. "I'd have no doubt of it. It must run in the Gentrys. Roman's father was always as strong a man as ever I knew."

Usaph nodded.

Daniel grew serious. "I would caution you all to be watchful when you're away from the fort. Always have your rifle to hand. As you may already know, we was attacked last spring as we made the journey in, and the savages killed four of us. . . . And after three days here, we found another of our men murdered in the woods over yonder, his scalp no doubt hanging this minute in a Shawnee lodge north of the Ohio."

"But what of the treaties?" Robert Sherrill asked.

Colonel Callaway snorted, tugging at a fleshy earlobe. "Treaties have been broken more than kept. 'Tis a mistake to be sure of anything when it comes to Indians."

"True enough," Daniel said. "On the other hand, there's been no trouble since then. No sign . . . And once winter sets in, I trust we'll be safe enough. I simply caution you to be on your guard."

Roman asked where Judge Henderson was, and Daniel said that he had returned to North Carolina on pressing business. His brother was still at the fort.

When they'd finally finished with their man-talk, Usaph sought out the Gentry cabin and was surprised to find the iron pots and skillets already hanging in the fireplace, and the ticks—now stuffed with sweet-smelling grass—placed neatly on the swept and scrubbed floor. Amelia's small framed looking glass, which she had wrapped carefully in quilts for its transport, hung on one wall, and the carved, mahogany Bible box rested on the floor beneath it.

While the girls placed wooden treenware and pewter mugs on a shelf they had put up, Amelia still scraped at the stained hearth.

"Damnation, 'Melia," Usaph said, laughing, "we'll likely only be here long enough to let me stake out the land we want and raise a cabin on it."

"That may be so, Usaph, but we'll not live like savages in the meantime."

He came to lift her gently to her feet. "That we won't," he declared. "I'll start on some bedframes tomorrow. But meantime, wash your face, woman. We're to be the guests of the fort this night. All of us. They're getting the coals ready now for buffalo meat and 'possums and rabbits aplenty.''

Amelia threw up her hands. ''And just look at me! Girls, see if I don't have a clean skirt in that pack over there. And, mercy me, I mustn't forget . . .'' She flew to retrieve the small leatherbound notebook and quill pen and ink pot that she'd guarded over the long trip.

She uncorked the ink, peering at the point of the quill to see that it was sharp enough, and then dipped it in. *September 26, 1775*, she wrote in her delicate hand. *We arrived at Boonesborough*.

In the next two weeks, with women and girls there, the small stockade had never seen such a spate of wash kettles and split hickory brooms, while the men exhibited a sudden craze for shaving and trimming of beards.

As the Gentry family settled into life at the fort, Usaph put to use his skills as a woodworker, turning out piggins and noggins, churns and washtubs, for all who needed them, in return for his share of the corn and vegetables. But every spare minute otherwise was spent looking over the land, deciding where he wanted to make his claim. As he had predicted, Amelia had refused to stay at the fort any longer than necessary.

''My lands,'' she fussed, ''just look at this place. Any savage with a mind to could walk right in if he felt like it. I guess I can close and bar my own door wherever we are.'' The Gentrys, she added, had come to make a home in Kentucke, and that was what they'd do.

Roman rode out with Usaph to show him the claim he'd made for himself upon his arrival the previous spring. It was a rich, gently rolling parcel of land, approximately six hundred acres in all, that took in the junction of Otter Creek and the Kentucke River—about a mile and a half above Boonesborough—and extended along each stream. With his responsibilities as head scout for the fort, Roman had no need for a cabin of his own, but he'd erected what was known as an improver's cabin to seal his claim. It was a symbol recognized by everyone on the frontier and consisted of a rough structure of poles, not more than four feet across, and without a roof. And he'd planted a few stalks of corn to complete the requirements.

He pointed out to Usaph that the land that bordered his own, which stretched still farther along the banks of Otter Creek, was not yet spoken for. And it only took a couple of hours of riding over the lush virgin land for Usaph to know that he'd found what he had been looking for.

The acreage was replete with tall cherry and walnut trees, groves of huge oak, ash, and beech, undergrown with the smaller dogwood, redbud, and tulip poplars. The soil was deep and loamy. Everywhere the eye turned brought forth new delights of luxuriant vegetation. Sweetbriar tangled beneath the nodding heads of giant sunflowers. Lacy ferns and green mosses stippled the banks of the creek, and there were three good springs—something that was vital in the selection of a homestead.

"Wait till you see it, 'Melia," Usaph enthused. "A rise that overlooks the creek . . . oh, not close enough to flood out. There's a spring out back of where the cabin will set, and two big sycamores that are a pretty sight. The trunks are rubbed white where the buffalo and deer have come up to scratch their hides after they've drunk their fill."

"When will you start?" Amelia asked, her cheeks fairly pink with excitement.

"Tomorrow. I've registered with the company . . . paid my money. And Roman and some of the others said they'd help." They were alone together in the cabin, and Usaph caught her up to kiss her on the lips.

The loft had proven to be too hot for the girls to sleep, and the four of them had ended up sharing the one room. Even now they could hear Priscilla and her friends talking just outside the window.

"I tell you one thing," he said. "I aim to build it big enough so's you and me can have our own room back." He slid his hand along the curve of her buttock, kneading it gently and pressing her to him.

Her eyes danced like a girl's. "Aren't you getting too old for that?" she teased.

"Are you?" he countered.

She drew a deep breath and touched his lips lightly with her fingertip before she answered in a whisper, "You hurry up with that cabin, Usaph Gentry."

Whether it was the unsatisfactory sleeping arrangements, the uncommonly good weather, or the fact that a dozen stout young men volunteered to help, the Gentry cabin went up quickly. It had two rooms below and a sizable loft, which Usaph had taken care to provide with enough ventilation. He even added a small porch for Amelia—a fact that was made much of. Everyone at the fort agreed that they didn't know of another cabin west of the mountains that had such a luxury. It took only a few days for Usaph to turn out the rough puncheon furniture that would have to do them until he had time to make proper pieces. They were able to move in by the last week in October.

"There's a world of work to do before winter sets in," Amelia told the girls, and the three of them set in to do it. One of the first things was to find a good place to set out the apple-tree seedlings that Amelia had heeled in as soon as they'd come to Boonesborough—laid them over on the ground by the cabin and covered the roots over with dirt temporarily so they'd live.

Usaph pointed out a good place, up the creek a ways from the house. Not as high as the land on which the cabin was built, it was still well drained, though covered with thistle and sweet-briar that would have to be cleared. Amelia and Kitty worked nine days cutting out the briars and digging out the roots, going home back-sore and exhausted, with scratched arms and blistered hands. There were times when Kitty had to press her lips together to keep from bursting into tears.

But finally they cleared enough space for the ten seedlings, and with Priscilla carrying water from the creek, Amelia and Kitty dug the holes and planted the young trees.

Amelia touched them tenderly. "They'll grow. You'll see," she said, though Usaph had already warned her that as late as it was, they might not get started well enough to survive the winter.

They tied up a hemp line to go with the wash kettle in the yard and set up the all-important ash hopper, which was crucial to the making of hominy and soap and other useful things. Priscilla couldn't do the hard tasks that her mother and sister did, but she took her turn at grinding the corn into meal, using a small hand mill. And she was learning to milk a little, though it was really Kitty's job.

The three of them gathered wild herbs, nuts, pawpaws, and wild grapes that had been sweetened by the first frost, all the time mindful of Usaph's warning that they must be careful whenever they strayed away from the yard.

"If you see or hear a thing that don't seem right, then yell a warning, fly to the house, and bolt the door and windows tight. I built it strong. No heathen's comin' through that door."

Meanwhile Usaph laid in wood for the winter and constructed a rough lean-to for the animals. He had already put together a passable wagon. But every minute he could spare, he worked doggedly at clearing a small patch near to the house where he would plant corn come spring.

Sometimes Roman would come to help. They'd take the bigger trees down then, hitching up Old Moll and Nell to drag them away.

One day Roman squinted at a clump of poplars at the edge of where Usaph had planned the first field. "We ought to girdle those," he said, wiping the sweat from his face.

Usaph considered it. "Make it easier to get out next year, wouldn't it?"

Roman nodded, and though they'd already put in a hard day's work, they went to work another hour, cutting away the bark in a ring around each tree to make it die.

"I almost hate to do it," Usaph said, peeling at the bark between the lines he'd cut with a hand ax. "But it's not an entire waste. I can use the poplar for something, I guess."

Each day, Kitty came to love the wild beauty of the place more. And as the weather stayed gloriously warm, she grew bolder. Unknown to Usaph and Amelia, she explored farther away from the cabin, sometimes going all the way down on Roman's land to where Otter Creek emptied into the river.

There were still late wildflowers in bloom along the shore, and great flat rocks that edged out into the creek where she could sit and feel the sun against her, watch the way it played along the surface of the rippling water . . . and on the splendid fall colors of the deep dense woods behind her. And each time she walked along the leaf-carpeted paths or sat out on the smooth white rocks, she felt again that it was untouched, that no one had ever been here before her.

Sometimes, close to the cabin, back where dense thickets shielded the creek, she and Prissy would stand watch for one another while they took turns stripping down and bathing, coming out of the cold water all covered with goosebumps, dressing quickly to run back home. One day, breathless and laughing, hair still wet, they came back to find Roman just arrived, their father on the front porch to greet him.

"Lord, look at 'em," Usaph said to Roman. "They've been in the creek in the altogether again. Just like their mother, for the world."

Kitty found herself blushing furiously as Roman looked at her, a slow smile coming to his face. "I was always told that it wasn't all that healthy to get yourself wet all over," he said, a definite twinkle in the blue eyes.

"Nor would any other than my females think so," Usaph shot back.

"I've heard that Ben Franklin has the same penchant," Roman offered, clearly trying to ease Kitty's discomfort. "Washes himself all the time. And it hasn't seemed to harm him."

Priscilla ran on ahead of her, while Kitty mumbled something about helping her mother and hurried off to dry her hair and make herself presentable.

Roman had brought the latest news from the east. Judge Henderson had held a meeting with a majority of the Transylvania Company's members, and it had been decided that the price of land would be advanced from twenty to fifty shillings per hundred acres.

"Damnation!" Usaph thundered. "Does that mean that they expect me to pay the difference?"

"I don't know," said Roman. "But there are mutterings. Over at Harrod's fort they're saying they didn't rebel against an English king to bow down to a judge."

Usaph nodded. "Richard Callaway told me that neither the Harrod people, nor Boiling Springs, nor St. Asaph's were much pleased when Henderson called his . . . what did Richard call it? His 'House of Delegates' meeting last spring. Said they didn't take it well to hear that the land they'd claimed really belonged to the Transylvania Company."

"I'd say they didn't. But it seems that the company has sent a delegate to the Continental Congress to persuade the members that Transylvania should be recognized as the fourteenth of the United Colonies."

"Is that likely?"

Roman shrugged. "They say that Tom Jefferson, for one, won't even discuss it except in the event that it be approved by the Virginia convention."

"And where do you stand?" Usaph asked.

Roman took his time answering. He sat on a rough bench with no backrest, leaning back against the cabin wall, looking out down the long stretch to the creek, which, through the brilliant orange and yellow trees, glistened like a ribbon in the sunlight. "I don't have anything against Henderson," he said finally, "though I have not been entirely comfortable with the idea of a proprietary government out here."

Usaph pondered that for a minute. "Well," he said at last, a frown creasing his forehead, "I guess they got me out here, and I'd best stand by them. For now."

"A man's got to do what he thinks he ought," Roman agreed. "They say that John Williams, an uncle of the judge's, is coming out soon. They've elected him general agent for the company. Maybe he can smooth things.''

Inside, Amelia had kept one ear open to the men's conversation. Now she took up the two large catfish that Usaph had brought in earlier—each stuffed with herbs and liberally encased in mud from the creekbank—and put them into the fireplace, carefully covering them over with hot coals. Once the mud had baked hard, it would be cracked off to reveal the succulent baked fish within. Wild greens simmered in a kettle. Kitty came out of the bedroom and began to mix up cornmeal and water for hoecakes, but Amelia took it away from her.

''Priss can do this,'' she said. ''You go out there and tell Roman that we're expecting him for supper.''

Smoothing her hair and the indigo linsey skirt that fell in soft folds about her legs, Kitty went out onto the porch. ''Ma says you're to stay for supper, Roman,'' she said, aware that her cheeks were abloom with soft color, and laying it to her cold bath in the creek.

''Tell her I thank her,'' he said. He looked at Kitty a long slow moment, and she could feel her blush deepen. ''It would seem this place agrees with you.''

''Indeed. I love it,'' she said.

All through supper, though Roman's face was as unreadable as always, she would find the blue eyes coming back to rest on her now and again, a kind of wonder deep within them.

✴ 4 ✴

KITTY LAY FULL-LENGTH ON THE SMOOTH, WHITE LIME-stone rock, her cheek pressed against the very edge, the fingers of her right hand trailing into the clear, cold water. The sun bore down, hot on her back, the weather still unseasonably warm with Christmas only two days away. She had put aside the woolen shawl she'd had about her.

Finished with the washing, and weary of grinding dried hominy into grits, she had slipped away for an hour to the place she loved best, here where the creek and the river met. She thought once again of the dance but two days ago, in one of the blockhouses at the fort, her cheeks brightening with the remembered pleasure.

Ezekial Turner had sawed a fine fiddle, and a Negro manservant had thumped out the rhythm on a makeshift drum while the settlers whirled and stomped their way through reel after reel. Kitty had danced until she was breathless, as had every female at the fort who was at all willing.

The men had turned out in their best and lined up, grinning and eager, hair slick and shining and beards trimmed. Flanders Callaway, dark and handsome, had pulled her onto the floor six times or more and danced that much again with Jemima Boone. Young Samuel Henderson, the judge's brother, had turned out to be a good dancer, and surprisingly enough, so had Israel Boone, who at sixteen usually seemed shy and awkward.

Kitty had been pleased to see Robert and Callie Sherrill having as good a time as any. Even her father and mother went out to the floor a couple of times. Roman, though, had sat in a corner the whole evening, watching the merriment, declining with a courteous smile whenever one of the Callaway girls had tried to coax him to dance.

She admitted now to some disappointment that he hadn't asked her for even one turn around the floor, though she had been aware of those intense blue eyes on her from time to time . . . especially when Pa had revealed that she'd always sung back at the Watauga socials, whereupon everyone insisted that she sing for them. Usaph had even tucked her dulcimore away, unknown to her, and brought it out then, to her surprise. The elongated, stringed instrument had been made for her by her father, who had acquired the art from his grandfather, who in turn had been taught by an old Frenchman originally from the Vosges mountains.

Kitty had sung shyly, her clear soprano lifting to the strains of "Barbry Ellen," all the time aware of Roman watching her from his place in the corner. He was unlike any man she had ever known before, so quiet and contained . . . so completely in control of himself.

The water, not far below her, rippled past with a lulling sound as she recalled the dance. She heard a bird call, soft and sweet, and a moment later another gave its answering cry. She should be getting back to the cabin, she thought. Ma might have missed her and be calling. But the sun was so pleasant that she lingered still, shifting her position to sit, cross-legged, looking down into the water to catch sight of a slow-moving turtle, its stubby legs moving awkwardly. She was still leaning forward, intent on the creature, when suddenly she was seized from above, a strong arm circling her roughly.

Frightened, she struggled against the iron grasp, her worst fears confirmed as she twisted to see the naked, oiled chest of an Indian, the gleaming dark skin of his head plucked clean of hair save for a thick, black scalplock.

"Pa!" Her shrill cry pierced the still air just as two more braves converged upon her. And then her mouth was covered and she was nearly strangling, the rank smell of bear grease in her nostrils, a hot terror scorching through her.

She was dragged a few feet, struggling all the way, but her efforts proved futile. Her arms were bound quickly to her sides, her feet tied securely, and a foul-tasting rag was stuffed into her mouth. Next she was dumped into the bottom of a crude canoe, really a hollowed-out poplar log, which had been hidden in the tall grasses by the riverbank. She could hear the slap of water and an occasional grunt as the rough vessel moved out into the current. But when she tried to lift her head, she felt a moccasined foot against her neck and lay quietly after that.

It was only a few minutes to the opposite shore—she could feel the canoe being hauled onto land, could hear the low, guttural exchange of the Indians—and the next moment she was hauled out and shoved sprawling. All of the bone-chilling stories she had heard—of dreadful tortures, of captives being made to run a gauntlet of savages armed with cudgels and knives, of poor wretches skinned or roasted alive, slowly so as to draw out their agony to the last possible moment—returned to torment her.

She had ended up on her back and was able to see her abductors clearly for the first time. All three were naked to the waist, coppery skin greased and gleaming, their lower parts clad in soft leather breechclouts and leggings. One wore a necklace of quail feathers, his features coarsely forbidding. The other two were younger, but equally frightening. One of them carried a rifle.

They untied her feet and pulled her upright, taking the gag

from her mouth, as if now that they were on the far side of the river, it didn't matter how much she might scream.

"Please . . ." It burst from her lips before she could stop it, but when the hard black eyes flickered over her contemptuously, she clamped her teeth together and vowed that no matter what they did, they would get no begging from her again.

Two of them hid the canoe, the older one barking out a few terse words, his face turned away for the moment. Impulsively she darted sideways, only to be jerked up short, the leather strip that bound her arms to her sides cutting cruelly into the flesh at her elbows. There was the barest hint of amusement in her captor's face as she realized she was tethered to him. Not only were her hands tied behind her back, but the strap around her upper body had a long thin line attached, the other end of which was fastened firmly to his sinewy wrist.

Once the canoe had been concealed in the bushes, the older one nodded and set out through the low brush. Kitty was forced to follow lest she be yanked down by the strap, and the others fell in behind her. While the gait he set seemed easy enough for him, it was difficult for her shorter legs; but she went ahead doggedly, knowing that if she fell or caused them trouble, it would go worse for her.

She must keep her wits about her, she told herself. There might yet be a way out of this, and she must find it. Ma would be calling her by now, and when she couldn't find her, she would fetch Pa from the field where he'd been grubbing out stumps. Pa would come after her.

No . . . It struck her cruelly. He wouldn't even know where to look. Nobody knew about *her place*. She had never told a soul, not even Priss.

Up ahead of her the Indian trotted effortlessly, and she realized that her breath was coming hard, burning its way into her lungs. She tried to slow it down, to make it deep and regular. She would have to pace herself or she'd never keep up. And the possibilities if that happened were too fearful to dwell on.

The terrain was rough, thick with trees and underbrush, yet the leader seemed to know exactly where he was going. She must try to figure out which direction she was being taken. That way, if she got free—*when* she got free, she corrected herself— she could find her way back.

She took a quick look to position the sun, blinking as the perspiration stung her eyes. It was slightly past her left shoulder.

She calculated quickly. That must mean . . . northeast. They were moving northeast.

A cold despair filled her as the significance of that burst upon her. The Warrior's Path. That's where they were headed—toward that ancient trace of the red men that bisected Kentucke and went right up across the Ohio. She had heard Roman and her father speak of it. Dear God . . . If they succeeded in taking her across the Ohio River into their heathen lands, she would be lost forever. Even should she survive . . . *she would never see her family again*.

Time after that became the effort to put one foot in front of the other, became brambles that tore at her clothing and limbs that whipped her long black hair and delicate skin, became an endless number of steep hills to be climbed and ridges to be slid down. They crossed shallow, rocky-bottomed creeks and sloughed through drifts of fallen leaves. Several times she fell, only to be dragged along the ground until her captor tired and turned back to set her roughly on her feet and yank her ahead once more.

The sun moved inexorably as the minutes became hours, but she had no concept of time or of the distance they had traveled; there was just the endless agony of going ahead, until finally she was hauled to a stop, her captors barking out a gruff command. She slumped to her knees, head bent forward, unable even to look around her at first.

After a while—she had no idea how long—one of the younger braves held a gourd filled with water to her lips and she drank greedily, realizing for the first time that her throat was so parched she could hardly swallow. She looked up into his face, realizing that if the circumstances had been different, she would have thought him a fine-looking man. But the black eyes fixed upon her were without expression. Was he giving her water, keeping her alive, so that they might have the pleasure of torturing her? she wondered.

The sun was almost down now, and she shivered in the rapidly cooling air as she watched him return to his comrades, who were seated a short distance away, eating something out of the leather pouches they carried at their belts. It was parched corn, she saw. They would take up several grains to shove into their mouths, crunching audibly, exchanging quiet comments as if it were a picnic. One of them even smiled.

Her strength returning, Kitty looked about her, noting they were in a clearing ringed close on by trees. She had been tethered to a sturdy sapling, limiting her movement to only a few feet in any direction. One of the Indians got up and moved to a sycamore tree a few paces away, and she watched as he reached into the hollow trunk and pulled out a packet.

In a moment he had unrolled the oiled-skin covering to retrieve a loose-fitting deerskin shirt, which he pulled over his head. He tossed the remaining shirts to the others, who soon followed his example, nodding while eating.

Her legs starting to cramp beneath her, Kitty edged to a sitting position, wincing with the pain that any movement set off. After a brief inspection, however, she decided that she hadn't yet sustained any grievous hurt—just suffered a hundred small scratches and bruises.

Cold through, she wished desperately for the woolen shawl she'd laid aside all those hours ago. The leaves and pine needles beneath her were welcome. At least they kept the full chill of the ground from her. She inched close enough to use the tree as a backrest, trying to restore the circulation in her numbed hands. A full bladder twinged insistently. She tightened her legs.

Her linsey dress was torn in numerous places; the top button of her bodice gone, to reveal the soft swelling of the tops of her breasts, the skirt rent from waist to hemline in one place. Her stockings were in tatters. She shifted to cover her legs better; there was nothing she could do about her bodice.

To her surprise, the one who had brought her water came now and pulled her up to untie her, freeing her wrists and then re-tethering her about the waist, the thin leather line secured in back. He shoved her back down again and cupped his two hands, muttering the same unintelligible words, or syllables, several times.

"Oui-then-eluh . . ."

She realized that he wanted her to cup her own hands, and she did, though they were stiff and numb from the long confinement. He took up the pouch at his waist and poured some of the roasted corn into them, then returned to his companions.

The last thing Kitty felt like doing was eating, but she realized she would need all her strength if she were to survive, so she took the hard kernels one at a time into her mouth, chewing them well and hoping she could keep them down each time she swallowed. The sun had set completely now, taking with it any lingering warmth of the day, and Kitty ate and shivered, watching the three Indians sitting some distance from her. Sooner or later they must sleep, she thought. And if they left her hands untied, maybe she could work the tether free and slip away. Perhaps they would not think it necessary to keep her secured this far from home.

Her bladder pained her insistently now, and she realized that it was only a matter of time until she would have to relieve it, no matter how tightly she kept her legs together. She rocked back and forth, glancing at the Indians now and again. She would not wet herself in front of these savages. The leather leash, she remembered, allowed her to move a few feet.

They glanced at her as she got to her feet, and one of them nudged another as she moved to put the sapling between them and herself. It was a slender tree, and certainly didn't offer much in the way of privacy, but she took advantage of it such as it was, lifting her skirt to show as little as possible, edging it up only as far as necessary to get her drawers down. She squatted quickly, releasing the warm, steaming flood.

She shivered as she put her clothing back in place, as much from the humiliation as the cold. Edging back around the tree, she found the three of them eyeing her solemnly, their faces blank.

She sank down and hunched forward, curling her body against her drawn-up knees, seeking what small warmth the loose leaves beneath her offered. She would not look at them, she decided. Let them sit and look at her all they wanted. Did they think that they would frighten her more that way?

As she continued to shiver, it occurred to her to wonder why they had not built a fire, as cold as it was, with the sky darkening now. Could it be that they were afraid to risk it? Afraid that someone might come after her and see the smoke and light? The thought cheered her. Undoubtedly, once Pa had not been able to find her, he alerted the fort. But that would have taken hours; a time before they realized she was gone. Probably an hour or two of searching. Then the ride to Boonesborough. Her courage began to waver. . . .

She heard the coarse, deep voice of the older of the braves, the one who seemed to be the leader, and she abandoned her decision not to look at them. Her captors were turning quick looks her way, with much gesturing toward her and low conversations. She steeled herself for whatever was ahead, reminded again of the stories of hideous tortures that had been inflicted upon white captives. Dear Lord, she prayed silently, a sudden wave of nausea assailing her, if I must die at the hands of these savages, then let me do it bravely . . . and quickly, please, when the time comes.

One of the younger men nudged the other, and when the leader nodded, the first one produced something from one of the pouches he carried. Carefully he cleared away the pine needles and leaves to make a smooth space, then flung the contents of his hand out before him. As the three huddled forward to peer at the ground, grunting, exchanging quick, short phrases, Kitty squinted in the gathering darkness, made out the objects of their curiosity—several small, smooth round stones, none bigger than a hickory nut. After nodding in agreement, the leader gathered up the stones and threw them out again to be studied with the same interest, but now the older man lifted his head to look straight at her, his eyes glittering in the dark.

It was with a sinking heart that she saw the remaining brave pick up the stones to take his turn. They were playing a game, she realized. And a new possibility burst upon her. A game whose prize was . . . *her*.

She drew her arms and legs in close about her, as if to make herself as small as possible, wondering miserably if she could work the tether loose and run now. But all three of them kept glancing at her. If she moved, they would be on her like hounds on a rabbit. And she watched in a kind of numb horror as the stones were thrown out once more and the thrower—the one who had given her the water—gave a hoarse cry of triumph.

The winner wasted no time. As the others hunkered where they were, faces impassive, he came straight to her and pulled her to her feet, touching a curious finger to one of her forearms, bending his head to peer at her violet eyes. But she couldn't hold back a gasp as, with that same air of curiosity, he began to unfasten the buttons left on her dress, clearly taken with the pale skin.

"No!" she cried, and pushed at him. But he seized her, holding her arms to her sides again as he finished what he had started, baring her from neckline to waist just as the moon emerged to bathe her exposed breasts with luminescent light, the nipples like dark rosebuds.

She tried to pull away, but he held her so firmly that she stopped struggling to stand proudly still. Though she was screaming inside, she made no sound, vowing once again that they would not make her beg or cry.

The brave's all but bald pate gleamed in the moonlight, and the rancid grease smell of him was nearly suffocating. His eyes were

deep-set, but now they opened wider as he stared down at her
fixedly, a kind of keening wail escaping him as, suddenly, he
drew back.

Confused, she watched as the others leaped to their feet to
join him, the three of them peering at her breasts almost as if in
fear, speaking their language in short, moaning bursts. She gathered the ends of her dress to cover herself, but they pulled her
hands away and continued to stare, shaking their heads and
keening still. Dear God, what was it? What had frightened
them so?

The birthmark. It was the birthmark they were staring at—
that small, rosy, crescent-shaped mark within the cleft of her
breasts. She fought back tears of relief, uttering a silent prayer
that whatever it was about the mark that had affected them,
would continue to keep them from her. With trembling fingers
she began to button her blouse again, and this time they didn't
stop her. Another of the buttons came off in her hand, but she
covered herself as best she could.

Warily she watched as the Indians argued, gesturing toward
her and scowling. Finally the older man brought down his hand
in a gesture of finality, uttering a sharp command. The other
two nodded, then came to bind her wrists securely behind her
again. She sank down, exhausted and cold but telling herself
over and over that she was still alive and unharmed.

The three braves stretched themselves out on the ground a few
feet away, and Kitty brought her legs up to curl herself into a
ball as much as she could, her teeth chattering in the cold wind
that had sprung up, listening to the far-off, mournful hooting of
an owl. After a while she dozed fitfully, jerking awake to shiver
miserably and then doze again.

With a start, Kitty opened her eyes as she had heard the dry
rustling of leaves and saw that one of the braves had gotten up
from his place and was now disappearing into the thick darkness
of the forest that ringed them, as if to relieve himself. The other
two did not stir.

Her arms had gone to sleep and she was trying to move them,
painfully aware of every muscle in her body, when she heard a
peculiar dull thud come from the direction that the Indian had
gone. To her surprise the other two were up instantly, leaping
to their feet, weapons already in hand. But before they could
move farther, the report of a rifle shattered the air, and the older
one uttered a piercing shriek, clutching at his chest as he fell
forward.

The remaining brave whirled, rifle in hand, and Kitty caught a flash of red hair and buckskin as Roman came diving headlong into the clearing.

"Roman . . . oh, my God, *Roman*," she whispered, her heart giving a great leap as he collided with the Indian to send the gun flying.

The two men locked together, the brave's powerful grip holding off the knife in Roman's hand. Falling to the ground, they rolled in a wild tangle of arms and legs that set Kitty gasping. In all the terrible hours, she had not given in to her fear, but now she had to bite her lip to cut off a scream.

Roman smashed at the Indian's cheek with his left forearm, and with the release of his right wrist, the knife flashed wickedly to bite into the brave's arm just above the wrist. The Indian howled, his lips drawing back, and Kitty moaned, faint as she saw the hand—nearly severed—flop uselessly, saw the sudden spurt of blood that sprayed upward. And in an instant Roman had driven the blade deep under the heaving rib cage.

The fallen man shuddered, working his lips, straining to stare at the white man above him. Then he fell back with a long grunt, to twitch and finally lie still.

Roman crouched above him for a moment, breath coming in deep, raspy intakes; then, satisfied that the red-man was dead, he pulled out the knife to give it a quick swipe against the dried leaves and grass. A second later he was beside her, cutting the leather strips that bound her.

"You all right?" he asked.

"I—I think so," she managed.

"Then come on. . . ." He lifted her to her feet and, grabbing her hand, hurried her from the clearing, stopping only to pick up the Indian's rifle and then his own where he'd dropped it just into the thick growth of trees. "There may be another party nearby. Two boys were taken close to the fort."

After that he said no more, and it was all that Kitty could do to make her legs work. But he hauled her along after him, and then, in the moonlight up ahead, she saw the big sorrel gelding. An instant later Roman had lifted her into the saddle and swung up behind her.

The well-trained horse moved silently, surely, winding through the trees as if he knew the way himself. And Kitty could feel Roman close up against her back, could feel the warmth of his body. Exhausted, relaxed, she let her head rest against his chest.

* * *

They had been riding for the better part of an hour when Roman turned the horse up a narrow draw that extended between two sharp ridges and ended with a sheltered overhang of white limestone rock. Dismounting, he lifted Kitty down, then hitched the animal loosely to one of the feathery pines that clung amidst the rocks, rising above the dried wild buck and cockleburs. Silent still, he motioned her back toward the shallow shelter that the jutting limestone shelf created.

Back there the ground was cushioned underfoot, thick with springy mosses, and Kitty huddled out of the freezing wind, her lips blue with the cold, her hands and feet numb. In a moment Roman brought a coarse woolen blanket that had been rolled up behind his saddle and handed it to her.

"Th-Thank you," she said, her teeth chattering as she draped it about her. "Will we be safe here?"

"Any to come up that draw"—he jerked his head to the front of them—"will have to do it one at a time."

They sat down out of the wind, and Roman placed his rifle carefully beside him. He pulled out a handful of jerked buffalo meat and offered some of it to her.

She shook her head and pulled the blanket closer about her, managing a smile for him. "I don't know when I've ever been so glad to see . . . anybody."

"It's my job," he said, and there was a downright grin on his face, the blue eyes laughing for a moment as they both remembered the other time he'd come to her rescue.

He set to eating the dried buffalo hungrily.

"You said two boys had been taken?"

He nodded. "Sam McQuinney and David Sanders. You know them?"

"Yes," she said.

"Henry Porter's oldest boy, Marcum, and the other two were exploring around. They'd crossed the river when Sam and David were captured. Marcum saw them taken. The Shawnees fired at him, but he got away to warn the stockade."

Kitty thought of the youths at the mercy of the Indians this night and she shivered. "How did you know that I'd been taken, too?" she asked. "Pa?"

He shook his head. "I didn't know. Daniel formed a party to go after the boys, but I struck out alone. I reasoned that they'd be heading toward the Warrior's Path. Before long I'd come on sign. I could tell there were three Indians and a captive. Figured they'd already killed one of the boys.''

She watched as he finished the jerked beef and then reached for his goatskin water bag. He undid the stopper and offered it to her. She took a couple of swallows, and then he drank, wiping his mouth with the back of his hand.

"Then you didn't know it was me they had until you came rushing in?'' she asked.

He was silent for a moment before he answered. "I'd been there a while.''

"Close by?'' she got out finally, thinking of what had happened in the clearing.

"A few feet away in the bushes.''

She felt her cheeks burn. "Why didn't you come in earlier?'' she asked, looking away.

"I was afraid they'd kill you before I could stop them. I had to wait for the right time.''

She sat huddled within the folds of the blanket, face still turned away as she wondered just how early Roman had been there . . . if he'd seen. His next words answered her, as if he realized that it was better for her to know than to wonder.

"I . . . was ready to come in before,'' he said slowly. "But then I saw that they were scared off.''

She nodded, cheeks still warm. "A birthmark.''

"Moon-shaped?''

She faced him. "Crescent.''

"I thought as much,'' he said. "I understand enough Shawnee to make out that they thought you'd been marked by their gods—the moon and sun figure in their religion. They decided they should take you back to one of their chiefs . . . or failing that, kill you so no unworthy male could take you for a wife.''

Kitty caught her breath; whatever embarrassment she'd felt before lessened in the harsh reality of what he'd just told her.

"I don't think they would have harmed you,'' he hurried on. "Not . . . that way. The Shawnee do not usually violate their female captives.''

He got up then, his moccasined feet making no sound as he left the shelter and went beyond her sight, moving within the cluster of pines that offered some small privacy. In a moment he was back. "I'll not risk a fire, and there's only the one blanket,'' he said, looking down at her.

"Oh . . . of course,'' she said, the full meaning of his words

coming to her. She got to her feet. "I'll just, uh . . ." She
looked toward the pines where he'd gone, and he nodded.

She went quickly, shivering in the deepening cold. She felt
shy about it, although she didn't know why. In the weeks coming over the trace, it had become commonplace to see one of
the party go into the bushes or seek the privacy of a broad tree
trunk. The obvious necessities had become a part of everyday
living. But now, as she squatted in the feathery shadows of the
trees, she was grateful for the pine needles that covered the
ground. At least Roman couldn't hear her. And hadn't she done
what she had to do before—practically in full sight of the Shawnee?

Hoarfrost gleaming underfoot, she hurried back, teeth chattering. She found Roman already stretched out with the blanket.
He lifted one corner at her approach and she slid in gratefully,
instinctively seeking the warmth of him.

She was still shivering too much to feel the quiver that went
the length of him as he opened his arms to her, and she burrowed
into him like a small animal seeking a nest.

"Oh, Roman," she said on a sudden impulse, "you could
have been killed back there. Trying to save me."

"Hush," he said. "Go to sleep."

She smiled in a kind of tired relief and closed her eyes. But
despite her weariness, maybe even because of it, she began to
be acutely aware of the musky scent of him, of the hard muscles
of his chest and thighs as he lay, half turned away from her. Then
she realized that he was holding himself rigidly straight, his
body tense.

"Roman . . ." She edged up to ask him what was wrong,
and her movement brought her full against the hard man-part of
him. Sensations that she had never experienced before coursed
through her; a delicious heat grew between her legs, and the
nipples of her breasts swelled to bursting.

There was a groaning rumble deep within Roman's chest as
his arms tightened and his mouth sought hers, his open lips
demanding entry as if he would drink her in and be drunk in
return. And all the while he pressed her to him with those strong
arms, the hard, big hands caressing her with a tender urgency.

The hidebound conventions of the East seemed far away. Even
in the settlements along the Watauga, it wasn't unheard of for a
girl to be rounding by the time she was properly married, and everyone pretended not to notice. The preacher himself showed no
undue concern as long as the young man did his duty by the girl.

But though Kitty was aware of all that, she had determined to let no man touch her until they were wed. She thought of that now, fleetingly, but Roman's hand was on her breast, his mouth still tasting hers, and there was a hot, sweet bubbling in her veins, as if she'd had too much of Pa's elderberry wine.

This was what it was like, she thought. And it would happen now. She wanted it now . . . her body aching with the need of his. But suddenly Roman wrenched his mouth away.

"Kitty," he gasped, shoving her away from him as if the very devil himself were driving him. "God's blood!" he swore, withdrawing from the blanket to sit, knees drawn up, his back against the hard limestone rock behind him.

Stunned, Kitty lay there for a moment, unable to speak. She couldn't make out his face—it was deep in shadow—but she saw the big hands on his knees, saw how they spread to grip the buckskin-clad legs as if he must hold himself to the spot.

The rising wind whispered among the pines, and nearby a cone dropped to the frost-covered ground with a muted rustling of needles.

"What is it, Roman?" she asked, her voice barely audible, her body still aching in the warm echo of their touching. And when he didn't answer: "Was it me? Did I do something wrong?"

"*You?*" he burst out. "My God! You are . . . the sweetest maid a man could ever want, Kitty Gentry. And I'll not dishonor you."

"But, Roman—"

"Go to sleep, damn it!" he cut her off. "That's what we both need to do." With that, he got up to move past her and out into the open, taking his rifle with him and stretching himself full length beneath one of the pines.

Kitty lay there, miserable and somehow shamed. All the bruises and scratches and small cuts she had suffered that day pained dully, and her ankle throbbed where she had twisted it sometime during the long day's march. She curled herself up as tightly as she could and closed her eyes, the scratchy blanket drawn nearly over her head.

The minutes passed slowly, and though exhaustion was so deep it hurt, she still did not sleep. After a while the cold bit into her, even with the blanket, settling into her very bones, it seemed. She shook as if she had an ague.

"Roman," she called finally, her voice small within the

woolen folds. "I—I'm s-so—c-cold . . ." She could hardly form the words, her teeth were chattering so.

After a long moment there was a tug at the blanket, and as he slid in beside her, he turned her as easily as if she were a baby, turned her so that her back was to him, and drew her into the warmth of his arms. Neither of them said a word, and after a while the paroxysms that shook her body quieted and she slept, never knowing what it cost him to keep her warm that night.

Once, he raised himself to look at her, moonlight bathing the wild tangle of her black hair, casting a pearly luminescence that played along the delicate curve of her chin, pooled in the soft hollows of her throat. The thick lashes lay heavy against her cheeks, and she gave a deep sigh, shuddering in her sleep.

He drew her closer and she quieted, but the burning for her forced a quiet groan from his lips. God, it had been so long since he had held a woman in his arms.

Kitty was so stiff and sore that at first every movement caused her to wince, but now, finally, she had settled in to the steady plodding of Roman's horse. The night wind had swept in colder weather, and the sun, even when it peeked through the clouds, seemed bleak and pale. The blanket was draped about her, Roman close behind her in the saddle.

Upon waking they had spoken little, and nothing of the night before. They'd hastily eaten the last of the buffalo jerk and gotten on their way when it was barely light, the hoarfrost still thick underfoot, mists rising in the hollows.

From time to time Roman dismounted to scan the ground or climb a steep ridge to let his eye sweep the horizon. Then he'd come back to swing up behind her and give that soft and easy cluck of his tongue to set the horse in motion. And now the hesitant sun emerged once again from a bank of gray clouds, showed signs of growing stronger as the morning wore on, and the big sorrel shook his head and snorted, his light red hide rippling.

The animal had covered the rough country well. He was one of a fine strain bred by the Chickasaws, Roman told her in a burst of conversation, in which they'd crossed Spanish horses from the West with their own native breeds. "Got him from an old chief a couple of years ago," he confided. "Traded him three pack ponies, an ax, and a rifle. I got the best of it," he added dryly. "The rifle sights weren't true."

"He's a good horse," Kitty said numbly, glad that she was

facing forward and he couldn't see her face. The dried buffalo lay heavy in her stomach, and nausea climbed up her throat. Memories of the night had begun to beat at her, to fill her with humiliation. She had been ready and willing, and Roman hadn't even wanted her . . . though he was kind enough that he'd tried to make her feel better about it. But that was the way of it, and she would just have to accept it, no matter how ashamed she felt.

The undigested dried meat caused a sudden roiling in her stomach, and she grew dizzy, leaning forward over the horse's neck.

"Are you all right?" Roman pulled the animal to a stop and in a moment was helping her to the ground.

She waved him away and ran into the screen of trees and bushes to drop to her knees and retch up the contents of her outraged stomach, heaving until there was nothing left to come up. Swaying weakly, she sank back on her heels when it was done, catching her breath as the queasiness began to subside.

What else could happen? she wondered miserably. If she'd wanted to shame herself forever in the eyes of Roman Gentry, she couldn't have done a better job.

After a moment she took up a handful of dry grass to wipe her face, then went slowly back to where he waited. He draped the blanket around her and insisted that she rest in the sunshine for a little.

They were in a circle of blackgum trees; a few brilliant red leaves clung to the branches yet, and the wind, still brisk, sent more fluttering to the ground. Roman made her take a drink from the waterbag.

"Better?" he asked.

She nodded.

He pointed far up ahead of them to a steep ridge in the distance that was covered with the pungent green of pines, a glimmer of rich gold here and there to mark the maples. "See that ridge off there? The river's just beyond that. No more than a mile."

"The Kentucke?" There was a soft little catch in her voice.

"That's right. We'll have to travel up it a ways, but that's it."

She drew in a breath at the thought that she would be home before too long. "Let's go," she said.

"Not yet." Roman's face was set into lines more serious than usual, even for him. "There's something I have to tell you first."

"If it's about last night, I expect there's no need." Her reply was quick.

"I think there is."

There was about him now that deep and quiet gentleness that Kitty had seen so often, yet he was the same man who had fought with unleashed ferocity in the clearing the night before. Blood, darkened now, still stained the front of his hunting shirt.

"Grant you, the circumstances didn't help"—a wry smile crossed his face—"but as I fancy myself a man of honor, it was greatly wrong of me to allow what happened . . . to happen. Since"—his eyes blazed, fiercely blue and honest—"I have a good wife who waits for me."

For a long moment Kitty was dumbstruck, could only look at him in astonishment. "A . . . a wife?" she stammered at last.

"Aye, back in Virginia."

"You never said . . ." It was almost an accusation, and she bit her lip to keep from saying more.

He looked away. "I never thought it necessary until last night."

They sat in silence, Kitty holding back the tears that were suddenly choking her. All she wanted in the world was to be back home on Otter Creek, to go up to her pallet in the loft, redolent of seasoned wood and the sweet, musky scent of dried wild rose petals which she'd gathered and sprinkled beneath the thin, grass-filled ticking.

"Could we go now?" she said.

He nodded.

❋ 5 ❋

THE FORT WAS ON FULL ALERT, AND SQUIRE BOONE, TAK-ing his turn as one of the three posted lookouts, saw the big sorrel gelding at a distance coming at an easy pace up along the riverbank.

"Roman's comin' in," he called out, shading his eyes in the

brightening sunlight. "Looks to be carryin' somebody up front o' his saddle."

The word passed quickly throughout the stockade. Ezekial Turner, who was making himself a new pair of moccasins, left the awl and buffalo hide lying on his cabin step, and Rebecca Boone and Elizabeth Callaway, who were cooking up a batch of soap in a big iron pot, left the bubbling mixture to see to itself.

In the cabin where the Gentrys had spent the night, and where Priscilla had just burst through the door to tell them that Roman was coming and somebody was with him, Usaph and Amelia just looked at each other for a minute, their faces telling the strain of the past twenty-four hours, despair struggling with the spark of hope that flickered now.

"Come quick!" Priscilla cried as she ran back out into the fort yard, pushing her way through the others who were turning out of their cabins. And as she caught sight of the horse and its riders coming through the gate gap now, she screamed out, "It's Kitty . . . Roman's got Kitty!"

The tall scout in buckskins, and the pale, obviously exhausted young woman with the blanket wrapped about her, were hardly on the ground before they were surrounded. Amidst lusty cheers and thankful smiles, Usaph and Amelia embraced Kitty repeatedly. Amelia's face worked painfully, though she set that strong little chin hard, and Usaph reached again and again to pat his daughter's face.

Daniel clasped Roman's shoulder. "Where did you find her?"

"Up northeast of here. Toward the Warrior's Path."

Daniel nodded, and Colonel Callaway crowded in close. "How many of them?" he asked.

"Three." Roman turned to retrieve the rifle he'd taken from the Shawnee. "Took this from one of them." He handed it over to the Old Colonel. "There might have been other weapons, but I didn't think it was exactly the time for a thorough search."

"How's the girl?" Daniel asked.

Roman's eyes went to Kitty, who was being hugged by Rebecca Boone at the moment. "She's bruised and scratched up some, but I think she's all right. Any trace of the others?"

Both Daniel and Colonel Callaway shook their heads. "We picked up sign more than once, then lost 'em," said Daniel. "We're fixin' to go out again."

Roman felt a tug at his arm and turned to find the McQuinney boy's mother at his side. She was a frail little woman, birdlike and red-eyed from weeping. The McQuinneys had only arrived at the fort a short time before.

"Mr. Gentry," she said, her chapped hands twisting and turning as if she couldn't keep them still, "have ye seen ary sign of my boy out there?"

"No, ma'am," Roman said, his voice soft. "But I'll be going out again with the others. We'll do our best to bring him back."

Kitty was being taken away now, clucked over by the womenfolk.

"Lord, the child is pale as a ghost," Elizabeth Callaway said. "Thank God Roman found her."

Rebecca Boone nodded. "What she needs now is to be quiet with her kin. She'll be all right after a while. If there's anything we can be doin' for you, Amelia . . ." she called. And Amelia Gentry gave her a grateful smile.

In the privacy of the small cabin, Usaph peered at his daughter anxiously, his eyes moist. "Did they . . . harm you, girl?" His voice cracked.

Kitty knew what he meant. "No, Pa," she said, and the moment the words were out, she heard the slightest expelling of her mother's breath.

"A few bruises and scratches . . . you'll be healed up in a week with not a mark to show for it," Amelia said, rearranging the blanket that Kitty still had draped about her shoulders. Her hand stayed for an instant as she caught a glimpse of the torn bodice, barely hanging together with only a couple of buttons left. "Usaph," she said, her voice carefully even, "why don't you go ahead out with the menfolk so she can get washed up some. And Prissy, you run ask Mistress Boone if Jemima could lend her some clean clothes to wear."

The minute they were gone, Amelia barred the door and came back to sit on the sagging, straw-filled mattress beside Kitty to hug her with her strong, sure arms. She drew back to touch one of the buttons with her forefinger, then looked her daughter straight in the eye. "There's not a thing you can't tell me," she said.

Outside, they could hear the sound of voices and the clang of the smithy's big hammer as he commenced to pound hot iron again. Light spilled in through the open window and made a square pattern against the rough floor.

"They didn't do anything, Ma," Kitty said. "They might have, but . . ." She told her mother the whole story, the part about the stones and the game they played, and the Shawnee unfastening her dress, then looking like he was scared to death when he saw her birthmark.

Amelia gave her head a shake. "Little did I know on the day you were born, and I looked down and saw that red splotch, that I'd ever be thanking God for putting it there. But I do." She squeezed Kitty's hand. "Whatever would have happened without it, would have happened. And we'd have lived with it. But"—some of the flinty set to her mouth softened ever so slightly—"I'd not have it be like that for you, Kitty, honey. Lord, Lord . . . it ought to be right for a girl her first time."

Roman's face was suddenly there behind Kitty's eyelids as she looked down at her lap, and a hot swelling gathered in her throat and spread until it seemed to fill her.

A fire burned in the fireplace, smoking slightly. "Well"—Amelia began to bustle about—"I'll just fetch in some water for the kettle, and you'll feel better once you're cleaned up. Looks like you've been dragged halfway to Pennsylvania and back."

Kitty managed a smile. "Can we go home after that?"

Amelia had started toward the door, but turned back to consider it. "Daniel says the Indians seem to have hit and run toward home," she said. "Besides, I don't think your pa's going to let a handful of heathens keep us away. If you feel up to it, I don't see why in the world not."

So they were back at the cabin on Otter Creek in time for supper. And while Amelia and Priscilla fixed it, Usaph went out to the shed, where the animals, in from the woods, waited patiently. Lady followed along after him.

Leaning his rifle against a rough-hewn post, he fed the stock corn nubbins and fodder, as the pickings weren't so good for them since the heavy frosts, and now the horses stamped against the soft earth, and the two cows made low, moaning sounds as they chewed, their udders full and ready. And though milking was a woman's job, Kitty's chore, Usaph drew up the three-legged stool and sat to press his head against the warm and hairy flank, coaxing the animal to let her milk down for strange male hands. "Saw, boss . . . saw . . ." In a moment the rich milk streamed into a red cedar piggin, to froth and steam in the chill, dusky air. His daughter, Usaph thought, need do nothing this night.

They were all tired, emotions drained, and they went to bed soon after they'd eaten. Kitty drifted off at once into a deep and dreamless sleep, wrapped in the safety and healing privacy of her own bed there in the loft. But Priscilla slept restlessly, plagued with visions of menacing red faces and reaching arms. Finally she started awake, perspiring freely in the frosty air that seeped in under the eaves and through the ventilation slots that Usaph had provided.

Damp, and now cold, she drew the bedcovers closer about her and peered through the darkness, trying to make out the form of her sister on the other side of the loft . . . trying to make sure that Kitty was really home. And safe. Trying to assure herself that the Indians had none of the Gentrys. Yet they had had Kitty. If it hadn't been for Roman, Kitty would have been gone forever. All of it opened up possibilities that the little girl had not considered before.

She slipped from her bed and, barefoot, felt her way down the steep steps lit only by the glow of the banked coals in the fireplace. She could hear her father's hearty snoring as she nudged open the door to her parents' tiny room. The half light fell upon the folded red coverlet draped over the blanket roll of the tall, four-posted bed, the one piece of what Usaph called "real" furniture he'd taken the time to make for the cabin. Amelia's blue-and-white pieced quilt was pulled well up to Usaph's chin.

With a mother's light sleeping habits, Amelia opened her eyes at once and edged up to put a finger to her lips. She slid out of bed, carefully tucking the quilts around her sleeping husband. And once safely out in the main room, the bedroom door shut, she peered into the woebegone face of her youngest daughter and put a hand to her forehead.

"You're not sick, are you, Prissy?"

Priscilla shook her head, wheat-colored lashes heavy on her cheeks, her face clammy and pale. "I had a dream. . . ."

Amelia set her mouth and nodded her understanding. "You've sweated right through your nightclothes. Let's get you into some dry things," she said matter-of-factly. And she went to the two rush baskets in the corner that held clean clothes, rummaging through them to find a pair of drawers and Priscilla's other nightgown.

The girl stripped down quickly, her childish figure shapeless as a boy's. As fast as she could, she pulled on the pair of drawers her mother handed to her, tying the drawstring about her waist, then she slipped the linen nightgown over her head and down.

Amelia threw a chunk of wood into the glowing embers and punched up the fire with the iron poker that Usaph had had the blacksmith make for them. As the flames licked up, a soft light spilled into the room to flicker against the rough table and chairs and around the log walls. Pegs held Usaph's coat and Amelia's hempen apron. Still others held shawls and linen bonnets and Usaph's stained felt hat. There was the soft sheen of pewter from a shelf, and above the stone mantel the long rifle had its special place, along with the powder horn and bullet pouch.

"I've got just a pinch of tea left from back home," Amelia said, putting her arm around Priscilla. "Might be nice if we had it now."

Priscilla nodded, and Amelia ladled some water into the iron tea kettle and hooked the bail onto the iron crane to swing it in over the flame. "Stay close by the fire. I'll be right back," she said, and went quietly into the bedroom, to return a moment later with the small tin of tea in her hand.

She sat down with Priscilla on the bare floorboards—which she'd finally scrubbed almost smooth—there before the stone hearth, the two of them in their pale, long nightgowns, Amelia's hair hanging beneath her ruffled cap. Priscilla lifted her face, cheeks pinker now, to gaze solemnly at her mother.

"What if Roman hadn't brought Kitty back? What if the Indians had got her for good?"

Amelia put her arm around the girl, who moved in even closer, and the two of them rocked gently. "That would have been terrible," Amelia said after a long moment. "But . . . terrible things happen sometimes, Prissy. And we would have had to stand it. Somehow." Her voice sounded hollow in the dim light of the room.

"What about Kitty?"

"She would have had to stand it, too."

They were quiet for a moment; the kettle had started to make a slight hissing noise.

"Do you want me to light the grease lamp?" Amelia asked.

Priscilla shook her head. The "Betty" lamps, as some called them—shallow little iron cups that held whatever grease was available, a lip at one end to hold a wick—smoked a lot, and she didn't like them. The two of them continued to rock gently, the warmth of the fire on their faces.

"What if the Indians had taken me instead of Kitty?"

"They didn't."

"But they might have."

"They might have." Amelia nodded. "But they didn't."

"What if . . ." Priscilla said after a minute. "What if they'd taken all of you and I'd been left . . . by myself?"

Amelia hugged her closer. "Why then," she said cheerfully, "you'd still have had your sister Faith, and Ben—you know the way to them. And there are the Callaways, and the Boones, and the Porters . . . Besides, Prissy, honey"—she grew deadly serious—"no matter what happens in the world to you, no matter how hard it is, you've always got yourself. Mind that, now. You're a Gentry. And a Sutherland from my side. You can manage with that if you have to. You remember that."

Priscilla nodded, her small face grave and somehow older.

"But then," Amelia continued in a lighter tone, "there's not a bad thing that'll ever happen to you in the world if your pa and I have anything to say about it. Kitty is safe. And you and I"—she grinned—"are about to have ourselves a fine cup of tea."

And once it was made, each cup sweetened with a spoonful of honey and lightened with a little milk, the two of them laughed softly and felt conspiratorial, and deliciously guilty, as they drank the last two cups of the precious brew.

Christmas was celebrated with a mixture of feelings by the Boonesborough settlers . . . joy that Kitty had been snatched back from the Shawnee and sorrow that the two boys were still missing. At the cabin on Otter Creek, Amelia had the Gentry dinner a day late, insisting that Roman must join them and waiting until the latest search party had returned to the fort, again with no sign of the boys.

She'd brought in some pine boughs and twined them over the shelves and the mantel the way she always had back home for the holiday. The Delft cups and saucers had been brought out, and the cabin smelled of a whole roasted 'possum, and fried rabbit, and persimmon pudding.

Roman arrived first, and Kitty was just as glad that Faith and Ben followed almost immediately, Ben sniffing appreciatively as he stamped in over the porch, clearing his boots of any remaining snow—a scant inch had fallen overnight. Faith was pink-cheeked, and she hugged her sister soundly.

"Kitty," Ben said, patting her lightly on the shoulder, "we thank God for your safe return, but in future think twice, little sister, before you go so far from the cabin." He was dressed in his best black wool suit for the occasion, the one he had always worn to Sunday meeting back on the Watauga, and now he hunched forward to peer down at her from his stringbean height, his eyes so colorless they all but looked pink sometimes. "Remember, you might not be so lucky next time," he added with a thin smile.

"It's true," Faith chimed in, touching a finger to one of the scratches that still marked Kitty's pale cheek. "Next time you might not have Roman to rescue you."

Kitty glanced at Roman, standing aside and looking splendid as he stretched out his hand to Ben. For once he had doffed the hunting shirt and wore a soft unbleached homespun shirt that lay open at the collar to reveal a touch of fine red hair. "You're right," she said. "It was foolish of me, and I'm very grateful to Roman."

"Enough talk about it," Usaph boomed as he came forward to give his son-in-law a friendly clap on the shoulder and kiss his older daughter. "Kitty's been through aplenty, and no need to upbraid her."

Faith still had on her dark blue woolen cloak, and as Usaph reached to take it, she hesitated a moment with the ties, an enigmatic smile coming to her lips. Since they had their own place to see to, the Tylers had not been overmuch at the Gentry cabin. Though Ben had been in contact with everyone, Faith had not seen her family or traveled in to the fort for nearly four weeks—a time that had brought about substantial changes in her figure.

As the concealing garment fell away, Usaph could only stand for a moment and stare, his jaw hanging. But Amelia, who'd handed Priscilla her big wooden spoon and started forward to greet them properly, fairly flew at her daughter. "Faith Gentry Tyler," she gasped, "you're carryin'. And getting along, too."

Faith nodded and grinned, wisps of thick, wheat-colored hair, exactly the same shade as Priscilla's, escaping from the fat braid that encircled her head. She stole a quick look at her husband, whose cheeks were reddening.

Amelia embraced her daughter, who was a head taller than she. "And why in the world didn't you *tell* us?" she remonstrated.

"Damnation, but that seems a reasonable question," Usaph bellowed. But he was grinning broadly, and the moment he could pry his wife loose, he swept Faith into his great bear hug and then held her out to look at her once again. "What were you aimin' to do, Faith, girl? Wait until the little one arrived and then bring him over to surprise us?"

"Him?" Amelia teased her husband. "If you can't get a son, you're bound on a grandson? Is that it, Usaph Gentry?"

Priscilla was dancing about now, her braids flying, and Kitty stole a look at her brother-in-law to see that he was smiling, a pleased look lighting the pale eyes.

"Why didn't you tell us?" Amelia demanded once more.

"Well . . ." Faith glanced toward Ben. "I thought you'd just worry. With the trip out here and all."

"You're *that* far?" said Amelia.

Faith nodded. "I thought for sure you'd see the last time I was over. But Ben"—her eyes flickered back to see how he was taking it all—"thought it wasn't proper to talk about before we had to."

"Fiddlesticks!" Amelia snapped. "Nothing more proper or natural in the world."

"Can I play with the baby when it gets here, Faith?" Priscilla tugged at her sister's elbow, and as Faith assured her that she could, Roman was shaking Ben's hand once again, a smile of genuine pleasure softening the hawklike features.

"It would appear that congratulations are in order," he said.

"But we'll want to know about it right off next time," Usaph laughingly warned his son-in-law.

Despite his natural rigidity, Ben was clearly pleased with all the fuss. "Yes, sir," he said.

While all that was happening, Kitty had reached out a hand to Faith. "I'm glad for you," she whispered, aware of such a sharp and inexplicable rush of anguish within herself that she could scarcely breathe for a moment. And then Usaph's big voice was booming through the cabin.

"We've been blessed for this holiday. And though we've come to it a day late, it's time for the eatin'. What about it, 'Melia?"

"It's ready. We just have to take it up. You menfolk get on to the table." And she proceeded at once to the big fireplace and began to turn the hot hoecakes onto a wooden platter.

Kitty and her sisters went to help, pouring milk, putting the pot of honey and the yellow round of rich butter on the table, fetching the hoecakes and cooked turnips. There were wild greens, which had simmered long in the big iron pot, seasoned at the last with the rich drippings from a whole roasted 'possum. And last of all there was the 'possum itself, surrounded by fried rabbit heaped high and carried to the table on a big wooden trencher.

Everyone crowded into the chairs, and Usaph said the grace, which included special thanks for Kitty's safe return and the blessing of a coming grandchild. Ben sounded a loud "Amen," and the eating began.

Kitty was glad there were so many there. It kept her from having to think about what to say to Roman. As she picked at the brimming plate that had been passed to her, she relived the moment when he'd first arrived and had stood for a moment, looking down at her, a kind of question buried in his eyes.

"I hope you're feeling better," he'd said. And she'd known that he was really asking if she had forgiven him for what had happened that night.

"I am indeed," she was quick to reply, and even managed a smile. No matter how she felt inside, she knew that Roman had not shamed her intentionally. And of all men, he probably would reproach himself the most if he felt that his behavior had been less than honorable.

Now, the sounds of laughter and the dull clinking of pewter filled the small cabin. There was much talk of the expected baby and a vigorous discussion of the best name for it, whether it be a boy or a girl. And then the spicy persimmon pudding, chock full of dried wild grapes, was served, and everyone assured Amelia it was the best they'd ever tasted.

As Ben finished off the last bit of his, licking his lips appreciatively, he mentioned that he needed to clear several large trees from his intended corn patch before the spring. Usaph volunteered his aid, and the two men looked inquiringly at Roman, who could always be counted on to pitch in a few hours, if he wasn't out scouting for the fort. But Roman shoved his plate away and shook his head.

"Wish I could help, but I'll not be here. I'm leaving first thing tomorrow for Virginia."

Usaph laid down his spoon. "Well . . . what in the world would take you back to Virginia with the worst of the winter settin' in?" he demanded. "Surely Daniel's not sendin' you on company business?"

"No," said Roman. "It's personal. And the best time to go. Once the first snow falls, the Indians generally keep to their towns north of the Ohio until spring. And . . . it's time I fetched my wife to Kentucke."

There was a silence. Kitty sat very still in her chair, eyes on her plate.

Amelia leaned toward Roman as if she might not have heard him correctly. *"Wife?"*

Roman nodded.

"You mean to say"—a grin split Usaph's face—"you've got a wife back in Virginia and this is the first we've heard of it?"

"Closemouthed is one thing, Roman Gentry, but not saying a word about a wife is another," said Amelia, half chiding.

Roman smiled his good-natured half smile. "It never seemed to come up in conversation," he said.

"I thought you and *Kitty* would get married," Priscilla piped.

"Oh, Prissy!" Faith said, and Kitty forced herself to laugh along with the others.

She heard the talk go on, Usaph asking who the girl was and Roman answering that her name was Sara. One of the Barkley girls, he added. Usaph said, Yes, he knew her daddy. And Kitty ached to escape to her spot and throw herself down on the smooth, cold rocks and dip her fingers into the icy water. Maybe, she thought miserably, it would have been better if the Shawnee had just taken her on to their camps north of the Ohio. . . .

But she had too much of her mother in her to entertain such foolishness for more than a minute. Roman had a wife, she told herself, whom he obviously valued. And that was the way it should be. There had never been anything more than kinship between them . . . that and a certain closeness at times. But nothing more until that night. And even that was really nothing. . . .

Usaph had brought out the long-awaited persimmon wine. "I'm not sure if we ever had more to drink to than today," he said, beaming. It was the first time he had worn a stock about his neck since arriving in Kentucke, and he looked very grand at the head of the rough table, his best red waistcoat stretching across the bear chest. He lifted the pewter mug, then hesitated. "Tell me now," he said with mock severity, "are there any more secrets to be out this day? Name them in case there's something more to raise this fine wine to." He peered down into the cup. "Well, fine enough, since it's all we've got."

"Make the toast, Usaph," Amelia prodded, smiling.

"Go ahead, Pa," Faith called out, her cheeks flushed prettily.

Usaph nodded, his eyes going to Kitty. "We've had a daughter returned safely to us—". His voice cracked.

"Praise be," Ben added.

"And," Usaph went on, his gaze moving to Faith, "come spring, from the looks of it, there'll be a grandchild at this table."

"Don't forget Roman's wife, Pa," Priscilla put in.

"I'll not, Prissy, girl." He grinned at her. "And Roman will be bringing his good wife to join us here in this fruitful and wondrous land. . . .''

They all drank, Kitty lifting her cup as high as any and welcoming the sharp new taste of the brew on her tongue.

After coffee in the Delft cups, the women cleared the table and went about the chores of cleaning up, and Usaph sought out Roman for a quiet exchange.

"It appears that you've set your mind on fetching your wife here as soon as you can. I understand that as well as the next man. But is it wise to travel those mountain passes when deep snow could fall without warning? You could be trapped up there. Might you not think about holding off till spring? 'Tis sure you couldn't start back before then anyway.''

Roman shook his head, a pair of small lines appearing between the red brows. "I'll get through all right, Usaph. I've waited a time to have Sara with me. Too long. And I'll not wait longer.''

It was December 27, the day after the dinner at the Gentrys and several hours after Roman's departure for the East, when a group of hunters from the fort came across the scalped and mutilated body of the McQuinney boy at the edge of a cornfield about three miles north of the river. There was no trace of young Sanders. And while officials of the company offered £5 for the scalp of each of the fleeing murderers, Colonel Callaway and Daniel privately shook their heads and agreed that the Shawnee were long gone, safe in their encampments beyond the Ohio. Even if the Sanders boy were still alive, they said, the chances that he would ever be heard from again were slim indeed.

✻ 6 ✻

WINTER SETTLED IN, BARE TREES STARKLY BEAUTIFUL against the sky and hills, naked branches relieved here and there with green patches of pine and spruce and cedar. The snow fell in deep, windswept drifts, and thin patches of ice froze in the creek where the water eddied in and stilled along the shoreline. Out back of the Gentry cabin, where the spring bubbled out of the ground year 'round, it became commonplace to see not only the smaller animals, but deer and elk come to drink, picking their way hesitantly, as if wary of the human smells about.

Usaph had heard stories of indiscriminate killing by some of the first arrivals on the Kentucke River last spring, and he refused to take advantage of the thirsty animals. "It don't seem right," he told Amelia.

"Fiddlesticks!" she said. "What difference does it make whether you shoot one here or half a mile away, Usaph?"

It just did, he told her. When he needed meat for the family, he took up his rifle and trekked the short way into the bright, cold woods where he felt he was not taking advantage. It was a fine point, he admitted to himself, but a point nonetheless.

Within the Gentry cabin the main room with its fireplace was always snug and warm, and mealtime saw ample meat and turnips and hoecakes. Amelia occasionally wished out loud for something green, and most of all for a bit of ham meat—civilized meat, she called it—to replace the wild-tasting game. But the boar and sow that roamed like wild things in the woods to root and grunt and then return for corn nubbins and slop from the house had to be kept for breeding. The spring would bring on a litter of fat piglets, and by next winter, Usaph assured her, they would have "civilized" meat.

With winter firmly upon them, Usaph at last had time to work on the furniture he'd promised. First he commenced on a much needed clothes press, and then he did a settle, working the wood patiently, his hands touching it as a man might touch a woman he loved. Once finished with those pieces, he proceeded, much to Amelia's delight, to make a fine chest out of cherry, cutting and fitting the dovetailed drawer fronts to perfection, rubbing the light reddish wood until it gleamed. Though he had never spoken of it, he had not forgotten the look on his wife's face when she'd had to leave her chest on the trail.

Amelia and the girls had their share of winter chores, too. Whenever they had an extra moment, they saw to the never-ending basket of mending. And they knitted, and spun, and wove cloth on the small loom that Usaph had put together for them. They had no flax or sheep's wool, but they had found tolerable substitutes for both. In the fall they had gathered wild nettle, which grew in abundance, and soaked the pods to retrieve the silky fibers within. For their wool they used buffalo hair, which was not hard to find; the big animals not only shed, but aided the process by rubbing up against trees. Though the herds had retreated a few miles from the settlements, there were still plenty of the woolly wads of hair to be found, and that and the nettle fiber combined to make a fair linsey-woolsey.

One day as Kitty worked at the spinning wheel, Priscilla suddenly rose from her chair where she had been stitching on her sampler, her eyes bright with wonder, finger outstretched.

"Look, Ma . . ." She pointed toward the wood box where a huge butterfly was perched on the rim, slowly opening and closing its wings.

"My lands!" Amelia exclaimed, putting aside the knife she'd been using to cut up a pair of rabbits that Usaph had brought in earlier. "What a pretty thing!"

She and the girls moved closer, Kitty caught by the brilliant yellow and orange and black of its wings. "How could it have gotten in here in the dead of winter?" she asked her mother.

Amelia gave her head a wondering shake. "Must have been a cocoon in some of that wood your pa brought in. It's been nice and warm here next to the fire. Likely thought it was spring and time to come out. Lord, Lord . . . it's a pretty thing," she said again.

Kitty nodded her head as she watched the delicate wings fold and unfold.

They could hear Usaph stamping his feet on the porch to clean them of snow, and in a moment he'd thrown open the door. With the flood of brilliant sunlight, the butterfly stirred and lifted, fluttering toward the bright light.

"It wants to go out," Priscilla cried, following after it.

"It'll die out there," Kitty protested.

"It'll die in here," said Amelia. "Best it die doing what it needs to do."

"What in the world . . . ?" Usaph stood aside to stare as the butterfly dipped and rose and cleared the open door.

Kitty hurried out, along with her mother and Priscilla, the three of them standing together on the porch in the freezing air to watch the lovely creature climb straight up into the sunlight.

"I've always been partial to them," said Amelia, her voice touched with awe. "Always thought that if God Himself decided to come down to earth, He'd come as a butterfly. I would if I were God."

Kitty stared up, losing sight of it in the light so bright that it hurt her eyes.

Despite their assurances that there had been no way to save the creature, Priscilla's eyes filled with tears and she sat glumly once they'd returned to the warmth of the cabin. Finally Usaph told them all to get their cloaks and bonnets and scarves.

"I've decided we should go into the fort this afternoon. Ben told me yesterday that the store had got in a new shipment. Who knows"—he bent to kiss his youngest daughter on the forehead—"there could even be some rock candy in there. Or some marchpane."

They all knew that no such luxuries were among the new supplies, but all the same, Priscilla dried her eyes and went to get her warmest cloak.

There were many such visits to the fort, which was the gathering place for all, over those cold months. It was quickly evident that, though no one worked harder than the settlers, no one welcomed a party more. Every couple of weeks, when the weather permitted, there was a dance or a social, and Kitty was much in demand to play and sing at the events.

She received three proposals of marriage that winter—two from eager, strapping young men who professed their undying love for her, and the other from a widower with grown children, a man as old as her father. She turned them all down as courteously and gently as possible.

The second week in March, as stubborn patches of snow were beginning to give way to a warming sun, Faith gave birth to a baby girl. Kitty stayed a week at the Tyler cabin until her sister was strong enough to take charge again. And though she enjoyed taking care of the new baby, she was nonetheless disappointed to see that the pale, bony little thing was a Tyler through and through. Nothing of the Gentrys about her. They named her Martha, after Ben's mother.

During the first week in April a group of new settlers arrived at Boonesborough, and a supper was planned to welcome them properly. With the chores finished for the day, the Gentrys arrived in late afternoon.

The huge old elm and the sycamores in the hollow were bursting with a rich and pungent green, the dogs barking and the fort yard stirring as usual. Several of the smaller boys chased about after a gray cat that one of the new settlers had brought in with him. Little Jesse Boone was doing his best to keep up with Junior Callaway, but he fell sprawling, his small face red with frustration as his nine-year-old sister Lavina picked him up and brushed him off.

Priscilla ran off to show Lavina her new doll with its stitched face, and hair from Old Moll's tail plaited into stubby braids. Amelia and Kitty, with aprons brought from home, headed straight to the blockhouse, where the women had gathered to prepare the meat for supper.

The Callaway girls and Jemima Boone came hurrying to Kitty as soon as they saw her, eager to tell her all about the new arrivals. Six families and as many unattached men had come in.

"There aren't any girls amongst them," Jemima revealed, a touch of disappointment in her voice.

"But one of the women, Mistress Maggie Hamilton," Fanny Callaway put in, nearly breathless with the telling, "looks like a girl herself, though her husband is old." She looked over toward the women. "She's not here yet."

"Rafer Moore," Jemima added, "was smitten the minute he saw her. Said it was a pure shame she's already spoken for."

"So it's lucky you didn't say yes to him," said Betsey.

Kitty couldn't help smiling. Rafer Moore was one of the young men who'd asked her to marry him.

"Betsey is afraid that Sam Henderson will take a shine to her," Fanny teased her sister.

"Don't be silly," Betsey said.

Fanny made a face. "Well, you like him."

"Yes, I like him." Betsey's dark eyes danced, her handsome

Callaway face suffused with color. "And he's asked me to save every dance for him tonight."

"Well, I aim to dance with Flanders, and as many times as I can," Jemima declared. "If he'll ask me."

"Oh, he'll ask you. He asks everybody," Fanny said, clearly hard put to understand why anyone would be interested in her older cousin.

Some of the men brought in a basketful of skinned and gutted game to be cut up, and the girls were called to help.

"Have you heard anything from Roman?" Jemima asked, hanging back a minute to speak to Kitty.

Roman's name had come up in the Gentry cabin often lately, with Usaph certain that he must be on his way back to Boonesborough by now. But over the passing of weeks and months, some of the sting had gone from Kitty's memories of the night they'd spent in the woods together. She had even come to feel a certain curiosity about Roman's wife. "No," she answered Jemima. "Your father's not had word from him?"

Jemima said he hadn't.

"Mind you put that big apron on," Amelia told Kitty. "No use to get blood all over your clothes."

Elizabeth Callaway had brought little Johnny over in his cradle, and he was sleeping peacefully, oblivious to all the commotion. Priscilla and the other girls her age had been charged with watching the younger children.

As Kitty went to one of the tables and began to cut up one of the rabbits, she glanced up to see a tall, full-figured, auburn-haired young woman in a fine cotton dress—the likes of which none of them could boast—coming in the door. It wasn't hard to guess that this must be the Mistress Hamilton who had turned the head of fickle Rafer Moore.

Amelia had commenced to cut steaks from a haunch of deer meat that one of the men had just brought in, and as Mistress Hamilton caught sight of the bloody flesh, she drew her skirts in close to her legs and stepped back a pace.

"I must say," she confessed to Elizabeth, averting her eyes, "that I've never been much of a hand at kitchen work. But I'll be glad to send my girl, Rainy, over here. She's a good girl," she rushed on. "Thank goodness Horace let me keep her. He sold all the others before we left home. I swear I don't believe I'd have survived the trip without her."

As the pretty young thing fled the blockhouse, dabbing at her nose with a lace handkerchief, Elizabeth stood looking after her and shaking her head.

"Mercy," Amelia said not unkindly, "I wonder how long she'll last out here?"

Elizabeth raised her fine dark brows. "Richard says that Horace Hamilton lost most of his money because of the war. Something about trade. Says he's come out here hoping to rebuild."

"Well," Amelia said, taking up her knife again, "I wish them well."

Kitty and Betsey exchanged glances, but just then the men started to bring in parts of the buffalo the hunters had brought back, and the work began in earnest. Though most of the butchering was done, steaks had to be cut, and the tongue and hump—which some considered the choicest parts of the beast—readied for cooking.

"Would you bring in some water?" Amelia called out to her daughter. And Kitty wiped her hands and went to take up one of the cedar pails by the door.

Priscilla, playing rag ball with little Jesse, gave her sister a wave as she started up the fort yard. Up ahead of Kitty an old grandmother came out of the Hawkins cabin, squinting in the afternoon sun. The Hawkinses had been the last family to come in last fall.

The old lady had just risen from her afternoon nap, and now came along the rutted and grassless path on her way to the blockhouse, a rough hempen apron over the faded brown homespun dress. Despite her advanced years, she was a spry little thing, with white hair wisping from beneath a lace cap as she continued with her measured pace. She spread her mouth in a toothless smile as Kitty approached her.

"Good day, Granny Hawkins," Kitty said. "How are you, ma'am?"

"Tolerable." She peered at Kitty. "I heered tell your sister birthed a baby," she croaked.

"Yes, ma'am," said Kitty. "A girl."

"A girl, were it?" The grinning gap of her mouth widened, the faded eyes beginning to sparkle. "Did she have ary bit o' trouble?"

"No, ma'am."

"Well, I'da been glad to help if she did. I've done a world o' doctorin' in my day."

"Yes, ma'am, I know that," Kitty said. "We would have come for you if we'd needed to."

The old lady nodded and continued on her way like a skinny bird, stepping carefully over the ruts.

With the clang of Winfield Burdette's hammer and the sizzle of hot iron echoing, Kitty went on down the path, noting the new stockade wall on the far side; sharpened posts that stood ten feet above the ground had been put in place to fill in the gaps between cabins over there. She wondered when the others would be put up.

She went through the gate gap, looking toward the garden in close to the fort. The peas and onions were already showing green. Though there would be a variety of meats for supper that evening, there wouldn't be a lot else. The potatoes were all gone. What turnips they had left were pithy. There'd be hot hoecakes and buttermilk and honey. And it would do. But it was heartening to see turned ground and growing things again.

She let her gaze move over the burgeoning clover that swept all the way to Hackberry Ridge, as the far, low-lying ridge in the distance had been dubbed, and she drew a deep breath and felt a sudden flush of pleasure at being alive, and safe, and where she was.

Down in the hollow, the water from the usable spring—the second one was sulfur water—bubbled out into a small clear pool, and Kitty dipped her bucket in and brought it up dripping, pausing to scan the horizon as she heard a male voice call out: "Rider comin' in."

She saw the black horse, a magnificent animal, coming at a smooth pace along the riverbank, and was sure at once that the rider was no one she knew. Dressed in buckskin, wide-brimmed slouch hat set to a jaunty angle, he sat his saddle as if he'd been born in it, his mount almost an extension of his muscular body. As he drew nearer to the spring, she saw a pair of dark gray eyes fix on her with an unabashed pleasure and a broad, well-defined mouth curve into a devilish, and altogether appealing, grin.

To her surprise, as the horseman drew abreast of her, he reined in, dismounting and sweeping off his hat to reveal an unruly thatch of dark hair that escaped its leather whang to curl about his ears and sideburns.

"Well, I'm damned," he said, still grinning, "if you aren't the prettiest girl I've laid eyes on from the Holston Valley clean to the Illinois country. . . ." There was the slightest hint of a burr in the rich voice. "And absolutely"—he expanded the outrageous compliment—"prettier than any I ever saw back east."

Even if she hadn't been standing dumbfounded, she'd have

had little chance to respond, because he clapped his hat on the back of his head at once and, without a moment's hesitation— or a word of permission from her—took the pail of water right out of her hand. "I'll just take this for you . . . Miss . . . ?" He looked into her eyes and waited.

"Gentry . . ." Kitty managed to get out, her heart giving a strange little flutter. "But . . . wait . . . there's no need . . ."

"Always a pleasure to assist a lady." He swung into an easy stride, and she had no choice but to fall into step beside him if she wanted her water back.

He was just above average height, though the broad chest and well-muscled arms and legs made him seem bigger. And as Kitty stole another look at him, she noted the fancy fringed leggings and quill-embroidered moccasins.

"It occurs to me, Miss Gentry," he said, those gray eyes laughing, "that a girl as pretty as yourself would have a fine given name, also. Now, what is it?" he coaxed.

"It occurs to me," Kitty said tartly, "that I don't know any *part* of your name, sir."

He threw back his head and laughed, white teeth gleaming and even. "Cullen Claiborne's the name, at your service." He peered down at her. "Well . . . ?" The black brows arched.

"Kitty," she said, grinning in spite of herself.

"Kitty is it? Kitty . . ." It came out of his mouth like a caress.

The young men who had been working the firepit had heard the lookout's call and, curious as always about a visitor, had gathered outside the gate gap. Now, one half-grown boy darted out to bring in Cullen Claiborne's horse, and Daniel and Colonel Callaway pushed through the knot of men, welcoming smiles on their faces.

"Cullen," Boone called out. "About time you paid us a visit."

"Daniel . . ." Claiborne returned the greeting, obviously in high good humor, and as Kitty hurried to keep up with him, she became more and more embarrassed at the questioning glances turned her way.

"Thank you, Mr. Claiborne. I . . . I'll take it now," she stammered the moment they were within the fort yard. She reached for the pail of water, but he swung it just out of her reach.

"Daniel . . . Colonel"—Claiborne inclined his head—"I'll be with you good men directly, soon as I deliver this pail of water to wherever this enchanting lass wants it."

There were nudges and grins among the young men. Even Daniel and the Old Colonel seemed to be having some trouble keeping their faces straight, and Kitty's cheeks burned.

"Down there . . ." She pointed in desperation toward the blockhouse where the women were, then fled down the path. Claiborne followed amiably, and his arrival among the ladies and girls set off a fair amount of tittering as he deposited the pail on a rough bench and doffed his hat.

"Cullen Claiborne!" Elizabeth Callaway's face lit up, and wiping her hands on her apron, she held out her arms. He came, grinning, to give her a hug. "I see"—she drew back to eye Kitty and the pail of water—"that you haven't changed a bit."

"I do hope not." He winked at her. "Tell me, who'd want to change a fine lad like me?"

"Get on with you," she said. "We've got work to do or there'll be no supper . . . or dancing."

"Dancing?" His eyes sparkled, laugh lines crinkling about the corners. "I'll go, then . . . if you promise to save a dance for me," he teased her.

Elizabeth laughed. "I'll leave that pleasure to Kitty here."

The bold eyes swept her way, and Kitty could feel a falling away at the pit of her stomach. "Aye," he said, grinning. "I'll have my dance with Kitty Gentry if I have to fight every man in Kentucke for it."

He started for the door but turned back so that he was beside her in an instant. "Are ye kin to Roman Gentry?" he asked.

She realized that her mother was watching the two of them and grew even more nervous. "Do you know him?" she asked.

"Aye," said Claiborne. "Are ye?"

"He's a cousin," she told him, and he nodded and turned away.

He gave a jaunty salute as he exited the blockhouse, and in spite of herself, Kitty looked after him through the open door, watching that easy stride that some might go so far as to call a swagger. Rebecca Boone, who had returned to her cabin to fetch a sharp knife, came out of her door, and Cullen caught sight of her and went at once to sweep her off her feet in a great hug.

"Rebecca, my love!" Kitty heard him sing out. And it was clear that Rebecca was as much under Cullen Claiborne's spell as any.

Kitty jumped as she felt a hand on her shoulder. "I think the girls could use some help over there," Elizabeth Callaway said, her eyes twinkling.

"Yes, ma'am," Kitty said, and went at once, her face hot.

Betsey Callaway was cutting up turnips. "Imagine that," she said as Kitty joined her. "Cullen Claiborne has come to Boonesborough. To stay, I hope."

"Who is he?" Kitty whispered.

"A scout. One of the best, according to Pa."

"You know him, then?"

Betsey grinned. "Just barely. Pa used to send Fanny and me to bed early those nights he came to visit back home. We heard Elizabeth say that he had a scandalous reputation with the ladies, and we weren't even sure what that meant back then. Still, we used to get all in a tizzy when he'd come, and both of us agreed that he was the handsomest man we'd *ever* seen."

"And still is." Fanny had come up behind them. "Now aren't you sorry you promised every dance to Sam?" she taunted her sister.

"I didn't! Well, not *every* dance," Betsey countered. "I think I could manage one for Cullen Claiborne."

But the object of the girls' conversation no longer had dancing on his mind. At that moment he was closeted with Daniel and the Old Colonel, the three of them hunched over a table, and for once Cullen Claiborne's handsome face had taken on a serious mien.

"The British are doing their damnedest to stir the Indians against the Kentucke settlements," he said flatly.

Daniel ran a hand over his thinning hair. "You're sure, Cullen?"

"Not a doubt. I ranged over the northwest country in the fall. Kaskaskia. Vincennes. Even went up around Detroit . . . though"—he grinned—"I didn't go into that British bear trap. It'd be hard to pass myself off as a Tory with this accent."

The Old Colonel and Daniel smiled, but their eyes still mirrored the gravity of the news.

"I got caught up there for the winter. Found myself a little cave and stayed there snug as a bear till I could travel again. The minute the ice started to break up, I headed down and crossed the Ohio below the falls. Come straight on down to Harrod's fort and Boiling Springs. Jim Harrod said he'd get word to Ben Logan down at St. Asaph's."

"How soon can we expect to see trouble?" Callaway asked.

Cullen leaned back in his chair. "Hard to judge." His eyes narrowed and a faint smile marked his face. "I had a little Wyandot girl . . . sloe-eyed little thing . . . helped me stay warm in that cave from time to time. According to her, the

British are agitating, but the Wyandot are nervous as whores at a Sunday meeting. They're not sure they can trust the British. Haven't made up their minds yet. But they will. They all want the same thing, them and the Brits. To drive the settlers out of Kentucke. And since the redcoats have their hands full in the East, they'll use the Indians. Won't be hard to get the Shawnee to go on the warpath. They'll do it at the drop of a hat. Could be this year, could be next, but they'll come.''

"Lord help us," the Old Colonel said.

"The Lord, and ourselves," said Cullen.

Daniel rose to walk to the open window and look out on the fort yard. The presence of womenfolk at Boonesborough was much in evidence now. Rain barrels at the corners of cabins, soap kettles about, and here and there a window that boasted a faded scrap of curtain . . . more than likely someone's petticoat once upon a time. The aroma of roasting meat was beginning to permeate the air.

He turned back to the table, his slightly paunchy figure silhouetted in the light coming from behind him. "How would you like to stay on here and scout for me?"

Cullen's eyebrows lifted. "I thought Roman was here."

"He is. Gone back east to fetch his wife. He should be back before long. But I can't think of a thing I'd rather have here at Boonesborough than the two best danged scouts on the frontier."

"I'll second that," Callaway chimed in, drawing his chin high, his strong face framed by the thick shock of silver hair.

It was Cullen who rose now, and glancing through the window, his eye fell on Kitty Gentry, who was coming along the path with one of the Callaway girls. No one had a better sense of womanflesh than he did. Despite her stout leather shoes, he caught a glimpse of slim ankles and let his gaze move upward to the lissome figure which, to his practiced eye, was clearly evident beneath the homespun waist and skirt. Her head lifted as she said something to her companion, the fine dark hair swirling about her face.

After a moment he turned back to the waiting men. "It occurs to me, gentlemen," he said, grinning, "that there's no place I'd rather be right now than Boonesborough."

A score of tallow dips lit the blockhouse where the dances were usually held, and as usual Ezekial was in fine fettle, his old violin tucked snugly under a bewhiskered chin, his bow sawing away at a foot-stomping pace. Since the place was used mainly for storage, it was easy enough to clear out, and a few benches had been placed along the walls where the older folk could sit and watch, clapping hands to the music if they were so minded.

The floor gleamed in the candlelight: in the fall, corn siftings had been spread at every get-together so that moving feet could polish the rough slabs of wood to an oiled smoothness. The air was close with the press of bodies, and absent of anything stronger to drink, the wooden dipper in the water bucket by the door was being passed freely; the younger boys were kept busy with refilling the pail.

After two dances Usaph and Amelia had retired to the sidelines to watch the young people, and to visit with Elvie and Henry Porter, who'd come in from their place. Old Colonel Callaway looked handsome in brushed buckskin, the candlelight burnishing his silver hair. Even Daniel looked splendid. Rebecca had prevailed upon him to don a pair of woolen breeches and a soft homespun shirt.

The ladies had brought out what finery they possessed for the occasion. There were bits of lace and long sashes and embroidered linen shawls in evidence. Kitty had worn her best indigo-dyed linsey dress, which she saved for special times, a length of precious velvet ribbon in her hair. But it was Maggie Hamilton's entrance in a tight-bodiced green satin dress and white silk slippers that brought forth admiring glances from the men . . . and looks of envy from the younger women.

It was the slippers more than anything that stung Kitty; she glanced ruefully at her own feet to see the clumsy leather shoes, polished so carefully with soot from the fireplace mixed with a little grease. She might as well have duck feet, she moaned inwardly, stealing a glance at Cullen Claiborne, who at the moment was dancing with Rebecca Boone.

Though Cullen had arrived with his dark hair damp and curling about his ears, fancy buckskins brushed spotless, he hadn't approached Kitty even once, despite his avowed intention to dance with her. To the chagrin of more than one young woman there, he'd stood about talking with the men, looking over the dancers appreciatively and tapping his moccasined foot from time to time. And when finally he had taken to the floor, he'd pulled a laughing Rebecca along with him.

But despite Cullen Claiborne's inattention, none of the girls had wanted for partners thus far. Quite out of breath from dancing with Flanders Callaway and the fickle Rafer Moore, not to mention two of the young men who'd come in with the new arrivals, Kitty had chosen to sit out the set. She watched the whirling figures as they went through the reel, bowing and skipping, partners holding hands as they danced down the line. Maggie Hamilton's husband, Horace, a thin and big-nosed man whose curled wig and silver buckles at knee and shoe looked out of place in the gathering, went through the movements stiffly, clearly only acquiescing to the desires of his young wife. Maggie looked to be less than half of her husband's age.

"Kitty . . . hello." Israel Boone popped up beside her, his wide, friendly face marked by a ready smile, voice raised to carry over the music.

"Israel . . . I haven't seen you for a while," said Kitty.

"I've been outside. It's hot in here."

Kitty nodded. She liked Jemima's older brother. He was outgoing and generous once you got to know him, she'd found, and fast becoming a man, though being a few months younger than she made her still look on him as a boy.

"Can I get you a drink of water?" he asked her now.

She smiled and shook her head.

The music had stopped, and she saw Rebecca laughing like a girl at something Cullen had said to her. They chatted for a moment, and then Rebecca went to join her husband, fanning herself with her hand. In the next instant Cullen turned to look directly at Kitty, as if he'd known exactly where she was every minute. As he started toward her, she felt as if she couldn't breathe.

Panicked, she turned quickly to Israel. "Dance the next set with me." The plea was delivered almost desperately, her hand touching his arm for an instant, and Israel's surprise showed in his face.

"Of course," he said.

And then Cullen was there, grinning and handsome and quite overpowering. "Kitty, lass . . ." Those bold eyes of his swept over her. "This afternoon I'd have wagered my last shilling that you couldn't look prettier. But I'd have lost. She's beautiful, isn't she, Israel?" He clapped the boy on the shoulder.

Israel nodded, understanding clearly beginning to dawn on him. Kitty felt the blood rush to her cheeks.

The music was beginning again, and Cullen held out his hand to her. "My dance," he said.

But Kitty lifted her chin and regarded him steadily. "I believe I've already promised this one to Israel, Mr. Claiborne."

Cullen just stood there, and Israel gestured toward the floor and extended his arm to Kitty. "Sorry, Cullen," he said, an innocent grin on his face.

Cullen's brows rose, the laugh lines about his eyes crinkling. "It's all right," he said good-naturedly. "But . . ." His hand came out to touch Kitty's wrist lightly and send strange little waves coursing through her. "I'll not take no for the next one." His eyes held hers, and for a second she couldn't move; then Israel pulled her on.

She felt giddy, barely hearing the music and going through the steps by rote until, piqued, she saw that Cullen had not sat out the dance after all but had come on the floor with Maggie Hamilton. And there was little doubt that Mistress Hamilton was enjoying herself no end. Her eyes were fastened on the handsome scout, and at every opportunity she kicked her heels high to show the delicate slippers and well-turned ankles.

What an idiot she'd been to turn him down, Kitty agonized. But then, as Cullen's eye caught hers when it was her turn to dance down the line, she perversely pretended not to notice. And after that she turned her full attention to Israel.

At last the set ended, and Kitty was relieved to see Ezekial go off to get a drink of water. Thanking Israel for dancing with her, she fled to Amelia. Usaph was off in a corner talking to Daniel and Colonel Callaway.

"Well, it looks as if everyone's having a good time," Amelia greeted her daughter.

"It does indeed." Kitty couldn't help but see how Cullen bowed over Maggie Hamilton as he handed her back to her husband. "Mistress Hamilton seems to show no signs of tiring," she added, a tart little edge to her voice. She could have bitten her tongue off the instant the words were out.

Amelia suppressed a smile. "Getting married doesn't turn you into an old woman." Her probing eye searched Kitty's. "She's still only a girl, don't forget."

Kitty nodded, ashamed of herself.

To her surprise, Cullen walked over to them and, before she could say a word, introduced himself to her mother. "Well, well," he said to Amelia, " 'tis clear where your lovely daughter gets her looks, Mistress Gentry."

Amelia smiled. "Daniel tells us that you're staying on to scout for the fort," she said. Surprised, Kitty raised her chin slightly to steal a look at him.

"That I am." Cullen's eyes moved over the room. "I can already see that I'm going to like it here."

Kitty set her mouth, wondering if he were looking for Maggie Hamilton again . . . Maggie and her white silk slippers.

Ezekial had picked up his fiddle once more and was calling: "Gents, pick your ladies!"

Cullen leaned down toward Kitty. "I do believe that this is finally my dance, Miss Gentry."

Kitty hesitated, that same panic settling into her again. Things were going much too fast with this charming stranger. "Well . . ." she stammered, "it's . . . it is hot in here. Perhaps we could wait for a later set. . . ."

"Fiddlesticks!" Amelia said. "When I was a girl, we could dance all night. Hot or not." And as if she'd read Kitty's mind: "We used to go out on the side porch of my father's house back in Virginia and dance in our stocking feet. It was better than slippers."

"That is a good idea." Cullen seized upon it at once, and to Kitty's astonishment, he was down before her in an instant, unlacing the ties to the heavy shoes. In another moment her slender and shapely feet were encased in nothing more than a pair of fine-knitted cream-colored stockings and Cullen was pulling her onto the floor.

At first she was mortified, but then she realized how light she felt without the shoes, and the floor was slick and smooth beneath her, and Cullen was grinning at her.

They bowed to one another and circled, hardly able to take their eyes off one another, and before long the other girls had kicked their own shoes away. The onlookers clapped their hands and called out encouragement as Ezekial fiddled to a near frenzy.

Cullen danced with no one else for the rest of the night, except for one set when Kitty pleaded for a short rest, and then he went to charm old Granny Hawkins, coaxing her to dance along the sidelines, his handsome head bent forward, sweeping the little old lady quite literally off her feet a time or two.

But as soon as Kitty had caught her breath, he was back, those eyes—the color of smoke rising from a hot campfire—demanding. And this time he danced her away from the others, into the shadowy corner where the tallow dips had guttered down, and his mouth brushed hers to set a fire raging through her. . . . But she pulled, trembling, back into the light.

Since Roman, she knew now what could happen. Cullen Claiborne was clearly a charmer and a ladies' man, not to be trusted. She would not risk her heart, or her virginity, so easily again.

PART TWO

❄

Early Summer 1776

❋ 7 ❋

WITH SETTLERS VENTURING INTO KENTUCKE IN IN-
creasing numbers now, a good many came to
Boonesborough . . . some to stay, taking up land,
others merely stopping on their way to other places—Fort Harrod or Boiling Springs. Those headed for Logan's fort usually
cut away from the Boone Trace south of the Rockcastle River.
New stations were springing up, two of them north of Boonesborough and halfway to the Ohio.

At the Gentry place, the corn was thrusting upward in a field
still marked by stumps. The vegetable patch was already yield-
ing up peas, green onions, and tender greens, and the young
apple trees in the fledgling orchard were alive and growing.
Amelia and the girls had found time to plant zinnias and phlox
and cockscomb out in front of the rough porch. And when Usaph
killed a bear, Amelia—who had always contended that nothing
made as good a soap as bear fat—got a predictable gleam in her
eye.

"Whitest fat I know," she declared. "Better than lard. I expect we'd best get a soap kettle set up."

Early in the morning she measured water into the big iron pot
in the yard, getting the fire going beneath it as Kitty and Priscilla
went to the ash hopper for the strong lye liquid that had gathered
in the bottom container, the result of rainwater filtering down
through the fine hickory ashes above.

Every woman had her own proportions for what she considered the best soap, and Amelia was no exception. She measured
carefully, boiling the water and lye mixture together until she
felt it was ready.

"It ought to be strong enough to float an egg in," she instructed the girls. "If we had an egg," she added wryly.

With a wooden ladle she scooped the rendered white bear fat into the hot liquid until she was satisfied she'd used enough, and Kitty and Priscilla took turns stirring as the mixture boiled slowly to a thick mass. When Amelia finally pronounced it perfect, a handful of dried lavender brought from back home, pulverized to a fine powder, was stirred in at the last minute.

"It smells good," said Priscilla.

Amelia nodded. "It'll smell even better after a couple of weeks."

Usaph had made a shallow wooden tray for them, and Kitty lined it with a worn linen bedsheet, and then she and Amelia carefully poured the soap in to cure.

They were cutting it the next day, Kitty leaning to dislodge a long-legged and quite dead insect from one of the soft soap cakes, when she looked up to see Cullen Claiborne riding toward them.

"Well, now," he sang out as he approached, his long rifle lying across the saddle in front of him, hat set to the back of his head, "that looks like enough to do for a while."

Kitty smiled and waved to him. Though he was out scouting for the fort most of the time now, he managed to come by the Gentry cabin at least once a week. And while Kitty remembered her vow, she had to admit to a certain weakening where her heart was concerned. Cullen Claiborne had proven to be a very persistent man.

The bodies of three fat squirrels dangled limply from his saddle. "Thought you might take pity on a hungry man if he came bearing gifts," he said to Amelia, grinning as he climbed down.

"Pity, is it?" Amelia laughed. "I don't know much that tastes better than a mess of squirrel fried up." She took the game from him to look them over admiringly. Men on the frontier prided themselves on being marksmen enough to "bark" a squirrel— the bullet striking a branch near enough to the head of the animal to kill it with concussion, thereby leaving the flesh unmarred. There wasn't a mark on any of the three, Kitty saw.

"I'll skin and clean them, Ma," she offered, and Amelia passed them to her.

"Do I get a bar o' soap, then?" Cullen called after her.

"If you'll use it," she shot back, laughing.

Usaph hailed Cullen from the field, where he was chopping grass out of the corn. He put aside his hoe and, taking up the rifle that was always with him, came to the spring at the back of the cabin, where Cullen walked to meet him. They dipped into the cool water, wiping the backs of their hands across their mouths.

"Lord, that's sweet," Cullen said.

"It is," said Usaph. He peered at Cullen as they walked toward the cabin. "Any Indian sign about?"

Cullen shrugged. "Only what you'd expect for this time of year. No big parties. Still, that doesn't mean there'll be no trouble."

Usaph nodded. The settlers had had their warning that the British were trying to set the Indians against them.

"Do ye ever think," Cullen said, his expression suddenly serious, "that you might take Amelia and the girls into the fort to stay until we know more of what's to happen here?"

"I've thought on it," Usaph said. "Talked on it, too. But Amelia says what she's said all along. That we come to Kentucke to make a home, not to stay inside a fort wall."

"But it wouldn't be forever," Cullen persisted. "Some have decided on it. Mistress Porter's come in to the fort for a while. With her young daughter and one of the boys."

"I guess," Usaph said with a sigh, "that you haven't known Amelia Gentry long enough to know that once she makes up her mind to something, it takes a bigger man than I am to budge her . . . little as she is."

With the smell of frying squirrel wafting through the doorway, they climbed up the stone step to the porch, where Cullen could see in to where Kitty was setting the table. For a moment his eyes rested on her long-fingered hands, small and delicate and vulnerable-looking. "Well, for God's sake, be ready," he said, his voice low. "All the time."

"I aim to be," Usaph replied. He patted the rifle, which he'd just leaned up against the wall beside the porch bench. "And I bought me another at the store to leave here at the house for the women . . . just in case there'd be a need of it."

In a little while Amelia stuck her head out the door. "Wash up and come to the table," she told them. And Cullen, no longer surprised by the request, followed Usaph, who grumbled all the way to the water bucket which sat on a flat rock near the porch.

"That is the world's cleanest woman in that cabin there," he said, grinning nonetheless. "She's near scrubbed the floorboards through."

They ate heartily, but once the meal was finished and Usaph was heading back to the field, Amelia gave her youngest daughter a look. "You can help me clear up, Priss," she said.

Priscilla made a face. "How come Kitty don't have to help?"

"*Doesn't* have to help . . . Because I expect it's Kitty that Cullen came to see."

Kitty blushed, but Cullen, grinning, caught Amelia up in one arm, Priscilla in the other, and kissed them each on the cheek. "Not a bit of it," he teased. " 'Tis really the two of you I came to court."

Priscilla giggled and Amelia pretended to be outraged as she set her hair right, pushing a loose pin back into the braided coil at the nape of her neck. "Get on, Cullen Claiborne," she scolded, "before I change my mind."

"Are you sure you don't need me, Ma?" It was asked dutifully, but there was a certain eagerness in Kitty's eyes that was not lost on Cullen. Amelia waved her away.

"I'm positive. Why don't you show Cullen how well the orchard is coming along?"

"She showed him the orchard last week," Priscilla called after the escaping couple.

Though Cullen laughed, he was groaning inwardly. He had not only seen the orchard a number of times, he'd seen the new herb bed and the vegetable patch, and they'd walked the long stretch down to the creek and back again until the path must be worn bare . . . all of those places in sight of the cabin, at Kitty's insistence. And though he'd managed more than once to maneuver her behind a tangle of wild elderberry or a thick tree trunk, managed to pull her against him for a quick kiss that only starved him for more, it was not likely he'd get it so long as Usaph was nearby in the cornfield, or Amelia hanging washclothes in the yard, or Priscilla ambling to the spring for a bucket of water.

Not that he didn't like all the Gentrys. It was just that at the moment he was a man frustrated. It didn't usually take him so long to get a woman to let him pleasure her. And maybe that was the trouble. Kitty was not really a woman yet . . . but he would make her one. She was ready, whether she knew it or not.

Chafing under the restraints of every visit, they had walked and talked. . . . Kitty told him about how they'd moved from Culpeper County and how she'd grown up on the Watauga, and he'd accounted for his twenty-four years. He was of Scotch-Irish parentage. "That's really Scotch," he'd hastened to assure her. "Not a bit of Irish about it."

His parents had been descendants of the original Scottish settlers in Ulster, he said. Presbyterians, they had fled the unrest in Ireland and come to North Carolina in search of religious freedom before Cullen and his three brothers were born. The Claiborne sons had grown up helping in the small cooper's shop his father had operated. And he could still, he boasted, make as fine and tight a barrel as ever a man saw.

And what had made him come out here? Kitty had wanted to know.

He'd shrugged, grinning. "Fate, I suppose."

The truth was, he'd been one step ahead of a furious father bound on setting his daughter's disgrace right or killing Cullen in the trying. And since Cullen had felt there was room for doubt as to who had actually fathered the babe she carried, and since he'd found in the full light of day and sobriety that the girl wasn't as pretty, or as young, as he'd first supposed, he'd hightailed it out of the county as fast as he could.

It was by accident that he'd run into James Harrod, who was heading across the mountains and into Kentucke on a surveying assignment. But Cullen, seizing the chance to put some distance between himself and the pursuing father, had joined up with the small party. And to his surprise, he had taken to the wilderness like a small boy to a creekbank. With the well-seasoned Harrod as teacher, he'd soon learned the skills of surviving in the wild land.

He'd been with Harrod in the first attempt to settle Harrod's Town in 1774. And when the Indians had driven them out, he'd gone off to fight them in Lord Dunmore's War, as it had come to be known. Kentucke had made its claim on him.

But there were other claims that could lay hold of a man, sometimes whether he wanted them or not. And now, as he looked at Kitty Gentry, her slender back pressed against the rough bark of a giant oak, the protective feelings she aroused in him bothered him. He was not used to worrying overmuch about the women in his life.

"I want you to be careful out here, Kitty, lass." It burst from him in spite of himself. "I can see no reason why you and your mother and Prissy don't come into the fort for a few months, at least until we see for sure whether the tribes are going to ally with the British."

Kitty's mouth set into lines reminiscent of Amelia's. "Who'd want to be cooped up in a fort when they could be here? There's been no sign of trouble. And we *are* careful. Besides"—she relented somewhat—"Ma said if it seems that the Indians are starting to move, Priss and I shall have to go in and stay until the danger's past."

"That's more to my liking. I . . . I'd not have Shawnee hands laid on you again."

Kitty looked up quickly. "You heard about that."

"Aye. I heard."

Her eyes searched his, the color of them deepened to a dark violet-blue. "They didn't—" She stopped.

"I know," he said quickly. "Daniel told me." He felt a rush of unaccustomed tenderness . . . and something more. He grinned. His hands were thick and square, but he touched her gently now, trailing a fingertip along her chin, bringing it up to touch her lips. And the hot and familiar and oh so sweet urge grew until he pulled her behind a tree and kissed her, his mouth rough in his eagerness, his hands groping at the small breasts beneath her bodice.

She didn't stop him until he'd found his way inside the rough, homespun cloth and felt the warm, naked flesh of her in his hands, found the rosebud nipples. But then she gasped and pulled away to rearrange her waist.

"Stop it!" she said, though she sounded out of breath. "Pa might see us."

"And if he couldn't?" Cullen challenged. He was breathing hard himself, felt as if he must burst. "If we were somewhere private?"

"Yes." She stood up to him, chin lifted proudly. "If it were the privacy of the marriage bed, Cullen Claiborne. I'll not be dallied with. Not even by you."

She started back toward the cabin, and Cullen hurried after her, falling into step beside her. "Dallied? How can ye say such a thing? Would I harm you, Kitty, lass?" He turned his best smile on her, but she went doggedly along. Jesus, but he had never before found himself burning for a girl who was so determined to guard her virtue. Sometimes he had half a mind to cozy up to Maggie Hamilton, whose every look said she was a woman in need of a good loving.

Despite his frustration, he reached out to catch her hand. "Kitty . . . Kitty, my lass . . . the prettiest girl in all Kentucke," he cajoled. "Will you save me the first dance at the fort next week?"

A small grin tugged at the corners of her mouth. "I guess I could do that"—her eyes sparkled impishly—"seeing as how nobody else has asked me first."

* * *

"So you're Kitty." The voice was gentle and pleasantly low as Sara Gentry reached out a hand that, though freckled slightly from her weeks of travel, seemed far too soft for frontier life. "I think I should have known you anywhere from Roman's description." Her young face, pale and flawlessly lovely, somehow fragile beneath the wide linen brim of her bonnet, broke into a smile of genuine pleasure. As their hands touched, Kitty knew at once that she liked her.

They were on the front porch, and Roman's hawklike features were wearing the familiar half smile as Amelia made him bend far down for another hug. She had just sent Priscilla running to the tiny springhouse, which Usaph had lately completed, to fetch some cold buttermilk. And in the yard, Usaph had taken charge of the horses.

"You look well, Amelia," said Roman. "And you, Kitty . . ." His eyes searched hers for a brief instant, and she smiled the reassurance that she sensed he needed, knowing in that moment that the past was past. She was just glad to have him back . . . and Sara with him.

There was an almost imperceptible relaxing of the lines about his mouth. "We could have gone ahead into the fort for tonight," he said, "but I know Sara's tired, and I wanted her to meet our Gentry kin first. But if we'll crowd you . . ."

"Fiddlesticks, Roman Gentry!" Amelia laughed. "I'd have been mad as a hornet if you hadn't brought her here first. And you know it."

He nodded, reaching out a protective hand to touch his wife's arm gently. "Then I'll leave you to get acquainted and help Usaph with the horses."

Sara Gentry's blue-gray eyes followed her husband for a moment as he went down off the porch, then she turned back to smile uncertainly at Kitty and Amelia. Though she was a good three inches taller than Kitty, there was about her a fragility that seemed intensified as she took off the linen bonnet to reveal pale golden hair, which shone almost silver in the afternoon sun. She wore it pulled neatly back in a bun at the nape of her neck, accentuating the slender and aristocratic nose, the high, delicate cheekbones.

"Let's go inside. You must be tired," Amelia said, ushering her through the door and waving her to the settle.

"I am," she admitted, then added hastily, "though I'm glad

to be here at last. I've heard so much of all of you. Roman spoke
highly of our Kentucke kin.''

"Mercy, if you can get that man of yours to talk much about
anything, you're doing more than anyone else can," Amelia
said, and the three of them laughed.

Priscilla came in the door, swinging the piggin of buttermilk
in her haste to get back to the company.

"Careful, Priss," Kitty warned, and took the milk from her
as the little girl gaped at Sara with undisguised awe.

"Roman never told us that you were beautiful," she said.

Sara just smiled. "I brought some things for you. For everyone. Presents."

"*Presents?* What, for me?" Priscilla fairly danced in her excitement.

"Priscilla," Amelia chided her, but Sara gave her head a little
shake and reached out a soft hand to the child.

"Ribbons for your hair. Roman told me about your braids."
She fingered one of them. "And I brought a length of calico just
for you."

"That was good of you," Amelia said.

"Roman told me how hard it was to get things out here. We
brought along some other dress goods as well. And potatoes
. . . and flour."

"Flour . . ." Amelia put a hand to her mouth and sat down
in one of the chairs by the table, where Kitty was dipping out
cups of buttermilk. "Lord o' mercy!" she said almost to herself. "I think I've nearly forgotten what a biscuit tastes like . . .
or light bread, for that matter."

But the best for Amelia was yet to come. In a moment Roman
had come into the cabin with a packet of letters from the two
oldest Gentry girls back in Virginia. Everyone was well. Miranda's husband was off fighting with the militia. Abigail had a
new baby, another girl. Usaph shook his head at that news when
he heard it.

"I suppose," he said, "that the good Lord knows what He's
doin'." He gave Priscilla a playful tickle that set her giggling.

Sara wanted to help with supper, but Amelia wouldn't hear
of it. "Not this time," she said. "After this, you'll just be
family and you can help all you like."

The meal finished, Usaph and Roman went out onto the porch
to sit in the deepening twilight and exchange news, while inside
the cabin, once the clearing up was over, the women unrolled
the packets of cloth, exclaiming over each piece in the flickering

light of the grease lamps. There were lengths of calico, and cotton gauze for petticoats, and a piece of blue-violet silk that Sara pronounced perfect for Kitty's coloring.

"Good cloth is hard to get back home," she explained. "Hardly any cotton to be had at all since the war. But my mother had some materials put back and said she doubted she would ever get 'round to using it all. I've got some pieces for myself, too."

"When we get the chance, we'll send our thanks," said Amelia. And after a few minutes she went off to empty the precious flour into a covered maple bin that Usaph had made for her, then put on the water for some sassafras tea.

Kitty ran her hand over the silk material. "I'll save it for a special occasion."

"Probably just wear it when Cullen comes," Priscilla said, rolling her eyes mischievously.

"Cullen?" Sara turned to Kitty. She was clearly feeling more relaxed with them.

"Cullen Claiborne," Priscilla got in before her sister could say a word. "He's a scout like Roman, and handsome, and all the girls make eyes at him, and all he does is try to kiss Kitty every time he comes and walks her down to the creek—" She caught her breath. "—when he thinks nobody's looking."

Sara suppressed a smile as Kitty fastened her little sister with a threatening look. "Why don't you go help Ma, Priss?"

"They think nobody sees them doin' all that kissin'," Priscilla got in.

"Priss . . ." Amelia called, and Priscilla made a face and went to help.

"Tell me about Cullen," Sara said to Kitty, and the two young women, left to themselves, sat in the corner of the cabin, whispering together and laughing.

It was decided that Sara would share the loft with Kitty and Priscilla, and a pallet was put down for Priscilla so that Sara could have her bed. Roman, in deference to being a married man with his wife in the house, stretched out before the fireplace instead of sleeping outside as he always used to do. It had started to rain, but that wouldn't have stopped him in earlier days.

The loft was redolent still of the sassafras tea they'd all had earlier. The root, brewed up fragrant and pink, thinned the blood and helped a body prepare for the heat of the summer, Amelia always said. But whatever its medicinal powers, Kitty just found it delicious, and she lay now, drowsy and content, lulled by the soft hum of raindrops against the roofboards. Priscilla had dropped off to sleep almost immediately, and it had been a long time since Sara had stirred.

"Kitty . . ." The voice came so small and forlorn in the darkness that at first Kitty thought it was Prissy, waking from a bad dream. Then she realized that it was Roman's wife.

"Yes?" Wide awake now, she turned toward the narrow bed that was nothing more than a shadowy blur across from her.

"Are you . . . ever afraid? I mean, out here?" It was as if the words tried to hide themselves in the warm night air, leaving room for denial once the morning came.

"Of the Indians?" Kitty asked.

There was a silence. "That," Sara's voice came finally, "and the rest of it. It's so enormous . . . so wild. It's as if it could swallow us all and not a trace left."

Kitty realized at once how it must seem to someone who had known only a town back in Virginia . . . someone used to cobbled streets, and stores, and churches with bell towers. She could remember the way it was back there. Before her family had moved to the Watauga.

"It won't take you long to get used to it," she said, trying to comfort Sara. "Pretty soon you'll start to see how beautiful it is. There's a place I wish I could take you. It's down on Roman's—and your—land. Where the creek empties into the river . . ."

"Where you were when the Indians captured you?" Sara asked.

"Yes," Kitty said, surprised that Roman had told her.

They were both quiet for a moment as the rain continued its soft drumming.

"I bet," Kitty said, "that someday you and Roman will have a house there."

"Perhaps we will," said Sara, and then she burst out softly, "Oh, Kitty, I'm glad Roman rescued you."

Kitty laughed. "So am I."

"Do you think that you could come into the fort with me?" Sara asked. "Just for a couple of days. Until we get settled and I get to know some of the people there?"

"Of course. If you want me to."

The next day Amelia said she could spare her, and Kitty went along with Roman and Sara into Boonesborough, where the entire stockade turned out to greet them. Roman had always been a favorite, and his pretty wife was made much of.

Sara seemed to bring out the best in even the roughest men at the stockade, and they minded their manners, and their tongues, when they were in her presence. Rebecca and Elizabeth lent their assistance, and Sara's things were unpacked and the cabin she and Roman had taken was soon livable. Usaph arrived, his wagon loaded with a puncheon table and chairs he'd turned out. The Boones contributed a stool, the Callaways some iron pots.

Cullen, who had been out for nearly a week, rode into the fort on the second day, and he and Roman wrestled and pummeled each other like two big kids, both grinning broadly, Roman's reserve breached for once. Afterward Roman brought Cullen by the cabin to meet Sara.

Surprised to see Kitty there, Cullen caught her up in an impulsive hug that left her flustered and blushing, but not at all displeased. And he worked his wondrous charm on Roman's wife, to leave her laughing and quite won over.

A meal was ready, and Roman insisted that Cullen stay to share it. Afterward the two men rode out along the river a ways, climbing down to let their horses graze in the deep clover while they sat at the crest of the steep bank to look down upon the clear green waters of the Kentucke. On the opposite shore a huge old turkey gobbler strutted and preened in the bright sunlight, tail feathers iridescent.

Roman told Cullen of the war in the East and the rumors of unrest among the Cherokee. "Some think the British are behind it."

Cullen nodded.

"Daniel says you wintered up around Detroit."

"Aye," said Cullen, "and I'd have sworn the damned English would have set the Shawnee to their dirty work by now. But I've ridden along the Licking, and the Ohio . . . everything looks quiet."

"Too quiet," Roman said.

Cullen chewed at a twig, his handsome dark hair curling about his ears. "Since you're back, Roman, to keep watch close around, I wouldn't be surprised if Daniel doesn't want me to head up north and see what's happening. Maybe go up in the Illinois country."

"Can you tear yourself away from Kitty?"

Cullen grinned, brows raised in surprise. "I wouldn't want to," he admitted.

Roman leaned back on his elbows, regarding Cullen Claiborne through half-closed lids. They'd fought shoulder to shoul-

der in Dunmore's War and shared many a cup together. There
were few men he liked better. But Cullen's careless ways with
women were certainly not unknown to him. "I would hope,"
he said, "that your intentions toward her are more honorable
than usual."

Cullen's head came up, and when he spoke, his burr was thick.
"Don't tell me, man, that ye've an eye for her yourself?"

Roman shook his head.

Cullen threw the twig aside. "I'm relieved to hear that. For a
moment I thought you'd quite reversed your ways, Roman,
m'lad. In the old days together I used to wonder if you used that
pecker of yours for anything better than a piss."

Roman's eyes narrowed dangerously. "Tumbling every female to cross your path makes you no more a man," he said,
his voice even quieter than usual.

The two of them had sat up stiffly to regard each other in a
way that was near to being a challenge. But after a moment a
grin broke over Cullen's face and he punched Roman playfully
on the arm.

"I'm casting no aspersions on your manhood, Roman Gentry.
In fact, now that I come to think on it, there comes to mind a
certain night . . . There was that pretty lass who served us roast
pork. Let me see now . . . we were in the ordinary at—"

It was Roman's turn to grin as he held up a hand to cut Cullen
off. "Guilty," he admitted. "But that has nothing to do with
Kitty Gentry, who, I would remind you, happens to be a kins-
woman of mine."

"I'm aware of that," Cullen said, "and it's reason enough
why I'd take no advantage of the lass." He smiled his most
engaging smile. "I'd admit this to no other man but you, Roman. I've taken no more than a kiss from her."

Roman nodded. "Well, then . . . so long as your intentions
are honorable, as her cousin I give my approval, for what it's
worth."

A pair of black-winged hawks flew low over the water and
circled away to dip down over the thick green tops of trees that
dotted the steep slopes of the opposite shore. The strutting tom
had disappeared into the reeds at the water's edge, but his guttural call echoed to them from time to time.

"And speakin' of who's the better man," Cullen said, "I
don't suppose ye've heard that at Harrod's Town come Saturday
there'll be contests . . . wrestling, shooting . . . racing?"

"Daniel did mention that."

"And I don't suppose you'd care to match your gelding against my black."

Roman turned to eye the animal. "Good-looking piece of horseflesh. Is he fast?"

"As a drunkard's fart," Cullen boasted.

Roman pretended to mull the matter over. "All right," he said at last. "And while we're at it, we may as well have a try at the shooting."

"Wrestling, too?" said Cullen, gray eyes innocent.

Roman nodded. "With maybe a small wager on the side?" He was grinning outright now.

"You're on!" Cullen whooped.

✳ 8 ✳

HARROD'S TOWN, A WELL-FORTIFIED STOCKADE COMplete with rough pole gates, was situated southwest of Boonesborough between Dick's River and the Salt River beyond. Cullen and Roman arrived the day before the scheduled contests, electing to camp outside the fort walls along with the other men who'd gathered for the event. There were representatives from most of the stations. The McAfee brothers had come from their places farther up on the Salt River. Benjamin Logan from St. Asaph's . . . James Harrod from Boiling Springs. There were even a few men from Ruddle's Station, all the way up on the Licking River.

The women of Harrod's Town, after coming out to cook, had retreated to their cabins within the stockade, leaving the rowdy gathering of males to themselves. There was a motley assortment, smooth-faced boys eager to prove their manhood come the morning, grizzled oldsters who'd come to watch and wager, and full-grown men who'd do a little of everything there was to be done. Cullen and Roman were well known to most of them and were hailed wherever they moved.

A roaring fire shot sparks high into the moonlit sky as jugs passed freely. Cullen had managed to talk the man who managed the company store back at Boonesborough out of some good corn liquor he'd had put back, and now he and Roman had had enough to make them mellow. Jim Harrod, the founder of Harrod's Town and a strapping fellow known both for his tenacity and temper—if the occasion demanded it—came over to shake hands and hunker down beside them.

"Heard ye were back, Roman," he said. "Heard ye brought your pretty wife out with you this time."

Roman nodded.

"Well, it's a good thing. Takes the womenfolk to tame us down, I expect. Now, if we could just get Cullen here to settle down . . ." He gave Cullen a playful nudge. "Behavin' yourself, are ye?"

Cullen laughed and passed the jug.

Nearby, a spotted dog darted in to snatch a piece of cooked rabbit from a one-eyed old hunter who sweated freely in his greasy buckskins. Taking shaky aim, the fellow let fly with his empty jug and, despite his drunken state, sent the thief yelping away in the night. The old man gathered himself up to fetch the meat back, then dropped into his place to gnaw at it with relish, dirt and all.

Benjamin Logan, a tall man of strong features, dark-haired and slim-waisted, made his way through the gathering and, catching sight of Roman and Cullen with Harrod, came to join them and share the jug. They were deep in a discussion of the possible consequences if the Shawnee were to join with the British, when suddenly a shout went up from the far side of the fire, down by the fort wall.

"Fight! There's a fight!" someone yelled.

There was little that these men loved better, and there followed an instant surge toward the commotion which was over near the fort gates, a great pushing and shoving and elbowing as each man scrambled for a better view. Quickly separated from Harrod and Logan, Cullen and Roman managed to maneuver their way to the forefront.

The combatants had wasted no time in standing head to head but were already down on the ground, thrashing about in a furious knot of arms and legs. They appeared to be well matched, both beefy as bulls and bellowing to match. One, nearly bald himself, was taking full advantage of his opponent's length of matted and dingy, light-colored hair, yanking out handfuls every chance he got.

"That's it, Chaney . . . Git'm by the hair!" someone shouted in the midst of whoops and jeers and catcalls.

"Use y'r thumb, Gawddammit . . . Go fer 'is eyes!"

"Shit! I think Chaney's pissed his britches!"

The crowd shifted to make way as the two men rolled and grunted and gouged. The hairy one bit deep into a smothering forearm, and the one called Chaney roared anew and brought a knee smashing into the biter's groin.

The crowd whooped and Cullen and Roman grinned at one another. No one interfered in a fair fight. Whatever happened, happened.

The one-eyed man they'd seen earlier was lurching about, swinging his arms wildly in his exuberance, and an irritated bystander caught him squarely in his broad behind with a moccasined foot to send him sprawling. Too drunk to get up again, he rolled over and sat there, his one good eye blinking, the crowd surging around him.

The fight continued, the man with the dirty length of hair getting the worst of it. Blood was trickling from his nose, and one of his eyes was swelled nearly shut. But suddenly he got his arms free and, bending almost double, whipped out a knife that had been strapped to his ankle, hidden beneath his leggings. The blade flashed blue in the pale luminescence of the moon, and that grimy ham of a hand moved faster than it seemed possible. With one stroke Chaney's ear was severed, to fall into the thick grass and quiver there like a piece of puckered chicken skin.

Chaney grunted and then began to howl, grabbing at the smooth, raw side of his head, beginning to ooze now—in a moment it would bleed freely—as the victor hauled himself to his feet to deliver one more well-placed kick.

Wiping his knife against his leggings, he gave his bloody nose a swipe and accepted the first jug passed to him, hefting it to take a strong pull, some of the clear liquid dripping off his chin. He took a cocky step or two, casting a contemptuous look back toward Chaney. "Goddamned whoreson's lucky I didn't cut off his pizzle," he boasted.

Chaney's friends had come to his aid, one pulling up a handful of damp moss from between the jutting roots of a nearby elm to clap the soft mass to the bloody wound in an effort to stop the bleeding. In a minute they helped him into the fort, where the women would see to him.

"Well, it wasn't a bad fight." Cullen grinned.

"No," Roman agreed. "Not the best I ever saw. But not the worst."

A man with a fiddle was prevailed upon to play, and struck up a lively "Sugar in the Gourd." And Cullen and Roman, enjoying the music, caught sight of the one-eyed man still sitting where he'd gone down. As if by common consent, they each took an arm and carried him to the fort wall to prop him against the sturdy logs. He muttered something unintelligible, leaned his head back, and went to sleep at once.

The excitement finally waning, those who had drunk too much went off to find a likely spot to stretch out and sleep it off, while the others, sober, or reasonably so, gathered to talk politics and war.

"The bloody British'll have the Indians on us, and here we sit on our asses, like turkeys in a roostin' tree!" declared one of the young men from St. Asaph's.

"He's right," someone else called out. "And if we ain't careful, we'll end up trussed, cooked, and et afore we know what's took place, by God!"

A young captain in the Virginia militia, who'd been sent out on a surveying mission to Harrod's Town, stood to speak, his military bearing evident, though he was garbed as the rest of them, in buckskin and homespun. His name was Clark, Captain George Rogers Clark. "A militia is what's needed here, gents," he advised. "An honest-to-goodness organized and trained militia. And I much doubt that will be forthcoming from the Transylvania Company."

"How do we know they can even make good on our land titles?" someone demanded.

"We don't," a man sang out.

To Cullen's surprise, Roman stood up, and heads turned toward him.

"What do ye say, Roman?" a voice called.

"You work for the company," another cried accusingly.

"I work for Daniel," Roman corrected him, and the gathering of men fell silent. "I'd get one thing said straight away. While I always thought the judge was a decent enough man, I have never held with the idea of quitrents or proprietors out here."

"That's it!" An impassioned youth shook his fist, and Cullen saw the grim looks of agreement around. Ben Logan was nodding his head.

"Virginia's charter gives it a valid claim to Kentucke," said Roman. " 'Twould seem the best thing for us if they decided to exercise that right."

"Well said, sir!" Clark's voice rang out. "Seems to me that what needs doin' is to seek the ear of the governor. Patrick Henry could certainly work some influence on the Assembly."

"Aye," James Harrod joined in. "Instead of Henderson's bein' left to present the company's claim unchallenged. Is that not what he's up to, Roman?"

"He's still in the East," Roman answered. "And I do believe for that reason. However, I trust that there are those in the Assembly who would be open to the idea that men should be free west of the mountains as well as to the east of them."

"I'll pay no quitrents on my land!" A man shook his fist.

"We not only need a militia, but, even sooner, gunpowder," Roman declared. "If a serious and prolonged attack should come from the Indians, we would soon run out. The company is doing nothing to address that need."

The approval of the men for overthrowing the claim of the Transylvania Company was overwhelming, but when arguments broke out over the best ways to seek the protection of Virginia, Roman sat down and quietly took another swig from the jug.

"Jesus!" Cullen regarded him quizzically. "A touch of corn liquor does oil your tongue, Roman Gentry."

Roman just shrugged and smiled his one-sided smile. "I had something to say and I said it."

The morning dawned clear and bright, and the fort women were out early, moving about the cookfires in their ankle-length skirts of blue or brown linsey, passing out hot hoecakes and honey and fried squirrel and rabbit. The men, somewhat subdued by their lively night, accepted the food with thanks.

Cullen's eye settled on a pretty young matron of plump face and flushed cheeks, a knotted white linen kerchief about her shapely shoulders. He winked and grinned, and in a moment she sidled his way with a wooden trencher of hoecakes dripping with butter. Once she'd moved on, Roman helped himself to some of them.

"There are times," he said, his mouth drawing wryly, "when your legendary way with the ladies does pay dividends."

Cullen laughed, his eyes still on the pleasant swing of the

young woman's hips as she made her way back toward the fort gates.

A few of the men were still stretched out and snoring after the prodigious drinking of the night, but most looked to be in remarkably good shape. They worked hard, and played hard when they got the chance . . . and today they would contest with one another with the same vigor. The one-eyed fellow, who'd slept sitting up against the fort wall where Roman and Cullen had left him, was not only up, but as Cullen said, "steady as a preacher" and at the moment finishing off a hearty breakfast.

A committee of five was in charge of the contests, and as they huddled to confer, those who hadn't yet answered the demands of nature were going into the bushes or beyond the nearest corner of the stockade—some of them the very same who'd made wagers on who could piss the farthest when the liquor had taken hold of them the night before. But now, cold sober, they took care to go out of sight of the ladies.

It was decided that the horse race would be first, and the committee spokesman, a red-faced, fat man with a chin like a turkey's, laid out the course. "You'll start right here," he said, "in line with this here sycamore. Keep to the open ground past that far grove of trees yonder and down the hill to that flat stretch along the creek . . . We got strips o' cloth tied to the tree where you cut back up through the hills there. And," he added, his eyes rolling officiously, "there'll be two men there to see that nobody don't take no shortcuts."

There were a few guffaws at that.

"Oncet you git up top o' the hill, you cut through them woods any way you please just so you come out on this side. . . ." He gestured toward the thick green trees in the distance. "Then you come right down to this here osage orange tree, and the first one to grab onto that bottle hangin' there wins."

"Bottle?" one of the challengers yelled, squinting to eye the dark brown bottle that had been tied to one of the tree's lower branches. "Where's the goose?"

"There ain't but two geese here at the fort," a committee member said. "And Mistress Brandley won't turn loose o' neither."

"You'll have to make do with that there bottle," declared the red-faced man.

The arrangement suited Cullen just as well. While he enjoyed a roasted goose as much as the next man, he had never taken to the practice of stringing a live goose up by its feet, greasing its neck with bear fat, and then having the racers yank at the slippery neck as they crossed the finish line until one succeeded in pulling off the head and thereby was declared the winner. Somehow it didn't seem the decent way to kill anything, though he'd never had nerve enough to voice that sentiment to another man.

"The race is near two mile in all," the fat man said. "And I'd git my horse ready if I's you, 'cause we're aimin' to start in a few minutes here."

Cullen grinned at Roman as they pulled their horses into line. A good twenty men and their mounts were spread out and ready, but Cullen had decided after looking them over that none could give his animal any serious competition except for Roman's big gelding and maybe a sleek little roan that one of the boys from St. Asaph's had brought over.

The fat man was priming and loading his long rifle, wrapping a greased patch of linen around the bullet to make it fit the barrel snugly, and then readying the long rod to drive it home. As the horses stamped and blew through their nostrils, Cullen sat his horse low, and out of the corner of his eye he could see that the women had come out to watch. He stole a quick look at the pretty one and grinned as she gave him an encouraging smile. At his stirrup, Roman was leaning forward and looking straight ahead, his face deadly serious.

The long rifle discharged into a bright blue sky, and with the sound, the line of horses leaped forward, haunches setting in and hooves digging at the soft earth. Just as Cullen had figured, he and Roman and the boy from St. Asaph's broke out in front, each striving for the lead. But they could do no better in those first minutes than stay evenly spread out, no one of them with the advantage. The boy had a switch in his hand and gave the roan a lick or two, but both Roman and Cullen just leaned forward over the withers and gave the animals beneath them their heads.

Cullen dipped his face low against the sleek, black neck. "Come on, my beauty," he crooned. "No horse in the world as beautiful . . . or as fast . . ." He cajoled the big stallion the way he might a woman when he had a hand on her thigh, the burr in his voice smooth as honey.

The cheering from the fort grew farther away, faded, and the hooves of the horses made a soft hammering against the ground, that sound hanging in the bright sunshine as if everything else in the world had ceased for that moment, just the silent straining of sinew and muscle, sweat beginning to break out on man and animal.

Still leading three abreast, Cullen and Roman and the boy raced their horses past the grove of black oaks and plunged down the hill, leaning far back in the saddle as the descent steepened, small rocks scattering beneath the animals' hooves. Then they all pulled up sharply and whirled their mounts onto the narrow flat stretch that bordered the creek. Cullen dug his heels in and tried to go ahead but had to haul his horse sideways to avoid a low-hanging branch.

"Damn!" He swore as Roman's big sorrel shot out in front of him, but he managed to beat out the roan. And as the three of them pulled farther away from the rest, he could hear the shouting back there, the high-pitched scream as a horse went down in its effort to make the tight turn.

The going was easy along the bank, Roman's sorrel no more than a length ahead of him, the roan still hot on his heels. In the distance Cullen saw the two posted men, one of them waving a hat, and he readied himself for the turn up the hill.

The horses slowed and dug at the steep bank, the boy from St. Asaph's yelling encouragement to his animal. Cullen and Roman cleared the ridge at almost the same instant and then broke apart to take different paths through the dense woods.

Cullen wheeled and dodged his mount, working reins and heels and knees skillfully, trying to avoid the stinging, supple limbs that striped his face whenever he wasn't watchful enough. One wrong move and a man could break his animal's neck. Or his own.

The big black stallion burst out into the open, and Cullen could see that Roman had come out of the woods slightly to the right and a quarter length in front of him. The boy from St. Asaph's was nowhere to be seen yet.

Now, Cullen leaned his face down on the lathered neck and cajoled in earnest. "Stretch out, ye black devil," he sang. "Win this race and I'll find you a ready mare to couple with as many times as ye've a mind to . . . do ye ken?" And he could feel the horse surge to close the distance, feel the powerful thrust of the haunches and the stout heart in a body that was stretched to its limit.

Slowly the black pulled abreast of Roman's sorrel and the two horses ran neck to neck, each animal giving every ounce of strength it had. Up ahead Cullen could see the bottle, brown glass glittering in the sun, and he set his eye on it, would not rest until he had it in his hand.

The two riders approached in a dead heat, and Cullen saw Roman lean to reach out his longer arm. In that instant he knew that he must lose with all things equal except their arm reach. Without even thinking about it, he hauled himself out of the saddle and, clinging precariously to one side, stretched his body out to feel his hand close around the glass and yank it loose a split second before Roman could reach it.

He tried to slow the animal down, making an effort to reseat himself that almost caused him to fall under the pounding hooves, but somehow he managed to stay on, clutching at the saddle and hanging grimly onto the bottle. Legs dangling, he finally brought the horse to a stop and promptly tumbled to the ground to lie on his back and whoop in triumph, waving the bottle above him.

Only an instant behind, Roman was down from his own horse and ran grinning to haul the victor up, Cullen's wide-brimmed black hat in his hand. "Here," he growled, his own chest heaving, "this came flying in my face just as you did your damnedest to break your fool neck!"

The two of them laughed, and Roman pummeled his arm. "Damned good race," he said, blue eyes alight in the sweaty hawk face.

The boy from St. Asaph's pulled up in a spurt of dust, and by that time the crowd at the fort had surged toward them to gather around and congratulate Cullen and look over both his horse and Roman's.

The two men walked the horses around the stockade to cool them down a little before watering them, and the comely young woman who'd given them the hoecakes that morning was standing near the gates as they came by.

"I doubt I ever laid eyes on a better horseman, Cullen Claiborne," she said, throwing him a coquettish smile.

Cullen's gaze rested on the ripe mounds that pushed her linen scarf upward. "I'm more than grateful for those kind words," he said, "especially from so pretty a lass." She threw him a bold look as the two of them passed on, leading the horses, Cullen grinning broadly.

Roman pretended to be crushed. "Not a word for the second-place rider," he moaned. Cullen snorted.

An hour later they competed in the shooting matches, and this time it was Roman who took the honors, putting a bullet squarely in the center of a circle drawn on the broad trunk of a tree fully two hundred yards away. Cullen's bullet had been a centimeter off, and he acknowledged his besting with good humor.

"Maybe," he jested, "we could find Mistress Wheatley and she could compliment you on your shooting."

"And how did you find out her name?" Roman demanded.

Cullen shrugged. "I happened on a chance to pass a few words with her."

Roman shook his head in wonder.

They wrestled each other through two matches to a draw, and finally, the games ended, they sat in the shade of a big elm outside of the fort, well content with the outcome of the contests.

"What do you say we start back," said Roman, squinting up at the afternoon sun. "We've got three good hours of daylight left."

Cullen eyed him. "To tell you the truth," he said, picking up a twig and chewing at the end. "I accepted an invitation to supper for us, Roman . . . at Mistress Wheatley's cabin."

Roman turned to stare at him. "What are you up to, Cullen? That woman is married and her husband much in evidence. I saw him this morning."

"True," Cullen said. "But the man has to sleep sometime. And there's nothing that says a lady can't walk out in the moonlight. Especially"—he grinned—"if she has someone along to protect her from harm."

"Depends on what kind of harm we're talking about."

"Just a *supper*, Roman . . . Who knows, she may even be a good cook."

"I thought," Roman countered, "that you were set on courting Kitty."

"I am," Cullen retorted with a look of total innocence, "but I told you before that I'd taken no more than a kiss from the lass. Christ in heaven, I'm no bloody churchman! How long would you expect a man to go without a bit of sweet flesh beneath him?"

Roman shook his head in defeat and leaned back against the tree trunk. "If her husband catches you, I hope to God he doesn't decide to shoot me as well. Just for good measure."

Cullen grinned. "He won't. I'll explain to him that you're as innocent as a newborn babe, Roman, lad."

During the weeks Sara Gentry had been at Boonesborough, she had done her best to accommodate herself to fort life. The women were generous with their help and friendship, especially Rebecca, Elizabeth, and Elvie. But it was Kitty whom Sara depended on. Sometimes she wondered if she could have stood it without Kitty. Kitty always seemed to know everything, all the things that Sara hadn't needed to know before.

Back in Virginia there had always been a couple of bound girls to see to household chores as she was growing up. And even after she'd married Roman, her mother had sent Letty along with her to the new house. She'd never had to make soap, or candles, or weave her own cloth, or even cook.

But now she threw herself into becoming a proper frontier wife with a determination that sometimes exceeded her fragile strength, to leave her exhausted and crying helpless tears when Roman was out of the cabin. And always, despite all she did to conquer her fear, there was that oppressive sense of the wilderness out there beyond the fort walls. Once she had tried to tell Roman how she felt, and he had laughed at her . . . gently, but he'd laughed all the same. Still, she was with him again, and that was what mattered.

She had held fast to her love for him four years before, when he'd stunned both his family and hers by throwing away everything he'd worked for—his prospering law practice, the growing respect of all who knew him. . . . He'd gone off to be with Daniel Boone, had gone with him into the wilds to warn Harrod and the others and then ride off to fight the savages in Lord Dunmore's War.

Her father, once delighted with the prospect of her marriage to a young man with such a promising future, grew furious at the very mention of his son-in-law's name and advised her to forget him. But she had not given up, not even when there were no letters over that last year. He had said he'd come for her when the time was right, and she had known that he would.

As Roman had clearly felt restless and caged before, he now seemed easy within himself. He was tender with her, and patient, never complaining at her ineptness . . . not even when she scorched his supper. She could see that he was happy in Kentucke, and she would do whatever she had to do to keep him that way, though his scouting terrified her. There were times when the thought of him out there, at the mercy of all she feared, was nearly unbearable.

Unable to hold it longer, she poured out her feelings to Kitty one day as the two of them sat having a cup of sassafras tea in the cabin. "Don't you ever feel that way when Cullen goes out?" she cried. "Aren't you frightened for him?" Kitty had confessed privately to her that she was head over heels in love with the charming Scot.

Kitty shook her head. "No," she said. "I suppose that's because I know that he—Roman, too, for that matter—is well able to take care of himself wherever he is."

"Oh, I wish I were as sure as you," Sara murmured. "I think I should die if anything happened to Roman."

Kitty quickly put her tea aside and reached for Sara's hand. "I understand that. But, Sara . . . Roman's the strongest man I know, except maybe for Pa." They were quiet for a minute. "You have to let him be that," she added.

Sara sighed. "You're right."

"Besides"—Kitty's eyes brightened—"it's not really how you see it out there. It's glorious . . . and free. And if I were a man, I think I should do just what Roman and Cullen are doing. How splendid to be able to ride wherever you wanted!"

Sara managed a smile. "To that place where the creek joins the river?"

Kitty nodded. "Sometimes now, when Pa is going down that way, he lets me go along."

"Why don't you have Cullen take you?"

Kitty's eyes opened wider, the rich color mounting to her cheeks. "I wouldn't dare," she admitted. "It's hard enough to say no to him in plain sight of the cabin."

The two of them giggled like the girls they both were. Sara wanted to know if Cullen had mentioned marriage yet, and Kitty said he hadn't.

May passed into June, and the crops were lush and green beneath the hot sun. Roman and Cullen were away from the fort for days, sometimes a week at a time, watching for Indian sign; but all stayed quiet. The waiting, however, seemed only to heighten the fears of some, and a few families from the newer stations left to go back east.

A convention to address the concerns of the settlers was called in Harrod's Town, and a number of men from Boonesborough attended. Roman was out scouting at the time, but upon his return he was met by Daniel and the two of them walked out beyond the springs.

"No war sign?" Daniel questioned.

"No."

Daniel gave a nod of his head. "Luck stays with us," he said.

"It does. And while that's so, let's see to getting some strong gates up now that the palisades are complete."

Daniel grinned. It was not the first time Roman had pressed him on the fort's security.

The breeze was warm off the river and stirred the deep green corn that grew in a large patch nearby them—the stalks were already higher than a man's waist. And farther off there were cabbages and turnips, sweet potatoes and greens . . . and onions and herbs to please the womenfolk, who declared they could not cook a tasty meal without them. Watermelon vines and gourds tangled their way around the patch, while in the shade of the corn, pumpkin vines grew.

Daniel stooped to retie the laces of one of his moccasins, giving Roman a sidelong look as he straightened. A sudden gust of wind stirred his sandy-colored hair, which he wore plaited and clubbed.

"What do you have on your mind, Daniel?" Roman asked, anticipating him.

"Jim Harrod rode over," he replied. "Brought news of the convention. Seems a majority voted to send a pair of delegates to the Assembly with a petition that Virginia disallow the company and claim its own right to Kentucke."

Roman mulled that over, facing with some hesitation the man who'd had so much influence on his life, who'd been to him at least an older brother, if not at times a father . . . and who also worked for the company. He concluded that he must say what he felt. "I'm sorry, Daniel . . . I think they're right." To his surprise, Daniel grinned.

"I find no problem in that, Roman. And take no offense at it. What happens out here will happen."

Roman nodded, relieved.

"They elected Captain Clark to go back and present their case," Daniel said.

"George Rogers Clark? A good choice," Roman said nodding. "I've met the man and like what he has to say."

" 'Twould seem that Clark was not the only man to seize their fancy. Jim Harrod told me that the other man picked to speak for them was you."

Roman's head drew back as he stared in surprise. *"Me?"* he got out after a moment.

"I know of no other Roman Gentry." Daniel grinned as if well pleased with the choice.

"But . . . but I can't go. Not now."

"Why not?"

The very idea had caught Roman off guard, and his answer was slow in coming. "It would leave you short-handed with only Cullen," he said finally. "There's a lot of territory to cover out there—even for two men. And who knows how soon the Indians may ally with the British and start to move against us?"

"All the more reason. If that should happen, we'd need a lot more powder than we've got. Go persuade *somebody* of that . . . the Assembly, or Henderson. Besides," Daniel snorted, "you don't suppose I have forgot how to scout, do you? I may be a mite thick in the middle, but I can ride a horse or walk a trail and read sign better than most. With Richard Callaway here, the fort will be in good hands while I'm gone."

Daniel turned to gaze at the upright log walls for a moment, a certain restlessness in his blue eyes. "I'd not mind to be out some again anyway. I'm mindful of the times I used to lie back in the clover and sing at the top of my lungs . . . not one to hear me except a buffalo or stray rabbit."

"Still . . ." Roman began, but his voice trailed away. While he was yet uncertain, there was a growing awareness of the honor done him, of the trust those men had placed in him. Not only Kentucke's future, but its survival could be at stake. Could he refuse to honor their faith to the fullest of his abilities?

"I'd say you got no choice," said Daniel, as if in answer to the unspoken question.

Roman lifted his head and looked out over Hackberry Ridge in the distance, his eye sweeping the wooded hills. Heat shimmered, the land giving off its rich, ripe scent.

"You need not fear for your wife," Daniel spoke again. "We'll see to her. You have my word on it."

But Sara Gentry had other ideas on the matter, and once she had partially recovered from the shock of learning Roman's plans, she confronted him. "I'll not stay at the fort," she declared with an unaccustomed firmness.

"Sara, I cannot take you along," Roman tried to reason with her. "We shall be traveling at top speed. I could not allow you to undergo such hardships there and back."

"I had not thought to go with you," countered Sara. "I've decided to stay with the Gentrys while you're gone, if they'll have me."

Agreeable to that, Roman rode out the same day to speak with Usaph and Amelia, and the matter was soon settled.

"We'd hear of nothing else," Amelia said.

Usaph agreed. "I have wood and to spare. I'll turn her out a bed. There's plenty of room in the loft with the girls."

"Ma and I can seam up a mattress," Kitty offered, clearly delighted, and Priscilla told him there was extra ticking.

"When do you leave?" Usaph asked.

"As soon as possible. I'd like to ride for Harrod's Town in the morning."

"Then I'll hitch up the wagon and we'll go fetch Sara and her things back today."

With Amelia and Priscilla off to the bedroom to look for the ticking, and Usaph out to round up the horses, Roman and Kitty were left alone for a minute.

"I'm very proud of you, Roman," she said.

He smiled, pleased.

The secret of that night was something still shared, but they had long since been able to put it behind them. They were both glad that nothing had really happened. Even so, there was a bond between them that neither could deny. Kitty could never forget that, but for Roman, she would have been swallowed up in the camps north of the Ohio, the unwilling bed partner of some Shawnee chief for the rest of her life. And as for Roman, he sometimes thought that this plucky Gentry cousin of his might be the only female in his life who had ever allowed him to be exactly what he was without trying to change him.

"Do you think the Assembly will act favorably upon the petition?" Kitty asked him now.

"It's my task, and Captain Clark's, to convince them that they must," he said. He sobered. "Kitty . . . it's not to my liking to leave Sara for so long. She isn't—" He searched for a word. "—as comfortable out here as you are. And not nearly so strong. Take care of her for me. Please."

Kitty's small hand reached out to grasp his at once. "I will, Roman. I promise you."

* 9 *

DANIEL MADE HIS WAY ALONG THE PATH TOWARD THE
Boone cabin, stopping to admire an unusually large
bearskin that had been fastened up and stretched against
the fort wall to dry. He grinned. Rumor had it that bear meat
increased a man's powers, and there might well be something
to that, he thought. He had had a steak from this very animal
not two days before, and last night with Rebecca had done nothing to disprove the theory. In fact, he was feeling uncommonly
fine of late.

There was food aplenty, the garden bountiful. And since it
was the middle of July, the corn was almost ready to lay by—
no more taking turns at hoeing out the grass. Come the last of
August or the first of September, there would be plenty of
roastin' ears.

It was a Sunday, and at the Bible reading earlier he had given
silent thanks that the long-feared Indian raids still had not come.
And now, as the sun dipped toward the west, he could hear the
soft lowing of the cows as they gathered outside the fort in the
hot, humid air, waiting to be milked. The women had just gone
out with their pails and stools.

Just ahead, he saw Rebecca come out of their cabin and hurry
toward him. Lord, but she was still a fine-looking woman, he
thought, his blood stirring pleasantly with the night's memory.
He put out a hand to her bare and freckled arm as she came
abreast of him, just to feel the warm flesh of her, but instead of
the smile he expected, he saw that her mouth was tight, the
wide-set eyes troubled.

"Daniel . . . ." She frowned. "I'm not sure where Jemima is.
She should have been back by now."

"Back?"

122

Rebecca nodded. "This afternoon she and the Callaway girls were complaining of the heat. They said they were going to take the canoe and paddle right here in back of the fort. In the shade of the bank and the trees there. They were just going to cool off. Jemima stuck her heel the other day on a cane stob, and she said it was painin' some. She was going to dip it in the water."

"They haven't come back?" Daniel asked her.

She shook her head. "I had to send Lavina out to do the milking."

"They're likely at the Callaways," he said, though he wasn't as calm as he sounded. And when he turned and saw Richard Callaway hurrying down the path toward him, there was a curious pulling in his throat.

"The girls . . ." Callaway got out. "They took the canoe. . . . Some of the men saw it caught up in the reeds across the river. John Gass is swimming across to fetch it back. Thought I'd best get you, Daniel."

Daniel nodded. "Turn out the men, Israel!" he called out to his son as he caught sight of him coming out of one of the blockhouses. Rebecca didn't say a word but followed tight-lipped as Daniel and the others hastened to the riverbank in time to see the empty canoe dragged up on shore. John Floyd, a surveyor for the company, and a good woodsman, was holding his rifle at the ready, his eyes on the opposite shore.

Flanders Callaway came running, followed closely by Sam Henderson; he had been shaving, and half his face was still lathered with lye soap.

"Betsey . . . ?" Sam said to no one in particular, his voice still holding the hope that what he'd heard wasn't true.

"See anything?" Daniel asked Floyd and Gass.

Floyd shook his head, and John Gass, standing beside him, dripping and still breathing hard from his recent exertion, shook his head, too. "It was just like you see it, Daniel. No sign of the little ladies."

Daniel gave orders quickly. Richard Callaway would lead a dozen mounted men and cross the river at the ford a little way downstream from the fort, then start working back upstream from there. Daniel would take several men, cross in the canoe, and work on foot, trying to pick up sign.

"I'll go with you, Pa," Israel Boone said.

"No." Daniel rested a hand on his son's shoulder. "We can't take too many men away from the fort. This could be a ruse to get all the men gone, and the Shawnee waiting to attack. You're a good shot. You stay here and take care of your mother.''

Sam Henderson lifted his hand, and Daniel nodded. Everyone knew that he was sweet on Betsey.

''I'd like to go with Daniel on foot if it's all right with you, sir,'' Flanders Callaway said to his uncle. The Old Colonel looked toward Daniel for approval.

''I'd be pleased to have him,'' said Daniel, nodding. If he remembered rightly, Flanders had favored Jemima at the dances for a while now. And, of course, the two other girls were his cousins.

They prepared quickly—long rifles and tow and bullet bags and patches. The women brought packets of buffalo jerk which the men tucked into the fronts of their hunting shirts.

Daniel and Rebecca stood a moment, not touching, an unspoken memory hanging between them. ''You will be careful, Daniel?'' Rebecca said, her eyes dry.

Daniel nodded. With their oldest girl, Susannah, marrying just before they'd come out here and staying behind, Rebecca and Jemima had grown even closer now, it seemed. He must not let any harm come to the girl. He wanted to pledge it but couldn't find the words, and so just nodded again.

Once they'd reached the far bank of the river, Daniel divided his group, taking John Holder—a well-favored young man who'd come in from Stafford County, Virginia, early in the year—and Sam Henderson with him one way and sending John Floyd with Flanders and John Gass the other. ''If you pick up sign, give a whistle,'' he called.

They went slowly, examining every blade of grass, every rock, every stalk of cane or reed. It was John Floyd who came upon the trail first, and almost as soon as the group had rejoined, Sam Henderson came upon a torn shred of linsey which he was positive was from the skirt that Betsey had been wearing earlier.

Colonel Callaway and his men caught up to them, and the Old Colonel wanted to ride right after the Indian party, declaring that his mounted men could overtake them easily enough, since they were clearly afoot.

Daniel shook his head. ''If they should hear you coming on them, Richard, it would be all over for the girls. They'd tomahawk them sure enough. No. Consider this. Cullen was heading north along the Kentucke,'' Daniel reminded him. ''If he'd seen any sign of Indians close on, he'd have come right back to warn us. They no doubt came by way of the Blue Licks, and will go back that way.''

''Along the Warrior's Path,'' Callaway agreed. ''Remember the Gentry girl.''

Daniel nodded. ''You stay away from the trail . . . cut away and ride at top speed for the ford at the Licking, where you can lie in ambush and wait for them to come to you. Meanwhile, we will follow their trail, with all caution. It's nothing to find them, but a lot to get our girls back alive.''

It was agreed, and Callaway and his men set off, while Daniel and his group proceeded on foot. Daniel was the center man on trail and directed the others to spread out on either side of him, spacing themselves twenty feet or so apart. ''We won't miss anything that way,'' he told them.

The going was rough, and Daniel, from long training, noticed every twig. Yet within him Jemima's sweet young face haunted him. And her mother's. It had been in Rebecca's look back there at the fort—the laying to rest of their firstborn back in Powell's Valley, his still body finally free of the torment the savages had inflicted before they'd mercifully killed him. There were times when Daniel wondered if she'd blamed him then. Or yet. He would probably never know.

They made five miles before it got so dark that Daniel called a halt.

''There are five of them besides the girls,'' he said, biting off a piece of jerked meat and chewing between sentences. ''Traveling fast. That's in case we're following. Probably good.'' He gave his head a hard nod. ''Makes it less likely they'll take time to do them mischief.''

In a little while they were startled by the sound of a dog barking, and with a wave of Daniel's hand the men fell in behind him as they approached the sound cautiously. To their surprise, they found several white hunters building a cabin in the thick woods. Apparently, the Indians and their captives had slipped right past them with neither knowing of the other. When the hunters heard what had happened, three of them volunteered to go along with the rescuers come morning.

At first light the trackers were up and off again. That day they covered thirty hard miles before the darkness made them stop again. ''But we're gaining,'' Daniel announced.

Early Tuesday they emerged from the thick trees onto the broad smooth trail of the Warrior's Path at a point not too far from the Blue Licks. They had hardly gone two miles when they came upon the carcass of a freshly killed buffalo. The great bloodied beast lay sprawled on its side, the tongue and hump taken. Flies swarmed to light and gorge.

"There's a stream up here a couple of miles. That's where they'll be," said Daniel. "They think it's safe to stop and cook after all this way. Still, we must go with all caution now."

It was as he said. As they approached the stream—a little creek that emptied into the Licking River not far from the Blue Licks—a wispy ribbon of smoke rose up ahead and to their left.

Daniel gestured, and they all drew back into the shelter of the forest, readying their rifles . . . pouring out the measure of powder, wrapping the bullet with patching, ramming the whole thing home with the rod, priming the pan. They were to a man skilled at doing it quickly and silently.

Daniel cautioned them to wait and then went ahead alone, crawling the last few yards, the rifle held carefully in the crook of his arm. Sweat flowed freely. God's mercy, but there'd been a time when he could slither through the grass on a lean belly, silent as a serpent and ready to strike . . .

He raised his head cautiously and, through the prickly branches of a blackberry bush, caught his first sight of the Indians. There were five, as he'd reckoned—four Shawnee and a Cherokee whom Daniel recognized at once—Hanging Maw—who'd come as a friend to the Boone cabin back in North Carolina. But then, Daniel reminded himself, another Indian, Big Jim, who'd been to his cabin, had not hesitated to torture and kill James. No mercy could be expected.

His breath caught in his throat as his eyes rested on the girls. They were on the far side of the campfire. Betsey Callaway sat with her back against the trunk of a white oak tree, the younger girls stretched out beside her, their heads resting in her lap. Daniel could just see a part of Jemima's face, the sweet curve of her cheek and nose.

He restrained himself from charging in, assuring himself that they were all right for the moment. Only one of the Indians was near them—clearly the guard, he had his rifle with him. But the others were all busy. One was gathering wood. Another put a spit through the buffalo hump to ready it for cooking. There was a sentry posted on a small mound to the rear, but the brave seemed more interested in lighting his pipe than keeping watch. He had laid his rifle aside. Hanging Maw was getting water from the creek. . . .

They thought they were safe, right enough, Daniel thought as he slid away carefully. He returned to the others and explained quickly. "We'll get up as close as we can and then charge in. "Flanders, you and Sam get to the girls as quick as you can oncet we've begun to fire."

The men nodded, and as they approached, crawling the last little way, the unaware Indians could be heard laughing and talking from time to time. Finally, only a few yards from the tree where the girls sat, silent signals were passed from man to man to be ready. Daniel, rising up, crashed through the underbrush into the open, his rifle blazing at the same time John Floyd let go with his. At almost the same moment, Flanders and Sam made a headlong dash for the girls, pulling Betsey and Jemima down, then yanking them behind the broad tree trunk. With a shrill cry, Fanny tripped and went sprawling as her cousin Flanders tried to drag her along. But young John Holder caught her up in his arms and whisked her to safety.

Meanwhile the other men had plunged into the clearing, long rifles ablaze to set the startled Indians fleeing. Daniel was sure he'd wounded one with his first shot, but the man had run like a young stag.

Flanders whooped at seeing Jemima and his cousins safe, and as several of the other men started after the fleeing Indians, Daniel called them back.

"All their weapons are here," he said, gesturing toward the rifles which the Indians, in their foolish assumption that they were safe from pursuit now, had carelessly left lying too far to grab once the shooting began.

"I got one of 'em," John Floyd declared, pointing to the blood on the ground where the brave had been standing.

Daniel nodded. "They'll be off in that canebrake over there. And let them go. Best we see to the girls and get them back home."

Sam Henderson and a smiling Betsey stood close together, speaking softly, words meant only for one another, while Jemima and Fanny stood near their rescuers, Flanders and John Holder. The girls' clothing was ripped and filthy. Jemima was wearing Indian moccasins—which she would later explain had been given to her by the Cherokee, Hanging Maw, when she refused to walk another step on her sore heel barefooted.

Daniel came to her slowly, looking down into a face that was streaked with dirt and tears. "Pa," she whispered, "at the first shot I knew it was you."

He hugged her close to him. "I expect your ma will be glad to see you," he managed to say.

Daniel's very first order upon reaching Boonesborough was that the stockade be fitted with stout gates front and rear as quickly as possible. And soon after their arrival with the girls, who were tired and bruised but unhurt, Callaway and his mounted band rode in. After waiting at the Licking ford and discovering nothing except the tracks of one retreating Indian, they had concluded correctly that Daniel and his men had already gotten the girls back and the Indians had scattered and run for the river.

A couple of days later Cullen came in to report that small bands of marauding Shawnee had struck around the stockades up on the Licking. Hunters had gone out and not returned, and several cabins had been burned. "One closer to home," he told Daniel and Colonel Callaway. "I come upon David and Nathanial Hart at their place. It was burned to the ground while they were out hunting a few days back. All the fruit trees they'd planted, pulled up."

"Well . . . ." Daniel pondered it, pulling at his earlobe. "They could well be making for their camps on the Scioto, and nothing heard from them again for weeks, or months . . . But if they've agreed to do the work of the British . . ." He shook his head. "Maybe better get word to our outlying settlers. Some may want to come in."

Cullen rode to the Gentry place first, but Usaph was adamant in his refusal to leave. "Look there at that." He pointed to the thickness of the cabin door. "A battering ram couldn't breach it . . . nor the windows once they're closed and fastened. No, by God, I'll not leave my stock and my crops. But Amelia—"

She cut him off in mid-sentence. "I'll take the girls and go to the fort if it looks like there's real danger. But until then, I see no reason to uproot us . . . or to leave you out here to see to yourself, Usaph Gentry. You'd probably starve to death. Besides, I can shoot a rifle as well as you, should there be a need for it."

Cullen and Kitty walked out together. "Take no chances," he warned her. "Stay close by the cabin. If there's trouble, I'll come for you."

The other settlers were mixed in their response. Some got a few things together and went into the fort at once, while others declared, much as Usaph had, that they'd come to Kentucke to make their home and would not be driven out. Henry Porter said he guessed he and his oldest boy would stay on awhile at their place. Elvie and the other children were already at Boonesborough. The Tylers decided they would stay. Ben's brother Todd had just come out from the East, and with two good shots at the cabin, they were not afraid. Besides, Ben reminded them yet again, they had the protection of the Lord and need not fear the savages.

A group of frightened people from Hinkston's Station—one of the small stockades up on the Licking River—arrived at Boonesborough, and as they told a tale of murdered hunters and burned cabins, the panic spread. Daniel tried to calm everyone and to persuade the fleeing settlers that they should stay. "We can take part of you here," he said. "And I know the others will be welcome at Fort Harrod or down at St. Asaph's with Ben Logan."

But they would not be dissuaded. And then ten of the Boonesborough people announced that they were leaving, too, among them Robert and Callie Sherrill. Within a couple of days, with tears and prayers, the entire party departed for the East.

"We are left with but thirty good riflemen to defend the fort should anything happen," Daniel noted.

Cullen shrugged and grinned. "I expect that thirty good Kentucke riflemen, if well placed, could hold off the whole Shawnee nation if they set their minds to it."

Despite the air of danger, there were others at the fort who had little time to dwell overmuch on the Indian threat. Betsey Callaway's abduction and the subsequent tender reunion with Sam Henderson had prodded that young man to action, and he had asked the girl to be his wife. She accepted at once, though the young couple's determination to be wed as soon as possible was hindered by Colonel Callaway's misgivings.

"There's not a preacher near," he objected, refusing to give his permission.

"But Papa," pleaded a tearful Betsey, "Squire Boone says he'll say the words over us."

It was true that Squire had just recently returned to the fort, having left to fetch his wife, Jane, and their children, but he wasn't exactly a real preacher, the Old Colonel argued. He was an elder, and did conduct services of a Sunday . . . but a wedding . . . ?

"Oh, Richard . . ." Elizabeth took up her stepdaughter's cause. "He'll do until a preacher comes along. And then they can be married all over again if it suits you better."

The Old Colonel finally relented. "But only if you promise to do it over when you get the chance," he demanded.

Betsey threw her arms around his neck. "Thank you, Papa," she whispered.

The vows were exchanged on the seventh of August, with a celebration befitting the first wedding in Kentucke. Samuel Henderson and Elizabeth—that was Betsey's real given name—Callaway were married at Fort Boonesborough before relatives, friends, and well-wishers. Fanny cried. So did Maggie Hamilton, who was fetchingly turned out in one of her best silk dresses. Maggie said she always cried at weddings.

The ceremony over, everyone gathered at the blockhouse, where the wedding feast waited. There was wild game of every description, but the Porters had contributed a hog, and the fresh pork was the most popular meat there. Everyone had to have a slice. There were vegetables aplenty from the garden, and ripe watermelons that had been cooled in the spring.

"Mercy, did anything ever taste so good!" Amelia exclaimed as she finished off the last bite of her pork. "You know, our sow dropped a litter of eight last month," she told Faith, who sat beside her jostling little Martha, soon to be five months old. "Come winter, we'll have all the pork we want . . . and enough for you and Ben."

The fiddlers were striking up—the fiddler from Harrod's Town had come over to join Ezekial Turner for the occasion—and Amelia took the baby from Faith.

"Go find Ben and get out on the floor," she told her. "I'll take care of her for you."

Faith hesitated. "Ben doesn't entirely hold with dancing," she said.

Amelia made a face. "Persuade him. A little dancing would do that man a world of good!"

On the opposite side of the blockhouse Cullen had seized Kitty and was whirling her about. Not bothering with the reel that was forming, he kept her in his arms and gradually guided her into a corner for a private word.

"I'm going to ride out. Just to make sure that everything is quiet," he told her.

"Do you have to?" she asked, disappointed. He had just come in to the fort after being gone several days.

"I'll only be away a couple of hours. Back in plenty of time for some dancing . . . and whatever else we might want to do."

He grinned suggestively, leaning over her, his gray eyes darkening to the color of wood smoke.

"Cullen," Kitty chided, though when he looked at her that way, when that hard-muscled body was so close to hers, it was difficult to think clearly, "everyone will see us!"

"No, they won't. They're all looking at the bride and groom." He brushed his lips teasingly across hers. "I expect to have every dance when I get back."

"You expect a lot, Cullen Claiborne." Kitty smiled at him, her heart giving that strange little flutter that his presence always induced.

"I do indeed," he said, and there seemed a world of meaning in his words.

While he was gone, she didn't lack for partners. Most of the young men were eager to dance, and since there weren't nearly enough girls to go around, she smilingly obliged. She even took a turn around the floor several times with Todd Tyler, who didn't seem to share his brother Ben's mistrustful view of dancing. But the truth was, she found him just as mirthless and self-righteous as her brother-in-law.

As good as his word, Cullen was back when he said he'd be, hair slicked down and curling about his ears. As Kitty caught sight of him in the doorway, she was reminded of the night she'd been so jealous of Maggie Hamilton's white silk slippers. But this time Cullen came straight toward her, maneuvering Rafer Moore, who at the moment was sidling up to her, a gleam in his eye, right out of the way.

"I do hope you're here for the rest of the evening, Mr. Claiborne," Kitty said, teasing.

"I am, lass . . . I am." He grinned at her. "Best take off your shoes, lest we dance them right off before dawn!" It was clear that he'd stopped outside for a moment with some of the other young men gathered there before he'd made his entrance. There was a hint of corn liquor on his breath.

In that next hour Kitty danced more, she was sure, than she ever had before. But both she and Cullen seemed tireless. Once in a while he would leave her to go outside, only to return a moment later, the dark eyes smoldering more brightly as they rested on her, the liquor smell heavier on his breath.

The bridal couple requested that Kitty sing for them, and Priscilla fetched her dulcimore. A silence fell as she stroked the strings. "As I walked out, one winter's night . . . a-drinkin' of sweet wine . . ." Her high, clear soprano rose to echo in the still hot air. All eyes turned toward her, but she was aware only of Cullen's. "Conversing with a handsome lad . . . who stole this heart of mine. . . ."

After that she sang "Fair Eleanor" and everyone's favorite, "Barbry Ellen," before she finally declared that she couldn't sing another note and they let her go.

Amidst great merriment and coarse jesting, friends of the young couple escorted them—bride first, as was the custom—to the cabin in which they were to spend the night. But Cullen and Kitty didn't go along. Instead, they walked out into the moonlit fort yard, going in the opposite direction from the raucous shouting of the bridal escort and away from the lively music and raised voices that echoed from the blockhouse.

Cullen held Kitty's hand wrapped tightly in his own and pulled her into the deep shadow beside a darkened cabin. Any restraint they might have shown was lost in the heady fumes of the liquor on his breath and the febrile knowledge that the bridal couple were retiring to their bed.

Cullen's mouth claimed hers, his tongue teasing entrance, and Kitty made no move to stop him as his hand slid inside her bodice to find her breast and gently tug at the nipple to send a hot pulsing through her. How could touching her there, she would wonder later, cause her to feel it in so many other places?

His kisses, his tongue, his exploring fingers, were fast weakening her beyond her power to resist, and she moaned softly as he dropped his head to kiss the tops of her breasts.

"Kitty, lass . . . my sweet lass," he murmured, and that wonderful laugh of his was in her ear, muted, joyous. He straightened to bring his hard thighs against hers, his hands pressing her body to his. It was almost as if there were no clothing to hold them apart, almost as if that wondrously hard man's body of his were pressed against her bare parts. She grew dizzy just at the notion of it.

She felt powerless to resist, and he was lowering her to the soft earth, bending to her as she arched to him . . . when suddenly she heard someone coming along the path and stiffened in a wild panic to pull herself upright, her heart hammering.

Rising quickly, Cullen pressed her back into the deepest shadow, back against the rough log sides of the cabin, his muscular body close up to shield hers.

"It's only old Granny Hawkins," he whispered after a moment. And Kitty could see past his shoulder to make out the stoop-shouldered old lady as she made her way along the moon-washed path toward her cabin, walking with that stiff little bird-like gait of hers, humming a tune as she went. It seemed to take her forever, but finally the old lady was beyond them and in a moment more had gone into the Hawkins cabin.

Cullen was still pressed against her. She could feel the rough texture of the logs against her shoulder blades, feel the rise and fall of the hard bands of muscle across his chest as he breathed. And though she still ached with that same sweet longing between her legs, it was as if she'd had a pail of water thrown on her. She couldn't believe they'd both gotten so carried away . . . and right in the fort yard where anyone could have stumbled upon them.

"Kitty . . . Kitty, lass . . ." He tried to find her mouth with his, but she twisted away.

"No, Cullen. We mustn't."

"I'll get my horse . . ." He pulled her against his demanding body to set wild new feelings warring with her resolve. "I know a place where we'll be safe, lass—a glen of grass so deep and thick, and the river down below . . ." He kissed her tenderly, for all the hot urgency his body showed. "I want ye, lass . . . do ye ken how I want ye?"

"Oh, yes," she whispered, filled with joy at what she thought he was saying. "I want you, too, my love. . . . Let's be wed soon, Cullen. Please, soon . . ."

It took a moment for the words to register, and then she felt him draw back a pace. "Wed?" One thick, dark eyebrow slanted upward as he peered at her through the shadowy darkness.

"Oh, yes, my love," she said, still caught up in her rosy dream.

"Wed?" he said again, glancing behind him as if the devil himself might be waiting for him.

For one long terrible moment, Kitty stared at him, realizing the mistake she'd made. The trembling that had but a moment ago been from desire now stemmed from a quick rush of outrage. His only intent had been to have his way with her. She'd been right about him from the beginning.

He flashed his winning smile, attempting to pull her back into his arms. "There'll be time enough to speak of weddings, lass," he cajoled. "Right now—"

She shoved his reaching hands away. "How dare you think you can use me as you please, Cullen Claiborne!"

"Kitty—"

"You're just exactly what everyone says you are. A man who's after just one thing, 'twould seem.'' She drew herself up to stand as tall as she could. "Stand aside and let me pass!" she demanded.

He stared at her for a moment, dark brows drawn together into an angry line. "Gladly!" he said at last, turning on his moccasined heel to stride away, leaving her standing in the darkness and already beginning to feel thoroughly miserable.

Cullen's horse picked its way silently through the thick grove of hickory trees and came out on the high bank overlooking the river. The water down below flowed sinuously, shimmering with a faint silvery glow, and Cullen, but a half hour from Kitty, stared down at it, frustrated and still angry.

There were names, he fumed, for a girl who'd deliberately tease a man to torment and then refuse to ease him without first extracting a promise of matrimony. Damn the lass, but she'd driven him crazier than any female ever had!

He swung down from the black horse and kicked at a rock to send it rolling down the steep embankment. With Kitty Gentry he'd ignored all he'd learned through hard experience. The young, unmarried girls were too much trouble in the end. There were always tears and recriminations . . . and more often than not an outraged father or brother to be dealt with. No. Give him an errant wife, eager to give as good as she got and keep quiet about it, or a widow whose empty bed needed filling for a night . . . or an Indian maid who pleasured a man and asked nothing in return.

True, the lass was enchanting; he'd not deny it. And she did seem able to call forth in him a tenderness, a protectiveness, that he'd never felt for another before her.

But marriage! God's tears! Marriage was not for him, no matter what he'd told Roman. He would never tie himself down to one woman, and that was the way of it!

He walked along the bank, brooding, so lost in his gloomy thoughts that, despite the rifle swinging from his arm, he'd have been easy prey for any Shawnee lurking in the nearby trees. But luckily he was observed only by a pair of curious raccoons, who cautiously lifted their heads above a rock to peer at him in the moonlight and then hurried away through the underbrush.

He made his decision and rode back to the fort when it was nearly dawn, the first faint signs of pink banding the eastern sky, the last of the partygoers straggling out of the blockhouse and heading for their cabins. He found Daniel, red-eyed from lack of sleep but mellow and smiling.

"I want to go out for a while," he announced.

"You just got back," said Daniel, surprised.

"I know. I still want to go. I think it would be a good thing if I rode up along the Ohio. Maybe even go across and up around the encampment at Chillicothe. Might get a better idea of what the damned savages are up to."

Daniel thought about it for a moment. "Might not be a bad thing," he said finally.

Cullen nodded. "If I come across anything that threatens the fort, I'll come back at once. Otherwise I might be out for a while."

The two men shook hands, Daniel eyeing Cullen's glum face. "I expect I don't have to tell you to be watchful up there."

"I'm a careful man, Daniel," Cullen growled. "Probably be safer up there than here." He had his things together and was gone within the hour.

"Rider just in from the East brought the news," Israel Boone told Usaph. "Brought a copy of the *Virginia Gazette* with him," he added, his wide face marked by a broad grin. He had come out to the Gentry cabin to tell them that the Colonies had declared their independence from England on the fourth day of July, six weeks past.

"Well, about damned time!" said Usaph, his grin as big as Israel's.

Amelia came out on the porch, wiping her hands on her apron. Kitty and Sara had been working on the hominy soaking in an iron pot in the yard, stirring the soaking kernels of corn in their lye-water bath, slipping the skins off the swollen white hearts. They hurried to wash their hands in the bucket of water by the porch, calling out greetings to Israel. Priscilla put aside the sampler she was almost finished working.

"The whole thing is in the paper," Israel told them. "They say Mr. Thomas Jefferson of Virginia wrote it."

"I've met Mr. Jefferson," Sara said, her ivory cheeks filled with soft color. "Roman knows him well. He read law under Mr. Jefferson."

They intended to mark the occasion at the fort, Israel told them. Colonel Callaway was going to read the whole text of it aloud that evening.

Once Israel had taken his leave, Usaph looked at Amelia.

There was nothing to stay them. With plenty to forage on, the stock would be fine until the next day, and since the cows were both due to drop calves soon, there'd be no milking to do. "Well," he said, grinning at her, "what are we waiting for? Do whatever you have to do and let's go, 'Melia."

A short while later, as they climbed into the wagon, Priscilla leaned close to her sister and whispered, "Maybe Cullen will be back." The little girl had overheard Kitty telling Sara about the quarrel.

"I don't care if he is or not!" Kitty hissed back. But it was a lie. The truth was she'd been miserable since he'd left without a word to her . . . without even saying good-bye.

On the way to Boonesborough she tried to decide what she'd say to him if they came face to face. Surely he was back by now. Still, that didn't mean that he could walk up and smile at her and everything would be all right, she thought.

But he was not back, and she tried to tell herself again that she didn't care. Not a bit.

The settlers assembled at dusk as a huge bonfire was lit and torches ignited. And in the light of one of them, Colonel Callaway stood tall and erect as always, his length of silver hair falling to his shoulders. In a strong and measured tone he read the stirring words from the front page of the *Gazette*.

A quiet hush fell over the gathering at phrases like "all men are created equal" . . . "unalienable rights" . . . "life, liberty, and the pursuit of happiness" . . . "free and independent states." By eastern standards there were many among them rough in speech and manner and dress, but they understood those words to the core of their souls. The future of Kentucke was still in doubt, hanging on the judgment of the Virginia Assembly. They might yet be the subjects of the proprietary government of Transylvania, but their hearts were with those men across the mountains who had taken a stand. And when the Old Colonel had finished, they cheered until they were hoarse.

Kitty sat apart on the grass, watching as the flames licked high in the night sky, and in a while Sara came to sit beside her.

"I was talking to Rebecca," she said. "I just happened to mention Cullen's not being here." She cast a quick look toward Kitty. "She said that he's gone up north of the Ohio, up around the Indian encampments. They . . . don't expect him back anytime soon."

Kitty sat very still, her hands in her lap. "Was that Daniel's idea? Or Cullen's?"

"I don't know," said Sara.

They were quiet, Kitty fighting back tears and sure that she had lost him forever. At that moment her intact virginity seemed small consolation.

Sara put a hand out to her. "It'll be all right. If ever I saw a man addled with love for a girl, it's Cullen Claiborne for you. He'll be back."

"Should I have let him?"

Sara thought about it for a minute, pale and beautiful in the soft light of the flickering flames. "I let Roman," she confessed.

"You did?"

Sara nodded.

"And were you sorry afterward?"

"No." Sara's answer was quick. "Though I admit there were times later when I wondered if Roman had married me just because of that. Because his conscience bothered him. He's so hard on himself."

"I know," Kitty said, remembering in spite of herself the night they had spent together. "But Roman adores you," she added firmly. "You should have seen how anxious he was to bring you out here."

"Oh, Kitty . . . dear Kitty . . ." Sara laughed softly. "I thought I was supposed to be comforting you."

They hugged one another.

✳ 10 ✳

SARA WAS OVERJOYED TO GET WORD FROM ROMAN. A LETter was delivered to the Gentry cabin by a man named Isaac Shelby, a surveyor headed for Boonesborough who had been prevailed upon by Roman to carry the missive to his wife and greetings to his kinfolk, as well as letters for Daniel and James Harrod.

"Was my husband well when you last saw him?" Sara asked, her eyes anxious.

"Indeed he was, Mistress Gentry," the surveyor assured her. A young man, he was not overly large, nor handsome—his chin took a decided slope—but his smile was infectious.

As Amelia apologized for the lack of buttermilk, since neither of the cows had calved yet, Usaph pressed a cup of blackberry wine upon Shelby, and one sip set his eyes alight.

" 'Tis plain that you know how to make a good wine, sir." His longish nose sniffed appreciatively as he took another sip.

"You are welcome to take supper with us and stay the night," Amelia told him.

"I thank you, madam. I shall accept that invitation with pleasure."

Sara had withdrawn to the relative privacy of the corner of the room where the flax wheel and weasel were. She'd broken the seal and begun to read her husband's letter, but now she hurried back, unable to contain her excitement. "Oh, you will all want to hear this," she said.

Kitty and Priscilla drew closer and waited anxiously.

" 'First August—1776. Richmond, Virginia,' " she began.

"That's a whole month ago," said Priscilla. "He might be finished and on his way home by now."

Sara nodded happily.

"Richmond?" Kitty questioned. "I should have thought he'd be at Williamsburg."

"He explains that here." Sara smiled.

My dear wife,

I write these lines hoping that an opportunity to send them to you will arise soon. Unfortunately, Captain Clark and I arrived at Williamsburg too late to speak to the Assembly before it had adjourned, but having received news of the Indian raids on the northern settlements and the abandonment of Hinkston's Station, we have hastened here to Richmond to meet with Governor Patrick Henry at his summer home nearby. We have had two audiences with him thus far, stressing not only the desire of the people of Kentucke to be recognized as a part of Virginia, but apprising him of our perilous position in regard to the Indians, who are without doubt being spurred to their barbarous acts by the British. We have made an urgent request for powder with which to defend ourselves against any future attacks.

Captain Clark has proven himself to be an eloquent and extraordinary man, who pleads our cause with uncommon persuasion, and the governor has lent a sympathetic ear. Though he can do nothing without the approval of the Executive Council of the Assembly, Governor Henry has arranged for us to meet with that distinguished body to inform them of our desperate need for adequate supplies of gunpowder if we are to defend the western settlements from the Indians and the British.

Meanwhile, Governor Henry has urged Captain Clark and myself to stay in Virginia until the next meeting of the Assembly which begins in October—"

Sara's voice faltered, and she glanced up, disappointment in her eyes, but then continued on at once. " '—then to present our request for recognition to the entire body of the Virginia legislature. We agree that this is the advisable course. But, dear wife, know that I miss you and—' " She smiled, the color in her cheeks deepening. "Well . . . this part is . . ."

"For you, of course," said Amelia. And while their guest expounded on the turn of events in Virginia, Sara quickly read through the rest of the letter and only looked up again as she neared the end.

"Roman says, 'My love and regard to Usaph and Amelia, Kitty and Priscilla. Stay well and safe, all of you, until such time as I shall see you again. I trust that will not be too long.' "

After supper, Usaph and Isaac Shelby discussed conditions in the East over pipes of fine cured Virginia tobacco brought in by the surveyor. Priscilla was putting the finishing stitches in her sampler while Amelia mended socks. But Kitty and Sara, having finished with the clearing up, excused themselves and went up to the loft, carrying along a stub of a candle with them. The flame flickered and danced from time to time as the breeze wafted through the vent holes.

"We're almost out of tallow dips," Kitty noted. "Ma says we'd best make some this week."

Sara nodded. She had been quiet all through supper, and Kitty peered at her now, coming to sit on the bed beside her. The mattress tickings had just been stuffed with fresh grass, and the smell was pleasant.

"Ma says Elvie Porter is going to give her a goose and a

setting of eggs next spring. We'll have feathers for our beds . . . though the grass does smell so good when it's new cut.''

Sara nodded.

"You're disappointed that Roman isn't coming home right away.''

Sara sighed. "Oh, Kitty . . . is it that plain, then?'' She didn't wait for an answer. "There are times,'' she rushed on, "when I don't understand him. He seemed anxious for me to come out here with him. But we'd hardly settled before he left me to return there. And now he's willing to wait until the legislature meets.''

"It isn't because he wants to be away from you, Sara. He's only there because what he's doing is so important.''

That smooth stretch of brow knitted, and Sara's eyes searched Kitty's. "You really believe that, don't you?''

"Oh, yes.'' Kitty's voice rang with conviction. "The future of Kentucke could rest with Roman and Captain Clark.''

"I wish that I could feel about this place the way all of you do,'' said Sara. "I confess that what I've wanted most was for Roman to tell me that he'd come to his senses and the two of us were going back home to take up our lives as they were before he left.'' She sighed. "But I think that isn't going to happen.''

"I think it isn't,'' Kitty conceded, and put out a quick hand in sympathy. She knew well what it was to ache over the man you loved. There had still been no word from Cullen, and each succeeding day brought the torment of wondering if something had happened to him or if he simply never wanted to see her again.

Sara managed a tremulous smile. "I suppose I shall just have to learn to love Kentucke as much as my husband does.''

The candle began to sputter as it burned closer to the end, and in a moment a sleepy-eyed Priscilla came up to get into her nightgown and crawl into bed.

Within the week one of the cows dropped her calf, but instead of the healthy heifer that Usaph had hoped for, the new arrival was a sickly bull calf.

"Damnation, 'Melia,'' he said, disgusted, "I don't know if the poor thing will make it through the day.''

"Well,'' said Amelia, "we'll do the best we can for it. Besides, our old red-and-white cow will likely do better. And at least we'll have some milk again soon.''

The new mother, as if sensing her offspring's frailty, did not attempt to lead the wobbly-legged creature from the shelter of the shed but nudged him toward her udder encouragingly. And by the next day the calf did seem slightly stronger.

The sky was cloudless, the breeze gentle, and Kitty and Sara decided that this was the day for their candlemaking. They assembled everything they would need in the yard, well out from the cabin and near the small dogwood tree that Usaph had left standing, at Amelia's urging.

The buffalo tallow was melted in one of the iron pots, the fire kept just right so it didn't burn and darken. There was flax in the field, but it wasn't ready yet, so the wicks were of nettle linen, spun into a tight twist and fastened in lengths to hooks that lined the underside of thin wooden strips that had been fashioned into a crossbar.

It was possible with the crossbar to dip all the wicks into the waxy hot tallow at once and then raise them to cool and harden, then dip again for another of the many coatings that were required to produce candles of a respectable size.

It was tedious and hot work, but the girls went at it cheerfully, Lady circling the pot from time to time, wagging her tail and nudging at their skirts to be petted until she finally trotted off toward the creek and the thick woods. Priscilla proved to be little help, since she was drawn to the shed and the new calf, and it was the middle of the afternoon before Kitty and Sara had finished.

Amelia came out of the cabin to look over the fat tallow dips, which had been hung to dry on one of the lower limbs of the dogwood tree. She gave the girls an approving nod. "You must be starved," she said. "Didn't even stop to eat. Go ahead in. There's some hominy and fried rabbit left. And some hoecakes. I just brought up a fresh bucket of water from the spring and it's good and cold."

"I am hungry," Sara admitted, tucking a stray wisp of fine blond hair into the bun at the nape of her neck.

"Where's Priss?" Kitty asked, catching up the hem of her apron to dab at the perspiration on her face.

Amelia gestured toward the cabin. "I finally got her to come away from that calf and put her to winding yarn on the weasel." Amelia was tanned and healthy-looking. Usually too thin, she'd even put on a few becoming pounds over the summer.

"How is the calf?" Sara asked.

"I don't know. Usaph's with it now. Think I'll walk over there and see."

Inside the cabin, Kitty and Sara found Priscilla turning the weasel halfheartedly. "I was coming back to dip candles with you," she said, "but Ma said I had to wind yarn." She screwed her face into such a look of misery that both Kitty and Sara laughed.

"I'll help you," Kitty promised her, "just as soon as we've eaten."

It didn't take them long, and once they'd finished, Sara volunteered to clean up, while Kitty went to keep her promise. "Look at this, Priss," she chided, "you have it all twisted."

"I know." Priscilla sighed. But in another moment they were giggling together as they tried to untangle the mess, Sara joining in from across the room as she scraped out the wooden plates.

Priscilla looked up at Kitty, her face round and pretty, framed by the wheat-colored braids. "If I had just kept it straighter—" she began, but stopped at a shrill, yelping noise from the outside, a peculiar high-pitched yipping that might have come from a dog. "Lady . . . ?" she got out, her eyes questioning.

But in some terrible way, Kitty knew that it wasn't, and in the next instant they heard Amelia's scream, wrenching from her belly and mixing with the roar of a rifle. The wooden plate in Sara's hands clattered to the floor as another gunshot reverberated, and Kitty darted toward the doorway, reaching the porch just ahead of the other two.

Her eyes swept the yard, trying to take in all of it at once. Her breath rushed from her as she saw Usaph, lying on the ground just outside the shed, that big, hardy body of his crumpled at an odd angle—still, Lord in heaven, so still, it came to her—his head tucked sideways as if he'd been trying to twist around to see the Shawnee brave whose oiled body gleamed above him. . . . Amelia was halfway to the cabin, running, her skirts flapping about her ankles . . . two Shawnee closing fast upon her.

As she caught sight of the girls on the porch, she waved for them to get back into the cabin and then threw up her small hands, trying to protect herself as her attackers overtook her and the knife wielded by one of them struck at her again and again.

As Kitty saw her mother fall, she was sure that Amelia was screaming, and then she realized that it was Priscilla who was making that awful sound . . . and maybe herself . . . She would never be sure.

"Ma!" the little girl shrieked, and Kitty caught a glimpse of her white face, the face that only a moment ago had been rosy and smiling. In that instant she knew what her sister was going to do.

"Priss . . . *don't*!" she cried, and made a wild grab for her as the little girl darted out. Too late. *"Prissy!"* she screamed again, and had started down off the porch after her when yet another Indian rounded the corner of the cabin and brought the poised stone ax around in a high arc, emitting the strange and triumphant yelping sound that they'd heard earlier.

And after that everything seemed to slow down, to move at a strange half-pace. Priscilla's beautiful fair head seemed to explode as the heavy ax made contact, and she was like a doll, broken now, flying slowly through the air to come to rest finally, almost gracefully, in the deep green grass. . . . A few paces away a Shawnee body gleamed, legs astride Amelia as his knife made its shimmering, endless circle, and then the mahogany-colored hand seemed to take forever to hoist aloft the bloody length of black hair. All of it fixed on Kitty's brain as if it were a scene caught on canvas—the cornfield and the vegetable patch over to the right past the shed, the black iron pot in the yard, the fat tallow dips hanging from the dogwood branches . . . all of it framed beneath that brilliant blue sky. . . .

But as the Shawnee by the shed came upright, heavy thigh muscles cording, the rifle in his hands swinging toward the porch, something within the deepest core of Kitty gave her the strength to move. She swung back just as the bullet penetrated the post beside her with a dull *thwack*, the pop of the rifle loud in her ears. Sara was standing ashen-faced in the doorway.

"Get inside!" Kitty screamed at her, but when the blue eyes just stared blankly, she sprang forward to shove Sara as hard as she could, sending her sprawling back into the cabin, then whirled to slam the heavy oak door and slide the thick bar into place.

"Help me get the windows closed," she yelled, but Sara had crawled into a corner and was huddled there making pitiful, whimpering sounds.

Kitty raced for the window on the front wall, catching sight of a pair of Indians out by the shed before she pulled the solid wooden cover shut and barred it. As she whirled toward the window in the back—Usaph had been proud of placing them so as to get a cross draft—she saw, to her horror, the gleaming pate with its coarse scalplock, one shoulder and arm already through. Without thinking, she reached for the first thing to hand, one of the stout hickory chairs Usaph had made, and she swung it with all her might against the intruder's head.

The brave jerked back, howling, and in an instant she had dropped the chair and slammed the window shut to fasten it. She never paused, but sprinted to the bedroom to get that final opening safely closed, and only then sank back against the wall for a moment, letting her eyes adjust to the dim light, her breath coming in hard gasps.

The gun . . . the gun . . . It hammered at her . . . the gun Pa had gotten at the company store just so there'd be one at the house when he was out. She was back in the main room in barely a breath, her hands closing about the heavy stock, lifting it down from its place on the pegs by the mantel. There was the bullet pouch, the extra powder horn . . . Could she remember how? God, help her remember . . .

She talked to Sara while she was doing it, as much to calm herself as to quiet Roman's wife, who was still huddled in the corner and babbling unintelligibly in her terror. "It's all right now. . . ." She lifted the brass cap from the hollowed-out place in the stock, assuring herself that the greased patching was there and ready. Tip the horn to pour in the powder just as her father had shown her. "Sara, listen to me . . . we'll be all right. . . ." Wrap one of the bullets in a piece of patching . . . detach the ramrod from the underneath side of the gun and drive the patched bullet down in the barrel . . .

It was hard for her because she wasn't all that much taller than the rifle, but she kept at it grimly until she had the bullet firmly seated. Pour a few grains of powder to prime it . . . "Pa said he built this place strong enough to stand off an army. . . ."

She went to one of the loopholes that Usaph had designed so carefully, removing the plug that fit from inside. The hole tapered to a slim, elongated opening as it reached the outer side of the wall, and she peered out into the sunlit yard. She could see the edge of the porch and out past it to the iron pot and the dogwood tree and beyond to the woods. As she shifted, she could just see the chopping block and the corner of the shed . . . not the wide double doorway, nor what lay in front. Neither did she allow herself to see the two still forms there in the yard. Later . . . later . . . she would face that when she could.

She heard rather than saw the Shawnee as he came down off the steps, and then he loped out into the yard, coming into full view. Feathers trimmed his scalplock and circled the thick neck. He held a rifle before him in readiness as he squinted back at the cabin, then turned to beckon the others, who must still be at the shed, she thought.

She heard the sudden bawling of the cow and the equally abrupt silence that followed as she carefully slid the end of the rifle barrel up and through the loophole. There was just enough room to sight down the blue length of it. She could still hear her father. "Truest sights as ever I saw." Be true now, she prayed as she lined it up in the square center of the Indian's naked chest.

When the rifle discharged, it sent her reeling backward to the floor, though somehow she managed to hold on to the gun. In an instant she had scrambled to her feet and was back at the hole to see the Indian lying full length on the grass, his dark-skinned legs jerking slightly. The sight sent a grim kind of pleasure coursing through her. Tears squeezed from her eyes, but she dashed them away as she worked feverishly to reload the rifle.

Ready again, she peered through the loophole to see the fallen Shawnee being dragged off toward the shed by two of his comrades. He was no longer jerking but bumped along the ground limply, like a sack of meal. She slid the gun barrel out. Hurry . . . hurry . . . they'd soon be beyond her line of vision.

She tried to brace herself better this time and quickly squeezed off the shot. Though she managed to stay on her feet, she was knocked backward several steps. But with the regaining of her place, a look told her that the ball had gone wide. The Indians were out of sight now.

Too fast, she chided herself as she reloaded. She'd have to be more careful. Couldn't afford to waste a shot. She scanned the yard once more and, when she couldn't see any of them, put the plug back in place for the time being.

Sara had stopped her babbling and was now crying softly, her long-fingered hands gripped together in her lap, her legs drawn up beneath her as if to make herself as small as possible. Kitty put the gun aside and dropped down beside her, her shoulder throbbing dully from the rifle's kick.

"Sara . . . Sara . . . ." She hugged her and smoothed the fine blond hair back from the colorless face. "Sara, I shot one of them. I think I killed him." For the first time, Kitty realized how hard she was trembling herself, and the two of them sat huddled together on the floor. "Do you hear me? I think I may have killed one of them."

Sara didn't answer, but her eyes blinked and she nodded.

Kitty stayed a minute more, which was as long as she dared.

"I have to keep watch," she told her. "I can't let them get too close. But it'll be all right. You stay here."

Her eye fell on the fireplace with its glowing coals left from cooking the noon meal, and she suddenly recalled tales of Indians climbing up on the roof to drop down the chimney. She hurried to throw a log onto the embers and start the flames licking upward. No Shawnee would come down that chimney, she vowed.

Next, she went back to the front loophole and took out the plug to look. There was nothing. The yard was quiet, the sun shining brightly. The tallow dips stirred ever so slightly in the breeze. But in the bedroom a moment later she spied one of them crouched out toward the young orchard the moment she pulled out the plug.

He made his way carefully past the blackberry bushes, his dark eyes sweeping the cabin from front to back. Unlike the others, who wore only breechclouts, his legs were covered with dirty fringed leggings. He held a heavy stone ax in his hand, and as she saw it, Kitty's heart constricted painfully. He was the one who had hit Prissy. . . . She couldn't bring herself to think the word *killed*.

With tears choking her, she inched out the tip of the gun barrel. Her legs stopped shaking and her hand was steady as she waited until he was a bare twenty yards away before she fired. And though the recoil of the rifle almost broke her shoulder, she stood stubbornly, determined not to fall back until she saw him fall first. And he did, headlong, like a tree that had been axed through . . . and never moved a muscle.

After that, Kitty went from one loophole to the next, watching on all sides of the house, pausing only long enough to make sure that the fire was burning well. She caught no sign of movement, but after a while, when she went back to peer out of the bedroom hole, the body of the Indian with the stone ax was gone. The others, she thought, had taken him off, as they had the first one.

When more than an hour had passed without catching sight of anyone out there, she went to sit with Sara, easing back against the rough log wall. It was dreadfully hot with the windows and door shut and the fire lit, and her blouse was wet through in back. Sara stared down at her lap, large beads of sweat standing out on her face. Kitty patted her on the shoulder.

A fly buzzed about the dim room, dipping to light, then flying again. Kitty closed her eyes, wondering if the Shawnee were still out there. Watching. Waiting. Maybe they had just decided to go. She hardly dared let herself hope that. Still, Roman had always said that Indians were unpredictable. . . . She mustn't take any chances. They could be hiding. Pretending to be gone to trick her and Sara into coming out.

But if she could hold them off long enough, it was possible that Ben might ride over. Or his brother Todd. Or someone from the fort . . . Cullen's smiling face was suddenly there behind her eyelids, and at that moment she would have given her soul to see him, to feel herself wrapped in those strong arms.

"Kitty . . ."

She started at the sound, turning quickly to find Sara regarding her solemnly, her face pale and sweaty. Kitty felt a wave of relief. At least Sara was able to speak to her now. There'd been a moment when she'd feared that Roman's wife had been terrified out of her mind. "Sara," she said thankfully, reaching for her hand.

"K-Kitty," she stammered, "I—I think I've wet myself."

Kitty stared at her a moment and then burst out laughing, hugging her, the two of them rocking. And Sara started to laugh, too, the sound painful and hoarse and racking, and both of them crying at the same time . . . laughing that awful sound and crying and holding to one another.

"It's . . . it's all right," Kitty got out finally, drawing back from the thin edge of hysteria and unknotting the kerchief from around her neck to wipe the sweat and tears from her own face, and then Sara's. "Come on . . ." She helped Sara to her feet, and arms linked, they went to get a drink from the pail. Then Kitty poured a small amount of the water into a washbowl, mindful of the fact that what was left might have to last them a long time.

"Wash up. I'll get you some dry things," she said. She went to the clothes press to find a skirt and a pair of drawers. Stockings were folded together and stored in a basket nearby. "These will do."

Sara stripped out of her wet clothes and washed and dried herself, her hands shaking still, her legs long and slim and white in the firelight. She pulled on the clothes that Kitty had handed her, then, still fastening the skirt, she looked toward Kitty, mouth trembling. "What will we do?" she asked.

"Well . . ." Kitty tried to think. "I know I killed one. Maybe two. And I think there were only two others. They could be gone. But we have to be careful."

Sara nodded.

"I'm going up to the loft," Kitty said. It had come to her at that moment. The ventilation slots that Usaph had built in were perfect for scanning the area all the way to the woods and the creek. "I can see better from up there. I'll be back in a minute."

The loft was dim and hot, though not as airless as the downstairs. Light threaded in through the thin, horizontal holes beneath the eaves, and Kitty determined to take full advantage of the view, going in turn to all four sides. Her careful gaze swept the orchard and the path to the creek. Nothing seemed out of place. The blackberry bushes and the slim young apple trees stirred in the breeze, and farther off the creek wound its way, silvery green and cool-looking. If Lady had come back, Kitty thought, she would surely have set up a wild barking at sight of Indians. Or if she had come back and they were gone, she could just be sleeping on the front porch the way she liked to do.

The view out toward the springhouse showed nothing amiss, and after a moment of steeling herself, Kitty moved to the side of the loft nearest the shed. Still not quite able to look, she closed her eyes and turned her cheek against the rough-barked log, breathing in the sweet, almost spicy smell of it. Surely she would not see Pa lying there when she looked.

But she did, and she could only bear a second of it before her eyes flooded with tears that scalded her throat and caused an awful ache in her chest. She wiped them away and forced herself to do what she must. She noted the shed and the shadows to the side of it, the cornfield and the vegetable patch . . . There was no movement except the stirring of the deep golden corn tassels.

Finally she came to the front of the loft, kneeling to look out over the front yard, moaning softly as she saw Priscilla there in the grass. She let herself look on to where her mother lay. It was all so still, so terribly still, and she was choking on the grief that rose within her . . . when suddenly she saw a movement, saw a finger curl.

She jumped, a thin cry escaping her. It couldn't have been, she told herself as her heart started to race. Her mind was playing tricks on her. There was no way her mother could have moved her finger.

She was frozen now, waiting, her eyes feeling as if they must burst from her head. A mud dauber swooped and made his graceful curves in front of her, but her gaze never wavered, fixed through the shimmering air on the still form of Amelia Gentry.

And then the hand moved slowly, feebly, opened and closed, and tears began to stream down Kitty's cheeks. *Ma is alive. . . .*

The words trembled within her as she raced down the steep stairs to clutch at a startled Sara. "She's alive. Ma's alive out there!"

Sara shook her head. Clearly she thought it was Kitty who had lost her wits this time.

"I'm going to get her," Kitty declared, starting for the door.

"No," Sara moaned. "For God's sake! They're out there waiting. . . ."

Kitty turned back long enough to grab the rifle and press it into Sara's reluctant hands. "It's loaded and ready. All you have to do is pull back the hammer, point it, and fire. Now, you wait by the door," she cautioned Sara. "I think they're gone . . . but if anything should happen out there, you just close and bar the door and don't open it except for me . . . or someone we know."

"Don't go," Sara pleaded, terrified. But Kitty already had the door open and was blinking in the sudden light, her eyes sweeping the yard.

With no sign of the Shawnee, she darted out, running in a half crouch to drop down by Amelia. "Ma," she said hoarsely, "it's me. It's Kitty."

There was the barest flicker of an eyelid and, as she caught her mother's hand, a faint pressure from her fingers. The front of Amelia's apron was soaked with blood, and as Kitty looked on the blood-crusted, wrinkled skin at the top of her forehead, where the hair had been slashed away, she came close to fainting—the white, blood-smeared bone of Amelia's skull was clearly visible. But with a mighty effort, she steadied herself. "I'm going to get you inside," she declared.

She caught her mother under the armpits and, calling on a strength she didn't know she possessed, pulled her a few inches. Amelia moaned.

"I'm sorry . . . sorry," Kitty babbled. "It won't be long. . . ." But it was harder every time, though she set her feet determinedly, straining and tugging for whatever headway she could make. Halfway to the porch she suddenly realized that Sara was beside her, her face so white she was green about the lips. Kitty could only nod, knowing what it had cost her to come out.

Together it was easier, and they got her inside the cabin at last, stopping to bar the door again before they took her into the bedroom and eased her carefully onto the bed.

"There's some linen in a basket over there," Kitty told Sara. "Get it, while I bring a basin of clean water. Lord, I wish we had some willow bark."

First they spooned some of the water slowly and carefully between Amelia's parched lips, and then when Kitty was satisfied that some had trickled down her throat, they stripped off her upper clothing and bathed her wounds, her breasts looking small and somehow girlish bared that way.

The knife punctures in her chest and midsection had stopped bleeding freely and now only oozed darkly. Kitty packed linen pads over each wound and bound the small-boned body with strips from a torn bedsheet. Then they stripped off the rest of her clothing and carefully eased her into a clean nightgown. Finally, Sara had to look away as Kitty draped a small square of wet linen over the top of her mother's head.

Amelia's eyelids fluttered and she tried to speak, but Kitty just squeezed her hand. "Rest, Ma," she said. "Sleep . . .''

After a few moments beside the bed, Kitty beckoned to Sara and they went into the main room. "I have to make sure about Pa and Priscilla," she said, her voice quiet and calm. "I'm going back out."

A small muscle twitched at the corner of Sara's left eyelid. "They're dead, Kitty. Don't go out again. Please . . .''

"I have to. We thought Ma was dead. What if one of them is still alive?"

Sara bit her lip and said no more, watching as Kitty took up the gun and headed for the door.

"Be ready to bar it," she instructed again. And then she was out and across the porch and into the lengthening shadows.

She looked down numbly at Priscilla, fighting back the hot surge in her throat. There was no doubt that her sister was dead. The whole side of her face was crushed in. They had taken her hair, too. Flies swarmed and lit . . .

Swallowing hard, Kitty quickly continued on her grim mission, her eyes sweeping the yard, expecting at any moment to hear the high shrill yelp and feel the ax against her own head. But everything was quiet as she approached the shed, except for the buzzing of the flies.

Usaph looked as if his neck were broken, and she closed the staring eyes quickly, leaning impulsively to kiss the cheek that felt cold. As she got to her feet, she caught sight of the cow lying sprawled, its belly slit, entrails roping out, the dead calf alongside.

The hot rush in her throat could no longer be denied; leaning against the side of the shed, she heaved up everything that was in her stomach, retching until only bile came.

Trembling still, eyes dry and burning, she started back to the cabin, and it came to her that if she lived—and she was fiercely determined to do that—nothing worse could ever happen to her than had already happened this day.

* 11 *

A S DUSK FELL, KITTY WAS RELIEVED TO SEE THE HORSES come up to stand by the shed. She had feared that the Indians had discovered and taken them. But with their appearance she knew what had to be done.

"We have to get to the fort tonight," she said.

The terror that had never been far removed from Sara's eyes in all those hours flared. "They could be out there . . . waiting."

"I know that," Kitty acknowledged. "But there are people at the fort who'll know what to do for Ma. She'll have a better chance. Besides, if we don't go while we can, they could be back at sunup . . . maybe more of them. It'll be too late then. We have to risk it now."

Sara was clearly reluctant but finally agreed.

As soon as it was fully dark, Kitty slipped out. The grass was already damp, the crickets chirping rhythmically as she stole across the yard. The moon was already up and casting its pale light. That could be a help, she thought. It would certainly make it easier to stay on the trail to the fort. But if the Shawnee were about somewhere, it would make it all the easier for them to see the wagon and its escaping women.

The mares stamped and shied as she approached, nervous with the blood smell in the air. "Whoa," she said softly. "Nell

. . . Moll . . .'' She reached out a hand to rub their smooth, warm necks, quieting them. She was careful not to look at her father lying nearby and willed herself to think of other things.

The spotted red cow had not come in. Probably the Indians had killed it, she thought, as they had the other. Neither had Lady come back. Kitty wanted to call her but didn't dare. It wasn't unusual, she thought, for the hound to take off for a day or two of hunting and then come home, her coat filled with cockleburs, wagging her tail and ravenous.

The wagon was at the side of the shed, and she worked quickly to get the animals hitched. She had never done it before, though she had seen her father do it a thousand times and knew exactly how. Still, it was not easy for her to handle the heavy doubletrees with their wooden bars and chains or to slip on the harness and back the big mares into place on either side of the rough-hewn tongue. And all of it was more difficult with the steady throbbing of her shoulder where the gun had kicked her.

But finished at last, she climbed to the seat and, clucking softly to the horses, drove the wagon right up beside the porch, her eyes sweeping the shadows, her heart pounding. Sara stood waiting in the darkened doorway—they had agreed not to light the grease lamps, so they wouldn't be such easy targets once the door was opened. "Here," she said, "I brought these quilts to put under her." She came out onto the porch and handed them up to Kitty, who hitched up her skirt to climb into the back and spread them in the wagon bed.

With a sunbonnet tied beneath Amelia's chin to keep the damp linen cloth in place atop her head, they carried her out, stopping to lower her to the floor every few steps; though there were two of them, her weight was limp and heavy. "Careful . . . careful!" Kitty warned once when it looked as if Sara might drop her end. There were moments when she staggered herself.

Once to the edge of the porch, Kitty braced herself to move onto the wagon bed, stepping backward. She tottered and almost fell, setting her legs and holding on to her mother determinedly. A small cry escaped Sara.

"It's all right," Kitty gasped. "I've got her." With a moment to steady herself, she met Sara's eyes, and with a nod of her head they sucked in their breath and swung the injured woman into the wagon.

Though Amelia's eyes were still closed, she moaned loudly, and Kitty, trembling, dropped down beside her, close to her ear. "We're going to the fort. You're going to be all right, Ma. Can you hear me? It's Kitty.'' There was a faint flicker of her mother's eyelids, but Kitty wasn't sure if she had really heard.

Sara had grabbed a light woolen blanket from inside the door, and they covered her with it now so she wouldn't get chilled in the night air.

"All right,'' Kitty said, "climb up. I'll be right back.''

She darted into the house to grab the gun and raced to the linen basket for the two sheets that were left there. Back outside, she passed the gun up to Sara, who sat hunched forward, her face ghostly in the moonlight, eyes down as if she dare not look toward the dark and endless trees out there ahead of them. Her hands were trembling visibly, but she took the rifle from Kitty without a word and laid it across her lap.

"I can't leave them that way,'' Kitty said, looking over her shoulder. She ran first to Priscilla to cover her gently, and then on to her father. Tears threatened to blind her, but she wiped them away determinedly. Ma was alive, and whatever strength she had must be used to keep her that way. She couldn't take time for tears now.

In a moment she was up on the seat beside Sara. Giving her a look of assurance that was far from what she really felt, she brought the reins down firmly to start the mares forward.

Those first moments were terrifying. The creaking of the wheels, which they had hardly noticed on their frequent forays to Boonesborough, now seemed to shriek out their presence, and they both started each time they scared up a rabbit or sent a raccoon scurrying away through a thicket. Kitty kept talking softly. It helped take her mind off the dark underbrush and the blackness that shrouded the trees, all those places where someone might be lurking . . . watching.

"It's not really all that far . . . through these woods, then along the river . . . skirt the cane . . . that stretch of hilly ground . . . remember? And wind back toward the river again and just keep going until we get there. . . .''

Once, a hoot owl called, and Sara jumped, her breath coming raggedly until she realized what it was and gave a strange, nervous little laugh. Kitty said nothing, but perspiration popped out suddenly on her upper lip, and her heart began to thump against her ribs. She knew now that Indians signaled to one another that way. Days after her capture, she'd remembered the call of a bird and its answer just before the Shawnee had crept up on her.

She held her breath, trying to pick up the pace of the horses a little. The trees pressed in on either side, the darkness deepening as the moon was covered over by a cloud for a moment. But no howling redmen leaped out at them; the woods were quiet but for the creaking wagon and the soft thud of the horses' hooves.

There was a certain relief in emerging from the trees and catching sight of the river. At least they'd made it this far, Kitty told herself. The water was almost black under the night sky, silvery ripples marking the current here and there, patches of gray mist hanging just above the surface. Mosquitoes rose out of the damp grass to sing close to the women's ears and bite. Kitty gave over the reins to Sara for a moment, stretching far back to pull a corner of the blanket over her mother's face. "Be easy, Ma," she said. "I don't want the mosquitoes to bite you."

The assault of the stinging insects didn't lessen until they'd skirted the low-lying cane bottoms and climbed to higher ground . . . though that brought its own problems. The wagon lurched over the rocky trail, and Kitty was at once concerned about the effect of the jostling on her mother. There hadn't even been a groan for a long time.

At Kitty's urging, Sara climbed awkwardly back to sit beside Amelia, speaking to her in a tremulous voice, pulling the blanket back from her face.

"Is she . . . all right?" Kitty asked her.

It was a long moment before Sara responded. "She's still breathing," she said.

Kitty held on to the reins grimly, her shoulder aching dully. That was enough, she told herself. For Ma to keep on breathing was enough for now.

At last they reached the final stretch. The banks climbed higher above the river here, worn smooth and kept free of trees by the countless herds of buffalo, deer, and elk that had taken the path regularly on their way to the salt-embedded ground around the sulfur spring out from the fort. The moon, unhampered by clouds now, lit the way ahead, gleamed off the dark backs of the mares. Though Kitty knew that before long they would be able to see Boonesborough, all the grief and shock and fear suddenly pressed in on her. The horror of the last eight hours was so overwhelming that for a moment she felt she couldn't get them any farther. Her hands felt numb from the pull of the reins. Her shoulders sagged.

She forced herself stiffly erect and began to sing softly, doggedly trying to remember all the words and every verse to "Goin' to London Town." And after a few minutes Sara, back beside Amelia still, joined in, her voice thin and unsure at first, and then steadier. "And we won't get home till dark, my dear . . . we won't get home till dark . . ."

It got them to within sight of the fort, the corner blockhouses and palisades outlined in the moonlight. Once they'd seen it, neither of them said a word. Their voices just trailed off in the middle of a line and they rode the rest of the way in silence.

There were supposed to be sentries on lookout all the time now, but they were almost on the stockade walls before they heard the sleepy male voice call out. "Hellooo, the wagon . . ."

"Open the gates," Kitty called back. "It's Kitty Gentry . . . and Sara. We've got my mother with us. . . ." And behind her in the wagon bed, Sara began to sob quietly.

Smoke from the grease lamps made the cabin murky and stung Kitty's eyes as she watched Granny Hawkins carefully peel back the linen pads that covered the stab wounds beneath Amelia Gentry's breasts. The old lady—acknowledged to be the most knowledgeable one at the fort when it came to doctoring—had been summoned at once after the arrival of the wagon. She'd come, skinny and birdlike, her clawed hands touching the injured woman gently, crooning her concern.

Rebecca had taken Sara off to the Boone cabin to try to quiet her weeping and get her into bed, and now Elizabeth Callaway touched Kitty's shoulder, shock and sorrow written on that patrician face.

"Won't you come with me to our cabin where you can get some rest, Kitty . . . my dear." Her voice threatened to break.

Kitty shook her head. "I can't."

"Fanny's still awake. You could rest in her bed and she'll climb in with Keziah. I'll come right back here once I see you settled. I'll sit right beside her. I promise. . . ."

"I thank you, Mistress Callaway"—Kitty didn't take her eyes from her mother's face—"but I can't."

Amelia's breath came harder, her skin waxen, but that tenacious spirit of hers still clung to life. Kitty sank down beside the bed to take a limp hand in hers, and it seemed to her that there was a feeble pressure, though the fingers felt deathly cold and Amelia's eyelids stayed closed.

Granny Hawkins, working with a surprising quickness, pressed a mass of dark, wet herbs against the stab wounds and bound them back up. Then, with a gesture to Elizabeth, the two of them eased off the bonnet and the damp square of linen to reveal the fearful sight of the scalped head.

Paling, Elizabeth stood back, her lips pressed tightly together, but the old lady looked closely at the dark, puckering edges of skin and the bared and bloodstained crown of Amelia's skull. She nodded her head and swallowed several times, chin bobbing.

"We need to peg her scalp," she announced. "I ain't never done it. I own to that. But I seen it done . . . back when I was a young woman. Back in Virginny on the outposts. The Indians would raid down, and I seen more than one head pegged."

"I don't understand," said Kitty.

"I got to take a awl, like as you puncture leather with for a pair o' shoes, and make holes right close together clean over this bare part . . . to relieve her some."

"Oh, my God!" Kitty moaned.

"I've heard of it, child," Elizabeth put in. "They say the French thought it was the best treatment."

"No . . ." Even the thought of it sickened Kitty. "No, you can't do that to her."

"I seen a woman," Granny Hawkins said, "most likely about your ma's age, live another twenty year after it was done. No hair ever grew back. She wore a little cap . . ."

"No! How could it possibly help? You'll kill her!"

"It could," the old lady acknowledged after a moment. "Or it could save her. I own I couldn't say for certain which. But if it does right, all them little holes ooze out and scab over."

Kitty felt as if she couldn't breathe, and she kept shaking her head, no, no, no. . . . She looked to Elizabeth Callaway for help, but in that moment the Old Colonel's wife could only look away.

"I don't know what to tell you," she said, finally meeting Kitty's eyes, "but it's the only thing I've ever heard done for a person scalped . . . but still alive."

Kitty felt a sudden faint pressure from the cold fingers against hers, and with a wave of horror it came to her that Amelia had heard . . . had understood. "Ma"—she leaned close, her voice cracking—"it's all right. Don't worry now. Just rest. I'll take care of you. I won't let them do anything like that. I promise you. . . ."

Amelia's breathing became more ragged and the fingers pressed again, feebly but insistently, her eyelids fluttering half open . . . and Kitty saw the clear recognition there.

"Are you—" Kitty's voice kept breaking so that she could hardly get the words out. "Are you trying to tell me that—you want to let her try it?"

Amelia's mouth opened and she tried to speak, though what came out was no more than an unintelligible whisper of sound. But Kitty, staring into the open eyes, saw the affirmation there.

She heard Elizabeth's long sigh and Granny Hawkins's swallowing, and after a moment she pressed her mother's hand and tried to smile. "All right, Ma. . . ." She felt she was choking as she said the words. The recognition in Amelia's eyes had already faded, and, half open still, they were dull now, her breathing labored.

"I guess you'd best get what you'll need," she said to the old lady before the agony inside her got too much to bear.

Granny Hawkins left the cabin with the promise that she'd be back soon, and Elizabeth stood beside Kitty, her ruffled cap askew, her long face sad.

In a moment they heard the sound of Daniel's voice just outside the cabin, and then Rebecca's. And in the next instant Rebecca entered the smoky room to lay a sympathetic hand on Kitty's shoulder.

She drew Elizabeth aside, and the two of them had begun to converse in low tones when Kitty, eyes fixed on her mother, saw that first faint tremor that coursed through the petite body . . . like a slight shudder, nothing more. And then Amelia's head drew back, her mouth open, soundless, her chest heaving. And Kitty screamed, as if she could scream for her, one sharp, awful sound.

The two older women were there at once, Elizabeth holding Amelia's other hand, Rebecca trying to cushion her head . . . all of them staring into the open eyes as a last, long breath escaped her lips and the tortured body arched, then settled back . . . and finally was still.

Elizabeth looked into Kitty's face, then back down. "God rest your soul, Amelia Gentry," she said softly.

After a long moment Kitty lay her head against her mother's chest, the grief within her dry and scorching, filling her. . . .

Israel Boone, along with several of the fort men, took word of the tragedy to the Tylers as soon as it was fully daylight, and they came to the fort at once, Ben tight-lipped, Faith red-eyed from weeping, the baby clinging to her, whining.

"Oh, my God . . . Kitty . . ." Faith began to cry the moment she caught sight of her. Fanny Callaway took little Martha outside, and the two sisters embraced, Kitty dry-eyed. She had cried out all her tears the night before.

She remembered being brought to the Callaway cabin, where her badly bruised shoulder had been rubbed with a soothing ointment. She had been plied with hot catnip tea, known for its soothing properties, and the Old Colonel had insisted that she be given a good swallow of his strong corn liquor. But nothing had helped until, tucked into Fanny's bed, she had given way at last and let the pent-up tears come. After that, exhausted, she'd finally slept.

Now it was she who tried to comfort Faith, as Ben stood by awkwardly, patting each of them and muttering words of faith to try to find some acceptance of what had happened himself. "God's will be done. He must know the reason . . . And we must accept."

He wrapped both of them in his long, skinny arms. "Kitty . . . little sister. Now we're here. We'll take care of you. Leave everything to me."

"I can't believe it yet," Faith said brokenly. "I just can't."

"I know," said Kitty.

"Where is Sara?" asked Faith.

"She's with Rebecca. I was just over there. They're going to keep her in bed today. But she'll be all right after a little rest. She helped me get Ma to the fort. I don't know if I could have gotten her here without Sara."

Faith shook her head and began to sob again.

Besides sending word to the Tylers, Daniel had sent riders to warn all the outlying settlers. Now, as the people began to trickle in, grim-faced and anxious, riding, walking, creaking along in makeshift wagons, Daniel called everyone to the northeast blockhouse.

Henry Porter and his oldest boy, Marcum, had just ridden in. Lureen Porter, after hugging her father, was now crying softly into Elvie's ample bosom—Priscilla had planned to spend the night with Lureen on Friday. The newlyweds, Betsey and Sam, stood quietly, while Maggie Hamilton dabbed at her face with a lace handkerchief and from time to time cast accusing looks at her husband, Horace. Squire Boone's wife, Jane—a freckled woman with big hands—kept her children close about her. Some found chairs, and others stood along the wall.

"I expect you've all heard what happened at the Gentry

place," Daniel began. He looked toward Kitty, who stood there, Faith and Ben beside her. "Words cannot express our sorrow."

The surveyor, Isaac Shelby, who'd brought the letter from Roman only days before, shifted from his place near the wall and extended his hand to Kitty, bowing in a formal but somehow touching gesture of sympathy.

"Amelia Gentry were a brave woman," Granny Hawkins piped. "I could take oath on that."

A tall, gaunt woodsman who was seldom seen at the fort doffed his hat, his mane of tangled hair unbound, and stepped forward to nod to Kitty and Faith. He held out a huge, bony hand to Ben, who accepted it gravely. "If there is a thing I can do to help you folks . . ." he said. "My name's Welter. Amos Welter."

"We all feel the same," Daniel called out. "But before we see what needs doin', there are things that ought to be said to the rest of you."

All eyes turned his way.

"My brother Squire and me rode out at daybreak and made a wide circle around the fort to pick up what sign we could. With Roman and Cullen both gone, we're short-handed. . . ."

Just the sound of their names made Kitty know how much she wished both men were there. Roman was her friend as well as kinsman. Even the thought of his seemingly endless strength made her calmer. And God knew Sara needed him. As for Cullen . . . Her heart twisted painfully. There were no words to say how much she wanted him, how much she needed his arms about her.

"We'll be out again," Daniel was saying. "But we are not sure yet what's afoot. My advice is to stay here at the fort until we know it's safe to return to your cabins. If you've got stock that has to be tended, drive it in. There'll be some of us to help you. And speaking now of that . . ." He looked toward Ben Tyler. "What can we do, Ben?"

Ben took a step forward, his light eyes paler than ever in the thin, sunburned face. "I'd be obliged if some of you men would go out with me to the Gentry place and help me bring in my wife's father and sister"—his voice quivered—"so that they, along with my mother-in-law, can have a decent burial here outside the fort."

"No!" It burst out of Kitty, and Ben, surprised, turned to stare at her, his mouth still open. There were low murmurs through the crowd.

"Kitty?" Daniel's eyes found her. "You have something you want to say?"

"Only . . . only that Pa and Priscilla mustn't be brought here. My mother must be taken back there . . . and all of them buried on our place."

"Now, sister," said Ben, his tone solicitous, "you're overwrought . . . and little wonder. Leave this to me."

Faith put a restraining hand on Kitty's arm, but Kitty shook it away. "No, Ben, I can't," she said. "I know what they'd want."

Her brother-in-law gave his head an impatient shake. "It's out of the question. I believe I know what's best here. When you've had time to think on it, you'll know I was right."

Kitty cast an imploring look toward Faith, who avoided her eyes, and then to Daniel, who looked as if he were about to say something. But the gaunt woodsman, Amos Welter, spoke up first.

"From what I heard," he said, "this little lady has been through aplenty . . . and been braver than most. I reckon she ought to have some say in it."

"That's what I think, too," Elvie Porter chimed in. "No offense to you, Ben," she added.

There was the soft rustle of a skirt, and Kitty turned to see Elizabeth Callaway edge through the crowd and come to stand beside her. "Amelia Gentry was my friend," she said. "I think what Kitty said is exactly what Amelia would have wanted."

Daniel looked back to Kitty.

"My father and mother always knew that there was a danger the Indians might come," she said, her lips dry and tight. "They could have come in here to the fort and been safe. But Pa said no heathen savages were going to drive him off his land. And Ma said we came to Kentucke to make our home and we weren't going to leave it. It wouldn't be right to bury them anyplace else. Please . . ."

There was a moment's silence. Daniel's high-cheekboned face was grave as he considered; then in barely a moment he gave a firm nod of his head. "There is sense to that." His eyes flickered to Ben. "I believe in the light of circumstance that Kitty ought to decide."

Rebecca had come into the blockhouse a few minutes earlier, standing quietly in back during the dispute. Now, at her husband's words, she smiled at him from across the room.

Ben's mouth was a thin line. "I still say it's adding undue risk for those who go. It would be a sight easier and quicker to just bring the bodies back here for the burial.''

"I'll go along," said Daniel, his voice steady.

"As will I," Amos Welter chimed in.

Isaac Shelby, solemn-faced, held up his hand. "I'd consider it an honor to be included," he declared with great dignity. And as he was saying it, others stepped to the forefront.

"I'll go along to say the words," Squire volunteered.

Daniel nodded.

Twelve men, besides Daniel, offered their help. The Old Colonel tried to, but Daniel convinced him that he should stay behind to be in charge of the fort should anything happen during their absence.

Ben was grim-faced when he realized that Kitty was determined to go along. "That's downright foolishness, sister. There's no way to know for sure that the Shawnee aren't out there waiting."

"I'm going," said Kitty.

Ben shook his head and cast a disapproving look at his wife, as if he held her responsible for the stubbornness of her sister. Faith appeared ready to burst into tears.

"I—I wish I could be there, too," she said, the words muffled, a guilty look stealing over her puffy-eyed face.

"I understand that." Ben softened to give her an awkward pat. "But I'm thankful you've got sense enough to know you can't. Now, why don't you go into the cabin here and see to Martha."

Faith regarded Kitty with a stricken look, but Kitty managed a smile. "Go ahead," she said, and Faith, crying now, went into the Callaway cabin where Fanny and Jemima Boone had been minding the baby.

There were no other objections to Kitty's going, and she sat on the seat beside Flanders, who drove the wagon that held Amelia's sheet-wrapped body. Daniel led the way, five riders just behind him, six bringing up the rear, behind the wagon.

The day was perfect, and as they rode, Kitty was strangely aware of how beautiful everything was, of the deep clear green of the river, the full and pungent cedars, the oaks, the creamy, patterned trunks of the sycamores. Trumpet vines were bursting with bright orange blossoms, and the goldenrod was in full bloom. It was as if she tried to fix it in her mind, as if she could record it for them . . . for Pa and Ma and Prissy, one last time.

As they approached the cabin, Kitty caught the faint, vaguely sweet scent of decay in the air, and she moaned softly, her eyes seeking the covered bodies lying in the hot afternoon sun. And as the wagon came to a halt, she could see that something, some animal probably, had pulled the sheet partly off her father's body.

Flanders gave her a hand down, but she didn't go any closer. She would spare herself that.

"Stay nearby until we satisfy ourselves there are no savages skulking about," he cautioned, the loaded rifle ready in the crook of his arm.

The men fanned out to make sure that all was clear, a couple of them going into the cabin to see that no one was hiding there, and in a moment Daniel came to stand by Kitty.

"Where would you like the graves to be?" His eyes, usually light-hearted, seemed heavy with memories of all the graves he'd dug or stood by. "I tell you true," he said, "I liked your folks. Roman will take this hard when he hears."

Kitty nodded, unable to speak.

She chose a spot past the orchard and somewhat higher, a small natural clearing bounded by a half circle of huge old walnut and cherry trees. From there, she thought, the cabin could be seen in the distance, at the rise of the gently rolling land . . . and the young apple trees were growing. And down the slope from the site, the creek rippled, several willows drooping gracefully along the banks.

The men worked quickly. Daniel and Ben and Amos Welter wrapped the bodies of Usaph and Priscilla so that they might be put decently into their final resting places. The others had begun digging the graves.

Kitty fetched a split basket from the side of the porch, somehow comforted by the feel of the smooth hickory splints—Pa had made it—and she walked out to the dogwood tree and gathered the tallow dips that still hung there—the tallow dips that she and Sara had made . . . dear God, was it only yesterday?

When all was ready, they called her and she went to stand beside Ben and Daniel, all eyes toward Squire Boone, who turned the pages of his well-worn Bible back and forth to various favorite passages:

"If a man die, shall he live again? . . . While the earth remaineth, seedtime and harvest, and cold and heat, and summer and winter, and day and night shall not cease . . . As for man, his days are as grass; as a flower of the field . . . For dust thou art, and unto dust shalt thou return . . . I send an Angel before thee, to keep thee in the way . . ."

The shrouded bodies were lowered into the rich dark earth, and Kitty dropped the first crumbly handfuls of dirt into each grave and then watched as the men shoveled them full, rounding over the tops and marking them with rough slabs of wood which they'd hacked out with an ax.

Ben, beads of sweat standing out on his face and darkening the back of his rough homespun shirt, came to put his arm around her awkwardly. "I didn't mean to speak harshly to you before, little sister, I only feared for your safety."

Kitty patted his arm. "I know, Ben. I know."

He went then to help some of the others clear out the shed.

Flanders sought out Kitty. "I found the dog out back of the springhouse," he said. "I'll bury her for you."

Kitty looked away for a moment. She'd known that Lady was dead when she hadn't come bounding up on their arrival. The Indians had killed everything. "If you would, please," she said. "I'd not like to have her just thrown out in the woods." Prissy had loved her. They all had.

Amos Welter approached her next, unkempt hair blowing about the gaunt-boned face. "I'm a right good hand with a chisel and hammer, Miss Gentry. If you'll tell me after we get back to the fort how you want them to read, I'd be proud to cut you some proper stones for your people out there."

"I'd thank you for that, Mr. Welter," said Kitty, "just as I thank you for what you've done today."

"No need," he muttered, and clapped his hat on his head and went to help at the shed.

The stench of decaying flesh carried on the breeze as the bloating corpses of the cow and calf, looped around by a couple of stout hemp ropes, were pulled out of the shed by the horses and dragged off a ways. Kitty covered her mouth and fled into the cabin to sit in the warm, dim light, her back rigid against the settle. Like something alive, the dry grief surged inside her, and her eyes moved over the blue Delft cups that had been her mother's pride and the worn wooden spoons that hung below the shelf. One of the pegs held her mother's apron, another Pa's old homespun vest. . . .

After a while she got up and began to gather some things to take with her. She put hers and Sara's clothes in a couple of large baskets, impulsively tucking the Delft cups and saucers between the folds of their skirts. Priscilla's recently finished sampler lay folded on a chair, and she brought that to place atop the clothes. She took up the carved Bible box, the Gentry Bible

within. She must record what had happened there . . . maybe
tomorrow, she thought.

She had fetched her mother's doted-upon books, bound them
with a leather strap, and was ready to take everything out to the
porch where the tallow dips waited—somehow it seemed important to her to take them—when she heard a shout from outside.

"Kitty . . . Kitty, come out here!"

She burst through the door to see a beaming Israel rounding
the corner of the cabin.

"Just look what I found!" he said. And the spotted cow before him came to a stop, her full udder swinging beneath her as
she planted her hooves and swung her head to low gently at the
big-eyed red calf that came awkwardly alongside her.

"They didn't get her . . . the Shawnee didn't kill her!" Kitty
cried.

"No." Israel grinned broadly. "She must have gone off by
herself to drop her calf. And it's a fine strong heifer."

Flanders came to join them. "We'll get them into the fort for
you," he said. "We'll put the calf in the wagon and drive slow.
Her mama'll just follow right along."

The calf made a funny sideways move, trying to play, giving
its head a shake, its tail twitching. And Kitty dropped to her
knees in the grass and put her arms around it. She had thought
she was all cried out, but tears came now . . . and they hurt.
But as she pressed her face into the soft warm neck, and breathed
in the newborn smell of it, and the rough little tongue came out
to give her cheek a lick, she was smiling.

* 12 *

AFTER TEN DAYS OUT, DANIEL AND SQUIRE RODE INTO the fort to announce that from all signs, the Shawnee party that had come into the area had been small and what was left of it was already back across the Ohio. Besides the Gentry tragedy, the only damage done had been the burning of a cabin south of McAfee's Station, empty at the time.

"It appears to me," Daniel said, "that we may owe their quick departure to the Gentry girl. There are times when an Indian would just as soon not go to a lot of trouble . . . and Kitty gave them more than enough."

The news that it was safe to go back home was welcomed, and some started preparations to leave at once, Ben among them. "Get your things together," he told Faith and Kitty. And once she'd done it, Kitty hurried to see Sara—the Boones had insisted that Sara stay with them until Roman came back from Virginia.

She was still pale, that certain fragility intensified, but her grip was strong on Kitty's hands. "I'll miss you," she said.

"I'll miss you." Kitty tried to grin. "But Roman will be home before long and you'll be back in your own cabin. And I'll be coming to the fort whenever Faith and Ben come. . . ."

Sara nodded.

There were no tears, but the parting wrenched at both of them. The friendship, already formed, had been tempered in those awful hours they'd shared, forged into a bond that each of them realized was as strong as either had ever had.

"You take care of yourself," said Sara.

"I will. And you, too . . . I'd better go. They'll be waiting for me." They hugged once more, then Kitty turned and ran from the Boone cabin.

* * *

The first few days at the Tyler place made it clear just how difficult it was going to be to grow accustomed to life with Faith and Ben. It was true that Kitty had stayed with Faith after the baby was born, but that had been different. She had known she was going home then.

The cabin was small and overcrowded with her presence. Since Ben's brother Todd was already sleeping in the loft, that left no place for Kitty except down in the one room with Faith and Ben and little Martha. And come bedtime, she would curl herself into a ball on her pallet, knees drawn up, listening to Faith's restless turning and, after a while, Ben's snoring, jumping up to answer the baby's thin wail when she was wet and needing drying.

Aware of the drawbacks of the situation, she did her best to give Ben and Faith time alone together, making it a habit to sit outside after the supper dishes were cleared and put away. She would take up the basket of mending and go out to the rough log bench beneath the spreading branches of the twin beech trees that bordered the side of the cabin, plying her needle as long as it was light enough. Afterward she would wait in the cool twilight, listening to the hum of the tree frogs and the soft lowing of a cow now and again. At least it gave her respite from Ben's everlasting dourness.

She had never cared very much for her brother-in-law, and daily living with him only intensified that. And if anything, Todd Tyler irritated her even more. He had an annoying way of chewing suddenly for no reason, solemn as a cow. He would chew and swallow when there wasn't a thing in his mouth except his own tongue. There were times when it nearly drove her crazy.

Her nightly hour or so of solitude helped her to deal with such minor irritations, though all too often Ben summoned her in before she was ready to come, calling her to one of the interminable daily prayer sessions he insisted upon. Not a crumb was consumed unless God's blessing be asked upon it, and the evening prayers were the longest of all. No one was excused. Even little Martha must be fetched, awake or asleep.

It was not that Kitty objected to a heartfelt prayer; there had certainly been those in the Gentry cabin. But there'd been a kind of joy and warmth in it all that was absent here.

Even to think of home brought a stinging grief, and she reminded herself that no matter where she was now, it wouldn't be easy. She would have to try harder.

To her dismay, the third week she was there, Todd took to

walking out to join her beneath the branches of the beech trees in the evening. She could hardly bear to have her only time alone intruded upon, but she reminded herself that he was Ben's brother and, as such, certainly as welcome there as she. She did her best to be pleasant to him.

One evening, in an attempt to make conversation, she told him how cute the baby had been in trying to hold on to and drink out of a wooden cup earlier that day. "She really was getting some of it down"—Kitty laughed at the memory—"but then she spilled all of it on me."

Todd just sat there looking at her soberly through those bleached Tyler eyes. He chewed on his tongue and swallowed. "Seems like a waste of good milk to me," he opined.

Ben called them in to prayers just then, and Kitty suddenly realized that she didn't even mind going. It was better than having to talk to Todd.

To her surprise, the prayers were cut short that evening, with Ben's announcement that there were important family matters to be discussed before they went to bed. Faith had just put the baby into her cradle, and as she turned back, Kitty noted the flushed cheeks and the looking away, while at the same time Todd was regarding her with a strangely knowing look in those pale eyes. Whatever the "family matters," she thought, it appeared that everyone already knew but her.

The coals were glowing in the fireplace, the grease lamps lit, and Ben settled himself into his chair, assuming one of his most serious airs. "I was to the fort a few days ago," he began, "and found out that Daniel is sending a courier east in less than a week. Todd will be going with him to take care of some personal business and bring our brother Latham back with him when he comes."

"Oh?" said Kitty, wondering what that had to do with her, and having to bite her tongue to keep from asking him why he hadn't told her he was going to Boonesborough so she could have gone along for a visit.

"Your sister and I have prayed over this matter, long and hard," Ben went on. "We've decided it's best, sister, if you go back with him."

It took a moment for his words to register. Faith was still looking away, Todd hunched forward in his chair, his hair light as straw. "Back?" Kitty got out, confused. "Back where? Back to the Watauga?"

"Of course not," Faith burst out.

Ben raised a hand to silence her. "We think it's best for you if you go to one of your sisters in Virginia. I'm sure either Abigail or Miranda would welcome you." He managed to make his voice firm as well as placating, bestowing one of his thin smiles upon her.

It was so unexpected, and overwhelming, that Kitty could only look from her brother-in-law to her sister, and then down at her own hands, which were clenched tightly in her lap.

"When you think about it, you'll see that we're right," Ben continued. "And Todd will see you safely home. . . ."

"Home?" Kitty flared, her head lifting. "Virginia's not home to me! Kentucke's my home. Otter Creek is my home." The thought of the cabin on the rise, the rolling hills, the creek, sent such a rush of longing through her that she feared it might shatter her.

Faith put a trembling hand to her throat, her hazel eyes filled with distress. "Kitty, you must see that there's no place out here for a young, unmarried woman who is"—she hesitated—"alone in the world. . . ." Her flush deepened.

"What your sister is trying to say," Ben intervened, "is that while we feel every obligation to you as family, it's not possible for us to keep you here with us. As you've seen, we're crowded for space. It was already arranged long ago that brother Latham would join us out here. Besides, Faith is right when she says this is no place for you now that Amelia and Usaph are gone."

"Ben's going to take care of the place for us," Faith put in eagerly.

He nodded. "You two sisters, and the two back east, will share everything equally when it's sold. Of course, it may take some time, but I assure you I'll send your share, and the shares of the others once it is. Todd, here, says that he might want to buy it once he's saved enough money."

Kitty had listened to this last with astonishment, and now she stood up slowly. The thought of Todd Tyler ever owning the place on Otter Creek—the land where Pa and Ma and Priss were buried—caused a revulsion so strong that she felt ill.

"I would never consent to selling Pa's land," she said, the quietness of her tone belying her inner feelings.

"You're overwrought," said Ben. "I fear I must insist."

Kitty's control snapped. "Since you don't own an inch of it, you have no power to insist on anything." She faced him down.

"Kitty!" Faith gasped.

"A sharp tongue in a woman is not a thing to be admired,"

Ben said coldly, telltale red spots beginning to speckle his thin cheeks. "I'll own that I don't hold with females inheriting, except through their menfolk, as should be. But Colonel Callaway says it's legal, strange as it seems. Usaph's papers on the place says 'heirs and assigns.' Still, as the head of the family, now that he's gone, I feel it's my duty to direct the matter in such a manner as will be right for all."

"I can decide for myself, Ben." Kitty stood her ground.

His face darkened, but before he could speak Faith lifted a hand to quiet her husband, and for once he let her talk while he stared stonily ahead. "Kitty, you're my sister," she said, "and I love you. And I know you've been through a terrible time. But you've got to face the truth. Ma and Pa are dead . . . and it's best for you to go back to Virginia and for the land to be sold so that you'll have your share of the money. It'll be a help to you until you find a nice young man back there."

Todd fidgeted in his chair, as if the rough homespun breeches that always seemed too big for him itched, and Ben sat tight-lipped.

"We're all tired." Faith tried to smooth out everyone's feelings. "The thing I want you to do, honey," she said to Kitty, "is to get a good night's sleep. And we'll talk some more in the morning. You'll see that we're right once you've slept on it."

But Kitty slept little that night. Curled up in the darkness, with only the soft glow of the coals in the fireplace to cast faint shadows about the room, the thin line she'd been able to hold against the pain, the loss, threatened to give way. Hot and silent tears choked her. She had never felt so helpless before, not the way she did now.

But what finally strengthened her in the hours before the dawn was her determination that Ben would not sell the Gentry place. She gritted her teeth and swore it to herself. Without the land, she would have given in and gone back east . . . though God knew that was not what she wanted. She wanted to go home to the cabin on Otter Creek, but that wasn't possible. Not now it wasn't. Not for a lone woman. But there must be something, she reasoned, that she could do at the fort to earn her keep. She was strong . . . and willing to work.

By the morning her decision was made, and she announced it to the others calmly. The three of them stared at her as if she'd taken leave of her senses.

"Of all the fool ideas!" Ben snorted.

"Honey, you don't mean that," Faith pleaded.

"I do," said Kitty, trying to summon a smile for Faith, who after all was her sister. "I appreciate your taking me in for as long as you have. I know you're crowded. But I'll have my things together within the hour. And if you'll be good enough to take me to the fort, Ben, I'll appreciate it."

"Kitty, we can't let you do this." Faith was near to tears, but Ben shot a stern look his wife's way.

"If she's not going to listen to those who know best for her, then she must suffer the consequences."

"Ben's right," Kitty told her sister, though from the look on his face, she could see that it did nothing to sweeten his mood. "I'll take my cow and calf with me," she told him.

The narrow nostrils pinched. "When the calf is weaned, I'll expect to have it back," he declared. "After all, Faith is due a share of the stock."

"You said you intended to round up the hogs from the woods."

"True. And when it's killing time, I'll see you get some of the meat."

"You've got the mares . . . ."

"That's a fact," said Ben, "but I can't see what use you'd have for them. If the time comes when you do, I'll bring one of them to you."

They stood, squared off at one another, Faith and Todd looking on in a kind of bemused wonder. But finally Kitty nodded. She had come to have a certain fondness for the little heifer, but she wasn't going to argue any more about it.

"All right," she agreed. "When the calf is weaned you can come after her. But mind that I get my share of whatever corn is left." And the words were hardly out of her mouth before she was off to pack her things.

Kitty rode in to Boonesborough sitting in the back of the wagon and holding on to the calf—no easy task since it had grown in size and strength in the two weeks since it was born. But the moment Ben lifted it to the ground, it joined its mother, which had followed along after it, and the two of them ambled off toward the river to join the other fort cows grazing there.

Without even a look at Kitty, Ben swung back up to the driver's seat and pulled the horses just inside the open gates, then climbed down again and started to put her things out on the ground. Her clothes were in the hickory basket, and she had the Bible box and books and the other things she'd brought from the Gentry cabin the day of the burial. Ben had raised no objection when he saw she was taking them.

He was hailed from several directions but replied only curtly as he hurried with his task. A young boy looked on in puzzlement. "Mornin', Miss Kitty," he said, lifting his shapeless cap as Kitty climbed down.

"Hello, Oliver," she said.

She kept her chin high as she saw Squire Boone headed their way. She would let no one guess how much she was shaking inside.

"Good day to you, Ben . . . Kitty," said Squire. "What in the world are you up to there?" he inquired of Ben.

"I'm leaving my sister-in-law and her belongings here at the fort as she has requested," Ben said shortly, swinging the last bundle to the dusty ground. "Sister"—he turned a stern but sorrowful eye on her—"if you should change your mind, my door is open to you until time to leave for Virginia. You send word and I'll come for you. In the meantime, I'll pray for you."

He nodded to Squire and in a moment was clucking to the horses, the wagon clanking through the gates and rolling away, little puffs of dust rising about the wheels. And Kitty just stood there before Squire Boone, who regarded her with a look of astonishment on his plain good face.

Someone had thrown a bucket of slops near the fort wall, and the sour, strong smell was heavy in Kitty's nose. Down the way, the blacksmith's hammer was clanging against hot iron, and she caught sight of Maggie Hamilton shaking a quilt outside her cabin door. Farther down still, the two younger Boone girls minded little Jesse.

"I expect if Captain Boone's here," she said, "he's the one I should talk to."

But the boy had already run to tell him, and Daniel was coming toward them along the path, his stride long for a man with a growing paunch. After a quick glance through the gates at the departing wagon and then a look toward Squire, Daniel greeted Kitty warmly, as if he found young women amidst their bundles and baskets left inside the fort gates every morning of the week.

"Oliver," Daniel called to the boy who stood a little apart, waiting to see what was going on, "you see to Kitty's things."

"Where ought I to take 'em, Cap'n Boone?"

"You can take them down to my place," Daniel directed.

"Oh, no, I couldn't," Kitty was quick to protest. "You already have Sara there. And with all the children . . ."

"Let's go talk," said Daniel, the sun slanting across his prominent cheekbones, accentuating the kind concern that filled his eyes.

Taking her by the elbow, he steered her into the nearest blockhouse, where they found Colonel Callaway going over some ledgers, scratching in figures with his quill. He stood once he saw Kitty.

"So, you've finally come in for a visit!" His smile was warm. "Everything well at the Tyler place? How's that little heifer of yours?"

"I . . . I brought her with me, Colonel," Kitty said.

The Old Colonel's bushy eyebrows lifted, and Daniel pulled out a rough chair and motioned for Kitty to sit down.

She told them her situation as simply and fairly as she could. "I'm not blaming Ben or my sister," she said. "Perhaps I'd feel the same way if I were in their place. But I don't want to go back to Virginia. And I don't want to sell any of the land that's coming to me."

Daniel considered that, nodding.

"I'm a good worker—" Kitty's voice caught in her throat, but she cleared it, began again. "I can earn my bed and food . . . I can work in the garden. I can weave and sew. My cow will give more than enough milk and butter for me, and I'll be glad to share. . . ."

Daniel and the Old Colonel exchanged looks, then Colonel Callaway shoved his chair back and came around the table to where Kitty sat. "Child . . ." His voice was gravelly as he put out a hand to help her up, catching her into a huge hug, the kind her father used to give her . . . and she could hardly keep back tears. He patted her with his big hand, the fingers callused and knobby but gentle as a woman's. "Now"—his voice was still ragged—"let's have no more talk of this. There's a place at our cabin for you. Why, we don't know what to do without Betsey, now that she's gone. Havin' you there will help. Come on. I'll walk you down and Fanny can see you get settled in."

"Colonel . . ." Kitty felt her lip tremble, knowing full well how crowded they were. "I'd not want to impose. . . ."

"Impose?" Those handsome features drew into an exaggerated frown, but the dark eyes misted. "Usaph Gentry was a friend. There is no way that his daughter could impose on the Callaways."

Daniel grinned. "I'll have Israel bring your things over."

And so it was settled. Fanny squealed her delight as soon as she saw Kitty, and Elizabeth hurried to embrace her, adding her insistence that Kitty stay as soon as she heard what had happened.

"Of course we've got room. There's Betsey's bed, now that she's married."

Kitty's protest that Fanny had taken that only brought Fanny's assurance that she didn't mind sharing a bed with Keziah again. Flanders and the oldest boy, Caleb, were living in the cabin next door, along with two young men new to the fort. The baby slept in the bed with the Old Colonel and Elizabeth. And the littler children had their trundles. It would be just fine, Elizabeth said.

Sara came hurrying the moment she knew that Kitty was within the fort walls again, and the two of them walked outside the stockade, to sit in the shade of the big elm, where they could speak freely. Sara was the only one Kitty could tell how much she'd really hated it at Faith and Ben's.

"I should have known and not let you go," Sara declared. The delicate color had come back into her cheeks, and she looked rested. "You'll live with Roman and me when he's back and we're in our own cabin again. After all, we're Gentrys. We're the ones you belong with."

"Well," said Kitty, "we'll see." Though the idea was tempting, her instincts told her that Sara and Roman deserved a little privacy after he came back.

October arrived with its warm days and cool nights, the trees along Hackberry Ridge and farther up along the river beginning to show the barest touches of fall color. Isaac Shelby decided that he would depart for the East before winter set in. The good-natured and well-liked fellow had suffered a series of stomach complaints and felt, for his health's sake, that he must return across the mountains. He called on Kitty before he left.

"I fear my constitution rebels at the limited fare here," he confessed with a wry grin. "But no doubt some good wheaten bread and real hen's eggs will set me right in no time."

Kitty wished him Godspeed and good health. She had not forgotten that he'd gone with her to bury her family.

One day Ben came in to the fort to see if Winfield Burdette could make him a piece he needed for his harness. Faith came along, her face working painfully at first sight of Kitty.

"Are you all right?" she asked as they embraced.

"Yes." Kitty drew back and smiled at her sister.

"If you'd want to come back . . . stay with us . . . I'll speak to Ben about it, honey. Maybe . . ."

Kitty caught up one of her hands. "No. But I thank you, Faith."

The rims of Faith's eyes reddened, and the two sisters embraced again. "I'm all right," Kitty assured her. "It's best this way."

The cornstalks in the field were cut and hauled in to stack against the fort walls—the fodder would make good feed for the animals come winter—and the men carted in the pumpkins, turning them over to the women to serve up golden and steaming. The juices, boiled down, yielded a tolerable molasses. The last of the vegetables were harvested and, those that could be, dried or stored away for later use. The extra game that the hunters brought in was salted down in barrels. And though the Callaways tried to treat her as a guest in the beginning, Kitty would have none of it. Her days were filled with work, both inside and out. But she welcomed it. Needed it.

She thought often of Cullen but couldn't summon the courage to ask Daniel if he'd had any word from him. With his long absence, she could only conclude that he had never really cared for her. Which meant that she'd been lucky, she told herself. She might have been left with a fatherless babe if she had been foolish enough to trust him. It had happened to more than one girl.

But there were times when, in her bed at night, giving way to an agony of imagining, she'd conjure up all the terrible things that might have happened to him. He could have been captured by the Indians and tortured to death . . . he could have been killed by a bear. Or a buffalo—bull buffaloes had been known to charge hunters. Or he could have been thrown from that beautiful black horse of his and left, bones broken, to starve slowly to death out in the wilderness. . . . A hundred awful possibilities would cross her mind, then finally she would turn her face into the pillow and cry silently. If she only knew for sure that he was all right, she could bear the thought that he didn't want to see her ever again, she'd lie to herself.

One breezy day toward the middle of October, she and Fanny took a couple of baskets and walked up along the riverbank, well within sight of the fort, to where a grove of hickory trees stood. They laughed and talked as they gathered the drying nuts from the ground. Though the kernels inside were small and tedious to pick out, they were delicious added to persimmon pudding, sprinkled over some honey-glazed squash, or eaten right out of hand. The hulls would not be wasted, either. They made a good light brown dye when boiled in water.

"There are lots over here," Fanny called as she got down on her hands and knees and scooped a bunch into her apron, drawing up the corners to make a pouch and then dumping the nuts into her basket.

Kitty did the same, and the rich smell of the woods—leaf mold, bark, and damp, rich earth—surrounded her. "They're big this year. Bigger than last," she said.

Fanny, that dark Callaway hair curling about her face, was chattering away about the corn shelling planned for Saturday when Kitty heard the sound of a horse's hooves, coming fast along the river. She lifted a cautious hand to still Fanny, then edged away from the trees for a better look, her apron held out before her, still filled with nuts.

Her heart began a slow hammering, her stomach squeezing in upon itself as she stepped into the open and caught sight of the black horse, its fine crested neck lathered, its sides dark with sweat. Her eyes fixed on the rider as he hauled the horse back on its haunches at the sight of her.

"Cullen," she whispered.

There were thirty yards between them, and Cullen sat there, hat shoved to the back of his head, motionless atop the sweating animal that stamped its hooves and blew through its nostrils. His face was marked by a stubble of beard, and those eyes, usually so filled with laughter, glittered with a dark anguish now as they fastened on Kitty for what seemed forever.

The corners of her apron slipped from her grasp, and the hickory nuts spilled onto the ground. She had on her oldest skirt. It was sun-faded, colorless, twigs and leaves clinging to it here and there. But the sun fell across that length of black hair, picked up the red hidden there, played across her face, thinner now, violet eyes blazing as she stared back at him.

And then Cullen was down and running toward her, and she met him in those last few steps, stumbling over the hickory nuts as she went, feeling herself caught up against his broad, hard chest. She could smell the horse and the sweat . . . and that wonderful man smell of him . . .

"Kitty . . . Jesus! Kitty, lass!" He kissed her, tender and rough at the same time, his beard scratching her. Then he drew back to search her face, touching it gently with his fingertips, wiping away the tears that she hadn't known were there. "You're all right, lass?" He peered at her. "My love . . . my heart?"

She nodded. "Yes, I am. But the others . . ."

"I know . . . Lord, I know." He drew her closer, pulled her head against his chest and ran his strong, square hands down the length of her hair. "I heard when I reached Harrod's Town . . . and came right away. As fast as I could without killing the horse." His burr was thick, and he kissed her again, as gently as if she were a hurt child, half crooning to her, patting her. "God forgive me for not being here when you needed me. But I'm here now. And we're going to be wed. . . . Do ye hear me, lass? We're going to be wed, for I'll not take no for an answer . . . do ye ken?"

Kitty lifted her head to look up into his eyes. She had known that she loved him, but never just how much until that minute. "I ken," she whispered.

❊ 13 ❊

CULLEN WANTED THEM TO BE MARRIED AT ONCE, THAT very week. But Sara, though delighted over the prospect, objected to the haste. "How can you have a proper wedding in three days?" she asked Kitty. "A wedding dress must be sewn. . . ."

"And a nightgown," Elizabeth put in, "and a cabin readied for you."

"And Roman ought to be here," Rebecca Boone added.

Kitty agreed with that, though she thought that any fuss might be unseemly with the deaths of her parents and sister so recent.

"That's not the way of it, child," said Elizabeth. "Life will go on quickly out here . . . and should."

There was solemn agreement in Rebecca's fine dark eyes.

"And if your friends and neighbors want to celebrate and wish you and Cullen well, would you grudge them that?''

"No," said Kitty, "I wouldn't." She set the date for December 23.

The women commenced at once on all the preparations. The length of violet silk that Sara had brought to Kitty from Virginia was seized upon and pronounced perfect for her wedding dress. And along with that, a wedding quilt was begun in secret, with each woman contributing a square of whatever design she chose and her name stitched in the corner. "Amelia would want Kitty to have a nice wedding," Elizabeth told the Old Colonel, "and I intend to see that she gets it."

Daniel was glad to have Cullen back, though the scout was able to tell him little for all his weeks away. He had gone across the Ohio and up close to the Shawnee camps along the Scioto and Miami—close enough to see the smoke from their campfires and smell the odor of their cooking meats. He had seen parties of five or six go out from time to time, apparently to hunt. But on two occasions British officers had ridden in to eat and smoke and talk with Cornstalk and his minor chiefs. They had come from the north—undoubtedly, Daniel agreed, from the British stronghold at Detroit.

Cullen was put to good use at once, going out for several days at a time, but Kitty always knew when he had come back in. She would hear his wild whoop and run to the door of the Callaway cabin to see him twirling that magnificent animal of his in a tight circle to finish with a flourish, hat swept off, that incredible grin of his flashing. He would beckon, and she'd run to be caught up on the horse before him, his arms tight about her as he galloped the length of the fort yard and back, whispering outrageous words into her ears . . . words that made her blush, made her heart tighten with love for him.

Two weeks before the wedding, she begged him to take her to Otter Creek. With everything quiet roundabout, he consented.

It was the first time she had been there since the day of the burying, and she led him first to the graves. True to his word, Amos Welter had cut and polished and chiseled three fine pieces of limestone; she got down on her knees, brushing aside the dry leaves, and ran her fingers over the names and dates . . . and over the perfect, lovely willow tree he had carved at the top of each one.

"I'm sorry, lass," Cullen murmured, standing beside her, his hair ruffling in the wind. "Oh, God, I'm sorry."

The pain was still sharp and deep, but she didn't cry, nor did she any longer wake up of a morning denying that it had happened. At least now she had accepted it. And she rose to stand beside him, realizing that one of the reasons she had come was to let them know that she was all right.

After a while they went into the cabin. Kitty didn't know if Ben might have gotten some of the things left there, but nothing seemed disturbed.

"I'd like to have these pieces that my father made, for our cabin," she told Cullen. "And I believe that Ma would want me to have the kitchen things."

Cullen pulled her to him and kissed her tenderly. "You show me what you want. I'll bring out a wagon. Flanders and Israel will help. We'll load up whatever you fancy."

She gathered together the big pots and skillets, the pewter and treenware, the huge wooden bowl gouged out of one solid piece of buckeye. She would, she said, like the linen press and the settle . . . and Ma's little looking glass hanging on the wall.

She took Cullen's hand and led him into the small bedroom, where they stood before the tall-posted bed that Usaph had made with such skill and love. "I want this for us," she said.

Since Cullen had come back, he'd not pressed her. Where once he had touched her breasts and slid his hand over her buttocks in spite of her efforts to stop him, now he just held her gently and kissed her with a kind of tenderness and patience that she hadn't known he possessed. And she understood the reasons . . . knew that he was giving her the time that she needed. But now, his gray eyes had gone dark and smoky.

"I love you, lass," he said, his voice nearly hoarse, a strange, wild set to his face. It was the first time he had said it right out to her, perhaps because he had said it so carelessly to so many others.

Their hands were still together, and she tightened her fingers on his. Afterward she would realize that she'd wanted him to bring her to Otter Creek because she wanted them to be together the first time here in this place that she loved best, here in this bed that she knew carried her parents' blessing. She'd been haunted by the knowledge that she'd refused him before, that she might have died that day, never knowing what it was like to lie with the man she loved. But now they moved together as effortlessly as the sun rising or rain falling to earth. . . .

He kissed her, the long-held need rising in each of them, his mouth moving to gain entrance, his tongue exploring, touching hers, sending shivers through her. She could feel the quivering that ran through those hard-muscled thighs, and he pulled her unresisting hand to touch him there, to feel the swelling fever of his need . . . and her own flesh leapt in response.

In a moment he had her out of her blouse, bared to the waist, and he lifted her straight up to press his face between her breasts, her fingers catching in that thick, dark hair, twisting, her breath coming in hard little gasps as he kissed and licked and began to do to her what a babe did to its mother. She hadn't known that a man did that to a woman . . . nor had she dreamed how it would feel.

She moaned as he slid her down him, bringing his hard, demanding mouth to hers again, the power that moved them both unleashed fully, like a river rushing toward the sea. He stripped the clothes from both of them as they approached a near frenzy for one another, then caught her up in his arms and put her on the bed and in an instant was atop her, parting her thighs to thrust between them.

She gave a small cry at the resistance her body gave to him, at the first pain, but as he drew back to thrust again, she brought her hips up to meet him, eager to break away that last barrier between them, hungering for the full length of him. And then she had it, the rhythmic pleasure filling her. . . .

She saw his face above her, grimacing, lips drawn back from those white teeth, almost as if he were in pain. And she understood, shared it . . . that nearly unbearable, sweet surging that carried her toward . . . she didn't know what.

"Cullen . . . Cullen . . ." she cried. A thin wail was torn from her as she felt her body quiver there at a glorious crest, poised and ready. And then the torrent swirled and pulsed within her . . . and somewhere in that long and trembling moment, she was dimly aware of Cullen's hoarse cry.

He slumped atop her, joined still, shifting his weight so he wouldn't crush her, and they lay that way for a time, racing hearts beginning to slow. After a while he eased away to lie on his back, pulling her into the curve of his arm, his lips touching hers as if to seal it all.

"Oh, Kitty, lass . . . there can be no doubt of it. Ye've captured my heart." He drew back to search her face as he said it, his voice a husky whisper underlaced with something close to fear at the revelation.

But Kitty just smiled and put her cheek against his. He had captured hers a long time ago. On that first day he'd come riding into Boonesborough.

"So that's the way of it . . . ." Daniel looked toward Roman, his face unreadable. "Virginia has disallowed the Transylvania Company."

"Aye," said Roman, glancing from him to Colonel Callaway and wondering how they would take to the news. Especially Daniel, since he had worked for the company.

He was backed up to the fire that crackled in the big stone fireplace of one of the blockhouses at Boonesborough, welcoming the heat from the blaze. The day had been raw and rainy, and he'd been chilled through upon his arrival a bare quarter hour before, riding into the fort just at twilight. He and Daniel had come to the blockhouse for a private meeting, with Colonel Callaway joining them almost immediately, at Daniel's invitation.

"Virginia disallowed the company's claim and declared her own," Roman said now to make sure that they understood the situation. "Mr. Jefferson offered the resolution at the beginning of the session. Captain Clark and I were heard, as were the representatives of the company. The legislators voted that Kentucke—henceforth spelled with a *y* at the end, not an *e*—is officially Kentucky County, of Virginia."

"Why the change?" Callaway asked.

"I don't know," said Roman. "It's that way on all the official documents, so I guess we'll have to get used to it."

"So," Callaway spoke again, "we are to be part of Virginia . . . and the new nation if the fight is won." There was an emotional quaver in his voice.

"We are," said Roman. "We are to have our own local organization and officials. Harrod's Town is the county seat. We must form a militia. Kentucky will have two representatives in the legislature."

"I hope you are not planning to campaign for one of those seats," Daniel put in. "We've needed you here, Roman."

Roman smiled, squaring around to warm his big hands before the fire. "No. I think I've had enough of the East for a while."

"What of the gunpowder?" Daniel asked.

"It's on the way. Clark is bringing it out."

The Old Colonel and Daniel turned to one another with triumphant grins.

"Aware that my kinspeople had been—" Roman's eyes darkened. "—massacred . . . that my wife and my cousin barely escaped with their lives . . . George was kind enough to insist that I come ahead over the mountains." He turned to stare into the flames. He had wondered a thousand times if he could have prevented it if he'd been at Boonesborough.

"It was bad, Roman," the Old Colonel said, his voice heavy with sadness.

Roman nodded, turned back. "Didn't Cullen pick up any sign? Was there no warning?"

"Cullen was away. North of the Ohio for several months," Daniel said. "But I was out. So was Squire. There seemed only four or five of them . . . traveling fast. It would have been uncommon luck to come on them before they struck."

There was a deep silence in the room, but for the crackle of a pine knot, a burst of sparks up the chimney.

"There'll be a lot you'll want to know. I expect your wife . . . and Kitty, can tell you the most of it," Colonel Callaway said, his silvery brows lowered, the deep-set eyes shadowed.

"And we can talk more tomorrow," said Daniel. "Meantime, I expect a visit with Sara and a good hot meal wouldn't go amiss right now."

"No," Roman said, "it wouldn't."

"Just tell us when we can expect Captain Clark to get the gunpowder to the settlements," Callaway prodded.

"Well . . ." Roman collected himself wearily, tried to pull his mind from the awful thing that had happened in his absence. "George and eight other men, including his cousin Joseph Rogers, set out at once for Fort Pitt. They're bringing the powder down the Ohio on a flatboat and then overland to Harrod's Town. We should hear something before long."

He took up the rifle which he'd leaned against the wall by the fireplace, then turned back. "Daniel . . . are you satisfied then with the way the legislature voted?"

Daniel pulled at an earlobe, a grin tugging at his wide mouth. "Long as I was working for the company, I thought I'd best say as little as possible on the subject. But now that I'm not . . . well, I'm satisfied enough."

The Old Colonel brought a hand of approval down on Daniel's shoulder. "I think we should drink to Virginia and the county of Kentucky," he said. "Your good wife will wait a moment more, eh, Roman?"

Roman nodded, smiling his one-sided smile as Callaway

fetched a jug of corn whiskey from a chest in the corner and the three men toasted Virginia and the new county, with Daniel insisting on another swallow to ". . . the defeat of the danged British!"

But at last Roman was able to get away, and now as he walked the length of the dark fort yard, the chill wind tugged at him. The rain had stopped, and he could catch the flicker of light from a grease lamp or fireplace here and there through the cracks in the cabins. As he passed he could hear the occasional sound of laughter, the smell of cooking food causing his stomach to growl with hunger. The news of his arrival had not yet spread, and he was glad. It would give him and Sara this night alone.

He bent his head low to clear the door of their own cabin, and she was waiting just inside, a glow about her face as she stood quite still and stared at him. He hesitated. With her pale hair and fair skin, she looked so lovely, so delicate, that he was suddenly aware of how big and damp and smelly he was. But in another instant she ended his dilemma by throwing herself into his arms.

"Roman . . . Roman . . ." She brought her sweet mouth up to his, and he kissed her eagerly, his body leaping after his long abstinence.

"Sara . . . my dear Sara," he murmured. "I've missed you. . . . After you sent word of what happened, I feared—"

She put her fingers across his lips. "Let's not speak of it now. We will later," she promised.

He nodded, wanting to take her right to the bed, though it didn't seem exactly decent to do it the moment he stepped in the door. Besides, she was clinging to him with a kind of desperation that made him feel guilty for being away from her for so long.

But in a moment, as if self-conscious, she drew back. "Look . . ." She gestured to the meat and potatoes and hoecakes that steamed before the fire. "Rebecca sent our supper over when she heard you were here. I've stayed with them, Roman, since . . ." She didn't finish that but plunged ahead. "But a few weeks ago I began to get ready." She looked about her. "I even kept the firewood laid."

He smiled at her, putting out a hand to touch her cheek.

"Come eat. I'll wager you're starving," she murmured, smiling shyly.

He admitted that he was, and the moment the food was on the table, he set about filling his empty stomach. But Sara ate little, content, it seemed, to watch him wolf down the food. While he ate she talked to him—not of the tragedy itself, but of some of the other things that had happened since he'd left, particularly about Kitty's having gone to stay with Ben and Faith and her subsequent refusal to go back east and let her brother-in-law sell the land.

"Good for her!" said Roman. He sobered. "After you wrote me, I went to see her sisters . . . told them the sad news."

Sara nodded, an odd closing off in her eyes. She toyed with the cup of milk by her plate, then brightened perceptibly. "I've saved the best news for last."

"Oh?"

"Kitty and Cullen are to be wed."

Roman put down his knife and stared at her. "They are? When?"

"Four days from now."

A certain surprise was laced through the gladness he felt for them. Somehow he had never thought that Cullen would put aside his wild ways. Though if anyone could entice him to do it, Kitty would be the one. "Well," he said heartily, "it looks as if I've arrived just in time, doesn't it?" He attacked the fried rabbit on his plate with renewed vigor.

Once finished, and Sara clearing the supper things, he was aware again of the stained and damp buckskins that were beginning to emit a rank odor in the warmth of the cabin. While he was not the zealot that poor dear Amelia had been on cleanliness, he reasoned that a wash once in a great while wasn't too harmful a thing.

There was a steaming kettle of water on the hearth, and he poured some of it into a washbowl, cooling it down enough with water from the bucket, then pulled his shirt over his head.

"I own," he said a minute later, soaping his chest, "that I had grown almost used to breeches and hose and buckled shoes again." He caught Sara's quick look and the hunger in her eyes for the East. "But I'm glad to be back in buckskins and linsey," he hastened to add, not wanting to leave her with any notion that he wanted to go back to stay. He kicked out of his moccasins and stripped off the rest of his clothing to continue his bath.

After he'd rinsed off the last of the soap, he commenced to dry himself with a length of soft linen that Sara had laid out for him. The fire was warm on his bare skin, the heat relaxing the muscles along his chest and back and tight flanks. He turned to find her looking at him, that same firelight playing across those classic features of hers, and his desire was evident, there for her to see.

She smiled and came to him, unfastening her waist. And in a moment he had pulled her to the bed in the corner and come down beside her.

He made love to her with tender care for all his urgency. It had always been that way between them. It had something to do with that air of fragility about her; he had always been afraid that he might hurt her. But it was good, despite the need he felt to hold the lustiest part of himself in check. And when she'd been satisfied and he had spent himself, he drew her in to his side and they lay there quietly for a time.

Then there was no putting it off longer. They had come to it now, finally. "Tell me what happened at Otter Creek," he said. And she did, recalling it all, crying sometimes, her willowy body quivering, sparing herself and him nothing.

He had been through Dunmore's War, had seen heads split like ripe watermelons, limbs severed. He'd seen the mutilated bodies of the victims of Indian torture. But few things cut as deeply as Sara's recounting of that day and night.

"I wasn't with Amelia when she died," Sara said. "Kitty was." She turned her face to him, her eyes red-rimmed but still beautiful, the thick blond lashes darkened by her tears. "Roman . . . Kitty kept me alive out there."

He nodded. "I thank God for it." He held her to him for a moment. "I'd like to see Kitty tonight. Would you mind?"

"No." Sara regarded him solemnly. "I think you should."

Roman mounted the stone step outside the Callaway cabin. Someone was still up. He could see the flicker of the grease lamps through the cracks. He knocked and in a moment heard Callaway's resonant voice.

"Who's there?"

"Roman."

The bolt slid back and the door swung open almost at once to reveal the Old Colonel, shirt open to bare his ropy neck.

"I know it's late," Roman began but Callaway cut him off.

"Not a bit of it. Mother there is still puttering about."

Elizabeth, who'd just put the baby on the bed, came to greet him, then both she and her husband stood aside silently. They understood that he had come to see Kitty—come to express his sympathy.

She had risen from her place by the fire as he'd come in, and she stood there now looking at him with those violet eyes, suddenly moist but not crying, one of her small slender hands held out to him.

"Roman . . . I knew you were back." She smiled tremulously. "But you didn't have to come tonight."

"Yes, I did. I'm a Gentry. And Gentrys see to their own." He covered the distance to her in two strides and wrapped her in his long arms. "I hear congratulations are in order."

"Yes. I'm so glad you got back in time."

"So am I," he said. He drew back to look down at her. "And where is that rascally friend of mine who'll have to answer to me if he doesn't do well by you?"

She laughed, the hint of tears still there. "Daniel sent him out. But he should be back tomorrow."

They stood there awkwardly, and it was in Roman's mind to tell her how sorry he was, but it was difficult in the cramped cabin—some of the littler children were peeking from their trundle beds.

"I'll get my cloak," said Kitty, as if she knew what he was thinking. "A breath of fresh air would be nice."

"Here, take mine," Elizabeth said. And Kitty did, though it swallowed her.

Outside, the moon had found a break in the dark clouds to cast swirling shadows across the fort yard. Kitty drew the outsize cloak close about her, and her dark hair swirled with the breeze as they walked.

"Kitty . . . Oh, God, Kitty, I don't know what to say."

"It's all right." Her voice was soft in the cold night. "I know what you feel already. You don't have to say it."

He nodded, and they walked on past the Boones' cabin and then the Hamiltons'. There were always dogs about the fort, and two of them bounded up now, breath steaming from their slobbery mouths as they wagged their tails, bodies loose and limbery. After a moment of sniffing, they loped away toward the shadowy far end where the heavy gates looked dark and solid enough to hold off an army.

"I owe you a lot," Roman said. "Sara told me she'd not be alive today if it weren't for you."

Kitty gave a deprecating shake of her head. "I was trying to save myself as well, don't forget that. Besides, there were times that day . . . and night . . . when Sara was very brave, Roman. I honestly don't know if I could have gotten Ma into the cabin without her help . . . or in the wagon later."

He felt a swell of pride in his wife. But a question was gnawing at him, and somehow it didn't seem impossible to voice it to Kitty.

"If I'd not gone," he said slowly, "maybe I would have been able to prevent it."

She swung to him, her small hand grasping his big, bony wrist. "Don't say that. Don't think it. Ever! You were doing exactly what you should have been. And from what the Colonel told us"—her voice trembled with conviction—"you did it well. You served all of us. You served Kentucky. You mustn't ask more of yourself than you've a right to."

"But if—"

She squared around in front of him, little thing that she was, facing off with her chin set. "If I had guessed sooner what Prissy was going to do, I could have grabbed her in time. If Daniel and Squire—or Cullen—had come riding out to visit that day . . . You could go on like that forever, Roman. A person wouldn't know whether to get up in the morning if he let *if*s rule him. And you're not to do it, do you hear me?"

"I hear." He conceded it meekly, smiling at the picture the two of them must present. Kitty, whose head came just past the middle of his chest, confronting him as if she were a foot taller and ready to take him on if he didn't listen to her.

A deep and good laughter bubbled within him, erupted. Anyone still awake who happened to overhear would have wondered what Roman Gentry was doing laughing out loud—a rarity in itself—on this damp and miserable night, and on an occasion that had to be a sad one . . . the first meeting with his cousin since the massacre at the Gentry place. But Kitty understood and grinned at him.

"I wonder," he said, "if Cullen knows what a splendid woman he's getting? As your male kin, I vow to thrash him within an inch of his life if he causes you any grief."

"I'll remember that," she promised, still grinning.

She was anxious to hear news of his trip. Though Colonel Callaway had told her of the outcome, she insisted on hearing Roman's account and listened with an eagerness that surprised him.

"How *fine*!" she exclaimed as he recounted that last day of debate and the vote affirming the Jefferson resolution. "Mr. Jefferson has proven himself a friend to Kentucky, 'twould seem."

He nodded and was about to go on with his account when

suddenly he realized that the wind had grown colder; small stinging bits of snow were beginning to swirl and glitter against the black sky. "There are times when I talk overmuch," he said stoutly as he took her elbow and started to guide her back toward the Callaway cabin.

"You? It's getting you to talk that is the problem, Roman, not stopping you."

He chuckled. "I should tell you that I brought letters from your sisters. I'll see that you get them tomorrow."

"Are they well?"

He nodded. "Abigail's husband is off fighting with the militia. Miranda has a new son."

"A *boy*? Pa would have liked that."

Everything was quiet. Even the dogs had gone to curl behind the woodpile out of the wind. Few cabins showed even a crack of light now.

"It grows late," he said, "and you'd best get in before you catch your death. It wouldn't do for the bride to be sick on her wedding day."

"I'll not be sick." She gave her head a toss and smiled up at him though the wind drove right into their faces. They had drawn even with the cabin door, and she gave him a quick hug. "Thank you for coming tonight, Roman," she said.

He nodded, backing away, then paused. "Sara holds you high," he said.

She looked at him soberly. "As I hold her." The wind caught at the folds of the big cloak, billowing it out to make her shiver, and she turned and slipped into the cabin.

There was a light covering of snow the day of the wedding. And since Christmas was only two days away, the blockhouse was decorated with pine boughs and huge cones and thick clumps of bittersweet. A heady punch made of persimmons and pumpkin sweetening and corn liquor steamed in a huge iron kettle, and since the corn crop had been ample, jugs of the pure, potent spirits lined the wall ready for the raucous revelers, who could hardly wait for the ceremony to be over.

Cullen was splendid in bleached doeskin liberally embroidered with quills. He'd gone all the way to Harrod's Town to have a woman who was especially skilled with the needle make the hunting shirt and leggings and moccasins for him—something of a luxury since doeskin didn't wear as well as buck. But it was especially soft and white when bleached out. Roman chided himself even for the thought that the woman at Harrod's Town just might happen to be the well-endowed Mistress Wheatley.

All the same, the tongue waggers at the fort were predicting that a womanizer like Cullen Claiborne would never be able to settle down to being a good and faithful husband. And even Elvie Porter said privately that she didn't know that it was good to marry a handsome man. "Seems to me like they'd think more of theirselves than of you. No offense to Cullen, of course. I guess a man can't help it if he looks good."

There'd been cheers all 'round, laced through with a bit of good-natured, if coarse, jesting as the groom entered the block-house. But now, as Kitty arrived, escorted by Colonel Callaway and Ben Tyler—who'd claimed the privilege as her brother-in-law—those gathered fell silent for a moment.

Most times it was not easy to shut them up. Working hard just to survive, living with the constant Indian threat, the settlers at Boonesborough seized upon any occasion for merriment with a vulgar kind of excess that sometimes surprised the more staid comers from the East. But now even the most boisterous among them fell silent as they looked on Kitty Gentry's radiant face, beheld that small, slender figure in the violet silk dress.

The gown was long-sleeved and cut right up to the throat; a wisp of lace circled the slender neck. Maggie Hamilton had loaned her white silk slippers—Kitty had had to stuff a bit of linen in the toes to make them fit—and Elizabeth had found a wide, white silk ribbon among her things to tie back the waist-length black hair.

"God save me, ain't she a beauty!" Ezekial Turner nudged the man who stood next to him, his voice barely a whisper. And far over to the wall stood Amos Welter, apart as always, dressed in the same greasy buckskins that he always wore. But as he looked at Kitty his eyes misted. Long ago his little blackhaired sister had been killed by the Indians in a raid along the North Carolina border. "I reckon that's a lot how she'd'a looked . . . if the savages hadn't killed her," he said to no one in particular. Over by Squire Boone, who waited to perform the ceremony, Sara and Roman smiled at Kitty and then at one another. Sara reached for her husband's hand and held it tightly.

But from the moment Kitty had entered the door, she saw only Cullen, and she went right to him, looking into those gray eyes that had charmed her from the first instant he'd turned them on her, settling her small hand into the crook of his elbow.

He grinned and leaned down to whisper, "I'm damned if you aren't the prettiest girl I've laid eyes on from the Holston Valley clean to the Illinois country."

Squire never believed in overlong ceremonies, so the actual wedding was over quickly. The twang of Ezekial Turner's fiddle filled the air the moment Squire had given Cullen permission to kiss his bride . . . and feet were already tapping and jugs being reached for. Well-wishers crowded in on the happy couple.

Faith was first to hug Kitty. "Oh, honey . . . I wish Ma . . . Pa . . ."

Kitty nodded, blinking back tears.

"I'm glad it's turned out the way it has for you. And I hope you don't hold anything against Ben. He was doing what he thought was right at the time."

"I know," said Kitty, giving her sister a squeeze. She would let no hard feelings mar this day.

"He killed hogs last week. Put by a couple of hams and some sidemeat for you once they're cured."

The Callaways and the Boones crowded forward to kiss and shake hands, the men thumping Cullen on the back. Elvie Porter bustled up to Kitty, her cheeks pink. "Come spring, if my goose raises a brood, I'll save a pair for you," she promised.

Sara and Roman had waited until most of the others were finished, and now they came forward. Roman bent to kiss Kitty on the cheek and drew back to look at her through those fierce blue eyes that somehow seemed even more penetrating than usual. "I wish you every happiness," he said, the familiar half smile breaking the somber cast of his face. And Kitty was filled with memories of all the things they'd been through together.

"I thank you, Roman," she said, and impulsively pulled his head down to kiss him full on the mouth.

"Take care!" Cullen feigned outrage. "I'll have you know, wife, that all kisses are mine from now on!"

Smiling full out, Roman turned to pummel Cullen, the two of them engaging in good-natured banter while Sara hugged Kitty. "You know how glad I am for you," Sara said.

Kitty squeezed her hand and turned to look at her bride-groom, at the handsome lines of his face, eyes laughing now at something Roman had said. She felt a rush of tenderness. I will be a good wife to you, Cullen Claiborne, she vowed silently.

Both James Harrod and Benjamin Logan had come to help celebrate the occasion—good-sized and well-favored men who moved with the easy tread of the woodsman. Logan bowed over Kitty's hand. "My best wishes, ma'am," he said.

"It does seem to me," Jim Harrod teased Cullen and Roman, "that ye've between you taken the two prettiest women in Kaintuck! I'll wager there are more than a few disappointed young bucks out there."

As soon as Kitty could, she disengaged herself for a moment to go over and speak to Amos Welter, who was leaning against the wall and looking as if he wanted nothing more than to escape back to his solitude in the deep woods. "Mr. Welter, it was good of you to come." She held out her hand to him.

He looked at it for an instant, then wiped one of his own, callused and none too clean, down the fringed sides of his leggings before he took it. "I don't reckon I'd'a missed it, Mistress Claiborne," he said.

The title took her pleasantly aback. "You're the first to call me that," she confided. It sounded strange to her, but she would grow used to it, she was sure. "I was out at the place," she went on, "and I saw the markers you made for my family. They're beautiful, and I thank you."

"No trouble," he assured her. "Just a little chippin' with a chisel."

"They're much more than that. You're an artist."

He grunted and shifted from one foot to the other. And fearing to make him uncomfortable, she said no more about the stones but urged him to help himself to the food and drink.

"Thankee kindly," he said. "And good fortune to you and your man."

Not long after, Kitty saw him slip out the door.

The ceremony had taken place in the late afternoon, and the wedding party had gone full blast for hours now, the tallow dips long since lit. Kitty had good-naturedly met the demands of all the young men for dances after that first dance with Cullen. And then later she'd sung . . . giving in to all the requests only when Cullen asked her to, singing the words she'd sung to him before: "As I walked out, one winter's night . . . a-drinkin' of sweet wine . . . conversing with a handsome lad . . . who stole this heart of mine . . .''

But now Sara found her and drew her away to the sidelines. "Are you tired?" she asked.

"Exhausted," Kitty replied.

"Good. We think it's time the newlyweds were escorted to their cabin. You first." She beckoned to the knot of young women who had been waiting, and they came giggling—Betsey Callaway Henderson and Fanny, Jemima Boone and Maggie Hamilton. Without giving Kitty a chance to say a word to Cullen, they whisked her toward the door where Elizabeth waited with their cloaks.

Kitty suffered herself to be drawn along with good humor, knowing full well what the procedure was. She had taken part more than once herself, back on the Watauga. She was just grateful that she and Cullen weren't to be taken to a bed in the loft above, as was sometimes done, with the boisterous wedding guests coming periodically to see how the frustrated bridal couple were doing.

"I saved you from the loft," Sara whispered as if she'd read her mind. "I insisted on the cabin."

"Thank you," Kitty whispered back.

Cloaks donned, the women went out into the cold, bright moonlight, the path dusted with snow, the brisk air refreshing after the stuffy blockhouse. The cabin that had been readied for the Claibornes was two down from the Callaways', and the giggling party was soon there, going in to find a fire burning smartly in the fireplace. Tallow dips had been lit in place of the smoking grease lamps, and the tall-posted bed—an almost unheard-of luxury on the frontier—was spread up with the quilt that the women had stitched. Kitty had already seen it, but she went to look at it again.

"It's beautiful," she said, "and I want to thank you all again. Jemima, this red bird is perfect . . . and the horse in this square looks just like Cullen's . . . And yours, Sara—"

"You can look at the rest of them in the morning," Fanny interrupted.

"That's right." Sara had fetched the white linen nightgown from the clothes press. "If we're not careful, the men will have Cullen here and you won't even be undressed or in the bed."

"Take off your clothes," Betsey ordered. "We'll turn our backs if you're shy."

"Don't forget to pee." Maggie Hamilton was dragging out the chamber pot from under the bed. "It's no good to do it when you have to pee."

They were all laughing, Kitty as well, but with cheeks aflame she did as they said.

"Goodness," said Betsey, "when they put Sam and me in the cabin, we found that they'd taken the lock right off the door and they deviled us all night. We didn't dare to touch each other until the next day when Sam had fixed it.''

Out of her clothes now, Kitty stood obediently while Sara slipped the nightgown over her head and down. A few scraps of lace had been found for the neck and wrists. "There," Sara said. "Now you look like a proper bride waiting for her groom."

"Who's going to bring Cullen?" asked Kitty.

"Sam for one," Betsey told her. "And Flanders. Israel and Tyler Hawkins, and Rafer Moore . . .''

"And two of the young men from over at Harrod's Town," Jemima put in.

"Roman would be right along with them, but he rode out to scout around . . . just to be safe." Sara grinned.

The sound of hearty masculine voices carried clearly on the night air. "Hurry," Jemima shrieked, "jump into bed!"

Kitty did, and Sara drew up the woolen cover. "We'll try to keep them from coming to bother you later," she said. The others were giggling and racing for the door.

"Wait! The chamber pot!" Maggie Hamilton shoved the pot hastily under the bed with her foot and paused just long enough to put out a soft hand to Kitty, her pretty face beaming.

Kitty felt a pang that she had ever said anything spiteful about her. "Thanks, Maggie," she said.

And then they were gone in a great flurry of new giggling, and in a moment, just outside the door, Kitty heard the rough voices of the men.

"Do ye feel up to it, Cullen, boy? If ye should need help, then, by God, I'm your man!" This loud declaration was met with great guffaws.

"I think I can manage myself, Thomas." Kitty smiled as she heard Cullen's voice.

"Sheeeit!" It was delivered in a high, nasal twang. "With all the skirts I hear tell you've lifted, I bet that pecker o' yours is wore plumb down! Likely no bigger 'n a corn nubbin by now."

"Not enough left to git it in!" another cackled. The others whooped and hollered at that. Clearly they'd all been at the jug.

"Now, boys . . . let's give him a chance." Kitty recognized Flanders's voice. "His lady's waiting."

"You sure you wouldn't rather go back to the party for a while?" Sam Henderson teased.

"Damned sure!" Cullen shot back.

Kitty could hear the fumbling with the door handle, and she popped her head under the blanket, giggling silently, undaunted by their ribald joking. Amidst the raucous laughter and a few more pointed remarks she heard the door open and close, and giggling still, she edged up a corner of the blanket until she could peek out to see who was there. It was not unusual for escorts of the groom, well drunk and overly exuberant, to bring the young man right in, strip him down, and forcefully put him into the bed beside his waiting, if well-covered, bride.

"You can uncover your head." Cullen stood there laughing at her and quite alone.

"Cullen!" She threw off the cover and ran to throw herself into his arms, the two of them hugging and laughing . . . kissing. "I was afraid they were coming in with you."

"I promised each one of them a jug of rum if they didn't."

"Where in the world would you get rum?" she asked.

He winked at her, gray eyes sparkling devilishly. "I haven't the least idea. But they're gone"—his grin was suggestive—"and the door is barred, Mistress Claiborne."

His thick dark brows arched, and he pulled her up to kiss her again, his tongue licking at hers. They had not been together since that day at the cabin; there had been no chance at the fort. "My God, I've hungered for you," he murmured, his lips pressed against her throat. "Here"—he tugged at the night-gown—"get out of this and let me lay eyes on that sweet body."

As he removed his shirt, she slipped out of the gown and stood there in the firelight, the flickering flames making shadows play along the supple curves.

"Lord save me . . ." He dropped to his knees in front of her, touching the small, high breasts gently, running the tip of his finger over the swollen nipples, tracing down the length of her flat little belly to cup the dark thatch in his strong hand. "Kitty, lass," he said hoarsely. "Kitty . . . my wife . . ."

✳ 14 ✳

THE WEATHER STAYED COLD AND BLUSTERY, BUT IN THE Claiborne cabin the newlyweds piled logs on the fire and laughed together and ate . . . and more often than not crawled again beneath the quilts, hardly able to get enough of one another. Roman, though he was newly home himself, insisted on doing double duty to give Cullen a few days' respite before he had to go out again—it wasn't likely that the Indians would venture down over the Ohio now that winter had begun in earnest. Israel and Flanders brought fresh meat for the young couple, and they came out of their cabin to mingle with their neighbors only often enough to meet what they felt was the minimum standard of decency. And even at that, there was a wealth of good-natured teasing.

There were times when Kitty lay beside her sleeping and, for the moment, satiated husband, listening to his deep, rhythmic breathing, looking at the thick, dark hair that curled about his ears, watching the way his upper lip puckered slightly as he breathed out . . . like a child's, she thought. And sometimes she would catch her own breath, considering that if Ben had gotten his way and she'd gone back to Virginia, she might never have seen Cullen again.

Once she told him that, and her husband looked at her out of eyes that held a sudden fire. "I'd have gone to the ends of the earth to find you!" he declared, his face filled with a solemn earnestness rarely seen on those handsome features. "If ye'd been spirited away to *England* and set down beside King George himself''—he warmed to the image—''I'd've fought the entire Royal Guard single-handed to claim you!''

Kitty burst out laughing and covered his mouth with kisses, setting loose that eager response she'd come to know so well,

194

welcoming the hot rising of him. He didn't wait long enough to take her to the bed but pulled her down before the fireplace, down onto the rough puncheon floor where the rag rug afforded little in the way of a cushion . . . though neither of them paid any mind to that. But on the first day of the new year their brief time for shutting out the rest of the world was ended.

Roman rode into the fort shepherding half a dozen gaunt-faced and shivering men, one limping from a cane stab wound in his heel, another with his head bandaged where a rifle ball had grazed his temple. They gathered in the blockhouse, venturing nervous, twitching smiles as they reached eagerly for cups of corn liquor and poured out their story to Daniel and the others.

They were from McClelland's—the last station north of the Kentucky River—driven out two days before by repeated attacks from the Indians. Most had headed for Harrod's Town and the bigger fort. These six had chosen Boonesborough because it was closer. Roman had come across them and brought them in.

Daniel and Roman, Cullen and the Old Colonel, drew aside to talk in muffled tones, faces set into hard lines.

"The Shawnee're out in force, then, winter or no?" Daniel asked Roman, who nodded.

"Sign everywhere."

"We must warn the settlers around to come in at once," Callaway said.

"I'll send someone." Daniel tugged at a fleshy earlobe. "Meanwhile, kiss that pretty little bride o' yours good-bye for a time, Cullen, boy. Best scout the river. Take the far side and go all the way to the Ohio. Roman, you range wide. I'd like to send the two of you together, but you can cover more ground if you go separate."

Cullen nodded and went off to get his things, and a scant half hour later Kitty watched as he rode through the gates, his black felt hat set to its usual jaunty slant. He turned to raise his hand and give her a wink, and she waved at him until Squire and Winfield swung the heavy gates closed and moved the massive oak bar into place with a dull thud.

The ground was frozen hard beneath her stout leather shoes, and the wind whipped at her cloak as she walked slowly back toward the cabin, the fort children playing noisily in the bleached and wintry sunlight. Little Jesse Boone darted up to her, bright eyes peering up from beneath the folds of his knitted cap, wind-stung cheeks pink, a thin trickle of snot edging from one nostril.

She smiled at him automatically and went on, listening past the shouts of the Porter boys for any sound beyond the walls.

She could picture Cullen leaning down close over the black neck of his stallion, going at a full gallop across the open ground to gain the shelter of the woods. He had made light of it to her. Maybe for her sake . . . or maybe because that was what Cullen would do anyway. But she knew from what little he'd said that no place outside those walls was entirely safe right now.

The echoes of that day at the cabin on Otter Creek sounded in some deepest part of her, and she stopped still in the middle of the uneven path, hearing again the rifle's crack and that high shrill yelp she could never forget, caught there with the memory of her mother's scream . . . shivering, but not from the wind. . . .

Young Jesse had run right out of one of his moccasins and had plopped himself down and struggled with the knot in the whang until his red cheeks puffed in frustration. And now he came to tug at Kitty's skirt for help but she didn't notice.

It was only when she felt a strong hand at her back that she was able to bring herself back to the present. She looked up to find herself staring into Roman's face.

"Kitty . . ." The blue eyes were reading her, as they always could, and the two of them just stood there for a moment, looking at one another. "There's no better man out there," he said finally. "But I expect you know that."

She felt steadied somehow by that deep, quiet voice. "Yes . . . yes, I do." She noted the tired lines about his eyes and mouth and reached out impulsively to touch the arm of his heavy deerskin jacket.

He smiled at her, then bent down toward the boy, who had stopped tugging at Kitty's skirt and was struggling manfully with the knot once again, the tip of his tongue caught between his teeth. "Let's see what the trouble is, Jesse," Roman said.

It took only a minute, and Kitty looked on as Roman loosed the knot and helped the child on with his moccasin, then laced and tied the whang firmly to bring a smile to the round little face. "Thankee, Wo-man," Jesse said, and raced away, the ends of his woolen scarf flying. Kitty smiled. Jesse still had some trouble pronouncing his r's.

Roman straightened. "Why don't you come back to our cabin with me?" he asked. "Sara would be glad of your company."

"You're going back out?"

"Once I catch a few hours' sleep."

Kitty shook her head. They deserved those hours alone. If nothing else, Sara could lie beside him while he slept. "You tell her I'll be over later," she said. She would not tell him to be careful. She knew he would be. She touched his arm once more, then turned away to her own cabin.

But Roman's well-deserved rest was cut short by the arrival an hour later of a courier from Harrod's Town who brought word that George Rogers Clark and the men bringing the gunpowder from Fort Pitt had been attacked by a band of Shawnee.

"The powder be safe at Harrod's Town now," said the leathery-skinned old hunter who'd been pressed into service. "But there's some killed . . . and they say Clark's own cousin was carried off by the bloody heathens."

"Joseph Rogers?" Roman groaned, remembering the clear-eyed young man.

"Major Clark said if you was tuh be here, Roman, he'd be obliged if you'd come."

"Major?" repeated Roman.

Tobacco-stained teeth flashed. "Cap'n got promoted."

Roman heard the muffled "Come in," and pushed open the door to see George Clark bent over the rough little table he'd commandeered for a writing desk, his quill scratching audibly in the uncertain light of a flickering candle.

"George," Roman said, and Clark lifted his head, a smile breaking across the long face, eyes that were almost as blue as Roman's lighting at sight of the tall scout.

"Roman . . ." He laid aside the quill and came to grasp Roman's hand in a strong grip. "By God, I'm glad you were at the fort when my courier arrived! Come . . . come sit. I've a drop of rum that won't go amiss this cold night." He pulled the chair he'd been sitting in—the one chair in that tiny cabin—close to the fire and waved Roman to it, going to rummage in a shadowy corner for a jug and a couple of wooden cups, which he examined with a grimace. He shrugged, wiping the cups out with his strong, thick fingers, and sloshed a goodly dollop of rum into each of them, passing one to Roman.

"I was writing up a report to Governor Henry." He gestured toward the table, and Roman nodded.

No more than a couple of years separated the two men in age, and they had taken a liking to one another in the months they'd spent in Virginia together. "I heard about the attack . . . and about Joe," Roman said. "God's blood, I'm sorry, George."

Clark took a swig of his rum and paced the length of the room like a restless catamount, shaking his head. "In hindsight, I ask myself if I should ever have brought the boy along. It'll be a bitter thing indeed to tell his father, my uncle. I am his namesake, ye know."

"I doubt you could have stopped the lad," Roman ventured, remembering the brash eagerness of young Joseph Rogers.

Clark's jaw set in a grim line. "I confess I hope he met a quick and merciful death. I'd not want my family to know what might have been done to him." His eyes, given to a slight droop at the corners anyway, were suddenly melancholy, heavy with personal loss. But his head came up, and he straightened his spine . . . ever the military man—self-disciplined, putting the common good ahead of his own family's loss. "The powder is safe, though. And now we must divide it amongst the forts."

"McClelland's is abandoned," Roman said.

"I know. Most of them came here. By God, but that just leaves three . . . With Jim Harrod back here, we've got Harrod's Town, Boonesborough, and Logan's fort. And God alone knows how many Indians between us and Fort Pitt!"

"And the Cherokee threatening the supply routes in over the mountains. We may be in for a lean time."

Clark began to pace again. "I've been put in charge of organizing the militia."

"I heard about your promotion. Congratulations, Major."

There was the barest flash of a smile and an acknowledging nod. "As the ranking officer I'll want all settlers into the forts without exception."

"Riders were already out warning them in when I left Boonesborough," Roman said. "Cullen Claiborne is scouting the north side of the Kentucky."

"Claiborne . . ." Clark paused. "I hear he's damned good. Maybe as good as you, Roman."

"He is that." Roman grinned. "And now a kinsman. He married my cousin Kitty something over a week ago."

"The young woman who accounted herself so well in the raid on the Gentry place?"

"The same."

A huge smile brightened Clark's face. "Well, you must give her my best wishes. Somewhere in my things"—he looked rather helplessly toward one darkened corner—"I believe I have a small bottle of peach brandy which I brought from home. I shall send it to them as a wedding present."

He seemed more relaxed, and came once again to sit on the edge of the bed, gazing into the fire. "Tell me," he said as if struck with a sudden notion, "would you accept a captaincy in the new militia?"

Roman's eyebrows rose. "That seems a considerable rank for a scout, George."

"You would take command at Boonesborough."

Roman was too surprised to answer for a moment. The gusting wind sent cold drafts of air through the cracks in the chinking, made the candle flame dance. "If I didn't know you so well," he said finally, "I'd think you were jesting. Daniel commands Boonesborough . . . and no one with more right. Or capability."

Clark leapt to his feet and went to his writing table to leaf through a stack of papers. "Oh, confound it, you're right, of course. Boone is well nigh a legend . . . and should be. But for all of it, the man is so lackadaisical. Great God, he didn't even have the *gates* up at Boonesborough until the savages came right to the shadow of the walls and spirited his own daughter away!"

"Daniel does things his own way," Roman conceded. "But he did bring the girls back unharmed."

"Aye," Clark said, "he did that." He finally found the paper he was looking for, and taking up his quill again, dipped the point in the inkpot . . . only to stay it just above the sheet, slying an eye toward Roman. "I take it your answer is no."

"It is."

Clark nodded and scrawled his name quickly across the bottom of the paper, sprinkling out a few grains of sand to blot it. "Here," he said, holding out the sheet to Roman. "Here then is his commission. You can take it back to him when you go, and tell him . . . tell him"—Clark stood tall, his lips pursed— "that I have every confidence in him."

Roman climbed down from the big sorrel gelding and knelt beside the small creek to crack away the thin ice at its edges, letting the animal drink its fill of the water first. He looked about, ever vigilant, his eyes sweeping the trees behind him where the bare limbs framed a leaden sky, his gaze moving across to the opposite bank, where the tangled underbrush came right down to the bank, dried and leafless, water maples and oaks beyond. He caught a faint stirring amidst the briars and spotted the disappearing blur of a rabbit's tail.

The sorrel, satisfied, snorted and shook his head, spraying

droplets of water over Roman, who grinned and patted the warm neck as faint fingers of steam blew from the wet nostrils. "Had enough, have you?" he said, and then dropped down to cup the icy water in his two hands and drink himself.

He sat back on his haunches, drawing a bag of parched corn from beneath his deerhide jacket and munching on the hard grains, holding out a palmful to the horse, who nibbled eagerly and nudged Roman for more. The peach brandy that George Clark had sent back for Kitty and Cullen was safe in the saddle-bag. Daniel's commission as captain in the Kentucky County militia and military commander of Boonesborough was there, too, and Roman pondered Clark's momentary hesitancy to give it.

George didn't understand Daniel, he thought. No more than that handful of others who criticized him. What they couldn't see was that Daniel, despite his white skin and blue eyes, was as much Indian in some ways as Attacullaculla, or even Cornstalk. Rebecca herself had accused him of it at times. "You'd rather be off in the woods, Daniel Boone, for all the world like some painted heathen, than at home tendin' the crops that feed your young'uns!" she'd declared more than once in Roman's hearing. And it was the truth. Daniel had not tried to deny it.

If he was a little careless in putting up gates, it was because he saw little reason for palisades or gates. To Daniel—as to the Indian—walls didn't make him feel safe. They made him feel hemmed in. Still, when the chips were down, there was no man braver or more steadfast. George would find that out. And God knew they needed such men now.

Once back in the saddle, Roman followed the creek bed for several miles to where a high, wooded ridge rose to his right. Leaving the gelding in a thick shelter of cedar trees, he crossed the creek, jumping lightly from rock to rock, and then climbed the steep slope, his feet slipping on the fallen and frosty leaves, using the saplings and lower tree limbs for handholds.

He approached the crest cautiously, dropping down to ease his head up and look around. To the right the land dropped gradually away to rolling hills etched in the subdued browns and ochers of winter. Left of him, trees grew thick and towering on the high plateau, dark vines clinging stubbornly to the bare branches. He was just ready to stand and have a good look around when suddenly he heard the whinny of a horse and the stamping of hooves through the trees.

It was too late to slide back down the hill without being seen, and he burrowed hastily into a deep drift of leaves next to him, pulling his gun along with him and hoping that the dry crackle didn't give him away as he caught a glimpse of six Indian ponies and their riders emerging from a point not twenty yards away from him.

Suddenly, almost in front of the lead Indian, a huge tom turkey came bursting out of the thicket, wattles purple-red, feathers flying, and the Shawnees, after one startled look, burst into laughter, nudging one another, their horses stamping about in circles. One took off after the big bird, getting off a skillful shot to bring him down just as the tom was launching himself into clumsy flight. The young brave, horse on the run, hung down out of his saddle to snatch up the still twitching turkey, emitting a thin screech of triumph as he held it high.

But Roman's attention was focused on the lead rider, who'd laid his musket across the horse in front of him, his vermilion-streaked cheeks rounding in a broad grin, hand upraised to the hunter . . . the otter fur wrap about his shoulders parting to reveal the scalp hanging at his belt. A bitter taste stung the back of Roman's throat. The scalp looked fresh, the hair long and tangled, the bloodstains on the warrior's leggings only half dry.

"Jesus! Who lived that way? Two fellows had put out a corn crop a few miles over there last spring, but both had gotten scared out and gone back east . . . And then it came to him. *Amos Welter*. Amos had a cabin up there in the hills overlooking the river, his place almost impossible to find if you didn't know your way in.

Roman hugged close to the ground, the dampness seeping into him as his body heat began to melt the frosty crystals of ice that had collected among the decaying leaves. In a moment the leader raised his hand again in a signal to ride and the group started down toward the creek.

When they were out of sight, he retrieved his horse and set out for Amos Welter's place. Roman recalled the last time he had been there, when Amos, tentative, almost embarrassed, had shown him the carvings he'd done in the rock cliffs nearby.

The cabin was nestled in a semicircle of limestone bluffs, and could only be reached by steep and overgrown paths. Half hidden by beech and oaks and cedars, it overlooked the rich, cane-covered bottoms below. Roman approached it now from the rear, and as he edged his gelding cautiously from behind a huge mass of tangled brambles, he drew a breath of relief as he caught sight of the slim finger of smoke that curled upward over the roof. Everything looked as usual in the thinning winter light. He chuckled softly. Amos was probably stretching his feet out to that fire right now, a cup of that wicked brew of his at hand.

But Roman had hardly put his horse two steps forward before he hauled up sharply and stared. There was something amiss. The smoke that at first glance had appeared to be coming from the rock chimney was really coming from somewhere to the front side of the cabin. The wind was curling it up over the roof.

He grasped his rifle firmly and swung down from the horse to run, lightfooted despite his rangy size, darting from one tree to another. Amos might just be burning some brush, he told himself. But then, he'd never known Amos to clear up much about the place. The wilder it was, the better he liked it.

Roman held to his caution as he edged around to the side wall. Now he could see the fire. It was up in front and had clearly been a big one, nearly burned out now, smoke drifting half-heartedly upward in the cold air, wind stilled for the moment. Looking at the size of it, a terrible possibility occurred to him, and he squinted at the smoking remains but failed to pick out anything that looked as if it might have been human.

Gun at the ready, he charged out from the side wall, his eyes scanning the line of trees, taking the last few feet in a rolling tumble that brought him behind the shelter of a big limestone boulder, coming upright to plant his feet wide and face the front of the cabin.

He stared, bitter juices scalding his throat once again, a crow scolding noisily from its bleached white perch. It took him a moment to be sure that it was Amos . . . that gaunt and naked body tied upright to a topped-off locust tree close to the cabin. But there was finally no mistaking the woodsman.

Roman sorrowfully noted it all . . . even the brown stains down his legs where Amos had beshit himself before they'd finished with him, his genitals gone, hacked away to leave a gaping wound. God, he would have hated that, Roman thought. However rough he might have appeared to some, Amos had been a private man of great natural dignity. Roman's eyes moved back to the contorted face, lips drawn back from teeth that seemed no longer human in their agony. It had taken Amos Welter a long time to die.

He took his knife out and cut the big woodsman down, easing the violated body gently to the ground. He hadn't forgotten that Amos had volunteered to help bury his kin when there could easily have been raiders about. And by tomorrow when he could get back from the fort with help, the animals and the carrion birds would have already been at him.

Once it was done, once he'd covered Amos over and packed down the earth and piled rocks up over it, he stood there in silence for a long moment.

He'd never known very well how to pray. It had always seemed to him that at a time like this God must already know it all, and to try to add anything to that was pure effrontery.

❊ 15 ❊

THE WINTRY WEEKS PASSED SLOWLY AT BOONESBOR-ough. The fort was full up with outlying settlers, and the close confinement and constant Indian threat wore everyone's nerves thin. Extra precautions were taken. Men with rifles at the ready accompanied the women outside the gates whenever they went to milk the cows or fetch water. The watch kept an especially sharp eye on the clearing right to the edge of the woods and along the river; sentinels on night duty learned to dread an overcast sky when they couldn't see what might be out there.

The horses were kept inside the compound now—they were too valuable to risk losing to the Indians—and the older boys were put to gathering up the droppings every few days and throwing them over the walls. The Porter boys, guffawing, allowed as how they'd just as soon clean up horse hockey as anything else, since there wasn't much to do cooped up the way they were. When their chores were done, there was no fishing through the icy skim at the edge of the river or taking the dogs off to tree a fat 'possum or stir up a covey of quail. The smaller children missed playing down in the hollow by the spring, but even they seemed to understand why they couldn't and didn't complain.

But the tasks of everyday living continued despite the ongoing Indian threat, and Kitty and Sara had fallen into the habit of sharing some of their chores. It was a pleasant way to pass the long days when Roman and Cullen were gone . . . and though it remained unspoken between them, it helped them not to dwell on the constant danger they knew their men faced.

They had spun and woven and knitted through the winter. Together, they had started a quilt for Sara. But today they were winding yarn on the weasel in the Claiborne cabin when Kitty's sister Faith knocked at the door and entered, red-nosed and shivering, a thick woolen shawl clutched about her. Though it was the first week in March, the ground was still frozen.

"Law me," she said, "but that wind is keen today!"

"You should have your cloak on," Kitty chided. "You'll catch your death."

"It's hard to stir a washpot with a cloak in your way." She sidled up to the fireplace and held out her hands to the warmth.

"There's some peppermint tea brewing," said Sara, smiling at Faith as she stopped winding to unsnarl a section of yarn. "That should warm you up some." She couldn't help but notice how red and chapped Faith's hands were.

"Wish I could stay for some, but once I get the washing done, it'll be time to start supper. I just came to see if you had a bar of soap you could spare me. I'll pay you back soon as I make up a batch."

"Of course." Kitty went to fetch one of the strong-smelling bars from the hickory basket in the corner.

"That yarn's a pretty color," Faith said, admiring the deep red-purple of a skein already measured and tied.

"Dried pokeberries," Kitty told her. "Boiled them in water, strained them out, and the dye was as good as if they'd been fresh off the bush. Surely you can stay a little. The tea'll be ready in a minute."

"I'd best not." Faith smoothed the wheat-colored hair that she no longer bothered to braid but wore pulled back severely and fastened into a flat knot at the back of her head. "I left Martha with Ben while I came over here. And if she acts up, it nettles him. Besides, she's sure to be squallin' to nurse any time now. I've tried to get her to take a little food off the table, but she doesn't want a thing but the teat." She thanked Kitty for the soap and, wrapping her shawl against the wind, went back to her washing.

"Sometimes I do wonder how in the world she can stand all

those Tylers," Sara said once Faith was out of earshot. With his pious pronouncements and dour air, Ben was not the most popular figure at the fort, and his brothers—Todd had returned with the oldest brother, Latham, just in time to be herded into the fort with everyone else—echoed his every word. "I can't even see a speck of Gentry in that little one of hers," she added.

"I know." Kitty sighed, her mouth settling into a line of resignation. "But she seems to fit in with their ways well enough, and I guess in the long run that's for the best. I expect it'd be awful to be married to a man you couldn't stand."

"I guess it would be." Sara kept the wheel of the weasel turning smartly, the little bit of hoecake and buttermilk she'd had earlier uneasy on her stomach. "It's hard for me to imagine . . . being married to Roman."

Kitty grinned at her. "Let's stop now and have some tea. I think it's steeped long enough." She tipped the heavy iron teapot forward and poured out two cups of the fragrant brew. "Lord, I'm glad I dried up a bunch of this mint," she declared, sniffing appreciatively. "It may not be real tea, but it is surely a comfort on a cold day."

Sara nodded and went to join Kitty at the table. "I wish the weather would break," she said, taking up the cup and cradling the warmth of it in her two hands. "Here it is March already. You'd think there'd be a warm day or two, just to let you know that spring is coming." She regarded the roughened skin on the backs of her own hands. They didn't look much better than Faith's. Kitty had told her to rub some 'possum grease into them, but the smell of it made her ill.

"Mmmm . . ." Kitty savored her tea. "I wouldn't mind a spring day myself." She peered at Sara over the rim of her cup. "You're looking a little peaked . . . Are you feeling all right?"

Sara shrugged. She felt well enough, she guessed . . . under the circumstances.

"I know what's wrong with you," said Kitty.

"You do?" Sara felt a quick rush of warmth to her cheeks.

"You need Roman to come back in soon."

Sara swallowed and nodded, sipping at the hot tea, vaguely disappointed that Kitty hadn't guessed. She did need to see Roman. She couldn't put off telling him too much longer. Every time she thought of it, a small flare of hope brightened within her that he would insist they go back home before her time.

The sound of good-natured male voices drifted in from the compound. The men had mustered to practice their soldiering again. Ever since the new militia had been organized, they'd gathered several times a week to march in close step; Sam Henderson, whom Daniel had made a sergeant, called out the commands.

It was done half in jest. They all knew that if they had to stand off the Indians, marching in formation would have nothing to do with it. But somehow it seemed to break the tension for them. Besides, some of them joked, how did they know the redcoats wouldn't turn up one day, a whole regiment of them, and they might have to meet them man to man? "Shit," another had responded to that, "if'n any Brits show up here, it's marchin' be damned! I'll be hyin' myself to the nearest loophole and aimin' my sights right square 'twixt the closest one's legs to separate him and his prime parts faster'n a hog can make wind."

Now, given the raucous shouts of laughter that echoed from the fort yard and Sam Henderson's good-natured call to "Straighten up there, boys!" it seemed fairly certain that they were indulging in more of the same coarse boasting.

Sara leaned back in her chair and tried to relax. Though the tea was good-tasting and hot, she felt the now familiar swell at the back of her throat, sweat popping out on her face despite the coolness of the cabin. And in the next moment, nausea deepening, she put down the cup so hastily that some of the tea sloshed out as she got to her feet and looked about helplessly.

"Sara, what is it? My goodness, you're white as snow!"

"Is the chamber pot under the bed?" she gasped, and without waiting for an answer she made a wild dash for it, throwing herself down and dragging it out just in time to heave up what little was in her stomach.

In a minute Kitty had wet a cloth and was down on her knees beside her. "Sara . . . poor thing . . . There, is that better?" She dabbed at her face.

Sara gave one final retch and nodded, embarrassed. "I'll be all right in a minute," she got out. "I usually get this over with in the mornings."

As Sam's voice, calling out drill commands, filtered in from outside, Kitty looked at Sara pointedly, the question in her eyes. "Sara . . . are you?"

Sara pressed the cloth to her throat. "Yes," she confessed, managing a smile.

"My lord, why didn't you tell me before?" Kitty was grinning.

"I wasn't sure myself till lately. My monthlies were never all that regular."

Kitty sat back on her heels and beamed. "How far do you think you are?"

The nausea passing, Sara felt a flush of excitement at being able to share her news. "Well," she said, "from when the morning sickness started, I think it must have happened the very first night that Roman came home from the East. That'd make me almost three months." The two of them laughed together, and Kitty hugged her.

"I'm surprised that Roman's been able to keep this to himself."

"He doesn't know yet."

"Doesn't know? For heaven's sake, why haven't you told him?"

Sara squared herself around and sat with her back against the leg of the bed, drawing her knees up beneath her skirt and hugging her legs. "He seemed so tired last time when he was in. All he wanted to do was sleep that first twenty-four hours. And after that there was so little time before he was gone again. I wish, Kitty . . . Lord, I just wish that we could go back home!" It burst out of her, and she couldn't call it back, though she wanted to. There was a look of surprise on Kitty's face as the silence hung in the room. Outside, Sam had stopped calling out drill calls, but Maggie Hamilton could be heard upbraiding her slave girl.

"Oh, Sara," said Kitty. For just a moment her fingers made contact with Sara's, and then she was motioning them both up. "Come on . . . it's too drafty down here on the floor. Settle yourself in the chair and maybe try a little more of this tea. Now that your stomach's emptied out, it should soothe you."

"Do you think so?" Sara asked.

Kitty nodded, wiping up the spilled tea and quickly pouring some more of the steaming liquid to fill Sara's cup again. "There, try that. Just a little at a time to see how it sets with you."

Sara sipped it and it went down well, clearing the rank vomit taste from her mouth. "Kitty—" She hesitated, then plunged ahead. "Don't tell Roman what I said before."

"I wouldn't," Kitty assured her. "But I expect it's natural that you'd want to go back long enough to have the baby . . . be with your mother and sister. I think Roman would understand that."

Sara nodded, bending down over her cup of tea lest Kitty read her eyes and see that she didn't just want to go back to Virginia for her confinement, but wanted with all her heart to leave this fierce, wild land forever and go home for good. She was overcome for a moment with memories of the house she'd grown up in. The leaf buds on the branches of the willow tree outside her old bedchamber would be swelling by now. Her mother would be mixing up a batch of her ''spring tonic''—a vile mixture of molasses and balsam and horehound with which she insisted upon dosing everyone in the household come March, from Sara's father right down to the bound girls, no matter their protests. And Papa would be going out to inspect the cabbage roses to see if they had survived the winter.

Sara realized that she would miss Kitty dreadfully if they should go back east. She had come to depend on her so. But she knew that Kitty would not go back, not even if she had the chance tomorrow.

She sipped the comforting hot tea and held back the threat of tears, admitting to herself at last that Roman wouldn't, either. Only a foolish, and pregnant, woman would think for a moment that he would. And in the end she would always do what Roman wanted—she and the baby. She would just have to learn to live with her fears . . . somehow.

Out in the fort yard the drill team had stopped for the day, to be replaced at once by some of the younger boys who marched back and forth in imitation, holding sticks for guns and showing off for the little girls who had gathered to watch and giggle. On the far side of the yard Faith lifted her head and smiled at them, then left her steaming washpot to enter the cabin and accede to little Martha's whining demands, yelping herself as the child bit down on a tender nipple. Out at the forge the blacksmith's hammer began to clang, the heated metal beneath it glowing red, small clouds of the smithy's breath forming to be spent in the cold air. But in a moment the normalcy of the fort was shattered.

Shouts rang out from the men on watch and then an instant later, musket fire, bringing Daniel running as cabins from one end of the fort to the other began to empty out.

''Secure that gate!'' Daniel roared as he saw the oak beam swing upward, the gates slightly ajar. A rough platform had been built to allow a look over the stockade walls, and he climbed up quickly, his eye falling on the crumpled form of a girl lying halfway down the path toward the spring.

"I . . . I think it be the Hamiltons' nigra girl!" the sentry nearest to him stammered out, his young face flushed and sweating despite the chill wind.

"Damnation!" Daniel swore beneath his breath. "Why in the world did you let her go out there by herself?"

" 'Tweren't his fault." Ezekial Turner, who'd also been standing watch, spoke up. "I didn't see her myself till she were clean outen the gate and headed down fer the spring. See that there bucket . . ." He gestured toward the pail that lay on the ground beside the still form of the girl.

Colonel Callaway pushed through the knot of people who'd gathered to see what had happened. He climbed up on the wall beside Daniel, taking in the scene in the clearing at a glance.

"An Indian come bearin' down out o' those trees." The young sentry gestured toward the nearby woods that spilled down from Hackberry Ridge.

"He were ridin' hard," Ezekial volunteered. "We got off some shots at him, but he swung a tomahawk upside her head."

"I think he was just aimin' to carry her off," the boy said, his baby face knotting up with regret. "Then when we commenced to shootin'—"

"It's all right." Daniel laid a quick hand on the bony shoulder. "You did as best you could."

Sam Henderson and Flanders Callaway came loping up from the back side of the stockade, the side nearest to the river. "He rode north along the bank," Flanders called out. "Just the one. We didn't see any more of them."

"That don't mean they're not out there," said one man.

There was a shriek from the back of the crowd that had gathered, and Maggie Hamilton pushed through, crying and demanding to know what had happened. "My God!" she wailed. "Is it Rainey? Did the savages carry her off?"

Her voice had taken on a shrill and uncontrolled edge, and Daniel quickly swept the knot of people, looking for Rebecca. Once he'd found her, he gave a quick jerk of his head for her to quiet Maggie if she could. That was all he needed now—a hysterical woman to set all the others off. That done, he beckoned to Sam and Flanders and the others who had fallen in, long guns ready, to follow him out and bring in the girl.

"I'll git my doctorin' things . . . in case she's still a-livin'," Granny Hawkins called after them as they went through the gates.

Kitty and Sara had gone to help Rebecca with Maggie, but

she wasn't paying much heed to their suggestions that they go back to her cabin and wait there for news of the girl.

"She must be all right!" Maggie appealed to them, her nose reddening in a pale face. "I only sent her for a pail of water."

"*You* sent her out there?" Horace Hamilton had come up behind his wife just in time to hear what she said, and he regarded her now with a mixture of disbelief and sorrow. "Why would you do that, my dear?" he asked, his bloodless fingers plucking helplessly at his waistcoat.

"Because we needed the water," Maggie declared tearfully. "I used up all she brought in this morning."

"Maggie"—Rebecca's voice was sterner than Kitty or Sara had ever heard it before—"you know that Daniel gave orders that none of us were to go outside the gates unless someone was standing guard!"

"I didn't think it would hurt anything. I told her to just run out there quick. . . ." Maggie's face went colorless as she saw the returning men.

Winfield Burdette, arm muscles bulging from his long years at the forge, carried the girl as easily as if she'd been a rag doll, her arms and legs bouncing lifelessly as he walked. Her kerchief had come off, was lying somewhere out there on the frozen ground, and the pulpy mass of flesh and blood where the side of her face had been showed the splintery white edges of protruding bone.

"Don't look," Kitty whispered into Sara's ear.

Maggie began to shriek again, her arms flailing, as Horace led her away. "There, there, my dear. Calm yourself," he murmured, but she only babbled something about the Indians coming to murder them all, while the rest of the little group stood there silently. Little Martha, still unsatisfied, whined and tugged at Faith's shirtwaist. Fanny Callaway twisted a length of her dark hair.

Rebecca's eyes sought Daniel's for a moment, and then she went along to do what she could for Maggie. Granny Hawkins followed, her old joints moving stiffly.

"I 'spect I kin mix up somethin' that'll help to quiet her," she croaked.

While volunteers saw to the proper burying of the girl, the rest were busy following Daniel's orders. The watch was doubled, guns were readied—flints checked, patches cut and greased, supplies of powder checked. . . . Though it was the women who usually carried in water, the young men and older boys did it now, bringing in a good supply; four men stood guard as they came and went—all just in case the Indians were preparing a direct assault on the fort.

It was with a certain relief that the settlers saw the cows come meandering along the river and out of the woods . . . come to stand at the gates and lick their raspy tongues out, lowing softly in anticipation of their portion of fodder and the relieving of their swollen udders.

"Damme, but I was afraid the Indians might have done for them," Colonel Callaway said. "Confounded savages don't even know enough to keep a cow for milk, but there's nothing they like better'n to slaughter the white man's cattle."

"That's a fact," Daniel said. He called out to the bigger boys: "Let's get 'em inside the gates now!" He turned back to the Old Colonel. "Be safer till we find out if they're out there in force." And the cows milled around in confusion, bumping into one another, heavy udders swinging beneath them as they were herded inside.

"Could have been just that one, Daniel. . . ." The Old Colonel looked hopefully at Boone. "A stray Shawnee that thought he'd carry off a pretty little girl to cook and sew . . . and warm his blanket for him."

"Could have been." Daniel nodded, but his eyes were sober. "I much doubt we'll have to wait too long to find out. It's not likely they'd move on us this close to sundown. But come morning, if they're figurin' on mischief . . ." He left the rest unsaid, and the two men went about the fort, seeing that all was as ready as possible should trouble come.

The women saw to their supper preparations as usual, after hanging quilts or blankets up against the back walls of their cabins which formed the perimeter of the fort. It was known that Indians would sometimes watch for the light that spilled through holes in the chinking and shoot at any moving figure they could spy. But as darkness fell, all stayed quiet and frosty, the moon rising in a clear, cold sky to cast long shadows out from every tree and bush and rise to make the sentinels on the walls jittery.

After a while the fort quieted; even the cows stopped their restless moving about, and the dogs curled together for warmth and settled down to sleep. But Daniel still prowled about, not ready to give up to his bed yet.

John Holder and Flanders Callaway were on the wall nearest

to the hollow, and now Flanders stiffened as he caught sight of a movement along the bank. "Look there," he cautioned Holder as he slid up his rifle. He got off a shot that reverberated in the still cold air and set the dogs up and barking. An instant later Daniel came running up.

"Somebody's out there, Daniel!" Holder whispered hoarsely as Boone hauled up beside them. "I seen 'em!"

"Two of them," Flanders said. "I think one is hunkered down behind that hillock out there. I lost sight of the other."

"God's blood!" A voice came out of the shadows. "Hold up on your rifle, Flanders! I think you came within a particle of my ear!"

"Roman," Daniel breathed, and the three men grinned at one another.

"It is." Roman's voice came out of the darkness again. "And that's Simon Butler behind that rise over there. Get that gate open. We're coming in."

Minutes later Roman and Butler were being pounded on their backs, safe within the compound.

"Why didn't you call out?" Flanders demanded.

"It didn't seem a good idea to make too much noise out there," Roman responded soberly. And Butler, a young giant of a fellow, fur cap pulled down tight on his head to accentuate the long and down-curving nose, gave an assenting nod.

"They're about . . . thick as fleas on a sore-tailed dog." The scout from Harrod's Town grinned, his voice edged with a kind of exhilaration, his eyes bright.

Daniel shook his head at the news. "John," he directed, "get back to your place on the wall. Flanders, you go rouse up Colonel Callaway. I expect he'll want to hear what Roman and Simon have to say. Then you get back to your post, too." And as the two young men headed off to do his bidding, Daniel ushered Roman and Simon into the nearest blockhouse, where the fire was still flickering.

"Simon, you old hoss, what are you doin' over this way?" Daniel threw a chuck of wood into the fireplace and poked at the glowing log already there.

"Thought I'd come a-visitin'." Butler grinned. "Didn't know ol' Chief Black Fish and his braves had fell on the same idee."

"Black Fish is leading them?" Daniel passed a hand over his wide mouth, eyes narrowing.

"I saw him myself," Roman said.

"How many would you say?"

"Fifty. Maybe more."

"I'd go along with that," Butler chimed in. "I laid up in a hollow tree and watched thirty-five or forty pass 'fore I dared come ahead. Once I'd run into Roman, we hid out together till dark . . . and then took our chance to come in."

The door opened and Richard Callaway came striding through, his back stiff as a ramrod, silver hair falling to his shoulders. "I was already up and dressing," he said. "I heard the dogs."

He greeted Roman and Butler warmly, but once Daniel told him of the situation, he could only shake his head soberly. "Then it looks like trouble come morning."

Daniel leaned against the big slab of wood that formed the mantel, looking down into the flames for a long moment. "Could be," he said finally. "But then"—he turned, grinning— "an Indian can get discouraged easy sometimes. I'd say we ought to go now and get what sleep we can, and just before sunup"— he winked solemnly—"we'll see if we can't discourage 'em a little."

Sara had decided to spend the night with Kitty, and the two of them, awakened by the barking of the dogs a short time before, lay close together, talking quietly and listening from time to time to see if anything was going on outside. They both sat up in bed at the sound of light footfalls along the frozen path, and a moment later a knock came at the door.

"Who is it?" Kitty called out.

"It's me . . . Roman."

The two women were up at once, Kitty pausing to grab a shawl from its peg and wrap it around her over the long white nightgown while Sara flew to the door and had it open in an instant.

"Roman!" She flung herself at him, her voice catching in relief.

He smiled and steadied her, closing the door against the gust of frosty air with one hand. "When I didn't find you at our place, I figured you'd be here. Sorry to get you up, Kitty."

"No bother," said Kitty.

Sara clung to him as if she were afraid he might disappear. "Oh, Roman," she burst out, "I'm so glad you've come in! An Indian killed Maggie's girl Rainey! Killed her right out there by the spring, the poor thing."

"I know." Roman regarded them solemnly. "Daniel told me."

"Are there more of them out there? What's going to happen now?" Fear quivered in her voice, but Roman stepped closer to the fire, drawing Sara along with him.

"Maybe nothing," he said in that calm way of his.

"But they're out there?" she persisted.

"Could be a few. But we're safe in the fort. Nothing to worry about."

Though Sara seemed to believe what he'd said, Kitty looked into his eyes and knew it wasn't the truth. "Can I fix you something to eat?" she asked him, trying to keep her voice light.

He shook his head. "I think a few hours' sleep will set best for now."

"The fire may be out at our place," Sara said.

"We'll borrow a chunk from Kitty," he answered.

Kitty took up the long-handled iron spoon leaning against the fireplace and scooped a bit of the live coals into a small covered pot, then passed it to Roman, who grasped the handle. "Have you seen Cullen?" She couldn't help asking it, though she knew that he would have said right away if he had.

"No. But I expect he's upriver a ways. Probably be in soon." His voice was confident.

Kitty nodded. It was hard not to worry. She had to keep reminding herself that if anybody could take care of himself out there, it was Cullen. He'd boasted more than once that the Indian hadn't been born that could best him.

"Wait," she said to Sara, "don't forget your cloak. It's freezing out there."

Sara followed her back to fetch the long woolen cloak that hung from one of the many pegs around the wall. "I'm going to tell him tonight," she whispered.

There was an eager nervousness about her, and Kitty smiled and squeezed her hand, wishing it could have been a better time for the news. But maybe a thing like that couldn't wait for the right time. Roman ought to know.

She said good night to them and bolted the door after they'd gone, going to stand before the fire and think of Cullen and wonder just what would happen when morning came. Sara was lucky, she thought. To be carrying her man's child and have him safe . . . for tonight, at least. She pushed aside the folds of her shawl and ran her hand down over her flat belly wishing that she were carrying Cullen's baby now . . . especially now. She shivered at the thought, giving in to the notion that something could happen out there and there'd never be another chance.

"Fiddlesticks!" she said aloud, sounding remarkably like Amelia. "You can't go through your life thinking 'what if.' " It was the same thing she had told Roman the night he'd come back from Virginia.

She laid another log far back in the fireplace and watched the flames curl up around it. Truth was, she'd probably have more children than they could accommodate before they were through. Ma had always laughed that she'd been caught before the door had hardly closed behind her and Pa on their wedding night. The Gentry women were fruitful enough, and with a man as willing as Cullen, it left little doubt of a houseful in good time.

She turned and faced the empty bed. Now her problem was to get some sleep. The morning would come soon enough, and she needed to be ready for it.

At Daniel's order, each cabin door was knocked upon well before dawn and the settlers instructed to gather in the fort yard once they were dressed. They came within minutes, puffy-eyed and shivering in the cold wind. Most of them had found sleep elusive anyway and seemed almost relieved to be up.

With no hint of light in the eastern sky, the slim crescent of a moon lying low on the horizon still, Daniel stood waiting, flanked by Colonel Callaway on one side and Roman and Simon Butler on the other.

"I guess we can quit our speculations," he announced soberly as soon as they had all gathered. "As you see, Roman come in last night . . . Simon Butler here along with him. And they tell us there are some numbers of Shawnee out there. Guess they come down to look us over," he added dryly.

"God protect us," Ben Tyler intoned, his head bowed. Toward the back of the small knot of people, Maggie Hamilton whimpered softly, and a few feet away from her stood Sara, a look of surprise on her face, her eyes seeking Roman's as if to ask why he hadn't told her last night.

"The fort is strong." Confidence rang in Daniel's voice. "Whatever mischief they've got in mind, we should be able to handle. But"—a sober grin marked his face—"if I know Indians, they're out there now wonderin' how many shootin' men we've got in here. And I expect it wouldn't hurt a thing if we was to convince them that there are more of us than they reckoned on."

Some of the younger men nudged one another and nodded.

Daniel pointed out half a dozen men, mostly those who weren't all that good with a rifle, such as Horace Hamilton, and directed that they be ready to fall in for drill as soon as it was light. "And set up as much commotion as you can in the doing of it. I want you to sound like a whole danged regiment to those that be listenin' out there. Daniel Morgan here"—he gestured to his middle son—"is aimin' to march along with you and beat on that potlid he's holdin' there, like as if it was a drum.

"As to the rest . . . I'll take five of our best marksmen and we'll man the walls, two of us to a side. But unless there's some move to attack, I want you others out in the yard in plain sight, in case Black Fish decides to send some of his scouts across the river to the high ground to get a look in."

"Bring every gun you have," Colonel Callaway put in.

"That's right," said Daniel. "If we don't have a man to carry it, then some of you women that's willing can dress up in your men's clothes. From a distance it'll fool 'em. Now go on about what you have to do. Just be ready by sunup."

The women cooked hurriedly, and the men gulped down buttered hoecakes and fried potatoes. There was little meat. Their supply was running low, and there'd be no more until it was safe to send a hunting party out again.

In her cabin, Kitty stopped for a moment to look ruefully at Cullen's clothes, realizing that they would swallow her; then she headed down to Elvie Porter, who quickly outfitted her in one of the boys' tow linen shirts and woolen breeches.

"Fits perfect." Elvie grinned. "Now tuck up that hair and put this here cap on your head while I find you somethin' to keep you from freezin' to death out there." She was back a minute later with a deerskin jacket that, while a shade too big for Kitty, would do.

"There now . . ." Elvie stood back to view her handiwork, squinting her eyes. "Cullen himself wouldn't know you from a hundred yards," she pronounced.

Kitty thanked her and hurried out, feeling self-conscious. She had never had on men's clothes before, and the breeches itched. But after only a few strides, she was struck by how much freer her legs could move than when they were caught around by her long skirts.

Rebecca and Jemima, dressed in Israel's clothes, were waiting in the fort yard along with several other women who had donned their men's apparel. Sara had gone off to help with the milking.

"Just take whichever one you want, ladies." Flanders grinned and gestured toward the extra rifles that had been stacked nearby.

A slender band of pink was showing at the horizon now. As the sun edged up, Sam Henderson began calling out his commands and the drill team began marching around the compound, eight-year-old Daniel Morgan Boone drumming a fine ratta-tat-tat on the potlid.

There was a general tensing as the light strengthened; Kitty's mouth was so dry she could hardly swallow. But the sentinels on the wall stood ready, as Daniel and the others watched for any movement. Down where the cows were, the women waited, Elizabeth Callaway setting aside the piggin of foaming milk to stand beside Sara and squeeze her hand in a hard grip.

As the minutes passed and no blood-curdling yell came, no horde of painted savages swarmed down upon them, the men began to grin at one another and the women breathed sighs of nervous relief. But everyone knew that they must not let down, that at most they'd only given the Shawnee pause to wonder at the wisdom of an attack on the fort.

They kept up their pretense through the hours, Kitty itching miserably in the woolen breeches, her arms aching from the weight of the gun. The sentries left their positions only long enough to go use the necessary house, or eat a quick bite of stew the women had made of the last of their meat—three squirrels and a rabbit—stretched with lots of potatoes and onions and turnips.

At last the long day ended, and as darkness fell, Ezekial Turner caught up his fiddle and played a quick jig, some of the men stomping a few steps to it. But for the most part they were all spent with the strain of waiting, of not knowing whether the Indians would attack or not, and wanted only to seek their own cabins and the comfort of a corn-husk mattress for a few hours.

Kitty was relieved to find her own fire still blazing—Elvie Porter had charged one of the younger boys with keeping it going through the day—and she sank into a chair before it, too tired even to get out of the scratchy woolen breeches. In a minute Sara came in with a trencher of leftover stew and steaming hoe-cakes and insisted that she eat.

"You all right?" Kitty asked between mouthfuls.

Sara nodded. "Roman's gone out . . . Simon Butler with him. They're going to see what's happening out there." Her voice was quiet, almost flat, but there was an unusual brightness about the blue eyes, as if she'd been crying.

"Roman will be careful," Kitty said.

Sara made no reply.

"Why don't you stay over again tonight?"

With a wan smile, Sara gestured toward the small hempen bag she'd left by the door. "I brought my nightgown with me."

They got ready quickly, and Sara climbed into bed.

"I don't take to Simon Butler all that much," she said. "There's something about him that's—" She searched for a word. "—wild."

Kitty snuffed out the grease lamp and climbed in beside her. "They say he's a good scout," she countered. "And we can use him right now."

Her arms and shoulders were aching from the long hours of holding the heavy rifle, her legs stiff and sore, and she curled herself into as comfortable a position as possible, watching the warm shadows that stretched across the floor from the fireglow. Sara was right, she thought. Butler did have a wild streak in him . . . big and unpredictable, violence just beneath the surface. She wondered if Sara knew that Cullen and Roman were not that much different. It was what made them so good at what they did.

"It must be so dark out there . . . ." Sara's voice was small. "I don't know if I can sleep."

"You can," Kitty said. "You need the rest. Think of the baby."

And, exhausted, they both slept, were still fast asleep just after dawn when Roman and Butler came into the fort, hollow-eyed with fatigue but grinning, to tell Daniel that their ruse had worked. The Indians had cleared out.

Ten days later word came to Daniel from his brother Squire, who some weeks before had taken his family and moved over to Harrod's Town, that he'd been wounded in a run-in with a Shawnee only a few yards from the fort gates. He'd suffered a glancing blow from a tomahawk down one cheek. "I expect to keep a goodly scar from it," he wrote, "but succeeded in sending the savage to his reckoning in the great beyond."

The messenger carried the additional news that Fort Harrod had been attacked but had held. The unnatural cold, so late in the year, had worked in their favor. The weather had turned so foul, Black Fish had taken his warriors and headed north.

PART THREE

❄

Spring 1777

* 16 *

KITTY DROPPED TO HER KNEES TO EXAMINE THE MOUND of green weedy shoots next to the cabin step, the sun warm on her back. Despite the muddy morass of the walkways and the filth that resulted from having the animals penned up inside the compound too much of the time, it was cheering to have things greening again. Nothing seemed quite as bad if the sun was shining, though just the thought of Cullen made her ache. He'd only been in briefly and then right out again. They'd hardly had time to talk . . . or touch.

Despite Chief Black Fish's retreat, small, roving bands of Shawnee continued to make life miserable for the cooped-up settlers. Hunting meat was still a dangerous task. No one could venture outside the gates for long with any degree of safety. And the acre of compound, which had always seemed a reasonable space before, was now full to bursting with people and horses and dogs . . . and sometimes cows, if there were any suspicion that Indians were nearby.

Kitty longed for the place on Otter Creek. Ma's flowers would be pushing up beside the porch. The apple trees would be budding. . . . Surely the Indians would leave them in peace sometime, she told herself. And when they did, she'd get Cullen to take her there. But for now, a flower bed right by the steps would be nice. Elizabeth had given her some cockscomb seeds, and she'd plant them as soon as the ground got dry enough to work a little.

"Kitty . . ."

She turned to see Elvie Porter, coming along the muddy path and doing her best to avoid the worst spots. Kitty got to her feet, grinning at the round-faced little woman who never seemed to change much no matter what happened. "Good day to you,

221

Elvie." She brushed at her skirt. "I've been down here deciding to put a flower bed in on this side."

Elvie nodded. "I've got some seed put back. Marigolds and dragonhead. Come down when you get a chance and I'll give you some."

"I will, thank you. Won't you come in and visit?"

"I guess not today. I've got a Lord's plenty work to do at home. Lureen's feelin' poorly. I declare, ever' one of 'em come through the winter without a sick day, and now here it is spring and her with influenza. Thought I'd step down here and see if Granny Hawkins can't mix her up a good tonic."

Kitty nodded. "Can I help you with anything?"

"Thankee, no. I'll put them boys o' mine to work if I can catch 'em." She grinned and went on down the path, and Kitty turned back into the cabin, leaving the door wide open to catch the sun and warmth.

Her old red-spotted cow was still giving a good quantity of milk, and now she skimmed a little of the cream from the pigginful she'd brought in earlier to let set. She had a few dried persimmons left, and cooked up and topped with a little of the cream, they'd make a treat. Maybe, she thought, she'd take some to Lureen.

She heard the sound of men's voices down toward the gates and wondered what was happening. Then a few moments later Sara, who was beginning to round nicely, came through the door in such a hurry that she almost tripped over the step.

"Be careful!" said Kitty.

"Cullen just rode in," she got out, breathless.

"Oh!" Kitty almost spilled the milk.

"He's up there at the blockhouse with Daniel and the others. Here, I'll do that for you. Go on up there if you want to."

Giving Sara a quick smile, Kitty hurriedly wiped her hands and then flew out of the cabin, keeping to the center grass where it was drier, dodging a cow pie now and again. Israel Boone hailed her.

"Cullen's in."

"I know." She grinned and went on.

There was a little knot of men around him, still outside the blockhouse door, and as he caught sight of her, he shoved his hat to the back of his head and elbowed through. "Excuse me, gents," he said. In a moment he'd scooped her up in an exuberant hug and kissed her soundly.

The onlookers elbowed one another and guffawed. There

wasn't a one of them that would have kissed his wife right out in front of everybody. Some of their faces reddened, but they all grinned.

Kitty was blushing herself, but she gave little thought to self-consciousness. She was too busy looking up into Cullen's handsome, tanned face to assure herself that he was all right.

"Bless me, lass," he whispered into her ear, "but you're a welcome sight!" He let loose with his great, hearty laugh, and giving her a final squeeze, set her on her feet before him. "Is all well with ye?"

"I'm fine." She grinned up at him.

Colonel Callaway was there, looking away tactfully, a twinkle in his eye, but it was only now that Daniel came hurrying from the direction of the necessary.

"Cullen . . . I hear you've got something to show me."

Cullen gave Kitty a gentle nudge and a wink. "I'll be along directly," he said.

Once Cullen had shown Daniel and the others what he had tucked in the front of his hunting shirt, the entire group pushed into the blockhouse, faces set with anger or scorn. They gathered around Cullen to ply him with questions as they examined the printed English handbills that exhorted them to come to Detroit and join with the British against the Americans. All who did, it was promised, would be well taken care of, but those who refused would meet their fate at the hands of the Indians.

Colonel Callaway showed his contempt by spitting into the blackened fireplace, a sour expression on his face as he commenced to pace the room.

"Lieutenant Governor Hamilton . . ." Daniel said.

"The goddamned Hair Buyer hisself!" Winfield Burdette balled his big fists.

The Old Colonel swung around, that silver length of hair all but quivering in his outrage. "Any white man that would pay for the scalps of others . . . !"

"For prisoners, too," Sam Henderson added.

"Goddamned pig-suckin' bastard!" someone called out from the back of the room.

"Well now," Daniel said calmly, "I reckon the governor can put out as many handbills as he's a mind to. Maybe he needs somethin' to keep him occupied up there in Detroit while he sends the Indians to do his dirty work for him. Where'd you find these, Cullen?"

"Right over on Hackberry Ridge." Cullen leaned against the wall casually. "There was some dropped near Harrod's fort, too."

Daniel tossed the handbill he held onto the table. "Well, I don't guess we needed anything to tell us that the British are behind our Indian trouble. We knew it already. So these don't mean a damned thing."

The men in the room eyed Daniel silently. Though he was no longer the Quaker he'd been born, he rarely used a word stronger than "danged."

"Set yourself down, Cullen." He gestured to the nearest chair. "There are more important things to talk about, such as how many of 'em you've seen. Where and when."

It was fully two hours before they'd finished and Cullen got away, to go to the cabin where Kitty waited for him, her face soft, her arms welcoming. He tossed the limp, furry bodies of a rabbit and two squirrels he'd brought with him into a corner and came to her, sweaty and eager. "Heaven help me," he said as he held her against him, pushing the folds of her skirt flat to cup his hand around her buttocks, "but I'm likely to burst if I don't get into you right this minute." They took to the bed at once, she as eager as he, their straining bodies joining in a quick, hot exchange that not only relieved, but drained them in its intensity.

Afterward, contrary to what usually happened, Kitty was the one to fall asleep in his arms, and Cullen crooked his head and looked down at her. A wisp of black hair trailed across a cheek still flushed with their lovemaking. He could feel the rise and fall of her chest as she breathed, and in that moment he was haunted by a memory he'd carried back to the fort with him. Something had happened out there this time that he couldn't get out of his mind.

He'd known on that day, nearly two weeks ago now, that Indians were close about and had headed up a ridge toward a small cave he'd discovered while hunting the past spring. It was hardly more than a hole in the rock, just enough space for a man to squeeze into and be safe for the night once he'd tethered his horse at a safe distance. But when he found it and pulled away the dried thistles and briars that hid the entrance, he took a step backward.

"Jesus!" he breathed.

The corpses of a young woman and an infant were there, obviously dead for some time but well preserved by the cold.

The side of the woman's waist and the upper part of her skirt were stiff and blackened with dried blood. Her head was turned so that she seemed to be looking down at the child held so tightly in that still arm.

Cullen stared at the pitiful sight, cursing under his breath. "Goddamn the bloody heathen who did this!"

He turned away for a moment, a fine rage gripping him. She must have been wounded, he decided, and had had just strength enough to drag herself and the baby into this little crevice to hide. The child, which looked to be only a few weeks old, must have been all right at the time. There was no sign of any injury. He turned back to look into that tiny face again, mouth half open, twisted as if it were crying right to the last.

Sickened to the depths of him, he wrapped himself in his blanket, pulling the briars up in front of him, and slept fitfully, propped against the rock and close enough so that he could have reached out and touched the cold bodies.

When morning came and he had made certain that it was safe, he buried the two of them in a shallow grave and then rode on up the ridge a piece until he found what he was looking for—a cabin up ahead amidst the tall poplars. He'd known that she couldn't have come far, carrying that baby and wounded as badly as she was.

He rode about the deserted place looking for whatever sign had not been obliterated by time and weather. The marks were faint, but he was sure a half-dozen or more horses had milled about in front some time back. Indian ponies. Unshod. Nearby, in the prickly branches of a hawthorn bush, he found a piece of a leather whang that looked as if it had been torn loose from a garment, and on the ground beneath it were a couple of stone beads . . . the kind the Shawnee were fond of decorating their buckskins with.

It was hard to know exactly what had transpired there. But somehow she had gotten away from them and was able to hide herself and the baby; that much was clear. God alone knew what had happened to her man.

Hours later that same day, his body stretched flat along a limestone ledge, Cullen watched as a lone Indian led his pony up to the bank of the creek that wound below. His eyes narrowed, blood beating at his temples as he saw the brave let go of the reins and kneel to drink. He was still full up with the last sight of that woman and her baby before he'd covered them over with half-frozen earth. He waited now with a deadly cold patience until the Shawnee had drunk his fill and stood upright once again, then sighted down the barrel of his rifle and squeezed off the shot.

The Indian flung up his arms and spun about, grabbing at the air as he pitched into the creek to claw a time or two and then lie still, a ribbon of red curling into the cold water as the pony reared and bolted away, running back the way it had come.

Up on the ledge, Cullen felt a vicious surge of satisfaction. "An eye for an eye," he muttered. But as he went to retrieve his horse, his stomach churned. He had killed more men than he could count, but he'd never shot one down in cold blood before.

When he reached Harrod's fort, he made inquiries to try to find out who the dead woman and her baby might have been. Jim Harrod recalled a couple who'd taken up land over that way and built a cabin. But when riders had gone out to warn everyone to come into the fort, they'd found the place deserted and concluded that the man must have decided to take his wife and go back east.

Now, lying beside Kitty, Cullen, who'd never been given to analyzing such things overmuch, pondered what he'd done out there. He had killed a man without knowing if he was guilty of any crime, had killed him purely on the basis of who he was. But the woman and baby had done no wrong, and they'd been shown no mercy. And maybe, because the Indian was dead, another woman, or man, or child, somewhere out there would live.

He only knew that it was a hard land. And he would do everything in his power, whatever it took, to make it safe for this woman who lay beside him. He looked down at her now to find those violet eyes open and full into his, a small smile tugging at the corners of her mouth. And he caught her closer in an embrace so tight she gasped for breath.

"Cullen, you're squashing me!" She giggled.

He gentled his hold, bending his head to kiss the hollow of her neck so that she wouldn't guess that there was a sudden, hot burning behind his eyes. If he hadn't known better, he'd have thought it was tears.

It was pouring rain the morning Cullen went back out again. He had left just before the gray dawn finally came; it was safer that way. And Kitty had reluctantly given in to his insistence that they take their leave of one another at the cabin instead of her waving him through the gates as she usually did.

Once he had gone, she sat before the fire for a while, listening to the rain against the roof and slowly sipping a cup of the hot "coffee" she made from ground-up persimmon seeds. Cullen liked it with his breakfast.

Lord, the cabin always seemed so empty whenever he'd just left. . . .

She set her mouth and put the cup aside to roll up her sleeves and go after the dirty plates and cutlery and crusty skillet, washing every piece clean and putting it back in its proper place. Then she turned her energy to the rest of the room, changing the linen on the bed, shaking the rag rugs out the door despite the peppering rain. Once the split hickory broom had been put to good use and every piece of furniture thoroughly dusted, she dashed out to the rain barrel at the corner of the cabin to fetch in more water, which she soon had steaming. Then, down on her knees, she scrubbed the floorboards until they were nearly white.

"It doesn't exactly seem the right day for it," Rebecca opined, stopping in just as Kitty was finishing up and looking down ruefully at the muddy puddles her shoes were making on the spotless puncheon floor.

"I guess it doesn't." Kitty laughed and, wiping her hands down the front of her apron, drew Rebecca into the room. She took the wet cloak from her and hung it on a peg behind the door. "Don't pay mind to that . . ." She indicated the muddy spots with a wave of her hand. "I'll likely scrub it again before the day is over."

Rebecca gave her an understanding look and took a seat. "I figured you could use some company this morning."

Kitty nodded. "Would you like some coffee? It's still hot."

"I would." Rebecca grinned eagerly. "I used up the last of mine weeks ago."

"I'll give you some grindings to take back with you," Kitty said as she poured a cup and passed it to Rebecca. "I don't fix it much for myself. Cullen likes it. Do you take a little milk with it?" Abruptly her hand flew to her mouth. "*Milk!* Lord help me, I got so lost in my cleaning I forgot all about the milking! I'd best get my pail and go."

"It's all right. Jemima went to milk ours, and when she saw you weren't there, she milked your old Red for you. Said she'd send Daniel Morgan over with it when she got it strained up."

Kitty turned away for a moment, nonplussed that she could have forgotten such a thing. "You tell Jemima that I'm obliged for her help."

"The first day always seems the hardest, doesn't it?" Rebecca's voice came softly, and Kitty turned back to look into her strong face.

"It does," she admitted. "It's always the time when I wish that Cullen were a cooper or a turner or a blacksmith . . . and could just stay here in the fort with the rest of us until the Indians get tired of their devilment and go back north."

"You don't really . . . any more than I wish Daniel had stayed a farmer. He wasn't suited to it and couldn't make himself be. His eye was always toward the far side of the mountains."

Kitty smiled and sat down across from Rebecca, the rain drumming against the cabin roof, the grease lamp flickering. "Did you ever get used to that?" she asked finally. "*Really* used to it?"

Rebecca pondered that, cupping the faintly steaming coffee between hands well marked with freckles. "I guess I did." She smiled. "At least it got . . . different after a while. In the beginning I felt like he'd just run off and left me to root hog or die." She laughed outright at that. "But then the young'uns come along and I had them . . . and I learned to manage without him, whether it was gettin' a crop in or havin' a baby. Once he was gone for two years. Come over here in Kentucky when there wasn't a sign of a cabin nor a stockade wall. Part of that time he was likely the only white man in the whole of it."

"Weren't you afraid that something had happened to him?"

Rebecca looked into the fire. "Squire went in and found him after a while. Brought word back that Daniel was fine. Then he went back and the two of them hunted and trapped through that next winter till they had a fine bunch of pelts. Only thing was, once they'd started back, the Indians surrounded them and took all the skins away from them. Let Daniel and Squire go without hurt, though . . . that was the most important thing. But Daniel was disappointed. He had debts to pay, and aimin' to pay 'em with the money he made off his trappin'.

"We always had plenty to eat, though. The land was good, and my family—I was a Bryan before I married—helped me with the crop until some of my young'uns got big enough. We managed. Ate better then than now." She grinned ruefully.

Kitty nodded, thinking how much she'd love a mess of green

beans or a skillet of fried apples. There hadn't been much but meat and hoecake for a long time.

"I'll be glad enough when we can get the garden planted," she said. The men had already started turning the soil, taking turns plowing or standing guard with rifles ready. It was the only way they dared be outside the gates.

"This rain'll set us back a few days," Rebecca said. "We'll have to wait till it's dry enough." She finished her coffee and set the cup on the table.

There was a great stomping outside the door, and after a knock and a call to come in, Daniel Morgan Boone, grinning and dripping, his hair slicked to his head, brought in the milk and set the piggin just inside.

"I thank you," Kitty said, but his mother was already shooing him out.

"Don't be messin' up Kitty's clean floor, now. Where's your cap?" she called after him.

"I don't need it, Ma." The door was closed and he was gone before she had time to say more, and the two women laughed.

"He looks like Daniel," Kitty said.

"Acts like him, too." Rebecca rose from her chair. "Well . . . I expect I'll walk on down to the Porters and see if Elvie needs any help this morning."

"Is Lureen still poorly?" Kitty had forgotten about the girl while Cullen was in.

Rebecca nodded. "She seemed some worse yesterday. Granny Hawkins was down there doctorin' her up last night. I told Elvie to send one of the boys down if she needed me or Jemima to sit with her."

"Wait," said Kitty, "I'll get my shawl and go with you." She drew the thick woolen shawl up over her head, and the two women braved the rain, which if anything was heavier now than it had been before. They hurried along the path, mud kicking up to spatter skirts and stockings, and as they drew abreast of the Porter cabin, they climbed the step together and huddled against the door to knock.

"It's me," Rebecca called out. "Kitty and me . . ."

In a moment the door was opened by one of the boys, who waved them in, then made his escape, sprinting down toward one of the blockhouses.

"Come in . . ." From the far corner of the room Elvie rose from her place by Lureen's bed. "Now just look who's come to see you," she said to her daughter in a voice slightly raised, as if she were speaking to someone who was deaf. "Rebecca and Kitty are here."

She made her way toward them, through the room crowded with two beds and a table long enough to seat the Porter brood. The door and window were closed against the rain, so the light was dim, but a tallow candle burned in a holder on the table.

"The smoke from the grease lamp was a-botherin' her," Elvie said as she took their wraps and put them aside. "Thought I'd burn what tallow dips I've got left. It won't hurt to humor her a little."

"I'll bring you some more," Rebecca said.

"How is she?" Kitty asked.

"Well, it seems like to me she's just a little bit better than she was last night." There was a forced air of cheerfulness about Elvie and a strange little rush to get the words out. And as Kitty drew closer to the bed and saw the shallow rise and fall of Lureen's chest and the hot, slick-shiny look to her skin, she felt a quick surge of foreboding, which she saw echoed in Rebecca's fine dark eyes.

"She was just restless as could be early on through the night," Elvie was saying, "but seems like she's quieter these last few hours."

The girl acknowledged their presence with the barest flicker of her eyelids and then turned her head away and slipped back into a febrile sleep.

"She's weak from the fever. I helped her up to use the pot a little while ago, and it was all she could do even with me a-holdin' her. But she's cooler than she was," Elvie went on with her determined brightness, though there was a noticeable droop about her shoulders, and deep lines seemed to have etched themselves almost overnight in that smooth plump face.

"Maybe so," Rebecca said, humoring her. "Now, Elvie, you're wore out and I can tell it. I want you to go on down to my place and get in the bed and rest yourself for a while."

"Why don't you go to my cabin instead," Kitty interjected. "There's no one there. You can sleep as long as you need to, and Rebecca and I will stay here and take care of Lureen."

Elvie was shaking her head.

"We'll call you if there's a need . . . I promise," Rebecca tried to persuade her. "And it will be better for you at Kitty's. My kids would likely be runnin' in and out. . . ."

"I'll not leave her," Elvie said. And from the set of her face and the way she folded her hands across her bosom, it was clear she could not be budged. But they finally talked her into lying down on the large bed over in the other corner of the room, and she was so exhausted that she fell asleep almost immediately.

Quietly, Rebecca and Kitty heated some water to lukewarm and wrung out a cloth in it to wipe off Lureen's face and smooth the light hair back out of her eyes. Kitty found a clean nightgown in one of the clothes baskets nearby. They stripped the girl down to bathe her hot body as quickly as they could, then put the fresh nightgown on her. But though Lureen opened her eyes once, she seemed all but unaware of their ministrations and, once they had finished, lay with her mouth half open, her breathing audible.

Rebecca shook her head. "Lord, Lord," she whispered to Kitty, "I don't know . . ."

After a little while Granny Hawkins, hooded and cloaked against the rain, came in with a poultice of dandelion and 'possum fat which she bound to Lureen's chest. Over in the corner, Elvie was sleeping so soundly she didn't even stir.

"I wisht we had some willow bark," the old lady said in her crackly voice, "or some angelica root. But maybe this'll help her some'at. You can't give up." The last was said almost to herself, her toothless mouth working. "You got to do with what you have."

She left, promising to return later with some medicine she was brewing at home. But she was hardly gone before Henry entered, slapping his dripping hat against his leg, a pair of fat, dead squirrels swinging from his other hand. His sons, clustered beyond the open door, seemed unmindful of the pouring rain.

"Me and the boys went over there to the woods," he said, dismissing the danger with a jerk of his hand. "Elvie thought some good thick broth might be just the thing to fix this little girl up." His eyes rested on his daughter for a moment, his round face red and soft. Then he glanced toward the other bed. "Both of 'em asleep, eh? Well, I reckon that's a good thing. Neither one of 'em hardly closed their eyes the whole of the night."

Rebecca patted his shoulder. "You and the boys go on down to my cabin, Henry. Jemima'll feed you."

"I thankee kindly," he said. And after one more look at Lureen, he went out the door.

The two women skinned the squirrels and gutted them and, once the meat was cleaned and cut up, put the pieces in a good-size pot half filled with water. Kitty added a little salt and a couple of the pithy potatoes she found in Elvie's vegetable bin, along with a small onion. "They'll cook soft enough to help thicken the broth," she ventured. "Make it taste better, too."

By the time the meat was cooked off the bones, Elvie was stirring and put out with herself that she'd slept so long. "Lord o' mercy!" she grumbled as she rose from the bed, wiping her eyes and looking immediately toward Lureen, who for the moment lay quietly—she'd been tossing restlessly and moaning just minutes before. "I must have slept half the day! Whyn't you wake me?"

"Because you needed that sleep," Kitty said.

"How is she?" Elvie asked, her lips drawing in to an anxious pucker.

"About the same," Rebecca said. "And you woke up just in time to try to get her to take some of this broth we made up. Henry and the boys brought some squirrels."

But no matter how hard Elvie tried, the sick girl pushed at the spoon feebly, choking and spitting out the broth whenever her mother succeeded in getting some of it inside her mouth. And finally Elvie gave up, sure that in a little while Lureen would wake up and eat.

Sara and Jemima brought in food for the women. And after a while Faith came with tallow dips she'd collected once the word had spread that Lureen fretted at the smoke from the grease lamps. Ben came along and knelt by the girl's bedside to pray for her swift recovery, and then patted Elvie, his thin face pale in the candlelight. "If there's anything at all that we can do," he said, "you just let us know." He turned to Kitty on their way out. "You send for us, sister, if we're needed," he said quietly.

All through that long afternoon and evening the women of the fort came to do whatever they could. They brought extra sheets since Lureen soiled herself from time to time and had to be cleaned, and they gathered up the dirty linen and took it with them to wash and stretch out before their fires to dry. Elizabeth and Betsey spelled Rebecca and Kitty so that they could go back to their own cabins and rest for a while. And whoever was there tried to see that Lureen swallowed the medicine that Granny Hawkins brought along for her.

Henry and the boys, well fed by Sara and Jemima, spent the night at Kitty's, while she went back once again with Rebecca to the Porter cabin to help Elvie keep watch through the night. And as she sat by the feverish girl, Kitty thought of Priscilla and what good friends she and Lureen had been, forever with their heads together, giggling. . . .

For some reason, she remembered that day in the blockhouse when she'd pleaded with Daniel to let her family be buried out there on the place. Somewhere in her memory there was the image of Lureen, standing silent and white-faced and alone in a corner. With everything else, she hadn't thought to speak to the girl that day. She wished she had now.

Lureen Porter died just before the dawn . . . slipped away quietly, although her mother, Rebecca and Kitty, and old Granny Hawkins had worked over her frantically for the last two hours. They'd kept hot compresses to her chest and bathed her arms and legs to get that awful fever down, and held her limp, hot body almost in a sitting position to help her breathe better. But finally the breaths came farther and farther apart, and at the last it was almost as if she sighed and it was ended.

Elvie bent over the bed for a full minute, rubbing Lureen's hand between her own, and then she finally went to sit before the fire, her face turned away as Rebecca pulled the sheet up over Lureen's face.

Kitty, hardly able to hold back tears, went to Elvie. "Do you want me to go after Henry?" she asked.

"In a bit . . ." Elvie rocked back and forth gently, though she was sitting in a straight-legged chair.

Granny Hawkins, her toothless old face gray as parchment, shook her head sadly, her hair wisping thinly from beneath the white mobcap. "If I could've just laid my hand on more yarbs and such . . . might be we could've saved her."

Elvie rocked still, just the upper part of her moving back and forth. "I always boasted of raisin' 'em all," she said. "Not a miss nor a stillbirth in the bunch . . . ever' one of 'em healthy." For the first time there was a hint of tears, her eyes reddening. "She was my only girl . . . Lord, help me . . ."

She gave way and wept quietly, covering her face with her hands. Rebecca went to stand beside her, trying to offer what comfort she could. After a minute Elvie wiped her eyes with the edge of her apron and gave her head a shake.

"Maybe the good Lord knows better than we give Him credit. I'm carryin' another. And if the truth be known, I was some put out with Henry over it. But maybe . . . it could be this'n was give to me to take her place, though I don't know how another could."

She rose from the chair. "Let's get her ready," she said, her voice infinitely tired. "I want her to look nice."

The rain had stopped sometime during the night, and the sun edged upward in a sky that promised to be brilliantly blue. Little specks of light shone through the cracks in the chinking, but Elvie didn't want the door or window opened just yet. In the flickering light of the tallow dips, the four women bathed Lureen and dressed her in her best linsey skirt and blouse and brushed her hair. Dry-eyed now, Elvie braided the fine strands into two golden plaits and tied wisps of faded blue ribbons to the end of each of them. Then she pulled a chair up beside the bed and sat down.

"Some of you can go get Henry now. Tell him I'll be right here a-waitin'."

* 17 *

WITH SARA STILL SLEEPING PEACEFULLY, CURLED IN the bed as if to protect her growing belly, Roman slipped quietly from beneath the quilt and dressed himself in the dim light of the cabin. He smiled, remembering the feel of that ripening body as she had turned toward him from time to time through the night. It was, he had discovered, eminently satisfying to touch that swollen abdomen and know that it was his child within there. Though he'd given little thought to it before, the prospect of becoming a father had pleased him as much as anything had in his whole life. And he felt a deeper tenderness for Sara because of it.

Fully dressed now, he stood to look down at her for a moment, edging the quilt up to cover her outstretched arm. Then he took up his rifle and let himself quietly out the door into the welcome freshness of the morning air.

The sun was barely up, still making pink streaks along the

edges of puffy clouds. He could hear the women laughing as they milked and the soft lowing of the cows at the front end of the compound, but he turned back toward the far corner and the necessary.

Warm weather had brought the usual stench. Flies buzzed and lit, and as Roman closed the rough wooden door behind him, he decided that it might well be an entirely unnatural thing for a man to have to relieve himself on top of someone else's voidings. Out in the woods such matters took care of themselves. A man went when he felt the urge, and nature took care of the rest. But civilization, he conceded with a dry chuckle—even that of this little stockade out here in the wilderness—undoubtedly demanded more restraint.

Finished, he emerged to find one of the Porter boys, George Henry, who apparently shared his feelings, edging out from behind one of the nearby bushes and lacing up his breeches.

"Mornin', Roman." George Henry grinned guiltily and dashed away.

Roman returned along the pathway, lifting a hand to Israel, who was just coming out of the Boone cabin.

"You fixin' to go out again?" Israel inquired, still chewing the last of his morning hoecake.

"I probably will tonight. After dark." He'd been in for three days, and that was longer than he usually stayed.

Israel brushed the crumbs from his mouth. "Simon Butler come in last night," he said.

"I know. I spoke with him."

They walked on down the path together, heading toward the front gates. Winfield Burdette, who was pumping the big leather bellows to put new life into his fire, helloed them, and Ben Tyler, coming along the path, stopped to talk.

"Faith says the cows are actin' up this morning," he told them once they'd all agreed that it was going to be a nice day. Since it had been quiet for a while, they had taken to letting the cows out to graze during the day. "Says usually our old Boss and the red heifer can't wait to get out and down to the river of a mornin', but this time none of 'em seem to want to go far from the gates."

Small warning bells were ringing inside Roman's head. He had heard more than one old-timer say that cows knew when there were Indians near. That they could smell them and were afraid. He'd never seen it himself, but he didn't think it should be dismissed lightly. With a quick nod of his head to Ben, he strode on down toward the gates, Israel right behind him.

The agitated cows were milling about slowly just outside the gates, the women standing with their pails of milk and shaking their heads at the sight. Flanders and a tall, lean-faced man named Goodman were on guard, rifles ready, as someone always was when the cows were sent out in the morning. Kitty stood back slightly within the open gate, a bemused expression on her face as her red-spotted cow bumped into the others in its eagerness to stay close to the walls.

"I don't know what's wrong with 'em," Flanders called out to Roman. "But I don't like it."

Roman touched Kitty's arm. "Get back," he told her. "And see that the other women stay well back, too."

A few of the men had begun to drift toward the gates to see what all the commotion was about. Ben had followed after Roman and Israel. Winfield had left his forge. And now Daniel, along with Simon Butler and the Old Colonel, came out of the nearest blockhouse and pushed through the women, who lingered still with their frothy pails of milk.

"What's wrong, Roman?" Daniel asked.

Roman explained, while Flanders and Goodman stepped in closer to hear what was said.

"Shit!" Butler spit out of the side of his mouth once he'd heard the problem, and swiped at his face with the back of his hand. "It just could be them cows know somethin' that we don't."

"Did you see *anything* suspicious before you come in last night?" Daniel asked him.

"Not a damned thing," Butler retorted. "But you know that don't always tell the tale."

Roman nodded.

"I've seen livestock act this way after a catamount had passed near," Colonel Callaway said. "Could be one prowled about last night. On the other hand"—his eyes narrowed—"if that's not the reason, we'd best find out what is before we risk gettin' somebody killed when the water's brought in."

More men had gathered now, most of them armed. A few, at Daniel's direction, had taken up places within the blockhouse at the loopholes. "Just in case," he said.

Silently Roman had been scanning the long length of Hackberry Ridge and the woods closer in, but he could see nothing amiss . . . no movement at all. And that made him nervous.

There should be something stirring this time of day—a porcupine, or rabbit, or groundhog maybe, heading down to the river for his morning drink.

"Two or three men generally go out for wood of a mornin'," Daniel said. "Usually there's some to be found close in to the river there." He jerked his head, and Roman looked out toward the open stretch along the bank that bordered the thick woods.

"Then it seems to me"—he pulled the powder horn from his belt and began loading his gun deftly—"it would be a good idea to do just that." He was quick at the loading from long practice, and in a few seconds it was done. "I'll go."

"And me," Flanders added instantly.

An ax was brought up to make the whole thing look right to anyone who was out there watching. Flanders took it, and Goodman hefted his long gun up into the crook of his arm. "Let's git," he said.

"I'll back you from the gate," Butler volunteered.

The three men walked out steadily at a pace not too fast, not too slow . . . nothing to signal that they suspected anything might he wrong. Roman was slightly ahead, with Flanders and Goodman to his left. Flanders began to whistle, and it was all Roman could do to keep from smiling at the young man's pluck. Still, there was that prickly feeling at the base of his skull . . .

They had covered sixty yards, the grass down from the fort green and rich, already up ankle high. The breeze fanned the smell of it against Roman's face as he gestured casually toward the others to cut over toward the river. "Once we're over there," he said quietly, "you two just go on about the wood gathering. First chance I get, I intend to slip into the woods. If there's trouble, you run for the gate."

But as he turned his head, he caught a sudden movement in the underbrush up ahead and shouted a warning, dropping to one knee and raising his rifle as the volley of shots rang out from the edge of the trees. Goodman gave a strangled cry and pitched forward.

Six Shawnee warriors, bare chests streaked with paint, sprinted from the wooded cover, howling as they charged. Roman took careful aim and fired, bringing down the lead Indian, while out of the corner of his eye he could see Flanders get off a shot that set one of them clutching at his arm.

Goodman, moaning, had managed to gain his hands and knees and was trying to crawl back toward the gates as one of the braves leaped on top of him and brought the heavy tomahawk crashing against his head to split it like a melon.

Shots were beginning to crackle from the fort now, and Roman heard Simon Butler's fearsome yell as he charged out with Daniel at his side and seven or eight others just behind them. With no time to reload, Roman and Flanders swung the butts of their guns like clubs.

The air was suddenly acrid with gunpowder as Daniel and the others moved past Roman and Flanders, past the body of Goodman. And it was in that moment that Roman knew what was happening—knew they'd been tricked. *"Daniel!"* he yelled. And as Daniel swung back, Roman saw in his face that he had realized it, too . . . maybe too late.

Shawnees, forty or fifty of them, poured out of the woods to the left and cut off their retreat. But Daniel lifted his gun high and rallied his men. "Back to the fort!" he called out. "Boys, we'll have to fight for it! Sell your lives dear!"

Those who had charges left in their rifles fired them, and those who didn't flailed away as Roman and Flanders had been doing. With no more than twenty-two men and boys in all who could handle a gun at Boonesborough, the handful of riflemen still within the fort gave a good support of fire, though they had to be careful not to hit their own men in the melee.

Inch by inch the beleaguered group in the clearing fought their way back, edging toward the safety of the gates. Roman heard Flanders grunt but had no time to look toward him.

A sinewy buck charged Roman with a knife, barely escaping the vicious swing of his rifle. They grappled, toe to toe, bodies straining . . . Roman looking full into the dark eyes that glittered with a kind of impersonal hatred. Sweat trickled from his temples and stung his eyes. The Indian had greased himself with bear oil, and it was hard to keep a secure hold on him. Roman could feel his fingers slipping. . . .

The Shawnee got his hand free and, off balance, slashed with the knife, but Roman jerked sideways just in time to avoid getting his throat cut. Instead, the tip of the blade sliced across the left side of his neck to inflict a stinging, shallow cut. He gasped but in the same instant swung the heavy stock of his rifle beneath his opponent's jaw and heard a satisfying crunch of bone. The warrior fell back to the ground and rolled, clutching at his shattered face.

Feverishly, Roman grabbed for his powder horn and started to load, backing up and kicking out at the next Indian to turn toward him, catching him full in the crotch to send him yelping. Jostled from all sides, bullets whining, he dumped in some powder. Jesus, it was hard to tell how much he was getting in; too much and the goddamned barrel would explode in his face! He fumbled with his shot bag, still swearing beneath his breath.

He had detached the ramrod from beneath the barrel when he caught sight of Daniel some twenty paces from him, saw him fall, wounded, face twisted in a grimace of pain as he grabbed for his ankle. In an instant an Indian had straddled him to grab at his hair, scalping knife raised.

Roman howled as he threw himself forward in a numb kind of horror, seeing the grimace of triumph on the vermilion-streaked face. Though he was flinging men out of his way, red and white alike, he knew there was no way he could get to Daniel in time, and he set his feet to shove the ramrod down the length of the barrel. If he could get off a shot fast enough . . .

But just then Simon Butler, no more than a few feet from Daniel, charged, roaring like a bull, to smash the Shawnee aside with his rifle. Dropping the gun, he swung Daniel up across his huge shoulders and started back toward the gates.

The Indians set up a shrill chant: "Boone . . . Boone . . ." They realized it was Daniel and were determined that he should not escape. Any brave who killed or captured the great Boone would be honored from that day forward as a mighty warrior within the tribe. Giving a high yelp, a huge Shawnee with shoulders broad as Butler's raised his musket and took dead aim on the escaping pair, but Roman had his gun ready and fired in time.

He hardly saw the man go down—the overcharge of powder had sent him staggering backward—but he righted himself and yelled to the others, "Close up, men!" And they did, rallying to his side with renewed vigor, cutting and slashing with knives, swinging their rifles as they inched back, yard by painful yard . . . until finally, with the help of the steady support fire from the fort, they were able to slip within the gates, ready hands reaching out to help them in. Ezekial Turner shot down an Indian right within the entry seconds before the gates swung shut and were securely barred.

The cows, which had been herded back in at sign of the first shot, were milling about the fort yard, wall-eyed with fear of the gunfire. Men shouted as they ran for cover, and Roman grinned as he heard Daniel, still atop Butler's shoulder, yelling orders that carried above the uproar. "Make sure all four blockhouses are manned! Don't let them get in close to the walls, boys! Dang it, Simon," he blustered, "will you put me *down*!"

With his wounded ankle, there was no way he was going to walk, so to save him the ignominy of being carried into the nearest blockhouse like a sack of meal slung over the big scout's shoulder, Roman offered his services. He and Butler made a pack saddle with their arms and got Daniel inside and into a chair.

The women and children had standing orders to gather in the blockhouses in case of attack. With stouter construction and greater ease of defense, it was safer for them there than in the cabins. In a moment Sara was at Roman's side, still in her long white nightgown, covered only by a shawl she'd taken up hastily.

"My God, Roman!" She stared at him, white-faced, lips quivering, "You're bleeding!" There was a faint edge of hysteria in her voice, and Roman took her firmly by the shoulders and gave her a gentle shake.

"It's nothing," he said. "Hardly broke the skin."

"But . . . but . . . ." Her eyes were fixed on his neck.

"See . . . ." He reached a hand up to wipe at the shallow cut, and Kitty was suddenly at his elbow to thrust a strip of linen into his hand to bind around it. "I'm all right, Sara. Take care of her, Kitty." He quickly knotted the linen around his throat and went to take up his place at one of the loopholes.

Israel had left his position to come anxiously to his father, but Daniel just gripped his son's forearm and grinned cheerfully, despite the pallor of his face. "Go back, son," he insisted. "A broke ankle's not likely to kill me. Get back there and fire away!"

Israel returned to his place just as his mother burst through the door of the blockhouse—she had been in one of the others.

"Now what did you want to do a fool thing like that for?" Daniel chided as Rebecca dropped down in front of him and started to unlace his moccasin and, finally, to cut away bloodstained leather. He stiffened at the pain but went right on talking. "You could have got yourself killed by a stray bullet, woman! Could be sharpshooters in the heights the other side o' the river—"

"Hush up, Daniel," Rebecca examined the wound as gently as she could, but sweat popped out on her husband's face. "Ball went clean through," she said after a moment, "but that ankle bone is broke for sure."

The sharp smell of powder filled the room. Maggie Hamilton, within the small knot of women and children gathered in the inner corner, snuffed miserably and scoured her reddened nose, wincing at each new burst of gunfire. Elizabeth, who was jiggling little John to quiet his crying, sent Keziah to bring some water from the bucket in the corner to Rebecca.

"No," Daniel argued. "Just bind it up. We might need that water to drink before it's over."

"I'll just use a little." Rebecca's voice was steady. "There's some bits of leather drove into the flesh, Daniel. We have to get 'em out or that leg'll swell up big as a tree trunk."

She touched his hand lightly, let hers rest there for an instant before she went to work, gently washing out the tiny bits of elkskin that had been driven into the wound. And though the sweat dripped from him and he flinched a time or two, Daniel directed his attention to the men at the loopholes. The firing had suddenly slackened off.

"Roman," he yelled, "what's happening out there? Don't let up on 'em!"

"They're drawing back, Daniel." Roman watched, peering through the loophole. "They're staying back beyond our range now. Just be wasting shot and powder on them."

He spied the sudden parting of a knot of braves closest to the edge of the woods, and a black horse with a white blaze emerged. The Indian astride the animal exuded an air of authority, a lone black feather jutting from his scalplock, and Roman recognized the powerful warrior chief at once.

"Black Fish." He turned back to Daniel, and the two of them exchanged a look that held a strange kind of satisfaction. Clearly the Shawnee regarded the men of the little fort as formidable opponents. They had sent no minor chief with their war party. Black Fish was said to be second only to Cornstalk himself.

As Roman put his eye back to the loophole, he saw Black Fish gesture to either side of him. The braves fanned out single file, spreading from the edge of the woods toward Hackberry Ridge, still just out of rifle range. "Jesus!" he muttered. There were more of them than he'd thought—looked to be between eighty and a hundred.

He relayed the information to Daniel, who beckoned Israel to his side at once with instructions to take messages to both of the back blockhouses, the ones closest to the river. "Tell them to be on guard, son. Could be some'll try to slip up from the banks there. They could be over the walls before we know it. Tell them I want no surprises from that way."

As the Indians stayed well back for the moment, the beleaguered garrison took advantage of the respite to check for casualties. One dead—poor Goodman's body was still out in the hollow—but of the others who'd been outside, it appeared that Daniel's wound was the most serious, though there wasn't one of them who hadn't suffered some hurt or other. Flanders had a knot on his forehead the size of a duck's egg. "I couldn't get my gun up in time, so I just bashed him with my head," he explained, grinning. And even big Simon Butler, who seemed to lead a charmed life, displayed a spot just above his left ear where a bullet had shaved a pathway through his thick hair as clean as a razor.

All in all they were lucky, Daniel and Roman agreed privately. Damned fools, Roman said, to get drawn into that trap. They should have known better. Daniel, who was still in considerable pain, grunted and nodded his head.

"I mistook the situation . . . ." He grimaced. "Thought there couldn't be more than a few of 'em out there, since Simon had just come in. They must of slipped in behind him last night."

"I should have gone out alone . . . made a run for the cover of woods . . ."

"And you'd be dead as Goodman out there," Daniel countered.

Roman shrugged and, since it was still quiet, went to see if Sara was all right. He found her with Kitty and some of the other women who were trying to cook a meal under the trying conditions of the crowded blockhouse. She was still pale.

"Is it over, Roman? Have they gone?"

"Not quite. But they pulled back a bit."

She attempted a smile. "Maybe they will soon, then."

He nodded. She seemed all the more vulnerable because she was trying to hide her fear from him. He felt that quick tenderness for her . . . and the child she carried. That was what had been in the back of his mind out there. There was no way he was going to let the Shawnee get past him. Not if he'd had to kill every one of them himself to prevent it.

Kitty brought him a piece of hot johnnycake and a cup of milk. He hadn't realized how hungry he was, and gulped it down.

"More?" Kitty asked, on her way to see if Daniel could eat something. But before Roman could answer, there was the sudden crackle of gunfire and he sped back to his post.

After several minutes of heated fire, with the advancing Indians taking cover behind stumps and hillocks, the Shawnees retreated once again to their line of safety and stayed there, watching.

The hours passed, and the war of nerves went on through the day until finally, with nightfall no more than a couple of hours away, Roman saw Black Fish suddenly raise his hand, wheel his horse around, and with the long line of warriors following, fade quickly into the woods.

"They're leaving!" Israel shouted.

The women rejoiced, Kitty and Sara hugging one another and laughing with relief. Flanders let out a big whoop, and an instant later the Old Colonel burst through the door of the blockhouse, waving his old leather hat in the air.

"By God, we held them off!" he chortled, coming to Daniel at once to see how the wounded leader fared.

"We should take out after 'em!" young John Holder announced, exuberantly. "Run 'em clean back up over the Ohio!"

The others razzed him at once, pummeling him good-naturedly and setting up a terrible uproar, while Daniel and Roman conferred quietly.

"I could slip out the back and keep down under cover of the riverbank until I gain the woods," Roman offered. But Daniel shook his head.

"Could be they're playin' the same game. Let's don't walk into any more snares, Roman. If they're gone, we'll know soon enough. No use gettin' anybody killed to find out. But truth is"—he ran his hand along the paining leg—"I'd bet money they're makin' ground in these last couple of hours before dark. Gettin' a head start toward home." He grinned. "An Indian'll look to his signs and such. If a job don't seem to be goin' too well, he'll put it off to a better day."

And by the next morning it was clear that Daniel would have won his wager. There was no doubt from the tracks that Black Fish and his warriors had headed home. The penned-up animals were let out to the river, and there was a collective sigh of relief within the little fort.

Though security at Boonesborough was kept tight, the next few weeks were free of harassment, and the settlers prayed that the Indians had decided to leave them in peace. Word came that Benjamin Logan had taken his people back to St. Asaph's. And the crops were growing. There were fresh greens now, and green peas, welcome additions to tables set with little more than meat and bread for so long.

An irritable Daniel had been confined to bed for a whole month with his ankle and then had walked with the aid of a stout-forked hickory limb for another. He'd only recently been able to put the crutch aside and, as he said, "walk like a man again instead of some danged, crotchety, wore-out old fella!" The hopeful settlers even risked having a dance—it had been a long time since they'd had any heart for one—and the men took turns dancing and manning the walls. Cullen wasn't in, but Kitty played her dulcimore and sang, and the fiddling went on until the morning light.

But within the week, Roman rode into the fort, with Cullen following before nightfall. Both scouts had seen the advancing war party and had ridden with all speed to warn the settlers to prepare for another attack within twenty-four hours.

✳ 18 ✳

KITTY SLIPPED AWAY TO A DIMLY LIT CORNER OF THE blockhouse and pressed her back wearily against the rounding surfaces of the log wall, aware of the faintly smoky smell of it. It was the first time she'd stopped in hours. The men at the loopholes and on the walls had to be kept in powder and bullets. And food when there was respite enough to eat it. There'd been times, during heavy exchanges, when the women had stood by, loading what extra rifles there were and passing them to the nearest man in exchange for the one he'd just fired. She'd stood behind Cullen, swapping rifles until the barrels got so hot that she'd had to snatch up a piece of cloth to handle them with or they would have burned her hands.

Even before the attack there had been more than enough to do. The animals had been gotten in. Water had been carried to fill up the rain barrels and as many other containers as possible. What vegetables were ready in the garden were gathered and brought into the fort. There was no one who didn't pitch in . . . even Maggie Hamilton had carried in cabbages. And finally, when they were as ready as they'd ever be, the waiting and watching began.

The Indians had come shortly after dawn. Swarming up from the steep riverbanks behind the fort like bees out of a hive, they had fanned out to take cover behind stumps and any little rise that would shield them from the hail of fire directed against them from the stockade walls. In a moment the three tiny cabins on the far side of the salt spring had been torched, black smoke billowing upward. And half-naked warriors, their chests and faces streaked with vermilion and ocher, raced through those fields that were just out of rifle range, slashing and chopping at the precious corn, while still others, mounted, burst from the woods to trample the stalks beneath their horses' hooves.

Within the fort the men at the loopholes and on the walls watched in impotent rage, silent except for the Old Colonel's quivering "Goddamn the heathens!"

Throughout the rest of the day the Shawnee had engaged in sporadic rampages through the crops between attacks on the fort, whipping themselves to a frenzy, emitting their high, yelping "Aieee!" But finally dusk fell, offering some hope of relief to the exhausted settlers, at least until morning.

Now, through the open door of the blockhouse, Kitty could see that it was growing quite dark. She stirred herself, making her way around the room to light several of the grease lamps. Elizabeth helped her, and they talked softly. Some of the women had brought out blankets and spread them to nap on the floor—though it was still warm with too many bodies, the heat generated by a July sun had abated, and a breeze wafted from the doorway now and again.

Tired men were in various positions at their posts. Flanders Callaway leaned up against the wall. Henry Porter looked to be dozing where he stood. But undaunted as usual, Cullen turned back to wink at her, and she went to stand beside him.

"Take a look," he said, boosting her up so that she could see through the loophole.

Campfires dotted the soft night, and as the warm breeze wafted toward the fort, the unmistakable aroma of roasting pork was carried with it.

"You remember them two pigs that got away from us when we was chasin' 'em through the woods?" one of the men called out. "Well, I think I know where they be. . . ." The remark was greeted with wry laughter.

Cullen set Kitty back on her feet. "Why don't you get some rest now, lass." He ran a finger lightly along her cheek. "They'll likely be quiet for the night."

"What about you?" she asked.

He grinned. There'd been no time for shaving, and his face was shadowed by a dark stubble; but his eyes danced mischievously. "If I could, I'd carry you off to our bed right this minute!" he teased, whispering it into her ear. And as if to emphasize it, his hand slipped expertly among the folds of her skirt to find her bottom and pinch it gently.

"Cullen!" She folded her lips together to suppress a giggle and looked around quickly to see if anyone had noticed. If they had, they were too tired to react. "You are impossible," she whispered.

"Am I now?" he whispered back, one of those dark brows handsomely aslant. They smiled at one another, hands touching tenderly. "You look tired," he said.

"So do you."

He nodded. "I'll take turns with some of the others. Go on now."

She did as he said, returning to her corner to spread out a blanket and lie down. Fanny Callaway, dozing close by, stirred. "Have they gone?" The girl edged up anxiously, rubbing at reddened eyelids.

"Not yet," Kitty whispered. "But it's quiet now. Go back to sleep."

On the other side of the room little Martha Tyler whined fretfully, and after a moment came the soft, sucking sounds of her nursing. Ben, who'd just come in from one of the other blockhouses, began to give his evening prayers and Kitty listened to the quiet but impassioned voice—"Lord, deliver us in this, our hour of peril"—adding her silent plea to his.

Someone said, "Amen."

With fatigue overwhelming her, Kitty was suddenly aware of how few of them there were . . . and how many savages were waiting out there. They might be overrun in the night. She curled to her side, holding herself . . . holding on. Cullen would watch—Cullen and the other men.

Sometime before dawn she came awake to a gentle shake of her shoulder and opened her eyes to see Elvie Porter's round face above her.

"Sara wants you to come," Elvie said, keeping her voice quiet enough so as not to wake the others.

Kitty sat up quickly. "Where is she? What's wrong?"

"She's havin' some pains."

"Oh, no . . . it's too early."

Kitty got up at once and followed Elvie; the two women picked their way among the sleeping people, the stale air of the blockhouse heavy with the smell of unwashed bodies and urine.

Outside, the stars were still bright, the breeze fresh and welcome as they crossed the front of the compound, past the heavy barred gate to the blockhouse at the opposite corner of the fort. A hound dog bolted up from his place behind a stack of wood and came to sniff at them and wag his tail.

"She don't want Roman to know about it yet," Elvie warned as they approached the blockhouse door. Kitty nodded and they went in.

The big room was even more crowded than the other had been, and every bit as odorous. Some of the people were beginning to stir. Winfield Burdette clutched a cup of something hot in his callused hand as he took relief from his post for a few minutes. Todd Tyler nodded to them from his loophole, his Adam's apple bobbing as he chewed and swallowed, and Kitty caught a glimpse of Roman's rangy frame stretched out to its fullest length as he caught a few winks on the bare floor.

Elvie led Kitty to the far corner where Sara sat with her back to the wall, her face drained of color. Rebecca was with her.

"Kitty, it's started," she said. "It's not supposed to be yet."

"I know," said Kitty, reaching for her hand.

"I don't want Roman to know. He's got enough to worry about." Sara's voice raised a pitch. "I can't stay here. I don't want everyone looking at me. I want to go back to the cabin. . . ."

Kitty looked to Rebecca and Elvie. "Let's take her," Rebecca said.

"Wait . . ." Sara caught her breath and slid her hands low on her protruding abdomen, her underlip tucked between her teeth. She grimaced and then, after a long moment, let her breath out and relaxed. "There," she said. "It's eased."

"Are they getting harder?" Rebecca asked.

Sara gave her head a shake. "I don't know for sure. Maybe a little."

At Sara's insistence, Kitty instructed Winfield to tell Roman when he woke up that Sara was with her and then the four women left the blockhouse and made their way to the Gentry cabin, staying close to the shadows of the buildings just in case there were sharpshooters across the river.

Moonlight slanted in through the open doorway, and Sara looked forlornly at the blackened fireplace. "The fire's gone out."

"I'll get a chunk," Elvie said. "We'll soon have it a-goin'."

"Don't light the grease lamp till I get some cover on this wall," Rebecca said. And while Elvie sped off for the fire chunk, Rebecca and Kitty quickly hung quilts across the back wall of the cabin to shut out any light that might make them targets. They had the lamp lit and Sara into bed by the time Elvie came back with the hot coals.

Sara had another pain.

"Could be false labor," Elvie offered. "Happens a lot with a first 'un. And it's awful early."

"When will we know?" Sara asked.

"We'll just have to wait awhile and see," Rebecca answered. "The pains could stop . . . and nothing happen again for weeks."

Elvie put on some water for sassafras tea, and once it was ready, Sara cradled the cup in her hands. "Oh, it tastes so good," she said. But the words were hardly out of her mouth before she had to put aside the cup and grab for her belly, holding it as it hardened, stiffening her back until the pain passed.

A sudden crackle of gunfire broke the stillness outside, and the women started. Rebecca hurried to peek out the door, then shut it and turned back.

"The sun's coming up. I expect the Indians are at us again."

Sara moaned softly, and Kitty took her hand. "The men will hold them off, just as they did yesterday," she declared, though her own heart was thumping against her ribs. "Don't fret over it. You've got to save all your strength for the baby."

"Here"—Elvie bustled about—"have some more of this tea. It'll help you to stay easy . . . and maybe the pains will stop."

But each new burst of gunfire caused Sara to stiffen fearfully, and the pains showed no sign of ending. "Oh, go see what's happening! Please, Kitty," she begged.

"If you'll try to be calm," Kitty said.

"I will. . . ." Sara's face was colorless, her lower lip quivering. "I just keep wondering if they're coming over the walls."

"They're not," Kitty insisted, her voice firm. "The men are

seeing to that . . . and you must see to yourself and the baby."
Sara nodded, her thin, pale fingers laced together tightly.

Rebecca followed Kitty to the door. "Try to find Granny
Hawkins and bring her back with you," she whispered. "Might
be she can do something. I don't hold a lot of hope for that baby
if she has it now. Six months is pretty risky."

Kitty sighed her agreement and turned to go, but Rebecca
caught her wrist. "Be careful out there. . . ."

Outside, Kitty pressed her back to the closed door and scanned
the compound. Out from the cabin and toward the center of the
sunny yard, a long-snouted hog rooted in the soft earth beneath
a wagon that held cabbages and a few turnips. The animal
seemed oblivious to the staccato bursts of gunfire, but farther
down toward the gates the cows milled about nervously, and in
the roughly built corral at the back of the fort, the horses whinnied and stamped.

It occurred to her that she hadn't even told Cullen where she
was going earlier, and as the exchange of fire trailed off, she
darted down the deserted yard, staying close to the cabins. There
were a few men on the walls, and they nodded grimly as she
approached. "I'd git inside one o' the blockhouses if I was you,
Mistress Claiborne," one of them called after her.

She found Cullen at his post, and he turned to her anxiously.
"I've been wonderin' where you were, lass."

She told him about Sara, and his thick eyebrows ridged as he
shook his head sadly. "She could lose it, then?"

"I don't know."

"Roman would take that hard, I'm thinkin'."

Kitty nodded. "How is it here?" she asked.

He shoved his hat to the back of his head. "Bloody heathens
are persistent this time, lass." He grinned engagingly. "But
we'll hold 'em. Never fear. Still . . ." Despite the grin, there
was something terribly grave about his eyes. "I want you to get
your pa's old pistol from the cabin and load it. Take it with you
when you go back. Do ye ken?" He seemed about to say more,
but a bullet splatted into the wood just outside the loophole, and
Kitty started, catching her breath at the sudden whine.

Cullen looked out quickly, then turned back, reaching out his
hand to touch those thick, broad fingers lightly to her lips. "Mind
you, do what I told you now," he said, his voice husky. Then
he gave her a gentle nudge away and slid his rifle barrel through
the loophole, squinting down the length of it.

"Stay safe," she said as she turned away, but her throat was

so tight the words came out in a whisper and she wasn't sure he
had heard.

The women were passing powder, their faces grim, but as
Kitty came by, Elizabeth called to her. "I hear Sara's started her
labor. How is she?"

"Scared," Kitty said truthfully. "We're still hoping it's false.
You don't know where Granny Hawkins is, do you?"

Elizabeth shook her head. "She's not here."

Outside once again, Kitty raced across to the opposite blockhouse, dreading to go in because Roman was there. She determined to do her best to avoid him. But if she couldn't, she'd just
have to make up something. After all, it was what Sara wanted.

Just as she came even with the door, she sucked in her breath
and took a quick step backward in time to escape being knocked
flat by Roman himself, who'd been on his way out. He grabbed
her by the shoulders, his piercing eyes as anxious as she'd ever
seen them.

"Sara . . . ?" he demanded. "One of the women said she
was feeling poorly. It's not the baby, is it?"

Kitty opened her mouth to reassure him, but those eyes of
Roman's were full into hers, and though she tried, the words
wouldn't come. She couldn't lie, not to Roman, of all people.

"She . . . didn't want you to know. She's having a few pains,
Roman. Not too hard," she added quickly. "We think maybe
it's false."

Just then there was a renewed burst of gunfire, and Kitty heard
Daniel yell: "They're tryin' to fire the fort! Don't let 'em get
close, boys! Roman, damn it, get back here!"

Roman hesitated only an instant. "You'll stay with her?"

Kitty nodded. "Rebecca is there. And Elvie, too." She directed the last at his back since he was taking the steep steps
three at a time to take up one of the positions on the upper floor.

The smell of burned powder was strong in the air as Kitty
flew to the nearest unmanned loophole and stood up on a keg
to look out. She caught the oily gleam of an Indian's torso as he
bent low over the neck of his white pony, urging the animal to
breakneck speed, a wavering trail of flame flowing from the
torch in his hand. The red streaks of paint down his cheeks
became clearly visible before he was brought down to roll like
a clumsy ball in the dust, the torch flying away harmlessly. The
horse reared and screamed, front legs pawing at the air, and
then found its feet to gallop off.

She got down, hands tight to her sides to keep from shaking, to scan the crowded lower room where most were doing something—cutting and greasing patches, passing up bullets, loading extra guns . . . They worked grimly, not talking, faces set into a pattern of gritty determination not unmixed with fear.

She found Granny Hawkins binding up a man's arm. Kitty told her quickly about Sara, and the old lady gave her mobcap a tug and took up her bag of "doctorin' things."

Outside, the high, yelping shrieks of the Indians filled the air, and the men on the walls shouted and cursed as they fired and reloaded. The dogs raced back and forth, setting up a terrible barking. Kitty and Granny Hawkins stayed near to the cabin walls until they reached Sara's cabin.

Rebecca met them at the door. "For goodness' sake, tell me what's happening," she whispered.

"They're trying to get close enough to torch the fort," Kitty whispered back, glancing nervously toward Sara. "So far, the men have held them back."

Rebecca's lips drew to a thin line, but she motioned Granny Hawkins into the room. "Her pains are coming some closer," she said.

Kitty pressed her hand, remembering what Cullen had told her to do. "I'll be right back," she declared, darting out the door and heading toward her own cabin.

It took her only a minute to find Usaph's old pistol in the bottom drawer of the cherry chest. The small bullet bag was beside the pistol, and she loaded it quickly, then tucked the bag into her skirt pocket and, gun in hand, hurried back to Sara's cabin.

Roman's wife was moaning softly as a pain seized her. Granny Hawkins bent over the bed, and Kitty took that opportunity to lay the pistol unobtrusively on the mantel. Pray God she didn't have a need for it.

Sara's water broke, dribbling, and they got her up to let her crouch over the chamber pot, steadying her while most of the fluid drained away. "Oh, God," she whimpered, her bared legs white and skinny.

"It's all right, honey," Elvie soothed. "Just let it come."

Granny Hawkins clucked her tongue and shook her head. "Nary a thing to stop this baby. . . . Young'uns are sometimes stubborn about when they decide to push into this world, and I've seed one or two of 'em live this early . . . one or two. . . ." She swallowed, the loose skin beneath her chin quivering. "Let's just get down to havin' it."

Rebecca had put a dry piece of linen on the bed, and they helped Sara back onto it, the shuck-filled mattress rustling as she settled down. Elvie heated up some soup left from the night before, but Sara refused to swallow any of it. She would only take a little tea from time to time. And as the day wore on, her pains came hard and close.

"It hurts," she wailed. *"It hurts!"* She was rigid, panting, sweat beading her face.

"She's tight. . . ." Granny shook her head. "If she could just ease herself some, it'd go better with her."

But Sara started up at every sound from the outside. And now running feet could be heard along the path, accompanied by deep male shouts. "Dan'l says look sharp back there, boys! He reckons they be tryin' to sneak up them riverbanks again . . . catch us nappin'!"

Sara stiffened with the fear she couldn't control. "Oh, God! What will happen to us if they get in? My baby . . . they'll take my baby!" She began to cry, moaning and rocking in the bed. Then another pain seized her, and for the first time she screamed, clutching at Kitty's hands.

"Sara . . . Sara . . . I know it hurts." Kitty held on. "But try . . . try to relax. Let the baby come. Don't worry about anything else. Roman and Cullen and the others will take care of it. They won't let them get past the walls."

"Push hard like I told you," Granny Hawkins encouraged her. "If'n you do, it won't be much longer." She pulled the sheet back for a moment to expose Sara's lower parts, her white belly bunched as if it were a big knot low down, knees drawn up to reveal the bloody mess beneath her. She couldn't seem to rest between pains but moved fitfully, straining to hear what was happening outside.

There was a knock at the door, and Kitty opened it a crack to find Daniel Morgan Boone there. "Do you want to see your mother?" she asked him, but the boy shook his head.

"Roman sent me to ask how Miz Sara is doin'." Sara let out a piercing scream just then, and Daniel Morgan dug the toe of his moccasin against the wooden step, shifting his thin shoulders.

"You tell him she's all right . . . and it shouldn't be much longer." He turned to run back, but she stayed him. "How goes it? Is Cullen all right?"

He nodded. "I think so. But the danged Shawnee just won't

leave off!'' There was a renewed burst of gunfire, and he darted away, agile as a young deer.

Back inside the cabin, Sara thrashed about on the bed and moaned. "Roman . . . I want Roman!" It ended in a high shriek as another pain wrenched at her body and contorted her face.

"He'll be here," Kitty tried to comfort her. "He can't come right now, but soon, Sara . . . soon."

"Push, honey," Elvie urged.

The pains came on top of one another now, and as Sara arched and screamed, Kitty prayed that Roman couldn't hear her. "We can see the head," she encouraged. "Only a little more. . . .''

"Push hard," Rebecca pleaded.

And with one great heave, sitting half upright and straining, sweat streaming down her face, the baby slithered out of Sara in a rush of blood and water, the little body coming straight into Kitty's waiting hands. Granny Hawkins gave a high cackle as the infant moved feebly.

"It's a girl!" Kitty called to Sara, who had fallen back to the pillow but now strained her head to see. "Wait—wait, we'll show you! Just a minute. . . .''

Granny Hawkins quickly took the baby up by its heels and gave it a sharp smack on its buttocks. It gasped and choked, fluid draining out of its mouth, and then let out a thin cry. She laid it up across Sara's flattened abdomen and, working quickly once again, tied off the ballooning cord and cut it. Then she handed the baby over to Kitty while she worked over Sara.

Rebecca stood waiting with a piece of soft linen, and after letting the new mother have a quick look, Kitty handed over the slippery infant and they took it to the table, where it was rubbed off and wrapped.

"She's a pretty little thing," Rebecca said.

"She is," Elvie agreed, but their faces were sober as they saw how poor the infant's color was and how it struggled to breathe. It seemed too weak to keep up even that first feeble crying and now lay quietly.

"Rub it some more," Granny Hawkins commanded as she worked over Sarah, darting quick, bird-like glances toward the child. "Don't be afeared you'll hurt it. You got to git that circulation goin'.''

They did as she said, rubbing the infant briskly with another piece of linen, but it responded only faintly, its breathing growing more shallow all the while. "Oh, God," Kitty prayed in a whisper only audible to the two women beside her, "don't let her die!"

"Git the brown bottle out o' my bag, there. See if'n you can't git a spoonful of it down its throat. Just a little at a time . . ."

Kitty sped to do Granny Hawkins's bidding and was back in a moment, trying to open the tiny mouth enough to let a drop or two of the pungent-smelling liquid roll back far enough on the tongue to cause it to swallow. It took several drops with no reaction except a slight heave as the medicine went down. Then it choked and jerked its arms out and, after a minute, mewed like a newborn kitten. But there was a terrible waxy cast to its skin, and as the minutes passed, Kitty watched in anguish as the breathing grew ever fainter. Finally the little chest gave one final heave and stilled.

Rebecca looked at Granny Hawkins and shook her head.

"Git some water," the old woman directed as she worked to help Sara expel the afterbirth. "Hot in one kettle—not hot enough to burn it, but right warm—and cold in t'other. Dip it in the hot first and then in the cold . . . see if'n that'll help."

"Isn't she all right?" Sara's voice rose sharply. "Bring her to me, Kitty! Please!"

"In a minute," Kitty said. "Just wait a little . . ." Elvie was already pouring the water into the big iron kettles and in another instant was ready.

They submerged the infant quickly, up to its neck in the almost hot water, and then pulled it out to plunge the limp body into the cold. There was no response, and they tried again—into the hot . . . into the cold. . . .

"There's something wrong with her!" Sara was trying to climb out of the bed, and Elvie ran to help Granny Hawkins ease her back. "I'll take care of her. . . ." Sara continued to reach and cry.

In desperation Kitty pulled up the dripping baby and, putting it back on the table, leaned down to hold the mouth open and breathe into it. She kept it up for what seemed a long time, until Rebecca finally pulled her away.

"It's no use," she said, her voice soft but strong enough to carry to Sara, who put her head slowly back on the pillow and opened her mouth in a soundless cry.

They stood silent for a long moment, unmindful of the quiet outside. And then as Granny Hawkins clucked over Sara and the other women helped to clean her up, Kitty carefully dried the baby, realizing with a stinging sorrow how very tiny it was and how much like Sara's the delicate features were. When she was finished, she wrapped it in a clean piece of a linen sheet, with only the little face showing.

"I want to see her," Sara said, pain and exhaustion and sorrow quivering in her voice.

And with Granny Hawkins nodding her scraggy-haired old head, Kitty brought the pitiful little bundle and placed it in Sara's arms.

Roman nudged open the door and stepped within the threshold, just standing there, his eyes seeking Sara, his whole body heavy as stone. As he watched she turned her head slowly, her hair loose and spilling over the pillow, her face so fine and pale that it frightened him. She held out a hand to him, her eyes brimming.

Kitty was at the fireplace, stirring the simmering contents of the iron pot that hung over the fire, but now she wiped her hands quickly down her apron. "I'll be back in a little," she said, looking from Sara to Roman and back. She slipped past him out into the twilight.

Rebecca had come and told him just a little while before. She'd waited until the shooting had stopped and the Indians had gathered up their dead and pulled back to Hackberry Ridge and beyond to disappear into the forest. And now he felt awkward and stiff as he went to sit on the side of the bed, as if he couldn't control his legs any better then he could what he felt inside him. But he leaned down and embraced his wife, holding her carefully while she sobbed against him.

"Roman . . . Roman," she got out between long, shuddering breaths, "the baby is dead. . . ."

"I know," he said. And the two of them clung to one another for a long time, just held each other without speaking as the shadows lengthened outside and the room grew darker. The cows filed past the cabin, instinctively going toward the gates to be fed and milked, and the warm breeze came in through the window, stirring the stale air of the room.

Finally he eased her back to the pillow and peered down through the deepening shadows to see the beads of tears still clinging to her lashes. He wiped them away gently. "I would have been here sooner if I could," he said. She nodded, and he got up to light the grease lamp.

"You look tired," she said, looking up into his face once he'd come back.

He managed a smile. "So do you. Have you eaten anything?"

She shook her head. "I can't."

He went to the fireplace and ladled some of the hot stew into a wooden bowl. Bringing a spoon, he came back to sit beside her once again. "I want you to eat a little," he said.

"No, Roman . . . I can't."

"For me," he insisted, blowing on a spoonful until it was cool enough and feeding her as if she were a child. "I want you to be strong and well again, and one day . . ." He couldn't finish, couldn't say, There'll be another child. . . . The words wouldn't come. The loss was too great.

He continued to feed her, and she swallowed obediently for a few spoonfuls but then pushed the spoon away again, shaking her head. He relented and put the bowl on the table.

"I have to go out," he said.

"No . . ."

He came back to sit beside her. "The Indians have pulled back. They appeared to be leaving. But we can't take the chance that they're setting up a trap. Cullen and I will have to make sure, as soon as it's good and dark."

"No . . . please, Roman"—she began to cry again—"don't leave me! Don't go . . ." She stretched up her arms to him, and he felt a terrible wrenching in his chest.

"I have to, Sara. Understand," he pleaded, "it's my responsibility. I can't ask someone else do it for me. Not even now."

The log in the fireplace hissed as a pocket of sap bubbled and darkened. Except for that, the room was quiet for a long moment. Then Sara wiped her reddened eyes, her face pinched and tired. "Please be careful," she finally got out, trying to smile.

"I'm always careful," he said soberly. "I'll likely be in by morning. Maybe before you wake up."

He kissed her gently, smoothing back the fine blond hair, his hand lingering for a moment, then turned and began to gather up the things he'd need.

As he collected an extra shot bag from its peg over the mantel, he spied the pistol lying there and recognized it as the one Usaph used to have. He glanced at Sara, wondering if she'd known it was there, then slipped it into the front of his hunting shirt.

When he reached the door, his rifle in the crook of his arm, he turned back for a minute. "You make sure you rest now," he said.

"I will."

"I'll send Kitty back."

He went out, closing the door behind him and carrying the image of that fragile face along with him. Rebecca had said she was fine, that there'd be other babies. Still, she was a delicate woman, unsuited to fort life. . . . A stirring of guilt for ever bringing her to the wilderness combined with his grief to make his chest ache. But in a year or two, he told himself, it would all be changed. The Indian threat would be ended. Towns would spring up. And she would see that it had been good for them to come here. And Rebecca was right; there would be other children.

He knocked at the Claibornes' door, and in a moment Kitty opened it. There were faint shadows of fatigue beneath her eyes, but she welcomed him with an outstretched hand.

"Roman, come in."

"Cullen here?" he asked, and then as he stepped in he saw the Scot slipping the strap of his powder horn over his arm. "Don't mean to rush you, but it's dark enough now."

"I'm ready," Cullen said. He hesitated, then reached out to grasp Roman's shoulder affectionately. "We're damned sorry that Sara lost the young'un, Roman."

Roman nodded his thanks. "If you could stay with her tonight," he said to Kitty, "I'd be in your debt."

"I'd intended to. I'll go right down as soon as you two are gone."

He took Usaph's pistol from the front of his shirt. "I think this belongs to you."

She nodded and smiled, taking the old gun and putting it on the table nearby. "I'll keep it handy."

"I think you'll find no use for it tonight," Cullen put in quickly. "If I had to wager, I'd say Black Fish has had enough. For a while, anyway. I'll bet he's hightailin' for the Ohio right now."

"I wouldn't be surprised." Roman turned away to the door. "I'll wait outside for you," he said, thinking they might want a moment alone together before Cullen left. But Kitty stopped him with a hand to his arm.

"Roman . . ." Her voice quivered. "Do you want to see the baby before you go? Elvie's got her, getting her dressed for the burying tomorrow."

Her. It echoed within him, and he was stung through by the knowledge. No one had told him what it was before, and he hadn't asked. Somehow, he had always thought of it as a boy. But a girl would have been fine. . . .

He didn't trust himself to speak. He'd seen death in more ways than most, but there was no way he could bring himself to look at that baby right now. He shook his head and went quickly through the door.

As soon as Roman and Cullen returned with the news that the Indians were indeed headed back across the Ohio, the gates were thrown open and the eager livestock let out to the river and the green grass. During the siege, one man had been killed, and now that it was safe, the settlers gathered at the small graveyard outside the walls to bury him and the Gentry baby. With that mournful task behind them, they took grim stock of the damage done to their crops.

"Well," said the Old Colonel, standing in the midst of cornstalks and pumpkin vines that had been trampled into the soft earth, and gazing sadly over toward the flattened patch that had, only two days before, been a thriving vegetable garden, "we can still plant turnips and greens. And potatoes could make it if the frost doesn't come too early this year. Maybe we can save enough of this fodder to feed the animals come winter."

But they all knew that the destruction of the crops promised a long hard time ahead. And it was difficult to predict just how soon the Indians might be back.

Daniel called for a courier to ride, with all speed, to the North Carolina settlements beyond the mountains and ask for whatever help could be sent to the beleaguered fort. Despite the danger, a steady and dependable fellow named William Bailey Smith volunteered and, with no more than an hour's preparation, set out at once.

A few hours later a hunting party went out for fresh meat with Daniel's admonition heavy in their ears: "Make every shot count, boys, 'cause there's danged little powder left."

✳ 19 ✳

"**T**HE PLAIN TRUTH OF IT IS, WE'D BE IN SORRY SHAPE if the Shawnee should strike again soon," Colonel Callaway said to Daniel, his handsome features doleful.

The heat of the afternoon sun caused the fresh deerhide that was stretched against the nearby stockade wall to emit a gamy odor, but no one cared or noticed in a compound filled with smells. The Old Colonel and several of the other men had converged upon their leader to discuss the perilous shortage of powder and bullets. Word had arrived that St. Asaph's had just barely survived a siege and a desperate Ben Logan had slipped out in the night to head back to Williamsburg to plead with Governor Henry to send protection to its westernmost county. With Harrod's fort, too, on short supplies and constant alert, it was clear no help could be expected from those garrisons.

"We must redouble our prayers that help comes from the East," Ben Tyler offered.

"Shit!" Winfield Burdette spit into the wiry grass beside the dusty path. "I'm as God-fearin' as the next man, but I'd feel some better if I had somethin' stronger'n a prayer in my shot bag right now. Just in case old Black Fish decides to pay us another visit come mornin'."

Ben favored the big blacksmith with a cold stare, his thin cheeks flushing, but Daniel lifted a calming hand. "We can take care of the bullets . . . just melt down a little pewter. It's the powder that's the problem, boys."

He leaned his paunchy frame against the palisade, waving a hand to clear away the flies that buzzed about, drawn to the green hide. "Actually, I could whip us up some gunpowder myself if I had the right makin's."

"You know how?" Colonel Callaway's question bespoke some surprise.

Daniel nodded. "An old-timer learned me when I wasn't no older than Daniel Morgan over there."

"What would you need?" Flanders asked.

"Oh . . . some charcoal, and brimstone . . . some saltpeter."

"I could make the charcoal," Winfield put in eagerly. A gleam began to steal into his eye. "And . . . by damn!" He brought one of his huge hands smacking down across his leather-clad thigh. "What all's in them old stores that Judge Henderson fetched in when he first come? Seems to me I recall some saltpeter."

"There was brimstone, too," Sam Henderson put in. "I remember."

Daniel's wide mouth broke into a grin, and he straightened up. "Well, what in the world are we standin' here for?"

An immediate search was conducted, and the precious ingredients were discovered far back in one corner of the magazine.

"God answers prayers in his own way." Ben shot Winfield a triumphant look, and the blacksmith grinned good-naturedly.

"That 'e does, Ben, my boy. And I thankee kindly," he added, turning his face up toward the blue heavens.

Ben shook his head and muttered something about near blasphemy, but Winfield just laughed and set to making the charcoal that Daniel would need.

The next day a call went out for pewter, and the women filed out of their cabins, bringing what they had to Winfield to be melted down, their faces grim as they relinquished pieces they had hauled over the mountains and through the wilderness.

"I'll not part with my charger!" Maggie Hamilton's firm declaration could be heard coming from the open door of her cabin, but after a heated exchange Horace came out into the fort yard carrying a basket containing the platter in question and several other pieces. Red-faced, he got in line with the women.

"I'll take it up with mine," Kitty whispered.

Horace shot her a grateful look as he held out the basket. She put the plates she was carrying atop Maggie's charger, then took it from him, whereupon he escaped as speedily as he could manage with dignity.

Sara, who had recovered quickly from the baby's birth—at least physically—looked after the rumpled figure, who still insisted upon wearing his knee breeches though his silk stockings all had holes in them now. "I guess I know how Maggie feels," she said. "I hate to part with these things. This mug"—she looked down sadly—"was a wedding present."

"I know," Kitty soothed. "These plates were Ma's. But we'll make do. When the Indians are driven back for good, we can always send East for more pewter."

Ahead of them, Faith delivered her contribution to the growing pile of tableware, and Jemima Boone added what Rachel had sent. Kitty unloaded the basket, and she and Sara watched for a moment as Winfield, sweating profusely, poured molten pewter from a heavy-lipped ladle into bullet molds.

"Come on . . ." Kitty hooked her arm through Sara's. "Let's walk down and visit with Elvie for a while." She was determined to keep Sara out and about in the sunshine a bit longer. "There's not a thing that we have to do before time to fix supper, at least nothing that won't wait. Besides, I expect Elvie could use some of that clabber I've got. The boys would probably like it."

The tension deepened as the settlers waited and watched and prayed for relief. Laughter, when it came, seemed forced. All of them were weary of being pent up and under constant threat, the sun unmercifully hot now as July passed into August. Though Black Fish and his band of warriors had not yet ventured back down across the Ohio, Cullen and Roman continued to warn of the numerous small groups of braves about. Sometimes the sentinels would catch sight of a pair, or as many as five or six, riding their ponies along Hackberry Ridge out of rifle range.

There were daily grumblings, especially from those who had land out beyond the fort that was going untended. "Here we be, cooped up like chickens in a pen!" Henry Porter declared, his usual good humor deserting him. "And likely the cabin I built with my own sweat . . . and a portion o' yours," he acknowledged to the men standing around, "is burned to the ground by now."

"It's them whoresons of Brits that've put 'em up to it!" declared a lean, hirsute old trapper, who'd barely gotten into the gates with his scalp intact but a week past.

But there were none of them so foolhardy that they would risk leaving the safety of the stockade to face the almost certain death that waited out there. Then, just when their spirits seemed lowest, forty-five mounted militiamen from the North Carolina settlements rode into the fort with William Bailey Smith leading them, their horses prancing to stir up small whorls of dust. They were greeted with loud hurrahs and not a few tears.

"Oh, thank God!" Rebecca Boone whispered, reaching out for Kitty and then Sara, to hug them soundly. Even Sara was laughing.

One fair-faced militiaman, his chin sporting hardly a whisker yet, leaned down from the saddle to pat Granny Hawkins in passing. The old lady was crying copious tears and wiping her nose.

"There, old Grandma," he said, his young voice quivering, "all's well withee now."

"I ain't a-cryin' fer myself," she quavered. "It wouldn't been no matter if'n I'd been skulped. But I'm beholden to you fer comin' to see that my grandson and his family be kept safe."

As the cheering went on and the fort men praised Will Smith for a job well done, the women set to work to feed the hungry militiamen with what limited fare they had to offer, and the welcoming went on far into the night.

They were only slightly less exuberant when they found that most of the men who'd come were on short militia duty and would be staying only a few weeks at best. At least they'd be able to hunt as much as they needed to now, and safely. The women could head out to the woods to gather wild greens, which were fine eating if they had a little 'possum fat to season them up. What little was left of the gardens could be tended. "And," Daniel said, "you can bet your shot bag that Black Fish already knows they're here. That can't hurt a thing, boys."

The situation improved even further when Roman came into the fort a week later with the news that a detachment of Virginia militia a hundred strong, under the command of a Colonel John Bowman, had ridden into Fort Harrod.

"I can't say that Bowman and George Clark took to one another on sight," he confided to Daniel. "Bowman is all military and some impressed with himself. Seemed put out with George's buckskins. But it's damned good to have a few extra guns out here." He also brought good news for the Callaways: two of Flanders's brothers were with Bowman's troop.

Letters, waiting back east for a chance to be transported, had been brought along by the military. Among them were two from Kitty's sisters in Virginia. She opened Abigail's first.

. . . it was on Christmas Day, dear sister, that he received the awful wound, and when word came that the surgeons had taken the leg, it was almost more than I could bear. Still, John is proud to have served under General Washington, a man whom he holds in high esteem . . . and prouder yet that they were able to carry the day at Trenton.

I pray God that you have been able to recover from your terrible ordeal the day that our parents and sister died at the hands of the savages. Miranda and I have decided that the land our father left out there should be yours entirely to do with what you wish. We have signed papers to that effect and filed them with the county clerk. In truth, dear sister, we can see nothing of civilization ever coming to that wild country, and we still yet beseech you to come back to us where you can be assured of a most warm and loving welcome . . .

Until such time as we can meet again, I remain

Yr devoted sister Abigail

It was the following afternoon before Ben and Faith came to see Kitty. Though it was only Friday, Ben sported his Sunday prayer-meeting clothes, his chin well-shaven and still faintly red from the strong soap and razor; Faith was in her best linsey skirt, her hair carefully braided. Clearly it was more than a casual visit.

Kitty ushered them into the cabin, and Faith sat down in one of the straight chairs while Kitty waved Ben to the only rocker. "Well, this is a nice surprise," she said. "Sorry I don't have any coffee makings left. I guess we'll have to make do until the persimmons get ripe this fall. But I just finished churning and there's fresh buttermilk in the crock."

"Thankee, no, sister." Ben spoke for both of them. Faith held her hands in her lap, fingers clasped in a tight knot. There was a moment of awkward silence, and then Ben cleared his throat, reminding Kitty of his brother Todd with all that chewing and swallowing.

"I don't suppose Cullen's in to the fort now," he said finally.

"No."

"Well . . ." Ben straightened himself in his chair and assumed his most righteous expression. "That's too bad, sister. I'd hoped he'd be here, for men understand such things better than women ofttimes. But since he's not . . ."

"Just what is it you'd like me to understand, Ben?"

Her brother-in-law seemed to struggle with the problem anew, swallowing again, but at last blurted it out. "About this land business . . . Faith and me have prayed diligently for guidance.

We have never wished to take anything from you, sister. Either of us would cut off a hand before we would claim anything that was rightfully yours. Still, we feel it is only just to claim the part that is ours. . . .''

Whatever hard feelings she had had for them before were softened by time . . . and by her happiness with Cullen. Now Kitty looked from one to the other, feeling somehow sorry for them. Despite her best clothes and done-up hair, Faith looked tired, as she always did, and there was about her already a hint of the old lady she would become, just beneath the lusterless skin. And poor Ben was so rigid there were times he looked as if he'd break. Kitty wondered if they ever giggled when they were in bed together, the way she and Cullen did. It was hard to imagine.

She realized that Ben was looking at her pointedly, waiting for her to say something. "I . . . I have no quarrel with that, Ben." She met his gaze squarely, seeing the flare of surprise in those pale eyes.

"Well . . . well"—he regained his composure quickly—"it is indeed good to hear you say that. While we agree that your sisters had the right to make the decision they did, we have the right to claim what is ours . . . no more, no less."

"I agree. I simply couldn't let you force me to sell what is mine, Ben. Especially when it is something that is so dear to me."

Ben ran a hand over his chapped chin. "I was perhaps a mite stern," he conceded. "I did not guess that you would be wed so soon. A husband to make proper decisions for you changes the picture somewhat."

Kitty's reply was quick and firm. "I don't need Cullen to make my decisions."

Ben's thin eyebrows rose and his lips pursed. "You were ever a headstrong girl, Kitty!" he flared. "I pray it does not one day bring you grief!"

"Strong doesn't always mean wrongheaded, Ben," Faith put in softly. "Ma was strong."

Ben got to his feet to pace the room. "She was," he said finally. "That she was. Though"—he had to get in the last word—"I always felt that Usaph humored her overmuch. But we didn't come to quarrel with you, sister. We'd like to mend whatever breaks are between us. And to show our good faith, we've decided to take our share of the land from that acreage that runs in a jag northwest of the main body of land. It's covered over with hardwood timber and will be a job for me and my brothers to clear, but this way will leave you the entire block of land that borders the creek on the one side and Roman's land on t'other. The cabin, and springhouse, and shed . . . if they're still standing . . . are yours.''

Kitty had not expected such generosity from Ben, and she was touched. "That's handsome of you, Ben. You have my thanks. And the cabin is still there . . .'' She turned impulsively to her sister. "Cullen was there only a few weeks ago. The Indians haven't harmed it.''

A slow smile broke over Faith's face.

"Well, then . . . it's settled,'' Ben said, nodding his head and grinning stiffly.

They left soon after, and Kitty took up her mending and sat near the open window, welcoming the soft afternoon breeze and wondering if the apple trees were still alive and thriving. Next year they might even bear fruit. And in Ma's little herb patch, the hyssop and costmary and lavender would have spread. Maybe by spring it would be safe to leave the fort, and she and Cullen could move to Otter Creek.

As fall came and the first touch of frost turned the leaves, it was apparent to the settlers at Boonesborough that what little of the crops they'd been able to salvage or plant late, right up against the fort walls and under the guns, would provide scant food for the winter. There were a few potatoes and turnips and pumpkins. Corn was in such short supply that long before spring hoecakes and johnnycake would have to become treats instead of the daily fare that they were now. A part of the precious grain would be saved to feed the cattle through the worst part of the winter. At least they would still have milk and butter, the women agreed. But it was hard to accept that they might be without the makings for bread before the coming winter was ended. They'd done without before, but there'd always been a platter of hot hoecakes or a thick-crusted johnnycake on the table.

The North Carolina militia troop had already departed for the East, and now word came that Colonel Bowman's troops were heading back across the mountains. Though not many of the Kentuckians had taken kindly to him—some said he seemed annoyed at having been sent to the frontier when careers were being forged and glory won on the battlefields of the East—it was nonetheless clear that the presence of the militiamen at Harrod's Town had been a deterrent to the Indians.

Flanders was greatly pleased when his brothers decided to transfer to Daniel's command and stay on. Both Micajah and James Callaway had become known and liked at Boonesborough, and the Old Colonel was glad to have two more of his family with him. Daniel accepted the transfers eagerly; it meant two extra rifles at the fort.

Once again, utmost caution had to be taken when anyone went beyond the fort walls. Still, there were edibles in the woods and, danger or no, the women of Boonesborough were not going to let them go ungathered. Each time they ventured out they took along baskets and piggins and big hollow gourds, and a dozen men would go to stand guard. Sometimes the older boys volunteered to help with the gathering, just to get outside the fort for an hour.

There were pawpaws for the taking. Persimmons and wild grapes, sweetened by the frost, were ripe and ready. The woods were filled with walnut and hickory trees. And the weather was perfect. Too perfect, some grumbled. The warm and sun-drenched days in the late fall provided too good an opportunity for the Indians to make one last strike before winter set in. Indian summer, Colonel Callaway and some of the others called it.

But despite the danger, Kitty looked forward to every foray into the woods. She felt exhilarated each time she walked through the gates and down through the hollow, smelling the mint that grew about the spring—it always seemed to have a stronger aroma in the fall. And she would have to keep herself from breaking away from the group to run toward the thick wood that bordered the river. It must be the way the livestock felt when they'd been penned up and were let out, she thought wryly.

Elvie Porter, eight months along now and round as a keg, insisted on going to help, and Kitty came upon her one day, sitting in a drift of leaves beneath a huge old walnut tree and scooping into her basket the fallen nuts that lay close about.

"Law me, I guess I'll have to get Flanders's brothers to get me up from here again," she said, laughing. The affable young men, one a year, the other two years younger than Flanders, and with the same dark Callaway looks, had obligingly set her on her feet the day before.

Kitty helped her for a while, and then Daniel Morgan—who had insisted that he was old enough to go out with the bigger boys—came bounding up to say that he'd found a good tree a little way toward the river, and Elvie told Kitty to go ahead. "I can get the rest o' these," she said.

"We won't be far," said Kitty.

Daniel Morgan ran ahead, plowing through the dried leaves, dodging trees and the thick, gnarled roots that protruded above the ground. Kitty followed more slowly, still thinking of the picture that Elvie had presented sitting there. A small grin tugged at her mouth. Would she get that big? she wondered, unconsciously slipping a hand to the belly that was still flat and hard, with not the slightest hint yet of what she carried.

She was only just sure. Cullen had been out for two weeks, and she hadn't said a word before he left because she hadn't wanted to disappoint him in case her monthly was just late.

"Over here . . ." Daniel Morgan's call broke into her thoughts, and she looked up, feeling the warmth of the thin sun as it filtered through the remaining leaves left on the branches. He was beckoning to her, waving his arms insistently, and she stepped up her pace to join him beneath the wide-spreading branches of another big walnut tree. "Just look at 'em all!" He gestured toward the fat walnuts, still in their browning hulls, that lay all about them.

"Mercy," said Kitty, "I didn't bring anything to carry them in."

"I'll go fetch us somethin'," the boy volunteered, and sprinted back the way they had come.

Kitty busied herself gathering up the nuts and putting them in a pile. It would be easy enough to scoop them into a basket or a gourd, whatever Daniel Morgan brought back. They had loaded up the wagon, which stood out in the cleared ground beyond the edge of the woods, with plenty of containers to carry back whatever could be found. These walnuts would be good cracked out, and the hulls wouldn't go to waste. They'd make a deep brown dye.

She could hear the voices of the men by the wagon, and the other way could just see through the trees to the river, making out the clear stretch along the bank and the dense growth that covered the opposite shore. She hummed softly as she worked, thinking still of the baby. It would be a good time for it to come, late spring or early summer. Warm-weather babies always did better.

She heard the crackle of a twig behind her, and in the next instant strong male arms encircled her from behind. She let out a startled shriek as a kiss was planted firmly behind her ear.

She twisted around, laughing, torn between outrage and delight as she looked up into Cullen's face, which at the moment betrayed an eminent satisfaction with himself. *"Cullen!"* she chided. "You nearly scared me out of my wits. Whatever possessed you to—"

He cut off her scolding with a kiss squarely on the lips. "Are ye not glad to see me, lass?" he asked innocently once he'd drawn back to look at her.

"I am," she said, laughing in spite of herself and looking around to see if anyone was observing them. When she only caught a glimpse of Daniel Morgan, heading away discreetly, she slid her arms around her husband's neck and gave him another kiss. "That should tell you," she said. "But it doesn't change the scare you gave me, Cullen Claiborne! You could have caused something terrible to happen!"

"Something terrible?" He grinned.

"Yes. You could've . . ." She paused and brought her chin up to face him directly. "You could have caused me to have a miss."

"Oh, I doubt—" He had begun it almost before she'd finished speaking, before he realized fully what she'd said. And now he stopped dead still, looking at her with those smoky eyes, lowering his brows with a long, questioning gaze before the self-satisfied grin returned.

His lean face was suddenly ruddy with color, and he stood there for a moment, beaming. Then he shoved the black hat to the back of his head. "Can you tell me what we're waitin' on?" he said. "Let's take up these walnuts and be on our way home, lass."

Kitty looked on in disbelief as he started to throw the walnuts into the half-bushel gourd that Daniel Morgan had put down before he'd run off. *"Cullen,* aren't you surprised?" she demanded.

"Now why would I be surprised?" His eyes twinkled. "I've done my part, have I not?"

She laughed and set to helping him with the nuts. And once they had filled the gourd, before he swung it up to carry back to the wagon, he reached out for her hand. "It's about time, Kitty lass . . . about time," he said, a great tenderness buried in his eyes, his voice as gravelly as if he were hoarse.

"I love you, Cullen Claiborne," she said.

"And I you, lass. . . ."

They went back to help Elvie up, and then everything was loaded into the wagon.

Once back within the fort, Cullen gave his report to Daniel, then hurried home to the cabin. He watched a minute as Kitty stirred the pot that hung over the coals in the fireplace, then closed the door and the window, leaving the room hot and still . . . and dark except for the glow from the cookfire.

He rubbed his hand along her back and shoulders. "Kitty . . . Kitty, my lass," he whispered, and pulled her against him, kissing and caressing her, drawing her hand to cover the hard swelling of him. "Feels like I've been wantin' to do this forever. . . ."

She pushed eagerly against him, and he took her to the bed.

He drew back once before he entered her. "It won't hurt you, will it? You or the bairn?"

"Not a bit," she whispered. "Ma said to my sister there wasn't a bit of use to pen up the mare after the stallion had gotten her. . . ."

With the first dusting of snow, news came that Cornstalk, chief of all the Shawnee, had been senselessly shot down and killed by a group of army officers. It had happened at Fort Randolph, located at the juncture of the Kanawha River with the Ohio. The mighty chief, his son, and a subchief had entered the fort under a flag of truce to talk peace with the Americans. A handful of officers, out of control, had murdered all three.

"Damme!" Colonel Callaway swore. "Were they trying to see the end of us here in Kentucky for certain?"

Daniel paced the blockhouse glumly. "Come spring there'll be hell to pay," he agreed.

But the two men were able to set aside their forebodings long enough to celebrate the wedding of their children, Flanders and Jemima. While the festivities did not include the usual feasting—food was in too short supply—there was plenty of music and the foot-stomping dancing that the settlers loved. And for spirits, Ezekial Turner brought out several jugs of new persimmon wine he'd made.

A few days later there was further cause for celebration. A messenger had come over the mountains with the word of Burgoyne's surrender at Saratoga. A roaring bonfire of dry cane was made in the center of the stockade, and there was merrymaking long into the night.

In the wee hours of the next morning, Elvie Porter gave birth

to a baby girl. Though the child was named Margaret, no one
ever called her anything except Little Lureen.

✳ 20 ✳

"WELL, BOYS, IT'S SETTLED, THEN." DANIEL addressed the men who had crowded into the
blockhouse to hear what the salt-making plans
were. "It's the best time to go. The Shawnee are likely settin'
out the cold weather up in their villages. And if they're not,
Cap'n Gwatkins and his men will be ready to send 'em hightailin'. We'll commence gatherin' what supplies are needed to
sustain us, and set out three days from now on the first day of
the new year."

The lean winter rations at Boonesborough had been difficult
enough, but now the last of the salt was gone . . . and conditions
no better at the other two forts. Both Logan and Harrod had
agreed with Daniel that something must be done. Even if the
beleaguered and pent-up settlers could tolerate the insipid winter rations without the addition of salt, meat couldn't be preserved without it, hides couldn't be cured. They must have it,
and it was there for the taking at the Blue Licks, forty miles
north of Boonesborough.

Fortunately, a small troop of militia had arrived from Virginia
two weeks before, and the captain who commanded it had agreed
that he and his men would take a turn at the salt making. The
first group, headed up by Daniel, would consist of thirty volunteers from among the three forts, who would boil down the
salt-rich water at the lower salt lick up on the Licking River.
After a full month Captain Gwatkins and his men would relieve
them. The crews would alternate from that point on until a year's
supply of salt had been made and sent back to the stations.

"Will you be going?" Kitty asked Cullen.

"Not this time. Roman will. And I'm just as glad, lass. It means I can come in oftener and see if you're fattenin' some." He put a hand to her chin. "It appears to me you're too thin for a woman carryin'."

"I'm fine, Cullen." She tried to reassure him, though all she had to do was look into Ma's old looking glass to see that what he'd said was true. The normal queasiness of pregnancy had been intensified by the daily diet of turnips and meat. Even the precious hoecakes seemed tasteless and unsettling without salt.

"You don't eat enough," he insisted.

"I'll eat more when my morning sickness is over. Besides, I drink plenty of milk when it comes in fresh. It seems to set well enough with me. Lord help me, don't go worrying over every bite of food I take, Cullen." She grinned at him and he relented, pulling her close to hold her tenderly.

The day the salt makers left was cold and windy, but the fort turned out to wave them good-bye. Daniel headed up the line, the others riding two abreast, half of them before and half behind the packhorses, which were loaded down with axes and shovels, huge iron pots and long-handled ladles. For food, they carried only a little of the parched corn and some of the precious meal. They'd depend on their guns for the rest of their sustenance.

"God be with ye," someone called out. And Ben Tyler answered, "Amen," lifting his hand to his brother Latham, who'd volunteered to go along.

Jemima's smile looked a little forced as she watched her new husband ride away, his brothers not far behind. And while Sara was never happy to see Roman go out, today there was a pinched look about her mouth. But for the most part it was a festive occasion. The children ran back and forth, whooping louder than the dogs could bark, and there were shouts of encouragement to the departing men.

"I'm a-countin' on a good, salty piece o' meat afore long," someone called out.

"A little seasonin' in the johnnycake wouldn't hurt a thing," yelled another.

They stood there watching, wrapped against the wind in deerskin jackets and fur hats, the women shivering beneath their long woolen cloaks. Elizabeth was drawn in close to her husband, whose long silver hair whipped about his ears, his nose reddening.

The gates finally shut, Rebecca stamped from one foot to the other, tucking her hands beneath her armpits to warm them.

"Lord, let's get in from here," she said to Jemima. "That wind's keen as a switch."

Kitty and Sara stopped off to see Elvie Porter, who hadn't wanted to bring the baby out in the wind.

"She's a colicky one," Elvie declared, bustling about to fix them some persimmon coffee and casting a glance at her new daughter, who lay in the middle of the bed. Winter babies always slept with their parents since it was too drafty and cold in a cradle near the floor.

"Are you feeling all right again, Elvie?" Kitty asked.

"Fine." Elvie poured the steaming coffee and lightened it with a little milk. "I'd appreciate it if she'd sleep a little better at night, though. Granny Hawkins brought me down some catnip this mornin'. Thought I'd make up some tea and see if I can't get a spoonful of it down her at bedtime."

Sara had been over admiring the baby, but now she joined them and sipped the strong brew. "I'd be glad to spell you with her sometime when you need me. With Roman gone for a month, I guess I'll have more time than I know what to do with."

"I'll remember that," Elvie said. Little Lureen had started to fuss and wave her arms in jerky little motions, and Elvie brought her over to the warmth of the fireplace and put her to a breast. "Thank goodness my milk is full," she said, looking down at the eagerly nursing baby. "Though I wouldn't be a bit surprised if it wasn't so many turnips that's givin' her the colic."

The work had gone well, Roman thought as he looked out over the salt spring. The men, early as it was, were already chopping and fetching wood to keep the fires blazing, and carrying water to keep the dozen or so kettles going. Their tracks crisscrossed in the light snow that had fallen overnight, all converging upon the huge black pots that sent billows of steam rising upward in the cold air. It took a lot of water—and back-breaking work—to boil out a bushel of salt.

Nonetheless, with their month almost up, they had managed to send three men back to Boonesborough with packhorses loaded down, and there were three hundred bushels waiting to go, far more than they thought they'd accomplish when they first arrived.

As if he'd read Roman's mind, Daniel sidled up, his expression one of satisfaction beneath the fur cap he wore pulled down over his ears. "I'd say we've done well enough," he declared.

Roman nodded, the two of them gazing out over the hive of

activity from their vantage point of the higher ground. Flanders, recovering from a mild case of scaldfoot, came limping to join them.

"How are they today?" Daniel asked, looking down at the ailing feet.

"Better," Flanders said, grinning. "I was lucky it wasn't worse."

"That you were," Daniel agreed. "I've seen some cry with it. Felt like cryin' a time or two myself." His eyes laughed.

Roman squinted up into the pale sunlight, scanning first the pewter blue of the sky and then the dense line of trees some little distance from them. The area where they were had been worn smooth and treeless by the tread of countless buffalo herds, coming for the salt. "I think I should go out today," he said.

Daniel nodded. "Tell you what," he said. "I'd planned to head over here to the west today and take a look around . . . maybe bring back a deer. Or a buffalo if I run into one. Why don't you go east, Roman. Take a good long sweep just to be sure everything's quiet that way. Might be a good idea if you took Flanders with you." He grinned. "Seems to me it'd be easier for his hind end to sit a horse for a couple of days than for his feet to carry him around here."

The two men were mounted and ready in a few minutes. The day stretched before them as they turned their horses eastward, the sun warming enough to make the snow start to melt. Though they didn't talk much, Roman found it pleasant to have Flanders along. He had always liked the Old Colonel's nephew.

They stopped around midday to water their horses and drink from a spring that bubbled up out of the rocks at the foot of a gentle rise. A handful of parched corn did for each of them, and they were soon on their way again, riding the crest of the ridges to look down on the valleys patterned with the dark and light of melting snow. The woods were quiet except for the soft thud of the horses' hooves and the scolding cries of a few hardy crows competing for the last of the clinging dried berries.

Before nightfall Flanders shot a rabbit scurrying off through the underbrush, and minutes later Roman brought down a hen turkey. With their supper and breakfast hanging from their saddles, Roman led the way up a steep ridge to an overhanging rock that formed a snug little cave. "We'll spend the night here," he told Flanders.

With a fire burning brightly and their stomachs full up with the rabbit they'd roasted on a sharp stick, the two men sat and talked some, the wind rising to stir at the bushes that protected the cave opening.

"So, are you taking to married life?" Roman asked.

Flanders grinned, leaning back against the cave wall, his bare feet stretched out to the warmth of the fire. "Guess I would be if I'd got enough of it."

"You could have stayed behind and let someone else come to make salt."

The young man considered that. "Yes," he said at length, wiggling his toes, "but I wouldn't have felt right about it."

From somewhere far off in the hills a catamount screamed, and the fire flickered.

"Panther," Flanders said.

Roman nodded, feeling somehow uneasy without knowing why. He got to his feet and, taking up his rifle, pulled his jacket closer about him. "I think I'll just take one more look around," he said.

"Sounded a far piece off," Flanders offered.

Roman nodded but went out anyway to check the horses, tethered loosely near the cave opening and sheltered by an over-hanging shelf of rock. His sorrel nickered softly at his approach, and he ran a hand along the warm neck, quieting the animal. The sky, stretching dark and heavy, had clouded over, and snow had begun to spit, swirling out there with the quickening breeze.

He walked out into it, out from the shelter of the ledge, making his way soundlessly among the shagbark hickories, their branches bare and stirring in the wind. Climbing to the highest point of the ridge, he scanned the valley below, the dark patches of trees, the new sifting of snow . . . standing there for a long time, the unease still pulling at him, though he could see nothing amiss. Finally he turned and went back.

He slept sitting up, wrapped in his blanket, his back against the cave wall, rifle at hand. They had scratched out a hole in the dirt floor and lined it with hot coals, then put in the plucked and gutted turkey, covering it over with more of the coals. He was aware of the odor of cooking meat from time to time through the night, and of the moan of the wind outside.

Both men were awake by dawn, and after stepping out to discover that several inches of snow had fallen while they slept, they dug out the turkey, which was black-crusted on the outside but juicy and tender to the point of falling off the bones.

"I do purely love turkey," Flanders said, swiping at his chin to catch the dripping juices.

Roman grunted his agreement.

Once they'd finished, they wrapped what meat was left in an oiled cloth that Roman carried in his pack and, taking up their rifles, went out to give each of the horses a handful of parched corn.

"I think we won't go straight back to camp," Roman said, remembering his uneasiness the night before. "Maybe we'll just swing back and forth a little, take our time and a good look around."

Hours later, with the sun straight up overhead and nothing come across except the trails of rabbits and other small animals, and now and again the delicate tracks of a deer through the fresh snow, they stopped at a small creek to water their mounts. Icy crystals glistened along the rocks at the edge, and the animals stamped their hooves and blew through their noses, breath steaming. Roman unwrapped the turkey leavings and they chewed at the cold meat, giving some more of their parched corn to the horses.

"Well," Roman said finally, squinting up at the muted sun, "two hours should put us back at camp. Let's ride."

Before long they emerged from the thick trees onto the wide smooth buffalo trail, and the snow stretched before them, unmarked. It was easy going, and Flanders grew talkative during the last hour, speculating on whether the relief party might have arrived in their absence. "I'd as lief go on back to the fort for a while," he said, grinning. "At least we'll be takin' plenty of salt back with us. I guess even turnips three times a day taste better with a little salt on 'em. Tell you what I miss the most from back in Virginia: fruitcake. With currents, mind you. . . ."

He launched into a description of the cakes he remembered, but Roman had hauled his horse to a stop and was staring at the horizon ahead of them.

"I expect it was the drenching with rum that made them so tasty . . ." Flanders was going on, until suddenly he realized that Roman had dropped behind him. He reined in his mount to look back. "What's the matter?"

"Look up there. . . ."

Flanders turned ahead, looking toward the clear afternoon sky and the broad path they rode; then he looked back toward Roman, his thick dark brows raised quizzically.

Roman's eyes swept ahead again. "The camp's not far up there. Where's the smoke from the fires? We should even be able to see some of the steam from the kettles." He dug his heels into the horse's flanks and passed the young man by. "Let's go!" he shouted over his shoulder.

With their horses at the gallop, they covered the distance quickly, cutting over to the shelter of the scrub and bushes and then, finally, bursting out into the open and hauling their mounts to a stop at sight of the deserted camp.

"Good God!" Flanders breathed. "What in damnation . . . ?"

They both swung down at once, Flanders walking among the places where the fires had been, now merely blackened heaps of ashes. The kettles were overturned and empty. The hard-come-by salt, which had been stored in a rough lean-to, was scattered over the ground and had partially melted the snow, giving it a strange gray look. Roman moved slowly, intent on reading whatever sign was there.

"What happened?" Flanders asked, his voice hushed.

"Indians . . ." Roman's eyes still swept the ground. "A lot of them," he added. "Maybe as many as a hundred."

"But—"

"Wait." Roman paced the area, looking for some sign of a fight. But there was none. Nothing. No bodies, not even a bloodstain or a spent bullet . . . not even a grain of powder where a hasty hand might have spilled a little in the loading.

Clearly, whatever had transpired had taken place on the day before. The cap of snow atop the overturned kettles attested to that.

"I don't believe a shot was fired," Roman muttered, as much to himself as to Flanders. He stood, chewing at his lip in his perplexity.

"That can't be!" Flanders protested. "Daniel would never have given up without a fight. You know that."

"Daniel was going out to hunt yesterday, remember? Maybe he wasn't here when it happened."

"Then where is he?"

Roman didn't answer, but went pacing slowly over the compound again. Surely there was something that would tell him, something that would explain what had happened. They couldn't have just stopped their work, waited while the Indians scattered the kettles and emptied the salt, then calmly climbed into their saddles and ridden away with the savages. It made no sense.

He stopped as his eye fell on the tip of a powder horn that had been half buried in a drift of salt. Scratching it out, he picked it up with a sinking heart. The initials D.B. were carved into the side of it. He heard Flanders, who had come to stand beside him, groan. Both of them had seen the horn countless times before.

"They've got Daniel," said Flanders.

Roman nodded. Only an act of will enabled him to push aside his personal feelings and think of what must be done now. His brain raced. Was there any way to mount a force large enough to challenge such a sizable warrior band . . . even if they could be overtaken in time?

The tracks headed north. Clearly they were pushing hard to get back across the Ohio, to lose themselves in the stronghold of camps that dotted the Scioto and Miami. And farther north there was Detroit and Lieutenant Governor Hamilton—the Hair-Buyer. . . . Hard currency awaited the delivery of American scalps . . . or prisoners. Jesus! Roman's composure came near to deserting him. It might just be that the scalp of Daniel Boone would be a prize that would bring a premium.

He shook off that thought and returned to his calculations. Gwatkins and his troop were at Harrod's Town. But they were green from the East, unused to the frontier. If only George Clark were available to lead them, Roman thought. He had not only the authority, but the drive and the skill as a commander to head up such an expedition. But George had returned to Virginia to see Governor Henry late in the fall, apparently on a matter of some importance. Besides, to take the strength of the militia troop away from the forts now would leave them all wide open to a concentrated attack, something that would avenge the death of Cornstalk in the minds of the Shawnee. Actually, God alone knew what might have happened already.

Roman slipped the leather strap of the powder horn he still held up over his shoulder and swung around to Flanders. "Mount up," he said. "We've got to get back to Boonesborough as soon as we can."

The little band at Boonesborough gathered in the blockhouse to hear the news, their faces registering a despair greater than any they'd known before. Cullen, who'd only come in to the fort twenty-four hours before Roman and Flanders, lowered his dark brows and stared grimly into the fireplace. Kitty, heavy in her fifth month, stood beside him. Israel Boone, his young face painfully controlled, stood with his mother.

"All of them taken?" The Old Colonel's voice quivered.

"Daniel? James? Cajer?" That was what the family called Micajah Callaway.

As Roman nodded, Flanders turned to comfort Jemima, who had begun to weep softly. Rebecca hadn't made a sound, but stood white-faced and still, leaning slightly against her son's arm.

Ben and Todd Tyler were visibly shaken. "God save him," Ben said of their brother Latham. "God save all of them . . ." he added brokenly.

They looked at one another blankly, red-eyed and bone-thin, worn out with winter and poor food and the fight to survive. "What in the world will we do without Daniel?" Henry Porter asked, voicing the question that had so far been unspoken. No one answered.

They broke into small groups to speak softly among themselves. Cullen and Colonel Callaway pulled Roman aside.

"It's hard to believe they didn't offer a fight," Cullen declared. "Are you sure, Roman?"

Roman nodded.

"That they could catch so many flat-footed . . ." Richard Callaway pondered it. "We can credit the scoundrels at Fort Randolph for this, I'm thinking! Damme, but I thought the Shawnee would wait until spring before they set out to avenge Cornstalk's killing!"

"I'll take word to Harrod and Logan, and alert the militia troop," Cullen said. "Then I'll ride directly back to Boonesborough."

Roman lifted his head. "If you should run into Simon, tell him we could use him here now."

"Butler's scouting at St. Asaph's," Cullen answered. "I doubt Ben Logan could spare him."

Roman accepted that word without comment, looking about the room for Rebecca now. He didn't see her, but Sara and Kitty stood nearby with the other women, who'd drawn apart to comfort Jemima and one another. One of the Porter boys came running in to inform Elvie that Willie and George Henry had gotten into a scuffle and spilled all the buttermilk.

"If'n they did," she snapped, nerves worn thin, "I'll take a strap to the both of them!" She hitched the baby higher on her hip and went out the blockhouse door.

"Where's Rebecca?" Roman asked Sara.

"She went to her cabin. She said she wanted to be by herself for a little."

"I'll be home in a while," he told her, then went outside to search in his pack for the powder horn he'd picked up at the Blue Licks camp.

At the Boone cabin there was no answer when he knocked. "Rebecca . . ." He leaned in close to the rough surface of the door and waited. After a moment he tried the latch and felt it give. "Rebecca, it's Roman . . . I'm coming in," he warned.

After the brightness of the sun on the snow-covered ground, it took a moment for his eyes to adjust to the dim light inside the cabin. The fire had died low and there was a damp chill about the place, but Rebecca sat in a rush-bottomed chair that the boys had made for her, her knitting in her hands, fingers moving with a deft sureness.

Roman stood gazing at her for a long moment, remembering how she'd looked when he'd first come to stay with her and Daniel. She'd surely not been old enough to be his mother, yet she'd not only made him welcome, she'd nursed him when he was sick and applied ointment to his scrapes and bruises . . . scolded him when he was ornery and heaped praise upon him when he did well. There'd been a time—he acknowledged it to himself now with a sheepish embarrassment laced with grief—when that boy, struggling with his growing pains, had even fancied himself smitten with the handsome young woman who was Daniel's wife.

"I've fallen behind on my needlework," she said, fingers still working doggedly. "The boys need stockings . . . so does Daniel."

Roman stooped to throw a log onto the fire and poke at it until the flames started to curl upward. "Looks like you could use some more light," he said. Hunkered down, he held a good-size splinter of wood in the fire until the end was lit and then rose to light the grease lamps around the wall.

She worked still, refusing to look up at him until he gently took the knitting away from her and put it into the basket beside her. Then those direct dark eyes lifted to meet his, and though her face was as thin as everyone else's, there was still that strong set to it to reassure him.

"Daniel will be back," she said. "You'll see. In a few days, here he'll come, grinning from ear to ear and filled with tales of what happened." She gave her head a shake. "It's not the first time he got captured. You know that, Roman. You've heard him tell about that time the Indians caught him . . . it was during one of those early times he come across the mountains."

Roman nodded. It was true. Daniel had been captured before and had gotten away with ease. But it had been years ago, in a time that seemed less perilous than now . . . before the women and babies and trains of packhorses loaded down with pots and pans and fruit-tree seedlings had convinced the Indians that white men were coming into their land to stay. And that the only way to stop them was to kill them.

"Indians take to Daniel," Rebecca was saying, her voice warming to her own words. "And he takes to them. I give him a week and he'll be back. I only hope . . ." Her voice quivered, lost a little of its assurance. "I pray he can bring the others back safe."

"I brought something for you." Roman slipped the strap of Daniel's powder horn from his shoulder, and Rebecca stood up quickly to grasp it, the smallest cry escaping her tight lips. "I found it at the camp where he'd left it," he went on. "I think on purpose . . . to let me know he'd been there."

Her fingers traced and retraced the letters carved into the horn, and her eyes were red, but not wet. "He'll want this when he gets back," she said stubbornly.

Roman hesitated, then put out a hand to touch her shoulder lightly. "I guess he will," he said quietly.

Heavyhearted and exhausted, he went to his and Sara's cabin to find the fire burning brightly, though his wife was not yet there. Something simmered in a pot, a thin mixture with a few pieces of shredded meat visible here and there, but he was too tired to feel any great appetite.

He sat down on the side of the bed, meaning to take off his moccasins, but leaned back instead. There hadn't been enough corn husks to provide a new stuffing for the ticking this year, and the mattress had flattened, but tired as he was, it felt like the finest goose down beneath him.

It was fourteen hours before he stirred again, rolled over on his side and opened his eyes to see Sara frying rabbit, a batch of hot hoecakes keeping warm.

He grunted, made a face at the awful taste in his mouth. "Is it morning?"

She smiled at him. "It is . . . and I was beginning to think you'd sleep right through breakfast. Look . . ." She gestured toward the food. "Israel brought this rabbit for us, and I've been saving some cornmeal for when you came in."

He swung out of bed, aware that his feet were bare. "It was

all I could do,'' Sara offered. ''I tried to get the rest off, but you were too heavy.''

His feet properly shod again, Roman sprinted down to the necessary house, relishing the frosty air, and was back by the time Sara had the food dished up.

''Have you seen Rebecca this morning?'' he asked between bites of the crusty rabbit washed down with huge gulps of persimmon coffee.

Sara nodded, faint lines etching the pale brow. ''She insists that Daniel will be back soon.''

''I know.'' He put his cup down. ''I'll be heading back out, Sara.'' He saw from the look on her face, from the way the skin suddenly seemed stretched taut over the cheekbones, that she understood his intention at once.

''You're going after them, after Daniel and the others.'' It came after a long moment, trembling and strangely resigned.

''I have to,'' he said. ''For Rebecca . . . and for myself.''

As Roman maneuvered the sorrel gelding from the thick stand of water oaks and out onto the flat stretch of bank along the Ohio, a startled deer burst from its cover and ran, causing the fowl at the river's edge to rise up in a great honking and flapping of wings. The water shone a clear gray-green in the midmorning sunlight, stretching wide toward the southern shore and moving with a vigorous current. If the warmer weather held, and the icy creeks and rivers that fed into it thawed even more, the Ohio could rise within hours and become a dark and raging stream, rushing to empty into the Mississippi many miles to the west. In that event it would be all but uncrossable for days, maybe weeks. Best that he cross it now, Roman thought, though it was hard to give up, hard to admit defeat.

He had tracked the war party without difficulty as far as the Ohio, but once across, he couldn't be dead sure just where they had come ashore. Even when he found tracks, they had all led in different directions, each one disappearing again into the network of waterways that fed into the big river.

With hope fading each passing day, he had taken a new tack and set out doggedly for those camps whose locations he knew, scouting them one by one, hoping to learn something, anything, that might give him a clue about what had happened to the captives. He found one of them deserted but for a few old squaws and a half a dozen old men. The others, while well populated, were all guarded so closely that there was more than one time when he came near to being discovered.

Now, he tugged at the month's growth of beard on his chin, dreading to go back to the fort and tell Rebecca and the others that he had not been able to find out what had happened to Daniel and the other men . . . that they would probably never know. It burned him inside, made his chest ache.

The grief he felt was so strong that it almost made him cry out with the pain of it, but he drew in a breath and swung down from his horse to squint across the width of the river once again. Not so wide as it was in some places, he observed with some satisfaction. On down by the falls it was fully a mile; here it was only three-quarters of that.

Spreading his piece of oiled skin flat on the ground, he placed his rifle, powder horn, and pouch of jerk and parched corn squarely in the middle. Next he stripped out of his clothes, moccasins and all, and deposited them atop the other things, shivering in the breeze that had seemed warm before. There was probably nothing, he pondered, that made a man feel as vulnerable as having his ass bared to the world, and it as white as a baby's where his clothes usually went. He wrapped the skin over and around, tied it securely, and fastened the whole packet to his saddle.

Some of the wild ducks, having decided that he was no danger to them after all, had settled back down to the shallows along the edge, and they only quacked mildly and paddled off a bit as he swung up into the saddle and urged his sorrel into the water. "Easy . . . easy," he soothed the big animal, gasping a little as the icy water inched up his legs.

The horse floundered in the soft bottom, then lunged free and was carried out into the deep, the powerful front legs pawing, head up and straining as Roman held on for all he was worth. The current was swifter than it had looked from the shore, and though the horse struggled valiantly, it was soon apparent that they were being carried downstream. Still holding on to the reins, Roman slipped out of the saddle and began to kick his numb feet and legs with all the strength he had.

The sorrel whinnied and strained, and Roman felt himself pulled under several times, his lungs bursting each time until his head cleared water. But now the reins had slipped from his stiff fingers, and as he came up he made a wild grab for the horse's mane and held on, gasping and choking and cursing.

Choppy little waves slapped into his face, threatened to engulf him, but he jerked his head upward, his lungs aching for breath.

The horse, game as always, put forth a steady effort, and after a few long minutes Roman could tell that they'd crossed the main channel and were coming into the calmer water toward the southern shore. "That's right . . . good old Chief," he managed to get out, though his teeth were chattering. "Almost there . . ."

He let go as the horse found its footing again in the soft bottom and made the rest of the way on his own, crawling up on the hard-packed bank to sprawl shivering and spent, as the horse shook itself mightily and snorted through his nose. Then, catching his breath, Roman rolled to his back to gaze up into the brilliant blue of the sky, welcoming what warmth the sun offered. After a moment he pulled himself to his feet, leaning into the wet hide of the horse and giving the big sorrel a grateful scratch between the ears.

"Might be just as well," he panted, "if we took our swims in the dead of summer." The horse's hide rippled beneath his hand, and the animal turned its head to nuzzle at his palm, looking for a grain or two of parched corn. "In a minute," Roman said. "In a minute."

He gathered up handfuls of the dry brush that edged down to the bank and began to rub himself vigorously with it, wincing at the roughness but pleased to have some feeling begin to return to the numb extremities. Despite the discomfort of it, he kept it up until his skin was pink and tingling, and only then unlaced his bundle, pleased to find its contents dry.

True to his promise, he offered the horse some corn, and then had turned back to take up his clothing when he heard a slight sound above the whisper of the current, a dislodging of a pebble or the cracking of a twig. He dropped his leggings and, still buck naked, grabbed for his rifle, his eyes sweeping the scrub trees and the outcroppings of limestone studded with brush. With another slight sound, he swung, hammer drawn back and ready to fire, when he saw the figure of an Indian, hands raised in friendship, emerge from the mass of greening blackberry bushes thirty yards away. The shambling gait was at once familiar.

"Three Toes," Roman called to the Cherokee, who had earned his name—and the limp—in a bout with a bear years before.

The Indian kept his hands out front, palms open to show his wish for peace, coming ahead with his head cocked to one side and a grin on his homely face, his eyes taking the measure of Roman's genitals and nodding his approval. "Firehair," he returned the greeting, nodding again.

"You are far from home," Roman said.

"Yes. We come to hunt. This many . . ." He held up five fingers to indicate how many braves had come with him.

"Where are the others?"

Three Toes pointed westward. "Three days, and I will meet them. At the stream of the Kan-tu-kee."

Roman nodded. "They went on without you?"

The Cherokee rubbed his bad leg, and Roman understood. Then he pointed a stubby finger at the fat groundhog that swung limply from his belt and raised his eyebrows questioningly. "You would eat, Firehair?"

Roman lowered his gun. "That is good of Three Toes," he said formally. "I accept the honor of his campfire and his food." And by the time he was dressed, the Indian had the fire going and the groundhog almost skinned.

Once it was sizzling on a green spit stretched across two rocks, the two men sat and talked, Roman warming now in the sun.

"Have the Cherokee come across Black Fish's warriors?" Roman asked, hoping that the Indian might know something. But Three Toes merely shook his head and poked at the fire.

"The Shawnee warriors took Boone," he went on, seeing how Three Toes's head came up, "and many other white men."

The obsidian eyes narrowed. "Boone . . . When? What place?"

"Back when the snow was still deep. At the Blue Licks." Roman watched him intently, searching for any indication that he might know what had happened. But the old warrior just hunched forward and began to rock, his craggy face troubled.

"Boone . . . Boone . . ." He shook his head dejectedly and rubbed at his bad leg. "Boone is gone," he keened, his face infinitely sad. "Attacullaculla is old and sick. Our people no longer heed his words. And Boone is gone. . . ."

❄ 21 ❄

H ER SWOLLEN BELLY FEELING THE STRAIN, KITTY tugged at the wooden churn, the milk sloshing within as she half dragged, half lifted it over the doorsill and out onto the step. Stopping to catch her breath, she straightened up to rub her back and slide her hands along the big muscles at the sides of her abdomen, grasping the whole aching thing as if it were a big watermelon beneath the front of her skirt.

Aside from the normal aches and pains of pregnancy, she had never felt better, though it was just as well that she didn't know the dire predictions being made by most of the female population of Boonesborough. There was sure to be trouble when the time came, they whispered among themselves, shaking their heads and clucking their tongues. Kitty Claiborne was sure as the world too small to be a good breeder.

"Some as are small have a world of trouble, and others don't," Granny Hawkins pronounced when asked for her opinion.

"Her mother did well enough, and her no bigger," Elizabeth countered, but few were convinced.

Kitty contemplated the churn now, wondering how hard it would be to lift it down to the ground, out into the bright sunlight and the warm fresh air. She turned her face up to the sun, thankful that the Indians had left them in peace for now, mindful of the green, growing vegetables and corn just beyond the fort wall. Only a few weeks ago they had been down to nothing but meat and what little milk there was—some of the cows had still been carrying their calves then, and left so bony and ill-nourished, they hardly gave at all. When word had come of the suffering and privation endured by General Washington and his troops over the winter at a place called Valley Forge in Pennsylvania, the settlers of Boonesborough had felt an instant kinship. But now the cows were fattening on the lush grass and there was milk again, and greens on the table, and berries for dessert. Fort Harrod had been able to send some meal to tide them over until their own corn came in, so there was bread again as well.

Kitty saw Israel Boone, arms filled with firewood, coming along the path toward the cabin. He called out to her, his engaging grin in place. "Brought you some wood, Kitty. I cut some for Ma and took some over to Sara. Figured you might could use a stick or two."

"I thank you, Israel," she said. The men of the fort always saw to her needs and Sara's when Cullen and Roman were out.

Israel laid the logs atop the pile at the corner of the cabin, brushed his hands down the worn linsey breeches, and squinted at the churn in the doorway. "Where are you aimin' to take it?"

"Right over there, where there's room to work." Kitty indicated the flat ground in front of the step. "Thought I'd do my churning outside since it's so pretty today."

He mounted the step to swing the churn down for her, then leaned up against the cabin to watch as, nodding her thanks, she tied up the loose ends of her apron, came down the step to position her feet, and grasped the dasher. As she began to move it up and down with long firm strokes, the milk bubbled and sloshed within.

"Neither of our old cows have freshened yet," said Israel.

"Mine dropped her calf two weeks ago, but it was dead. She's giving a goodly amount of milk, though. I'll bring some down later. Some butter, too." Israel said they'd be obliged.

Fanny Callaway, who had only recently wed John Holder, came along the path on the way down to the Callaway cabin and stopped to talk for a minute, then went on her way. Farther on down the compound, some of the fort children tossed a blown-up pig's bladder from one to another, and Winfield Burdette yelled at them to watch out as he worked at shoeing a particularly fractious horse.

"Is Rebecca all right?" Kitty asked.

Israel's face sobered. "I guess she is. She's decided on going back, Kitty."

Kitty nodded, working the dash a little faster. "I knew she was thinking that way."

Israel's broad forehead knitted. "She's finally give up that Pa's dead." He pulled at a worn place in the knee of the coarse linsey britches and looked away quickly.

Nothing so far had staggered the frontier communities like

the loss of Daniel Boone. While the grief for the other men was widespread and true, the shock of having Daniel taken from them was overwhelming. And as his widow, respect was paid to Rebecca.

Squire, hard hit by it, had come and stayed a few days with the family. The leaders of the other forts, Jim Harrod and Ben Logan, had each come to offer condolences. That was as it should be, the bereaved people of Boonesborough agreed. Scarcely a day passed that some grizzled old hunter didn't hello the gate and pass through to express his sympathy, often with tears in his eyes.

Now, Kitty could see Israel swallow hard, and it was a full minute before he turned back to her. "You'll be going back to North Carolina and your relatives . . . back to the Bryans?" she asked finally.

He nodded. "There are lots of Ma's kin back there in the Yadkin, aunts and uncles and cousins." He dug his toe in the soft earth. "I'm not all that anxious to leave Kaintuck, but I figure Ma'll need me."

"I expect she will," Kitty agreed. "But we'll miss you, Israel. We'll miss all of you." The dash was stilled for a moment as she looked over at the wide young face that in these last months had become a man's . . . vulnerable and touching still, but all the same, a man's.

He straightened, a tight smile on his lips. "I expect I'll be comin' back one of these days, when the time is right. Besides, we're not leavin' till day after tomorrow. No use to say good-byes yet."

He lifted a hand and swung off down the path. Kitty looked after him, feeling a great sadness. It must be awful for them, she thought. Not even a grave to go to. At least she had that. The savages hadn't robbed her of that.

She renewed her efforts at the dash, shifting her weight from foot to foot to ease herself some, feeling the baby kick vigorously. After a while she heard a footfall behind her and turned to see her sister Faith with two-year-old Martha toddling along behind her. The child stopped to pull at a bright yellow dandelion.

"What in the world are you doing?" Faith asked.

Kitty grinned. "Churning."

"I can see that. But why would you drag that heavy thing all the way out here, and you carryin'? Here"—she took the dash away from Kitty—"sit down on the step and rest yourself."

She began to apply the dash rhythmically, and Kitty, admitting that she was tired, lowered herself, not without difficulty, onto the step.

"How much longer do you have to go?" Faith asked.

"Four or five weeks, if I've counted right."

"Well, you'd best slow down a little from now on out."

Kitty nodded.

After a minute Faith stopped. "I think the butter's come," she said, and lifted the round wooden lid to peek down into the churn. "It is." As Kitty started to get up from the step, she waved her back. "Sit still . . . I know where everything is, for mercy's sake."

She went into the cabin and returned a minute later with a big burl bowl, a paddle, and a slotted spoon to skim up the butter with. Working quickly, she soon had the yellow globules lifted out of the buttermilk left in the churn, and she settled down beside Kitty to work the creamy mass, scraping the paddle along the bottom and folding the butter over and over, pressing the water out and tipping the bowl to let it dribble away.

Little Martha came whining to tug at the front of her mother's bodice.

"Will you get on and play now," Faith scolded. "You nursed not half an hour ago. Here . . ." She scooped up a dab of butter on her finger and stuck it in the child's mouth. "Get along now. Go out there and pull the dandelions. Gather 'em up for Mama and we'll have some for supper."

She watched the skinny little girl go out beyond the path, out onto the grass. "I declare, she keeps me sore as a boil all the time."

"Why in the world don't you wean her? She's plenty big enough."

Faith smiled sheepishly. "It keeps Ben off me. I tell him it ruins the milk for her if he does it. I'm not a bit anxious to get caught with another a minute sooner than I have to."

"Does it really ruin the milk?" Kitty asked.

"I don't think so."

The two of them laughed, and Faith put up a hand to groan and rub her jaw. "Law me," she said, "this tooth has been killing me for nearly a week."

Later in the afternoon, Kitty took some of the butter down to Sara, then fixed another ball of it and poured up some of the buttermilk for the Boones, as she'd said she would.

As she walked down toward their cabin, she recalled the

day she'd first come to Boonesborough. *You must call me Rebecca . . . it would please me.* That's what Rebecca had said to her. It was going to be hard to say good-bye to Rebecca Boone.

She found her alone in the cabin and determinedly bright. It was Kitty who broke down and cried when Rebecca went looking through a basket of things stored under one of the beds and came up with a baby's cap of fine bleached linen, all neatly hemstitched.

"I want you to have it," she said. "It was the nicest thing I ever had for my young'uns. An aunt of mine made it for the baby I had just before we come out here . . . the one that died. It never got to wear it."

"Oh, Rebecca . . ." Kitty hesitated, her eyes brimming.

"Take it," Rebecca said, her smile not quite steady. "I'll not be having any more, Lord knows." Her voice came near to breaking. "I was getting too old anyway."

Kitty had lain awake for a while now, listening to all the night noises. The soft chorus of the tree frogs drifted up from the woods near the river and was joined by a persistent cricket that had taken up residence within the cabin somewhere. The breeze tugged at a loose board on the roof, causing it to squeak, and Cullen, sleeping soundly beside her, drew in each breath with a heaviness that was not quite a snore. She wouldn't wake him. There was plenty of time.

She felt wrapped in the night, as if she were in a cocoon. She could sense the rhythm of the slight, hot ache that came in her back and hardened her belly now and again . . . a confirmation of what she'd known was going to happen. The baby was going to be on time. All through the day she had felt a surge of energy, as if her body were preparing for what was coming, and she had quietly seen that everything she'd need was ready, and then she'd cleaned the cabin and cooked up extra food for Cullen.

She had said nothing to anyone, not to Sara or Faith. Not even to Cullen, though she was glad that he was in. She had had a sense that this first part was for her alone and something special, before the women gathered to poke and prod and murmur words of encouragement.

Cullen stirred and turned away from her, hardly breaking the pace of his regular breathing, and she was glad that she could arch her back slightly when the pains came without fear of waking him. Each time, she'd put her hands on the distended abdomen as if touching the baby within her, aware of its struggle to be born.

After a while the pressure against her bladder made her uncomfortable, and she carefully eased out of bed to relieve herself in the chamber pot . . . not an easy task in itself, given the unwieldiness of her body. But just the effort, the stirring, brought on a sharper pain, and she saw that the urine was streaked with blood. She put a cloth between her legs before she got back into bed.

With the first faint signs of dawn, the cows began to move about and make low moaning sounds, eager to be milked and let out to the green grass and the river, and Kitty heard footsteps going past the cabin and down toward the necessary. A dog barked.

Cullen stirred sleepily and rolled toward her, nuzzling at her breast, moving his hand along her leg. She pushed him away gently.

"Don't get up yet, lass," he murmured.

"I'm not."

His hands sought her again.

"No, Cullen," she said, and he slowly raised up on an elbow to look down at her in the dim light. She had never put him off before.

Understanding dawned in his eyes. "Is it time, lass?"

She nodded, stiffening as the pain came, holding her breath through the contraction and then letting it out in a rush. They had grown gradually harder and closer. "Would you go get Sara, Cullen? And see if Elvie or Faith can come?"

He lit the grease lamp and dressed quickly, then paused only long enough to catch her hand between the two of his. "Is there anything you want me to do, Kitty, love?"

"No." She smiled up at him, hoping the baby would look like him. "They'll help me."

Sara came in a minute, looking pale and anxious, her hair caught up so hurriedly that thin strands of it trailed from the usually neat bun at the nape of her neck. She was followed closely by Elvie and Faith—Elizabeth was keeping the babies for them, they said—and they commenced to do all the things that women did at such a time . . . poking up the fire and putting on some water, slipping one of the pads that Kitty had prepared beneath her.

"How long have you been havin' pains?" Elvie asked.

"A good part of the night," Kitty admitted.

"My Lord . . ." Sara looked at her reproachfully. "Why didn't you send for me earlier? I would have come."

"They were easy. I knew there was plenty of time."

While Faith sat beside her and timed the pains with Usaph's old watch, Elvie cooked up a gruel of cornmeal and water. And in a minute Fanny brought in a pail brimming with milk from Kitty's cow. The word that Kitty was in labor had spread quickly.

Elvie mixed some of the warm, fresh milk into the gruel and sweetened it with a little honey. "It won't pass for grits," she said as she brought it to Kitty, "but it'll strengthen you all the same."

Kitty ate all of it, preparing herself for what she knew was ahead. The rhythms were quickening. She could almost feel the baby pushing to be out with each new pain.

"I told Fanny to send Granny Hawkins," Elvie said, and Kitty nodded.

"I'm going to get up and walk," she said. "Ma always thought it helped."

"It does," said Elvie. "If you feel strong enough . . ."

They got on each side of her, and she stood, the downward pressure so intense that she clamped her lips together, moaning. "It . . . seems so low," she got out. "Like it could come . . . right here."

"It's not ready yet, honey. It just feels that way," Elvie assured her.

She walked for a while, then finally, when the pains were bringing her almost to her knees, consented to lie down again.

"It's a-goin' fast for a first one," Elvie said.

The window was swung open to cool the room—June had commenced hotter than usual—and Kitty saw the flash of lightning still far off, heard the muted rumble of thunder. The night wind had brought clouds in with it.

"That rain's headed this way, sure as you're born," Granny Hawkins croaked as she entered the cabin in a great gust of air. Sara ran to shut the door securely, and the old woman came to lean down over Kitty and croon, her head shaking with its slight palsy. "Don't you worry, honey . . . nothin' to worry over." She turned toward Elvie. "Pains a-comin' hard, are they?"

Elvie nodded, and the two of them drew aside to talk, while Sara sat on one side of Kitty, Faith on the other, each taking a hand as a pain rose and held. Kitty gasped with the intensity of it, feeling the sweat pop out of her brow.

When it was past, Granny Hawkins leaned down over her,

spread her knees and probed, the taloned hands unbelievably gentle. After a moment the old lady cackled her approval. "It's right down there . . . head down the way it ought to be. Let's do some good bearin' down now as we go along."

The rain began, and as the pain took her over, there was a kind of withdrawal, the sense of the rhythm of it claiming her again. Even though it hurt terribly and there were times when she heard herself cry out, that was a thing apart. What was real and compelling was her body, working to expel the baby, because it was time. . . . There seemed a great and natural rightness to it.

Though she heard them talking to her, and she knew when Jemima came in for a few minutes to see how she was doing, it all seemed far removed. She was too wrapped in the process of giving birth.

Toward the last, she thought of her mother, tears brimming.

"Don't cry, Kitty . . . don't be afraid," someone said.

She wanted to tell them that she wasn't afraid, but she was too busy tensing herself for what she knew instinctively was the final push. She gulped in air, vaguely aware of the crash of thunder and the torrent of rain against the cabin roof, and closed her eyes to concentrate on what she had to do . . . straining with every bit of strength she had as the pain signaled. After what seemed an eternity, she felt her own torrent between her legs, felt the warm rush of water that carried the baby with it, and she shrieked in triumph.

"Catch it!" Sara said. "Oh, Lord, Kitty . . . it's a boy!"

Kitty opened her eyes and strained upward, trying to see.

"Wait . . . wait," Faith cautioned her, laughing.

"As fine a boy as ever I seed," Granny Hawkins said, lifting the infant up onto Kitty's belly where she could get a first glimpse of her blood-streaked son. He had a fine mop of black hair, plastered wetly to his head, and he had already begun to catch in his breath and howl, the little arms moving out to clutch at the air and quiver.

"Will you just listen to him?" Elvie exulted. "Don't even need a smack on the behind to git him started. Reminds me of Willie when he was born."

"Oh, Kitty, he's beautiful!" Sara said.

"Scrawny as a skinned rabbit," Granny Hawkins clucked, "but he's good-boned. Gonna be tall . . ."

As the old lady tied off the cord and cut it, Kitty couldn't take her eyes off the baby which still cried lustily, arms and legs catching in close to his body, that tiny underlip trembling. Never before had she felt such an outpouring of love for anything or anyone. It was so strong that tears stung her eyes.

"Don't cry," Sara said, but her face was radiant with understanding.

Kitty reached out to her, and they clasped hands. "He is beautiful, isn't he."

"Oh, yes." Sara's blue eyes glistened with tears, too.

"I don't recollect ever seein' a first'un come into the world with less trouble," Granny declared. "And I'll admit we didn't know as you'd do so well . . . you bein' such a little bit of a thing."

Kitty laughed out loud.

"We're just gonna clean him up a bit," Elvie said. "We'll bring him right back." And she and Sara took the baby away to the table where they could work with him better.

"I'll get his didies," said Faith. She knew that her sister had them ready and waiting in one of the clothes baskets.

Kitty had a mild contraction, and Granny Hawkins pressed at the stomach that seemed so strangely flat now. "Let's git that afterbirth," the old woman said. And with another light pain, and a slight bearing down, it passed.

Kitty let her head fall back to the pillow, exhausted and lightheaded, but still elated. She ached dully throughout the lower part of her body, aware of the mess she lay in.

"Rest easy now," the old lady said. "We'll git you fixed up in a jiffy here."

The baby continued to cry while it was being washed and dried, and Kitty looked toward them anxiously. "Are you sure he's all right?"

"He's fine," Elvie assured her. "Just mad as a hornet at havin' to come out of his nice warm place."

Once he was diapered and wrapped in a soft linen blanket, Sara brought him to Kitty, who reached for him eagerly.

"Put it right up close so's it kin feel your heart a-beatin'," Granny Hawkins directed.

Kitty put the infant to her breast, and he mouthed at the nipple and finally took hold and began to suck, quieting. The women brought a bucket of warm water and soap and cleaned Kitty now, removing the soiled wet cloths beneath her and replacing them with dry bedding.

"We'll take all this with us," said Elvie as she and Faith

gathered the wet things into a large bundle. "We'll get 'em washed up and dried as soon as the sun comes out."

"Martha's likely squallin' to nurse," Faith added. "I'll be back after a while."

Granny Hawkins checked on Kitty one last time, then began to collect her things and put them into her bag. "I expect your man would just as soon come in out'n the rain and see his young'un. I'll tell him on my way," she said.

"I thank you for your help," Kitty called out after her, and the old lady went out into the driving rain, smiling her toothless smile and bobbing that ancient head.

"Cullen hasn't really been standing out there in the rain, has he?" Kitty asked.

"I think he has. . . ." Sara smiled. "Part of the time, anyway. I saw him when I went to close the window some because it was raining in."

The door opened and Cullen entered, dripping and eager. He seemed unable to speak for a moment, then drew near the bed, awestruck as he looked down at his new son who slept now . . . the nipple slipped from his mouth, his fingers curled into tight little fists. "Oh, Kitty lass," he said, a kind of wonder in his voice and face, "ye did fine, I can see. . . ." And he bent down, wet as he was, and kissed her. Neither of them noticed that Sara had slipped out.

Elizabeth sent over a full meal, hot and ready. And later, after Cullen had eaten his fill and dried out before the fire, Kitty insisted that he hold the baby. But to her amusement, Cullen— usually so brash, so devil-may-care—seemed almost frightened. He only held the infant a shaky moment before passing it back to her.

"I can hardly get a handhold, he's so little," he said. "Michael Cullen Claiborne had best get some size on him before I do much holdin'."

"Michael Cullen?" Kitty asked.

"Aye. Does it suit ye?" Cullen's smoky eyes were filled with pride.

She smiled and nodded.

While Sara held Michael, Kitty fetched the cap that Rebecca Boone had given her and came back to slip it over the infant's head and tie the ribbons beneath his chin. "Look at that," she said. "It won't be too long before it fits."

"It's beautiful," Sara said. "Look at him. . . ." The baby pursed his mouth. "I think he knows he's dressed up."

Kitty laughed as the little features screwed up, face reddening. "And doesn't seem to like it a bit." She took off the cap and put it aside. But the baby squirmed and fussed, still unsettled, waving his fists. Sara shifted him up to her shoulder, crooning to him and patting his back, but the fussing developed into a full-fledged howl.

"Lord help me," Kitty said as she uncovered a full breast and reached for him, "he's just like his daddy . . . wants what he wants when he wants it."

Sara laughed. "I can't believe he's only a week old," she said. "Look at how fat he's getting."

"He should be. He nurses enough." Kitty looked down at him, feeling the strong tug at her nipple and that surge of love she always felt when she looked at his face. "Do you think he looks like Cullen?"

Sara tilted her head and considered that. "Yes . . . I guess so. It's hard to tell, he's so little."

The baby nursed contentedly, fastened onto Kitty's breast and oblivious of everything else, until finally, glutted, he let the nipple slip away, eyes closed, his mouth still puckered into a pink circle. Kitty put him into the cradle that Ezekial Turner had made for her.

"I'm only using it in the daytime when I can keep my eye on him," she whispered. "Even if it is summer. Two weeks ago I killed a snake in the cabin. I don't want him down so close to the floor without me watching. At night I take him in the bed with me."

As she came back to her chair, Kitty saw the look in Sara's eyes as she gazed down at the sleeping infant, and she realized what feelings Michael must engender in her after the loss of her own baby. She put out a quick hand to Sara. "I don't know what I'd do if you didn't help me so much with him," she said. "He makes a lot of extra work. I doubt I could get it all done without you."

That afternoon Roman rode into the fort and, upon hearing about the new arrival, came to the Claiborne cabin, an outright grin stretched across the usually sober face. "Well now . . ." He swung up the baby with a natural ease that surprised Kitty. "It appears that you and Cullen have done yourselves proud!"

"Roman Gentry," she said smiling, "will you tell me how

you come to be so good with a little one? Cullen is still afraid he'll break him."

Roman turned his pleasantly tanned face toward her, his blue eyes widening. "When I was with Daniel and Rebecca, it seemed there was always a baby to play with." He hoisted Michael up higher and jiggled him—which seemed to suit the infant well enough—and peered into the little face. "I do believe he looks like the Gentrys," he said solemnly, and Kitty laughed.

Before nightfall a courier brought the news that France had signed an alliance with the Americans against the British . . . that little over a month before, the Marquis de Lafayette had stood with General Washington as the troops were reviewed on a green field in Pennsylvania. And as the lean, handsome marquis had pledged the support of his king, the hurrahs of the men, according to those present, were all but deafening.

Boonesborough celebrated, too. With open cabin doors and tapers burning, and singing and fiddling far into the night. Michael was fretful with all the commotion, but once Kitty had him down, she pored over the letter that had come from Rebecca.

Dear Kitty . . . I am having Israel write this for me—since I never lerned how. I hope you have been safely deliver'd and you and your child have surviv'd well.

Our life here in the Yadkin is comfortable and the children are growing used to being gone from Boonesborough. My family here are glad to have us, it being some years since they set eyes on their grandchildren.

I am as resign'd as I will ever be over the loss of Daniel & will live out the rest of my life here I would expect.

yr devot'd friend
Rebecca

PART FOUR

❄

Summer 1778

✳ 22 ✳

THE VEGETABLE PATCH LAY LUSH AND GREEN IN THE HOT summer sun, bees droning and dipping down to the scattering of bean blossoms still left on the vines, then rising to soar toward the cornfield where green pumpkins the size of hog bladders lay thick among the stalks. What little breeze there'd been earlier had stopped, and Kitty could feel the perspiration trickle between her breasts as she walked down toward the spring in the hollow, a carry yoke over her shoulders, pails swinging from each side.

Security had loosened somewhat at the fort, as they had had no further trouble from the Indians since the salt makers were taken back in the winter. Though in general the women still went for water in a group, Kitty had used all of hers washing during the morning—keeping Michael clean and dry required a lot of washing—and the man on sentry had simply waved her through the gate with the mild observation that he would "keep an eye peeled fer ye."

She loved being outside the walls. It brought back memories of the place on Otter Creek. Cullen had promised that when he thought it was safe and Michael a little older, he would take the two of them there. She wanted Michael to know that that was home and one day they'd be going there to stay. Maybe, she thought, she would even take him all the way down on Roman's land to the junction of the creek and the river . . . let him see how beautiful it was.

A pair of crows set up a fine cawing and flew away as she approached the spring, and the heat shimmered before her, making the sky seem hazy. Her back and shoulder muscles ached as she filled the buckets. There hardly seemed a minute now when she didn't have something waiting for her to do. The baby did

make extra work, but he was worth it. And thank goodness for
Sara, who was minding Michael now.

The water sloshed and dripped as she fastened the pails and
then stooped to slide the shoulder yoke into place and straighten
up carefully. No use to fetch water if you were going to spill
half of it in the carrying, she was thinking . . . when her eye
strayed to the edge of the trees toward the river and her stomach
seemed to drop away as she saw the figure emerge—*God save
her*—saw the naked brown chest and the gleam of the head, bald
but for the jutting scalplock. . . .

She stood frozen for a moment, and then, as the Indian began
to sprint toward her, rifle in hand, she sucked in a breath and
threw off the yoke, turning to run in the same motion. But the
ropes tripped her and she sprawled headlong in the tall grass
and mint that grew there in the damp earth, oddly aware of the
smell of it . . . as if it would be fixed there forever in her mind
with the terror. Michael . . . Michael . . . It drummed within
her as she scrambled to regain her footing. She must get back
to her baby. . . .

As she hauled herself upright, her shoe caught in the hem of
her skirt and she could feel the material rip as she was brought
to one knee again. She twisted to see back over her shoulder,
her breath ragged, remembering the Negro girl who'd been killed
right out here. Her heart almost stopped as she realized how
quickly the Indian was closing the gap between them. He loped
toward her, waving his arms jerkily.

A cry went up from the fort, and at the same time the Shawnee
shouted something, a word that sounded almost like he was
calling her name . . . but that couldn't be.

She was on her feet now, but something made her look back
at him again, something about the way he was waving his arms
. . . about the scalplock, the color of it. It was wrong somehow,
too light . . .

"Kitty . . . Kitty Claiborne!" She heard him clearly now and
saw the light eyes in that dark lean face, studying it . . .

Recognition hit her like a blow to the chest just as the crack
of a rifle echoed from the fort and the bullet kicked up a plug
of sod not ten feet in front of its target.

She whirled toward the gates and screamed, waving her arms
frantically. "Don't shoot! For God's sake, don't shoot! It's Daniel!" She backed up, putting herself squarely in line with the
oncoming figure and holding her arms out from her to make

herself bigger, trying to block any more shots. *"Don't . . . don't shoot!"*

"Kitty . . ." Daniel, looking for all the world like a Shawnee brave, approached with his hands and rifle high to convince the fort sentries that he meant her no harm.

"Daniel, it is you!" She took in the leaned-down body and gleaming head, hairless except for the scalplock. "You're alive . . . my God, you're alive!"

That unmistakable wide mouth of his curved into a broad grin. "It would seem so," he said, then shouted toward the fort, "Hold up, boys! I'd hate for you to shoot me after I've all but wore myself out to get here!"

There was more shouting from inside the fort, and then the gates swung open and Squire Boone emerged cautiously, his rifle at the ready. He had covered about half the distance to them, squinting in the sunlight, when suddenly he dropped the gun to his side and set out in a trot.

"Daniel . . . praise God . . . Daniel!" he shouted. And coming together, the two brothers embraced, tears marking Squire's scarred cheek.

There was an outpouring of men through the gate now, the Old Colonel and Flanders Callaway . . . Sam Henderson and John Holder . . . Winfield Burdette and some of the others.

"I would have killed 'im dead, if'n it hadn't been for Mistress Claiborne," the on-duty sentry kept telling anyone who would listen.

Colonel Callaway and Daniel clasped hands solemnly. "I never thought to see you again," said the Old Colonel. "And for damned sure not done out like one of the savages!"

The laughter that ensued broke some of the tension, and Daniel was ushered back to the fort as Flanders and Winfield caught up Kitty's spilled buckets and refilled them to carry in for her.

Inside the gates, the people had begun to gather, and they stood nudging one another and muttering at first sight of Daniel, hard put to see in the Shawnee before them the leader they thought they had lost. But as recognition came, they fell still for a moment, stunned at this near return from the grave. Then Ezekial Turner let out a whoop. "It's him! Damnation if it ain't Daniel hisself!" And they all began to turn to one another and nod their heads, pushing in closer to see him the better.

Jemima came running, white-faced, and as Daniel clasped her to him, she sobbed with joy, unable to speak, she was so overcome at seeing the father she'd thought dead. Daniel leaned his head forward and patted her, his own eyes reddening.

Sara came up the path toward the knot of people, Michael in her arms. She stared at Daniel. "I heard all the commotion," she whispered to Kitty, "and then Willie Porter came running to say that Daniel was alive and back, and looking just like an Indian . . ." She seemed unable to take her eyes from him. Kitty took the baby from her.

"What of Cajer and James?" Flanders asked him.

"Can you tell us anything?" the Old Colonel put in.

Daniel nodded. "James was took to Detroit and I don't know his fate, but Micajah was well, though a prisoner, the last time I saw him at Chillicothe."

"My brother Latham," Ben Tyler pleaded. "Do you know what happened to him?"

"What about Rafer?" Blandford Moore pushed forward to ask about his son.

"I wisht I could tell you for certain," Daniel said, lifting his head and shaking it sadly. "Latham was among those of us took to Detroit."

"Detroit?" Ben swiped at his nose, and his brother Todd gripped his shoulder.

"You were took to the Hair-Buyer?" asked Winfield Burdette.

"Some of us. Latham was alive when the Indians hauled me off again. I can't say what happpened after." Daniel turned to Moore. "Rafer was in a party that split away early on from the one I was in. I never saw him again."

The sun was bearing down now, and they all crowded into the nearest blockhouse. "What happened at the Licks, Daniel?" Squire asked him.

"In good time," said Daniel. "Right now I must warn you that Black Fish intends to attack the fort again."

They looked at one another bleakly, suddenly silent except for Maggie Hamilton's "Oh, my God . . ." Horace put his arm around her, but she drew away.

"How soon?" Colonel Callaway asked.

"I don't know. I'd been bidin' my time to escape when I was took with a party of braves and squaws to make salt at a lick up on the Scioto. Chief Black Fish was along. After we'd been there a few days, a war party come in with their tails between their legs. Seems they'd raided over into Virginia and got the worst of it. I heard Black Fish determine that it was time to strike at Boonesborough, and I figured I must get away pretty quick.

"We'd started back toward Chillicothe when the dogs flushed up a flock of turkeys and the braves all took off after 'em . . . leavin' me behind with the women. I knew it was my chance, and I took it. I got here quick as I could to warn you."

"How many?" the Old Colonel asked.

Daniel shook his head. "I don't know for sure. Enough to give us some trouble, and I'm satisfied the English will give them all they need in the way of guns and supplies . . . maybe even send some of their own officers along with them."

Little Lureen Porter began to wail thinly, and Elvie shushed her.

"I know there are still questions yet, but I'd be obliged for a little time with my family. . . ." Daniel looked down at Jemima, who still stood within the crook of his arm as if afraid to let go of him. "Where's your mother?" he asked.

Jemima sniffled and wiped her nose on the corner of her apron. "Ma's not here. She took the others and went back."

There was a moment's silence while Daniel looked from his daughter to his brother. "Back to North Carolina?" he asked finally. "All of them?"

"She was sure you were comin' back at first," Jemima said forlornly. "She waited . . ."

"Rebecca give up finally. Just like the rest of us," Squire told him. "We all thought you was dead, Daniel. Rebecca thought it'd be best if she went back to her people."

Daniel tugged at an earlobe, and the lines of his face seemed drawn down. "Well," he said after a minute, "I don't expect I could blame her for that." He gave Jemima another hug, then drew himself up. "If there's aught to eat around here, I could put it to good use. I haven't had much but berries for four days. Got my powder wet crossin' the Ohio, and was travelin' too fast to set a snare and wait for somethin' to step in it."

"How'd you come by the rifle and powder, Dan'l?" Winfield Burdette called out.

"Well . . ." Daniel scratched at what hair he had left. "The fact of the matter is that after we'd been captured a while, old Black Fish took a likin' to me and took me for his son."

There were surprised looks all around and considerable nudging. "Just leave it to Dan'l," somebody said, grinning.

"If a way can be found, he'll find it," another agreed.

"Give me the name of Sheltowee. It means 'The Big Turtle,' " Daniel confessed, grinning himself. "That's when the old squaws plucked near all of my hair out the first time. Anyway, they had commenced to let me go hunting sometimes

. . . always keeping a close watch. But what they didn't know was I was taking half the powder they let me have and hiding it away. When I got my chance to run off, I took it and the gun they let me use.''

"That's the damnedest story!" Flanders laughed.

The baby had lain against Kitty's shoulder and fallen asleep. And while some of the women hurried to fetch what they had cooked up, Daniel admired the infant.

"He looks to be a fine, healthy boy," he told Kitty. "I'm proud for you and Cullen.''

The food was carried into the blockhouse and spread out on the slab table where Daniel attacked it with relish, the others gathering near to watch. But he had hardly wiped the last crumb away before the questions about the capture of the salt makers began again.

"I was took by surprise," he admitted, picking a sliver of venison from between his teeth. "I'd gone to hunt that morning and had killed a buffalo. I'd skinned it out and loaded the meat on my horse and was walking back to camp when I was set upon by four Shawnee. At first I thought I could cut the meat loose, climb on my horse, and escape, but the danged buffalo grease had froze my knife in the sheath, and before I could break it out, they had me.

"I was some shocked when they took me to their camp and I saw upward of a hundred of 'em . . . including Black Fish . . . all in paint. There was a handful of British soldiers amongst 'em, too.''

There were a few muttered oaths around the room.

"I knew enough Shawnee," Daniel went on, "to pick up most of what they were sayin'. And for the rest of it they had an escaped slave—his name was Pompey—that spoke for them. He understood Shawnee pretty good.

"Black Fish said he could not rest until Cornstalk's death was avenged. He planned to attack Boonesborough." Daniel shook his head. "I knew well enough that if he did, the fort would fall. With so many of us at the Blue Licks, there was no way it could hold.

"I lied to him point-blank. Told him that the fort was strong with men. That if he attacked, many of his braves would die, but he replied that it would be in a good cause . . . that maybe then Cornstalk's spirit could rest.''

Daniel was quiet for a minute, the deepset eyes distant. He drew a long breath. "I thought of all the women and children here, including my own. I saw nothing else to do. I told him again that it was a bad time to attack the fort, and that I would lead him to my men and have them surrender to him instead, provided he would give his word that they wouldn't have to run the gauntlet.''

There was a stunned silence in the room.

"You led them back to the salt camp?" Ben Tyler's voice came harshly, his thin nostrils quivering.

"Aye. I did. And to this day it's my firm belief that you would all be dead if I had not.''

Some turned away to talk among themselves, others came up to put a supporting hand to Daniel's shoulder.

Colonel Callaway sat, clearly troubled by the revelation, still and grave-faced for a moment. Then he leaned across the table to clasp Daniel's hand. ''After you were taken, I did what I could here at Boonesborough. But Will Smith was given military command. He had some business over at Harrod's Town. He'll be back in a day or so. I expect he'll want a full report.''

Daniel nodded.

Though Major William Bailey Smith—the man who had gone to North Carolina for help the year before—was still in fact the commander of Boonesborough, the people clearly looked to their restored leader to guide them now, and Will Smith himself seemed to give a tacit approval, deferring to Daniel in most matters. And while Daniel admitted that he was moved to set out at once to bring back Rebecca and the children, there was no way, he declared, that he could in conscience leave the fort while it was under threat of attack.

On his orders, repairs were begun on the neglected palisades and gates. Provisions were laid in . . . meat made into jerk or salted down, all the vegetables that were ready picked and brought in to store or dry. Guns were cleaned, flints changed, and patches prepared.

Roman came into the fort without knowing that Daniel was back, and at first sight of that Shawnee-style head above the frontiersman's worn buckskins, his jaw dropped. But then the keen eyes focused on the familiar features, and he swung down from his horse. The two men clasped one another, wordless in that moment.

But there was talk enough later. Roman brought news that George Clark and his men had come down the river from Fort Pitt with twenty families along, then had left the new settlers to start building cabins near the falls of the Ohio and had taken his men and gone on some miltary mission, the nature of which was unknown to those left behind. They did say that Clark had been promoted to colonel now.

With Cullen having come in the day before, the two scouts, and Daniel, and the Old Colonel closeted themselves, as they had so often in the past, to discuss what must be done in the present emergency . . . how to best protect the fort from the expected attack. Will Smith joined them but listened more than he talked.

"I'd give every piece of land I've laid claim to," Daniel said, "if George Clark and his boys was headed here. We could use them sure enough."

Roman shook his head. "No chance. I believe they headed downriver."

"Where's Butler?"

Cullen tilted his chair back against the wall and leaned his head against the rough logs. "I thought he was with Logan, but he's not. I'll wager he's with Clark."

Daniel's mouth drew down and he rubbed a hand over his chin. "How many men do we have now?"

"Thirty," the Old Colonel said, "and some boys."

"Well," Daniel said, his spirits lifting, "we've fought with less. Let's get off a courier to the Holston settlements asking for help of them . . . then on to Colonel Campbell in Virginia. We'll tell them that we're in fine spirits and intend to fight hard, but a few extra men wouldn't go amiss."

"Might be we could raise some volunteers from Harrod's Town or St. Asaph's," Cullen said.

He and Roman rode to the two forts, and in a few days five men had come in from Harrod's Town, and fifteen from little St. Asaph's, along with messages from Harrod and Logan expressing their delight that Daniel was alive and free. All in all, that swelled their manpower to fifty.

"While I don't feel entirely easy," Daniel declared, "I feel some better."

With everything done that could be done, and sentries on constant watch, there was nothing left but to wait through the long hot days.

Kitty kept herself busy with her work and the baby, who, oblivious to the threat they lived under, was clearly thriving and lusty in his demands for the breast. But there were times when she would catch herself listening for the slightest sound from beyond the compound, her eyes going anxiously to him in his cradle or on the bed. The thought that any harm might come to him was so sharp she could hardly bear it.

Cullen and Roman were out almost constantly, and Sara spent a good deal of time with Kitty and the baby. She had come to love Michael almost as if he were her own, and young as he was, he sometimes appeared to recognize her, cooing and smiling when she talked to him.

The days passed with still no sign of Indians, but one hot afternoon, scarcely a month after Daniel had returned, still another of the salt makers returned to Boonesborough.

William Hancock, hollow-cheeked and thin to gauntness, helloed the fort from across the river, and Flanders and John Holder went across in a canoe to bring him in. They had to help him the last few yards. He had always been a stout man but now seemed on the verge of collapse.

"Put him down here in the shade," Daniel directed. "Somebody bring him a drink of water."

Kitty, who had gathered with the others, watched as Will Hancock leaned weakly back against the rough logs of the palisade, his chest pumping, tears oozing out of eyes ringed about with dark circles. Though he didn't seem to bear any serious wounds, he was scratched and bruised. His clothing, which appeared to be the same he'd had on when he was captured, hung in tatters about the bony legs and arms.

"I been nine days in the comin'," he gasped out. "Bless God, I never thought I'd make it!"

"Thank God you did, Will." Daniel gripped that blade of a shoulder.

To Kitty's surprise, a sudden anger blazed in those cavernous eyes as Hancock gazed up at Daniel. "No thanks to you that I'm alive," he said.

There was a shocked silence all around.

"Take it easy, Will," Daniel said.

"He led the savages right to us," Hancock accused, his voice rising high and cracking. "Told us to put our guns in a stack on the ground."

"I did what I had to do." Daniel's rejoinder was quiet, his voice controlled.

"He's near out of his head with starvation and wanderin' around out there," Winfield offered.

"Let's get him inside where he can rest and eat," Colonel Callaway said. "He'll be all right."

"Mind you don't give him too much right off," Granny Hawkins cautioned, "it'll just come right up if'n you do."

But as Flanders and John prepared to hoist him up between them again, Hancock lifted a staying hand. "Wait . . . I got to tell you that Black Fish aims to attack."

"How soon?" Daniel asked quickly.

Hancock shot a scornful glance his way. "I couldn't wait around to find out just the exact day." He coughed, his chest heaving weakly, and then spat a gob of spittle sideways into the grass. "He was in a fine state when he come back from Paint Creek Town after you'd run off. First off he said there'd be no attack. But then the bloody British officers rode in carryin' presents . . . a dozen or more packhorses loaded down, and more promised. They palavered for days, and it was settled they'd attack. They're a-gatherin' now . . . probably three or four hunnert of 'em. . . ."

The numbers struck them all silent. Kitty looked into Sara's frightened eyes and then down at Michael, her heart squeezing at the curve of that tiny nose, covered now with a fine dew of perspiration . . . at the little mouth, so delicate yet, but unmistakably Cullen's.

"We'll be ready for them," Daniel said.

Despite the brave words, no one rested easy at Boonesborough during the next few days. Though they had checked every rifle and gone over every post in the palisades, everything was checked again, and the water barrels kept filled to their brims. As the corn ripened, they began to pick the ears, teams of men taking turns working in the fields or standing guard with rifles ready, while small patrols scouted the nearby woods and riverbank.

With all the corn safely in, the sheds full up, and more than one cabin loft stuffed to the roof, Daniel chafed at the waiting. With the approach of September, he declared that he had decided to take a party of volunteers and find out for himself what was happening.

"This is not the time to leave the fort, Daniel," Colonel Callaway objected at once.

"Believe me, it's the best way," Daniel insisted. "I know all their villages like the back of my hand now. And"—his eyebrows slanted upward above the deepset eyes—"if while we're there we get the chance to do them some mischief . . . steal some of their horses, or do some damage to their crops, it just might take their minds off comin' down here to do us harm for a while.''

"And if they attack while you're away?'' Callaway countered.

"They'll not get by me. We'll know if they're on the way. That's part of the reason for going.''

Will Smith remained silent, and Colonel Callaway paced the length of the blockhouse and back, his lips compressed, deep ridges between his silver brows.

"How many men would you figure to take?'' the Old Colonel asked finally.

"Twenty. But I'll leave Roman and Cullen here to scout.''

"Twenty men . . .'' The Colonel stared. "It would weaken us too much. They could take us like turkeys gone to roost! Damme . . . I'm dead against it!''

The two old friends of so many years faced one another for a long moment. Daniel was the first to speak. "I'm sorry, Richard, I aim to go.''

And that very afternoon he called everyone together and explained his intention, asking for volunteers. He got more than he could use, and picking his twenty, he directed them to get ready to ride. They would take little in the way of food. "We'll kill meat enough along the way,'' he said. "Be ready to leave at sunrise.''

Most of the fort turned out to see them go. And though Callaway's back was stiff, his face set, at the last possible moment he grasped Daniel's shoulder. "God keep you, Daniel,'' he said.

Daniel grinned and solemnly shook his old friend's hand. But Elizabeth, standing beside Kitty, bowed her head sadly. "I don't think Richard knows what to make of Daniel since he's come back,'' she said.

A new kind of waiting began for the penned-up settlers—the waiting for Daniel to return with word of what Black Fish was up to, or, worse, an attack before their full garrison returned.

"They won't get by Daniel,'' Roman assured them, and both he and Cullen scouted close in now, coming in and out of the fort almost daily.

"Won't it ever end?'' Sara asked Kitty.

Kitty, usually ready with quick answers of encouragement, just rested her free hand gently on the top of Michael's head as he nursed, felt the fine dark fuzz and the soft spot, the faint pulsing there. . . . "I don't know,'' she said finally.

But after an absence of just over a week, Daniel and the others rode in on a Sunday evening, all of them tired and dirty and hungry, their faces holding a grim answer.

"We crossed the Ohio and pushed on up on the Scioto . . . toward Paint Creek Town," Daniel said between huge mouthfuls of food. "But when we got there it was plain to see there wasn't a warrior in sight. I knew then that Black Fish was on the move, and we hightailed it back across the river and come upon him and upward o' four hundred braves encamped at the Blue Licks. There was maybe another twenty-five or thirty of the British. They were well provisioned with a whole train of packhorses . . . and gettin' ready to leave. We had to ride fast if we was to beat them here."

Daniel shook his head and looked up grimly. "I'd say they're not far behind, gents. Let's be ready for 'em."

* 23 *

A S DANIEL HAD PREDICTED, THE SHAWNEE CAME THE following day, not swarming up from the steep riverbanks as they had before, but riding into distant view at the top of Hackberry Ridge at a point opposite the fort and continuing down toward the clearing in two long, measured lines, horses held to a steady walk, British flags flying in the stiff breeze. The procession raised small clouds of dust, the morning sunlight highlighting gleaming coppery faces and chests streaked with vermilion, catching the color of the resplendent feathers that bedecked coarse black scalplocks.

As the lead riders reached the edge of the clearing, the lines divided and fanned out, still out of rifle range, circling around on either side toward the river until the stockade was ringed but for the stream side. And in the center out in front, down where the lines had split, Black Fish sat his horse, feathered staff in hand, the great war chief of the Shawnee clearly recognizable as his face turned in profile to outline the prominent nose and heavy line of his jaw.

From the outside the little fortress looked as if everyone were still asleep, but a quiet alarm had been called minutes before at first sight of the Indians, and the men and boys had taken up places in the blockhouses and on the walls, grimly silent in the face of the largest force ever to go against a Kentucky fort. In the southwest blockhouse Daniel and Cullen and Roman had gone up to the roomy loft for a better view, and now they watched through the loopholes, Cullen swearing beneath his breath.

"Would ye look out there," he said. "I spy Mingos, Wyandots . . . Cherokees in amongst 'em."

"Not to mention the redcoats," Roman added.

Daniel nodded grimly. "And a few green . . . Canadian. They've come prepared this time. But I own I thought they'd try to surprise us. Never expected them to come ridin' up in plain sight, takin' their own sweet time."

"They must have crossed upriver and come down under cover of the ridge until they were right opposite us," Cullen said.

As the three men watched and wondered at the unusual action taken by Black Fish, down on the lower floor, back in the inner corner of the blockhouse, Kitty finished nursing Michael and handed him over to Sara, fastening up her bodice with a strange inner calm now that the confrontation was really upon them.

The two women had planned it together, choosing the inner corner because of its greater safety. They'd brought the cradle and a basket of the baby's clothing and diapers from the cabin and put them there, along with the rocking chair.

Kitty leaned over to kiss her son's cheek, aware of the sour smell of him. There'd been no time to bathe him as she usually did right after breakfast, but, happily unaware of that, he lay contentedly against Sara's shoulder, eyes half closed as he burped noisily.

"I'll see to him," Sara promised, her face pale.

Kitty nodded and went to join some of the other women who'd set up a line to reload for the men the moment the firing started.

But to everyone's surprise, the Indians made no hostile move. And a minute later a low murmur ran through the blockhouse as a black man in Indian garb came walking slowly down into the hollow, a large square piece of white cloth tied to a stick which he waved back and forth.

"Pompey," Daniel said to Cullen and Roman. "Remember . . . I told you about him." He pulled back to address the other riflemen down the wall of the building. "Hold your fire, boys.'' And then to his son Daniel Morgan: "Run downstairs and tell them that, then go over to Colonel Callaway and Major Smith in the blockhouse across from us and tell them the same thing. Tell 'em we'll see what they have to say before we start shootin'.''

Daniel Morgan sped off to do his father's bidding as Cullen beckoned Daniel back to the loophole. Pompey had reached the big old sycamores and started on toward the spring, still waving the flag slowly back and forth, a cocky smile on his face, though his eyes were wide with fear.

''Cap'n Boone,'' he called once and then again. ''Cap'n Boone . . . Chief Black Fish have brought a letter fo' you from Guv'ner Hamilton hisself. He say fo' you to come out and he give it to you.''

Cullen drew back and eyed Daniel. ''I don't know that I would do that, Daniel,'' he said. And Roman shook his head in agreement.

Daniel pulled at his earlobe and considered the situation. Understanding the Indian mind as well as any white man alive, he knew that to answer right away would seem to be an admission of weakness. He waved everyone present to silence.

Pompey's black skin gleamed with perspiration as he grew ever more uncomfortable standing out there in the exposed position. He shifted from foot to foot. ''Cap'n Boone,'' he called out again. ''The chief, he say come out so's he kin talk with you.''

It was quiet out there, except for an occasional nicker of a horse or the stamping of a hoof.

Colonel Callaway came hurrying up the steep steps to the loft, his chest pumping with the exertion of running over from the opposite blockhouse. ''What do you make of it, Daniel?'' he got out.

But before Daniel could answer, Roman directed their attention back to the loopholes. ''Best take a look at this.''

Black Fish had climbed down from his horse and now reached for a blanket thrown over the flanks of one of the mounts beside him. With a peremptory gesture to the knot of subchiefs and warriors that surrounded him, he walked out alone, down into the hollow and toward the stockade.

Even with the years advancing on him, he was still a tall and powerful man, and his voice reflected that as he called out, the deep timbre of it carrying clearly on the bright morning air. ''Sheltowee . . . my son. I ask you to come speak. No harm to you . . . I have no weapons. You need none. You have the word of your father.'' He continued on, his stride wide and steady until he had reached the shade of the sycamore tree. There he spread his blanket on the ground and sat down, his back very straight, ignoring the slave Pompey, who stood off to the side and wiped at the sweat dripping into his eyes.

Daniel leaned his rifle up against the wall and removed the knife from its sheath at his belt and handed it to Cullen. "I'm going out," he said.

The Old Colonel, still trying to catch his breath, set his mouth stubbornly. "I'll go with you."

Roman had already put his gun aside without a word, and now, as Cullen started to do the same, Daniel shook his head. "Someone has to stay behind to help Will Smith in case something goes wrong out there. If you're determined to go with me, Richard, so be it. But you two stay here. I don't have a doubt that Black Fish's word is good, but if I'm wrong and we should be taken, give the order to fire away, boys. Pass that along to Squire and the others."

Daniel detached the ramrod from his rifle and took it along with him, calling for a piece of white cloth as he went down the stairs.

Left behind, Roman eyed Cullen. "I think one of us will be enough here," he said. "I'm going along with them."

"How come you and not me?" Cullen demanded.

The slow smile touched Roman's face. "Because I thought of it first."

After turning over his rifle to Cullen, he hurried down the steps to the lower floor of the crowded blockhouse, so intent on what he must do that he failed to see Sara back in the corner, her face pinched and colorless as, clutching the baby to her, she watched him go through the door. Outside, he overtook Daniel and the Old Colonel at the gates.

"I thought I gave you an order," Daniel said, his eyes twinkling.

"I decided not to take it," Roman returned agreeably.

Winfield Burdette lifted the thick wooden bar and swung the gate open enough for them to step through. Daniel went first, holding up his ramrod, which now had a strip of bleached linen tied to the end of it. "If things should go amiss for us out there," he whispered to Winfield in passing, "slam that gate shut and bar it." Winfield nodded grimly.

They walked abreast, Daniel in the middle waving the ramrod for all to see. Colonel Callaway seemed to have gotten his wind back, and they maintained an easy stride, careful not to acknowledge by even so much as a glance the long lines of warriors who eyed them silently. They knew that would be regarded as a sign of fear.

Black Fish at first gazed ahead impassively, but as they neared, that reserve was breached and the black eyes moved to Daniel, the furrowed coppery face setting into lines that revealed a mixture of gladness and grief.

"Sheltowee, my son . . ." He stood and embraced Daniel, tears marking the weathered cheeks.

"My father . . ." Daniel returned the embrace as Roman and Colonel Callaway looked on, the Old Colonel staring in open astonishment.

They had both spoken in the Shawnee dialect, but Roman knew enough of it to understand what they were saying to one another, and from Callaway's reaction, he was sure that the older man did, too.

"Why have you run away from your family?" Black Fish reproached Daniel. "There has been much grieving in our lodges for Sheltowee."

Daniel reddened slightly about the ears as the stately chief put a sorrowful finger out to the hair that had been allowed to grow back in the way of the white man.

"I wished to see my white family again," Daniel answered. "My wife and my children."

Black Fish drew himself up, the grief still strong in his expression. "Why did you not ask me? I would have let you come here to see them."

"I did not know that," Daniel said.

The deep-set, jet-black eyes of Black Fish flickered toward Roman and then to Colonel Callaway. "You have brought your lesser chiefs with you, Sheltowee?"

Though a muscle moved under Daniel's eye, his expression never changed. "I have," he said.

"They are known to me. The Cal-ea-way fought our people long ago . . . but he is a true warrior. The other is also true. He is the one our Cherokee brothers call Firehair."

Daniel nodded.

Black Fish turned and beckoned to his own subchiefs. Catahecassa—Black Hoof—came, tall and sharp-faced and sober, followed by Moluntha, who was just the opposite with his wide heavy face and body, his unfailing good nature. They were joined by Black Bird, the Chippewa chief. All sat down, legs folded in front of them, and Black Fish invited the three white men to do likewise. Though the Old Colonel's bones creaked noticeably, he managed to do it.

"I have come," Black Fish began formally, "to call upon your promise that you would deliver the fort to me in the heat of the summer, Sheltowee."

Roman could feel the slight tremor that passed through Colonel Callaway beside him, but the old man said nothing.

"You said," the chief continued, "that it would be a better time to take the women and children on their long ride. I have waited, as you counseled. And now the Hamilton chief of Detroit wishes it so. I have letter from him to you."

Daniel creased his brow and appeared to be pondering the whole thing. "I will take the letter back with me—" He paused as if still thinking, tugging at his earlobe. "—but I have been gone a long time from my fort, and in my absence the great Virginia father has sent a bigger captain here, and he may not want to surrender. . . ."

The faces of the four chiefs were guarded as they stared at Daniel, but he grinned at them disarmingly.

"Give me two days"—he held up two fingers—"and I will see if I can persuade him."

The breeze ruffled the red and yellow feathers that decorated Black Fish's scalplock, the hair standing straight and stiff, shiny with bear grease. A bee buzzed near, but he brushed it away. Finally he gave a quick jerk of his head. "It shall be as you say, Sheltowee." And with another of the peremptory waves of his hand, the letter from Hamilton was brought to him and he passed it over to Daniel as they all rose to their feet.

"I have brought forty packhorses to carry the women and children and the old to Detroit," he said. "You have the word of Black Fish, chief of the Shawnee, that they will be well treated there. And as a token of my friendship, I bring your white brothers seven roasted buffalo tongues." He gestured toward the seven braves who carried the tongues toward them, and the air was suddenly permeated with the mouth-watering smell.

"I thank Black Fish, my father," Daniel said.

Black Fish nodded, but his eyes glittered dangerously. "You must warn this great captain, Sheltowee, that if he does not surrender, I will put to death all within—but for the young squaws. Those I will keep for myself."

Daniel nodded, raising his hand, palm open to Black Fish, and then he turned away. Roman fell into step beside him, Callaway on the other side, and the three of them walked slowly back toward the gates. The seven braves who carried the roasted tongues followed several paces behind.

Halfway there, Daniel called out to those waiting and watching inside. "Be easy, boys. Black Fish has sent us a present." And when they were close up onto the gates, he instructed the braves to place the tongues, which were wrapped in leaves, on the ground, and they did as he said and turned back.

The gate swung partially open, and Flanders, Winfield, and several of the older boys came out to get the meat, grinning at Daniel and Roman and the Old Colonel. Squire came hurrying to give a quick nod of his head at his brother, a satisfied set to his mouth, while Ezekial Turner began to poke at the roasted tongues with the tip of his rifle as soon as they were all inside.

"Wouldn't be surprised if they ain't pizened," he observed, his whiskery face screwing up.

Daniel quickly drew Squire's hunting knife from its sheath and leaned down to cut a chunk of meat from one of the tongues and pop it into his mouth, chewing with obvious relish and licking his fingers. "Tastes prime to me, boys," he said once he'd swallowed. "If I was you, I'd eat up, 'cause it just might be some time before we get any more such."

He wiped his hands down his buckskin leggings. "Call some of the women to come get these," he ordered. "Scatter out a dozen men to keep watch and get everybody else together. We've got some talkin' to do."

"It looks as if we have," Colonel Callaway said, his dark eyes snapping. "How could you have told him that you'd deliver the fort over to him, Daniel?"

"I'd have told him anything, Richard, to keep him from attacking then."

The Old Colonel gave his head a shake, his face revealing the difficulty he was having in accepting Daniel's actions. "Seems to me that they wouldn't be here now," he said, "if you hadn't told them that."

"*We* wouldn't be here now if I hadn't told them that!" Daniel snapped. "Boonesborough would have fallen with so few here to protect it. Everyone would have been killed or carried off and the fort burned!"

Cullen came up to them. "Well now," he said, his burr thickening, "have ye forgot that the enemy is out *there*?" He jerked his thumb at the gates behind them.

"Cullen's right," Roman said. "There'll be time enough,

God willing, to argue who should have said what when this is over and the fort is safe."

"You're right," the Old Colonel said at once. "Gentlemen, I apologize."

Though Colonel Callaway had agreed to put aside the dispute until a more propitious time, there were others who were ready to take up the questioning when the letter from Governor Hamilton was read to the assembled group. In it, Hamilton made much the same offer that Black Fish had, promising that all would be treated well at Detroit in return for their loyalty as British subjects, and reminding Daniel that during his brief stay at that British stronghold, they had had a pleasant visit together and Daniel had promised to surrender his people peacefully.

"It's som'at strange to me that you'd be takin' tea with the Hair-Buyer, Daniel." Blandford Moore's fists were clenched in helpless anger. His grieving for his lost son had taken an obvious toll; lines etched deeply from nose to mouth.

"The man's a murderer!" Ben Tyler called out. "That's a fact well known to all. And I wonder that any God-fearing man would have aught to do with him!"

Daniel stood calmly under the onslaught. "I reckon if I found myself backed into a cave by a big old catamount and he leaped upon my chest, I'd do my best to make him purr . . . even if I had to scratch his head some to do it. Then oncet I got away with my skin whole, I'd blast away at him if I got the chance. It appears to me that any of you that wouldn't'd be a dang fool." He eyed his accusers squarely, including Colonel Callaway, who had remained silent. "I was doin' my best to protect this fort at a time when there wasn't enough of you here to stand off an attack. We've got fifty good guns, men and boys, here now. Seems to me our odds are a little better this way."

The militia commander, William Smith, sucked his cheeks in and rocked nervously on his heels, looking as if he didn't know what to do with this turn of events. "Surely," he offered, "we can keep peace among ourselves at a time like this."

Roman, tall and sober-faced, moved to stand beside Daniel. An instant later Cullen joined them, hooking his thumbs in the top of his belt and swinging around to confront those present with that jaunty and likable air of his.

" 'Tis my opinion," he said, "that no man among us has earned the respect, or the trust, that Daniel has. He could have been this minute back in North Carolina, safe with his family, if he'd had a mind to, instead of here seein' to his duty. Think on it, lads, before you go makin' bloody fools of yourselves.''

Will Hancock, who had recovered from the ordeal of his escape and journey on foot through the wilderness, scowled and muttered something unintelligible.

''If you've got something that hasn't set well on your system, Will, best spit it out now,'' Daniel said.

All eyes turned toward Hancock, whose face revealed the hatred he felt for Boone. But after a moment he looked away and gave his head a quick jerk. ''It may be this is not the time for it,'' he conceded.

''It's not,'' Flanders put in stoutly. ''Let's be damned glad we've got Daniel back among us now that we're threatened. We've never had reason to doubt him in the past, and I don't doubt him now.''

Daniel smiled at his son-in-law, while Henry Porter and Winfield Burdette and all but a few of the others began crying out their support for the man who had led them from the beginning.

''All right then, boys—'' Daniel held up his hands to silence them; it took a little time because they were anxious to show that they stood with him. ''—all right . . .'' He waved them down. ''Let's decide what we're going to do here,'' he said, clearly touched by their outpouring of respect. ''I can't promise we can hold against them. I don't know, and that's the plain truth of it. It's my feeling that we ought to try. But if we fail, you've heard what Black Fish says he'll do . . . and I've no doubt that he will.'' He looked out over them, his eyes resting for a brief moment on Jemima. ''I've no right to decide for you,'' he said, his voice suddenly husky. ''I expect you ought to talk it over with your womenfolk, since they should have a say in it, too. I'll abide by what you decide.''

There was a long moment of silence, when husbands and wives turned to one another, when mothers reached out to pull their children closer. . . .

''I'll not vote one way or t'other,'' Granny Hawkins declared. ''I've lived my life. Whatever happens now to me don't matter ary bit . . . 'cept I hope I kin go quick when the time comes.'' Her grandson leaned down to put an arm around the little old woman.

''Well, I know what I want,'' Squire said firmly. ''I aim to hold this fort while there's a breath left in my body.''

''Hear, hear!'' Flanders shouted, and he was joined by a chorus of assent.

It was decided then, and the men took turns standing watch

and sleeping. But the Indians, still in the position they had taken up just out of rifle range, went about their cooking and even playing games, laughing and at ease, as if they were back in their own villages.

By the following evening everyone's nerves had begun to wear thin with the waiting, when Black Fish surprised them all by walking right up to the gates of the fort with his small party of subchiefs and a British officer along with him . . . all under the protection of the white flag carried by Pompey. Daniel and Roman stepped out to meet the delegation, taking Major Smith—the "bigger captain"—along with them.

But the officer in command of the white members of the contingency, Lieutenant Dagneaux DeQuindre, virtually ignored Smith and introduced himself directly to Daniel.

"Lieutenant . . . ." Daniel acknowledged the introduction with a barely concealed contempt for the French Canadian under the command of Hamilton.

Black Fish seemed impatient with such formalities. "I have kept my word, Sheltowee," he said. "I have given you the time you sought to speak with your people. And now I would have your answer."

Daniel hesitated, and Roman thought he detected in him a certain amount of affection for the old chief, mixed with regret that it had come to this between them. But then Daniel drew himself up and faced the man who had called him son. "My people have determined that they will defend the fort while there is a man living," he said. "And I am with them. I will not return to the Shawnee. I must stay with my own people, as Black Fish must stay with his."

Clearly, it was not an answer that Black Fish had expected, and astonishment, then exasperation flickered over that usually impassive face. He stared at Daniel for a long moment, his black eyes beginning to burn with hard anger. "I have asked for his answer, and Sheltowee has given it," he said. "So be it!"

He turned and stalked away, but DeQuindre put up a hand for Daniel to hold, and hurried to overtake Black Fish, the two of them conversing just out of earshot. Black Fish was clearly furious, shaking his head several times, but DeQuindre gestured and talked, and finally the war chief nodded.

Through it all the lesser chiefs had stood waiting, faces set, their eyes expressionless. But in a moment DeQuindre and Black

Fish came back to the gate, the French Canadian calling out to Daniel that he would speak with him again.

"I had thought our business finished," Daniel told the thin-lipped officer. "But if you've got somethin' to say," he added cheerfully, "I expect now's the time."

"I do, Monsieur Captain," the officer said in his pronounced French accent. "There has been a misunderstanding between us. We have come to talk of peace, not of war. Chief Black Fish seeks peace. And Governor Hamilton wishes to avoid bloodshed if at all possible."

Daniel and Roman exchanged glances. "I expect Hamilton ought to," Daniel needled, "since George Clark has whipped the britches off you boys up in the Illinois."

But for a slight flaring of the nostrils, DeQuindre ignored that. "Chief Black Fish proposes that we meet in the morning to discuss a treaty of peace. Surely we are men of reason."

"We're always willing to discuss reason," Daniel parried. "Where would this meeting take place?"

"There . . ." Black Fish interjected, pointing a finger out toward the camp set up by his braves.

Daniel shook his head. "It will be better near the spring . . . under the sycamores in the cool of the shade."

Black Fish jerked his head in assent. "To negotiate a treaty, we must have nine of your chiefs present. It is required by our laws."

Daniel scratched his chin. "Nine of us will come," he agreed.

But once they were safely back in the fort, heated objections were raised. "Damme," the Old Colonel said, "but it seems to me that we're playing right into their hands. What if it's a trap? If they take nine of us at once, and leaders at that, where does that leave the rest inside?"

"He could be right, Daniel," Squire offered.

Daniel paced the blockhouse from one end to the other. "I admit it. Still"—he tugged at that earlobe, the way he always did when he was nervous or worried—"it's gainin' time for us, boys. And that's what we need . . . time."

"The spring is in good rifle range," Roman put in.

Daniel grinned. "That's right. That's why I suggested it. We can put several of our best riflemen in the front blockhouses, ready to fire on an instant's notice."

"Well . . ." Colonel Callaway scratched at his chin, his face lined with weariness. "Let's give it a try."

Together they decided who would go out there. Daniel, of course, and Colonel Callaway . . . Squire and Roman and Cullen. And Major Smith would go, in full-dress uniform. Indians did love a uniform, Daniel told him. The three others selected were not good shots, but tall and brawny fellows.

The settlers slept in the blockhouses now because they felt safer there but as night fell, Kitty left the baby with Sara, and she and Cullen went to their own cabin.

"I want us to be here together tonight," she whispered as she traced her husband's dark thick brows with a fingertip.

"So do I, lass. . . ." His voice was husky as he raised from the pillow and bent to kiss the milk-filled breasts, running a hand over the smooth stretch of belly and hips, rounder now than before Michael, actually more desirable to him.

"I swear to you, my love," he said, his voice cracking, "as long as I'm alive, no harm will come to you or the bairn."

The next morning, Wednesday, the ninth of September, Daniel gave orders that every woman who could should dress up in men's clothing—even shirts or hats would do, he said—anything to let the Indians think that there were a great many men in the fort. Kitty turned Michael over to Sara again and went to deck herself out in one of the Porter boys' things.

Final instructions were given to the sharpshooters. If treachery was suspected, Daniel told them, he and the others would take off their hats and wave them as a signal to commence firing. From the blockhouse vantage, they could see Black Fish and his party file out toward the spring and the sycamore trees, and Daniel gave the word to go out. The gates were swung wide deliberately and left open an extra minute as the men stepped out, the women who had dressed in male attire walking back and forth in plain sight— along with the men and boys not then at the loopholes—to make it look as if the fort were full up with defenders.

It was a beautiful clear day, the breeze blowing off the river. A pair of hawks swooped gracefully, one darting down toward the opposite bank after his prey, wings iridescent in the sunlight. The Indians had spread deerskins and panther hides on the grass beneath the leafy branches, and as Daniel and the others approached, Black Fish gestured for them to sit.

"It is a good day for making a treaty," he said, his anger of the previous day seemingly gone. "We will talk and eat, Shel-towee." He raised his hand and food was carried to them, great roasted haunches of deer and elk, bear steaks and buffalo humps. Delicacies such as they hadn't tasted in years had been brought from the commissary in Detroit—hard round cheeses, and smoked fish, and chocolate. And when an ample supply of whiskey was produced, there were grins all around, though Daniel managed a whispered warning: "For God's sake, keep your heads and your wits about you!"

They ate, pausing from time to time to wipe their grease-covered hands clean in the grass or against their buckskins, washing down the dripping meat with whiskey, the settlers careful to appear to be drinking freely but in reality managing to spill a good bit of the heady dark brew. The Indians smiled and appeared to be enjoying themselves greatly, Moluntha belching loudly.

As the day wore on, Colonel Callaway began to grow increasingly impatient, but Daniel signaled him to silence. It was the way of the Shawnee to take their time getting around to anything, he knew. And right now that suited him well enough.

After a while Black Fish began to recount a dream he had had the previous night. "I dreamed, Sheltowee, that you opened the gates of your fort and made your father welcome. That we feasted together to prepare ourselves for the journey to Detroit. Could it be that the gods were telling me something?" he asked, a certain guile stealing into his strong face.

"I, too, had a dream last night," Daniel countered. "I dreamed that Black Fish honored his son by leaving Sheltowee's white brothers in peace to till the land and raise their families."

Black Fish tilted that big head down and peered at Daniel from under the black brows, then he grunted and lifted a small gourd filled with whiskey to his lips. "It may be," he said, once he had drunk and wiped his mouth, "that yours is the true dream."

"That would please Governor Hamilton," DeQuindre put in quickly. "All he asks in return is the allegiance of the people of Boonesborough."

As the sun reached its zenith and moved on slowly, those inside the fort watched anxiously, squinting out of the loopholes to see as much as they could of what was transpiring in the hollow . . . and always on the lookout for the wave of a hat. But it seemed clear to the onlookers that Daniel and the others were drawing the whole thing out as long as they could.

"Lord, Lord," Elvie said to Kitty, "they must've eat enough to do them a week. And there the savages are a-carryin' in more."

Finally, late in the afternoon, Daniel and the men trooped back into the fort and everyone crowded around, eager for an accounting of what had been said.

"DeQuindre insists that Hamilton would like to avoid bloodshed," Daniel told them. "And Black Fish says he'll go along with that. They're writing up a treaty for us to sign in the morning."

"Treaty?" Blandford Moore sang out scornfully. "I don't know as I'd trust to any treaty that either the Brits or the savages sign."

"We don't have to trust 'em," Daniel answered him. "In fact, we'd be danged fools if we did. But we can let them think we're willing to meet their demands. We can even sign the danged thing if it'll buy us some time."

"Sign it?" Colonel Callaway was incredulous. "You can't mean that, Daniel."

Daniel paused, his own conflict written on his face. But he gave his head a nod. "Why not?"

"Because," snapped the Old Colonel, "we would be signing an oath of allegiance to the king of England!"

"Aye," Daniel said. "An oath that we don't mean and won't live up to . . . any more than Black Fish intends to live up to his part of it. Don't forget, I know the Shawnee. I know Black Fish. He's not going to go back beyond the Ohio and never trouble us again. Aye," he said again, bringing his hand down smartly against the tabletop, "I'm willing to sign it if it means even one life is saved here."

A hush fell over the group as they contemplated the choice. In the end, though there were some who still harbored reservations, it was generally agreed upon that any contract offered should be signed in the interests of buying time and safeguarding their home.

"We'll take turns at watch," Daniel ordered. "Otherwise, best get a good night's sleep. Tomorrow could try us."

"I don't like it, Daniel," Cullen said, pulling back from the loophole through which he'd just viewed the sycamores where the Indians already waited with what seemed to be a quiet patience.

"I don't, either," Roman said. "I can't put my finger on it, but something feels amiss out there."

Daniel nodded, plainly worried, and the three men walked the short distance to where the Old Colonel and the others waited for them.

"Let's keep our eyes and ears open out there, boys," Daniel said. Winfield Burdette swung open the big gate to let them pass through, and Daniel paused briefly by the big blacksmith. "Mind now, if a hat waves, fire away."

"We'll be ready," Winfield assured him.

As the representatives of the fort trekked down into the hollow once again, Cullen felt the prickly rising at the back of his neck that he'd had all morning, though he wasn't able to see a thing that looked suspicious, no matter how carefully he looked—until they drew closer to the sycamores and he realized that, except for Black Fish, almost all of the older chiefs who'd been present at the meeting the day before had been replaced by strong young warriors. He and Roman exchanged quick looks.

Once the greetings were over and the settlers had seated themselves, Daniel challenged Black Fish directly on the change. "Why is it that the old chiefs are not with us today?" he asked him. "Why have so many young braves taken their places? I count eighteen."

Black Fish nodded, his face grave, the fist-size scalplock carefully greased for the occasion. "They are here to represent the eighteen villages that sent warriors to join our army. They must witness the signing of the treaty so that they may go back and speak of it in their councils."

"Ah . . ." Daniel nodded, appearing to accept the explanation. But whenever he got a chance, he shot quick glances toward his men, and there wasn't one of them who didn't understand the danger they were in. Cullen could feel the ready intensity of Roman, who sat nearby, legs curled beneath him like a coiled spring poised to unwind.

DeQuindre read aloud the treaty that had been drawn up. It was brief and to the point, declaring the allegiance of the people of Boonesborough to the Great White Father across the sea, His Royal Majesty, George III of England, and their willingness to submit to the authority of his deputy in Detroit, Lieutenant Governor Henry Hamilton. In return, Black Fish and his warriors would retire to their lodges north of the Ohio, leaving their white brothers unmolested. The land that the Shawnee called Kan-tu-kee would be free for all, redmen and white alike, to hunt and trade peacefully within.

It was signed quickly, as if all involved wished to have it over as soon as possible. Black Fish, his face set and stern, raised his hand for the peace pipe to be passed. "We shall live as brothers," he said.

But as the pipe, decorated with feathers and beaded bands, was passed to Cullen by Roman, and he drew the strong tobacco smoke into his lungs, he wished fervently that he had slipped a knife inside his hunting shirt before he'd come out. And as he passed the pipe on to Squire, who was on the other side of him, he caught the guarded look in the deacon's eyes.

Once the smoking was finished, Black Fish rose. "To seal the agreement," he said to Daniel, "you and your people must clasp hands with mine. It is our custom." He beckoned to the young warriors, who sprang up and circled around to Daniel and his men, now on their feet and watching the proceedings warily.

There were two braves for each of them, and the two in front of Cullen suddenly grasped an arm on either side of him and attempted to drag him away, but he set his heels and managed to yank one arm free, swinging with his elbow to smash a nose squarely. With his free hand he snatched off his hat to wave it wildly as he brought his knee up to catch the Shawnee in the groin. The brave let go and grabbed at himself, his mouth opening wide to howl.

Cullen whirled, pulling his hat firmly down on his head, aware of the wild melee around him, the shouting and sound of blows intermingling with the crack of rifle fire from the fort and—as he now saw—from the line of Indians that had edged up from the riverbank where they must have been hidden and waiting since before daylight.

"Goddamn them!" he muttered. "They had it planned all along!"

He saw Daniel flailing away . . . and then caught sight of Roman, who had hauled up a short, chunky brave and now literally flung him into one of the others, who staggered backward and knocked down yet a third.

Some of the Boonesborough men had already managed to free themselves and were sprinting toward the gates under cover of the fire from the stockade. But the Old Colonel struggled in vain against his two stout, young assailants, and Cullen raced to assist him, hauling one of them around and bringing his two fists up under the brave's chin in a blow that dropped the Indian where he stood. Slipping free, Callaway stooped to grab up a slim length of tree branch and flailed away at the second Indian, connecting with a telling crack to the side of his head that brought him to his knees.

"Let's go!" Cullen shouted, and hauled the older man along with him. Roman suddenly appeared on the other side of them, and the three men raced past the spring and up the path toward the fort, bullets whining about them.

As they neared the gate, Cullen glanced over his shoulder to see Daniel just behind them. In that instant Squire, who was farther back, suddenly clutched at his left shoulder and went down hard.

"Get on in!" Cullen shouted, and waved Daniel on past him as he turned and headed back. But Squire had scrambled to his feet by the time Cullen reached him and was trying to run.

"Is it bad?" Cullen asked as he gave him an arm, the two of them running together.

"Naw . . . a nick," Squire grunted, though he was clearly in considerable pain. A red stain was beginning to steal through the linsey of his hunting shirt.

They were the last ones in, and Winfield slammed the heavy bar into place while eager hands reached out for Squire and eased him down.

Cullen raced for the northwest blockhouse, taking the steep stairs to the loft three at a time and grabbing for the rifle that one of the women pressed into his hands. Roman was already there before him, calmly easing the long barrel of his gun through the loophole.

"They're getting ready to charge." He jerked his head toward the wall, and Cullen looked out to see more than a hundred mounted braves, shrieking at the top of their lungs as they kicked their ponies into action and rode hell-bent for the fort, firing their rifles as they neared and veering away while another wave took their places.

"Make every shot count, boys," Daniel called out calmly. And Cullen, who'd glanced at him over his shoulder, drew in his breath as he saw the blood, deep red and oozing from the back of Daniel's head, glueing the sandy-colored hair into clumps and staining the back of his shirt.

"Daniel's hit," he said to Roman as he took careful aim and waited coolly until he was positive he couldn't miss that broad, paint-streaked chest fastened within his sights.

"Tomahawk shaved him," Roman said without looking up. "It doesn't seem too deep."

Cullen squeezed off the trigger and watched the brave tumble and roll; then he quickly reloaded. But after he'd fired the second time, he felt a tug at his shirt and turned to find Kitty behind him, a sheen of perspiration gleaming along her upper lip. She reached for the rifle in his hand and passed him a loaded one.

"Michael?" he asked as he took aim again.

"Safe," she said as she worked at reloading. "He's with Sara."

The next time he turned back to her, he smiled and winked. "It'll be all right, lass."

But the onslaught continued, the fearful howling of the Indians as they charged and the hail of bullets thwacking into the log bastions beginning to terrify some of the children, who could be heard crying down on the lower floor.

Most of the adults stayed calm under the attack, the men choosing their targets carefully, trying not to waste a single bullet, the women loading guns or comforting the frightened children. But, unnerved, Horace Hamilton paused, drawing the barrel of his rifle back in and leaning against the wall for a moment. "Good God, can we hold?" he cried out, trembling.

Daniel, nearby, put out a hand to steady him. "If the wind from all that flying lead don't blow the stockade down, we can." He grinned and passed on.

After what seemed an endless time the Indians pulled back, the sudden silence almost shattering. The men turned to nudge one another and nod. "By God, they ain't got us yet!" Winfield declared.

With a squeeze of Cullen's hand, Kitty hurried away to find Michael sleeping peacefully in Sara's arms, oblivious to all that had gone on around them. And Jemima found her father and insisted that he let her dress his wound, but he refused until he had sought out Squire.

The injured man had been carried to one of the back blockhouses and his wife was beside him, holding a pad of linen to the wound to stop the bleeding. Granny Hawkins hovered over him.

"Shit, Daniel"—Squire looked up at his brother—"if it ain't just like an Indian to shoot you so as the bullet don't pass clean through."

Daniel grinned at him. "Don't be worryin'. I'll get it out of there."

A fire had been started in the fireplace to heat water, and now Daniel stuck the blade of his knife into the flames for a few minutes. "Wisht we had some of that corn liquor Black Fish was passin' around yesterday," he said, a false cheeriness in his voice. "Here . . . ." He took up a small stick of wood from the basket by the hearth. "Stick this between your teeth and hold on. I'll be quick. . . ."

Squire stiffened as Daniel probed with a finger to see just where the lead was, and then as the knife blade entered the wound, he bit down hard, groaning softly and quivering from head to toe, huge drops of sweat popping out on his scarred face. But with a quick twist Daniel gouged the bullet free. Squire gave one final grunt, jerking, and then spit the wood from his mouth and let out his breath in a huge rush.

"The Bible says," he gasped out, "that the good Lord punishes the ones He loves best. I've about concluded that He must be purely partial to me.''

Granny Hawkins, who'd stood by and nodded her approval as Daniel had done his work, took charge now, binding the bloody wound with slippery elm bark, while Jemima finally persuaded Daniel to let her see to him.

"Call me at the first sign of them comin' again," Daniel instructed Cullen and Roman, who'd come to see how Squire was faring. "They're not through with us, boys. You can count on that."

❋ 24 ❋

THE AIR IN THE BLOCKHOUSE WAS CLOSE AND STALE, night air heavy with the odor of unwashed bodies and eye-stinging smoke from the grease lamps. But Michael looked up at Kitty from his cradle and spread his mouth in a smile, waving his dimpled hands at sight of her. He had awakened just minutes before, good-humored as always, and she had stood back and watched him, her own throat swelling with unshed tears as he kicked his legs in delighted fascination, his eyes trying to coordinate with the jerky movements.

Sara was curled nearby on one of the quilts, her fine pale hair coming loose from its pins and spilling about her face, faint blue circles beneath her closed eyes. She seemed undisturbed by the loud snoring from far down toward the other end.

Now and again one of the younger children whined or cried out and their mothers stirred to quiet them, but most of the others in the blockhouse—except for the men who took their turns at the loopholes—slept quietly in spite of the hard floor, exhausted with the last thirty-six hours.

They had withstood the repeated attacks of the previous day. There'd been times when Kitty had been sure that no fort could possibly stand against the sheer numbers that assailed it, yet somehow theirs had. But there'd been few of them within the stockade who'd been able to do more than catnap through the night, fearful with every creak of wood or moan of the wind that they would be overrun—though Daniel told them it was unlikely the Shawnee would come at them after dark.

Sometime before dawn their hopes had soared when they heard sounds of what seemed to be the whole army retreating—horses whinnying, guttural shouts, and loud splashing as they crossed the river, the brass bugle carried by the British soldiers resounding through the hills and hollows and gradually growing fainter in the distance, to fade away altogether.

"Goddamn!" Ezekial Turner whooped. "They've done turned tail and run!"

"I guess that'll show 'em!" someone roared.

But Daniel soon dampened their rising spirits with the prediction that it was nothing but a trap to draw them out come sunrise. Still, they wanted to believe that it was over. And when morning came and they saw the cleared battleground—not one Indian body felled the previous day left in the hollow or up on the plateau—it was hard not to cling to the hope that the huge war party had truly gone.

"They took all their dead with them," Ben Tyler observed. "You wouldn't expect a heathen to do that."

"They were afraid we'd scalp them," Daniel explained. "If a Shawnee goes into the next world without his scalp, he'll be forever dishonored. Maybe"—he rubbed at his chin thoughtfully—"that's why some white men seem to relish the practice and take as many as they can get. I never could warm to it myself."

Though the cows bellowed to be let out and the view from every direction seemed peaceful and quiet, Daniel insisted that no one stir outside the walls. And before the sun was straight up overhead, the attack he'd predicted came, beginning with a blood-chilling yell from the Shawnee, who'd doubled back to hide down below the steep riverbank and behind the stumps and hillocks of the hollow. Now a line of Black Fish's warriors emerged from the woods and commenced firing, digging their heels into the flanks of their ponies, charging the stockade with a ferocity unmatched even by the previous day's persistent attacks.

The garrison held firm, each person going about his tasks with the sureness born of recent experience. Lead balls whacked into the blockhouse walls and the outer bastions, where splinters flew and heads ducked. The men shouted and cursed, profane and exultant as they stood against the charge: "Goddamn the bloody heathens!" "Damn their eyes!" The women shoved the ramrods home and primed the pans. Kitty's nose stung with the sharp smell of powder, and her eyes watered and blurred. She swiped at her face repeatedly, leaving black streaks along the sides.

The charge was withstood, and the Indians fell back to re-form and come again, and still again, hurling themselves—some to their deaths—in a wild frenzy. But the fort stood.

It was later in the afternoon when Kitty, carrying powder from the magazine, saw one of the men on the walls go down. It was during a lull, and as he hoisted himself up to take a quick look out over the hollow, his head snapped back before she even heard the crack of the rifle and he fell right at her feet, a look of awful surprise on his face as he stared up at her, his mouth open and working as if he would tell her something important.

She dropped to her knees beside him, others springing to help, but his eyes were already dulling. He gave one final convulsive heave and lay still, the side of his head at the temple reamed open. All she could think of was how young he looked lying there, his corn-yellow hair bloodied.

It occurred to her later that she hadn't even been able to call his name. He was one of the volunteers from Logan's Station, and if she'd ever known it, she'd forgotten. And maybe, she thought, that was as bad as any of it . . . dying like that and nobody even to call your name.

Once dark had fallen, they'd buried him in one of the back corners of the stockade. There was no way they could risk taking him to the little graveyard outside.

Now, in the dim light of the blockhouse, the baby cooed up at her and laughed, oblivious to the danger beyond the walls. Kitty picked him up and settled back into the rocking chair, freeing her breast and bringing it to his eager mouth. He sucked vigorously, each tug at her nipple a squeeze of her heart.

It was quiet now, and she wished that Cullen were downstairs, here with them. But he ate and catnapped at his post in the loft above. And maybe it was just as well. He might not agree with what she had decided. It was probably best if he didn't know.

Michael finished nursing, tiny bubbles of milk blowing between the pursed lips as he let go, sighing, eyes closed now. And Kitty felt the warm flood as he wet his diaper. She should have had a pad under him.

She put him in the cradle and changed him quickly, bringing the cloth up between his legs and tying the soft linen ends together, wondering what she would do when his diapers ran out. There was no way to wash them now. Water was too precious to use for anything but drinking and cooking.

Finished, she smoothed back the dark tuft of hair, feeling the velvety smoothness of his forehead and thinking how beautiful he was. Tears welled in her eyes as she looked down at him for a long moment. Then she went to wake Sara.

Roman's tired wife started up at the touch on her shoulder, looking instinctively toward the cradle.

"He's asleep," Kitty assured her. "I nursed him and he dropped right off. Wet all over me."

Sara sat up and wiped her eyes. "You look tired," she said.

Kitty nodded. "So do you."

"Come on. There's plenty of room here." She scooted over a little. "Get some rest while you can."

"In a minute," Kitty said. "First, I want us to talk." She sat down on the quilt beside Sara, who drew her knees up and hugged them.

"What about?"

Kitty's hands were clenched together in her lap and she looked down at them, her throat tight. "The Indians could overrun us, Sara. And if they should, I'll not have them get to him. Do . . . do you understand?" she added, her voice a little unsteady, though she had thought about it through most of the day.

Sara just looked at her, and Kitty stretched out to reach for her woolen shawl, bundled up beneath the rocking chair. She had put it there when she'd first entered the blockhouse a little while ago, and now she unwrapped it carefully to reveal Usaph's old pistol.

Sara's face paled, but she didn't protest. Neither of them would speak aloud of the stories they'd both heard . . . of white infants tossed onto a bed of coals . . . or caught up by the heels to have their heads bashed against the nearest wall.

"I showed you how to fire it once before," Kitty said, taking up the gun. "Remember . . . you just cock the hammer and pull the trigger. I'll load it now. There's an extra bullet and some powder here in case you . . . you should want it for . . ." She left the rest unsaid, her eyes meeting Sara's and then dropping away to the pistol while she loaded it deftly.

When it was done, she wrapped everything as it was and slid it beneath the rocker again.

"If you see that we're lost to them, will you do it for me if I can't get to him in time?"

Sara hesitated only a moment, then nodded, a pulse beating at her throat, tears glistening. The two women embraced in the dim corner as the snoring began again.

It was Ezekial Turner who spotted it first and ran to fetch Daniel. "Best come take a look at this," he puffed, winded from sprinting down the full length of the fort yard. "The Injuns is up to some devilment sure!"

Daniel, accompanied by the Old Colonel, Roman, and Cullen, hurried toward the back wall, the leathery little fiddler doing his best to keep up with them. And once they'd seen the wide streak of silt drifting out from the bank to swirl and muddy the clear green water, widening still as the current caught it, they could only agree with Ezekial's assessment.

"What in hell . . . ?" Cullen said as he edged up to get a better look at it.

"Careful," Daniel cautioned.

"What is it?" Colonel Callaway asked. "What could they be up to down there?"

Daniel shook his head, a worried frown cutting across his brow. With the steep dropoff of the bank behind the fort, it was impossible to see what the Indians were doing below, but it was sure that they were up to something. "We've got to find out, boys."

Roman nodded. "I could try to slip through the gate on this side."

"No. It's too dangerous."

"If we had some way of getting up high . . ." Cullen mused.

"A tower," the Old Colonel put in. "We've plenty of logs in the compound. If we could erect something on the roof there . . ." He pointed to the cabin closest to where the silt entered into the river below.

"We could do it after dark," Roman said.

Daniel grinned. "Might be worth a try. Let's get everything ready."

And that night, with the logs to hand and the sliver of a moon affording enough light to work by without making them ready targets, the men erected a rough but sturdy structure atop the cabin roof. And come the morning, those up in it scrambled down to report that the Indians were digging away at the underbank and throwing buckets of dirt into the river, which had now muddied from bank to bank downstream.

"They're trying to tunnel into the fort," Daniel said, his face grim. "DeQuindre must have put 'em up to it. Indians don't take right off to hard labor."

They gathered in the blockhouse nearest to the tower to talk over the situation. Daniel, the Old Colonel, Roman, and Cullen were joined by Major Smith and Squire, pasty-faced and obviously weak from his wound but unwilling to stay down for long.

"What can we do?" Smith asked.

"Damned if I know," said Callaway, "except meet them head on if they succeed."

"We could take a group of volunteers and charge out there now, maybe take 'em by surprise," Cullen offered.

"And get half our men killed . . . and them with enough to set another crew digging and scarcely feel the loss." Daniel vetoed it at once.

"Daniel's right," Squire said.

Roman had been quiet, standing aside near the open door. Now he stepped out a pace and squinted over toward the nearest cabin on the back side, the one that held the makeshift tower on its roof. In his mind's eye he lined it up with the undercliff where the Indians dug laboriously.

"We could dig our own tunnel," he said, motioning them all out into the brassy hot sunlight. "Begin right there"—he pointed to the open space between the blockhouse and the cabin—"just this side of the cabin wall. Dig down until we're on a level with them . . . and then across, under the cabins . . ."

"Crosswise o' the way they're headed?" Squire asked.

Roman nodded, and Daniel's eyes lit up. "So they'll have to run square into ours!"

"That's right," Roman said. "And we could take them one or two at a time . . . no more than that could get through at once."

Cullen grinned. "By God, I think you've come up with it!"

"Let's tell everybody what's going on and organize squads to take a turn at digging. . . ." Daniel was already headed down toward the other end of the compound. "Winfield," he yelled as he caught sight of the big blacksmith, "collect all the shovels you can lay your hands on."

And so, in addition to their watches at the blockhouse loopholes and along the stockade walls, all of the able-bodied men of Boonesborough took their turn at digging daily in the close heat of September—sweating freely, yet trying to drink as little as possible of the precious water. The days became a blur of labor and sweat and sore muscles . . . and watching always.

In retaliation for the tower, which the settlers had found was an excellent and safe vantage point from which to fire, the Indians had posted sharpshooters along the heights across the river, and it became hazardous to move about freely outside in the daytime. Jemima was hit, but fortunately the bullet was all but spent and the wound was more embarrassing than serious. She'd been struck in the soft, round curve of her left buttock, and though it had frightened her badly at first, a tug of her thick linen drawers was enough to pull out the ball. Granny Hawkins dressed the superficial wound and declared her fortunate.

But the next evening, just before dark, Horace Hamilton was standing watch when a chance bullet struck the stone plug that was used to close the loophole when it wasn't being used. The piece of limestone shattered, and Horace dropped to one knee.

"Horace?" John Holder called. Kitty put aside what she was doing and ran to him.

"Are you all right?" She put an anxious hand to his shoulder.

Horace nodded quickly, his head bent forward.

"That was too close," she said. "It's a lucky thing you weren't hit."

He nodded again but stayed down on his knees, rocking back and forth. Kitty leaned down closer, gasping as she caught sight of the hole in the middle of his forehead, hardly as big as the end of her little finger, but ragged and nasty-looking. A trickle of blood snaked downward toward the bridge of his nose.

She called to them, and John Holder and Cullen and several of the other men gathered around.

"He's been hit," said Cullen.

"Must o' been by a piece of the stone," John offered. "The bullet broke it clean. I saw it shatter." And to prove his point, he gestured to the shards lying on the floor nearby.

"Well, whatever it was hit him a good lick. It's hard to tell how deep. Could be it just stunned him," Cullen said. "Let's get him back in the corner over here."

The men picked him up and took him over to prop him up against the wall.

"I'll go get some water to clean the blood off and something to bind his head," Kitty said.

Cullen caught at her arm, his eyes troubled. "Maybe you'd best find Maggie and fetch her here."

Maggie came, snuffling and wiping tears away but clearly relieved to see that Horace was sitting upright. "I knew you'd get yourself hurt up here!" she scolded. "Thank God it was a piece of rock hit you and not a bullet!'' She leaned down over him. ''It could have gone in your eye just as easy, and you'd have been blinded.''

But every time they tried to tend his wound, Horace waved them away . . . sitting there in his tattered stockings and frayed waistcoat, not saying a word but rocking still, blood and matter oozing from the small hole in his forehead, while Maggie sat beside him, telling him repeatedly how lucky he was.

Daniel came to see what had happened, and Cullen took him aside. ''I think the poor devil has taken one of those splinters of stone right into his head.''

They sent for Granny Hawkins, to see if the old doctor woman could do anything for him. After taking a look at the wound and hearing what had happened, she shook her head sadly. ''I don't know ary thing I could do . . . 'ceptin' pray.''

He died before midnight, sitting upright still, propped against the wall and leaning slightly against his wife. And instead of the hysterics that everyone expected, Maggie went from one to another of them, a drawn and desperate look on her face, telling them still that it was only a little piece of rock that had hit him.

Elizabeth Callaway finally got her to lie down and rest sometime before dawn, after the prayers had been said and Horace had been buried beside the young man from Logan's Station.

The direct attacks upon the stockade had grown less frequent once the Indians commenced their efforts to tunnel in. But while continued sniping from across the river still made any outdoor movements hazardous, it was the frequent gathering of braves, just out of rifle range, to taunt and yell and make obscene gestures, that really raised the ire of the men at the loopholes.

''Jist step a little closer, you hog-jawed bastard, and I'll blow your mangy balls clean off!'' someone would yell when he could contain himself no longer, and that was certain to set up a chorus of hoots and insults and dire promises.

''They're likely too little fer ye to hit,'' someone would take it up.

''Then I'll settle fer his goddamned pecker!''

''That's prob'ly too little, too!''

And always the Indians would laugh, most of them not having the slightest notion of what was being shouted but certain that they had made the Kentuckians furious.

Squire, skilled at gunsmithing and disgusted with the daily humiliation, determined to put a stop to it. He huddled with

Winfield Burdette to discuss the feasibility of building a make-shift cannon.

"By God, I believe we can do 'er!" Winfield chortled.

They constructed the crude gun of black gum wood banded about with an iron wagon tire, then loaded it with small pieces of metal and rifle balls.

"Make sure you've got a long wick tied into your powder, boys," Daniel cautioned. "The danged thing could blow to heaven and take all of you with it."

But as the word passed that it was finished, the men couldn't wait to try it, and everything was in readiness for the next day.

The taunting began as usual, and the sentries on the walls and in the blockhouses shouted back, scarcely able to contain their anticipation but putting up a good front . . . pretending to be as angry and frustrated as ever. And once the Indians were doubling over with laughter, the signal was given and the front gates swung open enough to aim the cannon quickly, its fuse already burning. By the time the braves saw it, they only had time for a startled yelp and a frantic dive for the ground before the explosion.

As the sod flew upward in a dozen different places, and the astonished braves hauled themselves up to hurry to a safer position—many of them limping, some being carried—the entire garrison exploded as well, in one giant cheer. Fortunately the Indians were too concerned with their own safety to see what had happened to the gun. It lay in pieces, splintered wood strewn about, but it put an end to the daily tauntings.

The incident lifted the spirits of everyone, but it was hard to stay uplifted for long when each day became a little more difficult. The lack of proper sleep, the long and exhausting hours were beginning to take their toll.

Though it had been overcast for days, the long-hoped-for rain hadn't fallen, and water was desperately low. In addition to the fear that they would run out of drinking water, the lack of clean clothing plagued the women, making it especially difficult for those with babies and small children.

Michael's diapers had long since run out, and Kitty had all but exhausted her supply of linens, cutting them into pieces of a suitable size. As she changed him now, Elvie and Faith looked on, the three of them commiserating over their common problem.

"I've got one more sheet left," Kitty told them. "When I use that up I guess I'll just have to let him go without."

Faith hitched up Martha's skirts to reveal the two-year-old's bare and skinny little bottom. "I figured it was about time she learned to use a pot anyway."

"You're lucky she's old enough," Elvie declared. "I already tore up one o' my mattress ticks. Nothin' left but a pile o' shucks beneath the bed frame."

Michael had soiled himself, and Kitty cleaned his plump buttocks with a rag dipped into a gourd half filled with clabber which she kept on the floor by the cradle. "Little Lureen's rash cleared up?" she asked Elvie.

Elvie nodded. "Since I started usin' the clabber on her. I'd have never thought of it but for you, Kitty. She was squallin' her head off. Red as a piece o' flannel."

"Buttermilk works almost as good," Faith offered, and Kitty and Elvie agreed.

Toward noon the long-awaited rain began to pepper down and the settlers gathered to peer out at it, some remembering that it was Sunday and declaring that it was fitting that God should send it on His day. Unfortunately the shower didn't last long enough to do much for the all-but-depleted rain barrels, and in the afternoon it was announced that water would have to be rationed out even more strictly than it had been up to now. A cup per person each day. But the sky was still overcast. Enough rain might yet come to help them, they encouraged one another.

Squire conducted services in one of the blockhouses that afternoon, and the weary people crowded in. "Lord, deliver us in this, our hour of need," he said. And those gathered whispered, "Amen."

Dusk came earlier than usual because of the overcast sky, and the campfires of the enemy winked and glowed with an eerie kind of beauty, dotting beyond the hollow toward the woods and fanning out toward Hackberry Ridge. Within the fort there had gotten to be a visible relaxing as night fell, an unspoken declaration that they'd survived one more day and, pray God, the Indians would leave them in peace, at least until the morning light.

A few brave souls went off to their own cabins, but most spread their quilts in the blockhouses, the women scolding at their younger children to go relieve themselves in the pot before they lay down. Kitty had just finished nursing Michael when a terrifying cry went up from the watch.

"Fire . . . Great Lord, have mercy on us! They aim to burn us out!"

The fearful words were passed throughout the garrison, sharpshooters springing to their posts to see the agile braves sprinting toward the stockade walls, flaming torches held high to cast bronze chests and paint-streaked faces into relief against the darkness.

Some of the runners were brought down with the hail of rifle fire that met them, but others got through to fling the sticky torches—wrapped with wild flax and the inner oily fiber of the shell-bark hickories that grew freely in the woods—against the palisades or up onto cabin roofs.

From outside came shouts of "Water . . . for God's sake, water!" And within the blockhouse Kitty quickly kissed Michael and passed him to Sara, their two hands meeting for a moment, both trembling. Then she turned and ran outside to help.

The cows were lunging awkwardly, and the horses in their makeshift pen reared and snorted as flames took hold in several places. Brilliant arrows, shot from down under the river cliffs, streaked through the dark and arced to drive into cabin walls or roofs, shafts quivering, smoke spiraling upward.

Some of the men had stayed at their posts to try to pick off the Indians who sprinted close enough to throw their torches. Others had run out, cursing and shouting, to join the women, all of them beating at the fires with brooms and whatever else they could get to hand. Kitty caught sight of Elizabeth Callaway, her mobcap trailing off one ear, flailing away with a hickory broom that looked as if it had caught fire itself.

The cry for water went up again, and Kitty heard her name called. She turned to see Betsey Henderson beckoning, and she ran over to join with Jemima and the Porter boys as they all formed a line to pass pails along, dipping deep into the water barrels for what little was left. Others came to help as they passed the buckets, careful in their hurry not to spill a precious drop.

As they succeeded in extinguishing one section of the burning wall, there were cries for help from in back of them. Kitty and some of the others ran that way to see several men sprinting bravely along the rooftops, wrenching out the flaming arrows as they fell and flinging them away into the damp grass.

Kitty drew near her own cabin and stood for a moment still, appalled at the scene before her. Suddenly a flaming, oily mass *whumped* into the cabin wall right beside her—fire dancing and leaping. She stared at it, gripped with a rage so powerful it all but choked her.

Her things were in there—the cherry bed and chest that her father had made . . . Ma's Delft cups . . . the Bible where Michael's name had been entered with her own hand after his birth . . .

"Damn them . . . *damn them*!" she shrieked, grabbing at the feathered end, yanking at the shaft with all her might. She lacked the strength to free it, but still she tried, baring her teeth and finally pushing it sideways with one great determined effort that snapped it off to scatter sparks and red-hot pieces. One big piece caught against her palm, the tarry stuff sticking to sear her flesh with a sickening sizzle that was lost in the scream torn from her lips as she finally shook it away.

For a moment the pain made everything in the world black, but she willed herself not to faint. She would fight with her last breath if it could save Michael . . . or Cullen. Dizzy and nauseated, she realized that fires were blazing in a dozen different places. For a moment she didn't feel the drizzle of rain, misty and fine against her face. . . .

Jemima passed her, forehead streaked with dirt, her skirt ripped. "It's raining, Kitty," she cried as she ran down toward the front blockhouse where Flanders was.

The drizzle thickened and the fires started to sputter out. And in a moment Roman came running through the compound to check the back wall. He stopped as he saw her standing there.

"Kitty . . . are you all right?" he asked, and then caught sight of her hand. "Oh, God . . . Kitty . . . Kitty," he moaned, catching her up as she fainted.

❋ 25 ❋

THE SAVING RAIN CAME DOWN STEADILY, DRUMMING against the roofs and dripping into catch barrels, while inside the blockhouse one lone grease lamp burned, casting shadows across the sprawling figures who slept, wrung out with exhaustion and relief. But in the darkness of the corner Kitty was awake, rocking silently, the pain in her bandaged hand bringing beads of sweat to her pale face. Having Michael hadn't hurt as much; nothing had ever hurt as much. But surely she hadn't needed to faint over it, she chided herself.

She felt embarrassed still because Roman had had to carry her as if she were a baby down the length of the fort yard. But thank goodness it had not been one of the other men who'd happened by to catch her—that really would have shamed her. Roman was her kin.

In that blur of pain, she'd been only vaguely aware of the people on their knees giving thanks for their deliverance or standing silently, too weary to cheer. But back inside the blockhouse she'd come fully to herself to find Cullen bending over her, that fine handsome face of his working painfully, as if he might weep, manly or no.

"Oh, lass," he'd crooned, his burr as thick as any ever heard from him, "how did ye do this to y'r wee hand?"

"I broke an arrow off. . . . It's not so bad, Cullen." She'd tried to put up a good front for him and for Roman and Sara, who hovered near, though after a quick glance she avoided looking again at the charred and blistered palm . . . fingers drawn in clawlike. She had heard that people the Indians burned at the stake drew up, their bodies hunched forward in death, arms and legs bent in close to make them as small as possible. Just the thought of that caused her to grow dizzy again.

Granny Hawkins arrived, and Kitty was unable to hold back a scream as the old lady examined her hand and then started to slather on a putrid-smelling green cream. Tears oozed from the corners of her eyes, and Cullen held fast to her as it was bound around with strips of linen, his breath coming as hard as if it were he who had the pain. Sara turned her face away, her fingers to her mouth as she cried in sympathy, and Roman stood by, his blue eyes filled with pity . . . and something else—a hard and flinty pride.

"It was a brave thing you did, Kitty Gentry," he said, calling her by her blood name, then a second later remembering to add, "Claiborne."

"More like foolish," she responded, though she managed a small grimace of a smile. "A few minutes more and the rain would've put it out anyway."

Elvie and Elizabeth had heard and come by then, and the women shooed the men away. "Go on now," Elvie said, "we'll take care of her. Do whatever waits you, or sleep if you can."

"The last thing she needs," Elizabeth agreed, "is two great men to watch every move she makes."

"You send if you want me, lass," Cullen said, lingering a moment.

"I will," she promised.

After getting her settled down on her quilt, the women went to make her some tea brewed up with special herbs that Granny Hawkins promised would help her to sleep. Kitty prayed that it would, anything to dull the pain that was like a wild animal gnawing at her hand.

The wind changed the pattern of the rain, dashing it against the blockhouse and then leveling out again to resume its steady drumming. Michael stirred in his cradle and found his thumb, commencing to suck with a satisfied sigh. Kitty caught the sour smell of milk, strong on him now since she had nothing else to clean him with, and tears welled in her eyes and trickled along her temples. She couldn't even pick him up without help now, couldn't diaper him—couldn't protect him if . . .

She stared upward through the tears and darkness, making out the smoky rafters above her . . . and she felt a kind of terror that was worse than the pain in her hand. She was aware of the savages out there, held at bay for the moment by the rain. But for it, the fort would have burned and the fate of all within would probably have been decided by now. Here within the stockade—which suddenly seemed all too flimsy—they might, right now this night, be the only Kentuckians left alive. Colonel Clark and his men could so easily have been overwhelmed; Fort Harrod could be gone, Mr. Logan's station lying in ashes . . .

For the first time she wavered, lost sight of why she was out here in this land that held such beauty and promise . . . and extracted such a price. How much more would she have to pay?

She tried to think of the place on Otter Creek, but she couldn't see it clearly anymore; it had been too long.

A shadow moved at her side, and she looked up to see Roman, reminded of how silently he had always been able to move. He had a small jug in his hand and a treenware cup.

"I had this put back," he whispered, hunkering down beside her. If he noticed the tears that she quickly wiped away, he made no mention of it. "Where's Sara?" He looked around for his wife.

"Gone with the others. They're making me some herb tea to help me sleep."

"I'd wager this good rum will do a better job of it." He tilted the jug, and it made a soft gurgle as the heady-smelling liquid poured into the cup. "Here . . . drink this. I've been saving it for a special time, and this seems as good as any."

Though most women didn't drink in the quantities that their menfolk did, there were few of them teetotalers, and Kitty was no exception. On cold winter evenings, Usaph had often mixed up a toddy for his wife and daughters, believing firmly that it would keep them from a chill. And though now she made a face at the straight rum, without water or sugar to soften it, she swallowed it down handily, without a cough and barely a catch of her breath to mark it.

Roman nodded his approval and took a drink from the jug himself. "It's smooth enough," he said, pouring a little more into her cup.

She sipped it this time, slowly, looking up at that hawk face in the shadows and glad that he had come. "I . . . I was thinking of them out there . . . thinking they may have overrun all the others and us all that's left." She could tell that to Roman, perhaps only to Roman. Not to Sara, who must struggle with her own fears constantly. Nor to Cullen, to add to his burden of worry over her and Michael.

He took another pull at the jug, wiping his mouth and smiling that crooked smile of his. "Not likely. Black Fish has more warriors behind him than I've seen mustered before. It's doubtful there could be other war parties abroad of a size to do much harm elsewhere. And right now, if I know anything about Indians, they're not feeling good. They're sure to take the rain as a bad sign from their gods, it coming just as they'd decided to try and burn us out. And they're out there now in it, wet as muskrats and without even a fire to take the chill off."

He poured a little more rum into her cup and she sipped again, the warmth of it beginning to steal over her. Though her hand still throbbed, it seemed more bearable, and the terror of being surrounded by over four hundred savages lessened when she could think of them as Roman had just drawn them, huddled in the rain, bedraggled and defeated for the moment.

"You think we can hold against them?" she asked.

"I do." His answer came quickly. "They've put their best against us already and we've held each time."

They were quiet for a moment, the wind gusting outside. Roman nudged at her cup. "Why don't you have a little more?"

She sipped at it again, the fumes of it strong in her nose, making her slightly dizzy, but comforting somehow. "I never drank so much at one time before . . . nor straight," she added.

He smiled. "I don't expect you ever needed to."

"If we do hold," she said suddenly, "if they go away and leave us in peace again, I'd like to go to Otter Creek."

He nodded. "The trees will be turning before long . . . down by the creek and over in the woods. The maples always seem the earliest."

"But the dogwood and the sumac are the prettiest." It came to her unbidden, the memory of it flooding through her with the soft warmth of the liquor She could see the porch and the wild morning glory that climbed along the side . . . and the woodpile and the springhouse, ringed round with mint.

There were footsteps down the loft stairs and Cullen appeared, surprised to see Roman there. "Thought ye'd gone off to sleep," he said.

"I had, but it occurred to me this might do Kitty some good." He held up the jug.

"How goes it, lass?" Cullen put a hand to her cheek, and she covered it with her good one.

"Better," she said.

He smiled at her, and across to Roman and the jug. "If there's any o' that left, I would welcome it myself."

Roman grinned and passed it.

"Rum," Cullen said, pleasantly surprised once he'd taken a deep swig of it. "By God, but it's tasty! Here's to the Gentrys . . . and the Claibornes." He tilted it again.

Once the women returned with the tea, the two men had already climbed back into the loft to be near their posts through the night. But they'd left the jug and what little was left in it behind.

"Lord, it's strong," Sara said, her gentle face screwing up as she swallowed a taste. Elvie laughed softly, and Granny Hawkins nodded.

"Aye," she said, rheumy old eyes dancing as they fastened upon the jug. "But right good for whatever ails ye." If pressed, she would not mind a sup of it herself, she allowed.

Elizabeth held the tea for Kitty, who dutifully drank the strong, sweet mixture. She was already drowsy despite the pain in her hand, which somehow seemed apart from her now. And whether it was the rum or the herbs in the tea that did it, she was able to doze . . . the pain and the whispers of the women far off, tugging her to wakefulness now and again.

The morning brought no lessening of the rain, and the mists had settled in over the river and spread over the hollow to hide the Indians from sight, which made the men on watch nervous.

"Goddamned heathens!" Winfield Burdette muttered, peering out into the fog. "Who knows what they might be up to out there? They could be ten feet from us afore we lay eyes on 'em."

"Aye"—someone else joined in the grumbling—"that's why I aim to shoot at whatsomever moves the minute I spy it!"

But the women rejoiced that the rain barrels were gradually filling, and they put out buckets and pots and pitchers to catch every drop they could.

With Kitty's hand hurting miserably, she attempted to nurse Michael, but to her distress, he pulled at the nipple and cried, getting nothing from breasts that felt sore and empty. She tried him on both before giving up, near to tears herself.

"It don't mean a thing," Elvie soothed her. "You've had a shock to your system. It'll come back. You ain't no different than ary milch cow that's had the wits scared out'en it by a big old catamount or such. It'll come back, I tell ye."

Faith, who'd only heard about Kitty's injury once she was up, and had come immediately to see about her, joined in. "One time when Martha was a little bitty thing, I caught the chills and didn't have a drop for her for a whole day. Had to spoon some clabber down her throat, and it gave her a terrible colic. But I was back to normal the next day."

Despite their assurances, Kitty felt no less distressed as Michael squalled, his small face red and his fists balled.

"Here," Elvie said, reaching for him, "hand him over here to me." She opened her blouse and put him to a full breast, which he promptly grabbed and began to suckle lustily.

"What about Little Lureen?" Kitty asked.

"She ain't woke up yet. Besides, there'll be plenty. Lord o' mercy, there are times I think I'm goin' to pop I've got so much still . . . and her near a year old."

After Michael had nursed his fill, and both Elvie and Faith had gone off to look after their own children, Sara brought in a little rainwater she'd caught in a pan and dipped a rag in it to bathe him. "It might be if it keeps on raining, we'll be able to catch enough for us, too," she said brightly. "Just enough to wipe off with."

Kitty sighed at the thought of it. There'd been times lately when she'd searched for a clean corner of her skirt—a spot not stiffened with Michael's urine or grease, nor black with gunpowder—to wet with her own spittle and wipe the dirt off her face and hands.

Along about noon Daniel was summoned to the tunnel by the

crew working there. Roman and Cullen went along with him, making their way down into the gloom of the four-foot-wide countermine that now extended well under the rear cabins. The workers, stripped to their waists and streaked with mud, were visible in the flickering light of a pair of grease lamps.

"Trouble, boys?" Daniel asked.

"Don't know." The answer came barely above a whisper, from a big beefy fellow from Harrod's fort. Setting his shovel aside to hook his thumbs into the top of his britches, he turned his heavy-jawed face Daniel's way.

"If'n you be right quiet, you'll hear it," said Winfield Burdette's boy Oliver, cocking his head to one side.

They made way for Daniel, Roman, and Cullen to come in closer and indicated a point several feet back from where they were digging.

"Listen," Oliver said.

As the three men waited, there was nothing but a lone drip of water to be heard at first. Daniel was on the verge of shrugging his shoulders and turning his back to them when it came—a hint of sound through the earth . . . a whisper at first, and then louder . . . the unmistakable scrape and thud of digging.

The men exchanged glances, and Daniel picked up a small rock that had been dislodged and used the sharp edge of it to mark the spot where the sounds were strongest. Then he motioned everyone from the tunnel.

Outside, the diggers hastily pulled on their shirts against the chill rain and waited expectantly. "You can put your shovels away, boys," Daniel said. "It's time for rifles now."

A round-the-clock tunnel watch was set up. Crews of four men each would alternate, ready to sound the alarm and take on the Indians the moment they dug through.

"I'll go with the first watch," Cullen volunteered.

"No," Daniel said. "I'll need you and Roman up here with me. We could be in for it now. Black Fish knows that we can hold off a few at a time trying to come through the tunnel. It's my notion that he'll hit the walls at the same time, likely with scaling ladders."

Roman nodded. "Divide us as much as they can. Probably try to blow their way in the postern gate with an outsized charge of powder."

"DeQuindre would put them up to that," Cullen agreed.

"Let's make sure we're as ready as we can get," Daniel said. He gathered the people together to apprise them of the peril of their situation and the need for unwavering vigilance, going about it with a calm and confident manner that helped to keep them from any undue panic.

"Lord protect us," Ben Tyler said.

"He will," Squire Boone returned, and they all went back to their posts.

As the day wore on, the mists thickened and rolled as the rain came down, heavier at times. The men on watch squinted, unable to make out anything beyond a few feet.

"Hell's fire," Ezekial Turner growled at one point, "they could have me by m'jewels afore I even knowed they was on me!"

The women who weren't otherwise occupied with children or other duties stood ready to help, quietly greasing patches and making sure that bullets and powder were readily available. And downstairs, Kitty had never felt so useless.

Late in the day Granny Hawkins came to change the bandage. "It's a-goin' to hurt," she warned, "but iffen we want it to heal up right, we got to do it."

As the cloth, which had stuck in places, was pulled away, Kitty came near to fainting again. And Sara, standing by staunchly, gripped her other hand, talking a steady stream of encouragement all the while.

"Don't look at it now . . . it's best not to . . . it won't take long. There, it's loose!" But Kitty couldn't keep herself from looking at the fearful blisters, some of them broken now, oozing and blackened raw flesh showing through.

Granny tried to ease back the stiff fingers, curled inward still, but the pain of it was so intense that Kitty let out a sharp scream in spite of herself, tears spurting from her eyes. She clamped her lips together, glad that Little Lureen Porter was already setting up a lusty howl at the other end of the blockhouse. Maybe the child's crying had masked her own cry and Cullen hadn't heard. She didn't want him to know.

Clucking her tongue, Granny let the fingers alone—but it was only for now, she warned. "Just as soon as you can stand it, you've got to begin workin' them fingers."

"I will," Kitty promised, tears streaming still as the old lady put some more of the green cream on the burn. "I'll try tomorrow."

"This hand's a-goin' to need a world o' care. We'll have to change it ever' day, and it still could end up drawed in and stiff." Granny shook her head, the wattle of flesh beneath her chin quivering. "I don't know. . . ."

With the fort shrouded in fog, there seemed little difference as night fell. The people gathered in small groups to speak softly among themselves, aware that it could be their last night, knowing that the morning would almost certainly bring an all-out attack. But when Cullen came down from the loft, he found Kitty sleeping soundly.

"She's worn out," Sara whispered. "Thank goodness she can sleep."

"Aye . . . poor little lass." Cullen looked down at his wife for a moment, then turned his attention to his son, who slept on his stomach, feet drawn up froglike. He rested his big hand lightly on the small back.

"Don't worry. I'll see to them both," Sara said.

He looked at her for a long moment. "You're a good woman, Sara Gentry. And stronger than ye give yourself credit for."

After he had gone back to the loft, Sara thought about what he'd said and hoped that it was so. She'd always been able to depend on Kitty. Now, Kitty needed to depend on her.

She couldn't bring herself to even look at the small store of torn linen sheets in back of the rocker, Kitty's shawl tucked safely beneath them, out of the way. She knew what was hidden within the woolen folds, knew that in some awful nightmare almost beyond her imagining, she might be called upon to use it. Could she?

She looked down at Michael in his cradle, the soft dark hair whorled at the crown, his dimpled hands brought in close. Her throat ached and she could feel her body trembling, her hands unsteady as she reached into her apron pocket and brought out her small comb. Releasing the pins from the twist at the back of her head, fingers unsteady, she took down her hair and ran the comb slowly down its length . . . smoothing out the tangles, gently working out the tiny snarls. She usually kept it shining, washed clean with rainwater, but now there was a heavy, oily feel to it. She would hate to die with her hair dirty, she thought wryly.

Still, there was the other . . . her secret hope that each day became more certain . . . Surely a merciful God would not start a new life within her and allow it to be snuffed out before it was fairly begun.

The rain ended sometime during the night, and just before dawn the brisk winds gusting from the south blew the clouds and fog away to leave the men on watch waiting for the sunrise with guns primed and ready. And as pink fingers of light streaked the horizon beyond the river, they strained to see, starting at the smallest sound. But there was nothing out there except the hollow and the woods beyond, and out in front of them Hackberry Ridge, gleaming in the first light.

"By Jesus, where are they?" someone called.

"I believe they've cleared out!" yelled Ezekial.

"Hold steady, boys," Daniel cautioned. "Let's don't get caught with our britches down."

But in a minute there was a joyous whoop from outside, and when Daniel and Roman and Cullen went running out into the muddy fort yard, they were met by Colonel Callaway and Squire, gesturing excitedly back toward the tower. The two men who'd been posted up there through the night were scrambling down now and in imminent danger of falling as they attempted to wave their arms at the same time.

"They say the whole tunnel has caved in!" Squire wheezed, holding his wounded shoulder and grimacing with the effort of running.

Roman and Cullen didn't wait to hear the report but climbed the tower themselves, nudging each other and grinning as they gazed down on the stretch of riverbank below them.

"Would you look at that?" Cullen said, slapping his thigh and laughing. The tunnel upon which the Indians had worked so diligently had collapsed into a watery mire of water and earth that extended from the river to within several feet of the back wall of the stockade.

They enjoyed the sight for a moment, the river flowing strongly, up a little from all the rain. And no matter which way they looked, the land lay peaceful, gleaming, washed clean under that bright sky. They turned to one another, the same question occurring to each of them almost at the same instant.

"God Almighty"—Cullen voiced it—"what about *our* tunnel? Ben Tyler and his brother were down there!"

But once they'd climbed down to the ground, they found Ben and Todd and the two other men who'd been with them grinning and glad to be out in the full daylight, quit of the damp darkness.

"Thank the Lord," Ben said.

"Looks like the cabins above kept ours from cavin' in," said Daniel. "But I expect we'd do well to commence fillin' it in quick as we can."

In a minute he conferred with Roman and Cullen, Colonel Callaway and Squire looking on. "I believe they've gone . . .

yet they've fooled us before. I can't discount that and maybe lose lives or the fort because of it.''

''Let Roman and me go out for a look,'' Cullen suggested.

Daniel pondered it, well aware of what the Shawnee's reaction must have been to the collapse of the tunnel after all their hard labor. It would have been taken as the final bad omen, a clear signal from the spirits. ''Well''—he chewed at a twig he'd plucked off one of the bushes behind them—''I'd not be surprised if Lieutenant DeQuindre ain't some put out with Black Fish about now.'' A grin spread over his face. ''Get on out there—but mind now, be careful. Let's don't get cocksure until we know for certain.''

Once the scouts were gone, the garrison waited quietly, few even venturing outside, as if they might at any moment hear the high-pitched whine of a bullet or the fearful yell of a Shawnee. No man left his post, and the women sat together, speaking little.

But about noon Cullen was sighted coming in along the riverbank, galloping his black horse the final way and waving his hat, a wide grin splitting his face. The men let loose with lusty cheers, shouting and whooping until they were hoarse . . . hauling him down from his saddle the moment he had entered the gate and pounding him on the back with such exuberance that he could hardly speak.

''They're in full retreat!'' he finally got out. And at Daniel's inquiry: ''Roman's staying out a little longer, just to make sure they don't take it in their heads to double back.''

Solemn and, for some, tearful prayers of thanks were offered. That done, the cheering broke out again and what spirits could be found were quickly brought forth and passed freely.

Sara and Kitty clung to each other and cried with relief. In a moment Cullen came to put his arms around the both of them at once. Then he picked up his son to delight the infant with his rough face and hearty chuckle, and held the boy high.

''You're a fine lad, Michael Claiborne. And you'll sleep in your own home, as ye should . . . tucked safe between your papa and mama this night!''

After nine days of siege, there'd been two killed within the fort and four injured. No one knew for certain how many Indians had fallen. The warriors, true to their custom, had taken all the bodies away with them.

A few days later a party of militia arrived from the Holston, much relieved to find that the little outpost had held. And hard atop that came word of George Clark's well-nigh miraculous exploits in the Northwest.

" 'E took Kaskasky, then Cahoky, and not content with that, slipped right over to Vinsins to catch 'em bare-assed and red-faced! By God, if 'e ain't the finest, bar none, that I ever seed! Ought to make him a goddamned gen'ral 'stead of a cunnel, and that's the plain truth of it!" The scabrous and scraggly-haired messenger who brought the news of Clark's remarkable sweep of Kaskaskia, Cahokia, and Vincennes was minus an eye himself, lost in some long-ago gouging, but the remaining one glittered in unabashed worship of his commanding officer. "There ain't nothin' the cunnel can't do once he sets his mind to it."

Ezekial took up his fiddle, and the settlers, feasting on deer meat and bear steaks that the hunters had brought back to the fort, tapped their feet and took their turns on the cleared blockhouse floor, stomping and whirling. Kitty watched from the sidelines, the pain in her hand still almost constant. But at least her milk was full again, as Elvie and Faith had said it would be, and Michael lay in her lap, well satisfied and lulled by the music.

Sometime during the celebration Maggie Hamilton approached the militia captain and asked that she be allowed to travel back with him and his troops once their sojourn in the western country was ended. There was, she told him, no more need for her to stay on now that her husband was dead. And she had never wanted to come in the first place.

❋ 26 ❋

THE SIEGE WAS HARDLY ENDED BEFORE WILL HANCOCK began to voice his criticism of Daniel again. And as he made his charges, his voice breaking at times with the intensity of his feelings, it was clear that the people of Boonesborough were confused and troubled about what they heard.

"I held my peace when the fort was in danger," he said. "But now it's time for the truth to come out. Boone was thick as thieves with Hamilton . . . and back at Chillicothe, he not only let hisself be called Black Fish's son, but he lived good whilst the rest o' us was treated like slaves. I say there was plenty o' times when he could've got away, but he didn't want to. He hunted and fished with 'em, fixed their guns when one of 'em broke . . . and he took hisself a squaw to wife."

"There's not a word of that true, Will Hancock," Jemima confronted him when she heard, fighting back tears.

"As God's my judge it is," Hancock declared. "I don't want to hurt you, Miz Jemima . . . I'm sorry fer that. But it's the plain-out truth."

Now that October was fast approaching, preparations for winter had begun. The men went about tightening up the cabins and chopping wood for the growing piles, and began to lay in a supply of meat to be salted down for the long cold months ahead. When there was time, they occupied themselves digging spent balls out of the stockade walls to be melted down and recast into bullets; over a hundred pounds of lead had already been gathered. The women had their share of readying to do as well, soap making and candle dipping and knitting warm socks and caps and gloves. Spinning wheels whirred as linens cut up for diapers or bandages during the siege had to be replaced. But in spite of all the activity, grease lamps burned late as people pondered and argued and found their loyalties divided over Hancock's charges against Daniel.

The subject of all the talk, hollow-cheeked and graying now, made one terse statement. "I have explained all I did before. I don't intend to do it again."

But that didn't stay the gossip or the doubters. "Seems I recall," Blandford Moore offered his opinion, "that his wife's people back in Carolina was of a Tory persuasion. It appears he may lean that way hisself."

"Hit's a fact," someone else put in. "I mind it myself. The Bryans was always firm for the English king."

"Daniel's no Tory!" Winfield Burdette put in hotly, and in the jostling back and forth, he and Blandford exchanged a few blows before those nearby could separate them.

Colonel Callaway, deeply troubled for some time now and haggard himself with the strain of it all, rode out early one morning, refusing to allow anyone to accompany him. "What I have to do, I'll do alone," he insisted.

Flanders shook his head and watched him go, and continued to keep his own counsel. Though no one could doubt how difficult it was for him with his two brothers taken captive, maybe dead by now, and caught himself between a man who had been like a father to him and another who was his father-in-law, Flanders Callaway refused to take a side. At least publicly. And if he ever expressed an opinion in his own home, it was kept between Jemima and himself.

Roman and Cullen sat late into the night talking over the whole thing.

"By heaven, I know Daniel too well," Cullen declared. "Whatever he did, he did because he thought it was the best way at the time."

Roman nodded.

"The women are outraged over the squaw—them and the psalm sayers too tight-assed to piss. But a man's a man, Roman . . . Daniel included. Has he said aught to ye of it?"

"No."

Cullen caught a flicker across that sober face. "You do believe Daniel, don't ye . . . Roman?"

Roman grunted. "Believe that he was fully loyal to Boonesborough? Of course I do. Daniel's no Tory. If he were, he'd be the first to tell it."

"What is it, then, man? What do I see in your face? Let's have it straight out."

They sat in one of the blockhouses, all to themselves, and Roman stretched out his long legs, holding his feet closer to the dying embers. The nights were growing cooler now.

"Roman . . ." Cullen prodded, and Roman lifted his head and drew a long breath.

"I probably know him as well as any except for Rebecca." He gazed into the soft glow of the smoke-blackened fireplace. "When I think of what it must have been like for him, Cullen—when Black Fish took him as a son . . . and Daniel was finally what he maybe always was in his heart—an Indian. God's blood"—Roman sat upright in the chair—"he must have loved it! The freedom of it. I think he understands them and the way they live in a way that none of us can. And it must have drawn him, must have seemed like heaven."

Cullen felt the truth of it, and he gave a short, hard nod, half angry at Roman for making him see it. "Are you saying he could have gotten away earlier?" he growled.

Roman shrugged. "Maybe. Maybe not. I'm not sure it matters. What's important is that when he knew the fort was in danger, he broke his neck to get here. And he directed its defense as well as he knew how . . . and I say, as well as any I know could have.''

"Aye,'' Cullen said, falling silent then to turn the whole thing over in his mind for a minute. "What do you suppose the Colonel is up to?'' he asked finally.

"I wish I knew.'' Roman rubbed at his chin, his eyes gone melancholy. "His nephews being taken was hard for him. And there were things that Daniel did that didn't set well with him . . . but I hate to see them have this falling out.''

Cullen nodded and, shivering, started to poke up the fire. "Well,''—his voice took on a cautious optimism—"with Daniel planning to leave in a day or two to go after Rebecca and the family, it may have all died down by the time they get back.''

But the next day around noon, the Old Colonel helloed the gate and came riding in. He'd been gone nearly a week, and his handsome old face bore the lines of fatigue and something else . . . a kind of resigned and tight-lipped sorrow. He didn't wait to rest but asked that the garrison be summoned to witness what he had to say to Daniel.

The people gathered outside the northwest blockhouse. The sun was pleasantly hot, and the women shielded their faces with linen bonnets. Kitty and Sara stood together, Sara holding Michael. Roman and Cullen were up in front, where the two old friends confronted one another.

"I take no pleasure in this,'' Colonel Callaway began, his voice quivering slightly but his shoulders squared, his eyes unblinking as he faced Daniel, who returned the gaze with an equally stony stare. "It may well be the saddest day of my life . . . but I've never shirked from what I thought was right, and I won't now. I've preferred charges against you, Daniel.''

There was an audible gasp from the onlookers, but Daniel stood unflinching, his expression never changing. Elizabeth Callaway was pale, her eyes searching her husband's face. Jemima began to cry, and Flanders put his arm around her.

Colonel Callaway took a folded piece of paper from inside his shirt and handed it to Daniel, who accepted it without comment, unfolding it to scan it only briefly. After that he let his hand fall to his side.

"As you see,'' the Old Colonel went on doggedly, "in accordance with his duties as a militia officer, Ben Logan has ordered that you be placed under arrest and brought to Logan's

Station to face a court-martial for your actions during and following the capture at the Blue Licks. You'll be confined to your cabin until time to leave at the end of the week, when you'll be taken there under guard. Roman . . . Cullen''—the Old Colonel turned to the two scouts—''Captain Logan has asked that the two of you assume that duty.''

Cullen and Roman exchanged looks. The Scot's dark brows were aslant with incredulity, while Roman's face betrayed no more than it ever did. But he was the one to recover first, and he took a step forward.

''I can't do that, Richard,'' he said, his voice filled with sadness.

''Nor can I,'' Cullen echoed him.

''Not even if Ben Logan means it to be an order?'' the old man challenged.

''Not even then,'' Roman said.

Daniel had remained silent throughout, but now he put out a quick hand to Roman's arm. ''Hold up there,'' he said. ''I expect I'd as lief ride over to Logan's Station with you two as anybody.''

''*Daniel,*'' Cullen tried to protest.

''No . . .'' He waved him to silence. ''Let's call it settled.'' He took a long look around the group of people who had followed him for so long, his head stubbornly high, and then he turned back to Roman and Cullen. ''I'll be goin' to my cabin as Ben Logan has requested, and I'll be ready to ride when the time comes, boys.''

Jemima ran to him and he hugged her, whispering something in her ear. Then he made his way through the knot of people, nodding to those who reached out to grasp his arm as he went, seeming not to see those who turned away from him.

Once he was gone, small arguments broke out. Voices were raised in heated exchanges. From the beginning there had probably been no two men on the frontier any more respected than Daniel Boone and Richard Callaway. And such a bitter division between the two old friends inevitably caused people to choose up sides.

''I hope you can understand,'' the Old Colonel said to Roman and Cullen, his face working painfully.

Roman hesitated, then nodded, morosely silent.

''I guess ye've done what you thought ye must,'' said Cullen. Some of Daniel's critics had begun to gather around Callaway now, praising him for the courage to take up the matter with the military establishment.

"The way I look on it, it's the only way for justice to be done," Will Hancock declared.

Alone in the cabin, Kitty took each finger of her right hand and pulled it straight, going slowly, one by one, and trying not to cry out. She clamped her lips over her teeth and moaned, faint with the pain of it.

Granny Hawkins insisted that it would help if she did it daily, though the burn was still awful-looking, crusted and oozing. There were times when Kitty doubted the hand would ever be right again. Still, she couldn't give up. And she couldn't depend on Sara and Elvie to do things for her for the rest of her life.

She trembled, looking away as she pulled and trying to think of something else . . . anything to take her mind off the pain. But all that would come to her was the rift between Daniel and the Old Colonel, and that was nearly as painful as her hand.

Jemima had appealed to her. "Kitty," she'd said, her voice trembling piteously, "you can't believe anything that Will Hancock says. Surely you can't. And how Colonel Callaway could ever do what he's done . . . and him once a friend of Pa's . . ."

Just the memory of Jemima's face grieved her. And it was no better with Elizabeth. She hadn't known what to say to either of them, except to mouth generalities about everything working out. And she certainly didn't know what to say to them today. Cullen and Roman had left shortly after dawn to escort Daniel to Logan's Station for the court-martial.

Actually, a good-size party of men had gone along—Colonel Callaway and Will Hancock to testify and the others because they were determined to be present at the outcome one way or the other. It was hard for the settlers to think of much else. And Kitty wondered how the whole sorry mess could ever turn out right for anybody.

She recalled the day that Ben had brought her to the fort and put her and her things out under the astonished gaze of Squire Boone. Daniel and the Old Colonel had made her welcome at once and without reservation. It would be impossible for her to ever separate their kindnesses to her that day . . . putting one of them over the other. She would not judge them now . . . either of them.

Elvie came in through the open door, carrying a pail half filled with milk, Little Lureen perched atop her hip. "I see you've been exercisin' them fingers," she said. She set the milk on the table and then put Little Lureen down on the floor. "Don't you be gettin' into nothin'," she warned the little girl, who toddled unsteadily toward a corner and plopped herself down to play with one of the balls of yarn piled in a basket.

"Let me see . . ." Elvie came to have a look at the hand. "I do believe it's a little better," she declared after a moment. "Here . . . let me help you bind it up again."

Kitty shook her head. "I've got to try to do as much as I can by myself." And she took up the strip of linen in her lap with her left hand and awkwardly bound it around her right one, finally tying the two long strips at the end by grasping one of them in her teeth and pulling. Elvie laughed, but her round face showed her approval.

"Did you see Sara?" Kitty asked. "She took Michael out for a walk. He's cross as can be. Makes me think he's trying to cut a tooth."

Elvie nodded. "She stopped down there to talk to Jemima. That poor little thing. She wanted to go along to Logan's fort this mornin', but Flanders wouldn't let her. Law, sometimes I think men don't understand a thing about women." She strained up the milk, then began to cut up a rabbit that Cullen had dressed out and left for Kitty.

In a minute Sara came back, Michael asleep against her shoulder. She eased him down in the cradle and he sighed, finding his thumb.

"Well, that's a relief." Kitty smiled. "He's been a handful this morning."

"He didn't want to give up," Sara said, tucking a stray wisp of hair up and smiling, "but he couldn't fight it any longer." She went to put the big iron skillet over the fire, spooning in some grease and letting it heat until it was smoking hot. When it was ready, Elvie slid the rabbit pieces in and they sputtered and popped.

"How's poor Jemima?" she asked Sara.

"About as you'd expect. And Elizabeth is no better. I talked to her a long time this morning. I never saw her cry before."

The three women were quiet for a moment.

"Well, I'm just glad that Rebecca's in North Carolina," Kitty declared.

Elvie shook her head. "Men just can't leave off rilin' things up. It's seemed to me all along that Daniel's done the best he could in a bad situation. But maybe if I was to've had a son took . . . or a husband, or nephew . . . I might feel some different."

Kitty had come to the table now, and she began to scoop some meal from the big gourd where she kept it into a bowl and then added a pinch of salt. The two women stood back and let her do it, respecting her wish to do as much as she could manage, awkward or not.

"Do you think that Daniel really took an Indian squaw?" Sara asked them.

"He could have," Elvie said instantly. "Law me, Sara honey, a man don't have his brain—nor his heart—betwixt his legs. There are times when what he's got there does just as it pleases. And if every man that's been up to that was to be court-martialed, there'd be few of 'em left to fight the war . . . east or west."

They had gathered from all three of the forts, and the air in the blockhouse was stale with the odor of greasy buckskins and tobacco smoke and spit . . . and the various personal, and some-times rank, body smells of the men who'd crowded in, deter-mined to witness the court-martial of Daniel Boone. As many chairs as could be rounded up had been brought in to be seized upon instantly. Those men without had jammed in to lean against the wall or hunker down on the rough puncheon floor, as Roman and Cullen had, near to the front.

Though Ben Logan had warned them to keep their strong spirits outside, more than one jug passed surreptitiously, to be quickly pulled at and then slipped beneath a chair once again. Tempers had soared so high, there had been several rip-roaring fights that turned the whole stockade out to watch. An eye had been gouged out. One old trapper had had his face laid open from forehead to chinbone. It was hard to find a man who didn't have firm beliefs on the subject of Daniel's guilt or innocence.

Logan read the formal charges himself, the deep clear voice reaching to every corner of the packed room.

"Number one," he said. "Charged that Daniel Boone, with twenty-six men at the Blue Licks, was surrounded by Indians ten miles below as he hunted near the Licking, and that he did then lead the Indians to his men and voluntarily surrender them.

"Number two: Charged that when a prisoner, he engaged with Governor Hamilton to surrender the people at Boonesbor-ough, to be removed to Detroit and live under British rule.

"Number three: Charged that returning from captivity, he encouraged a party of men to accompany him to the Paint Lick Town, thereby weakening the garrison in a time of peril.

"Number four: Charged that preceding the attack on Boonesborough, he was willing to take the officers of the fort beyond the safety of the walls to negotiate a peace treaty, and even to sign such a treaty, which swore allegiance to the British king.''

Ben Logan looked up from the paper he held in his hand, his dark eyes going to Daniel, who sat, thin and tired-looking, his face hollowed out and sharp. "How do you plead, Daniel?" he said, lapsing from his formal tone, his voice heavy with regret.

"Not guilty," Daniel said firmly, and his supporters were glad to see some of the old spark flaring in his answer.

"That's the way, Dan'l!" someone called out.

"Give 'em hell!" another shouted.

Logan looked relieved to turn the proceedings over to a young officer but newly arrived from the East. By his speech he was a man of some education, and obviously eager to prove himself.

The trial proceeded slowly, with several witnesses from Boonesborough answering general questions about the siege and Daniel's direction of the defense. Then Colonel Callaway testified, sitting stony-faced, only a slight involuntary movement of the hand at his side betraying the strain he was under as he faced up to the difficult duty he had taken upon himself.

He answered the young prosecutor's questions in a calm tone of voice for a quarter of an hour. It was only when the prosecutor asked him what had happened when Black Fish and his warriors surrounded Fort Boonesborough that the Old Colonel showed his outrage.

"Damme, the two of 'em embraced! Daniel and Black Fish. And Daniel called him 'father.' ''

Once the commotion had died down, the young prosecutor took a different tack. "Did you," he asked the Colonel, "have some problem in accepting the account given to you by Captain Boone of the circumstances surrounding the capture of the salt makers at the Blue Licks?"

Callaway nodded. "I did. And do now."

"Were not two of your own nephews taken that day"—he peered at his notes—"James and Micajah Callaway?"

"That's right, sir. And remain prisoners . . . if they still live."

The Old Colonel clenched his hands at his sides and looked down at the floor in front of him for a long moment, his bushy eyebrows working.

It was strong testimony, and obviously had an effect on the men gathered. But Will Hancock's words, coming next as he took his turn on the witness chair, seemed even more damning. He told once more of the favoritism shown to Daniel by the

Indians and his promises to deliver the fort to them. And he didn't miss the opportunity to add that Daniel had taken an Indian squaw to wife. When he'd finished, the room was still; the laughter and shouting of children playing with a hoop outside the blockhouse carried on the warm October air.

Logan's call for a short recess broke the silence, and the men elbowed out to go relieve themselves in the necessary or the bushes behind it, then gather to pass their jugs and their judgments . . . and argue still.

"What do ye think?" Cullen asked.

"I don't know," Roman replied, cut to the quick as he remembered how Daniel had looked in the blockhouse. Yet he could raise no censure for the Old Colonel, who stood apart now, seeking the shade of a huge elm, his handsome old face bearing the pain of the whole thing. They were each one of them right in their way, Roman thought sadly, in their view of things; but in the attempt to resolve their differences, the friendship they had shared for years would be shattered forever . . . no matter which way it went.

The court reconvened an hour later, with the first few minutes of spitting and swearing and settling in that was characteristic of most frontier gatherings. But no one had to tell the onlookers to be quiet after the prosecutor asked Daniel to take the witness chair.

"You've heard the charges against you," he said once Daniel had taken oath to tell the truth. "Does your plea of 'not guilty' mean that you deny them all?"

"No," Daniel replied, his wide mouth drawing down at the corners. "I don't deny a danged one of 'em. But it's in the why of it that matters."

"Can you tell us then *why* you led the Indians to the salt makers at the Blue Licks and surrendered them without a fight, Captain Boone?"

"Because I knew for a fact that my men would end up prisoners or they'd end up dead. Black Fish's scouts knew they were there. They would have been surrounded and massacred, every last man, if I hadn't persuaded Black Fish that it was better to take them prisoner. Besides that, he was set on attacking Boonesborough, and I knew the fort to be in bad order with so many of us away. It would have been taken easy. I thought to use some stratagem, and told the Indians that Boonesborough was very strong and had too many men for them."

"But when you were taken to Detroit, to that British stronghold, did you not tell Lieutenant Governor Hamilton that you were in sympathy with the British cause and would persuade the people of Boonesborough to come over to the British side?"

"I did. I aimed to make Hamilton think he could have Kentucky without a fight. I told him whatever tales needed to fool him . . . and hoped that if I convinced him of my friendship, he would turn me loose and I could get back to warn the settlements. He did try to buy me, but Black Fish had taken a fancy to me and wouldn't sell, so I was taken back to Chillicothe."

The prosecutor pounced on what he thought was an opportunity to shake Boone's testimony. "Captain Boone," he said, frowning, "do you really believe, or hope to make this court believe, that a man of Hamilton's rank—the lieutenant governor of Detroit—could be tricked into believing the tall tales of a militiaman?"

"Well . . ." Daniel took his time, cool and self-possessed. "It seemed to me a reasonable hope, since I would expect that the best of the British officers would be commanding armies against General Washington and not in some backwoods fort doin' his damnedest to keep George Clark and his boys from breakin' in through his back door."

There was a moment's silence, and then the room exploded in cheers, the men slapping their knees and shoving one another, their great guffaws bouncing off the log walls. Daniel was, after all, one of their own. Let this young coxcomb from the East with his fancy ways and words see what he could do with that! They nudged one another and winked as he reddened to the top of his collar and plucked a handkerchief from his pocket to dab at his brow.

Young though he might be, the prosecutor knew when to change the subject. "It has been testified to here, Captain Boone, that once you were back in the Indian village of Chillicothe, you were adopted by Chief Black Fish, and that it was common for you to hunt and fish with warriors . . . even to do them favors such as fixing their broken rifles. Did you not feel that that was being overly friendly for a man in the grasp of his enemy?"

Daniel took his time about answering that. "Well now," he said, "it could be. But then I've always believed that if a man was holdin' a tomahawk up to my head, I'd as lief make a friend of him as an enemy."

Again the onlookers roared and nodded their approval.

Even more flustered now, the prosecutor pressed on, his voice rising. "Is it not a fact that you could have escaped sooner than you did, Captain Boone?"

"I might could have," Daniel replied, his voice steady and sure. "But gaining the confidence of Black Fish held out hope of a peaceful settlement . . . without loss of life. Besides, don't forget that being there and trusted by him, I could not only learn his plans, but I came away with knowledge of the whereabouts of most of the villages north of the Ohio—information which I would expect could be of interest to some."

Daniel turned from the young prosecutor to face the officers gathered to sit in judgment of him, his jaw sharp as a blade in that gaunt face. He spoke directly to them. "I escaped in time to give Boonesborough notice of the attack and to help prepare for it. As to meeting with Black Fish, I aimed to gain as much time as I could, since help could have arrived at any time from the Holston . . . or Virginia. Talking won us four days, all of it done under twenty-five good marksmen who were watching from the blockhouses for any sign of treachery."

"But you signed an oath of allegiance to the king of England!" the prosecutor burst out, endeavoring to regain control of the situation.

"Aye . . . in the same attempt to gain time and save lives. I fail to see how that differed from the deception I practiced whilst I was with the Indians."

"And yet isn't it true that your wife's relations are professed Tories . . . that some of them are even now fighting with the British?"

Daniel's answer was without anger, and so quiet that those present had to strain to hear him. "I bear no responsibility for the politics of my wife's people, nor they for mine. I am not a Tory . . . nor a traitor. I am an American soldier who has done his best and now stands falsely accused. Whilst it is true that I used duplicity, it was to help my own people and for no other reason. Had it been otherwise, I would never have left the Shawnee, who were kind to me. Or once I'd run off from them, I'd have gone to Detroit, or returned to my family in the Yadkin.

"I did none of those things. I made straight for Boonesborough to do my best to defend it, and share in whatever fate the Almighty had decided for us. I would hope that that be sufficient evidence of my devotion to the American cause . . . but I will leave it up to your judgment."

There wasn't a sound in the blockhouse, the usually raucous frontiersmen struck to silence by the words. The Old Colonel sat with his head bowed, his knobby-fingered hands clasped loosely in his lap. Roman and Cullen looked at one another, and Roman nodded, sure that Daniel had defended himself well.

There was a sudden whoop, and a besotted old trapper, bleary-eyed from too much corn liquor and an excess of emotion, leapt to his feet. "I say three cheers fer Dan'l!" he shouted.

And it came, roaring up from their throats with a force that threatened to shake the rafters. *"Hip, hip, hoo ray! Hip, hip, hoo ray! Hip, hip, hoooo raaaaay!"*

The verdict was not long in coming. The not guilty pronouncement was delivered after a brief clearing of the block-house so that the members of the military court could confer. To show their confidence in Daniel, they announced that he was to receive a promotion to the rank of major in acknowledgment of his able defense of Boonesborough.

Outside, the firepits were ready and three pigs were being roasted along with a variety of game meat. Jugs were passed freely, and impromptu horse races and wrestling matches sprang up while well-wishers crowded around Daniel. Roman and Cullen worked their way over, and each of them shook his hand solemnly, noting the bitter sadness in his eyes still. Roman wondered if anything would ever take it away.

After a while Cullen sought out Roman, who was washing down a mouthful of roast pork with a swallow of rum. "I tried to find Colonel Callaway," he said, "but they tell me he set out for home . . . by himself."

Roman wiped a hand across his mouth and shook his head. "God help us, it won't ever be done between those two."

"I know." Cullen squinted against the afternoon sun, looking out toward the rolling hillsides dotted with orange and yellow and bloodred, now that the leaves had begun to turn. "I think I'll just ride after him. I figure it wouldn't hurt a thing for him to have some company on his way back."

Roman smiled and nodded.

✳ 27 ✳

THE THREE WOMEN MADE THEIR WAY DOWN THE FORT-yard path, a tentative but excited air about them. And as they came even with Kitty and Sara and Faith and the big black iron kettle filled with hot dye water, they smiled and stopped.

"That's a good deep shade o' blue," remarked one of them, a wisp of a woman with hair hanging limply about a pockmarked face. Casting an admiring eye toward the lengths of linsey and hanks of yarn already dyed and rinsed and hung to dry, she ran her hands nervously down a skirt as limp as her hair.

"It's the first indigo we've been able to get for a long time," Kitty replied, smiling.

"You must've come in last night after dark," said Sara.

Another of the women spoke up. "We did. And plain glad to get here."

It had been nine months since the siege ended, and once word of Black Fish's defeat—coupled with the news of George Clark and his ragtag band's retaking of Vincennes to capture none other than the Hair-Buyer himself—had reached the East in the spring, an influx of settlers had begun. Stockaded settlements sprang up, and some that had been abandoned in the face of the Indian threat were reclaimed. Hardly a week passed that didn't bring the arrival of several groups to Boonesborough.

Down the way, four or five men mounted the steps to Harley Bailor's store and disappeared within to bargain for supplies and tools to take with them when they pushed on to stake their claims somewhere in the rich wilderness—packhorses brought in goods from over the mountains almost regularly now to stock the fat old storekeeper's shelves. Winfield Burdette was kept busy at

363

his forge, hammering out plow points and other tools, and shoes for the horses.

The women exchanged names, the newcomers revealing that they had come from North Carolina and adding that there was a world of people back home who were bent on coming across the mountains to settle now that the Indians had been defeated. Kitty promised to give them some milk if they'd send one of their youngsters over for it.

"We'd be obliged," said the thin woman. And they made their way on down toward the necessary.

"Mercy," said Kitty, stirring the dye, "I don't know where we're going to put all of them."

Sara lowered a length of tow linen carefully into the dye bath, her smooth white brow creasing. "I just wish I were as sure as they are that the Indians are gone for good."

Nearby in the grass Michael, who had just passed his first birthday, made a wobbly attempt to hoist himself up onto shaky legs but failed, falling back onto his fat little bottom to make a face and wail. Martha, who was three now, patted her cousin and made faces at him until he was all smiles again.

"Looks like he's goin' to be walkin' soon," Faith said.

"I think he is." Kitty looked over toward her dark-haired son, her heart swelling with pride in him.

Faith, who was in to visit for the day, straightened and rubbed at her back, her greatly swollen belly pushing at her skirt. Though she'd tried to delay it as long as she could, she was resigned to the pregnancy. If she could manage to get three years between all of them, she'd confided to Kitty, she'd be satisfied enough.

"How long do you have to go?" Sara asked her now.

"Six weeks. I'm thinkin' "—she grinned at Sara—"that it won't be long before you find yourself caught again. Ma always said don't worry about a miss, that there'd likely be another'un before you were ready for it."

"I hope that's true," Sara said. She had been pregnant at the time of the siege but had lost it a few weeks later.

"Well," said Kitty, "we do seem to be a fruitful lot."

Faith peered at her. "Are you that way again, too?"

Kitty laughed and shook her head. "No. But besides you there's Jemima . . . and Melinda Hawkins. All of you big as houses."

They hung the last of the dyed pieces up to dry, fastening them to the log walls, draping some of them over bushes. Then they sat to rest for a minute, Faith on the cabin step, Kitty and Sara sunk down in the cool grass by the flower patch.

"Would you look at that. . . ." Kitty gazed ruefully down at the puckered scar that covered most of the palm of her right hand. Usually an unnatural white, it was now stained blue.

"You didn't burn it again, did you?" Sara asked quickly.

"No." Kitty started to giggle. "No. I just picked up this stirring stick by the wrong end. Lord, it's bad enough to have it all scarred up, but it'd be terrible to go through life with a blue hand." That set Sara and Faith laughing, too.

Kitty wiggled the blue fingers. Granny Hawkins's good doctoring and the painful daily exercises had made the hand fully flexible. Only the unsightly scar and an occasional aching when the weather was in for a change were left to remind her of the awful night when the Indians had tried to burn the fort.

Michael began to fuss now, and all of Martha's coaxing failed to restore his good humor.

"I expect he's hungry," Kitty said, and fetched him back to open her blouse and put him to the breast. He was beginning to eat soft foods but still got most of his nourishment from nursing.

"Has Jemima heard anything from Daniel and Rebecca?" Faith asked.

"I don't think so," Sara answered. "Not since she got word that they weren't planning to come back anytime soon."

"She sent a letter . . . telling them about the baby she's expecting," Kitty put in. "They say that Rebecca refused to come back. Someone told her about the squaw."

"That was a mean thing to do," Sara said, but Faith set her mouth stubbornly.

"Well . . . while I feel for poor Rebecca, it seems to me it serves Daniel right." There'd been no word still of the fate of Ben's brother Latham, and the Tylers had not forgiven Daniel for his part in that.

Kitty looked down at her nursing son, who looked so like his father, and wondered if she'd want to know about the Indian woman if it had been Cullen.

She had a sense that everything was changing too rapidly, and it disquieted her. Daniel and Rebecca back east . . . and all the strangers coming in. Even Squire had left again, gone with his family and several others northwest to land he'd claimed at a spot on Clear Creek, about twenty miles below the falls of the Ohio. And as for the Old Colonel, he had never seemed quite the same since the court-martial.

She tried to express her feelings to Cullen later, in the evening when Michael was at last down for the night and the dishes from supper cleaned and put away. But Cullen just shrugged.

"Did ye expect nothing would ever change, lass?" He went to sit on the step in the deepening twilight to smoke a pipe—he had taken up the habit now that tobacco was to be had again.

Kitty came to sit beside him, back a little so that she could rub his shoulders. He'd worked in the common corn crop, as was required of all now. With the new stations springing up between Boonesborough and the Ohio providing a buffer against those few instances of Indian mischief, there was less need for him or Roman to go out on extended scouting trips, and they were no longer exempt from their share of work in the fields. Roman didn't seem to mind, but Cullen clearly hated it.

The thick hard muscles were knotted beneath her fingers, but after a moment he began to relax. "Oooh . . . there now . . . That feels good, Kitty love . . ." From down the way came the sound of soft singing, a woman's voice. And toward the river the frogs chorused.

"You're right, Cullen Claiborne. Things do change. I've been thinking lately that—" She paused, then plunged ahead. "—that now they don't have such an urgent need for you to scout here anymore, we might think about moving out to the place. Out to Otter Creek. It would be wonderful for Michael, Cullen . . . and for us, too. You know it's what I've always hoped we'd—" There'd been a sudden stiffening in him, and she left off the rubbing of his neck to scoot down where she could see his face, see that quick avoidance in his gray eyes. "Cullen, what is it? Tell me. . . ."

He drew a long breath, the pipe aside on the step now, the smell of tobacco clinging to him. He looked away and then back, putting a finger out to touch her cheek lightly. "I should have told you before, lass . . . but I knew it would hurt. After the siege . . . You know that some of Black Fish's warriors split away to do what damage they could before retreating north o' the river?"

Kitty nodded, gooseflesh rising on her arms in the warm night air.

"The place," he said. "Your folks' place . . . They burned it."

She clasped her hands tightly in her lap, and they were silent for a long moment. One of the strangers at the fort walked along the path in front of the cabin and lifted a hand to them, his teeth yellow-white in a stubble of beard. Cullen returned the greeting and the man passed on, and they were alone there in the first darkness again.

"Burned right to the ground?" she asked finally.

"Aye. I'm sorry, lass."

"Well"—she was still cold and besieged by memories—"we could always rebuild it. We could still go. . . ."

"Aye." His voice came to her, and she couldn't really see his face now. "But do ye not know that I'd never be content to work the land, woman?"

He swung up and away, striding along in the direction of the main gates that were always open now. He would, she knew, saddle his black horse and ride wildly along the river. She had not been wed to him this long for nothing. It was what he did when he was restless or pressed.

She leaned her head against the door frame and closed her eyes, tears quivering behind her eyelids. A mosquito whined close to her ear, but she didn't brush it away. She was remembering the rich smell of the Gentry land on warm evenings such as this, remembering the taste of the spring water, and the sound of the creek at the shoreline . . . and that lovely, faintly blue haze that the tall grass took on when it bloomed and riffled in the wind. The pull of it for her was like the urge to be born, she thought, or to mate . . . or maybe even to die when you were ready, when you'd finally lived all you wanted to.

Her nose stung. And after a while she took up the hem of her apron and wiped it. The certainty that she would go back had been a thing carried within her all this time. She'd have to put it aside for now. But the land was still there . . . and it was hers. As long as she lived, nothing could take it from her.

Kitty would not allow herself to dwell overmuch on what had happened at Otter Creek. There was something else that she had been turning over, back in one corner of her mind, and she ferreted it out now and considered it seriously for the first time.

"I'm thinking to start a school here at the fort."

It was Roman to whom she first voiced what was quickly becoming a firm intention. She had gone out to the spring in the hollow to carry in water but had put her pails aside as she'd spied him, coming in from his stint in the corn.

He was sweaty and deliberate and brown as an Indian as he leaned to fill the dipper gourd with sweet water and drink his fill, his rifle hanging loosely in the crook of his arm. "A school?" he said finally, wiping his mouth, those piercing eyes narrowing as he considered it.

They went to sit in the shade of one of the big sycamores.

"What do you think of the notion?" she asked him, her eagerness coming through.

He smiled. "It seems a fine idea to me."

"Oh, Roman, it is! Ma was a teacher before she married Pa. And she taught all of us. I believe I could do it. I have all her books."

"I've not a doubt you could."

"I was thinking," Kitty rushed on, eager to tell him, "that one day Michael is going to need schooling. Oh, I know it'll be a while. But that set me to noticing how many children we have here at the fort who aren't getting any teaching at all . . . who can't read or write their own names . . ."

Roman unknotted the cloth about his neck and mopped at his damp forehead, laughing at her exuberance. "You don't have to convince me, Kitty. I'm all for it. What does Cullen think?"

"I haven't told him yet," she admitted. Cullen had gone out a few days before on a rare precautionary scouting trip. Though the Indians had for the most part stayed quietly north of the Ohio, there were some who warned that the heavy influx of settlers from over the mountains was sure to make them uneasy and lead to trouble.

"How soon would you plan to start?" Roman asked her.

"Why . . . as soon as I can." The words just popped out of her, and she hadn't felt so good in a while. "I'd need a little space for it. I know the cabins are full up, but surely there's someplace I could use."

Roman grinned at her. "Why don't we talk to the Colonel about it?" He hoisted himself upright. "Come on. Let's go."

"Now?" Kitty said, scrambling to her feet. "Right now?"

"Why not?"

She hurriedly filled her pails, and he took one of them from her as they walked back toward the fort gates. Cabins had been built outside the walls to accommodate the overflow of people. Washpots steamed, and several women hung wet clothing along the hemp ropes they'd strung up, one calling out a quick scolding to a scrawny, tow-haired girl who'd dropped a coarse pair of breeches into the mud beneath the line. The sweet smell of honeysuckle vied with the odor from the new necessary.

"I never thought to see so many people here," said Kitty.

Roman grunted. "I knew it would happen once they thought it was safe. They've worn out their fields from poor use back there. They know there's rich land for the taking here."

"Is it safe, Roman?" Kitty asked.

"For now." That was all he would say about it.

They found the Old Colonel at the Callaway cabin and told him of Kitty's plan.

"It's a splendid idea," he said at once, his eyes lighting with an enthusiasm that none of them had seen for a while. But in an instant the heavy lines that marked his brow deepened. "But damme, I don't know where we'll put you."

"Surely we could spare a little space in one of the block-houses," Kitty pleaded.

He chewed at a knobby-knuckled thumb for a moment. "Might be," he said almost to himself, "we could make room on the far corner there in back."

And so it was settled by the time Cullen returned to the fort. Some of the men and older boys had moved the supplies stored in that part of the blockhouse to the upper floor, leaving Kitty a bare corner of the large room to do with as she pleased. She'd gone through Amelia's books to see what she might use and had decided on *The Pilgrim's Progress* and an old hornback speller to begin with.

"Well, it looks as if ye've decided it all without me," Cullen said.

"You don't mind, do you? It just came to me and it all started to happen. . . ."

He grinned and patted her on her bottom. "Not if it suits you, and you have the time to do it, lass," he said, and she wondered if he wouldn't have been agreeable to most anything that would take her mind off moving to Otter Creek.

All that was left to do now was to take the word around that school was about to begin at Boonesborough and tell everyone what time to have their children at the blockhouse classroom. But to Kitty's surprise, she met with a certain resistance.

"I got to have Mattie to help with these here little'uns," one woman announced shortly, a whining baby perched atop her hip, while another who looked barely nine months older crawled in the dusty ground beyond the cabin door.

"It will only be for three hours a day," Kitty tried to persuade her. "And Mattie can learn to read and write . . . and do sums . . ."

The woman's eyes shifted away from Kitty's. "I'll think on it," she said, jerking her head to her daughter to grab the little one on the ground before he shoved a fat white grub into his mouth.

At another cabin a great solid man with hard-knuckled hands refused point-blank to let his four sons attend. "I was schooled myself," he declared, "and little good it's done me. What they need is the learnin' o' how to wield an ax to bring a tree down proper, and how to kill a hog so's the meat will be good, and how to work the land . . . That's the schoolin' they'll get. That and a strap to their backsides when they're in need of it!"

Still, there were plenty who agreed that a school at the fort was sorely overdue, and it was with a nervous energy and a fluttery feeling of excitement that Kitty rose before dawn on that first day so that she could get her morning chores finished before the class met. Sara would keep Michael for her.

"Maybe I should take him with me." She turned back, delaying at the last minute. "He might get hungry before I get back."

"He just nursed." Sara laughed at her. "Go on now and don't worry. If he gets fretful, I'll bring him over to you."

When she arrived at the blockhouse, the two little Hawkins girls were there and waiting, Granny Hawkins's great-granddaughters. And over the next little while four more children came in, two boys and two girls. The boys scuffed their feet against the blockhouse floor and seated themselves apart from the girls.

Kitty waited for the others to arrive, the minutes dragging on, the children present squirming restlessly on the rough benches that Cullen and Roman had made. She would have to caution the latecomers about being prompt, she thought. Three hours a day wasn't a lot of time to teach them all they needed to learn.

Finally, Phronie Hawkins, rough homespun skirt tucked primly about her legs, her scuffed leather shoes shined with 'possum fat for the occasion, raised her hand shyly. "Mistress Kitty . . . air we a-goin' to start with our schoolin' now?"

Kitty looked toward the open door and beyond to the sunny fort yard. Nothing was in sight but a rangy, skinny-ribbed yellow dog. She choked back the disappointment as she admitted to herself that no one else was coming. There were twenty-eight children of school age at the fort, and while she'd known that all of them wouldn't come, she'd surely expected more than this. But she managed to smile at Phronie and nod and commenced passing out smooth thin slabs of wood and small sharpened sticks.

"What are these fer?" one of the boys asked. Jason Roberts was nine years old and big for it. He stood, jamming his thumbs restlessly in the top of his britches, to regarding her with a challenge in his eyes—a look that said he'd as soon not be here, but his mother had made him come.

"You'll see in a minute." Kitty motioned him back to his

place on the bench. "Are there any of you who can read any
. . . or write?"

"I can do my letters," one of the little girls replied. "My ma
taught me."

"That's good. In a while you'll learn to put them together and
make words that we can all read."

The children slid their eyes toward one another and giggled,
and were boisterous when Kitty allowed them to go blacken the
ends of their sticks in the sooty ashes of the fireplace. They raced
back, pushing and shoving.

"One of the first rules is that you must learn to be quiet and
pay attention," she admonished them, not nearly as sure of
herself as she sounded. Maybe, she thought, she'd been foolish
to think she could do this. Six pupils today and maybe none
tomorrow—even Elizabeth hadn't sent her children. But she
pushed on resolutely, taking up one of the blackened sticks to
trace an A on the slab she'd chosen for herself to work on.

Though she had tried her best to remember the early days of
her own schooling and how her mother had gone about it, she'd
been unable to. But she'd thought out a plan for herself. It seemed
reasonable to start with the letters and go through them one by
one in order until the children were familiar with them.

"This is A," she said, holding it up so that they all could see
it clearly. "The first letter of the alphabet. You just look at it
now, and after a while you can all try to make one yourself."

They stared at it blankly and, prompted, repeated, "Aaaay,"
after her, looking bored.

Kitty caught a sudden movement out of the corner of her eye
as a small green snake slithered across the floor. Before she
could say a word, the second boy, Thomas Martin, younger than
Jason by a couple of years, spied it and, unable to resist, slid off
the bench and went diving after it.

"Git 'im, Tom!" Jason egged him on, while the girls squealed
and laughed, clapping their hands over their mouths.

"Thomas, come back here at once!" Kitty scolded, surprised
at how strident her own voice sounded.

The snake disappeared through a crack in the floor, and the
girls rolled their lips together and stifled their giggles as Thomas,
red-faced, came back empty-handed to take his seat again.

"You *must* learn to keep in your places." Kitty fastened the
boy with a steely eye. "All of you," she added. Though she
was beginning to feel that she'd lost whatever small control she'd

had in the beginning, she managed to feign a calm air again. "Let's get on with our alphabet now."

"Can I go get me a drink o' water, Mistress Kitty?" Deelie Clarkson's hand shot up. "Seein' as how I already know them letters."

"No," Kitty said shortly. She rubbed out the A with her finger and wrote a B in the same place, and the small faces looked up at her almost accusingly as she made them say it, "Beeee," and then went on to C and to D and the letters that followed them. She felt frustrated and angry at herself for ever thinking she could do it. It was clear they didn't want to know any of this.

"Now, this," she said, determined to carry it through, "is H. See . . . it's like two posts with a board in the middle."

Jason tilted his head and eyed the H, and then her, skeptically. "What's any of 'em good fer?" he demanded. "What's that 'ere aitch good fer?"

"Well—" She cast about in her mind for an answer to that, and suddenly one came to her. "—it's the beginning of Hettie's name!" She put out a quick hand to pretty little Hettie Langford's shoulder. The child was new to Boonesborough, as all of them were except for the Hawkins girls. "You add these letters to it"—she quickly finished writing the name on the slab of wood—"and you have 'Hettie.' If you wanted to write a letter to her, you'd put this at the top of it and she'd know it was for her."

They stared in openmouthed wonder at the letters and then at Hettie, who laughed happily, her cheeks pink.

"What's mine? Show me mine!" Jason jiggled his feet anxiously.

"I'd be obliged to see mine, too," Thomas sang out.

It was several minutes before Kitty realized that she had abandoned her carefully thought-out plan . . . that she was in fact sitting smack down on the blockhouse floor, her pupils off of their benches and gathered close about her as she wrote each of their names and they said the letters over to themselves, squinting their eyes as they tried to copy them.

But once it was ended and they had gone, she sat alone in the blockhouse, her hands covered with black from the fireplace, one cheek streaked with the sooty stuff. At that moment she wasn't sure if any of them would return the next day. She wasn't even sure if *she* wanted to come back.

But they did. All six of them. Ready to tackle their surnames and look with a certain wonder over the richly illustrated pages of *The Pilgrim's Progress* from which she read to them. The boys were particularly drawn to an engraving of two fearsome-looking lions, underneath which was written: "Christian discovers lions in his path." They begged to know how long it would be before she got to that part.

By the end of the week six more pupils had joined the class, including Elizabeth's Keziah and Richard, Jr.

New settlers were arriving at Boonesborough at an unprecedented rate, and whether they stayed or rested up a few days or weeks and then continued on with their journey, the sudden growth in population was creating problems that the small settlement had not had to face up to before. Colonel Callaway, besieged with complaints, decided to call a meeting to discuss the difficulties, and word was sent to the outlying homesteads.

Under a brassy August sky the wagons began to arrive early on the appointed day, rattling and creaking over the sunbaked ruts of what passed for a road approaching the fort. They lined up outside the log walls, horses stamping and blowing breathily, swishing their tails at the pesky flies. Drivers and passengers climbed down, calling out greetings to one another and to riders plodding in as the whole thing quickly took on the air of a social.

Within the stockade, the fort yard was aswarm with men who clapped one another on the back and passed jugs of whiskey. The children raced back and forth, the dogs barking excitedly at their heels, while the women greeted one another eagerly, glad of a chance to visit.

"My Lord, but it looks like that young'un o' yours has growed three inches just since we left outta here fer our place," Elvie declared the moment she set eyes on Michael.

"Little Lureen's grown, too," Kitty said.

Elvie nodded, smiling. "I hear you're the new schoolma'am."

"I guess I am." Kitty laughed.

Elvie had brought in all of Little Lureen's outgrown baby things to pass on to Faith, who'd had another daughter three weeks before. Once Kitty's sister arrived, she handed over the bundle. "I figured you might could use these," she told Faith, admiring the new baby, which rested in the crook of its mother's arm, its puffy little eyelids pinched tight against the sunlight.

"I can indeed, and I thank you," said Faith, shifting the baby up to her thin shoulder. Elvie asked her what the baby's name was, and Faith told her they'd decided on Charity.

Kitty took the bundle of clothing and put it just inside her cabin door. "I'll have these here for you when you and Ben get ready to go back to your place. I ought to gather up some of the things that Michael's outgrown and send them along, too."

"You'd best keep those yourself," her sister advised. "You're sure to be needin' 'em sooner or later."

In a little, Faith and Elvie went off to search out Elizabeth and say hello. Kitty sat down on the step once they'd gone, thinking still of what Faith had said. It came to her that she'd be just as satisfied if it was later rather than sooner. Not that she didn't want more children. She did. But it wouldn't hurt a bit to wait a little . . . now that she had the school going. And it was going well. Better than she'd dreamed possible that awful first day, which she could laugh at now.

After nearly six weeks she had fifteen pupils in the class and had abandoned most of the strict ideas she'd begun with. Now she only imposed enough rules to keep some semblance of order. Once, she'd even taken the children over to the woods, where they'd done their lessons beneath the shade of the great trees. Afterward they'd picked blackberries, hanging ripe and big as a man's thumbnail for the taking. She'd had Michael along with her that day, and he'd crammed his mouth full, grinning and happily oblivious to the purple juice that dripped from his chin and stained his cheeks.

The Skaggs brothers had been cutting wood nearby, and once during the morning while she was reading aloud from *The Pilgrim's Progress*, she'd seen the oldest boy, who looked to be about fourteen, edging closer and clearly listening while pretending to be busy with his work. Catching his eye, she'd beckoned to him to join the group, but he'd shaken his head and moved quickly away.

When she thought of it now, she was sorry she'd acted on impulse and glad that he'd refused. Hobe Skaggs appeared to be a hard man who subscribed heartily to the "spare the rod, spoil the child" philosophy. Not that he was that different from most. There were plenty of parents who quoted Scripture as their rationale for the harsh punishment meted out to errant offspring. But Pa had always said you could prove, or disprove, anything in Scripture if you looked hard enough.

She thought of her father now, the smell of roasting pork and venison and bear meat drifting to her from the pits heaped high with glowing coals where everyone's dinner cooked. His hands had been hard, too. Like Hobe Skaggs's. But they'd been gentle as a woman's when he touched his children.

It was Ma who had cut a switch on occasion, but as Kitty recalled it, what followed had been mostly a flurry of sound and a threshing of petticoats with little hurt to the Gentry girls except for their feelings.

Michael toddled to her now, his arms outstretched, and she caught his sturdy little body up to her, wishing with a sharpness keen as a knife blade that her parents could have lived to see him.

"Lordy, but your grandpa and grandma would've been proud of you!" She hugged him until he gurgled with laughter and patted at her face with his fat little hand, while the unmistakable smell told her that he'd messed his diaper. "One of these days, Michael Cullen Claiborne"—she tickled him and he squealed with glee—"you must start learning to use the pot!"

About the middle of the afternoon the men gathered down in the hollow beneath the wide-spreading branches of the huge old elm, where so much had happened before, to confront the problems, and the future, of the fast-growing settlement. The impromptu wrestling and shooting matches were abandoned as they came to sit themselves down in the welcome shade, wiping at sweaty faces and exuding a rank and funky mixture of smells—corn liquor and tobacco laced through with the aroma of grease-stained buckskins and stale linens and bodies in various stages of cleanness, from reasonable to downright filthy.

Roman had been showing Cullen the chestnut filly he'd just bought, but now they put the beautiful animal back into the pen that adjoined the fort wall.

"God's blood, but I'd hate for her to be spirited away by a stray Shawnee," Roman said as they walked out together and made their way through the gathering of men to lend their attention to the talk that had already commenced.

"We've got ourselves the beginnings of a town here," Henry Porter was saying. "And them of us that was here from the beginning must see what's to be done about it."

"That's the plain truth, Henry," Winfield said. "Harrod's Town ain't the only town in Kaintuck. Not by a long sight."

"So what've ye got in mind?" Hobe Skaggs called out.

"What is there fer to do but let 'er grow?" someone else joined in, which set up a fine argument from all sides. But though there were several heated exchanges, it was generally agreed that the use of the land immediately surrounding the fort must be better planned and more orderly in the future. Lots should be laid off and cabins built accordingly.

"My good wife," a deep voice boomed, "would appreciate

an additional necessary or two. And built farther away from the cabins, if you please. She finds the noisome odor offensive.'' The speaker was Josiah Langford, who'd come to Boonesborough but three months earlier with his family. Though he claimed to be a surveyor, there were some who suspicioned that he was just another of the greedy land grabbers flooding into the country, and he was not universally liked.

Ezekial Turner, well primed with corn whiskey, hitched his hempen breeches higher and slid his eyes toward the fellow. ''Shit!'' he said. ''In the start of it out here, a man could just bare his arse and do his business wherever he was a mind to.''

''He could if there warn't no Injuns about, 'Zekial,'' someone else chortled. ''Injuns about and a man might find his goddanged pizzle a-hangin' from a scalp belt right 'long side of 'is hair if he was too neglectful in takin' his drawers down.''

''I'd still just as lief have the necessary close to my cabin,'' yet another sang out, laughing along with everyone else and slapping his thigh. ''Stink an' all . . . jest in case the savages ain't full through with us yet.''

Langford spread his hands and grinned. ''Alas, the ladies come in and the demands of civilization with them, my friends.''

''Let's not be a-wastin' our time with talk o' necessaries,'' Harley Bailor the storekeeper said. ''A ferry's what we need . . . to bring goods safely across the Kaintuck when the water's high. I lost two full packs o' merchandise three months back, swept onto the Ohio like as not.''

That brought on several loud ''Ayes.''

''What sayee, Roman Gentry?'' Langford's big voice sounded again. ''I hear ye be an educated man and one of those responsible for Kentucky becoming a county of Virginia. What do ye say should be the first order of business?''

Roman looked up in surprise. ''Well,'' he answered slowly, ''it seems clear that we need to establish a township with trustees to control the planning and running of it. To do that means to petition the legislature.''

''There now,'' Langford said, obviously well pleased with the answer. ''There's a man who knows what he talks about.''

Colonel Callaway nodded and spoke up. ''There's time to do that if we come to an agreement on it. The legislature meets in October.''

''Well, by God, let's do 'er!'' Winfield Burdette roared.

And since everyone seemed to favor the idea, they cast votes for two representatives to take their request to the legislature.

Colonel Callaway and Roman were the overwhelming choices and, after some urging, agreed that they would go.

As the men milled about once the meeting was ended, Langford sidled up to Roman, fine beads of perspiration bathing the prominent jowls that, though well shaven, carried the shadow of a heavy beard.

"Well, Mr. Gentry"—he pulled a plain silver flask from the inner pocket of his woolen coat and held it out—"a fine day's work, wouldn't you say?"

"I expect it'll do," Roman said, shaking his head at the proffered flask.

"Come, come . . . have some," Langford urged. "It's fine brandy the likes of which you don't get out here often, I'm told."

"Another time," Roman said. "I've had a few pulls at the jug already."

Langford laughed and nodded and took a deep swig from the flask himself. He recapped it and slid the brandy back into his pocket, wiping at his mouth, a hearty smile still on his face. "There were matters of considerable interest raised here today," he said. "Talk of lots to be laid off around the fort here. I'd not be averse to acquiring some of this property myself. Nor would the idea of ferry rights go amiss with me."

Roman just looked at him.

"I'm an ambitious man, Mr. Gentry. I would"—Langford lowered his voice—"be willing to show my . . . gratitude to someone who might find himself in a position to aid me in those ambitions."

"Gratitude?" Roman's eyes had narrowed, but Langford rushed right ahead.

"Aye," he said, unctuous and oily. "I am very generous to those who do me favors."

Roman took a step toward the man, and Langford stumbled back a pace once he looked into those icy eyes and realized the peril he was in. His hands flew up as if to protect himself, but Roman merely slipped his fingers beneath the lapels of Langford's coat and hauled him up slightly.

Langford's face blanched. "Now don't misunderstand . . . I calculate there's enough out here to spread around." He still attempted to smile, and after a moment Roman let go of him in disgust.

"I'm willing to do you a favor right now, Langford," he said. "I'll forget we ever had this conversation."

Roman turned and walked away, and Langford looked after him, swallowing and sweating . . . and vowing to be more careful. Clearly, you couldn't do business with just anyone. It would appear that some of these men out here had become like savages themselves.

* 28 *

DANIEL RETURNED TO BOONESBOROUGH EARLY IN October. He rode in bringing with him a small party made up of his own family, some of Rebecca's people, and a longtime neighbor family named Lincoln.

There were greetings all around. Cullen and Daniel shook hands gravely. Winfield Burdette and Ezekial Turner and some of the other men of the fort crowded close to greet their old captain, while Flanders and Israel pounded each other on the back and grinned. Rebecca wept with joy as she embraced Jemima and looked for the first time on her new baby granddaughter.

They had arrived just before dusk, and it was early the next afternoon before Rebecca came down to the Claiborne cabin to search out Kitty and Sara and hug them with obvious delight.

"We would have come down to see you," Kitty explained, "but we knew you and Jemima would have a lot of talking to do."

Rebecca nodded. "And I had to rock my grandbaby."

She was ushered in and made comfortable, the teakettle put over the fire while she exclaimed over Michael and dandled him on her knee. Kitty told her all about the school.

"My goodness! It's hard to believe it's the same Boonesborough. A school . . . and all the new cabins outside there . . ." Rebecca's dark eyes sparkled, though she looked worn from her journey still. "Streets laid off . . . and with names. I could hardly recognize the place."

"It has changed some," Sara agreed.

"And real tea . . ." Rebecca cradled the cup that Kitty handed her and took a sip. There was a quick nervousness in her laugh, along with the gladness at seeing them.

"Harley Bailor got a little in and we splurged on a tin of it. Oh, Rebecca," Kitty said, "it's good to have you back."

"And good to be back," Rebecca said quickly. "Though I will own that I wasn't all that anxious to come at first. Daniel finally persuaded me." For a moment there was a fleeting look in her eyes that acknowledged the pain she had suffered, but she said no word of whatever problems she and Daniel had had. "We'll not be staying long at the fort, though," she added.

"Not staying?" Kitty's face showed her surprise.

"Surely"—Sara reached a quick hand to Rebecca's—"you'll stay until Roman gets back from the legislature."

"I don't know. I'd love to see Roman, but Daniel wants to get settled before cold weather sets in."

"Where do you plan to go? Harrod's Town?" Kitty asked.

Rebecca shook her head. "Daniel has a claim about five miles northwest of here. He likes the place . . . plans to build a cabin near a little creek up there."

"Well," Kitty said, beginning to smile again, "only five miles away . . . we'll still be neighbors."

"And Roman will ride right over to see you if you're gone before he gets here," Sara put in earnestly.

Rebecca nodded and set aside her cup for the moment to swing Michael up onto her lap again. And as Kitty poured more tea, and the women turned their talk to the children, Cullen and Daniel were walking together, out toward the river and along the edge of the woods where the richly colored leaves stirred in the warm October air.

Daniel, a bit grayer than when he'd left, looked lean and fit, though—as with Rebecca—there was about his eyes an echo of all he'd been through. But he was eager to learn of all that had transpired in his absence, and Cullen, who'd been along with the Boonesborough detail on the Chillicothe raid—led by Colonel John Bowman but a month past—talked with him now about the mismanaged affair.

"Bowman was bound and determined to do it, Daniel. And when he called for militiamen from each of the forts, I went along with our lads as scout."

Daniel nodded, chewing soberly at a sassafras twig. "I hear tell"—he shifted the twig to the corner of his mouth—"that it didn't go off too good."

"We were routed like dogs out to steal salt meat from a barrel,'' Cullen growled. ''And that with but a smattering of their braves to home. Most were off to a council meeting somewhere. Bowman botched his command. There was a time when I feared Jim Harrod would kill him, he was so angry.''

They walked a little farther along the bank, the sun high and warm on their backs.

''And have ye heard the rest of it?'' Cullen asked. There was in the question a certain hesitancy, and Daniel lifted his head and waited expectantly.

''In the fighting, Black Fish was wounded. . . . It was bad, Daniel. He surrendered himself. And . . . he asked for you.''

Daniel's eyes flickered, his cheeks tight and hollowed beneath those high cheekbones, but he said nothing.

''He's dead,'' Cullen added finally. ''He was supposed to be given medical aid, but somehow in the confusion of that whole mess, he was left behind.''

Daniel looked out over the river and after a time said only: ''I had not heard.''

He was silent after that, and in a little while Cullen walked back to the fort to leave him alone by the river.

Daniel stayed a long time by himself. It was well after dark before he returned to the stockade.

Cullen and a dozen other Boonesborough men volunteered to help Daniel and Israel build the new Boone cabin. Once it was done, they commenced on the good-size barn and the secure stockade that surrounded it all. And within two weeks of their arrival at Boonesborough, the Boones moved to what was already being called Boone's Station.

Snow was beginning to spit by the time Roman and the Old Colonel came home with the news that the legislature had acceded to their request. Boonesborough was now an incorporated town. Colonel Callaway, in recognition of his service to the fort from the beginning, had been awarded the right to operate a ferry close by.

The settlers listened eagerly to word of the new Virginia Land Law, which required that claims be registered in Richmond. ''But they've finally come to realize,'' the Old Colonel told them, ''that it's a hardship for most out here to make the trip all the way back. So they're sending four commissioners out to issue certificates on valid claims. First land court will be at Logan's Station, but they'll get around to us in time.''

The two men had brought in a good supply of lead and gun

flints and some powder, since it was certain that pack trains would not be bringing in supplies once the winter began in earnest. But in one of the bundles that Roman carried, there was a surprise for Kitty.

"Slates!" she exclaimed as she saw them. "And slate pencils! Oh, Roman, thank you! Now we won't all be covered with black from the fireplace every time we finish a writing lesson."

Within a few days of his return, Roman rode over to welcome the Boones back. After hugging Rebecca and wrestling Israel around the yard and swinging young Jesse up atop his shoulders, Roman and Daniel walked out to the new barn and climbed to the loft, where they sat on the edge, legs folded.

"It's good that you're back. You've been gone too long," Roman said.

"Aye . . ." Daniel took up a handful of the fragrant clover hay that he and Israel had cut and brought in for the horses to feed on over the winter. "It wasn't the best year I ever spent," he muttered, rubbing it back and forth between his palms.

"I heard that Rebecca wasn't anxious to come back," Roman said, choosing his words carefully.

Daniel nodded. "That's the truth. It took her a while to come 'round to it."

"She seems pleased enough to be here now."

"I believe she is."

They said no more about it, and Daniel flung away the handful of hay and shifted his position to let his legs hang off the edge of the loft. "I hear tell you was elected to the legislature again."

"That's right," Roman said, and launched into an account of the experience, ending up with the fact that Daniel had been named as one of the trustees of Boonesborough.

"Is that a fact?" Daniel seemed surprised.

Roman nodded.

"Who else?"

Roman named the other men chosen, finishing with Colonel Richard Callaway. Daniel's eyes grew distant.

"Well," he said slowly, "I'm appreciative of the honor . . . but I think I'll decline."

"I hope you'll consider it some more before you do."

Daniel gave his head a shake, and Roman knew that there was nothing more to be said about it.

Daniel asked after Sara.

"She's fine," Roman said, "though I expect she won't be

happy when I tell her that I've decided we should move to Harrod's Town in the spring.''

"Harrod's Town?''

Roman nodded. "It's the county seat, and I confess to some interest in politics.''

Daniel grinned. "I expect your pa would be glad of that.''

"I expect he would.''

They sat there for a moment, silent, Daniel pulling at the fringe on his worn buckskin jacket. "Kentucky is changin','' he said after a moment. "I guess the truth of it is there'll be more call for politics than scouts a day not too far distant. Time was when you could ride as far as you wanted to and not see a single cabin, nor washpot, nor privy. . . . Now they're all hoppin' in here like fleas headin' for a fat dog. Before we know it''—there was a certain disgust in his voice—"it'll be no different from back east.''

Roman clapped a steady hand to Daniel's back and grunted. "Maybe so . . . but it'll still be a while before we think we're in Philadelphia.''

Daniel acknowledged that with a dry grin, and in a moment Jesse came running to tell them that his mother and sisters had dinner ready.

It was a bleak, gray day, the wind gusting with a chill of winter already. Within the blockhouse classroom the grease lamps smoked and sputtered in the drafts and gave off just enough light to see to read. Kitty had just dismissed her class and was hurrying to gather up her things. Michael was at Sara's and probably fretful after all this time. Roman might have come back from Daniel's place; he'd been gone two days, and if he were home, Sara would have plenty to do without having Michael in her way.

The children had left the door of the blockhouse slightly ajar, and the keenness of the wind outside was evident as Kitty approached it. She stopped a moment to pull her woolen wrap closer about her throat.

Two women were coming along the path from the necessary. They didn't see Kitty, since she was still behind the door, but their voices carried clearly to her.

"They say he was a wild one before he wed, and it looks like he's took to his old ways again,'' one of them was saying. "Maybelle Shelton said she seen him comin' out of the Langford cabin twicet last week—and after dark.''

"Poor Mistress Claiborne . . . She seems like a nice little

lady. My old granny,'' the other woman added, ''always said a handsome man warn't nothin' but heartache, and I expect she was right.''

They passed on, unaware that Kitty had heard them. She stood there, fingers twisted in the woolen shawl, the words echoing hard-edged within her.

She fumbled with her books as she closed the blockhouse door behind her, then walked along the path toward Roman and Sara's cabin. There were a hundred reasons Cullen would be coming out of the Langford cabin, she told herself. Josiah Langford was off on one of his land schemes again, it was the talk of the fort, and Cullen more than likely had just taken some firewood in to Sallie. . . .

She thought of Hettie's mother . . . hair the color of cornsilk curling about her pretty face, dimples marking her cheeks. Hettie looked like her.

Kitty tried to put it out of her mind and hurried on to Sara's, where she found Michael asleep already. He'd taken some milk from a cup, Sara told her, and eaten some hoecake and potato she'd mashed up for him.

''Are you all right?'' Sara put an anxious hand out to touch her cheek. ''You look like you've got a fever.''

Kitty shook her head. ''I'm fine. Roman's not back yet?''

''No. Here, sit down. I'll take up some of this food I've cooked, and you can take it back for you and Cullen.''

''Cullen said he probably wouldn't be back until after dark.''

''Eat here with me, then.''

Kitty put her books aside, and together the two women sat at the table, Kitty pushing at the fried pork and greens with a piece of hoecake.

''I overheard something,'' she said at last. ''I heard two women talking about Cullen and Sallie Langford.''

Sara set down her cup of buttermilk and stared at Kitty. ''What did they say?''

Kitty told her.

Sara frowned. ''Who were they?''

''Oh, I don't know . . . they live outside. One of them is named Caldwell . . . or Cadwell . . . I don't know.''

''Well, they must have little to do to spread such word!'' Sara's usually mild voice took on a note of indignation. ''I'd wager Cullen was just trying to help Sallie Langford out while that man of hers is gone. You know well enough how the fort men have always looked after us when Roman and Cullen are away scouting.''

Kitty nodded.

''I wouldn't even think of it again if I were you.'' Sara jabbed at the pork on her plate with the tip of her knife. ''I used to borrow trouble worrying about Roman, when I was still back in Virginia and he was gone for so long. Part of that time I didn't even know where he was. But I knew that he would probably need . . . someone . . .'' Her voice trailed off, all of her certainty gone, and she put the knife down.

Kitty felt a sudden rush of memory and flushed. She hadn't thought of the night that Roman had rescued her from the Shawnee in a very long time.

She put her hand out to Sara's and squeezed it. ''I don't believe you ever had to worry about Roman,'' she said, and Sara smiled.

But once she was back home, Kitty couldn't get Cullen out of her mind. She tried to remember the last time they'd turned to each other in bed. The truth was, she was all too often bone-tired by bedtime, what with trying to keep up with her daily chores and teach school as well.

She thought of Sallie Langford again. She had beautiful hair . . . and hands . . . and a bound woman to do the cooking and cleaning and washing for her. Kitty looked ruefully down at her own hands . . . at the brown walnut stain on the index finger, and at the scarred right palm.

She shifted a little to see her face in the speckled old looking glass that had belonged to Amelia, narrowing her eyes to look at herself as if she were a stranger seen for the first time. There was about her, she decided, about all of them who'd been through it all—even Sara, as delicate and lovely as she was—a kind of neglected look . . . hair not quite shining, nails not trimmed evenly, skin allowed to roughen . . . It wasn't easy to find the time.

But that evening, once she had Michael down to sleep, she heated water in the big kettle and stripped to bathe in front of the fireplace, scrubbing her skin until she felt the warm glow. She washed her hair, rinsing and drying and brushing it until it lay long and black and lustrous over her shoulders. She was still brushing when Cullen came in, sitting there still before the fire with the brush in her hand, wearing nothing except a thin linen nightdress.

''Well . . . hullo,'' he said, his eyes taking her in, a sudden smoldering flare in the smoky depths. "I thought you'd be asleep."

"No," she said. "I wanted to wait up for you. Are you hungry?"

He shook his head. "Roasted a partner to these over my campfire." He dropped a pair of dead squirrels onto the hearth, then put his rifle on the pegs above the fireplace and slipped the strap of the powder horn off his shoulder to put it and his shot bag aside, his eyes flickering back to Kitty all the while.

She had wanted him to come, but now that he was here, all she could think of was Sallie Langford, and wonder if he'd lain with her. Suddenly the hurt and anger welled up as if to choke her. She grabbed the big apron that hung nearby and wrapped herself in it, tying the ends firmly, then turned her back on him.

"I'd best dress these out," she said.

Out of water after her bath, she took up a pail and went outside to the rain barrel at the edge of the cabin, shivering in the cold air. The stars were all splintery points, and moonlight bathed the fort yard. Her teeth were chattering as she came back—she'd gone in her bare feet—and she poured some of the water into a pot for soaking the squirrels once they were cleaned, then stood a moment, warming herself before the fire before she commenced skinning and gutting them.

She could hear Cullen moving about in the room behind her, looking at Michael, probably. He always went to bend over his son and lay a hand to that warm little body . . . And then she heard the soft tread of his moccasins coming close up behind her, but kept her head turned stubbornly away.

"Ye smell good," he whispered.

She stiffened as his arms went around her, but he turned her, his eyes questioning. She wanted to tell him in that moment, wanted to ask him if it was true . . . but she was afraid of the answer.

"It's been too long, lass," he growled. Fumbling at the ties of the apron to slip it away, he picked her up and carried her to the bed, kissing her mouth and her neck and touching her full breasts. And as he covered her with his body, her own need, long neglected, drove everything else from her mind.

When they were finished, both wet with perspiration despite the drafty cabin, they lay entwined, legs curled together. Cullen stroked her hair.

"Oh, Lord, lass," he said, "the feel of you could make a man weep with the pleasure of it!"

Kitty pressed her face to the warm flesh of his neck, and she could feel the pulse of his heart. "Cullen," she whispered after a moment, "there's talk of you and Sallie Langford." She was aware of that quickened beat as he pulled back and raised on an elbow to look down at her.

"Josiah Langford's wife . . . and *me*?" His eyes had assumed a round astonishment.

She nodded.

"In God's name, who'd be daft enough to say such a thing? Tell me and I'll thrash him within an inch of his life!"

She shook her head. "Just some women . . ."

"Women, is it? I might've known. Gossips at work!" He hauled himself higher in the bed. "Ye never believed . . . ye didn't, lass . . ."

Kitty couldn't answer.

"Good God, woman . . ." He was quiet for a minute, and then it burst out of him: "Don't ye know that ye're the only one to hold my heart?" There was such truth in it, his face naked with his inner feelings, that Kitty began to laugh softly. He reached a finger to wipe away her sudden tears, and he kissed her.

She slept after that, curled against him still, but he lay awake, staring into the gloom of the log ceiling above him and smarting with guilt. He'd been faithful the whole of his wedded life until Sallie Langford's swinging hips had proven more temptation than he could bear. Christ's blood, but a man's cock must surely be at once his greatest blessing and his most monumental curse as well! Once it started to rise up, it could make him careless of every vow he'd made.

He could hear Kitty's soft breathing, deep and peaceful. She had believed him. Thank God. And part of it had been true. She *was* the only woman to hold his heart . . . and the memory of the hurt, waiting there in her face and her trying to hide it, made his chest feel tight. He couldn't bear to see her hurt. There were times when he couldn't look at her hand because it made him recall the pain she'd suffered for weeks after the burn . . . moving the fingers of the poor blistered little thing and crying out when she thought he was too far away to hear.

He would stay away from the Langford woman, he swore it to himself now, avoid her as if she were taken with the pox. . . . Swaying hips or no.

❄ 29 ❄

"IT LOOKS LIKE WE DIDN'T GET HERE A DAY TOO SOON, don't it?" Hester Worthington grinned at Kitty as she slogged past the Claiborne cabin through snow halfway to her knees, water buckets sloshing at the rope ends of a carry yoke big enough to fit a man's shoulders. "Brrrrr!" She shivered. "There's ice formin' up in the pails already. If I don't git it inside right quick, I'll have to set it over the fire to thaw it out."

"The wind is bitter," Kitty agreed as she brushed the snow from her step with a stiff hickory broom. She watched the big, rawboned woman swing the pails sideways to enter the cabin next door.

The Worthingtons had arrived at Boonesborough only the day before, riding in half frozen and just ahead of the heavy snowfall. Foolhardy, some said, to come in this late. But they seemed an amiable, if oddly matched, pair. Pleasant Worthington—fully a head short of his wife and two stone lighter—was aptly named. And since the cabin next to Cullen and Kitty had been vacated recently, they took it gladly.

The Worthington woman stuck her head back out. "I hear you're the schoolma'am."

"I am," Kitty acknowledged.

"Well," Hester said, "I've never a child to my name. Wed a full fifteen years and never a thing to show for it. That's the way of it sometimes."

Kitty nodded. "Where are you from?"

"Virginia. Albemarle County."

"My family was from Culpeper County. I still have two sisters there."

"I've some cousins in Culpeper."

Kitty, finished with her sweeping, was beginning to shiver

387

uncontrollably with only her shawl about her shoulders. "If you need any help getting settled in, just let us know."

"I'm obliged." The woman gave a wave of her hand. "I expect we'd best get in before we freeze stiff."

Kitty stamped her feet, stepping back into the cabin and closing the door against a gust of wind that stung her nose. She had never known it to be this cold so early in Kentucky; it was only November. Usually it was into January before the snow and ice came.

Michael played with a rag ball that Kitty had made for him and clapped his hands and laughed at the sight of her. He had Cullen's way, she thought, as she saw his eyes sparkle and the small mouth curve into that familiar and winning smile that was so reminiscent of his father's. "My Lord, but you're going to please the girls when you grow up," she told him. "Mama's got to hurry. School's due to commence before long."

"Ma-ma . . . 'chool," he repeated, flinging the ball up onto the bed and then trying to reach it. It did seem to her that he was talking early.

There was a knock at the door, and Sara called out to Kitty and then came in, brushing snow from the bottom of her cloak and kicking her shoes together. "I thought you might want to leave Michael here with me," she said, trying to stop her teeth from chattering. "It's too cold to take him out."

"Oh, yes. If you can spare the time. I was going to bundle him up and bring him down to see if you could keep him. That blockhouse is probably cold as a tomb. And I don't want to risk him coming down with a fever or anything."

"I brought my mending," Sara said. "I'd just as well do it here as at home." She retrieved the ball for Michael, who by now was screwing up his face in frustration.

Kitty gathered up her things, drawing her heavy woolen cloak about her and raising the hood. "There's some stew there on the hearth," she said as she went out the door.

"We'll be fine," Sara called after her.

The snow had begun again, fine stinging little particles that drove up into Kitty's face and made her cheeks feel numb. It was deep enough to make it hard to walk. Her leather shoes offered small protection, and her stockings were wet and freezing just in the time it took her to cross to the back blockhouse. She dreaded the chill of it. She'd have to get the fire started.

But when she pushed the door open, she was met with the glow of a crackling fire. "Tolliver?" she said, surprised to see Hobe Skaggs's oldest boy.

"Yes'm," Tolliver said. He was at the age where he had started to grow in spurts, and his coarse homespun britches and the rabbit jacket looked too small for him.

"Did you do this?" Kitty put her things aside, then came to hitch her skirt up slightly and to back nearer to the fire to let the warmth thaw out her cold feet and legs.

He nodded. "Thought you might could use the chill took off the place before school commenced," he said.

"I thank you," said Kitty.

He stood there, hands restless at his sides. He would be fine-looking one day, Kitty thought, when his face all came together and his features stopped struggling to find their way to manhood.

"Is there something I can do for you, Tolliver?" she asked.

"Might could be." He looked away, and as she waited for him to say more, he suddenly snatched up another log and threw it onto the fire and began to poke at it with a vigor that almost put the whole thing out.

"There," Kitty said quickly, "I think that'll be enough wood on it for now." And as he rose up and turned back to her, face reddening: "What is it, Tolliver?"

"Might be you could teach me to read. And write." His eyes had assumed an earnestness that touched her.

"Does your father know you're here?"

"No'm," he said, but rushed on. "There ain't as much work fer me in the winter. I still got chores to do, but the wood is mostly chopped . . . and there ain't no time spent workin' in the corn nor the vegetable patch. I thought there might be days when I could slip in here and sit back over there and listen . . ."

Kitty hesitated. "I don't want you to get in trouble."

"I won't. My ma'd like me to be able to read. She's aimin' to talk to him about it. . . ."

His face still bore such a sober pleading that there was no way she could say no. "Of course you can come. Whenever you're able. But you make sure your ma speaks with him."

"She will," he assured her.

Kitty fetched him a slate and pencil and made his letters at the top. He had started to copy them and say the names by the time the other children arrived.

He was silent throughout the class, sitting far back from the younger pupils, but Kitty could see that he was absorbing everything, his eyes flickering with a bright intensity. And once the lessons were over and there were only the two of them left again, she stayed on for a little to work with him some more, struck by how quickly he learned.

"You can take the slate with you and practice when you get the chance," she told him as she gathered up her things to leave. Sara would be wondering about her.

"Yes'm," he said, sticking the slate quickly beneath his jacket.

He carried her bag of books back to the cabin for her. The snow had almost stopped, but the wind still swirled and stung.

"I'll try to come back tomorrow . . . if'n I can," he said.

"*If* you can, Tolliver," she said on a sudden impulse. "*If.*"

His eyes flickered in surprise, and then he gave a quick, short nod of his head. "Yes'm. *If* I can."

The grip of the winter deepened, until everyone agreed that they had never seen its like before. The snow lay fast. The little that was worn away by the normal traffic of the fort was soon replaced by periodic dustings. Ice lay thick and heavy on the river, with only a thin strip in the middle of it flowing, and finally that froze over. Water from the spring came out of the ground in a bare trickle to mound and freeze in strange shapes, and the men would chop out chunks of it to carry in to the women to put over the fire and melt down.

The animals huddled together and instinctively herded near the buildings for what little warmth they gave off. But it was hard to stay warm even inside the cabins. Kitty kept Michael bundled in his jacket and cap constantly. And at night, when in the stillness the trees in the woods would crack and groan with the bitter cold, she would put him between herself and Cullen so that their body heat would help to keep him warm.

Milking was the most difficult job for Kitty, since it required her to take her gloves off, and the cows weren't anxious to let their milk down when it was so cold. But her new neighbor Pleasant Worthington—a saddler by trade—had saved her feet by making her a pair of fur-lined leather boots. He'd made some for Sara, too.

"He's not worth a pound of spit for anything else, Pleas ain't," his wife confided. "Can't lay off a straight row of beans, nor chop a lick without riskin' a foot. Why, he's got no little toe on his right one. Cut it off before I made him quit choppin' wood and commenced to doing it myself. But when it comes to leather, that man can make anything. Saddles, shoes, harness . . . it makes no difference. He can do it all."

The Worthingtons' cabin was crammed full, what with Pleas's

leather tools and bench and the big loom that Hester had insisted on taking apart and bringing with her. She'd brought in a crate of chickens, too, and now, with a coop built for them outside of the cabin right up against the warmth of the stone chimney, the three hens laid eggs with astonishing regularity. "It's all that good corn they're gettin'," Hester said. "Thank heaven you all had a bountiful crop. I guess the good Lord doesn't send bad luck unless He's sent somethin' good to help you through it."

It was only on the best days that the children ventured out to school, and then Kitty held class in her own cabin because the big drafty blockhouse was too difficult to heat above freezing. On those rare times, the children sat as close around the fireplace as they could, reviewing the schoolwork they'd already done. Kitty had decided that if she could just keep them even until the weather broke and regular classes started again, she'd be lucky.

Despite the severity of the cold, the knitting and spinning and weaving went on as usual, and since Hester's big loom wove a wider strip of cloth than the one Kitty and Sara were accustomed to, she invited them to use hers, and they accepted gladly . . . the three of them working together.

Sometimes Elizabeth Callaway would join them, and as the time for supper drew near, they would cook together, sharing whatever meat their men had brought in and preparing pans of winter squash and corn pudding made light with milk and rich with Hester's precious eggs.

In winter, even those that were normal, it was not usual to stay up much past good dark, but on those nights they would, pooling their tallow dips and talking late, the women clearing up while the men passed a jug and made plans for the new ferry come spring.

Kitty's old red cow, somehow separated from the others, froze to death one night. And Granny Hawkins died, sitting huddled in her chair before the fireplace. Her grandson found her and swore that the old lady was smiling when she went. The body, well wrapped, had to be kept in one of the blockhouses for six weeks before the ground thawed enough to bury her in the grave-yard outside the fort.

But finally spring did come, with a sudden burst that seemed dazzling after the bitterness of the past months. And as the sun coaxed the land back to life, the trees greening and wild things stirring again, Roman and Sara made their preparations to move to Harrod's Town.

"I don't really want to," Sara confided tearfully to Kitty. "But Roman's bound to go."

"You might like it," Kitty said, trying to cheer her, though her heart wasn't in it. She didn't know what she would do without Sara. Sara was the one person she could always talk to—and, in truth, was dearer to her than any sister. "They say it's really nice at Harrod's Town," she encouraged, putting aside her own feelings on the matter. "And a lot more going on there than here. After all, it's the county seat. Besides, your sister and her husband are coming out that way, aren't they?"

Sara nodded, wiping at her nose and sniffing. "She wrote that Samuel figures there'll be plenty of work out here with the new land law going into effect."

"You see? You'll have them right in town with you. And Roman will have a better chance to do what he wants to there."

"I know. But Kitty . . . I'll miss you." Sara's lip began to quiver again, and the ache in Kitty's throat threatened to choke her.

"I'll miss you, too," she burst out.

They embraced, both crying now, and Michael began to wail himself, tugging at their skirts until they picked him up together and hugged him between them, laughing and crying at the same time now as he patted their cheeks with his dimpled hands. "Don' cwy . . . don' cwy," he told them.

"Will you come and visit?" Sara asked.

"Of course we will. Cullen's already said so."

"And bring Michael, too?"

Kitty nodded.

When Ben heard that Kitty had lost her old red-spotted cow over the winter, he and his brother Todd brought in the red heifer calf that Ben had claimed after the Gentry massacre—now a prime cow, just freshened—plodding along after the wagon.

"That's really good of you, Ben." Kitty touched a hand to his wiry arm.

"I figured it was only right, little sister," he said.

Kitty cooked up a meal for the two men and asked after Faith and the girls.

"They're fine as can be. The little'un is growing fast as pokeweed. Faith thinks she looks like Martha. I'd have brought them in with me, but Faith is feelin' poorly these mornings."

Kitty straightened up from the fireplace where she was taking up some more hoecake. "In the mornings? Is she carrying?"

Ben nodded, grinning. "We're hopin' for a boy this time."

He looked toward Michael with approval, a certain envy in his face as his nephew, well pleased with having company, stood on those sturdy little legs of his in an unconscious imitation of his father's jaunty stance.

Kitty turned back to her hoecakes, certain that Faith had not been pleased at being caught again so soon. "Well," she said, scraping the iron griddle, "I'll have to have Cullen bring me out to visit with her."

"She'll be pleased to see you," Ben replied.

Kitty took a day off from school toward the end of the week and went out to the Tyler place, to find her sister grudgingly resigned to the pregnancy. "At least," she said, "I'll have two girls the oldest as they all grow up. That'll give me some help in the house." Faith had finally lost the tooth that had given her trouble before. The gap was at the upper right corner of her mouth, and it made her look different. Older.

Going home, Kitty ran the tip of her finger over her own teeth, pushing at each one to find them strong and firm. And when she got back to the fort, she peeled a hickory twig to a ragged edge and scoured at them, glad of the sharp clean taste it left in her mouth.

Though she missed Sara and Roman dreadfully, Kitty found that it helped having Hester and Pleas right next door. Hester doted on Michael, stuffing him full of the treats she made daily. She'd spied a bee tree in the woods and cut it down herself, sharing the honey with Kitty and Elizabeth Callaway and several other women at the fort. And that morning the big, plain-featured woman was at the Claiborne cabin early, a steaming pan of pudding held carefully, her fingers cushioned against the heat by the end of her heavy apron.

"Elizabeth Callaway give me this receipt," she said. "She calls it Indian puddin'. I figured the boy would probably like it, and it was just as easy to make twice as much." She put the pan on the table and swung Michael up to her broad bosom, where he settled in happily.

"I thank you, Hester," Kitty said. "Cullen's got a sweet tooth as well."

"Elizabeth said he'd gone off with the Colonel to see about the ferry."

Kitty nodded.

"Where in the world are they aimin' to put it? Seems to me it'd be better to have it right out here in back of the fort."

"You'd think so," Kitty said, "but the men decided it'd be

better if they put it a mile or so upriver. Colonel Callaway put three men up there to clear away the trees. He and Cullen went up there this morning to start on the boat.''

Hester kissed Michael behind his ear with a great smacking sound to make him laugh. "Why don't you let him stay with Pleas and me till after you're finished with your teachin'? Pleas said he'd make him a stick horse.''

"You spoil him," Kitty said. "Both of you."

Hester grinned. "What in the world are they for but to spoil a little?''

Later that morning, after Kitty had dismissed her class for the day, she decided that she would go and see Tolliver Skaggs before she went to get Michael. The boy, who normally showed up several times a week for lessons, hadn't come by in over ten days.

It was the first day that the sun had felt really hot instead of just pleasantly warm. As Kitty passed through the open gates and started down one of the rows of cabins in the clearing, she could smell the soap that bubbled in a kettle out beyond a cabin step. Toward the woods she could see the cows grazing on the tender shoots of green grass, and pick out the red cow that Ben had brought in to her.

She passed the Langford cabin, which was now filled to bursting with a family just in from the East—Josiah Langford had finally come back, and he and Sallie and their daughter had left so suddenly no one even knew where they'd gone to. Still, Kitty never went near the place without experiencing a feeling of relief . . . and a twinge of regret that she had ever doubted Cullen. She was glad that she'd asked him point-blank. She might have gone on forever thinking that he'd had something to do with Sallie.

A little farther and she caught sight of Tolliver Skaggs chopping wood out behind the Skaggs cabin. Intent on his work, he didn't see her coming, but hefted the ax and brought it down expertly on the piece of wood poised atop the chopping block. The oak wood gave a loud crack and split evenly down its length, the two pieces toppling to the soft ground, which was strewn about with wood chips.

He had rolled up his shirtsleeves against the heat of the sun, and as he stooped to pick up the pieces and toss them onto a growing pile, Kitty saw the deep purple bruises on his upper arms . . . marks that looked as if made by a leather strap.

"Tolliver," she said softly, and the boy turned, his eyes widening at sight of her.

"Mistress Kitty . . ." He laid the ax aside quickly and at once pulled his sleeves down.

She pretended that she hadn't noticed the bruises. "I've missed you at class, Tolliver. Thought you might be sick."

"No'm. I mean, no, ma'am," he corrected himself. He looked down at the ground. "I've just been busy with work now that good weather's set in."

"Well, if you should want to come by the cabin after supper some evening, I'll make time for it."

"I don't know . . ." he started, and then his face took on a stricken look as he glanced toward the woods. Kitty turned to see Hobe Skaggs and the other boys, a good-size log atop their shoulders, headed toward the cabin. Tolliver wiped his hands down his britches legs. "You'd best go along, Mistress Kitty," he said, his voice taking on a low urgency.

"Why, Tolliver?" she demanded. "Did your mother not tell your father that you were coming for lessons?"

"No, ma'am." Tolliver bit at his lip and kicked at the chopping block with his toe. "Please go, Mistress Kitty," he said, such a look of misery on his face now that Kitty could have cried.

She nodded and turned away, but she'd only taken a few steps when an anger began to rise in her that Hobe Skaggs would prevent a boy as smart as Tolliver from learning all he could. She stopped dead still, then turned back. "No," she declared. "I'll not leave till I talk to him."

"No . . . don't! He'll only rail at you. And it won't do no good."

"*Any* good, Tolliver. It won't do *any* good. Well, maybe it won't, but at least I'll have had my say." She turned to face Hobe Skaggs, her feet set firmly apart, the hemp sack she carried her books in clutched tightly to her side.

The big man looked surprised to see her there as he and his other boys came up. At a signal from him, the log was heaved onto the ground to upend and settle, and by the time he wiped the sweat from his face with his rough shirtsleeve, his thick dark eyebrows had settled into a grim line.

"Mistress Claiborne . . ." He nodded.

"Mr. Skaggs, I've come to see why Tolliver has stopped coming to school."

"School? . . ." He peered at her and then at Tolliver. "*School?*" he roared. "Why, because nobody give him leave to go in the first place! And I'll have no son o' mine sneakin' around, a-doin' things behind his family's back!"

"I did have leave! Ma told me I could go!" Tolliver flared. He caught in his breath, stricken at having revealed that.

The other boys slid their eyes to one another and then to the ground, jamming their hands in their pockets as their father's face reddened.

"Damnation!" Hobe Skaggs cried. "If'n she did, it was pure foolishness, and I'll have no more of it! There's work to do and aplenty, and no time for such folderol!"

"Hasn't Tolliver kept up with his chores as well as ever?" Kitty demanded.

The color in Skaggs's face deepened, and he sputtered in his anger. "Just . . . just by God, whether he has or he hasn't would be my business, Mistress Claiborne, and I would ask ye kindly to leave before we have words that can't do nothin' but cause hard feelin's betwixt us!"

"I'll have to take that chance, Mr. Skaggs. And I'd like an answer to my question because it seems to me if he kept up with his work, you've no right to keep a boy as bright as he is from schooling."

"He did keep up, Hobe."

Kitty jumped, and all eyes turned toward the corner of the cabin as Lavinia Skaggs stepped around it and walked purposefully toward the little group, coming to stand beside her son.

"Tolliver never missed a lick o' work," she said. "And I did tell him he could go 'cause I wanted him to have the chancet to learn more'n we did."

"Woman, you git on back in the house and leave this to me," Skaggs said, his eyes narrowing.

Tolliver's mother was a reed-thin woman who looked bleached out from childbearing and miscarriages and hard work. But she summoned a fire now that Kitty wouldn't have believed possible, a defiance that her husband was clearly not used to. "I'll not," she said, and his jaw dropped. "I know y're his daddy. And while ye ain't been easy on a one of 'em, I know ye love 'em nonetheless . . . But Hobe, I don't know that ye understand what's the best for any of 'em, 'specially Tolliver. He wants to make somethin' of hisself."

"And he *can*, Mr. Skaggs," Kitty jumped in. "He learns so quickly."

"And just what good will knowin' a few letters do a man in this country?" Skaggs shot back at her. "A strong back and a will to work is all a man needs out here."

"That's not true. The frontier is changing," Kitty countered.

"Besides, there's no reason a man can't do all the things you're talking about and be educated, too. Look at my cousin Roman. He'd take a backseat to no man when it comes to working or shooting or scouting . . . and you well know it. But he's an educated man, a lawyer. Look at my husband. Cullen may not have gone to the university, but he's had schooling enough, and it hasn't hurt him a bit, now, has it?"

Skaggs set his lip glumly and didn't answer.

"Hobe," Lavinia Skaggs repeated, "the boy wants to make somethin' of hisself."

"What?" Skaggs barked. "Tell me what!"

"A lawyer," Tolliver replied at once. "Like Roman."

"Pshaw . . ." Skaggs turned his face away in disgust.

"He could do it," Kitty said. "Here . . ." She began to scratch through her book bag and finally dug out the worn copy of *The Pilgrim's Progress*. "I want you to listen to him read. He's learned in just these few months."

She held out the book to Tolliver, and he hesitated only a moment before he took it and opened it somewhere near to the middle and began to read in a sure voice: "Now Mercy began to be very impatient, for each minute was as long to her as an hour; wherefore she prevented Christiana from a fuller interceding for her, by knocking at the gate herself. And she knocked then so loud that she made Christiana to start. Then said the keeper of the gate, 'Who is there?' And said Christiana, 'It is my friend.' "

Lavinia Skaggs looked amazed, and her husband looked suspicious. "I wouldn't be surprised if ye ain't learned that by rote," he said. "Here . . ." He took the book and turned to a place near the end. "Read me that."

Tolliver took the book back and read the passage his father pointed out as surely and easily as the first, his brothers crowding near to gape at the picture opposite the page of an Elizabethan dandy done out in leather tunic and plumed hat, sword in hand.

"Well, I'll be damned!" Skaggs said, narrowing his eyes and staring at his son, dumbfounded. "Still yet"—he tried to hang on to his objections, scowling—"there's no excuse fer goin' behind my back."

"I told him he could." Lavinia Skaggs refused to back down. "And I'm a-askin' ye now to give y'r blessin' to it."

Skaggs looked from his wife to Kitty and back again, as if he were cornered by the two women. His features were still set into the same scowling lines, but there was a hint of capitulation in his eyes. "God's blood!" he burst out. "If I left it up to you, Lavinie, I'd be left with four schooled boys and not a one to lift his hand to help with the work . . . Aaaagh!" He flung his knobby-knuckled hands upward. "Ye can go," he said to Tolliver, "long's I see no slackin' o' y'r full share o' chores." He turned and stalked away before his son could say a word.

Tolliver grinned and reddened as his mother hugged him right out there for all to see. And one of the younger boys piped up: "Might be I could go, too."

"Might be," Lavinia said, "that we'd best give your pa a little time to study on that." She smiled shyly at Kitty. "Good day to ye, Mistress Claiborne."

"Good day, Mistress Skaggs. And thank you."

As the woman turned and started back to the cabin, Tolliver called after her: "I'll be back here quick, Ma. I just aim to walk a step or two with Mistress Kitty . . . if'n it's all right."

His mother waved her hand in assent, and he fell in beside Kitty, taking up her book sack for her.

"*If*, Tolliver," she reminded him. "Not if'n."

"I know." He threw a quick look back toward his mother, who was just disappearing around the corner of the cabin. "I'll say 'if' when I'm with you, Mistress Kitty, but when I'm with them I'll say 'if'n' . . . since I'd not want to shame them."

Tolliver walked along with Kitty as far as the fort gates before he turned back and she continued along the fort-yard path, well pleased with the results of her confrontation with Hobe Skaggs. She chuckled softly. She might yet get the rest of the Skaggs boys in school.

Up ahead she saw Hester, digging a flower patch in front of the Worthington cabin. Michael, a forked stick in his hand, scratched away beside her. She was just ready to call out to him and wave when she heard the shouting, coming from behind her and down by the gates. She glanced back to see the sudden gathering of men, Tolliver waving his arms and gesturing for her to come.

She started back, catching sight of Flanders, rifle in hand, and Israel Boone—who'd come over for the day—then John Holder, pushing his way to the center of the knot of men.

"Mistress Kitty," Tolliver called, "it's Big George. And he says . . ." Tolliver's voice trailed away, and she broke into a running step or two to bring her close enough to catch sight of the big Negro who was the object of all the attention. His right cheek was sliced open and bleeding freely, and there was a huge lump on his forehead.

It seemed suddenly difficult for her to breathe. Big George was one of a handful of slaves at Boonesborough now, and she'd heard Cullen say that Colonel Callaway had hired him out from his owner and set him to clearing trees up at the ferry site along with two other men. She edged in close enough to hear what he was saying.

"I fell in de bushes," he panted, " 'en I crawled clean away till I thought it be safe . . . 'en ah got up an' run, but I heered bad happenin's behin' me."

"How many were there?" John Holder pressed him.

Kitty felt a hand on her wrist and turned to find Elizabeth Callaway at her side, her face pale but her mouth set firmly.

"What's happened?" Kitty asked, hardly able to get enough breath to form the words.

"Indians attacked them . . . at the ferry site."

"Cullen . . . ?" Kitty's lips felt numb. "The others . . . ?"

"We don't know."

John Holder, now captain of the militia, was everywhere at once, shouting orders. Horses were being brought up, and suddenly Flanders was there in front of them, leading his rangy bay gelding. The animal, sensing the excitement, gave a sharp, high whinny and Elizabeth tightened her grip on Kitty's arm.

"They're likely hid out up there," Flanders said, trying to comfort the two women. "Both Cullen and Uncle Richard can take care of themselves."

"That's true, Mistress Kitty," Tolliver joined in.

Jemima came running awkwardly, her baby clutched to one side and squalling at being jounced so. Flanders leaned to whisper something in his wife's ear, then he gave the baby a quick pat before he swung up into his saddle, rifle crossways in front of him, and wheeled his horse around to follow the other men through the gates.

✳ 30 ✳

FOLLOWING THE ORDERS THAT CAPTAIN JOHN HOLDER HAD given out before he departed with the militia detail, Tolliver and some of the other boys raced to spread the word throughout the clearing. Within minutes the people came, straggling into the fort, most of them tentative in their disbelief, others aggressive in their haste. Many of them had never experienced the threat of an Indian raid before, and the faces of some of the women betrayed their fear. One young girl wiped at her red eyes and hiccupped regularly as her fat old aunt tried to comfort her. But a few of the younger boys, caught up in the excitement of the situation, turned cartwheels and emitted shrill war whoops until a land agent but newly arrived from the East, his nerves wearing thin, threatened to cut himself a hickory limb and give them something to whoop about. The boys quieted forthwith.

Kitty had gone at once to get Michael, and just holding him close helped to calm her. As she told the Worthingtons what had happened, Pleas squinched his small eyes even smaller and Hester looked worried.

"We'd best go down to one of the blockhouses," Kitty told them, "until we know that there's no threat to the fort."

"Fetch your gun, Pleas," Hester directed.

He nodded, his mouth puckering with determination as he headed back inside the cabin.

"Mind ye don't forget the powder," she called after him. A small shift of his shoulders was his only acknowledgment of her words. "Nor the shot bag!" she added.

"I'll not forget a thing," came his patient answer.

The two women started ahead, along the path. "He'd forget his head if I failed to remind him of it," Hester said.

Fanny Holder came out of her cabin, her young face pinched

and pale. She fell into step beside Kitty and Hester. "Oh, Lord, Kitty," she said in a half whisper, "I'm fearful for Papa. Cullen's young and agile and strong. He could get away. But Papa can't run so fast anymore. . . ." Her underlip started to quiver, but she stiffened it at once. And Kitty wanted to reach out to the girl, but her arms were filled with Michael.

"It'll be all right," she said, as much for herself as Fanny. "I doubt anybody knows more about Indian fighting than the Colonel. They couldn't get close without his knowing it . . . Cullen, either. Flanders thinks they've found a safe place to hide up there, and as soon as they catch sight of the men from the fort, they'll come out."

"I hope he's right," said Fanny, peering ahead to where Elizabeth and Betsey were herding the younger Callaway children into the blockhouse.

The boys had driven the cows into the fort yard, and they milled about and bawled nervously as the dogs that had helped herd them in darted back and forth through their legs. Several men had taken up watch on the front walls. It was all so familiar that Kitty felt a rush of bitter anger . . . and something else, a clawing fear that there were only so many times they could contend with the Indians and all of them—Cullen, Michael, and herself—escape unharmed. Clutching Michael closer, she stepped through the blockhouse door.

Almost everyone seemed to be doing something. Men were taking up places at the loopholes and checking their rifles. Boys and women were parceling out gunpowder and balls. Kitty saw Elizabeth Callaway and some others cutting and greasing patches. Michael, heavy on her shoulder, had fallen asleep despite the commotion, and Jemima, who had spread a quilt for her baby, beckoned to Kitty to come put him down.

"I'm tryin' to get this'un of mine to sleep," Jemima said, patting little Sarah. "She's fretted all day . . . like she knew something was about to happen." She looked up and her eyes reminded Kitty of Rebecca's. "I guess Israel will take the word to Ma and Pa . . . warn them."

Kitty nodded. "I expect he will. When he knows what's happened."

With Jemima watching the children, Kitty went to join the women who were readying patches. Hester and Betsey moved over to make room for her.

The time passed so slowly that Kitty wanted to scream, but she forced herself to join in the conversation while she cut patches with a practiced hand and passed them along to be greased. But all she could think about was the ferry site and what might be happening up there. Dear God, let Cullen be safe, she prayed silently. It was only a mile or so up there. Surely they would know before long.

She hadn't realized how rigidly she waited for the first signal that the militia detail was in sight until Ezekial Turner turned back and called out something. Kitty started up, a cry escaping her throat before she realized that he was only asking Pleas for a chew of tobacco. The other women pretended not to notice, except for Hester, who quietly reached out to touch Kitty's arm lightly before she went on with her cutting.

Finally, after it seemed that she'd been there forever, the smell of the grease pressing in upon her, a shout went up from Hobe Skaggs that the men were coming in. Kitty caught a sudden glimpse of Elizabeth Callaway's face . . . her white ruffled mob-cap framing those patrician features as she struggled to maintain her composure, a tiny little tic at the corner of her eye. And then Kitty darted toward the nearest loophole, trying to get up to see; but there were people crowding in ahead of her in the excitement, and she couldn't even get close.

She ran out through the door and headed toward the gates, strengthened at seeing Winfield Burdette there. "They're comin'!" he shouted to her, and she could hear the sound of the horses' steady pace, the squeak of leather. . . . They weren't riding in at breakneck speed. Obviously there wasn't a horde of scowling Indians at their heels. She felt a sudden and nervous relief that made her legs feel wobbly.

John Holder and Flanders were first through the gates, their faces so grim in the sunlight that some of her hope wavered. Flanders swung down and took her by the shoulders.

"Cullen? . . ." she got out.

"He's . . . he's alive, Kitty."

Her stomach seemed to fall away, and she couldn't move or speak for a moment. Cullen was alive, but Flanders's face still looked so awful.

He squeezed his eyes shut for a moment, swallowing hard, and then walked a few steps past her to Elizabeth Callaway. Her face was working strangely, her eyes fastened to the horse that was being led through the gate right then and the body that lay across the saddle.

Kitty's stomach churned as the rough saddle blanket that had been thrown over Richard Callaway's naked corpse slipped and the horse, skittish with the smell of blood, shied, tossing his head and neighing sharply. One of the men snapped down on the bridle and brought the animal under control, and the abused body was decently covered again—but not before Kitty saw the terrible mutilation and the bloody, oozing pate that made her want to scream out, the memory of her mother's poor scalped head sharp within her.

Kitty was aware of Fanny and Betsey's broken sobbing as she pushed through the gates, stumbling into the warm flank of another horse, smelling the pungent animal smell of hide and hair and stale urine . . . "Careful, Miz Claiborne," a male voice cautioned. But she had to find Cullen.

And then she saw him, slung over a saddle, his buckskin-clad legs dangling toward her. "Cullen!" she cried.

The man in front held up a hand to stop the horse, and she quickly grasped the animal's bridle and ducked beneath its head to the other side so she could see Cullen's face. "Cullen . . . Cullen," she crooned, the choking in her throat making the words almost unintelligible as she saw his eyes staring wide at her, no recognition in them. His breathing was hard, almost like snoring, and then with the shifting of the animal Cullen's head rolled slowly and she saw the tangle of black hair and blood and bone. God . . . no, please, God . . . It was all inside her, screaming . . .

Part of his head was gone.

Kitty poked at the fire and sat down to wait for the fresh kettle of water to heat, the anguish within her like one of the live coals in the fire bed. It was silent in the cabin, but outside a dog barked, and there was the tramp of feet from time to time and the soft echoes of hushed voices. She hardly heard them. She was preparing herself for what needed to be done.

Once Cullen had been brought to the cabin, it had taken three hours for him to die. And there wasn't a second of that time that she hadn't prayed silently that he might live . . . until those final minutes when his breathing grew so labored. Then she only pleaded that he might look at her with recognition, might know she was with him and see in her eyes how much she loved him.

But it hadn't happened. And once he'd drawn that last long tortured breath, she'd sent the women who'd come to help her tend him away and barred the door so that she could have this final time with him alone. She needed to accept it somehow. She couldn't yet, though there had been that small warning note

that sounded inside her head as she'd seen the familiar preparations to defend the fort. Still, she hadn't really believed that
anything could happen to him. Not Cullen, who was as filled
with life and living as anyone she had ever known. Cullen
couldn't be dead. . . .

She sat motionless, drawn far back within herself, trying to
come to grips with the agony that was so strong she could hardly
breathe. After a bit she realized that the kettle of water had
begun to steam, and she stirred herself to lay out a fresh linen
cloth to wash him and a bigger length for drying. She fetched a
new bar of soap from the soap basket and dipped some of the
hot water into a basin, cooling it to lukewarm with cold from
the water bucket—she wouldn't want it to burn him. Then she
carried it to the bedside and put it down on the floor.

After she'd pulled back the cover, she stood for a long moment
looking down at him, down the full length of his fine, muscular
body. There were two stab wounds in his chest, the edges puckered and red-purple in that soft mat of black hair that thinned to
a downy fuzz across his belly. But it was, she realized, the
crushing blow to his head that had snuffed out his life. As she
let her eyes take full measure of the body that had loved her so
well, she thanked God that the savages had not done to him what
they'd done to the Old Colonel.

She washed him, slowly and carefully, tears scalding now.
"Cullen . . . Cullen . . ." she whispered. The cloth about his
head was stained through, and she removed it, turning his head
so that she couldn't see the gaping hole. There still was that
awful heat within her, as if she were burning up with fever.

It was hard dressing him, but she didn't consider asking for help.
She was determined that they spend these last minutes alone. When
it was time, she would go for Michael—Hester had him—and she'd
take him with her to the graveyard out beyond the walls. Maybe
he would remember his father. She hoped he would.

Roman turned his head to listen, still as a statue against the plum
thicket. He picked up the sound of the single horse coming along
the path toward the creekbank and the self-satisfied grunt of the
rider that said he was well content with his full belly and the
safety of the Shawnee camp nearby. Maybe this time it would
be the one, Roman thought. The one he'd been tracking for
nearly two weeks.

He backed into the thick cover of the underbrush behind him,
crouching slightly to watch and wait. Before long the Indian

came into view, riding slowly toward the water with the careless ease of a man secure in his surroundings. Roman had watched others come down to drink or strip and bathe these last two days, sometimes as many as five or six together, but he still hadn't found what he was looking for.

The brave atop the blazed-faced chestnut was big and battle-scarred, his bare chest gleaming faintly in the dipping rays of the sun, ample evidence there of the several wounds he had suffered and survived. The marks would be, Roman knew, a matter of pride for him, proof of his bravery whether against man or animal. He made his little humming grunt again, picking at his teeth as the horse plodded past Roman's hiding place and then turned down toward the creekbank only a few yards away.

Roman edged out cautiously, careful not to rustle the thick branches, crouching low to the ground so that he could get a look at the prints left in the soft-packed earth by the horse's hooves. The blood pounded behind his eyes as he saw what he'd been looking for—that same star-shaped mark on the outer portion of the right rear hoof that he'd spotted at the ferry site and followed all the way into the heart of Shawnee territory. It was nothing more than a small pockmark, but it was unmistakable.

The brave had dismounted now and turned away from the water to relieve himself in the patchy grass along the bank. Seizing the opportunity, Roman moved silently out from the cover of the thicket, his hand closing about the bone handle of the knife at his belt.

The brave, intent on what he was doing, paid no attention to the horse's nervous sideways step but contemplated the stream that came from his penis, belching once, then grunting again contentedly an instant before the knife plunged deep up under his rib cage and into his heart, Roman's long lean finger digging into his throat to cut off the sound.

The Shawnee quivered and jerked, but Roman held him firmly until the big body sagged limply. Once he was sure the man was dead, he slung him up over his shoulder and carried him to the thicket. He would leave no telltale drag marks in the dirt. And his own moccasin prints would be lost in the crosshatch of tracks that already marked the path and the creekbank.

He looked down briefly at the dead man's face, the mouth contorted, eyes staring in a kind of innocent surprise. For the first time in his life he had to fight off a horrifying urge to run his knife around the Shawnee's scalplock and peel it away from the skull. He turned away quickly, sickened, wiping the bloody blade in the grass until it was clean and shoving it back into the sheath at his belt. That wouldn't bring Cullen back. Nor the Old Colonel.

The body well covered with brush, he turned back for the horse. The chestnut rolled its eyes and took a few skittish steps away as Roman advanced, and he slowed, holding his hand out cautiously. It wouldn't do to have the Shawnee's mount trot back into the camp riderless. "Whoa, boy," he said softly, hoping no one was happening along the path right then to hear. "Easy . . ." He gentled the animal until he could get close enough to slip a hand on the bridle.

The horse arched his neck and reared nervously, but Roman held him firmly. "Easy . . . easy," he whispered. "I don't smell right, do I? Too white. Easy, now . . ." He ran his hand across the withers and up the fine, well-set neck, a tentative understanding passing between him and the animal. He had always loved a fine horse, and they usually knew it. This one was a beauty. No more than two years old, he guessed.

His own sorrel was safely hidden in a sheltered copse of trees nearly a mile away to the north. In case he had to leave in a hurry, this one might well come in handy.

It didn't take him long to find a place that he thought suitable, far enough back off the well-defined paths leading to and from the camp. He left the animal loosely tethered and cropping at the tender leaves within its reach.

The sun was sinking rapidly now, the shadows deepening beneath the trees as he made his way back in the direction of the camp. He could hear faint sounds . . . the laughter of the squaws and the playful shouts of the children, and now and again he caught a whiff of wood smoke and roasted meat. He had not gone close up yet. It had seemed an unnecessary danger when he could hide out there by the much used creek site and know that the odds were in his favor that the man he was looking for, the one who rode a horse that left a star-shaped mark in the dust, would appear before long. But now, when he should be satisfied with the vengeance he had taken—all that one man could expect to take without trading his own life for it—he was drawn to the camp in spite of himself.

Once it was fully dark he crawled the last few yards cautiously, the glowing cookfires beacons as he edged along up a slight rise that would give him a good view of the camp. As he lifted his head cautiously, he could make out the rectangular lodges, little more than dark shadows beyond the firelight. To his right a group of braves took their ease after the evening meal, smoking and talking.

In a moment the rhythmic sound of a drum began, and the plaintive, cracking voice of an old brave rose and fell as he sang of better times and lamented the fate of the Shawnee, some of whose septs, or clans, had already gone westward to escape the onslaught of the white man. Roman spotted him sitting cross-legged before the largest of the lodges, a blanket drawn lightly about his shoulders as if his old bones were cold with age. "The trees will never grow so tall there," he sang in the Shawnee dialect, "nor the streams run so deep. . . ."

There were cockleburs beneath Roman, and he could feel them stick and prickle through his linsey shirt. But he lay motionless, suddenly beset by a great sadness. For a moment he had been tempted to tear the scalp off a man back there. Cullen and the Old Colonel were dead. And Black Fish. And old men sang of the beginning of the end of a proud people.

His eyes were drawn to the copper-skinned and smiling squaws who saw to their children now that the men had eaten, scooping up bits of meat, dripping from the pot, to thrust into eager mouths . . . chewing the meat themselves for the littlest ones. Roman caught sight of a slender young squaw who bent down to tickle the fat stomach of her little boy and laughed. The sound came to him gentle on the night air, and he thought of Kitty. . . . The boy was just about Michael's age.

Kitty . . . God, poor Kitty. He could see her face still as it had looked when he'd ridden into Boonesborough, Cullen's horse in tow.

He'd set out from Harrod's Town that day in good humor. Sara's sister and brother-in-law had finally arrived, bringing along with them a few things that were still luxuries in the West, and Sara had insisted that he take a little piece of chocolate and a chunk of sugar to share with Kitty. "Michael will love the chocolate," she'd declared. "I doubt he's tasted it before."

The arrival of her kin had seemed to make Sara better content with living at Harrod's Town, which was at the root of his good spirits. And he'd not been unhappy with Jim Harrod's urging him to run for election to the fall legislature.

But about four miles short of Boonesborough he'd caught sight of Cullen's big stallion, mud spotting that magnificent black hide, reins dragging free, and a cold dread had settled over him.

With Cullen's horse secured to a lead line, Roman had begun to work back and forth cautiously, picking up clear sign now and again of unshod Indian ponies. But it was not until he came upon the ferry site that he could make out something of what had happened. If he was right, two had been killed or badly injured and two more taken captive. Some of the sign had been obliterated by the tracks of the horses from the fort, but he could pick out that star-shaped mark on one of the Indian ponies' hooves again and again.

He'd ridden on to Boonesborough then as quickly as he could, cursing himself for having fallen under the same sense of false security as everyone else and dreading what he would find there.

As he approached, the cabins in the clearing looked deserted. A faded curtain flapped forlornly at an open window, and a little farther on the fire beneath a washpot had burned to cold ashes; the clothing was still soaked, unwashed. But in a minute a towheaded boy carrying a bundle of quilts and a cooking pot darted out and ran alongside of him.

"Mr. Gentry . . . that 'ere horse be Cullen Claiborne's, ain't it?" He jerked a thumb at the big black.

Roman nodded, recognizing the boy as one of the Willard brood. "Has there been some trouble here, boy?"

"Cullen Claiborne's dead. Him and Colonel Callaway. The Indians kilt 'em yesterday."

Roman reined in his horse. Despite all his forebodings, he was unprepared to hear what he'd just been told, and he sat motionless for a minute, trying to absorb it, the grief of it piercing him.

"We'd best git on inside," the boy prodded him. "Most folks are skeered to come out till they know the Injuns is gone. We're a-sleepin' on the blockhouse floor . . . and Ma sent me fer some more covers so's it won't be quite so hard fer tonight."

Up ahead of them the gates swung open and Winfield Burdette's big voice sang out. "Come on in, Roman. You, too, Eathan," he added. "Your mama's gettin' fretful about you."

People pressed around as Roman rode through the gate and dismounted. Winfield pumped his hand. "I'm damned glad to see you," he said.

"Lord above . . . he's got Cullen's horse with him," someone called out.

They made way for Flanders, that handsome Callaway face unshaven, revealing the toll the last twenty-four hours had exacted of him. "Roman," he said, "do you know about—"

Roman nodded, reaching a hand to grasp Flanders's shoulder. "I'm sorry."

John Holder clasped Roman's hand next. "You're a welcome

sight, Roman. We can surely use you right now. I didn't dare keep my men away from the fort long enough to make sure the savages have headed back north.''

''I'll be going out,'' Roman said, his eyes narrowing as he remembered the star-shaped mark in the dirt back at the ferry site. He reached up for the soft leather pouch that hung nearly empty from his saddle. ''If one of you could see that this is filled with parched corn for me, I'd appreciate it.'' Tolliver Skaggs threw up his hand and Roman tossed him the bag, then turned back to John Holder. ''Send word to Harrod's Town of what's happened. And make sure Sara knows that I'll be gone for a while. Her sister's with her—''

He broke off as he saw Kitty coming along the path toward him, leading Michael by the hand. She faltered as she saw Cullen's horse, stood still and white-faced; but the boy, catching sight of Roman, pulled loose and darted ahead. Kitty recovered herself quickly to make the last few steps with her head high and a brave set to her chin that Roman thought might break his heart.

He realized that Michael was tugging at his leg, and he swung the boy up to hug him. ''Well, now, Michael,'' he said, his throat tight. He wished Sara were here. She would know what to say.

Michael, looking confused and a little relieved, as if he'd been afraid that everyone else he loved might just suddenly be gone, clung to Roman for a minute and then reached out toward his father's horse. Cullen had taken him up front of him on the saddle many times, and the little boy was used to the big black.

Roman put the child down and turned to Kitty. ''I found him out there,'' he said of the horse.

Kitty nodded. ''Cullen's dead.''

''I know.'' He was suddenly aware of how young her face looked, pale with grief, those violet eyes blazing with it. But there had always been that strength about her. Like a willow tree, he thought.

They understood each other too well to need many words. He just leaned to put his arms around her, and in a minute she whispered: ''Maybe we could walk back toward the cabin, Roman. I'd not want to cry out here . . . not for all to see.''

He could feel the pain of that moment still now, so strong and sharp that it took a minute for him to pull himself back to the present and realize that something was happening in the camp before him. Several drums, throbbing insistently, had replaced the old man's soft lament, and some of the warriors had begun to dance slowly, the women watching from their places.

A big brave led the dancing, eagle feathers trimming his scalplock and bear claws strung into a necklace that hung almost to his waist. His moccasined feet slapped the packed, bare earth rhythmically. And now he raised his voice in a high chant, the muscles in his chest and back rippling, the powerful naked thighs cording, as he sang of the strength of the Shawnee nation . . . a clear rejection of the old man's sad song. Roman could understand most of the words.

"We will drive the white man back across the mountains, my brothers," he chanted. "We will fall upon them as my namesake the eagle falls upon his prey and tears it with his beak and talons . . . as we fell upon the Cal-la-way and the Black Hat . . ."

Roman's head lifted, his heart commencing to pound. The Cal-la-way was what they'd called the Old Colonel, and the Black Hat must have been their name for Cullen.

The warrior threw back his head, his arms uplifted to the night sky, and a fierce cry burst from his lungs. "Aaaiiiiiii!" He held it, his face contorting, then he darted toward a pole that had been hidden in the shadows and snatched something from it to leap back into the circle of the dancers again, waving what was in his hand wildly. And Roman's stomach heaved as he saw the scalp stretched over a hoop to dry, recognized the length of silver hair. . . .

There was a great clamor now as the other braves joined in the chanting, those who were still sitting leaping up to dance. And Roman, whatever feelings of pity he'd had before wiped out now by a lust for blood vengeance, slid his rifle up and took aim. He watched the warrior's head move in rhythm, waiting for the precise moment when he knew his sights would be exactly dead center of the gleaming forehead . . . and then he squeezed the trigger.

He didn't wait to see the brave go down. He knew when he got the shot off that the man was as good as dead, and he was on his feet and running in an instant, aware of that moment's grace of stunned silence. And then the guttural shouts began and the shrill cries of the squaws as they snatched up their children.

Branches whipped his face as Roman ran, a high keening setting up now behind him, mixed in with the angry voices of the men and the soft, loping sound of the swift, moccasined feet that pursued him, much too close for comfort. He sucked in air, trying to get his bearings in the dark. A bullet whined past his ear . . . then another and another as the cry went up that told him he'd been sighted.

He darted sideways and suddenly found himself pitching forward down a steep hill, sliding and rolling his way precipitously to the bottom, the hard edges of stones and gnarled roots digging into him during his headlong descent. The abrupt landing knocked the wind out of him, but he struggled up, gasping for breath, relieved that he still had a firm hold on his rifle. Before he could reload, however, a howling brave charged into him out of the darkness, knocking him down again.

The two of them grappled, Roman still half dazed from his fall, defending himself by instinct. And then the sharp pain of a knife blade penetrating his upper arm acted to clear his head as he jerked away, managing to grab on to the rifle, which had fallen free but was tangled between their legs. He swung it up and around in a wild arc that caught the Indian squarely above one ear and felled him like a tree that had been cut through with an ax.

He ran then, his senses honed to a keenness born of danger, a certain exhilaration surging within him. They might kill him, but he'd make them work for it!

He knew where he was now. The fall had at least done that for him. He'd seen the steep bank before it was good dark, and he knew that he was now headed back toward the creek, on the smooth trail that led from the camp. The clouds moving in had made it easier to fade into the shadows. Still, they were bringing up the horses now—he could hear the high whinnies and the stamping of hooves. If he tried to outrun them in the open, he was lost.

He plunged into the thick undergrowth, going more slowly but knowing that to keep hidden was his only chance. He could hear them, thrashing about and calling to one another. Once he could have reached out and touched one of the horse's hooves as a determined brave jabbed his way through the bushes with a long pole. Roman crouched motionless, blackberry brambles scratching his face. The pole jabbed in twice, missing him both times, and the Indian moved on.

As Roman crawled ahead cautiously, he thought of Cullen and the Old Colonel . . . and of Kitty and Elizabeth Callaway. Then Sara's delicate face came to him with a bittersweet clarity that filled him with a determination to survive. If he died here, Sara would never even know what had happened to him. At least Kitty and Elizabeth knew.

Through the branches he could see the creek ahead, and he realized that the body of the brave he'd killed earlier was only a few feet away. The sounds of his pursuers were strong; if he could but get to the horse he'd hidden earlier, he might have a chance.

The wound in his arm had begun to throb, and he could feel the blood soaking through his sleeve. He explored the ground about him, his fingers discarding the twisted vines and creepers until he fell upon what he was seeking, a cool, damp, spongy wad of moss. He scooped it up and pressed it firmly against the wound, a fine clammy sweat popping out on him with the pain of it. He always carried an extra leather whang or two, slip-knotted to his belt, and in a moment he had freed one and bound it securely around the sleeve to hold the moss in place, tying the ends with fingers and teeth. Not too tight—mustn't cut off the circulation. He didn't want to end up losing the arm.

He waited for the moon, which had emerged from the clouds, to be covered over again, setting himself to dart out of the concealing brush and across the creek to the opposite bank. But before he could move, a hound bitch from the Shawnee camp came loping along the path, tongue lolling, several male dogs not far behind her.

She whirled toward him, panting, caught by his smell, and began to paw at the bushes, sticking her head so close to him that he caught a blast of foul hot breath in his face and felt a drop of saliva on his hand before he jerked back. The movement excited her more, and she began to bark shrilly as the male pack caught up to her and milled about. The collective barking fast became a frenzy.

"This way!" Roman heard the shout go up in Shawnee. "The dogs . . . the dogs have come upon him!"

Four or five braves came running along the path, and Roman closed his hand about the bone handle of the knife at his belt, determined that before he breathed his last he would take as many of them with him as he could. The dogs leapt and whirled, their shrill barking growing even louder, and through the branches Roman could see the Indians before him, rifles ready, so close now that he could pick up the glitter of the dark eyes.

One of them muttered an oath as the bitch darted between his legs, almost tripping him, and he kicked out viciously to send her yelping away. The male dogs circled and barked, confused now with the scent of the female and the smell of the white man in the brush. After a moment of hesitation, nature won and they sped after the bitch.

The braves had spread wide to plunge into the thicket, and Roman tensed his muscles, ready, a sharp regret filling him that it must end this way. There was a fleeting thought of Sara . . . and of the children they would never have now. And of God. And then there was no room in him for anything but what he must do. He was resolved that he would fight to the death here rather than be taken alive back to the camp to face a long and painful death.

He could smell the rancid bear grease that oiled the body of a brave no more than three feet from him, and though his blood raced and pounded in his ears, he felt calm. He waited those interminable seconds, waited for the next step when he would stand up to plunge the blade through the Shawnee's throat. But suddenly there was a commotion over to his right, a grunting exclamation followed by a sorrow-filled cry. "Meshewa . . . Aaaeeeii . . . Meshewa!"

They had found the dead brave.

The Indian, almost stepping on Roman's hand as he sprang away, veered toward his comrades to help them carry the body of their dead brother back to camp. Roman let his breath out and pressed his face into the damp earth, the sudden relief and the loss of blood making him feel weak.

When he was sure that they were all far enough away, he moved out swiftly, running along the creekbank and making his way silently through the trees. Once he'd recovered the dead Indian's horse, he vaulted to the animal's bare back and gripped its warm sides with his legs, urging it forward with a soft command. And a short time later he sat motionless atop the animal, peering down from the edge of a high wooded ridge, the sudden wash of moonlight revealing the line of warriors below him . . . at least twenty of them, mounted and heading south.

After they had passed, he pulled at the reins and dug in his heels to head the chestnut north toward the place where his sorrel was hidden. There were times, he thought wryly, when the longest way home just might be the best.

When Roman arrived back at Boonesborough, he found Sara waiting for him. Upon getting word at Harrod's Town of what had happened at the ferry site, she'd insisted on going back to the fort to be with Kitty. Jim Harrod had sent half a dozen men along to escort her.

"We have to get her to agree to come back with us," she said to Roman as she examined his arm wound, which was healing nicely. "Try to persuade her."

Roman nodded. But when the subject was broached, he found Kitty firm in her refusal.

"I'm grateful to Sara . . . and to you, Roman"—she turned a face toward him that was thinner than it had been, the fine skin beneath her eyes still faintly circled—"and I've really considered it. But I think it's best for Michael and me if we stay here."

They sat outside the cabin, the twilight casting a soft light over the fort yard. The gentle sound of Sara's voice drifted to them as she readied Michael for bed.

"Sara will worry about you," Roman said.

"There's no need. I have Michael . . . and the school to keep me busy."

They were quiet for a minute, and Roman stretched his long legs out from the step. "Still . . . a change might be good."

Kitty shook her head, smiling at him, her eyes too bright suddenly. "No. I need to be here where everything is the same—" She faltered, picked up again. "Michael and I will need to be here."

PART FIVE

❋

Autumn 1780

✳ 31 ✳

Harrod's Town was a bustling settlement now, complete with a land office and a county magistrate. Hunters and trappers in their familiar buckskin and linsey strode the dusty streets, leading packhorses loaded down with deerhides and beaver and sometimes a buffalo hide or two to sell or trade at the general store. Bright weskits and woolen coats, even a wig now and again, were not uncommon sights, as lawyers and surveyors and land agents and moneylenders arrived in greater numbers.

The stout fort had withstood its sieges, and the people— particularly those battle-worn survivors of the early days—had to varying degrees developed confidence in their ability to withstand whatever nature or the Indians might confront them with. But the cocksure and the mildly confident alike had found their feelings of security seriously shaken earlier in the year by the fall of Ruddle's Station up on the south fork of the Licking River, followed immediately by the quick defeat of nearby Martin's.

The small stockades hadn't had a chance against upward of seven hundred Shawnee and Great Lakes Indians accompanied by a handful of British regulars hauling artillery with them. Those that hadn't been killed on the spot had been taken prisoner and marched north of the river. The old and the young and the weak—any who'd been unable to keep up—had been tomahawked and scalped and left along the way.

A boy who'd managed to play dead had escaped to bring the word to Harrod's Town, weeping in the telling of it. Every last member of his family had either been killed before his eyes or driven away to captivity.

"By the Almighty," declared the fat storekeep, giving voice to their deepest fears, "even could we all squeeze within the fort walls, wooden gates are no match for a cannon, no matter how solid they be.''

Men found themselves looking out toward the hills and hollows more often after that, pausing as they passed the time of day with a neighbor or straightening as they did their daily chores to gaze out toward the deep wilderness that still surrounded them, eyes sweeping the land as far as they could see. It was an uneasy habit that they'd fallen into over the past months. Even General George Rogers Clark's return to Kentucky to lead a raid north of the river against the Shawnee towns of Chillicothe and Piqua had not brought back the old complacency. And now, on this warm October day, with the colors of fall merging in the distance, there were few out and about who hadn't noted the lone rider coming in, a lean figure in buckskin who sat his horse with an easy grace.

As the horseman drew closer and was recognized, the word passed. "It's Boone . . . Boone is coming in." And those newly arrived from the East turned to stare, small boys running to see the man they'd all heard so much about. Others who knew the aging scout lifted a hand and called out greetings, their faces sober.

"Ho, Dan'l. Proud to see ye."

"Sorry about y'r brother."

Roman had only gotten the word a day or so earlier that Daniel's brother Ned, who'd brought his family out from North Carolina the year before, had been killed by the Indians. It was heavy in his mind as he welcomed Daniel to the Gentry cabin.

"I had some business to see to and thought it a good chance to visit," said Daniel.

The two men clasped hands gravely, Daniel's face pinched and lean.

"I had intended to set out for Boone's Station in the morning," Roman said.

"You heard, then?"

Roman nodded.

Daniel shook his head wearily. "I have not had the best of luck at the Blue Licks."

"It happened there?"

"Near there."

Roman grasped the older man by the shoulders and drew him inside. "Come in. I've a jug of good whiskey on the shelf."

"I'd not object to a drink of it," said Daniel.

The cabin was roomy compared to Boonesborough standards,

with a large central room and a smaller bedroom off to the side. A fire burned in the stone fireplace.

"Sara's over at her sister's," said Roman as he reached for a couple of pewter mugs and uncorked the jug.

"And how is your good wife?"

"She's well, so far. She miscarried last spring, but we hope that this time . . ."

Daniel nodded. "I wouldn't want to put her to any extra trouble."

Roman handed him one of the mugs. "You'll stay the night, or for however long you're here. She'd never forgive you if you didn't."

Roman settled himself across from Daniel, and the two men drank, quiet for a minute, the whiskey potent and smooth.

"When did it happen, Daniel?" Roman asked finally. "The news of it was sketchy at best."

"Two weeks ago now. Ned and me had made some salt at the Lick, then started back by way of Hinkston Creek," Daniel said.

Roman nodded.

"We'd stopped off to rest our horses a spell when I spied a bear directly across from us, beyond the creek and movin' into the trees. I got off a shot . . . too hasty, I expect. Only wounded him. I left Ned there on the creekbank. He was crackin' hickory nuts between two rocks. I remember he said they was as tasty as he'd ever had." Daniel paused and wiped a hand across his mouth.

"I'd just gone a short distance, trackin' the bear . . . that's when they came upon him. I heard him shout out once. But when I got close enough to see, it was clear that they'd done for him. They thought it was me, Roman. They kept hollerin', 'Boone . . . . Boone . . . We've killed Boone!' "

Roman was silent, remembering how much the two brothers had favored one another.

"I hid in a canebrake till they were gone," Daniel said. "When it was safe, I went back for Ned's body. . . ." His voice had begun to quiver, almost broke. "They had taken his head, Roman."

Roman had known Ned Boone well . . . and liked him. He swigged at his whiskey and turned away for a moment, staring morosely into the fire as Daniel swiped at suddenly reddened eyes. Then both men turned as Sara's light step was heard at the threshold.

"Roman," she called, "I heard that Daniel—Oh." She broke off, a gentle smile overtaking her face at sight of him. "You're here."

She advanced into the room, her full skirts hiding her pregnancy, but her eyes revealing the secret with a serene, almost determined contentment that said this time it would be all right.

Daniel had risen, and she held her two hands out to him. "We were so sorry to hear about Ned."

"I thankee kindly," Daniel said.

"Do sit down. And tell me of Rebecca and the children."

"Thank Providence, they are well." Daniel held out his mug as Roman poured him another drop of whiskey. "They send their regards."

"And have you been to Boonesborough recently?" Sara pressed, eager for news.

"Aye. My granddaughter is growing well enough." He smiled. "Rebecca says she is a pretty child. I agree."

Sara laughed. "And Kitty . . . how is she?"

"She continues to teach the school there." Daniel shook his head. "Kitty Claiborne has had her share of sorrow . . . and borne it better than most."

Sara nodded. "All the same, I worry for her. I intend to send a letter the next time Roman goes over there, asking her to come visit if a safe opportunity presents itself."

Sara set to frying up some meat, and Roman and Daniel sat quietly.

"It has been a hard year," Daniel said finally. "Cullen Claiborne and Richard Callaway . . ." His face was turned away and Roman could not see his expression, but his voice was infinitely sad. "Ruddle's and Martin's . . . and brother Ned."

Kitty stood in the cabin doorway and looked out toward Michael and young Georgie Walters playing in the rich, fall sunlight of the fort yard, their throaty giggles drifting to her. Nearing two and a half now, Michael was a sturdy and handsome child, taller by an inch than his playmate, though Georgie was six months older. She watched for a moment as the youngsters wrestled and tumbled. Michael's dog, which he'd dubbed "Bear"—a half-grown, shaggy red-brown pup that Henry Porter had brought in to him—darted in to poke a soft wet nose into the tangle of arms and legs, the long sweep of a tail wagging frantically. Kitty shook her head. The animal already showed signs of eating her out of house and home. But Michael loved the beast.

She turned back into the cabin, setting a basket of butter beans down on the table, and absently tugged back an errant strand of hair that had escaped the severely tight bun she wore now. She didn't even glance toward Amelia's old looking glass, though it was only a step away. The bone-thin face, all cheekbones and eyes, held no fascination for her. There were times when it hardly seemed to be her but in fact looked more like the Kitty of '77, when they'd all nearly starved.

Hester and Elizabeth were forever after her to eat more. But food, except for seeing that Michael had plenty, seemed unimportant. And she was strong and healthy, with rarely a sick day. Right now, after stooping to pick the beans, her back ached dully, but it was only that small hot pain that said her monthly would probably be on her by nightfall. She guessed it was time for it. There was no need to keep track anymore.

Hester called out a greeting and came into the cabin carrying a large bunch of bittersweet. "There's aplenty of it along the wood's edge," she said. "I put some in a pitcher top of my mantel, and it brightens the place some."

"I thank you, Hester." Kitty reached for a burled bowl to hold the orange berries, then settled herself and began to hull the butter beans. "I picked enough for both of us," she said, and Hester nodded and began to help.

"I see that Georgie Walters came over to play with Michael," she said.

"His sister brought him over. I told her she could leave him awhile. Michael likes to play with him." Kitty glanced out the door once again to catch sight of the two boys. Michael was marching Georgie ahead of him, stick gun in his back, Bear bringing up the rear. Michael liked to pretend that he was a scout . . . "wike Papa." When he'd say that in his brave little voice, it would bring tears to her eyes.

"I believe I saw his pa over here again last evenin'. Sittin' on the step with you."

Kitty sighed. "He was," she acknowledged. "But I doubt he'll be back. Jonathon Walters asked me to wed, and I said no."

Hester stayed her bean hulling. Her thumb poised against a fat lima. "He's a fine-looking man. In his prime."

"I know."

"And I note that you didn't run him off as fast as you have all the others that's come swarmin' like bees tryin' to light on a hive."

The truth was, there'd been a moment when Kitty had been tempted to say yes to Jonathon Walters. He was a good man, unlettered, but naturally bright, with a solid and dependable air about him. A widower himself, he needed a mother for his three children. Georgie was the youngest; the two girls were five and seven. Kitty had entertained the fleeting thought that he would be happy to settle with her and the children at Otter Creek once the Indian threat lessened . . . if it ever did.

Hester had resumed her bean hulling but continued to shoot sideways glances at Kitty. "So why did you turn him down?"

"I feel no need for a husband." Kitty's voice was firm. "Michael and I manage well enough."

It was true. The trustees paid her a few shillings a month for keeping the town records in order. The older boys in the school kept her in meat. She had the cow that Ben had given her, and her little vegetable patch. Actually, when Jonathon Walters asked her, but for that wistful thought of Otter Creek, she'd known that she couldn't.

She filled her days with work, going about it doggedly so that she could shut out the pain of Cullen's death. But there were nights—no matter how tired she was when she went to sleep—when she still dreamt of him . . . waking to turn her face into the pillow and cry or lie dry-eyed, staring at the smoky rafters. And though the waking hours might be a little easier to deal with now, she knew that she wanted no man to touch her, and she had not yet come to the place where she'd marry for any other reason. Maybe she would. But she was not there yet.

"Well," Hester observed, "I note you haven't sent Todd Tyler on his way."

Kitty moaned. "How can I? He's kin. Besides, he's not courting . . . he just comes to visit with Michael and me when he's in to the fort."

"Pshaw!" Hester dismissed that notion crisply.

Kitty remembered it the following day when Todd showed up at the cabin carrying a dead 'possum by the tail, obviously expecting to be asked to stay to supper.

"I come in to pick up a couple of barrels from old man Thomas. He's still cooperin', ain't he?"

"I'm sure he is," said Kitty.

"Ben needs 'em," he explained, grinning at her as if he'd said something clever. He stood there, awkwardly after a minute, chewing at his tongue and swallowing. "I come in so late in the day I figured it'd be safer was I to spend the night here and go back tomorrow. I can sleep down at one of the block-houses.''

Kitty looked down at the 'possum. It had been a hard day. She'd been right about her monthly, and her lower parts felt swollen and tender. Michael had tipped over the pail of milk, and she'd had to scrub the floor twice to get it all up. Hester had brought over some of their milk, and Kitty had planned to have it along with hoecake and butter beans left over from the day before for supper. As tired as she was, the thought of dressing out the 'possum and cooking a big meal wasn't welcome, and she certainly didn't relish the idea of an evening with Todd. But as she had told Hester, he was kin.

"Well"—she grasped the animal by the tail, managing a po-lite smile and trying her best to appear grateful for the meat—"it's a fine fat one. I believe there are still some greens left out there in my vegetable patch. I'll go pick us some and use part of the drippings to season them.''

Todd rewarded her efforts with a hearty appetite, declaring that it was maybe the best 'possum he had ever eaten. And after he was finished, he sat back and picked at his teeth as she readied Michael for bed. "I spied a persimmon tree thick with fruit back there a ways in the woods as I come in," he said. "I figured before I go back home tomorrow I might just go over there and bring you back some.''

"That would be nice," Kitty said as she tucked Michael into his trundle bed.

"Be-ah . . . Be-ah come in?'' He grinned at her with Cullen's grin.

"Bear," she said, emphasizing the r sound at the end. She was proud of how well he could talk already.

"A dog belongs outside, boy," Todd spoke up.

"Pwease . . .'' The small face turned up to Kitty with an earnestness that made her chest feel as if something warm had melted inside it.

"After he eats," she answered, brushing back his thick shock of dark hair and kissing him. It was forever in his eyes.

Once she had fed the big dog, she let him come into the cabin, and he trotted right to the side of Michael's bed and curled up, his tail making a soft thump or two against the braided rug as the boy's hand, still dimpled as a baby's, stole out to pat the shaggy head.

Todd watched Kitty as she cleared up. "I was never one to let a dog in the house," he said after a while.

Kitty shrugged. "Michael sleeps better when the animal is beside him." And as if to prove her point, she glanced over to see that her son had fallen off to sleep already. "I remember," she said, as much to make conversation as anything else, "that Ma used to let Priss and me, and Faith while she was still at home, bring in Lady to sleep in the loft with us sometimes."

Todd nodded. "I do recall that hound o' Usaph's. Still . . ." With that Tyler air of certainty, he fastened her with his light eyes. "I don't take to a dog in the house."

Kitty made no answer as she scoured at the wooden plates, steam rising from the soapy water.

"I would say," Todd went on, and she could tell that he was chewing at his tongue and swallowing by the long pause, "that what the boy needs to settle him down is a father."

She turned to look at him, surprised despite Hester's warning, aware of the pale hair and lashes and the clothes that never quite fit . . . as if he weren't enough man to fill them. The thought of Cullen's hard-muscled body came unbidden, like a physical blow, opening her to the pain she could usually keep sealed away. Oh, God, she missed him! The loss was so strong, she had to bite at her lower lip to keep from crying out.

She cast about for something to say that would head Todd off, but it was too late.

"I have laid claim to some good bottom land up the river a ways, not too far from yours. Betwixt us, we would have a fine spread of acreage. And I confess"—he reddened slightly—"that before I knew about Cullen and you aimin' to marry . . . the thought had crossed my mind."

He leaned up in the rocking chair and nodded his head firmly. "Now that he is gone . . . I have concluded that it would still be a good thing. I will make you a decent and faithful husband, and I will be a father to your boy."

Ben and Faith and the children came in to the fort a few days after Todd's visit. The Tylers were part of the stubborn few who had stayed on their places through the uncertainties of the summer. "If the Indians have commenced to haulin' artillery with 'em, we're as safe here as we would be at Boonesborough anyway," Ben had declared when pressured to move his family in. And they had had no trouble.

Though Kitty had not seen her new nephew since he was born two months before, she knew that they had not come to show her how little Latham—named for Ben's brother, captured at the salt licks—was growing.

But as she made much over the fat baby, Michael dutifully showed the two little Tyler girls the top that Pleas had made for him. He spun it on the plank floor for them but turned his back scornfully as the little one held out a corn shuck doll for his inspection.

"Boys don't play with dolls, Charity," Martha scolded her sister.

Michael grabbed for his sweater, letting out a shrill whoop and racing for the door. Ben looked after him, disapproval written on his spare features.

"Go ahead with him," Faith told the girls. "Mind you watch your sister, Martha . . . see that she keeps her bonnet on."

"Yes'm," Martha said, taking the toddler in tow.

"Michael is good to stay right out in front there," Kitty said for Ben's benefit.

Once they were gone, the meaningful looks that Faith and Ben cast at one another weren't lost on Kitty. Ben clasped his hands behind his back and pursed his lips as he backed up to the fireplace. There was a hint of winter in the air. They had had one hard freeze already, but today the sunlight was crisp and clear.

Kitty tried to stave off what she knew was coming. "I just let school out and haven't started a thing to eat yet. Let me put Latham down here, and I'll just start us something. . . ." She had moved to pick up the basket of yellow summer squash on the table when Ben held a hand up to stay her.

"I would take it kindly if you'd set and talk with us first," he said.

Kitty wiped her hands down the rough linsey of her skirt and, resigned, nodded.

The two women sat, but Ben continued to stand, clearing his throat and fastening Kitty with those pale eyes. "Something has come to my ear that has puzzled and grieved me mightily, little sister," he said.

"I expect you're talking about Todd." Kitty faced it squarely.

"I am. When your sister and I heard that you had turned down his honest proposal of marriage"—Ben's thin nostrils pinched tighter and he shook his head in clear exasperation—"we could not believe it."

"Honey . . ." Faith put her hand out to her sister's. "I don't think you've considered everything. Todd's a good man . . . honest and hardworking as Ben.''

"He would make you a good husband," Ben put in.

Kitty sighed. "I'm sure that's true. But I don't want to wed him.''

"Why in the world not?" Faith demanded.

"Because I don't—" She hesitated to find the right word. "—care for him.''

Ben snorted. "What kind of foolishness is that? A woman alone . . . with a boy sorely in need of a father.''

"Michael is a very obedient child," Kitty said firmly.

"Kitty," Faith pleaded, "how long do you think you can go on by yourself?''

"Michael and I are fine," she said stubbornly.

"Why must you ever be wrongheaded?" Ben began to pace back and forth. "Think of the boy.''

Kitty stood firm. "I know what's best for me. And for Michael.''

There was a moment's silence, and then Faith squeezed Kitty's hand. "We are only thinking of your welfare. I ask myself what Ma and Pa would have wanted for you . . . and I know they would have had you safe in your own home, with a man to see to you.'' Her eyes had reddened as she spoke of their parents.

Ben turned back, his face softened some. "I understand that you have grieved for Cullen, little sister. But there is a time for grief to end. I was not overly concerned when I heard you had turned others down. Because I knew that my brother—decent and God-fearing man that he is—had it in his mind to ask you. It is something that would please Faith and me. We have worried for you, widowed and with a boy to raise alone. . . .''

Kitty sighed. "I appreciate that, and I thank the both of you.'' She cast about in her mind for something to say that would make them feel less that she had rejected the whole Tyler family with her refusal of Todd. "I . . . I'm honored that he asked me,'' she lied, "but . . . I'm not ready to enter into a marriage with anyone.''

Ben had worn his best black coat, and his thin fingers worried the lapels as he looked down at her gravely, considering what she had said. "Well . . .'' He sounded more reasonable than usual. "I'll tell brother Todd that you still yet need a little time to adjust yourself. You could set a date for the spring. . . .''

"No!'' Kitty's voice was sharp, but she couldn't help it. She felt besieged. Two proposals of marriage in as many days. And now Faith and Ben trying to push her into accepting Todd, with whom she could hardly stand to be in the same room, let alone the same bed . . . not that she wanted any man in her bed!

She rose from her chair, struggling to regain her composure. "I know you both mean well, but I have no need, nor desire, for a husband. Since that is settled, I'll start frying up some pork for us. Hobe Skaggs butchered a hog and sent us some. Faith"—she turned to her sister and tried to smile—"maybe you could slice up that squash."

"Aaagh!" Ben threw up his hands in disgust. "There are times when I do believe your sister is daft! You talk to her!" he said to his wife, and stalked out.

Pressing her lips together, Kitty flew to the meat crock that she kept in the corner farthest from the fireplace and brought back the piece of salted pork that Tolliver had brought her. She began to slice it determinedly, not looking up even when she felt Faith's tentative touch on her arm.

"Oh, honey . . ." Faith took the knife from her and laid it aside, then drew her around to hug her.

They clung to one another, tears stinging Kitty's eyes.

"I know how hard it's been for you," Faith said. "I know what Cullen meant to you."

The tight knot of her grief twisted within Kitty. "I didn't think I could stand it when he died."

"But you did."

"Yes. Because of Michael."

"You would have managed it anyway. You're like that, sister. Always were."

Faith drew back, holding Kitty at arm's length and studying her face. "How old were you on your birthday?" she asked finally.

"Twenty-one," Kitty whispered.

"Lord, Lord . . . twenty-one years old and look at you." Her gaze took in the linsey dress dyed as dark as Kitty could get it, and she touched her hand lightly to the black hair which was pulled back so severely even the natural waves were straightened out of it. "Look what you've done to yourself. Got yourself up like an old woman."

"You wear your hair pulled back."

Faith's own eyes filled as she gently brushed a tear from Kitty's cheek, and she gave her head a shake. "I was never as pretty as you."

"That's not so—" Kitty began, but Faith shushed her.

" 'Tis," she said firmly. "But the truth is, were I to lose Ben, God forbid, I'd need a man to help me feed these young'uns of mine." She looked toward the bed to baby Latham, who'd fallen sound asleep. "And I'd probably fluff myself up as much as I could to get one."

They both laughed.

"Do something for me," Faith persisted.

"What?"

"Just think about what Todd asked you. He's not Cullen. I grant you that. But he might be what you and Michael need. Will you just think about it?"

Kitty hesitated, knowing that if she agreed, Faith and Ben would tell Todd and she would only have to deal with him again some time in the future. But the look on her sister's face was so earnest that she couldn't say no.

"I'll think about it," she said finally. "But that doesn't mean—"

"I know. Just think about it. That's all." Since Faith had lost her tooth, she usually kept her lips together or put her hand over her mouth when she smiled. But now her grin was free and wide. "Here"—she took up the knife—"I'll slice up this meat, and you can see to the squash." She set to work with a sure hand. "Do you have any onions?" she asked. "Ben purely loves a little onion fried up with his meat."

* 32 *

WITH THE WEATHER HOLDING COOL AND CRISP though Christmas only ten days away, Kitty decided to risk a trip to Harrod's Town. It seemed safe enough with the Shawnee demoralized for the time being by George Clark's raid. The Kentuckians had destroyed their crops and stored supplies of food to leave the Shawnee braves occupied with the task of feeding their women and children over the winter. Sara had been begging her to come for months, and Roman had suggested that she make the journey under the protection of a party of Boonesborough militiamen who were heading over to the fort for a much touted shooting match. The prize for the affair was a spanking new Pennsylvania rifle with a silver inlaid stock, which prompted more than a little good-natured boasting and betting among the Boonesborough marksmen, anxious to test their mettle against the Fort Harrod men.

Roman came over to Boonesborough himself to make the trip back with her and Michael. And Pleas had made sure that they wouldn't catch a chill on the way: he had made a new deerskin jacket and leggings for Michael, and a soft leather cape with the fur left on and turned inward for Kitty.

A fair-size crowd turned out to see the party off. "Show 'em over yonder what good shootin' be!" someone called out to the young man who was thought to be the best shot at the fort now.

"Shit!" Ezekial Turner spat a dark stream of tobacco juice out of the side of his mouth. "We need Dan'l . . . or Roman to shoot fer us. How 'bout it, Roman?"

Roman shook his head and smiled.

After two days of leaden skies, the sun was a welcome sight, though the wind was still cold. It was early yet, the mist barely lifted from the river and the hollows as the group gathered just outside the fort gates. Tolliver and two of his younger brothers waved. Hester handed Michael up to Kitty, who settled the youngster on the saddle in front of her, but Roman maneuvered his horse over beside them.

"Let him ride with me for a while," he said. Michael held his arms out at once, and Roman swung the eager little boy over.

Leather saddles creaked as the militiamen mounted up, and as Kitty saw John Holder lift his hand in a signal that they should move out, she leaned down to say a last good-bye to Pleas and Hester. "I thank you both for looking after the cow and Cullen's horse for us. And Bear," she added. They had had to fasten the dog in the cabin until they could get away. The animal followed Michael everywhere.

Kitty felt an unexpected exhilaration at the thought of seeing Harrod's Town for the first time. It was almost a shock to realize that, but for a few trips out to Faith and Ben's place, she had been at Boonesborough for four years, and a good part of that time cooped up within the fort walls.

She had thought that Michael would get restless on the long trip, but he clearly loved it. Sometimes he rode with her, but more often he was with Roman, smiling and waving to her from time to time. John Holder set an easy pace, and Kitty was reminded once again of how beautiful this land was with its gently rolling hills and high ridges, well timbered with magnificent trees, the ground covered with frosty drifts of leaves that still held a hint of red-brown and gold. The sight of it set up an ache in her for Otter Creek and home. She would go back one day, she promised herself again. She would go home.

They spotted five or six great shaggy buffalo, grazing along the edges of a canebrake. Several of the young men hefted their rifles, and one of the huge beasts was brought down with a terrible bellow that set the others stampeding away.

They soon had a fire going and buffalo steaks sizzling atop wet forked sticks set into the ground; the smell of the cooking meat was tantalizing.

"I hate to see one of them killed now," Roman said as he hunkered down to wipe the blade of his knife clean in the dried leaves beside him. "You don't see them very often anymore. They've moved westward."

Michael seemed at first puzzled, and then greatly pleased, at the idea of rolling up in fur robes and sleeping in the mouth of a cave, a fire burning brightly nearby.

"He's got a lot of Cullen in him," Roman told Kitty once the boy had finally given way to sleep.

"He has," she agreed, smiling as she tucked the robe closer about him.

They arrived at Harrod's Town late in the afternoon, and as they rode in along the rutted streets, Michael stretched his neck to gape in amazement at all the strange faces. His world up to now had been the fort walls at Boonesborough. He knew everyone who lived within the compound, and not a few of those who lived close by outside. But now Kitty could feel him press back against her with an unaccustomed shyness. She gave him a gentle squeeze to reassure him.

John Holder took his men off to report to James Harrod, and Roman and Kitty and Michael continued on to the Gentry cabin, where Sara was waiting eagerly.

The two women flew at each other on sight, hugging and laughing, wiping tears away.

"My Lord, you're thin!" Sara scolded. "Are you eating enough?"

"Yes . . . yes, I'm fine."

"And just look at *you*!" Sara clucked over Michael. "You've grown so tall!" At first he hung back, pressing into Kitty's skirts. It had been nine months since Sara had been at Boonesborough, and that was a long time out of his life. Clearly he was having trouble remembering her. But after a few minutes of Sara making over him, he began to grin and adopt that squared-off-shoulder look that was so like his father.

He let Sara help him out of his jacket, and she hugged and petted him and grasped Kitty's hands again and again as if she couldn't get enough of them. "I'm so glad you've come."

"You look wonderful," Kitty told her, taking in the rounded belly that, at six months, could no longer be hidden by her full skirt. Her face was fuller than Kitty had ever seen it.

Sara laughed. "I'm getting downright fat."

Roman went to show Michael where the necessary was, and Sara whisked Kitty into the bedroom where she could use the pot.

"Do you want to rest?" she asked. "You must be tired."

"A little," Kitty admitted. In truth, every bone in her body ached and she wasn't sure she ever wanted to sit a saddle again; but she declined Sara's offer. "I don't want to waste a minute of this visit," she said.

Sara brought in a pan of hot water and Kitty washed up, splashing the water up on her arms and face, shivering in the cool air of the room. "Mercy, that feels good." She grinned, looking around as she dried her face on a linen towel and slicked back her hair, catching any small errant strands and tucking them firmly into the knot. "You have a lot of room here," she said.

"Yes. More than at Boonesborough. Enough for you and Michael if we can persuade you to move over here with us. The loft is good-sized."

Kitty smiled at that. "You'll be surprised at how much space the baby will take up. They don't stay little for long, you know. Look at Michael." She took fresh clothing out of the pack she'd brought along and began to dress.

"Won't you stay?" Sara pressed. "Roman and some of the other men could get your things over here. I bet Flanders would help. Israel, too."

"I expect they would. But I can't leave Boonesborough, Sara. If I did, who'd teach the school?"

"*Someone,*" Sara insisted. "It doesn't have to be you."

"Yes, it does." Kitty buttoned her blouse, a quiet edge of truth entering her voice. "I'd be lost without it."

Sara peered at her, and Kitty could not avoid meeting those clear blue eyes. "Are you all right?" Sara asked.

Kitty nodded. "As right as I *can* be." She didn't mean for her lip to quiver, but it did, and the two of them hugged again, though hugging was hard with Sara's belly in the way, and that made them laugh.

"Come on," said Sara. "My sister wants us all to have supper with her and Samuel."

Marietta Brewster, ten years older than her sister, was a tall, slender woman with a nervous air about her and hair as fine and blond as Sara's. Though her features were not quite as delicate, there was definitely a family resemblance.

"I'm so glad to meet you at last," she told Kitty. Despite the high-strung look of her, she seemed accustomed to taking charge. "I've everything cooked and ready," she said. "Let's just sit down and visit until the men get here."

Roman had taken Michael and gone to fetch Sam Brewster from his law office—actually nothing more than a tiny cabin where he shared space with a pair of surveyors—but it wasn't long before the three of them were back. The portly lawyer, ruddy-faced and balding, was holding fast to Michael's hand as they entered the Brewster cabin and promising that as soon as they finished eating, he'd take him over to see a litter of brand-new hound pups he'd found in the hollow of a sycamore tree.

Michael turned a pleading eye toward his mother, but Kitty shook her head, laughing, understanding her son's unspoken question. "I think Bear is enough for us, Michael."

Marietta and Sara wouldn't allow her to do a thing, and as they put the dinner on the table, Kitty had time to admire a fine mahogany lowboy and a pair of side chairs and a candle stand. Though her own bed and chest at home were the envy of Boonesborough, they were certainly not as fine as these pieces. The lowboy had fancy brass pulls on the drawers.

"Had those rafted down the Ohio to the falls and from there overland," Samuel told her. "There was more, but those scoundrels that I paid dear to get our things here left a sideboard and a credenza and who knows what else at the bottom of a dropoff . . . smashed to pieces. At least that's what their story was. I wouldn't be surprised if they didn't sell the things that were missing. The thieving blackguards!''

Roman put a hand to his mouth to cover a smile, but Samuel's quick eye caught the gesture.

"Roman told me that they'd never be able to get them all the way here," he said dryly. Then he grinned amiably. "I suppose we're lucky we were able to have these few pieces. Still''—he shot Roman a look—"that sideboard was made by one of the finest craftsmen in Philadelphia. And I wouldn't be a bit surprised to go to the settlement at the falls someday and see it sitting smack dab in somebody's dining room.''

Roman grinned unabashedly now. "Old Chief Moluntha may have it in his lodge by now. His squaw's likely got it shined up with bear grease. Maybe keeps her cookpots in it.''

Samuel let out a hearty belly laugh.

Michael tugged at Kitty's skirt. "Pup-py . . . Unca Pweas . . .''

"Oh''—it dawned on Kitty what he was saying—"you want to take one back to Uncle Pleas.'' As he nodded, eyes shining, she pushed the hair back out of his eyes. "I think not, son,'' she said.

Marietta called that the food was on the table, and they all sat down to eat.

Roman and Michael had bedded down on pallets in the main room, letting Kitty and Sara have the bed in the bedroom, and now the two women giggled in the darkness, quilts pulled high to muffle the sounds of their laughter. Kitty had been recounting Todd Tyler's proposal and describing the way he had chewed and swallowed . . . "like a cow belching up its cud,'' she said.

But in a moment she sobered. "Lord, I ought to be ashamed of myself. He means well. I shouldn't make fun of him.''

"But you couldn't *marry* him!'' Sara protested.

"No. Though I promised Faith I'd think about it.''

"Thinking and doing are two different things. But Jonathon Walters now . . . that's a different matter.''

Kitty was silent for a minute. "I'm not ready to give up Cullen yet, Sara.''

Sara found Kitty's hand and squeezed it. "Time . . . that's what they say: time takes care of everything. Do you think it's true?''

"I don't know.''

There'd been a plaintive note in Sara's voice that hung in Kitty's mind. "What about you?'' she asked after a moment.

"Are you content here now that Marietta and Samuel have come?"

Sara hesitated. "I'm content to have this baby kicking strong inside me," she said. "I know that this one will be all right. I can feel it."

"I'm glad about that, but it's not what I asked."

Sara was still again for a long moment, and Kitty waited.

"There's a barber set up here now," she said. "Can you imagine? And a widow lady is taking in sewing. You could almost think you were back home. And then something happens, and you know that out there beyond the last street, it's a savage place still . . . and it can come right in and touch you close to home"—her voice dropped to a whisper—"it can make you feel that you've not really known the person you love best. Kitty . . . I saw Roman kill a man." She shivered, as if the pile of quilts that covered them weren't enough.

"What man? Where?"

"Right here in town. A man . . . one of the trappers that come in and out all the time, had brought in a live catamount, trussed up to where it could just barely move. He'd staked it out and was tormenting the poor beast. Cutting it and burning it with a stick he'd hold in the fire he'd made there. It screamed, Kitty, like a child, or a woman . . . and twisted about so . . .

"Marietta and I had been walking. We were back in the crowd that had gathered, and we'd turned away, sickened by the sight, when I heard Roman's voice. He hadn't seen us there. He was telling the man to put the animal out of its misery. When the fellow refused, Roman raised his rifle and shot it through the head himself."

"As he should have. Don't you think?"

"I don't know. Maybe so. I guess it was a brave thing to do . . . especially since some in the crowd were egging the trapper on. But I've never been brave. Not the way you are . . . or Roman."

"That's not so. You were brave enough to help me get Ma to Boonesborough," Kitty said, her voice a soft whisper.

"I didn't have much choice. I would have been more afraid to stay there by myself than to go."

The wind rustled the bushes outside the cabin, but there was no other sound. Roman and Michael had been quiet for a long time now. There was just Kitty and Sara and the darkness.

"Roman killed the man?" Kitty asked after a time.

"Yes. He came at Roman with his knife, and the two of them

fought . . . rolling on the ground . . . God, it was awful! And Roman took the knife from him and killed him, right there. I could see the man's mouth open and close, and I couldn't look away, no matter how hard I tried. . . . His head was jerking, and Roman pushed the knife in again . . ." Sara was crying softly now, and Kitty sat up in the bed and cradled her in her arms.

"Hush . . . hush . . . You don't want him to hear you."

"No," Sara said.

Kitty held her there, wondering if gentle Sara could ever really understand about Roman, or the other men like him who'd come out here and matched this land, able to pay the price for it . . . sometimes for the rest of them. . . .

"What did you do?" she asked finally.

Sara sighed. "Fainted dead away. When I came to, I was back here on this bed, Roman bending over me. He was so concerned . . ."

"Of course."

"But just minutes before, he'd killed that man."

"Because that's what he had to do," Kitty put in quickly. "Would you have wanted the man to kill *him*?"

"Oh, God, no! I just never thought of Roman as someone who could kill someone else . . . I mean, not like that," she wailed. "I know during the siege he had to . . . all the men had to . . ."

"Sara, Sara . . . just be glad he's alive. And strong. And able to do whatever he needs to do for you and this baby you're carrying. I wish to heaven that Cullen had been able to kill the Shawnee before they killed him. He would have, too, if there hadn't been too many of them. And—" Kitty's voice broke, but she went on. "—he would have come to me, and he would have loved me . . . and he'd have gone to Michael's bed and touched his back in that gentle way he had. . . ."

Sara caught in her breath. "Oh, Lord, Kitty . . . I'm sorry."

"Don't be." Kitty hugged her. "Just thank God for what Roman is, and for every minute you have with him."

"You shame me. . . ."

"Never, Sara . . . dear Sara. Forgive me if it seemed so. I'd just have you know how strong you really are. A thousand times more than when Roman first brought you out here."

Sara giggled suddenly in a kind of high-pitched relief, a hand to her mouth to muffle the sound. "I must have looked scared to death that day when we came to the cabin at Otter Creek."

"You did. But look how far you've come since then. You lived through—*we* lived through what happened out there." Kitty made her voice steady when it threatened to break again. "And you survived the Shawnee . . . and losing the baby, and the near starving to death . . . I always knew that if I needed you, you'd be there, Sara. And now, look at you—here in Harrod's Town in a cabin with *two* rooms, and a healthy child within you. . . ."

Sara squeezed her hand, and Kitty lay in the darkness, aching with the thought of how good it would have been if she could have had another of Cullen's in her belly before he was killed.

But she had Michael. Thank God for her son . . . for Cullen's son.

Before Kitty left for home, Simon Butler, who was going by the name of Kenton now, came by to pay his respects. Since he had hardly ever done more than aim a perfunctory if polite nod her way before, his appearance at the Gentry cabin especially to see her was something of a surprise.

The huge hook-nosed scout pulled a dun-colored slouch hat from his head to uncover the thick shock of hair that was barely controlled by a leather whang. "I heard you was here on a visit, Miz Claiborne," he said, bending down slightly so that he wouldn't tower so above her, "and I come to offer my services to escort you back to Boonesborough, should you have the need. I expect to be riding that way in the next day or two."

"Why, that's very kind of you Mister . . . Kenton." She had almost said Butler. "I intend to start back the day after tomorrow with Captain Holder and his men. I'm sure that John would be glad of your company."

"I expect he would, Simon," Roman said.

Kenton nodded. "I'll see him directly, then."

"Would you take dinner with us?" Sara asked him. "Everything is just ready to take up. I'll set another plate."

"Thankee, no, ma'am. I've et already and need to go down to the blacksmith and let him have a look at my animal's right front shoe. I think he's fixin' to throw it," he said to Roman.

"Another time, Simon," Roman said.

Kenton nodded and donned his hat once again. At the door he turned back for a moment. "I never got the chance to tell you before, Miz Claiborne, but I'd as soon had your husband cover my back, times when we was out there together, as any man I ever knowed." He ducked through the door then, gone before Kitty could say a word.

Later, Roman explained that when Kenton had first come into Kentucky, he'd been on the run, thinking that he'd killed a man in a fight. Sure that the law was after him, he'd gone by the name of Butler for nearly ten years, and no one the wiser.

"But then last spring he came upon a group of men along the Boone Trace," Roman told her. "And he realized that one of them was his own brother. He found out that the man he thought he'd killed wasn't dead at all."

"So it was safe then to reveal his true name," said Kitty.

Roman nodded.

James Harrod came, too. The next day.

"I'd not let Cullen Claiborne's widow come and leave before I paid a call," he said. Looking fit and trim, the fine webbing of leathery wrinkles about his eyes deepening as he laughed, Harrod caught Michael up and raised him nearly to the rafters. "If you're not the spittin' image of your pa, I've yet to see it!"

The big frontiersman, garbed in a well-worn linsey hunting shirt and leather leggings, dug into a pouch at his belt and brought out a curved piece of bone about six inches long, its surface polished smooth and incised with a small, rough likeness of a buffalo on one side and an elk on the other. "You'd not lose this were I to give it to you, now, would ye, boy?"

Michael's eyes widened and he shook his head solemnly.

"I picked it up one time at Big Bone Lick . . . up there a ways close to the Ohio"—he gestured expansively—"about halfway twixt the Kentucky and the Licking. There's bones there of creatures y' could hardly imagine. Rib cages bigger than this cabin. I figure this'un to be a part of some great giant of a beast long dead. Might could be a little toe, eh?"

He winked at Michael and held the piece out to him, and the little boy grasped it eagerly, turning it back and forth to gaze with fascination at the animals scratched there. Kitty reminded him of his manners, and he breathed an awed thank-you.

"I'll see that he doesn't lose it," she said.

Harrod accepted Roman's offer of a drink of rum and told them of the word, just arrived, that the legislature in Richmond had acted to divide Kentucky into three counties. "We're in Lincoln County now. Boonesborough and Logan's Fort, too. All south of the Kentucky River."

"Lincoln? For General Benjamin Lincoln under Washington?" asked Roman.

Harrod nodded. "North and east of the river will be Fayette County. Y'd think if they intended to pay tribute to our most famous French ally, they'd use his full name, now, wouldn't you?"

Roman smiled. "The Marquis de Lafayette County could be a little long."

"And some o' our good citizens would have the devil's own time in sayin' it!" Harrod chuckled. "As for the rest of Kentucky, it's to be Jefferson, and that's an honor well deserved."

With uncharacteristic enthusiasm, Roman clapped Harrod on the back and nodded. "My God," he said, "but nobody deserves to be remembered in Kentucky more than Tom Jefferson. He's been a friend to us more than once, when we needed it most."

"He has that," Harrod agreed.

"Here . . ." Roman hefted the jug and signaled Sara to fetch more pewter mugs from the shelf. "We must have a toast at this news. Sara, you and Kitty . . . Michael, too . . ."

Sara clucked her tongue. "Michael? You'd best ask his mama about that."

"Just a sup?" Roman looked to Kitty, who smiled.

"I expect a drop won't hurt him," she allowed.

"Not a bit!" Harrod roared, lifting the boy once again. "When I was a lad not much older, I use to sneak a bit from my father's spirits at every chance!"

Roman passed the mugs, and with Harrod still holding Michael on one arm and his rum in the other, they lifted their cups. "To Kentucky and her three counties . . . and to what lies ahead for her," Roman said, piercing blue eyes lit with a vision of his own.

"To Kentucky," Harrod joined in.

Michael coughed at the pungent taste, his eyes reddening. But he laughed, and the others joined in as Kitty took the mug from him.

They left for home the next day, Kitty and Sara both crying in those last minutes.

"I know that Marietta is here, thank God, to see to you when your time comes. But if you need me, just send word and I'll come," Kitty assured Sara.

"I will." Sara kissed Michael. "You keep your cap pulled down so you don't get an earache," she cautioned.

True to his word, Simon Kenton was mounted up and ready. And the Boonesborough men were going home well pleased. Their young marksman had won the prize rifle.

* * *

With the welcome end of winter the sun took on its spring warmth, the days lengthening. The cows began to drop their calves, and Kitty's red cow came in one evening with a spindly-legged little brindle heifer following along after her. The next day Elizabeth Callaway's old cow dropped twins, a male and a female.

"Would you look at that." Elizabeth pointed them out to Kitty. The two calves, good-sized for twins, bumped and shoved at one another awkwardly, their raspy little tongues licking out as they vied for their mother's teats. "They're not what I'd have ordered up." Elizabeth sighed and gestured toward the heifer. "A freemartin sure. Good for nothing except to butcher for the beef once big enough. I could have used another good milch cow."

"It's too bad," Kitty agreed. "Is your other cow about ready?"

Elizabeth nodded. "She should be dropping any day now. Maybe better luck with her. I'd hate to end up with two bull calves and a freemartin, though maybe I can do some trading with someone who needs the beef. Meantime, Jemima and Fanny between them are keepin' us in milk, bless 'em. With my young'uns, we need a Lord's plenty."

"Hester is giving Michael and me part of hers until I can wean the heifer," Kitty said.

Elizabeth nodded. "I sorely miss Betsey. She was always a help to me. Used to bring over milk every time she had extra." Elizabeth's daughter and her son-in-law, Sam Henderson, had moved away that summer. Sam's older brother, Judge Richard Henderson, had come to Boonesborough—for the first time since the Transylvania days—to buy corn for his latest venture, which he called French Lick, down in the Tennessee country. Betsey and Sam had decided to go back there with him.

The two women fell into step as they went back along the path. Elizabeth had aged in the year since her husband's death. The lines from nose to mouth had deepened noticeably, and the hair that peeked from beneath the white mobcap had grayed. But she was still a strong woman who managed her family well.

"Have ye heard aught of Sara?" she asked. "She should be coming close, shouldn't she?"

Kitty nodded. "I keep expecting to see Roman ride in here any time now. She was due a full week ago."

"I pray she gets a live baby this time," Elizabeth said.

"She's confident that she will."

"I've known women to lose two or three in a row and then settle in to have a dozen healthy ones," Elizabeth offered hopefully.

But as a week went by with no word, and then another, Kitty began to worry.

"She's likely just a little late," Hester soothed her.

Kitty nodded. "But it'd be hard for her if she lost it. She was so sure . . ."

The next day, as Kitty was gathering up her books and stuffing them into her old hemp bag, she was surprised to see Keziah Callaway come running back fully five minutes after class had let out. Now that the weather was warm and sunny, the children usually couldn't get out of class fast enough, but the girl seemed clearly in a hurry to get back as she burst through the blockhouse door, dark hair flying.

"Did you forget something, Keziah?" Kitty asked.

"No, ma'am," the girl panted. "My ma says . . . you'd best come, Mistress Kitty."

Alarmed at the urgency in Keziah's voice, Kitty took up the bag and followed her. Outside, the sun was still shining brightly, though a bank of dark clouds to the west threatened, and the wind was beginning to gust.

"Is something wrong with your mama?" Kitty called. The girl was running ahead, fleet as a young deer.

"No, ma'am." Keziah beckoned Kitty on with a wave of her hand.

They found Elizabeth by one of the front blockhouses, her face somber as she talked to a homely stringbean of a youth, whose homespun breeches were an inch or more short on him. He hitched at them nervously as Kitty neared, slying his eyes toward her and then back to Elizabeth as if he'd as soon be someplace else.

Elizabeth broke off with whatever she was saying as she caught sight of Kitty and her daughter. "Kitty . . . Lord, Kitty"—she shook her head—"there's bad news. I knew you'd want to know. This young fellow is Larkin Moser . . ."

Kitty nodded to the youth. "Bad news?" She looked at first one, then the other of them, puzzled.

"When I heard he'd just come in from Harrod's Town," Elizabeth explained, "I thought I'd just inquire if he knew Roman and Sara . . ."

The young man's Adam's apple bobbed noticeably. "I expect there ain't many over there that don't know of Roman Gentry and his missus. And I surely ain't happy to be the bearer of sad tidings. . . ."

Kitty sighed and turned back to Elizabeth. "She lost the baby, then." She shook her head, grieving already for the both of them. Dear God, Roman would take it hard, too.

"No'm," Moser spoke up. "The babe is fine. But poor Mistress Gentry died in the birthin' of it. Folks sure hated it. She were a nice lady."

The clouds had rolled quickly, driven by the wind, and the sun was suddenly darkened as Kitty leaned back against the blockhouse wall, chilled in the burst of cool air.

"I am sure enough sorry."

Elizabeth, her long face marked with the sadness of the news, reached out to squeeze Kitty's arm. "He says it happened nearly two weeks ago," she said.

The fire had died to the soft glow of banked coals, and Kitty lay in her bed, staring up, dry-eyed now, into the smoky darkness and listening to the rain that lashed the roof. For some reason she thought of Michael, asleep long since, thought of the night she had started in labor with him. It had been raining then, too. Was it raining, she wondered, when Sara had her baby? When Sara died?

The visit to Harrod's Town kept coming back to her. Sara's face, rounder than she'd ever seen it. Maybe it had not been good health, but swelling. She'd heard Amelia talk about that long ago, about a woman who'd died in childbirth because "the poisons had built up in her." She should have seen that, should have said something. Maybe if they'd known . . .

It hit her afresh, and the tears came again. Sara . . . dear, sweet, lovely Sara . . . "God rest her soul," Kitty whispered.

Elizabeth had gone with her to find John Holder, and upon hearing the news, he had volunteered to head up an escort party himself. "Fanny and me thought the world of Sara Gentry," he said.

It was settled that they'd leave in the morning, and Kitty chided herself now that she needed to sleep if she was to have strength enough for the journey. Everything was ready. Hester would keep Michael for her.

She closed her eyes and tried not to think of anything. The rain drummed at the cabin, assumed a kind of rhythm that she lost herself in . . . until the knock at the door jarred her, brought her bolt upright.

"Who is it?" she called, up and reaching for her shawl. She heard Michael stir and roll over.

"Roman." The answer came back, muffled with the sound of the rain. But Kitty recognized his voice and caught her breath as she flew to the door to draw the bolt and fling it wide.

"Roman . . . oh, Roman," she said. For a moment she could hardly recognize him, his face was so gaunt, skin stretched taut, his eyes burning as if with a fever.

The rain drove through the open doorway, cold and stinging, and she grasped his arm and tugged at him until he stepped inside. Then she shoved the door shut behind him. He was soaked, water dripping from the brim of his hat, trickling onto the floor beneath his moccasins.

"Lord, Lord," she said, "come in here to the fire." She took up the iron poker at the side of the fireplace and poked at the coals, stirring them up until they started to smoke. Then she laid a piece of wood on top, and turned back to him. "You're soaking wet. I'll get you some of Cullen's things—"

"No." He stopped her. "I'll dry." He took off his hat and his buckskin jacket and put them aside, drawing near to the fire that was beginning to curl up and crackle.

"I know about Sara, Roman." She pressed her lips together, tears stinging her eyes.

He nodded, seemed unable to speak at that moment, staring still into the fireplace.

"I only learned of it today. I was planning to leave for Harrod's Town come morning. Oh, God, Roman . . . I can't believe it. I'm so sorry. . . ."

She began to cry softly, and Roman's head came forward slightly in such a gesture of grief that Kitty instinctively reached out to him. But it was like touching stone . . . the center of him encased in the hardness of his grieving. And in a moment she drew away.

"I'll fix you something to eat," she said, laying another log on the fire now that the first one was catching.

"No, don't," he said. His voice sounded hoarse. "I'm not hungry."

"I have a little coffee."

He hunched his shoulders and nodded.

As she put fresh water into the iron pot and hooked the bail onto the crane to swing it over the flame, she kept stealing looks toward him, worried at the state he was in. It would have been better for him if he cursed or cried.

"Is the baby all right?" she asked finally.

His eyes flickered toward her and then away. "She seems healthy enough."

"A girl . . ." Kitty sighed. During her visit to Harrod's Town, Sara had confided that she'd like it to be a girl.

Michael stirred again in his trundle bed, and Kitty went to cover him. He lay curled on his side, one hand tucked beneath his face, his breath coming sweet and regular. He would like having a baby in the house, she thought. God knew that Roman couldn't take care of that child. And if anything had happened to her, she'd always known that Sara would take Michael. She would do no less for Sara's baby.

She made the coffee and Roman drank it, sitting now, his long legs stretched out toward the fire, moccasins steaming faintly.

"We can go to Harrod's Town tomorrow and bring the baby back here," Kitty said. "You need not worry over it. I'll take good care of her, Roman."

He looked up at her, really looked at her for the first time since he'd come into the cabin. "Here? You'd take her?"

"Of course. Sara would have done the same for me."

He shook his head slowly and looked back into the fire. "No," he said wearily. "I thank you, but it's all decided. I only came to tell you about Sara . . . and say good-bye."

"Good-bye?"

"Marietta and Samuel are taking the baby. They've had enough of the West. They're going back, and I'll be going along to see that they get there safely."

She'd been standing by the table, but she took a step closer to him there by the fire. "Marietta . . . I hadn't thought—"

"They have no children. They wanted her, and it seemed best to me."

"But . . ." It was all too fast for Kitty to absorb. "You'd not get to see her if they take her east, Roman."

His hands, long lean fingers, were clasped across his chest, as if he were holding that terrible grief closer to him. "I don't expect I'll be coming back for a while, Kitty . . . maybe never."

She sat down in a chair, the rain still coming down hard outside, the rhythmic beat against the roof the only sound in the room but for an occasional hiss of burning wood.

"When Cullen died," she said after a while, "I thought it would kill me. But it didn't."

"It's different," he said.

"Why?"

Roman looked away, gave her no answer.

"Talk to me, Roman," she begged him, but he kept his face turned away.

Not for years had there been a time when the two of them couldn't talk to one another, when they did not understand one another, and she refused to accept his silence now. She dropped to her knees beside his chair.

"For God's sake, Roman—no . . . for *your* sake . . . or *mine*," she cried, her voice laced with sorrow and pain and something close to anger, "talk to me!"

"Have done, Kitty!" he exploded, blue eyes blazing.

"I'll not!" She gave him as good as he'd given. "Didn't I love her, too?"

He grimaced, a low and terrible sound wrenching its way between his lips. "Yes . . . for Christ's sake, yes! But you didn't bring her out here to die!"

She drew in her breath. There it was.

She grasped one of his big hands in the two of hers. "You were ever the one to torture yourself, Roman Gentry . . . but I can think of no better time than this to break yourself of the habit. Sara wanted to be wherever you were."

"She hated Kentucky! She was so fragile, never strong enough to be out here. But I . . . so claimed by this land . . . the wonder of it, the promise . . . I could not even entertain the notion of going back." He swore under his breath and tried to pull his hand away, but Kitty hung on fiercely.

"I'll not have you blame yourself . . . and for naught, Roman! The truth is, Sara told me how content she was when I was with her last at Harrod's Town." It was a lie—there was no gainsaying it. But it was needed. And Usaph Gentry had always said that God understood necessity better than anyone. " 'Tis enough to bear the loss of her without whipping yourself to a fine guilt you have no cause to carry."

His eyes narrowed, and for a moment he looked away from her, and then back, brows drawn nearly together. "She told you that?"

"She did. She was so happy about the baby . . ." That, at least, was the truth. "And glad of Marietta and Samuel being nearby." As she got on safer ground, Kitty's sureness grew. "And she was well pleased with the cabin. We couldn't talk enough of it . . . all that room!"

He was silent, the grief and guilt and exhaustion all written on his features; his eyes seemed set deeper in the sharp planes of his face. Still, Kitty could feel the easing, however slight. He settled against the chair back, some of the rigidity going out of him, and in a moment he brought his free hand over to grasp her right hand and turn it up, looking for a moment at the scarred palm.

"Does it hurt you still?" he asked.

"No." There were times when it felt stiff, and she would go back to exercising it again, but she didn't tell him that.

One of the logs in the fireplace shifted, and a shower of sparks shot up the chimney.

"Do you remember after Cullen died . . . when I asked you to come to Harrod's Town with Sara and me?"

Kitty nodded.

"You told me then that you had to stay here."

She nodded again.

"Well, I understood that there was a need in you to do that. There's a need in me, Kitty, to do this. I have to leave Kentucky."

She pressed his hand, and there seemed no reason for more words. She got up after a moment and went to fetch some quilts from the chest at the foot of the bed. "You can stretch out here before the fire," she said.

He waved a hand. "I can go down to the blockhouse."

"No. I doubt there's a fire there. And you're still not dry. Stay here."

She went to check on Michael again, then put aside her shawl and climbed into bed. Roman was still sitting in the chair when she finally dropped off to sleep.

When she woke to the gray dawn, the rain still pounding against the roof, she saw that he was gone, the quilts still folded and where she had left them.

❄ 33 ❄

WITH A FIRM SET TO HER SHOULDERS AND A DISBE-
lieving shake of her head, Rebecca Boone settled
herself into the rocker and stared up at Kitty.
"There's no way I could be convinced that Roman Gentry's
gone from Kaintuck for good," she declared. "Why, he could
no more go back east to stay than Daniel could."

She'd come over to Boonesborough with Israel and Daniel
Morgan—who was twelve years old now and leggy as a colt—
to visit with Jemima, and had walked on down to see Kitty.

"You didn't see him," Kitty said, pouring two cups of buttermilk and passing one to Rebecca. "He's so stricken. Blames
himself for Sara's death."

Rebecca's dark eyes filled with sadness. "Lord help the poor
man." She cupped her hands around the buttermilk, looking
down into the pale depths of it. "He was always that way, you
know. When he was a boy, he took everything on himself."

Kitty nodded.

"Still . . ." Rebecca sighed. "He'll come back when he's
worked the grieving out of him. You'll see."

Kitty noted the few threads of gray beginning to gleam in
Rebecca's brown hair. She seemed slightly heavier than when
Kitty had last seen her. And there were a few more lines around
her eyes, but the face was not much changed from the one Kitty
had first seen six years before, despite all that the Boones had
been through.

"I heard," Kitty said, "that Daniel was appointed county
lieutenant for Fayette."

"Aye. And well pleased with it, I vow. Pleased, too, with
being promoted to lieutenant colonel in the militia, though he
won't own up to it." She grinned. "Daniel has never been much

446

to puff himself up about anything. He's off now to Richmond as county representative in the Assembly. I do just wish that he'd known about poor Sara before he left, though. At least he could have gone to see Roman if he'd known he was back there, too.'' She finished the last of her buttermilk and put the cup aside.

"Lord, Lord . . . the loss of Sara Gentry is a hard one. But when a woman starts a child, she can surely never be certain of the outcome.'' She went to stand and look out the open doorway, her back to Kitty. "Though, I guess,'' she went on, almost to herself, "that I birthed mine as easy as most.

"My ma was with me when I had James. Said I popped him out at the last like a watermelon seed spit between gapped teeth.'' She laughed and turned back, freckled cheeks slightly flushed. "I hope I haven't forgot how.''

Kitty looked at her for a long moment before it dawned on her what Rebecca was saying. *That* was why she looked heavier. "Rebecca . . . you're carrying.''

Rebecca nodded. "I thought surely I'd be done by now. Me or Daniel one. Looks like few of them get finished, though— the men.''

"Oh, Rebecca . . . it's wonderful!'' Kitty went to hug her.

"That's what Jemima says. But I expect it'll be some confusing for my grandbaby when she gets old enough to realize she's got an aunt or an uncle younger than she is.''

Kitty laughed. "Now you know it's not all that uncommon. Plenty of times it happens. What does Daniel think of it?''

"He seems pleased enough with his part in it.''

"And I'd wager you will be, too. Once it's over.''

"Maybe I will. I didn't know at first.'' There was an earnestness to her strong face and a light in her eyes. "I felt it quicken last week . . . and it seemed like it was a kind of''— she groped for a word—"*testimony* . . . like in church. Oh, Lord, that doesn't make a bit of sense, now, does it?''

She looked away, as if embarrassed by what she'd said, and Kitty wondered if she thought again of her firstborn, poor boy, tortured to death by the Indians . . . or of those dark days when everyone, even Rebecca herself, had given up Daniel for dead. Or maybe she was haunted still by the memory of helping prepare Ned Boone's headless corpse for its final rest at Boone's Station not too many months before.

Kitty recalled with a sharp, sweet clarity when she and Cullen had forsaken the greater safety of the blockhouse and risked sleeping in their own cabin, though the Shawnee threatened in force beyond the walls. They had lain together, and for those precious moments death seemed powerless over them. If such an act filled a woman with life, then *testimony* was as good a word as any for it, she thought.

"Yes, it does," she told Rebecca softly. "It makes sense enough to me."

Rebecca smiled and said she guessed she wouldn't mind another cup of buttermilk if Kitty had it to spare. And after she'd drunk it, Kitty walked back along the path with her toward Jemima's.

Kitty straightened up to ease the pull on her back muscles and wiped at the sweat that stung her eyes, looking down the row of beans ahead of her to see how many weeds yet awaited her hoe. With the heat of the afternoon at its fullest, it did seem a pure foolishness, she thought, to be out working the vegetable patch. But there was so much for her to do before school in the mornings. And if she tried to hold class in the afternoon, the children would fidget and fret in the sweltering blockhouse and not get a thing done. Maybe, she sighed, she could get up a little earlier . . . though very much earlier and it would still be pitch-dark.

She bent to the hoeing again, quick strokes chopping out the pesky weeds that seemed to spring up almost overnight in the rich dark soil. Her scarred right palm pained a little with the constant friction. It never seemed to callus over as well as the other one. Sometimes it would blister after hoeing and the like. But her garden had never looked better, she noted with some satisfaction.

The potato tops were green and full, and the beans were ready and waiting to be picked. Maybe she would take some to Jemima, she thought, who was sick in bed with a fever . . . though she'd been much relieved to hear at last that Daniel was safe, and that was a Lord's blessing.

Over the weeks of spring and summer, word had filtered over the mountains of the fighting in the East. The British, commanded by the turncoat Arnold, had set the Marquis de Lafayette and his troops retreating. It was said that the members of the Virginia legislature had been forced to flee from Richmond and, but for those captured by the enemy, had reconvened in Charlottesville eight miles to the northwest.

But though the frontier patriots had been undaunted, Jemima and the rest of the Boone family had spent several anxious weeks until a surveyor traveling through Boonesborough and on toward the falls had delivered up a torn and dirty letter from Daniel assuring them of his safety. Kitty knew that the letter must have eased Rebecca's mind some. The poor woman had gone through times enough when she didn't know if her husband was alive or dead, and there had certainly been other occasions when she'd borne a babe without its father home. If Daniel was to make it this time, he'd best be doing it, Kitty thought wryly, since Israel reported that his mother expected to deliver any time now.

God keep her in that hour, Kitty prayed, memories of Sara coming to her. The loss was still overwhelming. There were times when she thought if she could just have been there at the last, she might have been able to do something to save her.

She put her hoe to a stubborn weed, bringing the sharp blade up to chop doggedly at the thick, tough root of it again, when she heard her name called out and turned to see Todd Tyler, his placid old buckskin gelding plodding along behind him. He dropped the reins to the ground and threw up his hand in greeting.

"Thought that was you over here," he said, grinning, his fair hair nearly white in the sunlight.

"Todd . . ." Kitty nodded. "What brings you to Boonesborough today?"

"I was over to Estill's Station and thought I'd stop in here on my way home."

Kitty had heard that Ben's brother was courting a woman over at Estill's—a small stockade some fifteen miles from Boonesborough. Since Todd's declaration the year before, he had not again mentioned marriage to her, and she was glad.

He reached for the leather canteen that hung from his saddle. "I just this minute filled this at the spring," he said, holding it out to her across a row of onions.

She nodded her thanks and drank, realizing how thirsty she was. As she handed it back, she noted how his chest and shoulders had filled out with the hard work of clearing his land. He was in truth, she thought, not a bad-looking man. Certainly better-looking than his brother.

"The shade of that tree yonder looks inviting enough," he said. "Why don't we set awhile?"

She hesitated. "Well . . . I'll be pleased enough to rest, but I need to finish up with my hoeing first. It'll be time to start supper before I know it. And you're welcome to stay for it," she added quickly, "if you're minded to."

He stepped across the onions and took the hoe from her. "You go set. The sun is hot."

She watched him for a moment as he put the hoe in motion, head forward now, intent on the work. And then she walked toward the shade, feeling the dampness of her blouse across the back, the trickle of perspiration between her breasts. The breeze stirred, and she welcomed it, sinking down to the thick grass and cupping her hands in her lap. She saw that her right hand *had* blistered, on the pad just below the middle finger. The blister had broken and it stung.

Todd worked in steady, sure strokes, and in a surprisingly short time finished the weeding and came to sprawl down beside her, sweaty and grinning.

"I do thank you for the help," she said. "It would have taken me a good while longer."

He nodded, leaning back against the rough bark of the thick tree trunk, which for some reason made her feel slightly uncomfortable. After a pause, he swallowed and chewed and said: "I must own that I come to see you a' purpose, Kitty."

Kitty's disquiet grew as she was struck suddenly with the notion that what she had heard about him and the woman over at Estill's might have been false. She had gotten almost at ease with him in these last months, and she hoped that he would let it stay so.

"As you know"—Todd cleared his throat, coughing and har-rumphing nervously—"I have given some thought to taking a wife. It is not something which I would enter into lightly."

"I . . . I'm sure that's true." Her misgivings were in full force now.

"And when I asked you last year and you said no . . . I was sincere in my offer, which is why I thought it only right to make sure you haven't changed your mind in the meantime. . . . Have you?" The recent coughing seemed to throw him into a great spasm of swallowing and chewing as he looked to her for an answer. And yet, somehow Kitty didn't mind it anymore, was ashamed of herself that she had ever been so hateful about him.

"No. I haven't changed my mind," she said, her voice soft and filled with the knowledge that she was probably a fool to turn him down. But it wasn't in her to marry him. She was sure now that she would never marry again. Not Todd, not anyone.

"Well then, that being the case"—he cleared his throat once more—"I have decided to ask Miss Phronie Sweeton from over at Estill's Station to wed."

A big grin had spread across his face, his cheeks ruddied up, and Kitty was filled with such a relief for herself and a sudden gladness for him that she impulsively leaned forward and gave him a hug, which set him chuckling softly. "Oh, Todd," she burst out, "I *am* pleased for you! I know Faith and Ben will be, too!"

"I expect they will," he said.

Phronie Sweeton had been to Boonesborough a time or two, and Kitty remembered the tall, sober-faced, but not uncomely girl. A nose that was a little too long and thin, maybe, but a fine, full-hipped body. She'd make a good wife for Todd.

He waited for her in the shade of the tree while she picked enough beans for herself and Jemima, then the two of them started back toward the fort together. The rich smells of searing meat and thick-crusted johnnycake drifted from the cabins that stretched out now almost to the woods, and Todd said he guessed he'd take her up on her invitation to stay and eat with her because he was hungry as a bear just waking after the winter.

"Hester is keeping an eye on Michael for me. I'll get him and start supper."

Todd nodded. "I expect I'll visit with the men for a while, then be on down directly." He stopped and lifted a hand to shade his eyes from the sun, peering off toward the river, and Kitty followed his gaze to see a rider coming. "Looks like Israel Boone," Todd said.

"It is Israel. . . ."

The horse was coming at a fast trot, and as Israel drew closer, Kitty could see the pale flecks of lather that speckled the dark hide. He didn't see them but urged the animal on through the wide gate.

"Something must be wrong," said Kitty.

They hurried to Jemima and Flanders's cabin. Elizabeth Callaway was standing in the doorway as if ready to leave. Everyone knew that she didn't stay around when Jemima's Boone kin came.

"Israel is here," she said to Kitty. "He says Rebecca's in labor and not doin' so well."

Todd said he would wait outside in case there was anything he could do, and Kitty slipped past Elizabeth to find Israel insisting that Jemima, who was clearly ill yet, lie back down.

"I've got to go to Ma," she said stubbornly, her eyes bright with fever.

"You'll not," Israel said. "You'd be little good to her, sick as you are."

"He's right," Kitty said. She went at once to the bed and pressed Jemima back to the pillow, straightening the long white nightgown and pulling the linen sheet right up to her chest. "There are well people here if there's need for us. What's wrong, Israel?"

"Ma's been laborin' a long time, Kitty . . . since yesterday." That wide, friendly face of his was pinched with worry, his chin shadowed with a stubble of light-colored beard. "The girls—neither Lavina nor Becky—don't know what to do."

Lavina, Kitty recalled, couldn't be much more than fourteen or fifteen now. Becky was younger.

"Ma don't look good," Israel said, passing a hand across his scratchy chin. And Jemima pressed her lips together, tears welling in her eyes as she struggled to sit up again.

"Now you lie down there," Kitty scolded her. "I'll go back with Israel."

"I'll go, too."

The voice had come from the doorway, and the three of them within the room looked up, surprised to find Elizabeth Callaway still there, and still yet more astonished that she had offered to go.

Under their combined gaze, she clasped her long-fingered hands across her waist and gave a diffident shake of her shoulders. "I've helped bring my share of little ones into this world, enough to know what I'm about."

"Oh, I'd thankee kindly if you would, Elizabeth!" Jemima's voice broke, and she started to sob.

"Hush now." Elizabeth advanced into the room. "Everything will probably be fine by the time we get there. And your ma setting up in bed with the new babe in her arms. Now don't worry yourself. I'll get my things," she said to Israel, "and be ready in a hurry."

Smiling, Kitty walked outside to find Hester there with Todd. "I've already heard," Hester said. "You get whatever you want to take with you and go. Michael's with Pleas . . . and Todd can help us eat up that mess o' food I've started."

"I'm obliged to you, Hester," Todd said solemnly. "Might be another time. For now, I expect I'll ride along to Boone's Station. 'Twon't hurt to keep the ladies safe company along with Israel."

It was nearly dark when they arrived at the small stockade. Daniel Morgan, fresh from a trek into the woods to bring down some supper meat, held the gate open for them as they rode through, then fastened it carefully behind them. The Boone family had suffered too many losses, and Daniel himself was too great a prize to the Shawnee, for his family to be careless now.

The main cabin lay directly ahead, with a good-size barn and several outbuildings to the right and back. They all climbed down from their horses, Todd helping Elizabeth, who groaned slightly with the unaccustomed strain of riding. Jesse, who was eight now, but as active as ever, bolted up to them in the dusky fading light, half grinning and breathless, a little pale with all the commotion. "Lavina said I was to set out here a while," he said.

"Well, let's go see what we can do," Elizabeth said.

Kitty was the first one into the dimly lit interior of the cabin, and as her eyes adjusted, she saw the two girls, Lavina and Becky, before the fireplace, their young faces pasty with uncertainty as they ladled out some hot water. Rebecca was on a slab bed in the corner, knees drawn up beneath a light linen cover. There were deep, shadowy circles beneath her eyes. She looked exhausted, but as she caught sight of Kitty she smiled weakly.

"Kitty . . . I'm glad you come along with—" She broke off as she saw Elizabeth Callaway in the doorway, struck silent for a moment, and then she held out her hand and Elizabeth came quickly to take it, the two women holding to each other for a long moment.

Rebecca's nose reddened, her eyes blinking, and Elizabeth had to clear her throat twice before she could speak.

"How is it with you, Rebecca?" she got out at last.

"Not well." Rebecca looked from Elizabeth to Kitty. "I think it's turned wrong," she whispered.

"We'll see." Elizabeth gave Rebecca's hand a shake. "If need be, we'll turn it right. I've done it before." She lifted her head and peered about the room. "Let's get some light in here."

As the Boone girls hurried to light the grease lamps, Rebecca was struck by a contraction and drew her legs higher beneath the cover, turning her face toward the rough log wall behind her, holding her breath against the pain until she couldn't stand it and gave way to a hoarse moaning.

Israel had just stepped inside the doorway; he waited until the pain was finished, looking away toward the fire, then dumped five plump squirrels on the hearth and came to take his mother's hand. "Daniel Morgan got our supper for us," he said.

"I declare," she said, pressing her lips into a grin for Israel and squinching her eyes against the sweat that had popped out on her, "he's near as good a shot as you or your pa."

Israel nodded, struggling to keep the smile on his face. "We'll be outside if you want us, Ma."

"I'll remember."

Once he'd gone, Kitty set the girls to cleaning the squirrels. "Fry up all but one of them," she directed. "There are a pair of hungry men and the boys out there. Stew up the other one for your mother. She needs to keep her strength up."

Lavina nodded, the light from the grease lamps limning the wide, strong face and dark eyes that were so reminiscent of Rebecca's. "I'll cook up some turnips and onions with it, too," she said, beginning to look less frightened now that there was someone else to take charge of things.

Elizabeth and Rebecca had been conversing in low tones, but as Kitty neared the bed, Rebecca was struck by another pain. Arching upward, her hands on the distended belly, she clamped her teeth together and pushed, grunting and straining, the guttural sound she made drawing out finally in a long, low wailing.

"Oh, Lord," she gasped as soon as she could speak, "it's not moving a bit. It's been the same since way last night sometime. I've had enough of them to know."

"I'm going to try to see how that baby's layin'," Elizabeth declared. "I'll need some lard or 'possum fat," she told Lavina and Becky. "What do you have over there?"

As Elizabeth prepared, Kitty found a well-worn linen towel in a basket and brought it back to dry the sweat from Rebecca's face.

"I told you I might have forgot how," Rebecca said, still trying to smile as she looked up at Kitty.

"Don't worry now. It'll be all right."

Elizabeth came back to the bed, her fingers and most of her hand well greased with lard, and gestured toward the linen cover. "Hold that up," she said.

Kitty lifted the cover enough for Elizabeth to work. Someone had put a square of dressed buckskin under Rebecca, and the soft leather was stained with blood and water.

Rebecca tensed as Elizabeth probed between her thin, vein-marked legs.

"I'll be easy," Elizabeth assured her. "I'll try not to hurt you."

"Why didn't Jemima come?" Rebecca asked, obviously trying to get her mind off what was happening.

"She's down with a summer flu," Kitty told her. "Nothing to worry about. Elizabeth and I thought it'd be better if we came."

Rebecca's head drew back as another hard pain hit her.

"He's tryin' to come breech," Elizabeth said, sweat popping out on her own long face, her fingers still groping.

Rebecca twisted and cried out, arching and straining.

"Don't—don't push," Elizabeth cautioned. "You can't bring him that way. You're just wearing yourself out."

"I'll . . . try . . . not to," Rebecca gasped out. "It's . . . hard . . ."

As Elizabeth worked to turn the baby, Kitty gave a silent thanks that the older woman was there. While she had heard of babies being turned before, she had never done it herself.

"There," Elizabeth breathed, "he's moving a little. . . . Lord, there's not much room."

"He?" Rebecca looked up at her, a sudden light in the tired eyes.

"He, right enough. I could feel his man parts a minute ago. . . ."

Rebecca gave a glad cry as another pain claimed her, Elizabeth cautioning her not to push again, and working still to inch the baby into a better position. "Almost," she said. "Almost. . . ." She looked toward Kitty, nodding her head. "We just might do this."

The two Boone girls left the cooking supper to see to itself and came to stand close together near the bedside, the younger one, Becky, holding fearfully to Lavina as they watched and waited. Kitty held Rebecca's hands, and the laboring woman twisted and cried out with the pain as Elizabeth still worked, drenched with sweat herself now.

"He's coming . . . coming 'round!" Elizabeth shouted. "I can feel the shoulder . . . Thanks to God, the head!"

Rebecca was laughing and crying, raising herself to a half-sitting position. "I can do it now," she said, and in a moment her eyes flared wide with the pain and she pushed, biting at her lip, her face reddening. She panted when it lessened, catching her breath and beginning again.

"The head's coming!" Elizabeth looked at Kitty and began to laugh, tears mingling with the sweat on her face. And just then Rebecca gave a great, joyful shriek and the baby slithered out into Elizabeth's waiting hands.

* * *

Once Rebecca and the baby were cleaned up, the waiting males trooped in to see the infant, who seemed none the worse for his mother's difficult labor.

Todd stooped to get a good look at the sleeping baby, then raised up and chewed and swallowed and grinned. The younger boys pressed in close.

"He looks like Pa!" Daniel Morgan crowed.

"I think he looks like *me*," Jesse countered.

"*You* look like Pa. . . ." Israel and Daniel Morgan chorused, the two of them pummeling Jesse good-naturedly.

They quieted at once as Lavina scolded them. "Ma needs her rest. Hush up, now!"

Once they had eaten, the men and boys went off to sleep in the barn, and Kitty and Elizabeth bedded down with the girls.

The next day, when they were sure that Rebecca and the baby were doing well, Todd and Israel escorted them back to Boonesborough, where they delivered the good news to Jemima. It was three weeks before Daniel returned from the East to greet his new son.

* 34 *

P REPARATIONS FOR WINTER AT BOONESBOROUGH WERE gone about in high spirits once word arrived from the East of General Washington's victory over the British. The commander in chief of the American army, with the support of Lafayette, had pressed Lord Cornwallis to the sea at Yorktown. At last the war was over.

With corn cribs full, the stalks were cut and stored for fodder. Ricks of wood, standing in wait for the cold weather, were topped off. Tolliver Skaggs had cut most of Kitty's, but Hester had insisted on adding some more to the pile.

The women went about their usual gathering of nuts and persimmons. Kitty and Hester dried beans and onions, stored potatoes and turnips in baskets, and pounded hominy into meal for grits. Though they had both knitted all summer, there were still yet more stockings to be done. Michael never seemed to have enough stockings, Kitty complained.

With the first snow, the people of Boonesborough settled in for the winter with high hopes for the future, a sentiment shared by most other Kentuckians. With the war won, the British would stop stirring the Indians against the frontier towns and settlements, and now, maybe, they could get about the business of tending their land in peace, their towns growing and safe at last.

It was a better time for Kitty. She had begun to lose that bone-thin look, the angular hollows of her face softening now. There was a quiet contentment in teaching the children and having good friends close around her . . . and it was enough, she told herself. In truth, Hester and Pleas had become her "family." The hours that she and Michael spent with them that winter gave her a feeling of regained security. She still missed Cullen, but she had learned to live without him.

Pleas would play his old mouth organ, Michael snugged into the chair beside him, while the women did their mending, or knitted, or roasted chestnuts to be served up dripping in butter. Sometimes, they would be joined by Elizabeth, Jemima and Flanders, Fanny and John.

But spring came quickly that year, bursting upon them to melt the last vestiges of snow. And when the first days of March brought its painful memories, Kitty went to the small cemetery beyond the walls. Though it had been two years, the old rush of grief coursed through her, in that moment as sharp as it had been in those first days.

There were no flowers blooming yet, but she found a few immature clover heads and picked them to put in with a handful of tender green willow-branch ends, placing all of it on the earth beneath which Cullen lay. She could close her eyes and see his face clearly. She'd heard it said that sometimes when people you loved died, you couldn't quite remember their faces after a while. But with Michael before her, there was no danger that she could ever forget Cullen's face. He'd needed no portrait to leave behind.

Kitty folded the last of Michael's clean clothes and put them away in the clothes press, keeping out a pair of his breeches and sighing as she saw that a knee needed patching. She shook her head, smiling in spite of herself as she put them in the mending basket.

The afternoon was warm, and Pleas, who'd been promising Michael he would teach him to fish for days now, had taken him off to the river an hour earlier. They had only gone a little way up from the fort, and Kitty, remembering how Michael's eyes had lit up at sight of the cane pole Pleas had made for him, decided to walk out and see how they were doing.

She passed through the gates and walked down through the cabins. The mother of one of her students waved to her, and she stopped to talk a minute, then walked on to the river, going along the top of the steep bank until she saw Michael and Pleas below.

Michael looked up, chortling as she made her way down to the level strip at the water's edge. "Look, Mama . . . I fishin'!"

"I can see you are." She smiled at the determined way he gripped the pole. "Have you caught anything?"

"Not yet," Pleas spoke up, "but he's learnin' so fast, I expect he'll be catchin' our supper afore we know it."

Michael beamed.

Tolliver and his brother Jeremiah hailed them from above and came sliding down, pebbles and twigs flying, poles in hand. As they began to turn up rocks along the bank, looking for worms to bait their hooks, Kitty settled herself on a smooth flat piece of limestone near Michael, conscious of the beauty of the river. The sun glittered off the blue-green water, and the warm breeze rippled the clear surface from time to time, the slow-moving current flowing gently around the gnarled end of a tree stump. It made her feel lazy, almost sleepy. Fall had always been her favorite time, but it was undeniable that spring was lovely. She thought of the flower beds she'd planted in front of the cabin. The seed should be sprouting before long. Her onions and peas were already up in the vegetable patch.

Michael yanked his pole to find that his bait was gone, and Pleas put another worm on for him. "You'll be ready this time . . . and when you feel 'im give a nibble, all you have to do is give 'er a yank and haul 'er in."

"I will," said Michael, nodding his head vigorously.

Tolliver and Jeremiah, having gotten their worms, came back along the bank, and Jeremiah suddenly lifted his arm to point out toward the middle of the river and slightly upstream. "Lookee there," he said. "Somebody's done lost his raft."

As Kitty's eyes picked up the three logs, lashed crudely together with wild grapevines, she felt a prickly rising along the nape of her neck. The makeshift raft bucked gently with the flow of the water, then caught in an eddy and swirled closer to shore.

Jeremiah began to tear off his heavy shoes, keeping a sharp eye on the raft as it turned slowly, moving ever closer until it snagged on the tree stump not six feet away from them. He let out a triumphant yell, stripping off his stockings, and then waded in, whooping and shivering as he dragged the logs up on the bank. "Lookee, Tolliver . . . look what we done found!"

As Michael put his pole aside, curious, Pleas caught sight of Kitty's face. "What's the matter?" he asked.

"I hope nothing. Tolliver, go see if you can find John Holder and get him down here to see this."

And minutes later John Holder, along with three of the town trustees and a dozen others who'd dropped their work and come along to see what all the commotion was about, stood bunched together on the bank, looking down at the crude raft. Some of the newcomers looked at one another and shrugged, clearly at a loss to see what was so important about three logs tied together with vines. But those who had been there from the beginning knew.

Winfield Burdette spat a great blob of tobacco juice toward the water's edge. "Shit! I thought we was finally quit of the goddamned red-assed heathens!"

And John, his face grave, wiped a hand across his mouth, raising his head instinctively to sweep the far bank with his gaze. "Indians are about, right enough."

There was a sudden hush, and then a young girl who had stood in back of the men suddenly gasped: "Lordy me, I better go tell my ma!"

"Hold up!" John called as some of the men started to bolt up the hill. "Don't be goin' off half-cocked, now. Could be no more'n a stray hunter or two. Just pass word o' this. And take no more risk than you have to. Those that want to can come to the blockhouses to sleep." He turned back to Kitty. "You did right to send for me. Let's hope it don't amount to much."

But the next day their worst fears were confirmed when word came that a war party of Wyandot had killed a young woman just beyond the gates at Estill's Station, and a Negro man working nearby had been carried off. Captain James Estill and his entire garrison of twenty-five men had given chase, but the large band of Wyandot had turned back and fought ferociously. Estill was killed, along with twenty others . . . only five lived to tell of it.

When Kitty heard the news, she thought of Phronie Sweeton Tyler, Todd's wife of half a year now. Poor Phronie had had a father and two brothers at Estill's.

In those next weeks at Boonesborough, every precaution was taken. Powder and shot were checked and more brought in from Harrod's Town. Not everyone could crowd into the fort, but those who continued to live beyond the walls kept a sharp eye toward the river and the woods, ready to run for the fort gates at a moment's notice. Those crops that still needed planting were done in shifts, part of the men working, part standing guard with rifles as they had in the old days. Even the weather seemed to have turned against them; the usual spring rains were nowhere to be seen. June had come, with no rain since back in April, and the men were carting river water to keep the corn alive.

Indian threat or no, Kitty was determined that her vegetable patch was not going to burn up. She made innumerable trips from the spring to the patch, carrying buckets of water to save her beans and turnips and potatoes and the little herb garden she'd put in. Hester's patch was right beside Kitty's, and they carried and worked together . . . sweating and groaning after so many trips. Sometimes Hester would insist that Kitty sit out to rest while she carried an extra load.

July commenced with no relief, and one day, as Kitty and Hester started toward the spring, empty buckets swinging from the ropes of their carry yokes, they saw a lone rider coming fast. Hester squinted, wiping away the sweat that dripped from the end of her nose, her mouth set across in a straight line. "I hope to the good Lord that's not bad news," she said.

With the sun broiling down on them, the two women stopped where they were, looking on as the rider hauled his horse up to talk with the riflemen on guard. After a few words, elbows flying, he slapped his hat down against the animal's flanks and sped on toward the fort. The guards sprinted out toward the cornfields where a dozen men were working, and one lanky rifleman veered wide to meet Kitty and Hester.

"Were I you ladies," he said, "I'd leave off with my waterin' and get on inside the fort. The Indians have kilt Nathanial Hart not a mile from here!"

Kitty straightened from her washpot and looked up at the sky, at the clouds building into a forbidding dark mass, and prayed fervently for rain. The crops were just barely hanging on. The corn would be ruined if it went another week without it. An interrupted washing would be a small price to pay.

She bent over the worn wooden washboard that had once belonged to Amelia Gentry and attacked the grass stains on Michael's shirt, rubbing persistently as she thought of all that had happened in the past two weeks. Nathanial Hart had been a man well known and well respected. That he and his brother had had a share in the old Transylvania Company had never been held against him, in fact was long since forgotten by most. Everyone at Boonesborough and beyond had been horrified by his killing at the hands of the savages . . . and he was hardly in the ground before there were scattered reports of others—a lone settler found fastened to his cabin by a lance, hanging upside down, body mutilated; a woman struck down within sight of her small station.

The fort was crowded now with outlying settlers who had once again come in for safety. The Tyler men had refused to leave their places. "I'll not abandon my crops to the savages' pleasure!" Ben had declared. But Faith had brought in the children. Todd's wife, Phronie, well along with her first pregnancy, had come with her, and until three days ago they had all been crammed into the cabin with Kitty and Michael, the children whining and fighting constantly. A family in the clearing had left for Harrod's Town, where they thought they'd be safer, and the Tyler women had jumped at the chance to take their cabin.

"If there's sight of Indians, we'll hie for the fort," Faith promised. "But meanwhile," she added, grinning, "there'll be a little more room to turn over." The women had shared the bed at Kitty's, every night Faith giggling that with Phronie's big belly it was like four of them instead of three.

It did seem, Kitty thought, that despite all the people who'd poured across the mountains, they were no safer now than that little handful of them had been back in '75. Surely it must end sometime.

A great flat drop of rain hit her nose, and she gave a little cry, peering up at the sky only to have two more splat against her forehead and cheek. "Lordy me!" she shouted, waving joyously to Jemima, who was halfway down the fort yard and had flung aside the piggin she was carrying to dance up and down. Winfield Burdette, working at his forge, let out a roar that could be heard from one end of the stockade to the other.

As the huge drops thickened, Hester came running out of her

cabin, waving her arms and grinning. "Look at it!" She held up her big hands to catch the rain. "Thank heaven for it! We won't have to carry water today!"

The cabins had emptied out, people spilling into the fort yard, heedless of the wetting they were getting, laughing and slapping each other on the back. Kitty could feel the rain trickling down her neck now as she clasped hands with Hester; the fire that she'd built outside to heat her wash water was fast dissolving to a smoking black heap.

"Where's Michael?" Hester asked her.

Kitty gestured toward Bear as he came bounding up, Michael not far behind him.

"It's waining, Mama!" the boy shouted. "Aunt Hester, it's waining!" Kitty nodded and laughed as Bear gave a great shake, then resumed wagging his long sweep of a tail.

Through what was fast becoming a downpour, Kitty's eye was caught by a tall figure, over by the front gates and starting to move down the path. But she shook her head; it couldn't be. . . .

"Can I stay out in it, Mama? Can I get wet? Pweeease . . ."

"Lord, let him," Hester said. "A little water won't hurt the boy none. Won't hurt none of us after how long we've waited for it."

Kitty smiled, but her eye was pulled back to the figure in buckskins, caught by that long-legged stride. . . . Her breath came in a rush. "Roman," she whispered. And then in a great shout: "My God . . . it's Roman!"

She caught up her skirt and ran, drenched now, the rain nearly blinding her, waving aside Winfield and Fanny Holder, running right by Elizabeth Callaway. . . . And then she could see Roman's face, see that crooked smile of his, and with a few more strides she had thrown herself against him so hard it would have knocked over anybody smaller. "Roman!" she cried.

He lifted her right off her feet and swung her around, the rain beating at them, and Kitty wasn't at all sure that some of the moisture running down her face wasn't tears.

"My God, Roman . . ." She tilted her head back to search that achingly familiar hawk face of his, trying to see if he was all right. "I'm so glad you've come back," she said, until that moment not knowing how much she'd missed him.

He set her on her feet, grinning down at her. "So am I."

Michael sprinted up, stopping just short of Roman to peer up at him uncertainly. It had been a long time for a four-year-old to remember.

"Don't tell me this is Michael!" Roman said, and as the boy nodded, he shifted the small pack he carried farther to his back and caught him up. "Why, you're half grown!"

They walked back toward Kitty's cabin together, Roman stopping along the way to greet his old friends despite the drenching rain. Jemima had run to fetch Flanders, who came out of their cabin with his face lathered up to shave.

"My God, Roman, it's about time to see you back again!" he shouted against the downpour. The two men embraced, pounding each other on the back, and then Winfield came roaring up, his huge hand outstretched. Elizabeth ran to hug Roman and warn him that he was not to dare leave before he came to see her. Then she broke for her cabin, sodden skirts slowing her progress.

But finally Kitty and Michael and Roman gained the Claiborne cabin and burst in, dripping and stamping. Bear sneaked through the door behind them and gave a shake that sent water flying everywhere.

"*Bear!*" Kitty wailed.

"He didn't mean to, Mama," Michael defended the beast, who settled immediately close to the fireplace and put his big head down between his front paws to look suitably chastised.

"Lord help us, we'd better get out of these wet things." Kitty laughed, still hard put to believe that Roman was really standing there dripping onto her scrubbed floor. "Let me just see if I can't rig us up a little privacy. Michael," she directed, "you know where your things are."

"Yes'm," Michael said, starting to peel out of the sopping shirt and breeches. He was not yet self-conscious about that sturdy little body, and bared himself with an unconcerned grin that made Roman smile.

"Michael," he said, slipping out of the elkskin-wrapped pack and lowering it to the floor, "you have grown considerably in the time I've been away."

The boy nodded proudly, then bounded across the cabin to the basket where his clothes were kept, his small penis bobbing as he went. Kitty paused in her efforts to hang a quilt across one corner, casting a look toward her son and holding back a grin.

"And since you *are* such a big boy now, you could take your clothes behind the quilt here and dress," she said.

"Are you going to?" he asked Roman solemnly.

"I expect I will." Roman's answer was equally sober. "And

once I unroll this pack to search out some dry clothes, I just might find something in there for you."

They took turns, Michael going first, clearly intrigued with the idea since he'd never gone off to put on his clothes out of sight before. He giggled the whole time he was there.

After a while, once they were all changed and his mother was about cooking a meal, he clutched the dried rabbit's foot that Roman had given him in his fist and curled up contentedly with Bear in a corner.

"I heard it hasn't been so good here," Roman said to Kitty at last. He had sat silent for a time, the way he always did, long legs stretched out from the chair. Kitty, nearby at the table, cut up potatoes to fry as the rain settled into a steady, life-giving watering and pelted softly against the roof.

"No." Kitty had propped the window partly open for air, and the damp breeze cooled her face from time to time. "Last fall," she said, "when word came that the war was ended, we were sure that the Indians would be little threat to us without the British to spur them. It hasn't turned out that way."

Roman sipped thoughtfully at the wine Kitty had poured for him. "No. The fact is, the British have redoubled their efforts. They've poured in guns and powder . . . new knives."

Kitty put down the potato she was holding. "But why . . . with the war lost to them?"

"Because if they could go to the treaty table in Paris having control of the West, they'd have a good chance to retain claim to it . . . all or part."

"My God, I never thought of that."

"They'll do their damnedest."

"Is that why we've had trouble with the Delaware and Wyandot, then, as well as the Shawnee?" Kitty jabbed at a potato with the point of her knife.

Roman grunted. "They'll use whatever tribes they can stir against us."

Kitty noted the *us*. Rebecca had been right. Roman had not been able to stay away from Kentucky. "Will you be going back to Harrod's Town?" she asked.

He cocked his head to one side, the light falling across the hills and hollows of his face, catching the fiery red of his hair. "I thought," he said slowly, "that with the Indians about again, Boonesborough could maybe use a good scout."

She had resumed her peeling and stayed her knife now, surprised and pleased. "You're going to stay here at the fort?"

"For a while," he said.

It was not until after they'd eaten, and Kitty had cleared up and put the dishes away, that she asked him about the baby.

He looked into the fireplace, the cookfire settled to glowing coals. "She's a beauty," he said, the deep-set eyes proud and sad at once. "Looks like her mother."

"What did you name her?"

He was silent for a moment. "I let Marietta do it. She liked the sound of Hallie."

His face didn't change, but Kitty could feel the pain in him still, and she understood that coming back must have set it loose again. Just the way it had been with her when she'd gone to stand at Cullen's grave to mark the second anniversary of his death.

"What about you?" he asked suddenly, as if he'd known what she was thinking. "It is better than it was, isn't it?"

She smiled at him and nodded. "Yes, it's better. It gets better."

Roman walked down the darkened fort yard, the fresh dampness of the breeze welcome, most of the cabins dark and quiet now. He had stayed later than he'd intended. But he had felt a welcome ease there with Kitty. He'd never had to pretend anything that he didn't feel with her, or hide anything. Kitty had always understood.

It had occurred to him as they'd talked that her loss had been as great as his own. And yet that stubborn little mite of a Gentry had stood her ground and faced it head on. He had turned his back and run.

When he'd first gone east, he had thought there would never be a coming back. But then, when news of what was happening in the settlements began to filter through to Virginia, there had been no doubt in his mind about what he must do. At least, he thought, he could be of some use out here again. . . . There was some stirring in him of the old dreams he had always had for this country beyond the mountains. Goddamn the British! They must not end up with Kentucky.

A hound came trotting up to him and gave his hand a lick, and as he walked on, there was a kind of swelling inside him, an awareness that he was really back. He sucked in the smell and feel of it, looking up now at the endless blackness of the sky and knowing that it would rain again soon. He was conscious of the resonance of that rich land, in the same way that he could close his eyes and feel the current of the river just beyond the bank.

He would check on his horses—he had brought several in with him—then climb up into one of the blockhouse lofts and spread his blanket down. In the morning he would talk to John Holder and see if he couldn't use another scout.

❈ 35 ❈

ROMAN COMMENCED SCOUTING FOR THE FORT IMMEDI-ately. John Holder was overjoyed at having his services, and it was soon as if he'd never been away. He would go out for several days at a time and then report back to John, as he once had reported to Daniel—he had gone to Boone's Station at the first opportunity and found the family in good health, the newest member, young Nathan, fat as a bear cub, and his father proud enough to have another son at the age of forty-seven.

"I'd not be surprised to have half a dozen more," Daniel teased Rebecca, who simply smiled.

Whenever Roman came back in to Boonesborough, he brought fresh meat with him—a turkey or 'possum, two or three squirrels, or a brace of rabbits to give to Kitty, who always insisted that he stay to eat with her and Michael.

"I'd not intrude upon you," he'd said once, and she had scolded him roundly.

"Roman Gentry, how in the world could you intrude? Sit down at once and let me feed you before you grow any leaner."

This time he rode in with a young buck deer slung back of his saddle. Kitty ran to fetch Hester and Pleas, and the men skinned and gutted the animal, Hester and Kitty standing by to help with the butchering.

"You must take half of it," Kitty insisted to Hester. "We'll salt down what we don't eat tonight."

And that evening the four of them, along with Michael, gathered at Kitty's table and ate prime venison and summer squash and fresh greens until Kitty was certain that she would pop. She even passed up Hester's egg custard—those few scraggly chickens that Hester had kept alive during the "hard winter," as everyone called it now, had reproduced at a rate that had her giving chicks to any and all who wanted them. The custard was Michael's special favorite, and the boy ate his fill, with Roman and Pleas not far behind. Bear feasted on the scraps once everyone was finished.

As the women cleared up, Pleas got out his mouth organ and blew and sucked away at it, stamping his foot as he played, Roman smiling and Michael clapping his hands.

The grease lamps flickered with the breeze from the window and the open door, and in a moment Tolliver Skaggs appeared in the doorway, framed against the darkness.

" 'Twould seem a fair revelry's afoot in here," he called.

"Tolliver . . . come in," Kitty insisted, wiping her hands on her apron as she finished up. "Come join us. Look, there is some of Hester's egg custard left." And he came, happily devouring the rest of the custard. And when Pleas commenced to play again, he clapped his hands and sang with the rest.

After a particularly fast piece, Pleas paused to regain his wind, declaring that he must have a drink of something before he could continue. Kitty brought out some blackberry wine and passed it around. Even Michael had a sip.

They had all grown used to Roman's taciturnity, and it was almost a surprise when he spoke up. "Why don't you play the dulcimore for us, Kitty?"

"Dulcimore? So you *can* play it," Hester said. "I've seen that thing hanging back in the corner there. Why have you never got it down?"

"Oh, it's been years. I've forgotten most I ever knew . . ." Kitty protested.

"We'll entertain no excuses," Pleas said. "Fetch it for her, Tolliver."

"You must, Mistress Kitty," Tolliver joined in, jumping up from his place on the floor to get it.

"Pleeease, Mama," Michael piped.

She agreed at last, tuning up the strings and then strumming hesitantly for the first few chords, her voice lifting finally, echoing clear and sweet in the small cabin. She could feel the rush of blood to her cheeks.

She sang "Frog Went a-Courtin' " and Michael looked on in wide-eyed amazement that his mother could do anything so wondrous. He soon caught on to the um-humms, and joined in at the right places, nodding his head, his baby falsetto ringing.

"Another . . ." Pleas leaned forward in his chair once she'd finished, his squinty eyes nearly closed in delight. "You must give us another."

Kitty protested, but they all insisted, and she sang a plaintive, old country ballad about being far from home. But that finished, she put the instrument firmly aside.

" 'Tis quite enough. I've grown too old for such. Best leave it to the young girls."

"Pshaw . . . I don't know when I've heard such foolishness!" Hester laughed at the notion. But Kitty didn't answer. Her eyes had met Roman's and been caught by a strange look there, as if he'd just come upon something that he hadn't seen before.

"Young man"—she turned to Michael, somehow unsettled by the playing, resting her hand gently upon the tousle of black hair—"I expect you and Bear had best go curl up now."

"Sing again, Mama . . ." Michael pleaded. "Once more . . ."

Kitty smiled, but shook her head firmly.

"Go along with ye," Pleas said. "I'll play one to lull you to sleep, then we'll be off ourselves. The sun comes early." He winked at Michael, who nodded solemnly.

The boy went off to pull his trundle bed out from under the big one, and Kitty and Hester both kissed him good night. Bear settled down beside him, and before long, he'd drifted off, listening to the soft strains of Pleas's mouth organ, his cheeks still pink with excitement.

"God love him," said Hester.

Tolliver made his good-byes and left, and Hester and Pleas rose to go as well.

"That was a prime buckskin on that animal you brung in," Pleas said to Roman.

"Take it," Roman said at once. "You'll get more use of it than I would."

The little man, bandy legs set, nodded. "Thankee kindly. I'll make ye a good hat fer it."

"Good enough," Roman said.

Once they were gone, Roman lingered as Kitty gathered up the cups from which they'd had their wine. "Would you like some more?" she asked.

He shook his head.

She began to wash and wipe them. "I'm glad Tolliver came by tonight," she said. "He's a nice boy."

"He seems so," Roman said, his voice absent, as if he were absorbed in something else.

"I'd love it if you'd talk to him sometime, Roman. He's very bright. It's a shame that he can't go off to school. The plain truth is, I've taught him all I can . . ."

Her back was to him as she stretched up to the highest shelf, and she stilled suddenly as she heard the soft fall of his moccasins and an instant later felt his hand on her arm, turning her gently toward him. And it was as if she'd known that he would do it . . . or in some strange way had a sense that it had happened before, long ago . . . yet she knew that it hadn't.

She stared up into his eyes, seeing the wonder there, standing perfectly still as he pulled the pins from her hair and let the wealth of it free about her face.

"You're too . . . beautiful"—the word did not come easily to him—"to pull it back so."

His face was dark as an Indian's from the sun and the wind, the eyes fiercely blue, and for a long moment his gaze held hers as if she were bound by it. And then he turned quickly and walked out of the cabin, leaving her to stand there, trembling suddenly, as if she'd had a terrible fright.

In a minute she went to bolt the door, then took care of the last-minute chores as if nothing had happened, banking the fire with ashes so it would not be burned out when time for cooking breakfast came, checking on Michael to see him slumbering peacefully, readying herself finally for bed . . . though once there, it took her a very long time to get to sleep.

In the morning she was up early, rising with the first pink streaks of dawn. Lord knows, she thought determinedly, there's plenty to be done before class.

She ran the tortoiseshell comb through her hair, starting to twist the black length of it back as she had every morning for over two years, but her fingers tangled in it and she went to stand in front of Amelia's old looking glass and peer at herself.

She drew the hair into a loose coil and pinned it, her cheeks suddenly coloring as she saw the natural curl of it spring out around her face. It might not hurt, she told herself, to let it be a little looser. Some even said that to pull the hair too tight could make a person bald. And while she had never thought of herself as vain, she surely didn't want to wake up one day and find herself bald.

* * *

It did not take long for word to spread after a courier came riding hell-for-leather toward Boonesborough from the south, waving a tattered hat and yelling hoarsely the moment he was in sight. He had come from Hoy's Station to warn that Indians had struck at the small settlement. They'd carried off two prisoners, boys who'd not been quick enough in getting within the stockade.

"They circled fer a while, the bloody heathens . . . just out o' reach of our rifles, haulin' poor Lem and Squire Loftus . . ." He paused to gulp in a breath, his lean chest pumping as he told his story to John Holder and the men gathered around him. "Had 'em trussed up at the end o' rawhide tethers. Lem fell oncet . . . but he got up agin . . ."

"Where are they now?" John asked him.

"They had started off northerly, last I seed 'em. I stayed to the canebrakes and whatever cover could be found. Come roundabout to git here, but that's a damn sight better 'n goin' home to my young'uns without m' hair."

"How many?" John pressed.

"A devil's plenty . . . upwards o' sixty, maybe seventy, I'd reckon."

The Boonesborough men conferred gravely. John Holder said he would not take too many rifles away from the fort and leave it unprotected. Roman had been out now for five days and no word from him. "I wish to heaven that I could talk to him," John swore, and looked off toward Hackberry Ridge, the sun turning it to a fine shimmering green. "It could be the savages will double back and hit right here. Still . . ." He struggled with the decision. "I could take a small party and pick up others at McGee's Station . . . and Strode's. That would appear to be best. Should we get lucky, we might recover the two boys. Sixty . . . seventy! God Almighty!" He shook his head. "We'll do what we can."

"I'll go," Flanders said.

And while other volunteers were chosen and readied themselves to ride, the people who lived outside the stockade were snatching up their guns and what few things they felt they had to have and now came streaming through the gates to the safety of the fort. Hoy's Station was too close for comfort.

Hearing what had happened, Kitty ran to look for Faith and Phronie and came upon them just inside the gates. Todd's wife had given birth to a baby girl ten days before and had the infant clutched to her now, the pale little thing mewing like a kitten, its small face screwed into a tight knot of features. Faith had little Latham in her arms, the two girls hanging to her skirts.

"Dear God, I am fearful for Ben," she said, her voice barely more than a whisper. The oldest, Martha, set her thin little lips, but the younger girl began to whine softly.

"I know," Kitty said, refusing to put a reason to the nagging fear that plagued her. The fort was strong enough to withstand an assault, she told herself, as long as the Indians didn't have artillery, and there had been no mention of that.

She leaned down and picked up Charity, who was still whining and rubbing at her rabbity little eyes. "Come on back to the cabin with me," she told Faith and Phronie.

"Should we not get into the blockhouse?" Phronie looked from one to the other of them, the skin across her nose and cheekbones discolored still from her pregnancy, puffy circles beneath her eyes. She had had a hard time with her labor, and the poor girl was not yet over the deaths of her father and brother, who'd been killed in the Estill massacre.

"We'll come if there's a need," said Kitty. "But meanwhile the children will be better off at the cabin . . . and you, as well, Phronie. At least you can rest. Hester is there with Michael now."

Preparations were made in case of an attack. Powder was brought out, patch bags filled, flints picked so there'd be no chance of a misfire. The women poured molten lead to make bullets. Phronie stayed at the cabin with the children, but Faith went to help Kitty and Hester and the others.

Cooped up in the fort, they waited the rest of that day and the next, sleeping little through the night. The men took turns at watch, everyone ready at the slightest warning to take up their places. But the following morning, just after dawn, the entire place was turned out when the fort was helloed and the shout went up that Colonel Boone was riding in, a small party of men behind him.

"Dan'l!" was the cry from many a throat as the veteran woodsman led his horse through the gate, Israel following close behind him. Several there pressed in to shake Boone's hand, and Israel, always a favorite at the fort, returned their greetings with his ready smile.

Kitty, who'd just finished with her milking, came with some of the other women, edging around until she could see between the broad backs and elbows and rifles.

"By God," Winfield Burdette said, "it's good to see you, Daniel."

"And you as well. How's your boy?" Daniel asked quietly.

"Tolerable well, as you can see." Winfield pointed out Oliver, who was grinning broadly.

The cows just beyond the gates milled about and rolled their eyes at the horses, shying away to lumber awkwardly toward the river, where the mists still hung heavy and cool, the grass beaded with moisture.

"We got word that Hoy's is under siege," Daniel said. "We'd be obliged for whatever men can be spared. There are others riding from Lexington and Bryan's Station and Harrod's. Ben Logan has been sent word."

Winfield told him what had taken place, and Daniel listened attentively, tugging at his earlobe. "Then you don't know where John Holder might be right now?" he asked when the blacksmith had finished.

"No." Winfield spat to one side and swiped at his mouth with the back of his hand. "We just know that the fellow from Hoy's thought the savages had left and started north."

"Well then," Daniel pondered aloud, "we are left with this, aren't we. The Indians may have played one of their tricks, falling back as if to leave, and then waiting until all at Hoy's thought it safe to come out, only to find themselves at risk. Or if they did head north, with John behind them, he could find himself greatly outnumbered should he attempt to recover the stolen boys."

"What'll we do, Dan'l?" someone shouted. But before Daniel could answer, a cry went up from the lookout that another rider was coming in fast.

Kitty shifted slightly, stretching so that she could see through the open gates. She caught a glimpse of a long, lean frame stretched down tight over a chestnut horse, and her breath caught in her throat, a sudden relief flooding her. "Roman," she whispered, realizing how worried she had been for him.

"It's Roman!" The cry went up. "By God, it's Roman!"

Kitty took an eager step forward as Roman gained the fort and came down from the saddle of the sweating animal in one fluid motion. The men surged around him, as they had about Daniel, and she found herself jostled back against the rough surface of the stockade wall. She set the milk pail down, steadying herself, her eyes still fastened on him.

She felt a hand on hers and looked up, startled, full into Hester's face, who turned her gaze to Roman and then back again to Kitty.

"I've been wonderin' just how long it would take. . . ." She left the rest unsaid, but Kitty stared at her a long moment and then gave her head a toss.

"Fiddlesticks, Hester Worthington! Don't be silly!"

But even as she said it, she was aware that Roman had seen her there . . . saw him lift his head, eyes glittering in the morning sun as they met hers, and something that she'd thought long dead, turned to ashes, flared so hot and bright within her that she must deny it to herself—or admit that Hester was right. And that was impossible. She was not some foolish girl who had such feelings anymore.

"Cullen is dead," Hester said softly. "And Sara . . . God rest them both."

Vexed, Kitty pressed her lips together and hugged her arms to her sides. Of course she loved Roman, had always loved him . . . but it wasn't *that* way. Hester simply didn't understand how close they had always been.

Roman had passed through to Daniel, only a few paces away from her now, but he didn't look her way again. He nodded soberly to Boone, and the crowd hushed, pressing in from the fringes to gain a better ear.

"We've come close to being bamboozled by them, Daniel," he said at once. "The raid at Hoy's was only a feint, meant to lead us away from where the real force is . . . gathered about Bryan's Station right now."

One of Daniel's sandy eyebrows cocked upward. "The men from Bryan's are supposed to be on the march to Hoy's already," he said.

"I couldn't get close enough to tell. If they are, then Bryan's has fallen by now."

There were mutterings in the crowd, and Daniel shook his head, his wide mouth drawing down. "How many would you reckon?"

"Hard to guess," Roman said. "You know the acreage of corn close on the fort . . . and the trees there by the trace. The brush is high. Too much cover. But I think there were a goodly number hiding out. I pressed on to Lexington, but found Levi Todd and his men already on the way to Hoy's. They've sent a rider to try to overtake him . . . and word to head off those from Harrod's Town, as well."

"Well . . ." Daniel shifted the rifle that rested in the crook of his arm, pondering their next move. "I would guess our support to be sorely needed by now. Let's send word to warn Ben

Logan. And as he should be passing here as he comes"—Daniel lifted his head and looked about him at the men gathered—"I'll ask all those that are able-bodied to ready yourselves to ride without delay."

There was a great stirring and jostling as men set their shoulders and declared themselves.

"Give me a few minutes and I'll be ready enough, Daniel!" Winfield called out.

"And me as well!" Oliver joined his father.

There was a great guffawing as Winfield caught his son in an affectionate armhold. "You think y'r man enough, do you?"

"Aye!" Oliver shouted, a half-scared grin on his face.

Winfield sobered. "Well, maybe y'are, son . . . just maybe y'are."

The men began to shift away to prepare for the foray to the besieged station. Daniel and Roman conversed quietly, and Kitty took up her pail and hurried back to the cabin.

Faith had already heard the news and carried it back to Phronie, who, baby at her breast, looked anxiously toward the door as Kitty came in. "Has there been any further word?" she asked, her face pale and pinched with worry over Todd.

"No," Kitty said, mindful of Michael and the two girls, who played quietly at the moment in the far corner. "The men are getting what they need to take along."

Phronie looked down at the baby, who sucked contentedly at the blue-veined breast. "I do pray for the safe deliverance of those poor people who are threatened at this moment," she said.

"Amen," Faith and Kitty joined together.

They knew as well as any that taking so many men away from the fort would leave them in some jeopardy themselves, but no mention was made of it. As Faith started to strain up the milk, Kitty heard Hester haranguing loudly and hurried to see what had happened. She found her, hands on hips, confronting her husband just beyond their cabin steps. Pleas, looking entirely pleased with himself, had his rifle in hand, a shot bag and sheathed knife at his belt, and a powder horn slung over his shoulder. He wore his old leather hat pulled firmly down on his head and carried a small hemp sack, which appeared to be filled with provisions.

"He's set on goin'," Hester appealed to Kitty, "and will no doubt come home minus a foot instead of just a toe. Shoot it off himself like as not," she continued to scold, casting an irate look toward him that Kitty realized was a mask for her concern.

"They said all able-bodied men, Hester," he retorted patiently. "Were I to stay behind, I should have to go about in one of your skirts henceforth."

Hester threw up her hands. "You're bound and determined, then?"

"I am."

"Well . . ." She looked down at the ground, her nose reddening suddenly, then at last back at him, "you just mind you be careful, then!"

Pleas grinned. "I'll be careful, Hester." His eyes were squinched, and he reached suddenly to pat her arm awkwardly. "You be careful yourself, woman." With a cocky set to his hat, he winked at Kitty and turned away down the dusty path.

"Wait up, Pleas Worthington," Hester called after him. "There's some johnnycake still warm on the hearth that you can put in your bag." But he stumped ahead with that bandy-legged gait of his, tossing her a look over his shoulder and grinning still.

" 'Tis in here already," he called back.

Roman, coming the other way, clapped a hand to Pleas's shoulder as they passed. Catching sight of him, Kitty felt a quickening of her heartbeat and a rush of blood to warm her cheeks. All due, she thought, to Hester's silly tongue. After all, she had never been more at ease with anyone than with Roman. He knew her as well as any in the world. . . .

She turned an accusing eye toward the big woman, who at once looked away innocently. And then Roman drew even with her, standing tall, his face sober. "I'd have a word with you before we leave," he said.

A glance back through the cabin door revealed Phronie still nursing the baby and Faith busy scolding Martha and Michael, who between them had just turned over a cup of buttermilk and now disputed loudly over which one was at fault.

Hester, still standing there, looked at Roman and then back to Kitty. "You could step in our place," she said. "I was just this minute headed down to see that Pleas don't forget to take a skin o' water with him." Then she flew off, stealing looks over her shoulder as she went.

"I'd think we could talk right here as well as not." Kitty attempted a small smile, determined to set Hester's foolish notions to rest in herself. "Do you think there is much danger for us here within the fort?"

Roman didn't answer but reached out to take her hand and lead her toward Pleas and Hester's cabin. The quickened heartbeat turned to a slow hammering, to make her sure that she had taken leave of her senses.

The light slanted in, dust motes shimmering. Everything was neat, pewter plates in a row on the shelf, cockscomb in a bowl on the table. The place was redolent of honey and sugar from the maple trees, of rich eggs and cream . . . Hester was forever cooking up something sweet.

Kitty looked up at Roman but found the intensity of those blue eyes, which all of a sudden seemed to burn hers, too much to bear. She looked away, but he wouldn't let her. He caught her face in his two hands and tilted it up toward his.

"There is something that needs saying. . . ."

"And is it so important that we must say it now?" She heard the words, and it was almost as if someone else were speaking them.

"Aye," he said.

She stared up at him, thinking suddenly of Cullen and the days and weeks after his death when she had shut away that deepest part of her, building up the layers of her own grief to protect her from ever feeling so much again. She did not want to risk it. But the barriers were crumbling in spite of her, and it terrified her.

"Please," she said, not knowing herself whether it was a cry for him to stay or go. But he stood his ground and made her look into the blue fire of his eyes.

"I love you, Kitty Gentry," he said. "Love you to the bone of me, and I could not leave without saying it." He looked at her a long moment and then, nodding as if he'd done what he must do, let her go and turned away toward the door . . . was almost there, when:

"Roman!" she cried, and it was as if a river, long dammed, had been loosed within her . . . and part of it was squeezing from her eyes. "Roman, wait!"

He turned.

They stood there looking at each other, each of them knowing in that uncanny way they sometimes did what the other one was feeling in that moment. He came back slowly, reaching out to touch her hair.

"You changed it," he said.

She nodded, wanting to put her hand on his but shy suddenly at touching him. She shivered as he trailed his fingers gently down her cheek, bringing them finally to rest against her mouth, holding them there . . . still . . . still . . . that look of wonder in his eyes again.

And then, the last barrier gone between them, he pulled her into his arms, sure and strong, lifting her against the hard-muscled length of him to make her gasp, that deepest woman part of her, denied so long, leaping with new life. He kissed her, his mouth laying claim to hers, hot and tender, rough and sweet at once. And she was filled with the taste and smell of him, musky and wild as the land. . . .

When they had parted their lips at last, catching in their breath, he swung her up and hugged her again, throwing his head back to laugh a great resounding laugh.

"I don't know how this has happened," she gasped, laughing, too, but crying as well.

"Nor do I," he said. "I've been such a fool as to be blind to it until that night when you sang." He wiped her tears away and kissed her again, his tongue recklessly demanding the taste of her once more, which further fueled the fire that both knew could not be quenched in what little time was left to them.

"Roman Gentry . . ."

Winfield Burdette's deep bellow startled them as it echoed from the fort yard, and Roman let her go reluctantly, going to the door to open it and answer. "Here," he said.

"Daniel says to tell you it's time."

"I'll be there."

He turned back to her for a moment. "I have to saddle up the sorrel. I trust him most on such a ride."

"Oh, God, Roman . . ." She started to say, Be careful, but she knew he would do what he thought he should . . . and do it well.

He came back to hold her again for a moment, gently, her head against his chest so that she could feel his heart beat. "I'll be back in a few days," he said, letting her go finally.

She nodded, holding back that rush of sweet words she longed to say to him before he left. There would be time enough later. He took her hand and they walked out together.

Michael, who had come to sit on the cabin steps, saw them and, as Roman beckoned, came running to squeeze himself between, the three of them walking down toward the gates.

Roman went to saddle up the sorrel, while Kitty and Michael waited with Hester and Elizabeth. Mrs. Skaggs was there to see Tolliver off, and he came to speak to Kitty, eager to go, his face flushed with excitement. It was the first time he'd been considered old enough to go out with the men.

"I would not think we'd be too long, Mistress Kitty," he said.

"You look out for yourself," Kitty told him, hugging him soundly.

"I will," he said, blushing red as a rooster's comb.

Pleas mounted his old black horse and waved a hand at Hester. And in a moment Roman was back, leading the sorrel gelding. He dropped the reins to hunker down in front of Michael.

"You mind you take care of your mother, now," he said. And Michael nodded, caught up in the air of excitement, his eyes wide and solemn.

The men were mostly mounted now, and Roman raised full up and smiled at Kitty, neither of them touching, just that look into one another's eyes to pledge their wondrous discovery.

"I'll be back," he said, and then swung up into his saddle and rode through the gates to take his place with Daniel.

Those that were left behind, the women and those males too old or too young to go, stood to watch until the riders were out of sight. But in a moment Elizabeth Callaway's strong voice rang out. "Let's get this gate closed and barred . . . and set about posting lookouts night and day."

"Aye," Hester joined her. "If the red heathens should dare this way, we'll show them there are women here can shoot as well as any man."

❊ 36 ❊

"GOD BLAST THEM INTO HELL!" ONE OF THE BOONESborough men breathed, staring at what lay around him.

They had all hauled their horses to a halt, faces grave, at the destruction that the savages had wrought. The cornfields of Bryan's Station had been trampled, the vegetables pulled out of the ground. What had been a healthy stand of hemp was now nothing more than burned and blackened stubs. Cows and hogs and sheep lay here and there, legs jutting oddly as their bellies swelled and flies buzzed at their gaping throats. Some had had haunches cut away for meat, but most lay untouched except for the killing.

Daniel cast a sober look at Roman. "Let's hope we don't find worse within the fort," he said.

"I'll have a look," Roman told him, and Daniel nodded. Both men knew that the silent and peaceful-looking stockade ahead could be filled with Indians, waiting to open fire when they drew close enough.

With only slight movements of the reins, Roman guided the well-trained sorrel through the tangle of uprooted potato vines, skirting the dead and bloating carcass of a brindle cow to gain the open ground. Pausing, he leaned to rub the warm rich neck, whispering the horse's name, the animal's ears flickering at his touch. Then he flexed his knees and put the gelding to a gallop, the splendid animal reaching its full stride quickly.

He flattened down in the saddle, tucking his head low, cheek resting close to where his hand had touched only a moment before. If there were Indians at the loopholes, he reasoned grimly, they'd surely not be able to resist such a tempting target for long. Still, there was a certain comfort in the knowledge that few of them were good enough shots to hit him at the speed he rode. He'd simply veer away and head for the woods to circle back to Daniel and the others.

He had cleared nearly half the open ground, the morning sun catching him in its full light, when a shout went up from the palisades ahead. Roman broke into a grin. He'd recognized the voice of Aaron Reynolds, celebrated far and wide for his ability to outinsult, outcuss any man on the frontier.

"It's Roman Gentry, or I'm much mistaken!" Aaron whooped. "Were I a dog-eatin' fartbag of a yellow-hided Shawnee lookin' down the barrel of this rifle, I could this minute put a ball clean through your gizzard and out your pizzle in a wink!"

Roman laughed, hauling the horse back to an easy trot, then snatching off his hat to wave it back and forth above his head. Aaron, he decided, must be toning down his language for the benefit of ladies present.

A lusty cheer rose from the battlements. "Come on in, Roman," Captain John Craig called out. "I hope my eyes don't deceive me, and I do indeed see Daniel Boone out there a ways!"

The gates swung open, and Daniel and the others trotted in close after Roman, to be greeted by Craig, the fort commander.

They were pressed upon from all sides, dogs barking raucously, men of both sides hailing friends.

Levi Todd and men from Lexington were there. "Word of the savages' treachery was got to us in time," he told Roman. "Thanks to you and the two brave lads that managed to slip from here and come for help. Will Ellis and his boys got here first, with us not far behind."

It was still early, and the women laid out food while the men gathered to eat and tell the tale or hear it. They had been geared and ready to ride to the relief of Hoy's Station, Captain Craig related, when a nine-year-old boy reported that he'd seen "four heathen Injun's a-comin' " and had hid himself forthwith in the tall cane till they passed.

Quietly, the men of Bryan's Station had taken up their posts and watched, seeing faint signs that suggested there were many more than four of the savages out there. They pretended not to know and commenced their game of waiting.

"Our women, bless 'em"—Craig's voice rang with pride—"were the bravest of us all. With no more water in the fort, and us sure to give our knowledge away should we men attempt to gain some, our ladies walked out to the spring, cool as you please . . . like it was any other day."

The game had continued until Captain William Ellis and seventeen mounted men had come to the relief of the besieged station thirty-six hours before, dashing their horses through the hail of Indian fire to gain the gates without a single loss.

"With their presence exposed," Craig continued, "Simon Girty—curse his white renegade hide!—took cover behind a stump not five yards out and demanded we surrender. Said artillery was on the way and should arrive by nightfall, and he could not be responsible for our lives should we elect to hold out still."

There was a sudden quiet . . . not a man present who didn't remember Ruddle's and Martin's and the bloody horrors there. But after a moment the irrepressible Aaron Reynolds had them whooping with laughter as he related how he'd stacked two whiskey barrels within the wide stone hearth and climbed atop them to stick his head out the chimney and hurl invective at Girty and his band.

"My woman, used as she is to my rough talk," one laughing stalwart joined in, "clapped hands over ears and run for cover!"

Aaron grinned. "Oncet I was finished explainin' his pedigree to 'im, I set my dog to send him scramblin' back to his whoreson of a brother.''

"I barely got the chance to officially refuse surrender," John Craig put in, and those crowded into the blockhouse set up a renewed chorus of loud guffaws.

The fort was hailed and more help arrived before the men had finished eating the buttery hoecakes and ham served up by the women. The commanders greeted one another gravely, since they knew they must now decide what to do. John Todd—Levi's brother—and Stephen Trigg were lieutenant colonels, as was Daniel, and the three of them conferred, though there was no one there who did not feel free to offer his advice. Colonel and militiaman were more often than not friends and neighbors, working side by side, a fact that tended to blur the distinction of command.

"They appear to have headed along the trace toward the Blue Licks," Daniel said.

John Todd nodded. "I'd say we must press after and hit them hard."

A Major Hugh McGary of the Lincoln County militia spoke up with the word that Ben Logan was confident of rounding up four hundred men or more from the southern settlements and would be coming soon. " 'Twould seem best to wait till they arrive," he said.

John Todd cocked an eye at McGary. "Why wait?" he countered. "One day lost could enable them to cross the Ohio and gain the safety of their villages."

"Aye!" came the uproar from the men gathered close about.

"We've enough brave men to whip them soundly!" Captain Craig insisted. "I say let's proceed at once!"

Craig had put no particular emphasis on the word *brave*, but Roman saw McGary's face darken instantly and realized the man had taken insult.

"Do you mean to call me *coward*, sir?" McGary demanded, his hand straying toward the pistol at his belt.

Some of McGary's friends moved to calm him as Craig's bushy eyebrows rose in some surprise. "Upon my honor, no!" he burst out. "We are all free to state our opinions here, Major."

Daniel stepped between them. "To argue amongst ourselves would seem naught but a waste of precious time, boys."

There were nods of agreement around and calls of "Dan'l's right."

A count was made. One hundred-eighty-two men were ready

and eager to ride, and the decision was made that there were enough of them to set out after the savages. Logan and his men could be sent ahead at once when they arrived.

The troop rode off grimly determined, and confident as well, moving at a steady speed that was meant to guard the stamina of horse and man over the miles ahead of them. The sun was straight up overhead, beating down to cause the sweat to gather under hatbands and trickle into eyes and ears. But the leathery frontiersmen paid little heed to sweat or heat. Once in a while one of them would swear mildly as he slapped at a particularly voracious blackfly or mosquito. Sometimes one would swing down from his mount to relieve himself quickly at the side of the trail and then haul himself atop his animal and fall in beside the nearest rider.

The trace they followed clearly bore the marks of the retreating Indians. Roman and Talliaferro, one of three fort scouts with the troop, split up to ride ahead, as protection against the main body of militiamen riding unawares into an ambush. Several hours passed before Roman circled back and found the group stopped to water their horses from a shallow creek that ran along a rocky bed. He swung down from his saddle to let his own animal drink. Daniel and his gray were nearby.

"I'm thinking they want us to follow," Roman said, and wasn't surprised when Daniel narrowed his eyes and nodded.

"I've been feeling some disquiet myself. Most times when you can see too easy where an Indian's been, it's because he aims for you to."

Oliver Burdette whooped as he sat right down in the middle of the creek bed, letting the cool water sluice around him. And Israel, not far away, swiped his dripping neckerchief over his sweaty face and head, then came to stand beside Daniel and Roman, his light hair slicked back and wet. His father laid a hand on his shoulder.

"Are you feeling well enough, son?" he asked. Israel, who had just recovered from a summer fever, grinned and said he was.

Daniel and Roman spoke of their misgivings to some of the other officers.

"We must use all care," John Todd declared.

"Could be they're in too much of a hurry to get away to take the time to cover their tracks," Colonel Trigg offered. "With scouts ahead, we should be safe enough against treachery."

They mounted up and set out again, following the ample signs relentlessly.

The Licking River was divided into three branches, and late in the afternoon they crossed the south fork near the junction with Stoner's Creek and came upon the burned-out remains of Ruddle's, a grim reminder of all that had transpired there. It was clear that the Indians had made camp within the walls—which bore the gaping holes and splintered wood of their British allies' cannon fire—to eat and rest as they'd come this way again. There'd been no attempt made to conceal the remains of camp-fires where the haunch bones of part of Bryan's Station's cattle lay, picked clean of meat. After a look around the settlers pressed ahead, stopping finally at sundown to rest the horses and draw up a rough battle plan.

Roman hunkered down away from the others, looking toward the last band of light that bathed the rolling hills and valleys to the west, etched faintly in red and purple. He thought of Kitty . . . God . . . please, God . . . He tried to find the words to ask for her safekeeping, something always hard for him to do. Surely that power to which others turned so easily must know what his feelings were.

It had taken so long for him to realize the truth. And he could not yet, perhaps never would, question it too closely lest he find the love he felt for her had been a part of him, buried too deeply for acknowledgment, since that night long years ago when he had held her in his arms.

He had been a husband to Sara, loved her and grieved for her . . . and borne his guilt, enough to last even him a lifetime. Now he was alive again, and he would not question it. He only knew that his love for Kitty Gentry was stronger than anything he'd ever felt.

"Roman . . ."

He looked up, startled. Israel had come to tell him that it was time to ride again. He got to his feet, hearing the groans of some around him as they put tired muscles to the test once more.

Though it was good dark now, they were unwilling to call it a day yet, going carefully, the great trees looming black and endless. Mosquitoes settled down in earnest, merciless in the hot damp air, and the horses swished their tails from side to side as their riders slapped themselves and muttered curses.

From time to time a fat 'possum or a rabbit would skitter away to rustle the underbrush, and once Roman startled a deer to send it crashing away. But mostly it was just the silence and the night . . . and weary men.

After three hours they stopped to sleep, taking turns at guard. Roman, head cushioned by a thick drift of old pine needles, dreamt of Kitty . . . waking to imagine he could feel the touch of her mouth against his.

Roman and Talliaferro lay stomach down, side by side at the crest of the hilltop, eyes sweeping the river below and the hilly reaches beyond it. The main fork of the Licking curved back upon itself, the great horseshoe bend peaceful in the morning sunlight. The water was deep and swift here, except for the narrow ford that was in a direct line from where he and Talliaferro lay. And on the far side the rocky, almost barren land lay all but closed within the pincers of the river bend, the open end holding scrub-covered ridges.

"I ain't set eye on a living thing yet," Talliaferro said, shifting to scratch vigorously at his crotch and taking oath that the lice would eat him up one day.

Roman merely grunted and kept his eyes to the scene in front of them, scanning the land close around the salt springs. His gaze shifted to take in the higher ground, cropped down and trampled, and the ridges where scrubby oaks stood stubbornly amidst twisted cedars.

"If there was aught to see, 'twould stand out clear enough in such barren country," Talliaferro insisted.

Roman shook his head. "There are ravines behind that ridge, filled with saplings and brush. . . . They drain to the river as it curves either way."

"You think they may have set theirselves in wait, then?"

"It could be," Roman said, and a moment later he narrowed his eyes as, high up in the line of trees, he caught sight of an Indian, then another . . . stopping to talk and gesture, turning to look back across the river and gesture again. "Shawnee," he muttered, knowing that Talliaferro had seen them, too.

They watched as the redmen fell into an easy trot along the buffalo trace that wound up and over the hill. In a moment both had disappeared from view. The nickering of a horse signaled the approach of the militia troop, and Roman and his companion slid down from their perch and went to tell them what they'd seen.

"It appears to me, Colonel," Talliaferro said to John Todd,

"that they be hightailin' it fer the Ohio and them two nothin' but stragglers tryin' to ketch up."

"I don't think so," Roman said, catching Daniel's eye to see agreement there.

"They intend to fight us, John," said Daniel.

Major Hugh McGary looked skeptical, but Colonel Trigg turned a worried look toward the river. "What makes you think so, Daniel?" he asked.

"Because for some time," Daniel told him, "they have been treading in one another's tracks to make us think there are less of them."

Some of the men looked down at the well-trampled ground beneath their feet, squinting about but unable to distinguish between their own marks and those left by the marauders now.

"Well"—McGary tossed his head back, chin up, the light hair curling about his ears—" 'twould seem to me we'd as well meet here as elsewhere."

"No." Roman challenged him. "There are ravines back there which make too good a place to lie in wait."

Daniel shifted his gun and nodded. "It would be safer were we to cross the river higher up a ways and strike the trace again in the high ground to the north of here. That would take us around an ambush, should there be one set."

"And lose us precious time!" countered one of the other officers, a Major Silas Harlan. McGary sided with him at once.

"Right enough. And let them escape across the Ohio safe in their mischief!" he added. "By God, let's at least move down to the ford and see what the situation is! If they're lingering about, we should see some sign of them, I say!"

After their few hours of rest, the men were fired up for vengeance, and there was a great chorus of agreement as the word was passed from one to another. "Aye, by God," they said. "Let's at least see what's about!"

"I don't see what harm that can do," Todd insisted, and his brother Levi nodded.

"We can regroup and confer again at the ford. If they're about, the sight of us may just flush them out," he said.

The horses picked their way, hides rippling in the morning light, blowing through their noses as they smelled the water ahead. The salt spring as they came near lay blue as the sky mirrored in it. The river just ahead looked clear and cool.

"Prudence may be the better part here, boys," Daniel counseled when they'd gathered to confer again. "The crossing upriver could take a little longer, but my judgment says it's safer in the long run of things.''

The men looked across the river, scanning the peaceful-looking heights, some of them grumbling that they'd come too far to detour now. But John Todd deferred to Daniel.

"By my soul," he said stoutly, "Daniel Boone's been too long in this country to doubt what he says in such a matter as this. If you think there's too much risk, we'll do what you say is best.''

"Aye," Trigg joined in, along with several of the other officers. But McGary's face had flushed, and he turned a scornful eye toward Daniel.

"It could be we'd be safer at home in our beds. Has your age begun to make you overcautious, Boone?" he sneered.

Roman, holding himself in check, saw the flicker of Daniel's eyes, but the veteran woodsman answered calmly. "We've important business here at hand," he said. "Let's not forget that Logan should be moving up with reinforcements before long.''

"To what end," a man from the ranks cried out, "if the bloody heathen butchers have made good their escape!''

"I believe us to be outnumbered," Daniel insisted. "And we stand before a place hard to put to charge. If you are bound to cross the river, then let's choose a better place.''

"Daniel is right," said Roman. "We should go upstream and circle 'round.''

McGary muttered something about "damned cowards," and Roman, furious, took a step toward him with the full intention of teaching the man a lesson then and there; but the Todd brothers quickly intervened to press him back.

McGary's slur had stung Daniel as well, and his usually mild manner deserted him now. His eyes glittered dangerously as he stared down the hotheaded major. "If you are determined to meet the enemy at this great disadvantage," he growled, "go on . . . I can go as far into an Indian fight as any other man!''

"By God, what have we come here for?" McGary shouted.

"To fight the Indians!" somebody yelled, fired up.

"By God, then, why not fight them!" McGary leapt into his saddle to wave his rifle overhead and yell out: "All who are not damned cowards follow me, and I'll soon show you the Indians!" And with that he spurred his horse forward into the shallow ford.

It was a challenge that few of those proud and independent men found easy to refuse, and a good number of them, fully

more than half, spurred their mounts to follow him, yelling
encouragement to one another and snatching off their hats to
wave above their heads.

"God's blood!" Roman swore while the officers looked on in
open-mouthed astonishment. Daniel shook his head.

"Damned hotheaded fool!" John Todd muttered, hauling his
own horse around to mount and waving his hand for all to follow. "If there is an ambush, we'll find out soon enough," he
said to Daniel. "We can't let the blithering idiots go charging
up there alone!"

The rest of the troop followed after McGary and the others,
crossing the river, Trigg and Todd shouting that they should wait
up. "At least form lines and proceed in good order, man!" Todd
shouted to McGary.

There was a great circling and stamping, horses bumping one
another, until finally the three commanders shouted orders that
their own troops should come behind them to form three columns . . . Todd in the middle, Trigg to the right, and Daniel to
the left. McGary and Major Silas Harlan, flushed and intent,
vowed they'd take twenty-five volunteers and form an advance
guard, and there were enough at once willing to follow them.

Roman fell in beside Daniel. Glancing back, he caught sight
of Israel and Tolliver Skaggs side by side. Tolliver looked scared.
"This is a fool's errand," Roman said to Daniel, who nodded,
his wide mouth set grimly.

Once beyond the miry land close on to the riverbank, they
dismounted, checking rifles and throwing their reins up over
their horses' necks. His sorrel would come to him with a whistle, Roman knew. Ready, they proceeded on foot, crossing the
gravelly stretch that led toward the open end of the horseshoe,
pressing on toward the ridges, the land rising steadily.

McGary and Harlan were leading the advance group ahead,
Roman still cursing them both beneath his breath for the arro-
gant asses they were and calling himself six kinds of a fool to
be following them. But there were good men up there who'd
fallen in with them, carried away by McGary's vainglorious pos-
turing and the fever of the moment. He'd not desert them.

As they climbed the hill toward the ridge, a silence settled in,
unbroken save for the soft tread of moccasined and booted feet
against the sparse-grassed trail. The men, who only moments
before had shouted out their eagerness to charge ahead, were
now tight-lipped as they neared the top of the rise. McGary and

the advance group crested the hill first, and McGary threw up his arm in a cocky wave that said everything was clear.

Passing the crest himself now, Roman saw the deep ravines sixty yards or more ahead, quiet and innocent in the sunlight, the tops of saplings and brushwood that lined them unstirring in the morning air. Maybe, he thought, he *had* been wrong . . . maybe the Girty brothers and their British commanders had thought it best to push on toward the Ohio. In which case he would be glad enough to eat his dish of crow, even for a man he. disliked as much as Hugh McGary.

The advance group had come abreast of the ravines now, and McGary turned around and flung his head up, grinning superciliously and signaling that the columns should come on up, the stillness broken at last with the sheepish laughter of the men.

"God save me, I nearly wet m' britches!" Pleas Worthington admitted, and those around him whooped and hollered and shoved him playfully.

"Best not tell Hester that!" Winfield joshed him.

But the smiles froze on their faces, laughter sticking in their throats, as suddenly a clatter of gunfire erupted up ahead. They watched in horror as the advance was cut down nearly to a man. Two or three were seen to drop forward and scramble backward.

There was no time to see who'd lived or died, for in an instant the Indians came swarming up from the ravines and from a hollow still farther to the right, charging, hordes of them, rifles blazing.

"God help us—we are done for!" someone cried. But Daniel's voice rang out, calm and steadying.

"Keep cool, boys!" he called. "Get down! Fire as you can . . . cover each other!"

The air was filled with high yelping war cries, warrior faces streaked with ocher and vermilion, the colors deep and brilliant in the morning sun.

There were screams and curses as men were hit, but Boone's men responded well, dropping down on one knee to take aim. Most of them were crack marksmen, the others good enough. And in that first rush they not only held their own, but seemed to be pushing the line of Indians back. Roman fired and reloaded, ramming the ball home with a quick thrust, to bring the rifle up and fire again.

But to the right the Indians had quickly flanked Stephen Trigg's column, and the colonel was hit almost at once, staggering backward, blood gushing from his chest and back. He twisted, open-mouthed, then pitched down dead.

"Colonel Trigg is down!" someone shouted. And the badly demoralized men tried to fall back slowly, but the Indians were in behind them now, catching them in a deadly crossfire. The panicked troops, comrades falling around them, broke and ran, trying to get back to their horses and the river.

The Indian line was still giving ground on the left. Unaware yet of what had happened on the right wing, Daniel urged his men on, using an extra-long fowling piece with deadly accuracy. But in that haze of smoke and stinging powder, Roman glanced back over his shoulder to see that Trigg's unit had broken, the savages hitting full at John Todd's middle line, both front and rear.

"Daniel!" he shouted, pointing, then turned to fire quickly at a brave who was bearing down upon him.

"God save us!" Daniel whispered as he saw Todd's men breaking.

Just at that moment Hugh McGary, unhurt, dashed up, face blackened with powder. "Boone! For Christ's sake, man, why are you not retreating? There are Indians all around you!"

Roman saw that it was so, and the Indians out ahead of them, seeing their advantage, charged full as others came from side and rear, casting aside their rifles as they fired to take after the retreating white men with tomahawk, knife, and stone ax.

"Get to the horses if you can!" Boone shouted. And it was every man for himself, shooting and clubbing their way . . . the smell of powder and blood everywhere, the air torn with the screams and whispers of dying men.

Roman heard a bellowing roar and swung about to see Winfield Burdette pick up one of the Wyandot braves and break his back with a terrible cracking sound, throwing him aside as if he'd been a sack of meal. Oliver, at Winfield's side, stared ashen-faced at his father, but it wasn't until the burly blacksmith swung around that Roman saw what prompted the wordless horror mirrored in the boy's eyes. Half of the big man's lower jaw had been smashed away with an ax blow.

Winfield stood there, looking at his son, eyes bulging as he tried to speak through that bloody mass of flesh, something that Roman thought must be his tongue moving in that awful gurgle of sound. And in that same instant a ball slammed into him and he pitched forward, reaching out to Oliver as he fell.

The boy leaned over his father, snot running from his nose

and mingling with the spit and tears on his face. "Oh, Lord . . . Lord . . . oh, Lord . . ." He said it over and over.

"We're cut off," Daniel shouted. "Let's try to the west—through the trees, boys! There's a ford near the mouth of Indian Creek. Get to it if you can. . . ."

Roman looked back down the hill they'd climbed, seeing the wild melee of men and horses, the screams of each alike in some agonizing way. He couldn't catch sight of his sorrel.

With Winfield dead, he yanked Oliver to his feet and shoved the rifle the youth had dropped back into his hands. "To the west, boy," he ordered.

A dappled horse came galloping, wild-eyed and terrified, and Daniel managed to grab the dragging reins and haul it to a stop. Israel was only a few steps away, and Daniel pressed the horse upon him. "Take it, son . . . and ride."

But Israel shook his head and dropped down to get off a shot. "I'll not go without you," he declared.

"I'll be along right after you. Get on, now."

But Israel shook his head again, pouring his powder with a steady hand to reload quickly. "Give it to Roman," he said. "You and me will go together. . . ."

Seeing Oliver still standing there, Roman took the reins when Daniel pressed them into his hand, and in a moment was shoving Oliver up onto the saddle. "Ride now if you value your life!" he shouted, and brought his open palm down hard on the animal's flank to set it running toward the trees to the west of them.

Israel had waved his father past him, dropping down to get one more shot off and cover Daniel's retreat, when suddenly he grunted, rocking back with the impact of the ball that caught him full in the chest.

"Israel!" Daniel turned back, calling out anxiously to his second son.

Israel struggled to regain his knees, one hand outstretched before him as if to hold off the howling Shawnee brave bearing down on him now, shiny, new British-steel tomahawk upraised. Daniel tried to get in a position to get off a clear shot, but Roman, nearer, darted in to set his feet squarely and fire away point-blank.

He swung back to see that Daniel had already reached his son and was gathering him in his arms. Israel looked full up at him with that wide, likable and open face of his, blood coming from his mouth, a bright red river at his chest.

"Israel . . . Israel," Daniel said brokenly.

"God . . . oh, God . . . *goddamn!*" It was hardly more than a whispered growl, but it burst from Roman, tearing from the depths of him, an agony of prayer and cursing at once as he saw how bad the wound was.

Daniel struggled to pick up the dying boy, but Israel, his life's blood pumping from his chest, moved his hand in a feeble gesture meant to tell his father to escape while he could. "You'll be all right, son," Daniel lied. "You will. . . ." And Roman bent to help him.

Together they moved off through the trees, carrying Israel between them, his breath a bubbly wheezing now. Once, Roman caught sight of an Indian off to the right of them and shouted a warning, realizing that he had failed to reload his rifle. He sank down to the ground, Israel beneath him, while Daniel swung his own rifle around and took the deadly aim that he was noted for. The man pitched forward, facedown.

They both reloaded quickly, and as they leaned to Israel again, Roman realized suddenly that the bubbly sound had stopped.

Daniel, on his knees, knew it, too, and he stayed there still for a long moment, hunched forward, tears running down his leathery cheeks. "He would not leave me . . . and I'll not leave him," he said finally, his voice stony. And Roman's face was wet, too, as they picked up Israel Boone's still body and started stubbornly ahead again.

They heard shouting in the woods around them now and again but managed to elude the bands of exulting Indians, staying to the thickest cover they could find. In a little they stopped to rest, dropping down in a shallow sinkhole and pulling brush over themselves.

The air seemed too close to breathe, rage and sorrow and exhaustion beating at Roman. He leaned his head back against the damp earth, the rich funky smell of it choking him, all the screams and curses echoing in his ears still. God spare him from the images that filled the dark place behind his eyelids. . . .

But in a moment the sharpness of the grief he felt for Israel cut through it all to make him think of Daniel . . . and Rebecca. Dear God, they had to tell Rebecca. . . .

Daniel stirred, and Roman opened his eyes, peering through the darkness to try to see his face; but it was hard to see the features clearly beneath all the brush above them.

"I don't know that we can get him back just now," Daniel said.

Roman knew that it was so. "We could leave him here, covered over," he said. "And come back . . ."

"No. They might find him, and I won't suffer that. There's a cave, not far. Maybe there . . ."

And when they thought it was safe, they started out again, carrying Israel between them. The cave, near the river, was one that Roman had never found, though he'd hunted and scouted the area many times. It was clear that the Indians knew of its existence—there were evidences of old fires and a few broken arrowheads strewn about the packed earth floor. He wondered why Daniel had thought Israel's body would be safe here.

But then Daniel beckoned, and Roman, too tall to stand upright, ducked down and followed him to the darkened depths at the rear. "Look here," Daniel said, pulling aside a few loose rocks to reveal a narrow shelf.

Roman nodded, and without a word they retraced the distance to bring the body back and put it in the niche. Daniel touched Israel's face tenderly before they piled up the loose rocks to cover over the opening.

They only waited a little, knowing that they dared not risk staying longer. And when they failed to hear any sound outside to hold them off, they clasped hands . . . as men who knew they might not have the chance again.

"We must cover ground for our lives now," Daniel said.

✳ 37 ✳

THE NEWS OF THE BATTLE OF THE BLUE LICKS WAS BITTER indeed for Boonesborough. As the first survivors began to straggle in and tell the tale, a few of them on horseback but more walking in, footsore and haggard—ghost-ridden almost, as if they carried the spirits of their dead compatriots with them—the women watched eagerly for sight of their own or begged for word when they didn't find them.

"God help me, did ye see aught o' my Johnny?"

"Might ye have word of Will?"

The cries went on, and the returning men did their best to answer, though too often they had to deliver the terrible news that yet another father, or son, or brother, had been added to the growing list of Boonesborough dead.

Marcum Porter was among those lost and Elvie and Henry heard from one of the Williards the grim details of how their son had died.

There seemed hardly a family untouched by the tragedy. But Kitty was relieved to hear Oliver Burdette say that the last time he'd seen Roman, he was alive and unhurt. "It was him that give me the horse that got me back."

"Last I seen o' Roman he was with Dan'l and Israel," Ezekial Skaggs added.

She was determined to hold fast to that. During the long nights when the women had manned the loopholes to watch and wait, she had realized just how much she loved him . . . loved him in her heart and mind and soul. And she wondered why it had taken her so long to acknowledge it.

The kinship between them had been more than Gentry blood, more than the need they'd felt for one another that night in the forest. There'd been a bond between them that had only deepened with the years. A part of her had always belonged to Roman; she knew that now. And she pondered how that could be true if she'd loved Cullen—and she *had* loved Cullen . . . loved him deeply. It was a puzzle, and she didn't fully understand it no matter how many times she confronted it again.

Her father had always said a woman would worry a thing to death. " 'Tis in the nature of the female, God bless 'em," Usaph would say. "Give a man a horse and he'll not go lookin' it in the mouth—but a woman will have to see the creature's teeth every time!"

Kitty steeled herself against doing that now. That she'd been able to love two men as fine as Cullen Claiborne and Roman Gentry could only be counted good fortune beyond measure. Now she could only pray God that Roman was safe. The alternative would be too cruel. Even the thought of it was almost past bearing.

But as the hours passed and more survivors straggled along the river road toward the fort, two or three at a time, there were

more and more women at Boonesborough who no longer had
reason to hope. Hobe Skaggs had to tell his wife that Tolliver
was dead, cut down at the ford when they were almost to safety.
And it was one of the Hawkinses who brought the word to Hester
that Pleas had been killed.

"He was beside me when it happened. And—if 'tis any comfort to you," he said, " 'twas over quick for him. My sympa-
thies to ye, Mistress Worthington."

Word of it reached Kitty just as she'd taken some broth to
Oliver, who'd come down with an ague as soon as he'd returned.
She went at once and found Hester at the cabin alone, turning
over Pleas's leather working tools in her hands, gently touching
the unfinished pieces at his workbench. Her face, usually so broad
and strong, was somehow narrowed, pinched in upon itself.

"Hester . . . oh, Lord, Hester, I'm so sorry." She put her arms
around that tall, broad-shouldered woman who seemed so fragile
at this moment, and they hugged and swayed, both crying.

"I could not believe it would be that word," said Hester.
"Not with the sky so bright and blue . . . 'Twould seem it
should have rained this day, or stormed. In warning."

She sobbed, and Kitty let her, knowing it was best, until
finally she could wipe her eyes and catch her breath. "I guess
he wasn't worth a lot . . . to any but me," she said. "He couldn't
do spit"—she gave a sad little laugh—"but leather, you know
. . . there was nobody his equal when it come to that."

"I know." Kitty's answer was soft.

Hester sat down in the rocking chair and folded her hands
across her lap. "When I was a girl—Lord help me, I was a head
taller than any in Albemarle County—I baked up a rhubarb pie
for a pie supper we was havin' at the church. Pleas bought it.
And, oh my, his friends did tease him unmerciful . . . said I
was the long and he was the short of it."

Kitty smiled.

"My folks didn't take a bit to him, neither. Said a girl like
me ought to have a great strappin' man, not a little banty cock
of a fellow. But we—" Her voice cracked and she swallowed
hard. "—we liked each other well enough. . . ."

Kitty made some coffee, and in a little, some of the other
women came, bringing a pot of honey with them, or a little
packet of tea, or a dish of hot stew. Elizabeth and Fanny and
Jemima walked down. Mollie Hawkins came. And Faith and
Phronie. A few of the women who'd lost their men came, too
. . . and some spoke of what they would do now. Lavinia Skaggs

came and she and Kitty held each other's hands and cried. Kitty had meant to talk to Roman about the possibility of Tolliver going to Harrod's Town to read law under one of the judges there.

Kitty stayed with Hester that night. She was going to leave Michael with Faith and Phronie, but Hester wanted him to come, too. "Pleas loved that baby," she said. "And so do I." The three of them slept together in Hester's bed.

But as the news continued to filter in of the enormity of the settlers' defeat at the Blue Licks—at least a third of the men who had ridden off from Bryan's Station that day killed, Colonels Todd and Trigg dead, and Daniel's fate unknown—Kitty found it harder to cling to the certainty that Roman was alive and would be coming back.

She kept as busy as she could. School must go on. And poor Hester needed all the companionship she could get. But it was in that sudden hush that fell just before dawn that Kitty would wake to stare into the darkness, hard put to fight off despair. It was then that she admitted to herself that Roman should have been back by now, if he had survived the battle.

Then, toward the end of the week, just as she had let school out and was gathering her things, she looked up to see Daniel Morgan Boone standing in the doorway of the blockhouse. Her heart constricted painfully at sight of the tight, drawn look of that young face. She couldn't speak but just put out a hand to rest it on one of his bony shoulders, dreading what he might tell her.

"I come to bring word to Jemima," he said, his eyes red-rimmed, as if he'd gone too long without sleep or had cried when no one was looking.

The latter thought brought on a trembling that Kitty held tightly within her. She could only look at him mutely and wait.

"Roman asked me to tell you—"

"Roman!" His name burst from her, echoing in the hot close air of the blockhouse, and her fingers dug into the thin shoulder. "Oh, my God . . . you've seen him?"

"Aye," the boy said, and Kitty had to sit back suddenly against the rough table that served her as a desk, the strength suddenly drained from her. "Him and Pa," Daniel Morgan went on. "They've gone to join Colonel Logan and his men. Headed back to the Blue Licks to bury what dead they can. They aim—" Daniel Morgan's voice broke, but he went stubbornly ahead after a moment. "—aim to bring Israel back to bury at Boone's Station if they can."

"Israel . . . Oh, not Israel!" Tears stung Kitty's eyelids, and she leaned against the edge of the table, still for a moment, Israel's face sharp and clear in her memory. Lord, it was too cruel. So many dead, men and boys she had known and loved as friends. All of them dead. It was too much . . . too much.

"How is Rebecca?" she asked finally, the thought of that poor woman's sorrow making her own pain seem small.

"Tryin' to hold up." Daniel Morgan shook his head. "If truth was known, I expect Israel was always her favorite of us all."

Kitty looked at Daniel Morgan, remembering the shy six-year-old he'd been when she'd first come to Boonesborough. She felt a sudden rush of relief that he hadn't been quite old enough to go along with the others when they'd ridden off. If he had, he might be dead now, too.

Impulsively she leaned over and hugged him. He blinked and reddened, but his mouth, wide like Daniel's, edged up slightly at the corners.

"Was Roman all right when you saw him?" she asked.

He nodded, still red in the cheeks. "Roman's like Pa," he said. "Both of 'em tougher'n bull elks."

It was the next morning when John Holder and Flanders rode in, Fanny and Jemima weeping with relief at seeing their husbands alive and unhurt. But the news they brought was not good. The small group had ridden into their own ambush. Four men had been lost.

It did seem, Ezekial Turner opined grimly, that there wasn't a hell of a lot to fiddle over these days.

Hester Worthington loomed up in the open doorway suddenly, eyebrows arched high, fine hair escaping to wisp about her ears. "He's here!" she called to Kitty, who was bending over the hearth to stir a simmering pot of rabbit stew. "Roman's here and comin' down the path right this minute!"

Kitty's stomach seemed to turn over, a small sound escaping her as she caught her breath and whirled around to straighten and face Hester. She had waited and worried for days, and now all she could do was gape foolishly at the big woman and repeat his name, as if she'd lost her wits. "Roman? . . ."

"Aye." Hester pursed her lips and smiled. But Kitty still stood there, all but covered with an oversize dun-colored apron, cheeks flushed from the heat of the fire. Hester gave her head a shake and gestured toward the rough hempen garment. "Will ye get that off and go!" she said. And Kitty snatched off the apron at last, handing it and the long-handled spoon to the big woman as she sped past.

Once she had cleared the steps, she saw him coming toward her, and she went a few paces along the path, then stopped. The waning sunlight burnished the red of his hair and caught in the week's growth of beard. His buckskins were torn and filthy, yet there was something in the way he strode down the path so determinedly that reminded her of that day long ago when he'd first come up to the Gentry place on the Watauga . . . Lord, how long had it been? Seven years. And for some reason, she felt as shy as she had that day. Maybe because what she felt at this moment was so much that she must stand very still or it would shatter her.

He covered the ground between them with a few long strides and then stopped just short of her, no more than a foot between them, looking at her soberly, lines in his face that hadn't been there before.

"Roman," she whispered, and he reached his hand slowly to wipe a tear from her cheek.

"Don't cry," he said.

"Why not?" She smiled, her lips trembling.

"Because I can't bear to see you cry." He reached for her, still so solemn, eyes deepset in those marvelous caverns of his face, wrapping her in his long arms to hold her close to his chest. And all the sadness and the tears, the horror and death of those past days, seemed far away. She was filled with the knowledge that she was where she belonged.

Since there were people out and about the fort yard, they did not really kiss; Roman only brushed his lips against hers in the barest, sweet touching, and then Michael came running up to tug at his leg.

"Roman . . . you're back!" he shouted, capering about, Bear lolling his big tongue out and wagging his tail at the boy's excitement. "Will you take me hunting? Will you?" Roman had promised to take him to the woods and show him how to set a snare.

"I will. How about tomorrow?" He squatted down to be on an eye level with the youngster.

"Early?" Michael pleaded.

Roman nodded. He straightened to smile at Kitty and take Michael's hand, and the three of them moved toward Hester, who was still standing there outside of Kitty's cabin.

"Hester," said Roman, "I'm sorry about Pleas."

She nodded, patting at her skirts with big-knuckled hands.

"I'll be all right. And I thank God that you've come back safe."
Her eyes were suddenly moist, but she cast an affectionate look
toward Kitty and then turned her attention to Michael. "You
there, Michael Claiborne . . . would ye know anyone would like
to help me eat up a persimmon pudding that's goin' to waste at
my place?"

"*I* would," Michael cried at once, and Hester took him in
tow and headed next door to her own cabin.

"I've more than enough stew," Kitty called after them. "I'll
bring some over."

Hester replied with a wave of her hand, and Kitty and Roman
went into the Claiborne cabin. As Roman found a chair before
the fireplace, Kitty hurriedly lit a couple of the grease lamps
against the deepening gloom.

"There," she said, "now at least I can see you." She turned
to him, so filled with gratitude that he was safe that she couldn't
speak for a minute. Afraid that she might cry, she began to poke
at the stew, which was thick with vegetables and shreds of squirrel meat. "Daniel Morgan said you went back to the Blue Licks
. . . afterward."

There was a long silence, except for the scraping of the spoon
against the pot bottom. After a moment Kitty turned back to
him again, seeing the deep fatigue that pulled at his face and
added a hoarse edge to his voice when he finally spoke.

"With Ben Logan and his men. We buried all we could find
. . . in a common grave. And piled stones over it."

He didn't tell her of the bodies bloated and rotting in the
August heat after five days, mangled by wild animals, unrec-
ognizable. . . . Kitty would hear of it later, from others who
had lived through it, too; but not from Roman. It was as much
as he could ever say about that terrible task.

"Israel?" Her voice was soft, hesitant. "Could you . . . did
you bring Israel back?"

He nodded.

"Poor Rebecca," she said. "And Daniel." She went to kneel
beside him. "Are you all right?" She lifted her hand to his face,
let her fingers touch the fiery red beard.

"I am now," he said, and slid his arms around her to lift her
against him, half into his lap, his mouth finding hers to linger
there and send a warmth flowing through her that was so sweet
she could hardly bear it—all the tenderness and love and promise
there in it . . . and the pain and sorrow of what had gone by.
Tears trembled on her eyelashes and fell.

"No . . . don't," he said, rubbing his face against hers, the rough beard scratching gently. "I would close my eyes and see you while I was gone—before the battle, when we could rest . . . afterward, when Daniel and I were hiding . . ."

"I was afraid for you."

He smiled that one-sided smile of his. "I was determined to come back. I want us to wed." He caught her face between his two hands and looked into her eyes. "Would you . . . will you? Maybe you need some time to think about it," he broke in before she could answer.

She pressed her fingers against his lips to prevent him from saying more, her heart almost stopped inside her. "I've had all the time I need. Yes, yes . . . yes, Roman!"

"God's blood!" he said, grinning, a great breath bursting from him. "Kitty . . . Kitty Gentry . . ."

They held to each other and kissed, the slow tenderness giving way to a quickening of blood that brought a groan from Roman and caused Kitty to draw back, suddenly shy again, as a girl before her first time. "You must eat now . . . and rest. We've time enough for . . ." She could feel the heat in her cheeks.

"Aye." He grinned at her. "Time enough to get this brush off my face"—he rubbed a hand over the beard—"and scrape some of the stink from me. And find a preacher," he added.

"There isn't one here now."

"Then we'll get one. From Harrod's Town."

She nodded, smiling at the impatience in his face that made it look younger than his thirty-one years.

"First though," he admitted, the grinding fatigue overtaking him again, "first a little sleep."

"Let me fix you a plate. You need to eat." She turned back toward the hearth, but his hand on her arm stayed her.

"No. Just sleep. I'll go down to one of the blockhouses."

"No, you won't. I'll turn back the bed."

"No," he argued. "I'll not risk a word said against you."

"There won't be," Kitty insisted. "I'll sleep over at Hester's." She pulled back the blue-and-white woven coverlet that had belonged to her mother and plumped up the feather pillows. "There . . ." She came back to tug at him.

"Kitty, look at me. . . ." He stared ruefully down at the filthy buckskins. "I'll ruin the bedclothes."

She shook her head, smiling. "They'll wash, Roman. I'll get my nightgown and the stew."

He sat down on the side of the bed, reluctant still, but tugging at the laces of his moccasins, while Kitty flew about gathering up her things.

She made two trips, the last to fetch the hot kettle of stew, and found him sprawled back crossways on the bed, still fully clothed except for the moccasins, his head to one side, mouth open slightly to make a soft snoring sound as he breathed. She tiptoed up to cover him lightly, tears welling again, the knowledge strong in her that they'd been coming to this day since the moment they'd first laid eyes on each other. She didn't understand how that could be, with all the other—with Cullen and Sara—but it was the truth, and there was nothing in her that wanted to deny it.

Kitty insisted on having two weeks before the wedding. "There are things I must do, Roman, my love . . . I'd not want to stand before the preacher in this." She looked down at the dark-colored dress she wore, typical of the dark browns and blacks she'd attired herself in since Cullen's death. And Roman reluctantly agreed, since it appeared it would be hard to obtain the services of a man of God before then anyway. Most of the preachers were busy consoling the families who'd lost men in the battle—seeing to the needs of grieving widows and in some cases having to find the nearest relative to whom they should deliver an orphaned child or children.

Hester volunteered her services, and the two women entered into a frenzy of cutting and fitting and sewing. Kitty had managed to save a little money from her small monthly stipend, and now she used it to buy several good lengths of cloth from old Harley Bailor's general store. For her wedding dress she picked a lightweight linen that had been dyed a pale blue.

"You must have new nightdresses, too," Hester declared, and would brook no argument when she dug into her own pocket and brought up the coins to pay for the material and laces. " 'Twill be my gift to you."

They worked at Hester's cabin, laying the cloth out on Pleas's old worktable—Hester had packed all his tools away—and taking charge of readying Kitty for the wedding seemed to help the big woman some in her time of bereavement.

"Have you let Roman lie with ye yet?" she asked outright one day as they plied their needles.

Kitty shook her head, feeling her cheeks redden, but Hester leaned forward, the needle stilled for a moment.

"Tell me why in the world not," she demanded.

"Well . . . it hasn't been easy," Kitty admitted, the blush deepening, "but Roman is anxious that there be no gossip against me."

"Bosh!" Hester's black eyes snapped. "Let the tongues wag all they want. They will anyway, ye know. I'd not waste a day were I you. Pleas and me went at it ever' chance we got, and I'm glad enough of it now."

It *was* growing harder, Kitty admitted to herself. The week yet to go seemed an eternity, and every evening, after Roman had eaten supper at the cabin, he would kiss her good night with that steely misery plain in his eyes before he went down to the blockhouse to sleep. But Michael's presence in his trundle bed, usually just drowsy and calling out good-nights to Roman as he left, had helped them to observe the proprieties.

But that very evening, Hester asked Michael if he didn't want to come over and have supper with her and spend the night. "You can bring Bear with you," she said, and as Kitty cast an accusing look her way, Hester's eyebrows arched innocently.

Michael looked toward his mother and, when she nodded, agreed readily. "I be back in the morning, Mama," he assured her, squaring up his small shoulders, his voice taking on as manly a tone as a four-year-old could muster, "and help you carry the milk."

Kitty smiled at him, her heart swelling with that familiar aching pride, and Roman looked on approvingly.

"He's a fine boy," Roman said once Hester and Michael had gone.

"Yes," Kitty said as she laid out the treenware plates and set the cutlery on the table. "I've been thinking that to have a sister would be good for him."

Roman lifted his head and looked at her a long moment, knowing what she meant. "Hallie," he said, smiling.

"Yes. She belongs with us."

He nodded, still grinning. "I'll go fetch her. Before winter."

Though Kitty had fried up a chicken and cooked some summer squash and green beans, neither of them ate much. "You weren't hungry tonight?" she asked as she cleared up.

"I had enough," he said. He sat close by, smoking his pipe and watching her, his eyes caressing her as she moved about in front of the fireplace.

She dried the plates and the cups and put them on the shelf, then wiped off the table, finding it hard to breathe suddenly, she was so aware of him there . . . long legs stretched out, muscular thighs outlined beneath the tight-fitting leggings, his face turned toward the fire now so that she could see that hard, clean line of his profile.

When she'd finished, she took up her mending and sat across from him but put it aside in a moment, all thumbs, the thread snarled and knotted. "Mercy," she said, knowing his eyes were on her and looking up to see the blazing blue heat there. Her heart was pounding against her ribs so that she was sure he must hear it.

"I'd better go now," he said. "If I don't . . ."

He didn't move despite what he'd said, and their eyes held, such a trembling set up in her that she tucked her hands beneath her armpits to hold herself still.

"Don't go," she said.

"God's blood!" he exploded, all that fierce sense of honor struggling in his face, "would you make it that hard for a man, Kitty Gentry?"

"Aye," she said softly, and he stared at her for a moment and then was up and to her in an instant, pulling her into his arms.

"Kitty, my own . . ." His mouth was strong and sure on hers, and he lifted her so that she was pressed against that hard male part of him. She thought she would die with the wanting.

"Roman . . . Roman," she gasped while she could still think, "wait, love . . . wait." He set her on her feet and she sped away to the door, shoving the bolt home, then turned back to him.

He walked to her slowly, reaching out to untie the white linen scarf that crossed over and fastened at her waist. The bone buttons of her bodice gave way to his sure fingers, and in a moment her breasts were bared to him. He touched them, a wonder in his eyes, moving fingertips causing her to moan as they brushed at the birthmark, lingered at her nipples.

"I was determined not to die out there, Kitty . . . not before I held you." He picked her up in his arms, his mouth finding her lips, her throat, as he carried her to the bed and laid her down. And in those next minutes they discovered each other, touching, caressing. Kitty took in the lean length of him, the fiery red fuzz that furred his chest and belly and legs, not shy at looking at the full power of his manhood . . . just as Roman explored every inch of her, touching the curve of her hip and thigh, coming again to the swell of her breasts with their fine pointed nipples, entering her mouth with his tongue. . . .

"I love you, Roman," she whispered as she felt him part her thighs. In the next instant, as they were joined, she heard him gasp out his answering pledge, and she was lost then in the fierce, wild pleasure of it. Time grew somehow meaningless, as if they were back in the forest all those years past, except that now there was no bar or guilt, nothing that kept them from belonging to each other. Though in one way they always had. And that was part of it, too—all the years of closeness, of knowing each other better than any other. . . .

When it was over they lay cradled together, holding to each other, Kitty's face wet with tears.

"If I should live to be a hundred, I'll not forget," Roman said, stroking her cheek gently.

They made it do them until the wedding, when Roman stood up, tall and solemn and looking unnatural without his familiar buckskins, garbed in a black frock coat and a blue woolen weskit that was almost the same shade as Kitty's dress. She carried a small bouquet of blue salvia and wore borrowed kid slippers with silver buckles.

"Johnny Callaway said you're my papa now," Michael said, confronting Roman, the confusion he felt at that twisting his small face. "Are you?"

Roman hunkered down to him so that they could talk man to man, the wedding party in full swing about them. "Well, I know that you had your own papa . . . you remember?"

Michael nodded, though the truth was, Cullen was only a shadowy figure to him now, more the words of his mother than any real memory.

"I'd not ask you to put that aside entirely. But with him gone, I'd be proud to have a boy as fine as you for a son, Michael."

Michael stared at him a long moment and then threw his arms about Roman's neck and held on tightly.

It was two weeks after the wedding when Roman took Kitty to Otter Creek. She cried at sight of the burned-out cabin; vegetation had grown up to nearly hide the ruins of it. But the orchard was there and flourishing, branches hanging full with ripening fruit, and they made love beneath the leafy covering, cushioned by the mosses and the grass.

They knew each other so well by now, and made full use of that knowledge, until Kitty begged him to come into her. But even then Roman took his time, carrying them both finally to such pleasure that they cried out together in that last, shuddering moment and lay still in each other's arms, locked together yet and drenched with sweat.

And a little later, when they'd rolled apart and looked up through the apple-laden branches above them, the blue of the sky showing through the green, Roman told her of his plans to build a house for them as soon as it was safe enough, down at the junction of the creek and river. "Maybe next year, even," he said. For a moment she couldn't make a sound, and then she gave a happy shriek and fell upon him, covering his face with kisses to set him laughing.

"Oh, Roman," she said, sobering, "I did not think that I could . . . that I would ever—" She stopped, voice quivering, and he hugged her to him.

"Nor did I, my love," he said.

And a little later, as they lay there, content, Kitty quietly pressed her hand against her belly and smiled. She *knew* somehow what had happened this day . . . could feel it . . . was positive of it. Roman's baby had started in her.

Though the entire frontier had been cast into despair and grieving after the terrible losses at Blue Licks, the settlements rallied quickly with the news that General Clark was at Harrod's Town and calling for volunteers to sweep north of the river and carry out the settlers' vengeance against the Indians.

"By the Almighty," George Clark had been heard to bellow, "we'll see that they pay a price for it!"

Kitty knew that Roman must go, and helped him collect what he would need to take with him.

The Kentucky men gathered, a thousand strong, to carry out the retaliatory raid. Roman elected to serve under Daniel, who commanded a detachment. They burned Chillicothe, and Piqua Town on the Miami, laying waste to crops as they went. And while many of the Indians were able to scatter into the forests to escape the deadly long rifles of the Kentuckians, it would be some time before they would be a threat to the whites again. They would have to see to their own survival with winter coming.

The skies were gray and heavy with snow the day that Roman came home, but to Kitty it could have been springtime. And when at last they could be alone, after they'd held each other, Kitty took his hand and pressed it to her stomach as she told him. She'd been right about the day at Otter Creek.

PART SIX

❊

Summer 1785

* 38 *

THE TWO-STORY CABIN, BORDERED BY BEDS OF FOXGLOVE and cockscomb and love-in-a-mist, sat on the high ground overlooking the junction of the river and Otter Creek, far enough back to be safe from spring flooding but close enough to enjoy the view of the clear green streams and wooded stretches beyond. It was what was called a double cabin, constructed of square-hewn logs with two large rooms on either side at the ground level, divided by a "dogtrot"—an open corridor about ten feet wide that ran right through the middle of the structure from front to back and was covered overhead by the second story. It was a pleasant place to sit in the summer since it caught the breezes from the river, and Kitty had been especially pleased with it because Roman had hauled in flat rocks from the creek to pave it instead of leaving it with a dirt floor, as most dogtrots were.

The barn and the springhouse and the corn cribs were a few hundred yards from the house, and Kitty emerged from the barn now, a foaming bucket of milk full to the brim in her hand. From where she stood, she could not quite see the spot where she'd been surprised by the Shawnee braves and carried off back in 1775; there was a grove of tall trees that blocked her view. But to her left, plain enough, lay a good-size crop of corn, green fronds stirring in the breeze; and on the far side of the corn, the lush green tobacco plants stretched nearly to the woods, welcoming the morning sunlight. The vegetable patch was closer in to the house.

If she turned, back along the creek she would see the Luttrams' two cabins—with seven boys out of a brood of eleven, it had eased the family's crowding to put up a second cabin for the four oldest boys. The Luttrams had lost the legal claim to their

507

land—as had too many others because of poor surveying or improper filing—and Tom Luttram had been glad to come and work for Roman for a yearly stipend and a portion of the crops. He was a good, hardworking man, and his boys were cut from the same mold, Roman often said.

Kitty thought of Daniel and Rebecca, who had lost their claim to Boone's Station. "I'd counted on staying this time," Rebecca had confided to Kitty, fighting back tears. Daniel had simply set that wide mouth of his and, without a word, moved his family a few miles away to Marble Creek where he had a patch of land, leaving behind the graves of Israel and his brother Ned.

The Boones were coming today, and Kitty would be glad of the chance to see them. Daniel was now talking of moving to Limestone, up on the Ohio. If they did, it might be a long time before she got to see Rebecca again.

"Chester says there might could be a hunnert people here come afternoon. Is that a fact, Mistress Kitty?"

The voice came from behind her, and Kitty turned back to see Celie Luttram, at twelve already taller than she was herself, coming through the barn door with full buckets of milk in either hand, her round face flushed and freckled, straw-colored hair braided into a fat rope that hung down her back. Chester, two years older than Celie, was her favorite among her brothers, and she was forever quoting him.

Kitty laughed, set upon by a mild panic just at the thought of that many arriving. "I hope not a hundred, Celie," she said. "I'm not sure we'd have enough food for that many. Let alone be able to bed them."

She looked over toward the spot where Roman and Tom Luttram and the other Luttram boys tended the glowing beds of coals above which three nearly grown pigs and two sides of beef and a deer roasted slowly. The turkeys and assorted smaller game meat that the boys had brought in would be added to the spits later in the day. She could see Roman, shoulders squared and head high, the very stance of him saying that he was well pleased with this day.

It had been his idea to have a party. It would, he declared, be a good idea to celebrate the boys' birthdays with a get-together on the day in between—Michael had been seven yesterday, and Trace would be two years old tomorrow. What better chance to assemble family and friends? Plus, he'd added, it would be nice to invite a few of the men he'd served with or met at Danville last May when he'd been elected delegate to the convention held there.

"I'm going to take this milk to the kitchen, Celie," Kitty said, the very thought of how many her husband might have invited setting her in motion. "You take those two buckets on down to the springhouse and put them with the rest. Maybe there'll be somebody here with a taste for sweet milk this afternoon."

She hurried on toward the house in time to see Michael emerge from the dogtrot, a piece of johnnycake in his hand. His eyes danced as he grinned at her. "We could use some water inside," she told him.

"Yes'm," he said. "I'll carry some in soon's I help Lonnie fetch some wood down to Papa and Mr. Luttram."

Lonnie Luttram was just a year older than Michael, and the two of them did their chores together. Bear came bounding up to the boy and trotted along after him as Michael loped toward Roman and the others, breaking his stride to leap upward, like a young deer feeling good. Kitty smiled.

Entering from the dogtrot, she went into the kitchen, which was bigger than the whole cabin had been back at Boonesborough. She could never quite take it for granted after being cramped for space for so many years. The stone fireplace took up most of the wall opposite the door and had a real oven built right into the masonry. To her left an opening led into a dining room, while to the right the front wall boasted of two large windows that allowed enough light into the room. Roman had insisted that all the rooms throughout the house have enough windows—fitted, of course, with hinged wooden covers in case of an emergency. But there'd been no Indian trouble nearabout since the raid on the Shawnee towns after the Battle of the Blue Licks, though there had been scattered reports of killings and thefts elsewhere from time to time.

At the kitchen table Hester was feeding young Trace Able Gentry the last of his grits. At two, though he still had his baby fat, the unmistakable body build of his father was evident, as well as the bright blue eyes and thatch of red hair. There were times when Kitty wondered how she could possibly have borne two sons so like their fathers; but however it had happened, she gave thanks for it.

"This young man is in fine fettle this morning," Hester announced as she scraped the bowl for the last spoonful and popped it into the boy's mouth. "I do believe he's ready for all the goings-on today.'' The big woman looked on fondly as the boy gave his mother a toothy smile, grits dribbling from the corner of his mouth.

He climbed down from his chair and came toward Kitty, holding up his arms. True to his father, he didn't talk a lot yet; other than ''Ma-ma'' and ''Pa-pa,'' he could say ''Bear'' better than anything else. Michael came out ''Mike-oh'' and Hester ''Hessa.''

Kitty put the pail of milk aside to catch him up and hug him, suddenly filled with the sight of him and the memory of Michael bounding along with Bear at his heels a moment earlier, of Roman standing out there, of the land and the river and the house . . . ''Oh, Lord, Hester''—it burst out of her—''I do love it here!''

Hester, who'd been wiping the crumbs from the table, straightened and smiled. ''I do, too,'' she said, an unaccustomed softness in her voice. ''And I'm glad enough you talked me into coming along,'' she added.

Trace's great wet kiss had left a sticky spot of grits on Kitty's cheek, and she took up the corner of her apron to wipe it off. ''You're not sorry you didn't accept 'Zekial's proposal, then?''

''Pshaw! That old fool?''

''Hester!'' Kitty laughed. ''He's a good man.''

''Good enough,'' Hester conceded.

''He's coming today, you know.''

Hester gave her head a toss. ''And I'll greet him as a friend,'' she said.

There was the squeak of wagon wheels outside and the stamping of hooves amidst the calling of children's voices. ''That must be Faith,'' said Kitty. ''She promised they'd come early so she and the girls could help us.''

''My lands, they must've started before daylight!'' said Hester.

With Kitty still carrying Trace, the two women went out to greet the Tylers. The older kids were already down, and Ben was reaching up to take their youngest, Charles Willis, from Faith so that she could get down from the high seat more easily.

''Well, little sister . . . Miz Hester,'' Ben greeted them, grinning, ''it appears to be a fine day for a get-together.'' He clung to Charles Willis as the boy squirmed and squealed in pleasure at seeing Trace. The two of them were nearly the same age. Charles Willis would have his second birthday next month.

Faith looked nice in her best dress, her hair braided and wound around her head the way she'd worn it when she was a young girl, her face a little fuller, cheeks pink. Kitty put Trace down beside Charles Willis, who'd succeeded in squirming his way out of his father's arms, and hugged her sister soundly.

"I dressed out three chickens, and there's a basket of green beans, some onions, and squash there in the wagon," Faith told her, her smile broad enough to show her missing tooth. "See if you can get all of it down for your Aunt Kitty," she directed Latham. And Michael jumped up in the wagon bed to help his younger cousin, with Lonnie Luttram pitching in.

"I brought our aprons," Faith assured Kitty. "Mine and Martha's. We'll set Charity to watching these two young'uns for us." She cast a pleased look toward her youngest son, who was already following Trace off into the dogtrot, the two of them headed toward a small wooden wagon that Roman had made for the boy.

With the vegetables carried inside, the women commenced their chopping and peeling and cooking, Faith oohing over the five cakes that sat in a row on the kitchen worktable.

"Real cakes!" she exclaimed, clapping her hands together. "Martha, look at them! I'm not sure if you've ever tasted one. Have you?"

"No, ma'am," Martha said. At nine, Martha was tall for her age. A pale, shy girl.

"Where did you get the flour?" Faith demanded. Real wheat flour was hard to come by since, in the beginning, the soil of Kentucky had been so rich that planted wheat resulted in rank and luxuriant growth but no grain heads. It was only now, after ten years, that some were trying wheat again, in fields that had been worn down some by corn.

"Roman got it for us," said Kitty. "He was over at St. Asaph's, and someone had brought some in from the East. He persuaded the man to sell him a little. And we used every pinch of it in those cakes."

"We had some sugar left from the sugarin' in the spring," Hester added, "and we cooked it down with butter and milk for the icing. Go on, taste a little crumb of it there," she urged them. And they did, Faith oohing and ahing again.

In a little while Celie and her mother came in to help. Polly Luttram walked slowly, huge with her twelfth child and due to deliver any day.

"You don't need to do a thing," Kitty told her.

"Not feelin' as poorly as you are," said Hester.

But Polly, a stout woman of strong features, with the same straw-colored hair as all her children, got herself lowered into a chair and laughed good-naturedly. "Lordy me, my hands still work. Fetch me some o' them potatoes to peel, Celie. Then help Mistress Hester with them pans o' squash there. I do hope," she confessed, "that I hold off till tomorrow at least." She smiled. "I'd purely hate to miss the party."

It was about midday when the Porters arrived, Elvie as plump and smiling as ever, gray patches at her temples now and occasionally a look in her eyes that let Kitty know she still felt the loss of her son Marcum, killed at Blue Licks. They were soon followed by John and Fanny Holder, who'd brought Elizabeth and all the other Callaways along with them. Jemima and Flanders were living over in Fayette County, but they'd loaded up their children—four by now—and had come over to Boonesborough the day before so that they could come along with the others.

Ezekial Turner arrived, sweating in his best black wool coat. He sought out Hester and told her that he'd not mind a cool drink and maybe they could set a spell and catch up since the last time he'd seen her.

"You'll find the spring right down the hill there, 'Zekial Turner. And as sweet and cold a water as you'd want. As for me"—she tilted her nose coolly—"I've plenty to see to if all these people are to be fed. Look there . . ." She pointed toward the pair of wagons just coming into sight and several mounted men not too far behind. "There are more comin' right now."

Roman looked around him at old friends and neighbors as they sat, satisfied, in the thick grassy shade beneath the trees at the side of the house or moved back and forth to the rough tables loaded down with food. A good many of their visitors had brought something along with them—a pan of cooked rhubarb, or a blackberry cobbler made with cornmeal and molasses, or a whole roasted 'possum—which should, he thought, have eased Kitty's mind some about having enough.

His eyes sought her out, close up to the house talking to Rebecca, and he felt that familiar swell of pleasure in just looking at her. She was wearing the slippers he'd sent to Philadelphia for, and she looked so graceful, as if she were light as a feather in them . . . and she damned near was. It was always a wonder to him that such a delicate-looking, fine-boned little body could house a strength, at least in spirit, the equal of any he knew.

A few of the younger men were out toward the barn, running foot races and whooping good-naturedly, while some of Roman's fellow delegates from the May convention took their ease in the shade. Ben Logan stood deep in conversation with Daniel. And Isaac Shelby—who, on his way to Boonesborough back in '77, had accepted the hospitality of Usaph and Amelia Gentry, and later volunteered to help lay their bodies to rest—was helping himself to another scoop of cobbler, his wife Susannah at his side. After distinguishing himself at the battle of King's Mountain in South Carolina during the war, he had returned to Kentucky and made it his home.

Michael walked near and Roman reached out to clasp his shoulder. "Stay here a minute, son," he said. Kitty had seen and smiled as he signaled to her to bring Trace.

"Friends"—Roman's voice lifted and carried, heads turning toward him—"and kinfolk," he added as he caught sight of Faith straightening up from the water bucket and looking to him, gourd dipper in hand, "I'd think a word or two might be the thing on this occasion."

"A word or two is 'bout as much as we ever git from you *anytime*," Ezekial sang out. And as Roman smiled, the others laughed. The youths who'd been wagering on the outcome of their races straggled in, sweaty and red-faced, flopping down in the shade and waiting to hear what Roman had to say.

"We"—Roman looked toward Kitty, who'd drawn near with Trace in her arms—"are proud to have you all here today. Most of you know my family. But for those who don't, this is my son Michael . . ." Michael grinned broadly, not the least embarrassed, glancing briefly over his shoulder at Roman. "And this young man's name is Trace." Roman reached for the boy and swung him up. "We're celebrating their birthdays today. Michael's yesterday, Trace's tomorrow. And I guess it's only right to thank my good wife publicly"—his eyes sought Kitty's—"for a pair of fine boys."

There were cheers from among the men, and the women smiled and nodded to one another, some clapping their hands.

"There's food enough," Roman continued, catching sight of Hester and Faith as they started bringing out the cakes. " 'Zekial's brought his fiddle along. And down there in the barn you'll find several kegs of spirits."

A few of the younger men, laughing and jostling one another in high good humor, set off for the barn to fetch the kegs up to the house, while the women gathered to admire the cakes. Everyone would get a taste.

Roman set Trace down, and Michael grabbed the little boy's hand, grinning as Hester beckoned. "I'll get him a piece with frosting on it," he declared, half pulling, half carrying his little brother along. Trace, though smiling still, looked slightly confused by it all.

Roman and Kitty were left alone beneath the branches of the big sycamore at the corner of what Kitty called "the yard." He took her hand in his and felt the deep stirring that she produced in him, something of the spirit, if truth be known—but physical, too . . . most assuredly physical.

" 'Tis too bad you'll be in the barn with the men tonight," she teased, reading him as she always could, her violet eyes deepened by the shade, her mouth pert as she grinned at him. There were times, he thought, when she looked almost as young as that first time he'd laid eyes on her . . . and surely even prettier.

They stood there a moment more, holding hands still. "Where's that dulcimore of yours?" he asked.

"Roman, don't you dare! 'Zekial's fiddle playing is enough."

"But I love to hear you sing. And I'd wager our guests would, too."

"In front of all these people?" She shook her head stubbornly. "I'd be too nervous to open my mouth."

He would have said more, but in turning his head he caught sight of two men just down from their horses and coming toward him—a pair, he noted, mildly disgruntled, that he was sure he hadn't invited. James Wilkinson, who'd attained the rank of brigadier general during the war—some said undeservedly— strode along surely, garbed out in clothing more suitable for a Philadelphia drawing room than a Kentucky outdoor get-together. He had come west to operate a mercantile business in Lexington, and the ladies surely loved him in his silk hose and fancy weskits. Even Kitty, Roman observed wryly, was smiling at him. Beyond a doubt Wilkinson was a handsome-enough man, his reputation for charm not undeserved. Still, there was something about the man that put Roman off.

What surprised him now was Wilkinson's companion. He hadn't seen Josiah Langford about for some time and had been pleased enough at the absence. The low opinion he'd formed of the man when he was at Boonesborough had not changed a whit . . . and neither, he noted, had Langford's considerable paunch.

"My dear Mr. Gentry"—Wilkinson beamed, his dark eyes alight—"we were traveling this way, Mr. Langford and I, and thought to throw ourselves upon your hospitality. And now we find this delightful gathering. . . ." He looked about him, at the boys who had resumed their foot races, and then over toward the side of the house where Ezekial was just drawing the bow across his fiddle to set up a full chord. "I do hope we're not intruding."

Roman remembered his manners. "Of course not. We're celebrating the birthdays of our sons, and all are welcome here this day."

Wilkinson inclined his head gracefully. "And this"—he turned that handsome smile immediately to Kitty—"must surely be your lady. I had heard she was a beauty, and now see that that was hardly praise enough. Mistress Gentry," he said, catching her hand up to kiss it, "permit me to introduce myself . . . once an officer under General Gates, now but a poor merchant, and content to be so out here in this rich land of Kentucky. General James Wilkinson, entirely at your service."

Kitty's cheeks colored prettily. "I had guessed as much, sir," she said. And as she drew her hand back, the palm tilting upward to reveal the scar, Wilkinson's eyes flickered as he saw it, but the unctuous smile never changed.

"Mistress Gentry is no stranger to me," Josiah Langford broke in. "I had my family at Boonesborough for a time, and my sweet daughter Hettie still talks of her most accomplished schoolma'am."

"How is Hettie, Mr. Langford? And your wife Sallie? Well, I hope."

"Well, indeed. The two of them. Hettie nearly as tall as her mother. We make our home in Lexington now. Ah, things do change, don't they." He leaned forward slightly, fleshy jowls showing the dark shadow of his overcoarse beard. "I'm quite sure that Boonesborough is the poorer for Roman having spirited you away."

"There was little spiriting." Kitty smiled up at her husband. "I came most willingly. And glad enough to turn the education of the children over to a capable young schoolmaster from Richmond. 'Tis enough for me to see to Michael's lessons, and those of the Luttram children when they care to join us."

"Aha!" Wilkinson said. "You *are* still teaching, then." He turned to Roman, shaking his head and chuckling. "Our good wives and mothers, eh? What should we be without them, we poor menfolk?''

"What indeed?'' Langford joined in.

Kitty smiled politely and glanced toward Roman. "Hungry, I expect,'' she said, "which you gentlemen must be now. Pray do go and join our other guests and help yourselves.''

Roman nodded. "Some good corn whiskey is being passed.''

"You're most kind.'' Wilkinson bowed again, and Langford smiled his jowly smile.

Roman watched them as they walked away, glancing down finally to see that Kitty was doing the same. "So that is General Wilkinson,'' she said, her voice low enough that none could hear but him. "Lord, but he is a peacock, isn't he? And Langford . . . I confess I never cared for Mr. Langford.''

Roman wanted to kiss her, right there for all to see, but he contented himself with a smile.

It was later in the afternoon, when the stomachs were full and the fiddling and dancing ended for a while, with the ladies collected in the shade at the far side of the house and the younger children napping, that some of the men gathered in the house, in the dining room, to sit around the long table. The door into the kitchen stood open, and the breeze had free passage from front to back windows. The bare floorboards, wide and gleaming, seemed cool without the rugs that would be there in the winter. Pewter mugs lined the sideboard, and, at Roman's direction, the men helped themselves and passed a jug of brandy, the talk turning to politics.

"By the Eternal,'' Isaac Shelby said, "we are besieged by matters domestic and otherwise. The Indians to the north of us, biding their time, and now the damned Spaniards would close the Mississippi to us, deny us the right to raft our goods down to New Orleans and those lucrative markets. . . . Gentlemen, 'twould seem that seeking statehood for Kentucky is the only sensible solution, since our mother state of Virginia is so preoccupied with her own problems that she cannot concern herself with ours.''

"That is your position also, is it not?'' General Wilkinson addressed Roman.

"It is,'' said Roman, "and well known to all. It is at the heart of the election next month for delegates to the convention in August.''

"And you are standing for that election here in your county, I understand,'' Wilkinson said.

Roman nodded. "And you, General . . . you have been out here a year or so now. Surely you have formed some opinion on the matter by now."

"Well . . ." Wilkinson leaned forward, elbows on the smooth cherry tabletop, looking about the gathering to bestow his ingratiating smile. "There can be little question but that Kentucky's future is bright indeed. Just what course it will or should take will likely be decided by wiser, and older, men than I. However, to press for separation from Virginia seems to me to be the first step, I would certainly agree to that."

"But there are those aplenty who don't see it that way," argued one of the delegates from the May convention. "Those who think 'twould be ruination to leave the protection of Virginia."

"*Protection!*" Ben Logan growled. "What protection is there to be had of them, tell me that?"

"They are hard-pressed, I grant you, with the war debt hanging over them," said Isaac Shelby, "their attentions turned to the problems of the new nation . . . still, they send us not the smallest help."

"Aye," Logan said, "and the savages are about whatever mischief they can manage still. John Floyd shot down from ambush. Walker Daniel killed in the same way."

Roman saw Daniel shake his head and look down at his hands, folded hard-palmed and leathery in his lap. John Floyd, appointed the first judge of the Kentucky judicial district only a few weeks before his murder, had been a good friend of his. And Walker Daniel had laid out the town of Danville, where district court and the conventions were now held.

Isaac Shelby lifted his mug and took a long swig, pursing his lips and snuffling as he set the brandy back on the table before him. "Ah, gentlemen, these very outrages have awakened painful memories for my dear wife. If you'll recall, her own father, Nathanial Hart, was slain in much the same way some years back."

"Aye . . ." came from several throats at once.

"Yet," Logan continued, "those in power in Richmond say that we should refrain from crossing into Indian territory again to punish the savages, by God!"

There were nods and glum looks from about the room, and one of Roman's fellow delegates from the convention began to rummage in his pocket for his pipe. Remembering his duties as host, Roman went into the kitchen and brought back a lighted taper, which he passed around to those who would smoke. The rich smell of tobacco soon permeated the room.

"Gentlemen"—Wilkinson puffed delicately at his own pipe, a costly thing, carved and elegant with its long stem held out from him—"methinks that the Indian problem will solve itself. What with new settlers pouring in over the mountains and rafting down the Ohio almost daily, it would seem that soon the sheer numbers of the white man would be a discouragement to the savages."

Langford, whom Roman had learned was working for Wilkinson now, was seated beside his employer and nodded his head to set his heavy jaws awaggle. "They will see that they have lost, good sirs," he seconded the general.

There was the flicker of an eye here, the slanting of a brow there, the unspoken agreement of those gathered to the woeful ignorance of the Indian character that Wilkinson and Langford had just revealed. But Wilkinson, wily enough to realize at once that he had made a mistake, met Roman's gaze full on, waving his hand expansively.

"But, of course, I would never presume"—he smiled effusively—"to second-guess some of the men in this room who have contributed so much to this promising country. I defer to your better judgment, gentlemen, whatever it may be. In fact," he said, jumping to his feet, "while I have a sup of this good brandy left, I would claim the privilege of drinking to men of such stature in the opening of this fair land that I cannot express my admiration of them enough. . . . Gentlemen, I give you Mr. Boone . . . Mr. Logan!" He turned from one to the other of them, basking in the smiles of the assembled group and the cheers around, the raising of mugs. "And let us not forget our good host, Roman Gentry!"

As there was a smacking of lips and audible swallows, Ben Logan acknowledged the toast with a polite smile, while Daniel gave a short hard nod and a modest wave of his hand, as if to dismiss the whole thing. Still, Roman thought, the others about the room were beaming as they resumed their seats. Wilkinson was a master indeed at backing away from a misspoken word.

"You've said not a syllable on these weighty matters thus far, Dan'l," Henry Porter sang out from his place at the far end of the table. "What sayee on pressin' for Kaintuck to become a state, full equal o' the others?"

Daniel gave a deprecating shake of his head. "I have neither talent nor taste for politics, Henry. I would leave such to Roman, here, and trust his judgment full well.''

Roman felt a sudden pang as he looked at Daniel, past fifty now and preparing to move on again. The last few years had not dealt kindly with him.

Recently Roman had tried to loan his old friend money, but Daniel had been immovable in his refusal. ''By the Almighty, Roman''—he'd grinned with a touch of his old spirit—''I'm not too old to start afresh! They say Limestone is bulging, what with that being the first jump-off place for those comin' down the Ohio. And plenty of land to be surveyed about . . . I do have some knowledge of that trade, you know. I thank you, kindly enough . . . but never fear. We'll be all right.''

Throughout the house the soft voices of the women echoed, punctuated now and again with the higher pitches of the children, as they all prepared to settle in for the night. Some few were sharing the beds, but the rest cheerfully made do with quilt pallets spread out on the floor wherever a likely spot could be found.

Trace, overexcited still from the long day's events and all of the unfamiliar faces, fought sleep stubbornly, holding out as long as he could, until Kitty took him to the old cherry rocker in Roman's and her bedroom. Now she breathed a sigh of relief as he slept at last, his small body settled into her shoulder, his breath moist and sweet on her neck.

''Mercy me,'' Hester whispered to her, ''I thought he never would give it up. Here''—she reached out to take him carefully—''let me put him down for you.'' She hugged him up to her wide bosom and carried him to Michael's old trundle bed to ease him down beside Charles Willis, who was already sleeping soundly.

''Why don't you go ahead up to bed,'' Kitty suggested softly as she got up from the rocker.

''What about you?''

''I'm just going to make one more trip around to see that everybody has what they need.''

Hester nodded, and they went together into the sitting room, where the simple but well-made furniture was cast into shadowy relief by the single lit taper. The narrow steps, which led from that side of the house to the second story, were snugged flat against the wall just to the right of the door that led out onto the dogtrot, and Hester mounted them now, giving a tired wave of her hand by way of good night. Kitty stayed a moment to exchange a word or two with Fanny Holder, who sat on a pallet, comforting her little girl, who was not much older than Trace and now whined softly.

"She's gettin' a sty on her eye, poor little thing," Fanny said.

Kitty crossed the dogtrot to go into the kitchen, and returned to the sitting room a minute later with a thin slice of potato and a strip of cloth. "Here . . . let's bind this on that eye. It'll soothe her, and draw the fever out by morning."

The pretty child, who favored her mother—a Callaway sure enough, Kitty thought—squirmed about at first, and then quieted as the wet, cool piece of potato soothed the irritated lid.

"Where's Elizabeth?" Kitty asked as they finished tying the remedy in place with the soft cloth.

"Upstairs, I think. Said she was going to sleep in with Hester."

Kitty smiled and nodded as she made her way to the steps. The upstairs was as shadowy as the lower floor had been; a grease lamp or two burned still, along with a taper here and there, just in case someone needed to get up through the night to use the pot. Kitty found Rebecca in the hall that ran above the dogtrot.

"You still up?" she said.

Rebecca nodded. "Nathan was as wild as a March hare. Didn't want to settle down."

"Trace, too," Kitty agreed.

"Jemima finally told him to come in there with hers"— Rebecca jerked her head toward one of the bedrooms—"and thank the Lord they're all asleep now."

"What about you? Do you have a place?"

"There's room in there, but I'm not all that sleepy myself."

"Neither am I," said Kitty. "Come on. Why don't we go down to the kitchen."

There was a second set of stairs—identical to the ones that Kitty had just climbed, but on the opposite side of the hallway— which led down into the dark dining room. The two women took it now, led on by the soft glow from the kitchen that came from the banked coals in the big fireplace. Kitty lit two of the grease lamps and motioned to Rebecca to sit down.

"Would you like some buttermilk?" she asked.

"Lord, no. I'm full as a tick."

They sat at the old kitchen table, its worn walnut top mellowed with hard use and scrubbing. Hester had put a bowl of cockscomb in the center of it.

"Michael went off with the men and older boys?" Rebecca said.

Kitty nodded, smiling. "He begged Roman to let him come. Told him if he stayed here at the house, he'd likely as not end up having to sleep in the same bed as Trace, who'd pee on him sure during the night."

Rebecca laughed. "And Roman gave in."

"Yes," Kitty said. "He spoils both of them."

"And doesn't seem to make the least difference in them."

"Not a hair. You'd think Michael was his own blood son."

The room held the lingering odors of some of the foods prepared earlier that day—onion and cabbage and turnip mingled with the touch of wood smoke. Upstairs, everything was quiet now.

"What of Roman's daughter Hallie?" Rebecca asked. "Do you hear much of her?"

Kitty thought of the letter come but a month ago, in the drawer of Roman's desk. "Marietta writes news of her once or twice a year." She sighed. "We wanted her, you know."

Rebecca nodded.

"But we hadn't considered how much it would hurt Marietta and Samuel if Roman took her away from them . . . or Hallie herself. They're the only parents she's known. Roman saw that once he was there. I was disappointed when he came back without her. I had counted on having the child. I have always wanted to do that for Sara. Dear Sara . . . Still"—she brightened after a moment—"I've promised Roman a dozen, and fully intend to keep that promise."

Rebecca laughed. "He's happy," she said. "I see it in his face."

"He's doing what he's wanted to do."

Rebecca's eyes grew thoughtful, and for a moment she looked toward the dark windows as if she could see through the walls and the night to the rolling hills and valleys, the giant trees, the springs and creeks and rivers, that had beckoned to Daniel since before she had known him. "I never thought that Roman would be content to give up scouting . . . to not be *out there* most of the time."

Kitty shook her head. "He loves it still. But the dreams for it, for Kentucky, were always there. Even in the beginning. I always knew that."

They were silent for a moment, the soft humming of crickets and the higher pitch of the tree frogs drifting through the open windows with the breeze.

"You're lucky, Kitty," Rebecca said at last, her head forward slightly so that her face was in shadow. "It's a blessing for him, and for you. It's all changed so out here, and Roman able to change with it. Daniel . . ." She shook her head and sighed. "It's hard for Daniel to adjust to it."

"He's still set on going to Limestone?" said Kitty.

"Aye. What with all the travel on the river now, he has some notion of opening a tavern. Would you believe it? Daniel, a tavernkeeper?" Those strong, square shoulders of hers lifted just slightly. "Maybe it's for the best," she said. "I've trailed about after him, the children and me, all these years. I expect I can stand one more move . . . if Daniel can just find some contentment there."

* 39 *

KITTY BROUGHT ROMAN HIS STEAMING MUG OF COFFEE in the sitting room, the strong brew giving off a generous whiff of the brandy she'd added. That was the way he liked it, no matter how hot the weather. With brandy or rum. And because of his fondness for it, she made sure that she had a supply of coffee—which could be had from the general store at Boonesborough—on hand all the time. It had become almost a ritual with them of an evening—Roman content with his pipe and his cup, sprawled back in the stout Windsor chair, Kitty nearby with her mending or knitting. And it seemed doubly pleasurable to her this night, since Roman had just returned from Danville after serving at the convention, riding in just in time for supper.

The boys were asleep at last and Hester had only gone up to

bed minutes before as Kitty settled into one of the cherry rockers and took up her basket of socks to be darned.

"Now"—she looked up to meet Roman's eyes and smiled, happy to have him home—"tell me everything that happened in Danville."

He chuckled, removing the pipe stem from his mouth. "Everything? It would bore you for certain, my love. Much of it was standing about waiting for all the delegates to assemble."

Despite his reply, he was pleased with the outcome. She could tell it by the way his lanky frame draped over the chair, by the relaxed lines of his face and the way he savored the brandy-laced coffee when he took it up to have a sip. She waited patiently, working the soft yarn back and forth across the wooden darning egg that filled out the toe of the sock, knowing that Roman might take his time but would eventually tell her all she wanted to know.

"There were thirty delegates in all," he said. "Ben Logan was there . . . and Levi Todd. George Muter was elected presiding officer."

"*Judge* Muter?" Kitty interrupted. She remembered Roman introducing her to a Judge Muter while they were still living at Boonesborough, a husky man of ruddy complexion and a great, gusty laugh.

Roman nodded. "And Wilkinson was there."

Kitty looked up in some surprise. "So the general is interested in politics as well as the mercantile trade!"

" 'Twould seem so . . . or it could be that he's interested in whatever pie he might stick a finger in. Popinjay that he is, though, I will say that he worked as hard as any. He's an intelligent man, I'll give him that," Roman said.

He watched her work, raising his mug to take a long drink and drawing a contented breath once he'd swallowed. "There was a goodly amount of agreement amongst the delegates," he continued, "which means that the people must share our views on statehood or they wouldn't have elected us. We worked the first few days on a paper which set out the difficulties in being separated from our seat of government by nearly five hundred miles and from the nearest Virginia settlements by a mountain range. With that done, the course we should follow seemed clear enough."

He was silent for a long moment, looking down into the bowl of his pipe and then puffing rapidly at the stem end as if it weren't drawing properly.

"And . . ." Kitty prodded him gently.

"And"—he removed the pipe stem from his mouth and looked up at her solemnly—"we drafted a petition that, while acknowledging our debt to Virginia, outlined those difficulties in detail and requested that the legislature consider the separation of Kentucky from the parent state and admission to the Federal Union on Virginia's recommendation."

It suddenly seemed monumental, though they had talked about it many times, to hear it said right out like that. "You've done it, then. . . ." She put aside her darning and leaned toward Roman to find his free hand.

"We've *begun* it." The sober set to his face suddenly gave way to his one-sided smile, and he held fast to her hand.

"And when will the petition be presented?"

"In the fall meeting of the legislature." He let go, smiling still, but two small vertical lines had appeared just above the red brows, midpoint of his forehead . . . a sign that Kitty knew meant he was struggling over some part of it.

He took another drink of the coffee and set the mug back down on the table beside him. "But here I am just home, and glad to be," he said. "Surely there are better things to talk of than politics. The boys seem well enough. What have they been up to since I've been away?"

"One of Trace's jaw teeth came through," she said. "I think he was so excited to have you home that he forgot to show it to you. He has everyone else. Whether they wanted to see it or not," she said, laughing. "And as for Michael . . . two days after you left for Danville, Michael and Lonnie Luttram caught a rabbit in the hollow part of that big old sycamore tree down by the creek . . ."

Roman nodded.

"Only," Kitty went on, "the 'rabbit' proved to be a skunk."

Roman shook his head, and though he grinned roundly, his expression still held a good amount of sympathy. "I'd wager that's a lesson they'll not soon forget."

"I wouldn't be surprised." She grinned back at him. "Polly made Lonnie sleep down at the barn for a couple of nights. She was sure that the smell would make the baby sick." Polly Luttram had had a baby boy a few days after the party, vowing to Kitty and Hester eighteen hours into her labor that it was the last one she intended for Tom to get on her—that shortly before she gritted her teeth and, grunting and groaning, pushed out her twelfth.

Despite his amusement at Michael and Lonnie's mishap, Kitty saw that the small lines were still there in Roman's forehead, and after a few moments she asked him directly: "What is it, Roman? What's troubling you?"

His eyebrows climbed upward. "Nothing," he dissembled.

"Roman . . ." Her voice was soft, but she fastened him with a questioning gaze that would not be turned aside. And after a moment, he grinned wryly.

"Good Lord, Kitty Gentry, it's a fortunate thing that I'm a faithful husband to you. You'd be sure to find me out were I not."

"I would indeed!" she said with mock severity.

He shrugged and gave in to her. "I was elected to present the petition to the legislature, along with George Muter. But I'm beginning to wish I had declined." His pipe had gone out, and he tapped his thumb at the bowl impatiently.

"But, Roman, I don't understand. Why?" She picked up the wax taper and held it while Roman sucked at the pipe until smoke billowed about his head. He nodded his thanks and sat back. "You haven't answered me," she reminded him, and he burst out laughing and swept her onto his lap.

"Roman!" She did her best to muffle the involuntary squeal, giggling and holding the burning candle away from them.

Still grinning, he took it from her and set it back on the candle stand. "I had no idea you were going to turn into a nagging wife," he said, "but if you must know my every thought . . ." He paused and sobered. "I wish I'd declined because I'm just now realizing how much I'll miss you . . . and the boys. These last twelve days have seemed long enough, and then some, to be away."

"Oh, Roman," she said, looking into his eyes, the love she felt for him so strong that she thought she must surely weep with it . . . or shout. How could anyone ever be so lucky? She drew the tip of her finger down the hard edge of his jawline. "You must go, you know," she said, her voice serious now. " 'Tis an honor to be chosen. Besides, you're the best one to present the petition."

He smiled. "You could be prejudiced, my love." His forehead wrinkled, those red brows of his drawing closer together, and he tapped the pipe stem lightly against his front teeth as he considered the consequences if he went. "There's the gristmill . . . I had intended to begin work on the sluiceway this fall, while the river is low." Some weeks earlier Roman had announced his intention to build a gristmill at the junction of the river and the creek. "It's the perfect spot for one," he'd said. "And we can grind not only our own grain, but the grain of farmers 'round about for a small fee, or share."

"Well, you can still start on it," Kitty said. "There's time enough before you'd have to leave. And Tom Luttram is dependable. He and the boys can carry on with it once you've gone."

"Hmmmm . . ." He pondered it, nodding his head. "I guess I could." He put aside his pipe and drew her closer, kissing her neck while his hand cupped through the thin linen of her blouse. "Perhaps we should think about that tomorrow, though."

"I doubt Hester's asleep yet," Kitty whispered, the familiar warm stirrings between her legs growing ever stronger. It had been impossible to sit in his lap and not know that he was stirring, too. Twelve days *was* a long time to be apart.

"Well, then . . ." There was a sudden gleam in the blue eyes, and he grinned as he set her on her feet and rose to take her hand and lead her toward the door, tiptoeing with a comical exaggeration as they escaped the house. But once beyond the dogtrot and out under the deep reaches of the night sky, he pulled her along, running lightly, both of them stifling their laughter as they raced down the hill toward the spring and beyond.

They veered away from the spring and headed toward the woods, stopping finally by the clump of huge elderberry bushes down that way, breathless and laughing still. Roman caught her up to bring her against him. "Lord, Lord . . . I do love you," he said, coming down on the soft, sweet-smelling grass and drawing her down with him.

"Roman," she chided half-heartedly, "we can't do it *here*!"

"Why not?" He pulled her beneath him, grinning down at her, and the laughter bubbled in her throat again, low and heady with the wanting of him.

"Someone might see," she whispered, arching to him in spite of herself as he undid her buttons, his hands finding the all-too-willing flesh.

"Who . . . tell me, who?" His mouth found hers, tasting her.

"Someone," she gasped between kisses. "One of the Luttrams, maybe . . ."

"No, they're all asleep. Besides, we've got the bushes to hide us." He drew his head down to kiss her throat, his lips moving in a line to the soft hollow of it. "It may well be," he growled, "the best use an elderberry clump has ever been put to."

And in another second she had thrown prudence to the winds and pulled him closer.

Roman returned from the East with good news. The legislature had looked upon the petition of the Kentuckians with favor, though they had attached some considerations to their ultimate approval. In the bill that was passed, the legislators declared that the matter of separation must be subject to agreement—no later than June first of the following year—by the Continental Congress that Kentucky would be admitted into the Federal Union at "some convenient time in the future." And they directed that yet another assemblage of delegates must be held at Danville on the fourth Monday of September, to speak for "the good people of the district" and declare in due form whether it was indeed their will that the district become a state, independent of Virginia.

Roman was well pleased, both with the results of his efforts and to be home again. Tom Luttram and his sons had kept the place in good order, the work on the gristmill was proceeding nicely, and everyone looked forward to the arrival of the big grinding stones, which Roman had ordered while he was in the East. They would be sent down the Ohio and then overland.

Spring passed and summer came quickly; the boys' birthdays were marked with a party again, this time without Daniel and Rebecca, who were living in Limestone now. It seemed hard for Kitty to believe that a whole year had gone by since she and Rebecca had sat in the kitchen, talking late into the night. She would miss her.

With the passing of Trace's third birthday, Kitty had begun to wonder why she hadn't conceived again. Surely, she laughed as she confided her disappointment to Hester and Polly Luttram, it was not for lack of trying.

"An old doctor woman I knew years back told me if Pleas and me did it on the night of a full moon," Hester offered, " 'twas certain to take. But as you see, it surely did *me* no good."

"Lord love ye," Polly said, "be grateful for a little rest in between. Just look at me," she lamented, gazing down at a belly that was clearly rounding again despite her vow during her last labor . . . the result of which perched on her hip now, saliva drooling down his chin as he got his pudgy little fingers entwined in his mother's hair and hung on to make Polly's eyes water.

The three women had gathered at the far side of the house to admire Hester's bed of Sweet William and foxglove. Out of the corner of her eye Polly caught sight of her eldest daughter, carrying a basket of eggs from the barn. "Celie," she called, "put them in the kitchen for Mistress Kitty and then come here and spell me with this young'un." She turned back to the two women. "My back is purely killin' me."

"Here," said Hester, "give him to me."

Despite what they'd said, Kitty still hoped that she would get pregnant before too much longer. A girl would be nice. She knew that it had hurt Roman to have to give up Hallie. Maybe, she thought, if they had a girl, it would help make up for it.

Right now, though, Roman seemed happy enough seeing to the crops and conferring with the millwright who'd arrived from Pennsylvania to oversee the final stages of the mill's construction. Walter Maynard, a pink-cheeked and plump little man who filled his short breeches nearly to bursting, settled happily into the routine of the place, bragging on Hester's cooking and invariably reaching for seconds and sometimes thirds. Work on the mill proceeded rapidly.

The millhouse, a hewn log structure about sixteen by twenty situated at the river's edge, was virtually complete now, except for the grinding stones—which still hadn't arrived—and the erection of the big wheel. And on the day that it was to go up, everyone gathered at the riverbank to watch.

The millwright, wire spectacles askew on his face, scurried about with surprising agility as Roman and Tom Luttram shouted out orders to Earl Thomas and James, the two oldest Luttram boys, who were urging the four-horse team forward. And as the animals haunched down, digging at the soft earth with their hooves, ropes and pulleys creaking, the big paddle wheel was hoisted up and swung in.

"Don't force it!" Maynard cautioned. "Careful . . . careful . . ." With plump hands gesticulating, he oversaw the fitting of the hub onto the big spindle, which hooked to the gears that would in turn rotate the stones once they'd arrived and were set in.

"If he don't watch, he's goin' to fall in sure," Hester told Kitty. "But if he did, he'd likely float easy as a bottle cork."

"Now," Kitty teased, "I do believe Mr. Maynard has an eye for you."

"Bosh!" Hester drew herself up and pursed her lips. "It's my corn puddin' that interests him. Besides"—she smothered a sudden burst of laughter—"I much doubt he could get it out from betwixt those fat legs—far enough to do any good, leastways."

"Hester!" Kitty grinned, and Polly, standing nearby, doubled over with merriment.

The wheel finally in place, Michael turned a limbery cartwheel. Trace, watching, made a valiant try at one himself but landed flat on his back to set up a loud wail and bring Bear trotting up to lick at his face, tail wagging.

"Lordy me, you're goin' to kill yourself." Hester clucked her tongue over him, and Kitty hurried to pick him up and pat him.

"It just takes a little practice. . . ." Michael darted in to console his little brother. "Maybe best done in the hay pile," he added.

As a big boy now, Trace bit back the pain of his skinned elbows and set his mouth stubbornly against any more tears. Kitty smiled as she watched him give his freckled nose a swipe and then wiggle down to go running after Michael and the other boys.

It was after the wheel was in place that Roman commenced campaigning for the convention, passing out handwritten papers that stated his position clearly in the towns about the county. Flanders Callaway, on his way down to Crab Orchard to buy a horse from a man there, visited for the night and declared over a cup of brandy that Roman would win if he didn't lift a finger. "There's no man the people of Madison County trust more to speak for them," he said.

Roman dismissed that with a shake of his head.

A letter had arrived from Daniel, Flanders told them. The Boones were well, the tavern he'd opened prospering. But the Indian trouble grew worse daily up there. Horses stolen. A boy too far from his cabin carried off. A man out working his land found with his head split open and his scalp gone. And hardly a week passed that some tale of settlers attacked on their way down the Ohio didn't reach Limestone. "Daniel says they grow bolder all the time. He thinks we'll have to do something about it, or the day will come again that none of us will be safe."

On the same day that Roman received the news that he had been elected a delegate to the September convention, the millstones arrived and the upcoming convention was all but forgotten for the time being. The stones were set in place within twenty-four hours, and for the first time the water was channeled upward along the sluiceway, narrowing in until it came with a rush; the big wheel shuddered for an instant and then began its slow turn with a creaking *whoosh* of sound, the spray flying.

The word spread quickly that the Gentry mill was in operation, and with the corn crop not too far from harvest, there were settlers who rode over or stopped Roman in the dusty streets of Boonesborough—which was an open town now, the pickets and gates that had made up the fort long since torn down—to tell him that they intended to bring their grain out to him and inquire about a price.

One fellow, as lean and worn as the plow points he'd brought in to have ground down, accosted him at Oliver Burdette's blacksmith shop. "I've little in the way o' hard currency," the fellow said, his underjaw thrust forward as if he'd learned to expect a fight for what he got. Roman remembered seeing him before. He'd come out only a year or so earlier, he and others like him— men who'd heard of the rich land of Kentucky and come over the mountains without tools to work it or two bits in their pockets to buy any, with little more than a brood of children and a wife old before her time . . . but determined to carve out a better life.

"No matter," Roman said mildly. "We'll grind on the shares."

The man shoved his hands into his breeches pockets and eyed Roman suspiciously. "And how big would you reckon your share to be, Mr. Gentry?"

"Whatever you think is fair," Roman shot back at once. And the narrowed eyes flew open, Adam's apple bobbing a time or two before the fellow nodded his head in a quick jerk and went on about his business with Oliver, who was stifling a grin.

Roman had brought in his chestnut stallion to be shod, and he led it now across the straw-strewn dirt floor to one of the stalls and took off the saddle. It was the horse with the pockmark in its hoof that he had tracked all the way to the Shawnee camp where he'd seen the Old Colonel's scalp . . . and barely escaped with his life, thanks in part to the animal, he thought now as he ran a hand over the sleek withers. The stallion had put his mark on his get surely enough; there were half a dozen on the place now that were the image of him. But Roman was still partial to Sundowner, as he called him. There hadn't been a horse since the Chippewa gelding he'd lost at the Battle of Blue Licks that he prized quite as much.

The blacksmith shop was filled with the mingled scents of hay and smoke from the forge and fresh horse droppings. Roman lingered by the stallion for a moment until he heard the man who'd spoken to him earlier call his name.

"Name's Morgan," the fellow said. "Enoch Morgan. And I take some pride in bein' an honest man, Mr. Gentry, so I'll say right out that I didn't cast my vote for you this last election. But"—his Adam's apple rose and plunged again—"I expect I will next time." With that he turned and made his way to the broken-down wagon outside and hauled himself up to creak and wobble away, his old horse plodding ahead beneath the brassy afternoon sun.

"Well," Oliver said, grinning, "looks like you won yourself a constituent, Roman."

Roman shoved his old leather hat back and looked after the wagon, watching as the wheels churned the dust to a fine cloud. It was not, he thought, the way he would wish to win votes. Still, he would do his best to make it easier for men like Morgan to get on their feet. A free way down the Mississippi for their goods would go far in helping, provided the Continental Congress could be dissuaded from bargaining away to the Spaniards the Westerners' rights of passage. It was one of the reasons that Kentucky must become a state, with a full voice in such matters.

When he arrived home, he remembered to tell Tom Luttram to let Enoch Morgan set his own share rate when he brought his corn over to be ground.

The day was fast approaching when he must leave for Danville, and Kitty busied herself with getting his clothes in order. It simply wouldn't do, she told him—as she told him every time— for a delegate to the convention to appear in anything but his best black woolen frock coat and his newest weskit.

"I'd as soon go in my buckskins," he groaned, grinning to show that in the end he would give in to her, as he had each time before.

But on the eve of his scheduled departure, a courier arrived with a brief message from Ben Logan, scrawled on a piece of paper, directing him to report to Limestone immediately. And signed as it was with Logan's full rank, "Benjamin Logan, Brigadier General, Kentucky Militia," instead of just "Ben," Roman knew at once what it meant. With or without Richmond's permission, they were going to move against the Indians.

The rider who'd brought it stayed barely long enough to gulp down a plate of food before he went on his way again, tipping his sweat-stained hat to Hester and Kitty on his way out. Now Roman stood looking down at the missive one more time before he passed it to Kitty to read.

"Michael"—he strode out into the dogtrot and called to the boy—"you and Lonnie go see if you can catch up Sundowner for me. I'll be down in a little to saddle him."

He turned back to the door to find Kitty standing there, looking out at him. "You're going?" she said.

"Of course. A militia scout is under as much obligation to obey his general as any other."

"But the convention, Roman . . ."

"Will have to wait."

The coat, and the weskit, and Roman's best linen shirts, were forgotten as Kitty went to put half a cold johnnycake and some ham into a sack for him. She grabbed up two ripe apples from a bowl on the table and put those in, too.

Roman took a few minutes to tell Tom Luttram what had happened and instruct him to see to the place during his absence, then he came up to the house, leading the chestnut stallion.

He swung Trace up. "You be good, now, will you? And do what your mama tells you?"

"I will. . . ." Trace threw his arms about his father's neck and hugged him as tightly as he could, his little face screwed up with an unfocused awareness that there was something different in his father's leaving this time. Roman hugged him back, then kissed him and set him down.

"And you, son"—he turned to Michael—"I know I can depend on you."

"Yes, sir, Papa." Big as he was now, Roman caught Michael up in a bear hug, too. Then he turned to Kitty.

"Looks like buckskins after all." He grinned down at her.

It was a strange feeling for both of them, being pulled back to something they'd thought long behind them. The sound of the iron oven door clanged in the kitchen, where Hester, who'd made her good-byes already, was putting in a pan of apple Betty to bake. And down toward the Luttrams' cabin Celie and one of the younger girls were spreading wash out to dry on the bushes. The cows grazed near the woods. As the warm breeze stirred the tendrils of hair about Kitty's face, Roman could see the apprehension in her eyes, though she managed to smile confidently.

"I'll be back—" He said it firmly, pausing for a moment

before he finished. "—just as soon as I can." He leaned down to kiss her, and she held to him for a moment.

"Be sure you take care of yourself, Roman Gentry," she whispered.

He swung up on the stallion, putting it to the trot, and before he reached the far trees he turned once and waved. He was strangely excited. It had been four years since he'd ridden north of the Ohio with Clark after the Battle of Blue Licks. Four years of being a farmer and a politician. He was thirty-five years old. Was his eye as sharp, his hand as fast?

"Yes, by God!" He said it aloud, suddenly exhilarated at the prospect of testing himself, aware of the hard muscles of his stomach and thighs. He had not gone to fat as some men did when they started to add a little age.

He grinned, kicking his heels lightly against the red-brown flanks to spur the horse ahead, leaning down to clear the limbery branches that whipped by. He had made his choices, and he was well pleased with them. But right now he felt again that wild calling that had drawn him so totally when he was younger. Still, he was able to laugh at himself a little now. Given the path he had set his foot to, he was going off on what could well be his last time to ride out against the Indians, his last hurrah. . . . And he knew it.

The common room at Daniel's tavern, though furnished with the plainest of tables and chairs, was spacious and cheery, the white oak floors scrubbed with river sand until they gave off a soft gleam. Pewter mugs were lined along a broad shelf, and iron pots clustered on the hearth of the huge fireplace. Daniel had clearly prospered since coming to Limestone, Roman thought. "Clean beds and good food," an old riverman had assured him as he'd ridden into the busy town and asked his way. "And Dan'l be the best surveyor around here. Much in demand, 'e is, good sir!"

Roman regarded his old friend, across the table from him now, and decided that he had never seen Daniel looking as content with life. The old woodsman sat with his chair tilted back against the log wall behind him, his hand cradling a noggin of rum punch against a middle that had gained a few inches in girth since Roman had seen him last.

"I receive more in the way of surveying than I can do. And have been able to lay a few claims for myself and children," he said.

"A few claims!" Simon Kenton, who was seated to Roman's left, snorted. "You are looking, Roman, at a man who is fast becoming wealthy . . . in land, at least."

Daniel grinned, and Ben Logan, who was opposite Kenton, nodded. "Aye," he said, "and I know of no one who deserves it more."

Though the hour was late, there were still two gentlemen at a table not far from the fireplace, a pair of river pilots on their way down to Louisville, as the town at the falls had been named. Rebecca approached them now to see if they wanted any more of the good stew she had served up earlier or another mug of punch; but they declined and, yawning, soon mounted the steps to one of the plain rooms above, bidding the proprietor and the three others at table good night as they went.

"And you . . ." Rebecca came up to Daniel and the rest, smiling but obviously worn from the long day. "Can I fetch you some more punch?"

"We can fetch our own," Daniel said, reaching a hand to rub at her shoulder. "Why don't you go ahead to bed?"

"But what of Major McGary?" she asked. "Won't he expect to eat when he returns?"

"McGary is here?" Roman asked, aware of Simon Kenton's muttered oath. Hugh McGary had not been too popular among his fellow officers since his part in the Battle of Blue Licks.

"Aye," Daniel said. "He came in yesterday. But a plate left before the fire will do well enough for him," he told Rebecca. "I expect he's out gaming. They say he's a taste for it."

Rebecca nodded. "As soon as I help Eulie finish, then, I'll go up . . . and I'll bid you good night now, gentlemen." She smiled at the men gathered at the table with her husband, all of them old friends.

Daniel watched her as she joined the girl, who was emptying the leftover stew into a smaller pot. "With none left to home but the three youngest, I thought 'twould be well to buy her a girl to help with the work. But I declare she works harder than the wench still."

"That is like Rebecca," Roman agreed.

The men sipped their strong drinks, and once Rebecca and the girl had departed and they had the place to themselves, their talk turned to the task at hand.

"There is evidence and to spare," Logan said, "that the Wabash tribes—the Miami and Piankeshaw and Wea—are negotiating with the Shawnee to form a confederation."

"Aye," said Kenton. "And if that plan goes unchecked, there'd be worse than hell to pay."

Logan's dark brows drew nearly together. "Detroit is still yet occupied by the damned British despite the Treaty of Paris naming it American territory. And 'twould seem that the Brits are up to their old tricks again. Two braves were captured near here with brand-new British rifles in their possession. By heaven"—Logan's scowl deepened—"'tis easy enough for them in the East to speak of their 'invasion law,' which declares it illegal for us to cross the Ohio to protect ourselves! 'Twill not be *their* women and children under the knife!"

Roman nodded. "George Clark has gone already?"

"Aye," Daniel said. "Two weeks past. Marching toward the Wabash camps. He will strike there while we hit the Shawnee towns."

"We'll ferry our men across the river under cover of darkness," Logan said. "Try to surprise them if we can. And take as many prisoners as possible. That way we can trade for white captives."

"How many men?" Roman asked.

"Between seven and eight hundred," Logan answered, a proud gleam lighting his dark eyes. "We had to beat the bushes to turn out George's troops, but I did not need to ask twice to have Kentuckians rally against the Shawnee."

As if by unspoken agreement the men raised their drinks again. Kenton, elbows planted on the table before him, hunched forward grinning, his eyes alight with the prospect of riding with his old friends once more. "By God, it occurs to me that, but for Ben, we are like to have the best noses in Kaintuck!" He touched a finger to his own downturned beak while eyeing Daniel's humped appendage and Roman's sculptured hawk face. "It may well be that a fine nose gives a man an edge in the wilderness."

As the others broke into loud guffaws, Logan considered it. "You may be right," he conceded wryly. "As I recall, George Clark is no slouch when it comes to noses, and he hasn't done so badly, either."

"Never mind, Ben," Roman consoled him. "You're surely the handsomest one amongst us."

✳ 40 ✳

THE TASK OF FERRYING THE ASSEMBLED MEN AND HORSES across the wide and deep Ohio was one that took up an entire night and the better part of the following day, so that once under way, the full complement had only drawn above the mouth of Eagle Creek to reach the gap in the river hills before darkness set in and they must make camp. And as Roman and Kenton readied themselves to head right out again, the men around them grumbling about food rations already, Roman slapped at a mosquito and grinned at the big hook-nosed scout. "I'd just as soon have sat down to one of Hester's meals myself," he admitted ruefully, looking down at the nearly empty cup of cornmeal and maple sugar and water, most of which he'd just swigged down.

Kenton grunted, wiping out his own cup and tucking it back into the front of his hunting shirt. "Might not be roast pork and sweet 'taters," he said of the dry mixture they carried in their saddlebags to mix with water when a quick meal was needed, "but it'll hold us till we git the chance to eat proper."

After a word with Logan, they fell into step and headed for their horses. They hadn't bothered to hobble them, and Sundowner nickered softly and took a few steps forward as Roman drew near.

"Good-lookin' animal," Kenton said. "We ought to race sometime."

"You'd get beaten," Roman bantered.

They swung up into their saddles and lifted a hand to each other as they headed in different directions. Though there were guards posted, it wouldn't hurt to scout about a ways, Daniel had said, just to be safe before they settled down for the night.

But in the next few days the army was confronted with nothing worse than the persistent mosquitoes and the unusually hot weather, which caused the troops to mop at their faces with their shirttails and swear. And then one steamy afternoon Daniel and his men broke away from the main group to head for a small Shawnee camp he recalled that lay just to the east, only to find the place seemingly deserted. It was a hunting camp, not always inhabited, but when Roman swung down to rake back the dirt and ashes from what appeared to be an old campfire, he squinted up at Daniel.

"Still warm," he said.

"They knew we were near," said Daniel. And as some of the troopers stamped about, checking each of the lodges to be sure that no one was hiding within, he eased up in his stirrups, deep-set eyes sweeping the surrounding countryside. There were hills farther east, and to the north of the camp a creek meandered through a canebreak.

Roman lifted his head as he heard a dog bark not far up above them along the creekbank, and his eyes met Daniel's. The old woodsman had already lifted his hand to signal the men.

"All right, boys, mount up," Boone called. And they gathered, horses stamping and jostling, to await his orders as the hound's high voice sounded again and was joined by several others. "Where there's dogs, there's like to be Indians," Daniel said. "Remember, we'll take prisoners where we can . . . but see to yourselves."

At Daniel's command they moved out cautiously, spreading wide. Just as they caught sight of the dogs, four or five Shawnee sprinted through the trees, and another, tall and big-chested, jumped from behind a huge boulder. He stood upright, looking straight into Daniel's face across the hundred yards that separated them, black eyes glittering with recognition before he broke for the cover of the tall cane.

"Mind that fellow!" Daniel shouted, his voice cracking strangely. And the Shawnee swung his rifle around to get off a shot as he ran, muscular legs moving effortlessly.

Roman heard the whine of the bullet as it passed between Daniel and him and, almost as soon, heard that peculiar *thwack* as flesh was struck and the gasping grunt that followed. A quick backward glance revealed one of the younger of the volunteers, slumped forward in his saddle, clutching at his midsection.

Another bullet slammed into a nearby tree, splintering the wood with a loud *twang*, and Roman was down and running, memory stirring. Big Jim. It had been a long time, but that's who it was. The brave who'd called Daniel friend . . . who'd visited the cabin on the Yadkin and then had tortured James Boone to death in Powell's Valley, more than thirteen years before.

The Kentuckians were down from their mounts and taking cover now to return the fire that came from different directions. Roman plunged into the thick cane at the point where he'd seen the big Indian enter it just seconds before. The stalks pressed in around him, towering over his head, and he moved through the thick growth as silently as possible, eyes searching the soft damp ground underfoot, picking up the almost imperceptible mark that a moccasin had left at the root of a stalk in passing. The air was so thick and hot that he had to try hard not to pant, controlling his breathing. And then not far ahead he heard that slightest sound, a root snapping, and he braced himself as, suddenly, that big body came crashing through toward him, ax raised.

With a kind of cold satisfaction, he swiveled the barrel of his rifle upward, pulling the trigger as he ducked sideways, the sound bursting in his head as he remembered James Boone's face—the boy had had Rebecca's eyes and Daniel's steadfast gaze. One summer he had helped James to build a tree house, and together, on a day heavy with the smell of honeysuckle, hidden there in the cool green leaves, they'd watched as two baby robins emerged, blind and featherless, from their pale blue eggs . . .

The Shawnee gasped, clawing at his naked chest, which was suddenly smeared with red. He threw back his head to wail out a prayer to his Great Spirit that was almost a triumph . . . a song . . . rising and falling in the air that was nearly impossible to breathe. And then he fell, stiff cane stalks cracking, a faint smell, almost as sweet as honeysuckle, drifting upward.

In a moment Roman realized that Daniel was behind him, face grayed, the skin stretched taut about his mouth. "I thank you for James," Daniel said, looking down at the man who'd taken that young life. He wiped his eyes and blinked. "One score settled, I'd reckon. I'll tell Rebecca. Though right now, it don't seem to give me much."

The Kentuckians were dispirited when, after several raids, they had found few prisoners to take and had only been able to burn a few villages, destroying crops as they went. But Logan decided to lead an advance group against the Indian town of Mackachack, and one morning just after dawn the troops charged, howling at the top of their lungs as they went in.

What few braves there were scattered out in the tall grasses and were soon rounded up to join the squaws, and children, and old people herded into the middle of the town. It had been the same wherever they went. But now Roman was surprised to see old Chief Moluntha, who came shuffling out of the milling group, smiling his toothless smile and lifting his hand in greeting. He was dressed in a loose-fitting white robe, a battered old black cocked hat atop his head.

"How'd'ee do?" he called, catching sight of Roman and Ben Logan, his shambling gait setting up small puffs of dust about his moccasined feet. "Baawd-ler . . ." He spied Simon Kenton and addressed him, as best he could, by the name Simon had used for so long before he admitted to Kenton.

All three of the men lifted their hands in reply. "Moluntha," Kenton said. And then to his two companions: "He don't seem much daunted to be took prisoner."

"No," Logan said, "and with reason. He's come in to Limestone more than once to negotiate with officials for an exchange of prisoners. But some of the younger braves in the tribal councils have been slow to go along with him. Still, the old man's trying."

Despite Moluntha's greetings, he could speak or understand little English, and Logan called for an interpreter. "Get Breedlove up here," he ordered, and the call went back for a man among the troops who'd been at the salt licks and taken along with Daniel back in '78. Nearly four years of captivity before his escape had been ample time to learn the Shawnee tongue well.

"Where are your warriors?" Logan asked once Breedlove had explained to old Moluntha that the general wanted to ask him some questions.

"Gone," Moluntha replied in the Shawnee tongue, gesturing to the west. "Many days ago."

"Where?" Logan wanted to know.

"To fight with Miami, and Wea, and Piankeshaw . . . against the Long Knife."

"The Long Knife . . . George Clark," Roman said, the men exchanging glances.

"Claarrrk . . . Claarrk . . ." Moluntha nodded, small dark eyes all but lost in a face that had wrinkled to a fine webbed mahogany.

"Ask him how many warriors went to join the Wabash tribes," Logan directed.

Moluntha extended his arms, the sleeves of his loose robe stirring in the breeze. "From all Maykujay towns . . . all Wapatomica towns . . . many warriors gone . . ." With his complicated calculations, they finally figured out that he was saying upward of four hundred braves had gone to join Chief Little Turtle on the Wabash.

An old squaw had hovered near during the entire questioning, watching Moluntha with anxious eyes, gnarled fingers plucking nervously at the beading on her tunic. *"Keewa?"* Roman asked the old chief, using the Shawnee word he thought to mean "wife" and gesturing toward her.

Moluntha grinned and nodded, grunting his satisfaction with his old woman. And Roman, in his less than perfect Shawnee, tried to tell her that she had nothing to fear. His attempt seemed at least partially successful. Though she continued to cast sidelong looks at the Shemanese from time to time, she no longer appeared to be so worried for her mate.

Logan, after issuing strict orders for the care of the prisoners, detailed half a dozen privates with seeing to the safety of the old chief, then he and Kenton prepared to head back to the main camp where Daniel was, to tell him the news of Moluntha's capture. Surely it would give them some bargaining power when the time came to talk of exchange.

Still a fine-looking man with only a little spread through his middle and a touch of gray creeping in at his temples, Logan swung up into the saddle with a suppleness nearly the equal of the young militiamen under his command. "Are you riding back with us?" he called to Roman.

"If you don't need me, I'll stay here."

Logan nodded and headed his horse out, and all but those who'd been ordered to stay fell in behind him. Kenton lifted his hand to Roman and put his horse to the gallop. He would scout ahead.

Roman's stomach was growling—though the sun was high in the sky, he had not yet eaten—and he dug through his saddlebags for some jerked beef and parched corn and sat down in the shade of a tree to chew at it . . . watching with some amusement as Moluntha calmly cut a leaf of tobacco into small pieces, taking his time to stuff the bowl of his clay pipe until it suited him, patting at the cut leaf with a knobby old finger.

Once the old man was satisfied, he took up a dry twig and lit it in the cookfire, where the squaws had begun to prepare the noonday meal, laying the burning twig to the pipe bowl and sucking at the stem until white smoke wreathed his head.

He smiled and offered the pipe to his guards, who nodded and grinned and took a puff themselves. They were farmboys, young and friendly, their faces showing their amazement that a chief of the Shawnee could be so little different from their old grandpas back home. Moluntha, Roman thought, had never been the fierce war chief that Black Fish had been. There had always been something likable about the old fellow.

Finished with his meal, Roman tossed the last small piece of jerky to one of the dogs that lurked about, then hauled himself up to walk down to a spring that bubbled out of the rocks not far away. The water was cold and clear, and Roman drank deeply, wiping his mouth with the back of his hand, his head coming up in a moment at the sound of hooves in the distance. One horse, he thought, coming in at a good clip from the south. And once the animal had come into view, he recognized the rider, swearing under his breath. McGary . . .

He'd given the man a wide berth whenever he could throughout their duty north of the river. He'd never liked him, and time had not changed it.

As he turned into the bushes to relieve himself, he wondered what McGary had come for. And in a moment the sound of the major's voice, raised and demanding, drifted to him.

"Are you questioning my authority, private?"

"No, sir." The young militiaman's answer was low enough that Roman could just barely make out the words.

"Then stand aside!" McGary barked.

The man was an ass, Roman thought as he directed his hearty stream into the tall thick grass. Always flaunting his rank.

"Goddamn you, answer me!" McGary's voice carried to Roman again after a little, and he hurriedly finished with what he was doing. God's blood! What was the man up to?

"Were you . . . ?" McGary shouted.

Roman could see that it was Moluntha who was being confronted, and uneasy now, he quickened his pace toward the old chief and the circle of young militiamen set to guard him, who were regarding one another with confusion now in the face of McGary's high-handed ways.

Moluntha's squaw was hovering anxiously again.

"I said, were you at the Blue Licks?" McGary demanded, moving closer to Moluntha as if to threaten him. *"Answer me!"*

Roman felt a sudden throbbing at his temples and shouted out a warning. "McGary . . . hold up!" He was no more than twenty-five feet away now. But the old chief, trying his best to placate the officer, nodded his head and smiled amiably, holding out his pipe in a gesture of friendship. . . .

"Damn you!" McGary shouted. "I'll give you Blue Licks!" Face purpling, he snatched up a small ax of the kind used by the squaws to cut up meat and, to Roman's horror, swung it in an arc that ended against Moluntha's skull.

There was that instant of silence as the old man fell, everything quiet and suddenly still under the bright noonday sun. Roman had stopped dead in his tracks, too stunned to move . . . only the beating at his temples marking time. Then Moluntha's old squaw uttered a high thin wail that tore at the ear as she threw herself over her husband.

McGary, still in a rage, swung the ax again and hacked at her, the blade glancing against one of her thin old hands, and the keening gave way to a guttural cry of pain.

With a roar, Roman flung himself forward, lunging against McGary to bring him down hard, the ax flying into the grass, both men grunting as they grappled and rolled. McGary kicked out, arms and legs flailing as he tried to loosen Roman's grip at his throat; but the fury in Roman made him oblivious to the blows that McGary managed to get in. It was only when he heard the shouts of the militiamen and saw that McGary's face was turning blue, eyes bulging, that he finally let go.

McGary sucked in air, saliva dribbling at the corners of his mouth, his chest heaving until he caught his wind again, face reddening now and mottled with white spots. "I'll . . . I'll see you . . . court-martialed for this . . . Gentry!" he gasped. "Assaulting an officer!"

Roman had gotten to his feet and looked down at the man with contempt. "I doubt it," he said. He actually held the rank of major himself, though it was not something he thought about often.

The captured braves being kept at the far side of the lodges, out of sight of what had happened, seemed to know anyway and set up an angry and at the same time mournful chanting. And some of the squaws took up the keening as they saw to Moluntha's woman—three of her fingers had been severed with the ax blow. As they stanched the flow of blood and two of the younger women hurried to bring willow bark and brew a tea to help her pain, Roman stared down at Moluntha, his wrinkled old face still amiable in death somehow . . . his brains spilled out in the dust like hog entrails.

McGary had gotten to his feet now, and Roman turned back to him, sorry that he hadn't gone ahead and killed him. "Goddamn you," he said, and drew back his fist to catch the man squarely in the jaw and send him sprawling again before he turned and walked away.

The heat of October had given way finally to cool nights and days of pleasant sunshine, the trees just tinged with faint color after a light frost. What the old-timers called Indian summer, Roman thought as he guided Sundowner through the trees and thick underbrush. But there was no need for even those up along the Ohio to fear for a late attack this year. Logan's troops had burned Shawnee villages and destroyed their crops, had brought back seventy-five prisoners to trade for white captives. And there wasn't much in it that Roman felt good about. He had fought his share of Indians in his time, had gone at them as hard as any. But to ride against squaws and old men left little in the way of satisfaction. Moluntha's killing had left a bitter taste in his mouth.

Logan had been beside himself when he heard the news, striding back and forth and vowing to have McGary up on charges in the face of his explicit orders that prisoners not be harmed. But Roman doubted that much if anything would be done to McGary in the end. The truth was, most white men would not be that much concerned over the death of one old Indian.

He guided his horse through the trees and brush to emerge onto the hard-packed trail along the riverbank, catching a glimpse of the tail end of a big snake, iridescent in the sunlight as it slithered away. He was on his own land, by God, and the Kentucky River had never looked so beautiful to him, clear blue and sparkling. Before too long he would be riding up that stretch that led to the house and the mill, would be able to see it in the distance. And he had never been so happy to come home.

There was Danville and the convention still, but he would have a few days with his family before he went, would hold Kitty and hug his boys and eat some of Hester's good cooking. His "last hurrah" was ended, and he was glad enough of it.

Kitty saw him as he rode up that final stretch, between the river and the woods, and came running, her face flushed. God, she was beautiful . . . For a long moment after they'd kissed, she put her hand against his cheek and studied his face, as if to make sure that he was really all right.

"Roman . . . Roman . . ." she whispered. And then the boys came running, Michael whooping and tugging Trace along.

Ben Tyler had brought a wagonload of his corn over to be ground and came to slap Roman on the back and welcome him home. Tom Luttram, and James, and Earl Thomas came out of the millhouse. Tom shook Roman's hand.

"Has the water stayed high enough all along?" Roman asked him, eyeing the wheel as it swished and turned, that blue water foaming to white.

"But for a few days," said Tom. "Then came a good rain, and we've not missed a day o' grindin' since."

It was at supper that Kitty told him about news of the convention. "They didn't have enough for a quorum, with so many of you off with George Clark or Ben, so they say that those in Danville have met every day just to keep it official until the rest of you could get back."

"Do you ha' to go, Papa?" Trace put his spoonful of mashed potatoes back on his plate and regarded his father soberly.

"Of course he has to go," Michael told his little brother scornfully. "He was *elected*, Trace."

Roman smiled. "I expect I can wait a day or so," he said. "Maybe we can go out and shoot us a turkey for Hester to cook."

Hester, carrying a huge pan of hot persimmon pudding to the table, grinned and nodded.

"Can I go wiv you, Papa?" Trace begged.

"You think you're big enough, do you?" Michael teased.

"I *am*," Trace returned soberly. "I could hold Papa's p-powder horn for him." He stuttered, he was so anxious.

"Well . . ." Roman studied his son for a long moment. "Maybe it's time. Let's give him a try, Michael."

"Roman," Kitty said, "he's too young!"

"It's only to the woods over here. We'll see to him, won't we, Michael?"

And as Trace, without a word, drew in his breath, blue eyes shining fiercely, the barest grin on his face, Michael, grinning broadly himself, reached over and rumpled the red hair. Roman looked across the table at Kitty and smiled . . . conscious that in a little they would be lying beside each other in bed.

With some of the delegates needing to get their crops in yet, and others delayed in getting back from the Clark expedition, the proceedings at Danville did not obtain a quorum until after Christmas. But with the delegates fully assembled at last, it took little time for them to complete their task. A bill was drawn up and passed that declared it "expedient for, and the will of the good people of the district" to separate from the state of Virginia and become an independent state.

It was too late, they agreed, to meet the exact terms set out in the Act of Separation drawn up by the Virginia Legislature. It would be all but impossible, given the distance involved and the slowness of communication, to present the matter to the Congress and gain a favorable action upon it in the time left to them. But surely, Isaac Shelby declared to Roman over a bowl of steaming punch in the common room at Grayson's Tavern, there would be no problem.

"The esteemed legislators at Richmond are reasonable men," he insisted, leaning back in his chair and puffing contentedly at his pipe. "They must take into consideration the circumstances which brought about this delay."

But the convention was hardly over before word came from the East that the Assembly had passed legislation that demanded that yet another election and convention be held in the fall, with approval by the Congress prior to the next July fourth.

"And if that, gentlemen, isn't enough," Roman told Shelby, Ben Logan, and Harry Innes, who had come to the house at Otter Creek to discuss the matter, "there's a proviso that sets January first, 1789, as the earliest date for separation."

"Damnation!" Shelby swore. Roman rose to pace back and forth before the fire.

"Well—"he turned and faced his friends"—we must start all over again!"

Kitty entered the dining room just then, carrying a tray set with rum and cups. "Don't let me disturb you," she said, observing the grim set to her husband's face and knowing her appearance ill timed.

"My dear Kitty," Shelby said, "you could not."

"Isaac"—she smiled at that dear man, who had changed little in the years since she'd known him, but for the hairline that was beginning to recede a bit and the decided paunch—"you were ever the gallant."

Harry Innes, the congenial attorney general, chuckled. " 'Tis true, Isaac . . . by God, it is!" he teased, slapping his thigh and turning for confirmation to Ben Logan, who nodded.

"And how is Susannah?" Kitty asked Shelby as she put the tray on the table. "I heard that she's expecting again?"

"Round as a watermelon and due any day," Isaac replied, undaunted by the teasing of his friends.

"You must let us know afterward," said Kitty.

"I will indeed."

Kitty threw a look toward Roman as she headed for the door. "I will leave you gentlemen to your politics," she said apologetically, but saw that her husband's eyes had softened once they'd met hers.

"Thank you, my dear, for the tray. Perhaps a cup or two will make us all feel better," he said. But once she'd left the room, he turned back to the others, frowning again.

"I'm much afraid we've lost our chance to do it easily. But do it we must, however long it takes!"

Despite Roman's glum disappointment over the setback, he was at least partially pleased at the outcome of McGary's court-martial, at which he had testified. While the punishment was little enough, Major Hugh McGary had been stripped of his rank. It was, Roman confided to Ben Logan, probably the best they could have hoped for, under the circumstances.

❉ 41 ❉

EARLIER IN THE DAY IT HAD RAINED, JUST ENOUGH TO settle the dust in the Lexington streets, and now the August sun broke through the clouds. Kitty straightened her best bonnet and tucked her hand into the bend of Roman's elbow as they waited at the corner of Main Street and Cross. She was as excited as the others in the crowd that had gathered outside the two-story, double log courthouse. Though she went over to Boonesborough often, it was a real treat to get to Lexington, which was growing, it seemed, at an incredible rate.

Levi Todd, standing with them, pulled out his timepiece and peered down at the enameled dial. "With a population in the district now of seventy-five thousand or more, surely a newspaper's long overdue." He gave a quick and hearty laugh. "And it does look like John Bradford intends to keep us waiting as long as possible for the first edition." The handsome militia major with the roundish face and expressive dark eyes, one of Roman's fellow survivors of the Battle of Blue Licks, had kindly insisted that the Gentrys stay at his home during their time in Lexington. "I hear," he continued, "that John's having to do the job without help since his brother Fielding is laid up with a summer ague."

Roman nodded, smiling down at Kitty. He looked splendid, she noted proudly, in his dark blue weskit. "It would have been handy to have Bradford run off some handbills for me when I was running for delegate last month instead of having to copy them all by hand," he told Todd.

"Indeed," Todd agreed. "And 'twill be the quickest way to inform the people of what's taken place once the convention has been assembled and action taken."

"What's this I hear of conventions and action?" Isaac Shelby called out, edging through the crowd, his wife Susannah following after him.

"Isaac!" Levi Todd tipped his hat to Mrs. Shelby and clapped the rotund surveyor-farmer—and sometime delegate—on the back. " 'Tis about time you got here. We feared you were going to miss the auspicious moment."

"One of our horses pulled up lame," Isaac explained, pulling a linen handkerchief from his coat pocket and mopping at his damp forehead, "and we found ourselves dependent upon the generosity of a fine fellow whose place was nearby when the mishap occurred. He kindly offered us the loan of one of his animals, which we shall return on our way home."

He bowed over Kitty's hand in that courtly way of his. "Kitty, my dear, 'tis good to see you," he said, and then turned to shake Roman's hand. " 'Twould seem, friend Roman, that we shall once again share the duties of the convention next week," he said, beaming.

Roman nodded. "I heard you'd been elected . . . and glad of it."

The Shelbys had been invited to stay at the Todds' house, too, and Kitty had been looking forward to seeing Susannah again. "How well you look!" she exclaimed as they embraced.

"And you, dear Kitty," Susannah Shelby said.

They inquired about one another's children as the men spoke of politics. Susannah, hazel-eyed and fair-haired, laughed merrily. "The three of them are all fine . . . for once. I vow, motherhood seems to agree with me, Kitty." The Shelbys had produced three offspring in their four years of marriage, and it did indeed seem to agree with Susannah Shelby. Rosy-cheeked, her face glowing, she looked about. "And did Mistress Todd not come along?"

"No," said Kitty. "She said that she would see the paper in good time. I tried to stay and help with the preparations for supper, but she insisted that she and the servant girl could take care of everything. She's nice. You'll like her."

Susannah nodded and smiled as a cheer went up from some of the men nearer the courthouse door.

"Here'ee comes, by God!" a male voice bellowed.

"Pass one this way, John Bradford!"

"The first'un! Right here in m'hand!" someone chortled.

And another shouted, "Let's hear it, boys!" which set off yet another rousing cheer.

There was a great jostling and shoving, but Roman pushed up to the front where Bradford, a man of stout limb and back, with a lower lip that stuck out determinedly, was handing out copies of the *Kentucky Gazette* to the first subscribers. "It's a good day for Kentucky, John." Roman's voice was quiet enough that it carried only between himself and Bradford.

"Aye . . . ." Beads of perspiration dotted the forehead of the new editor and publisher of the first, and only, paper in the district. Bradford grinned, handing several copies to Roman. "I'll see you at the Todds' this evening," he said.

The first edition consisted of two sheets of coarse paper about ten and a half by seventeen inches, still slightly damp from the press, the print a little smudged in places. The news items offered were several weeks old, but there were beaming smiles all around.

"Aha! An editorial!" Isaac Shelby peered at his copy. "Listen to this: 'My customers will excuse this, my first publication, as I am much hurried to get an impression by the time appointed. And my partner, which is the only assistant I have, through an indisposition of the body, has been incapacitated of rendering the smallest assistance for ten days past.' "

"He says"—Levi Todd took it up—"that future issues will be published weekly on arrival of mails from the East."

As the men perused their copies, Kitty and Susannah looked over the sheets that Roman had given to them. "Look!" Kitty pointed out the advertisement excitedly.

JUST OPENED. REASONABLE TERMS FOR CASH AT HOME OF MR. JOHN CLARK IN LEXINGTON . . . COMPLETE ASSORTMENT OF LINEN & STUFFS—COFFEE, TEA, CHOCOLATE, MUSCAVADO SUGAR, PEPPER, ALLSPICE, NUTMEG, GINGER, INDIGO, RICE, CHINA & QUEENSWARE, GLASS TUMBLERS, WEST INDIES RUM, WRITING PAPER, COTTON CARDS, EIGHT PENNY NAILS, & ETC.

"Oh, I should like to buy some ginger before we return home!" said Susannah.

And that evening at the Todds' house, with all still gathered about the table after a sumptuous meal, she and Kitty agreed that their host must have availed himself of some of the West Indies rum offered, judging by the freeness with which the pewter pitcher filled with that heady brew was passed. Kitty had a sip herself.

"A fine day indeed!" Levi Todd raised his cup to John Bradford, and all joined in.

Bradford, looking as if his stock were too tight, grinned and nodded his thanks. "I wish brother Fielding could be here with us, but I fear this rich food would be too much for him yet."

"A good dosing with comfrey tea would get him on his feet in no time," Jane Todd offered. She was a plump, pretty woman, who after a little excused herself to see that her children were tucked into bed.

Kitty went along with her upstairs and held the baby, who was just seven months old, before he was put down for the night. His sister, a lovely, dark-eyed child, hovered nearby.

"Mercy," said Jane Todd, throwing a smiling glance at her daughter. "Barely seven, and she's a little mother already . . . and a help to me, God bless 'er. Go fetch your sampler and show it to Mistress Gentry before you get into bed, Hannah," she directed. And the little girl shyly brought her needlework for Kitty to admire in the light of a flickering taper.

Before Kitty went back downstairs, she availed herself of the privacy of the room that had been assigned to her and Roman for the night and made use of the chamber pot under the bed while she assured herself that her monthly hadn't started. She had fully expected that it would be on her before now. But she was just as pleased that it had not. Far better to have it wait until she returned home.

Mellow with good food and the sip of rum, she came back downstairs and stood in the doorway of the dining room, catching Roman's eye and returning his smile. She looked about her, suddenly aware of the commodious log house with its soft rugs on the floors, catching the gleam of silver on the well-set table, the glass-fronted china cabinet . . . And she could not be unmindful of the reason they were gathered there. Kentucky could boast of a newspaper now.

For some reason she thought of Boonesborough—not the bustling little town it was today, but the tiny little fort she'd first laid eyes on, surrounded by a vast wilderness. The cabins that Rebecca had led the women to had been rude indeed compared with this house, yet the sight of them had been full welcome to that weary party, glad to have reached their new homes at last. She could see her mother yet, rolling up her sleeves and scrubbing away at the rough puncheon floor. . . .

"Kitty . . ." She was so deep in that memory that she started when she heard Roman's voice and looked up to see him nod his head toward John Bradford, who, cup in hand, was looking toward her.

"I did not want you to miss my toast, Mistress Gentry," he said, smiling. And with a murmured apology, she hurried in to sit beside Susannah Shelby and pick up her own cup, which still held a drop of rum.

"I have already toasted our illustrious host," Bradford said, pushing back from the table and standing up. "And now I would drink to the two other gentlemen here this evening." He tilted his head toward Roman and Isaac and raised his rum high, eyes glittering with an inner vision. "Gentlemen . . . I make a prediction this night. When Kentucky does at last become a state, one of you shall be its first governor." And he lifted his cup and downed the rum in one swallow.

With the featherbeds from the boys' room airing in the sunshine, and the linen curtains soaking in an iron pot out back of the house, Kitty twisted the wooden bed key—a handy device of smooth maple, with a hand grip at one end and a slot at the other—tightening the stout ropes that stretched across the bed frame and looped about the pegs along the rails. "Lord," she said as Hester came bustling into the room, scrub bucket in hand, "I think Trace must commence to bouncing in this bed the minute the door is closed, the way these ropes are sagging."

"Michael's are just as bad." Hester cast a baleful eye at the older boy's bed. She grunted as she set down the bucket of steaming water. Her own good cooking was starting to tell on her; the once angular face had begun to take on a becoming roundness, and with no little grumbling about it, she'd had to let her waistbands out not too long since.

As Kitty tugged and pulled, Hester came to take the key from her. "Here, let me finish," she said. "Sit down there and rest yourself a minute. You've been goin' since mornin' without a break."

"So have you," said Kitty. Still, she did sit down in the walnut rocker, the close, still air of the upstairs bedroom making her feel suddenly light-headed. She reached for the handkerchief in her apron pocket and dabbed at the film of perspiration on her upper lip as Hester tilted her head around and peered at her.

"As I think of it, you've been a little peaked for a day or so now," she declared. "Hardly ate a bite of supper last night."

"I'm fine," Kitty insisted. "It's just the hot weather." She'd told herself that every day for the past week. She would not let herself get too excited. She'd been disappointed before.

Hester squared up and faced her, the thick brows drawn upward. "Have you had your monthly?" she demanded.

Under those probing dark eyes Kitty busied herself with rubbing away a finger smudge that one of the boys had left on the polished walnut armrest. "Hester, every time I feel a little tired or lose my appetite—just from the heat—it doesn't mean that I'm carrying."

"No," Hester agreed, "but *have* you?"

"Have I what?" Kitty was beginning to grin in spite of herself, and Hester's eyes lit up.

"You *haven't*!" The older woman dropped the bed key and clapped her hands to her mouth in delight, laughing through her fingers. "Lord, Lord, I would dearly love to have a baby in this house again!"

Kitty forgot the smudge on the armrest and jumped up. "Oh, it would make me so happy . . . and Roman, too, I do believe," she said. Then, trying still to hold back that trembling hope: "But it may not be. . . . I've been late before. And it's too soon to know for sure."

Hester tilted her head back and peered. "I swear ye've the look of it about you."

"Stop it," Kitty said, grinning all the more. She snatched up the bed key and started tightening the cord once more. "And not a word about it before him. I'll not have him going off to Danville to the convention wondering about me. He needs nothing on his mind except the business of Kentucky right now."

The sound of the boys' voices echoed from the yard, and in a moment the quick stamp of feet below in the house and then on the stairs. In a second Trace burst into the room, hair askew, his lips drawn into an exaggerated pucker.

"You surely have not been trying to eat persimmons, green as they are yet?" Hester confronted him.

He shook his head. "There's a bug down there," he gasped out, his blue eyes shining in his sweaty and freckled little face, "a big, long one. . . ." He measured off a distance with his hands that grew bigger and bigger until his arms were wide and Hester was shaking her head and grinning. "And . . . and Michael says," he stammered, "that . . . that it'll sew my lips together sure!"

"I was only teasing him!" Michael laughed, following quickly on the heels of his little brother.

"Michael," Kitty chided, "whatever are you telling the child?"

Michael's dark eyes sparkled. "It was just a Devil's darning needle. And they *do* say that," he defended himself.

"But you know that it isn't true."

"Yes'm," he said, still grinning. "They won't really sew your lips together, Trace. Don't be a dunce!" He rumpled the boy's hair, and Trace gave his head a toss and glared, still unforgiving.

"Come on," Michael coaxed. "I saw a big old turtle down by the creek yesterday. Let's go see if he's still around. Come on . . ." He tugged at Trace's arm, and in a moment Trace gave in and allowed himself to be taken along.

"Mind you don't let him fall in a deep spot," Kitty called after them. She stood there a moment, looking toward the doorway through which the boys had just gone, before she went to Michael's bed to tackle the sagging ropes. A girl would be nice, she thought. For a change. Still . . . to have three sons wouldn't be a bad thing, either.

She tugged at the rope and twisted, suddenly vexed with herself. Lord, here she was getting her hopes up again and would probably end up disappointed. Still, she permitted herself the thought, she had never been *this* late before.

"I came across the cradle just the other day," Hester offered innocently. "Up in the loft over that back room."

"Hush!" said Kitty.

But during the three weeks that Roman was away at Danville, she became more and more certain, and when one morning at the table she looked down at her johnnycake and grits and fried pork and had to flee the kitchen to throw up, there was little doubt left.

"Now I guess you'll tell him when he gets home," Hester said, coming after her to bring a wet cloth.

"I guess I *will*." Kitty managed to grin, taking the cloth to press it to her pallid face, which still held a faint tinge of green. The two women sat there together and laughed, tears in Kitty's eyes suddenly.

She dashed them away. "Lord, I'd come to think that I never would again—"

"Well, it looks like you are. And Roman ought to be comin' home soon, oughtn't he?"

Kitty nodded, so happy she could hardly stand it.

It was pouring rain when Roman rode in, wet through and slapping water with his leather hat; such a satisfied gleam in his eye, Kitty thought, that she could almost believe someone had already told him, if she didn't know that that was impossible. "We've had not a word from Danville," she said. "Tell us of the convention."

"All in good time, my love!" He laughed, his red hair escaping to curl about his ears, the way it always did no matter how tightly he tied it back. "I am starving!" he declared, and while he changed into dry clothing, Hester commenced to slicing up salt meat. Soon it was sizzling in a black iron skillet, potatoes frying in another. He came back to wrestle both of the delighted boys about the kitchen, Trace squealing and giggling, Michael whooping, until Kitty and Hester threatened to banish the three of them from the room until the food was ready.

Roman ate with an uncommonly good appetite, pushing in great forkfuls of the potatoes and meat and washing them down with a cup of strong coffee. The boys insisted that they were hungry, too, and must eat with him, though it had hardly been two hours since the noonday meal. Kitty smiled to see Trace doing his best to hold his fork exactly as Roman did. And for once the youngest of the Gentrys even picked up his napkin and wiped his mouth with it instead of using his sleeve when no one was looking.

The rain had stopped, the clouds breaking apart, by the time the meal was ended. Once the table was cleared, Roman came to where Kitty stood on tiptoe to put the cleaned plates back on the shelf. He took the last one from her and slid it easily into place.

"Come walk with me," he said.

She glanced toward Hester, who was busy scraping the last of the potatoes from the heavy skillet. "I'll be back in a little," she said, and Hester threw her a knowing look and jerked her head toward the door to hurry them on.

They took the path along the creek, which was considerably wider than it had been in the old days. Roman had had tobacco planted on the old place, and Tom Luttram and his boys drove the wagon back there from time to time to see it. The rain had cooled the air, and there was a fresh sweet smell from the water, the wet leaves of the trees on either side of them glistening yet with moisture from the sudden downpour.

"You seem in a fine mood, Roman Gentry," Kitty declared, smiling up at him as they walked.

"I am that," he said. "Glad to be home with my good wife and sons."

"Is that all I've come to be to you, then?" she teased. "Just your 'good wife' . . . keeping your home and minding your children?"

"Aye . . ." His eyes lit mischievously. "How else would you have it, Mistress Gentry?"

"After being gone three weeks, I should think you'd be wild to tumble in the bushes," she carried on the banter, and got more than she bargained for when he picked her up as if to carry her off.

"The bushes, is it?" He grinned.

"Roman"—she giggled like a girl—"put me down. For mercy's sake! I think they can still see us from the house!"

He gave her a firm kiss on the mouth and set her back on her feet. "As a matter of fact," he declared, "I *am* wild to tumble you in the bushes, or our bed, or anyplace else that would accommodate us. But first we must talk."

"I think we must," she said, savoring her secret. But when he turned a quizzical look her way, she returned it with one of innocence. Her news could wait until she'd heard whatever it was he was so anxious to tell her. "Well, out with it," she prompted, smiling. "What happened in Danville that has pleased you so?"

He lifted his head. "The convention has asked that I plead our case for statehood before the Congress."

"Roman . . ." Kitty caught in her breath and held it for a moment. Of course, she thought, near to crying with the burst of pride she felt in him, he would be the one to do it. "Oh, Roman . . ." She reached her hand out to him, a full and trembling smile on her lips, and he caught her up and kissed her again, swinging her around. Then he sobered suddenly and set her on her feet.

"It's a weight to carry. . . ." He shook his head.

"Oh!" she scoffed. "If anyone can persuade them, you can." She grasped his hand again, and they walked along the path, avoiding the puddles from the rain.

"I shall do my best," he said finally, and she smiled at him.

"Your best is good indeed, Roman Gentry." She tilted her head to one side and studied that great hawk face of his. He had changed greatly from the sober-faced young man who'd come riding up to the Gentry cabin back at the Watauga. And she loved him so much in that minute, walking there along the rain-washed banks of Otter Creek, that she thought she might die of it.

"I'll be leaving in a week or so for Philadelphia, where they've convened. And I've decided that you and the boys must come with me."

She missed a step, almost stumbling, but his hand tightened on hers. "Come with you?" she gasped. "To Philadelphia?"

He nodded. "With the winter setting in soon, it's unlikely that I'll be back before spring. I expect," he added wryly, "to do a good deal of cooling my heels in outer chambers."

His suggestion had taken her quite by surprise, and she wasn't sure yet how she felt about the matter.

"You haven't been back east once since you came out, and the boys not at all," he reminded her.

"That's true," she said. "But Trace is still awfully young for such a trip. . . ."

"But tough as a catamount cub," he insisted. "No," he said, "I think it will do them good . . . and it will certainly do me good to have the three of you along. Philadelphia is a beautiful city. You'll love it."

They continued on down toward the old place, with Kitty trying to digest this latest turn of events and Roman telling her of his plans. "We'll go back across the mountains, and once in the East, will take coaches on to Philadelphia, where I'll lease a house for us. When my business is finished, we can go to Pittsburgh and float down the Ohio.'' He grinned, obviously well pleased with the idea.

They came too near to a covey of quail, and the startled birds flew upward in a great whirring burst. And a little farther on an otter slithered off his rock and into the creek.

By the time they reached the old place, making their way through the high grass and on toward the apple orchard, she realized that it was Roman who had talked all the way, and she who had listened . . . hard put to accommodate it all just yet.

''I should have James and Earl Thomas come down here and cut some of this.'' He gestured toward the fine rich grass. They had built a small shed not far from the site where the old cabin had been, and used it to store hay for the winter.

Running ahead, Kitty spied an old basket that the boys had left under one of the trees. She picked it up and started to gather some of the apples that had fallen to the ground. ''Hester and I must come down here and take up some of these to put in the root cellar,'' she called.

''There'll be little time for that,'' Roman reminded her. ''We leave in a week, remember.''

She nodded, and he leaned down to scoop up an apple and toss it into the basket, his eyes taking on that devilish gleam she recognized so well. ''You have warmed my blood indeed, 'good wife,' with your talk of tumbles in the bushes.''

The sun was fully out from the clouds now, the air steamy, and Kitty could feel her breasts, already full and sore, swelling with her need of him. ''The bushes are wet still,'' she said, smiling up at him, their eyes still caught.

''Aye . . . but the shed over there is dry.'' He ran his fingers over her aching nipples to make her catch her breath. ''And, if I'm not mistaken, there'll be a pile of old hay left . . . to tumble in.'' He laughed, his teeth strong and white in that bronzed face, taking her willing hand in his and drawing her along.

With Roman sleeping peacefully beside her, his breathing soft and deep, Kitty lay awake long into the night, thinking yet of their loving down at the old place. Maybe it was the life inside her that had made it even better than usual. She'd heard women say that it was that way for them. ''When you're first carryin','' they confided. ''And when y've startin' into y'r change,'' some of the older women would put in. ''Law, it's like y'r a female critter with her heat upon her!''

She ran her hand over her still flat belly. She had not told Roman about it. She had needed this time to think first. She was not afraid of making the trip east with him. She was a good breeder; the baby she carried was secure. Now that it was there, she would carry it and deliver it well. There had been many a babe come squalling into the world beside a buffalo trail in the early days, most half grown and hearty now, she told herself. And it *would* be lovely to see Philadelphia.

Roman stirred and caught his breath and turned over on his side, the deep regular breathing returning almost at once. She wanted to reach out and touch his back but knew it would wake him. The years out in the wilderness had made him a light sleeper.

She had made up her mind. She knew she could not go with him, and it came to her how much she would miss him . . . gone until spring. But his attention must be to the affairs of Kentucky now, not on her. And if he knew of her condition, he would worry over her; she knew him too well to think otherwise. He had fretted over her the whole time she was carrying Trace, and she never more well.

No . . . she would tell him in the morning that the children were too young yet, Trace especially, and that she would go with him next time he went east. Maybe they could go next year or the year after. And she could visit her sisters in Virginia.

Her biggest problem now was in keeping him from guessing before he was safely gone. No matter how sick she got, she would not throw up in front of him, she vowed. Not if she had to stick a cork in her mouth to keep from it.

❊ 42 ❊

WITH TWO FULL WEEKS LEFT BEFORE CHRISTMAS, winter had settled in early and hard, ice already frozen solid for several feet out from the shoreline of the river. The trees were stark against the sky, only here and there a lone stubborn leaf left, shriveled and brown, shivering in the wind. But as Kitty gathered her woolen cloak about her and emerged from the dogtrot, she was glad to feel the sun against her face. It had warmed some overnight, and the wind was not as keen as it had been for the past two weeks.

Earl Thomas and James were chopping wood at the far end of the yard, adding to the already huge pile, and they waved a hand to her, James pulling off his cap and tugging back that fair Luttram hair of his while his brother hefted a big piece atop the chopping block.

" 'Tis some warmer, don't ye think, Mistress Kitty?'' James called.

"It is and welcome.'' She lifted a hand to them and continued on down toward the river. She walked out along the bank every afternoon. She had never been able to stand being cooped up in the house all day, no matter how cold the weather. And now the child inside her shifted, as if to give its approval, and she smiled. She had felt that first faint stirring last week.

Hester fussed over her constantly, but she was fine. It was true that she tired more easily than she had when she was carrying the boys, but she was older, she reminded herself. She'd be twenty-nine in April. And her mother had always said it went some harder once you got close on to thirty. Besides, this baby was going to be bigger, or else she was carrying a lot of water. Faith, who'd brought the children and come to spend the day two weeks back, had insisted that she must have miscounted.

"My lands, just look at you! You must have figured wrong. Looks to me more like five months than four. But you look good, honey." She'd hugged her.

She saw Trace coming along the path toward her now, bundled into his woolen coat, his red knitted cap pulled down around his ears and nearly the same color as the few tufts of hair edging out about his face. Lord, he was a dour little thing, she thought, her heart catching as she looked into that glum little face.

"Trace, where's Michael?" she asked before she caught sight of her older son, coming from behind a big clump of elderberry bushes and loping along to catch up with his brother.

"Wait up . . . don't be mad, Trace," he called, grinning good-naturedly.

"Michael won't let me go wif 'im . . ." The little boy looked up at his mother, his face screwed up. Bear, switching that long tail, came up to circle around Trace, bumping against him, and the boy pushed him away.

"Lonnie and me are going down the creek a ways and fish through the ice," Michael explained.

"Lonnie and I," Kitty corrected him. "Are your chores all finished?"

"Yes'm."

"All right . . . but mind you be careful. The ice could be melting some today." She bent down to take Trace's small chin in her hand and kiss him soundly. "I think you'd best not go with your brother," she said.

"I'm big enough," he declared, stretching himself tall and sticking out his chest as far as he could get it. Michael laughed, and Bear circled still, panting, while Trace slid his blue eyes upward, scowling at his brother.

"Maybe next year you will be," Kitty said firmly. "Now why don't you go along up to the house. Hester's in the kitchen, and she's got something in the oven that you'll like. Go on, now. . . ."

He nodded glumly and started slowly along the path, as Michael, Bear at his heels, ran off the other way. "I'll be back before supper," he shouted.

"See that you do," Kitty called after him.

She continued on her walk, smiling and shaking her head. Trace had begun to think that he should do everything that Michael did, and was apt to sulk when he couldn't. And Roman seemed the only one who could clear up the gloom and make him smile. It was clear that he missed his father. As she'd tucked him into bed last night, he'd asked her when Papa was coming home.

She missed Roman, too. Dreadfully. Those first weeks after he left had been so busy . . . drying beans in the sun, storing away the last of the potatoes and turnips in the root cellar, packing the rest of the apples with straw between them. There had been nuts to gather, and persimmons. Tom and his boys had killed three hogs as soon as the temperature had dropped low enough, and the meat had been cut up and salted down and sausage made to take off to the smokehouse with the hams and sides of bacon. There was always so much to do to get ready for winter that the days had passed quickly. But now . . .

She reread his letter every night before she went to sleep. It had arrived three weeks ago, and at least she knew that he was safely in Philadelphia, and that he missed her, too. She had written back. But heaven only knew how long it would take for him to get it. Her letters must go across the mountains, while he could send his down the river if he could get them over to Pittsburgh. And even when he got hers, he would not find written there what she wanted most to tell.

But it was clearer than ever that he must keep his mind on the business that had taken him east. He'd had a meeting with the Virginia delegation, he'd said. And he was trying to get in to see General Washington, who had chaired the special convention that had drawn up a constitution for the government. Right now there were simply thirteen states, each of which acted on its own, and the new constitution appeared to be badly needed if the government was ever to function. But it did seem, he'd said, that the mind of the Congress was more on getting the new document ratified by the various states than on any other business. Still, he hoped to bring the matter of Kentucky statehood to their attention soon.

Kitty passed the mill, the big wheel stilled for the winter; the small icicles that had formed along the paddles were melting where the sun hit them, glistening and dripping. It was her habit to walk to the junction of the creek and the river, and she continued on today. The fresh air did the baby good, she was convinced. Hester fussed over her and insisted that she should take it easier, but she had not cut back a bit on her regular routine. Still, the extra weight so soon was beginning to tell on her.

She stood down on the point for a few minutes, enjoying the sunshine and watching as the water from the creek rushed between the flanks of ice on either side and flowed out wide to merge with the main current of the river. The water was not as blue as it was in the spring and summer. In winter it grayed down, the depths of it displaying a cold brilliance, especially when the sunlight hit it.

She must keep herself busy, she thought. And there was plenty to do, even if they got snowed in. Michael and Trace both needed new breeches and shirts, and the baby must have didies and blankets and belly bands. She smiled and slipped her hand inside the woolen folds of her cloak to press it to her swollen belly. Lord, it must surely be another boy; no girl would have her that big so soon.

She started back, careful of the slick spots along the way. She didn't need a fall. In the distance she could hear Bear's throaty bark and thought she heard Michael shouting to Lonnie.

Halfway back along the path another sound—hardly a sound, more a whisper of it—caught at her ear: a half whimper carried on the breeze off the river. Like a small animal or a child far off, she thought. She glanced sideways toward the river, out over the ice toward the flowing water. And suddenly her breath froze as her eye fastened on that tiny patch of red, there at the edge of the ice where it was jagged . . . as if it had . . . *broken*.

She was screaming as she ran, awkward and lurching, shrieking like a wild thing as she reached the ice and started out, slipping . . . almost falling and then righting herself . . . instinctively slowing as she felt the ice beneath her crack and start to give. She dropped to her knees and stretched out forward, as flat as she could, feeling her big belly bunch and knot beneath her as she slid on it inch by inch toward that red woolen cap. . . .

"Trace . . . Trace!" she screamed, and caught a glimpse of movement out at the edge, a sudden clawing of small fingers that slipped and slid and disappeared. And then she saw his head bob up once, the bright blue eyes wide open and filled with terror, his mouth and nose never above the waterline as he struggled and slipped from view again.

Frantic, she propelled herself forward recklessly, the upper part of her plunging into the water, feeling the cold of it like a hammer blow as her face and head and shoulders went under. She groped with both hands in the icy depths, hanging off the shelf of ice, praying, Please God . . . please!

She felt something within her grasp and pulled upward, but it came away, and through that watery gray, cold place she could see the red cap rise and fall away. She groped again, trying desperately to see down beneath her. And then suddenly there was something between her fingers. . . .

Hair! Dear God . . . she had her fingers twined in Trace's hair. And despite the numbness of her hands and arms, she held fast, determined not to lose him, groping with her other hand until at last she had an arm. She tried to move backward and could feel the ice crack again, her head still submerged, her lungs near to bursting . . . Please God!

She tried again, jerking her body convulsively, and managed to clear her face and gulp in air as she pulled Trace up . . . inching backward, the thinning ice cracking dangerously, until she was out of the water and had his head out. Oh, Lord, he looked dead. . . .

She pulled him up slowly, gasping and crying, easing that little body along until she had him back from the thin edge, terrified as she looked down at that small still blue face. And it was only then that she heard the shouting from the shore. Earl Thomas and James were there, and Tom had come running.

"Good Lord!" he shouted. "Ease out there, James. Pass the boy back first. Chester!" he bellowed back toward the barn where one of his younger sons was cleaning out the horse stalls. "Bring blankets! Quick!"

"Lie still, Mistress Kitty," James called to her, slithering toward her, belly down, until he could stretch out his arms for Trace. "This ice could go. . . ."

"Get him back." Kitty was shivering violently. "We've got to get the water out of him." There hadn't been the slightest movement since she'd gotten him out, and she could barely hold the screaming back, the litany drumming inside her: Please God . . . don't let me lose Trace . . . Trace . . . Trace . . . God in heaven, don't take him from me. . . .

She watched him passed back carefully, and by the time James had helped her in far enough that Earl Thomas could grasp her hand and haul her the rest of the way, Tom had laid Trace out on his stomach and was kneeling over him, pressing with his big, flat hands against the little back.

Trace's head was turned to one side, and Kitty dropped to her knees and peered anxiously into his small face. His eyes were closed, the lids puffy.

"Is he breathing?" she pleaded. Tom Luttram didn't answer but kept the rhythmic pressure going as young Chester raced up dragging a mildewed, hole-filled blanket that he'd found in the barn.

"Get y'r ma and Miz Hester," Tom directed without missing a beat. "And more blankets," he called.

Kitty had not been able to take her eyes off Trace's face, and now she clapped her hands to her mouth as she saw the slightest twitch in one of the swollen blue eyelids. She waited a long moment, not breathing herself. Please . . . please . . . And after what seemed another eternity, he coughed feebly and then gagged, water draining from the corner of his mouth.

"Oh, God, God . . ." Kitty said aloud.

"He's comin' around," Tom said.

The boy heaved, and vomit followed the water as Earl Thomas let out a triumphant whoop. Kitty could only begin to cry anxiously, still not sure that he would be all right.

But in a moment his face was screwing up, patchy spots of color coming back, and he opened his eyes and looked full into hers. "M-Mama," he bawled, and Kitty pulled him into her arms and began to rock back and forth, there on the cold ground, with the Luttrams trying to wrap the moldy blanket about the two of them . . . tears running down her face.

"She's goin' to lose it sure, 'less we can git it quieted," Polly Luttram whispered to Hester. The two of them passed back and forth from Kitty's room to the fireplace in the small hours of the night, candles casting flickering streaks of light into the darkened corners as they carried warm flannels to lay against her belly. It was the best thing they knew, they said, to stop the dull pains that stirred from time to time, down low in her back and deep into her abdomen.

She lay as still as she could, hesitant even to move. She could not bear to think that she might lose this child before Roman even *knew*. She watched the shadows dance as the air in the room stirred the candle flame. But Trace was safe—thank God for that—sound asleep in his bed upstairs and seemingly none the worse for his ordeal.

Once they had gotten him to the house, Hester had stripped him of the icy clothing and stuck him immediately into a washtub filled with warm water and more than a little rum poured in. Kitty hovered anxiously to be sure that he was really all right before she'd let Polly get her out of her own freezing apparel and into a nightgown. And she'd come back to hold Trace in her arms, his tired little face pressed right into her neck before she'd finally consented to let Hester take him. The pains had started by then.

Polly Luttram came now to take away the cooled flannel and gently press the hot one to her middle, pulling the woolen blanket back up over her.

"Are you sure Trace is all right?" Kitty asked.

Polly nodded. "Hester just come back from seein' about him. Said he'd crawled over in bed with Michael, and the two of 'em sleepin' like babies—" She caught herself as if she feared to mention babies now.

"Am I going to lose it?" Kitty asked after a moment.

"I don't know," said Polly, her face earnest. "But"—she brightened—"you ain't lost it yet."

"I'm bleeding."

"I know. But not much. Mercy sakes, I've spotted with more than one o' mine and carried 'em still full time. Don't fret yourself now."

In a little Hester brought her some willow-bark tea and she drifted off to sleep fitfully, to dream that she was down in those icy depths again, knowing that Trace was down there somewhere, too . . . groping frantically but unable to find him. And she would start awake from time to time and have to be assured again that he was safe.

But toward dawn she fell into a deeper, more restful sleep, stirring a little when she had a pain and drifting off again. Finally, with the sun high, she woke up to find Hester coming into the room with yet another flannel.

"Hester," she said, her voice still heavy with sleep, "you must be exhausted."

Hester shook her head. "Polly and me spelled each other after you settled down a little. How do you feel?"

"A little pain just then." Kitty made a face. She'd hoped they'd be gone. "But not as bad."

"That's a good sign. Now mind," Hester scolded, "that you don't set your foot out o' that bed. Except to use your pot, and I'll help you."

Kitty nodded, and Hester went to bring her some hot grits from the kitchen. And in a little while the boys came in, Trace covering her face with wet kisses.

"He says he was goin' fishing through the ice . . . with a stick for a pole," Michael said, shaking his head and grinning.

"Michael wouldn't let me go wif 'im," Trace offered soberly. And, while Kitty knew that she should probably punish him, she pulled him close and hugged him.

"Don't you ever, ever, *ever* go near that river or the creek again unless someone older is with you . . . not until you're twenty-one years old! Do you hear me, Trace Able Gentry?''

"Yes'm." A small grin stole across that freckled little face. And in a moment Hester came in with the grits and shooed the two of them out so that Kitty could rest.

The pains had stopped by early afternoon, and Kitty waited, hardly daring to hope. But when morning came and they still had not returned, and all the spotting stopped, she began to cry with relief. And Polly Luttram, who'd come over to see about her, smiled broadly.

"Now, now . . . don't be a-cryin'," she cautioned. "You might start 'em up again." She and Hester kept Kitty in bed for a whole week before they'd let her up.

With pale pink peony shoots beginning to thrust their way out of the ground at the far side of the house, and several new calves already dropped and following their mothers on wobbly legs up to the barn, Tom and the boys spied out several big maples and set to tap the rising sap, which was boiled down into syrup and deliciously sweet sugar. And Hester outdid herself baking up cakes and puddings, and frying batter cakes—Michael's and Trace's favorites—of cornmeal and buttermilk and eggs, dropped onto a sizzling hot-iron griddle and served up browned and swimming in butter and syrup.

"Lord, I always know that winter's ended when I set down to a trencher o' batter cakes," Hester said.

With the sun giving off the pale golden warmth of spring, Kitty sat outdoors most afternoons and mended the boys' socks and embroidered little jackets for the baby. Sometimes she walked down to the river, careful now because she was so big and apt to lose her balance easily. "I swear, if I fell over I don't know if I could get up," she told Hester and Polly, laughing. But after her close call when Trace had almost drowned, she'd had no trouble at all except for carrying all that weight, as small as she was.

"Lord in heaven," Polly had remarked, "that baby's comin' out big as a bull calf!"

"Unless it's two of 'em, it is," Hester rejoined. To which Kitty had declared firmly that she couldn't recall any twins in the Gentry family.

Privately, Hester and Polly agreed that they were worried about her delivering a baby so big. But Kitty was blissfully un- aware of their forebodings and would have been unperturbed even if she'd known of them. She had had no trouble at all with the others, and she expected none with this one. And since she had until May, there was plenty of time for Roman to get home before the event. She couldn't wait to see the expression on his face when he first laid eyes on her.

It had been several weeks since she'd had a letter from him, and that a month old from its date. He'd written that he could not help but grow more discouraged daily over the prospects of getting the Congress to act upon the matter of Kentucky statehood within the deadline that the Virginia Legislature had set.

"I wish that I had never accepted this responsibility," he wrote. "The months have dragged on with little to show for their passage . . . and I do miss you, my dear wife, more than I can ever tell."

It seemed to her certain that the matter had been settled by now, and Roman *must* be on his way home. She couldn't help keeping an eye peeled for him whenever she was where she had a view of the trail from Boonesborough, though she knew that it might be a *little* early yet. But soon, she knew, soon . . .

One balmy afternoon, as she sat out on the big wooden bench beneath the sycamore tree, stitching at a tiny cap, she looked up and caught her breath as she spied a rider coming along the river trail. But after a second, during which her heart seemed to beat a hundred times, she pressed her lips together in disappointment. That was not Roman's lean, lanky figure atop the horse.

The man astride the animal, shorter in the leg than Roman and thicker through the midsection, looked to be uncommonly well dressed for the district. Kentucky men, even when they were done out in their best, tended to be conservative in their attire.

She watched as he spurred the horse forward and soon covered the distance to the house, her initial impression borne out as he trotted up. Ruffles peeked from beneath the opening of the gray, double-breasted, woolen frock coat. His shoes were fastened with ornate silver buckles, and his stockings, while suitable for traveling, were still of the softest cotton. He swept off the large hat, brim cocked both front and back, to reveal a thick head of curling hair, well powdered above a face that could only be described as handsome, and raised his eyebrows in an expression of doubt as his eyes fastened upon her.

"Madame," he said with a heavy French accent, "I was

given directions in Boonesborough to the Gentry place, and they seem to have led me here. . . ."

"This is the Gentry place, sir." Kitty smiled politely.

"Ah!" He looked relieved. "I have come to see Meestress Kitty Gentry, eef you please."

"I'm Mistress Gentry," Kitty said, only to see the stranger's dark eyes widen as he took in her obvious condition once again. Recovering, he began to smile broadly.

"*Mon Dieu* . . . I did not know . . . Roman did not tell me that you were soon to present him weeth—"

"*Roman?* You know my husband?" Kitty asked anxiously.

"*Oui.* And I carry a letter of introduction, madame. You must think me a perfect fool. . . ."

"No, no . . . Oh, please come in. Bring your things." She gestured toward the large pack that was strapped to the horse in back of the saddle, getting herself up from the bench with some difficulty.

"Oh, I fear I impose." He spread his hands, fingers wide. "Roman should have told me."

Kitty laughed. "Nonsense." A traveler was seldom turned away in Kentucky, whether friend or stranger. "Do come along. A letter? You say you have a letter for me . . . from Roman?"

He nodded, turning to Tom Luttram, who'd just come striding up to see who the visitor was. "Henri Malroux, monsieur, at your service," he introduced himself, explaining quickly that since business had brought him to the district, Roman had insisted that he call at the Gentry home. And in a moment Earl Thomas was leading his horse away toward the barn and James was carrying his bundle inside the house.

As Hester bustled around and started supper now that they had a guest, Kitty couldn't wait another minute and begged to be excused long enough to read Roman's letter.

"Of course, madame." His smile was boyish, though he was not much shy of Roman's age, she thought. "Take all the time you need," he urged.

Once in the privacy of her room, her fingers trembled as she broke the seal, her heart squeezing at sight of that strong scrawl.

My dearest Kitty,

The bearer of this is Monsieur Henri Malroux, whom I first made the acquaintance of at the home of Mr. Alexander Hamilton, and then had the good fortune to discover was living at the Boar's Head Tavern, just across the hall from the room that I must call home in these many months since I could be in my own. He has been a friend, helping me while away the lonely evenings with games of whist . . . in which, I confess, he is more often than not the winner. You will find him a fine fellow.

I had thought to be leaving for home by now, but, alas, there is still more to be done. I have succeeded in getting the ear of General Washington, who favors the acceptance of Kentucky's petition, and the matter will go soon before the Congress. I pray that there will be a speedy, and favorable, resolution. Doubly so, since I have been approached by the Spanish minister, Don Diego Gardoqui, who urges that I use whatever influence I can bring to bear that Kentucky declare its independence and separate from the Union, for which he promises the friendship of His Spanish Majesty and a speedy restoration of our right to use of the Mississippi. While the prospect of free trade with New Orleans is tempting, I am sure you knew me well enough, dear wife, to guess that I cannot sanction, much less urge, such an action. It has been, and still is, my unswerving view that Kentucky's future lies with the United States of America, and any suggestion that we should align ourselves with the Spanish, who clearly wish to use us to protect their own possessions to the south, is abhorrent to me.

In all conscience, I feel that I must report this overture on my return, and I am fearful that if the Congress does not give its immediate approval to our petition, there will be those impatient men at home who will press that we accept the Spanish offer, Wilkinson among them. I will fight that to the end.

It is wet and cold here, and I long for the hills of home where, I am sure, the trees are greening and the days bright. But most of all, I need to see our sons . . . and most, most of all, to see you, my dearest Kitty, and hold you close. What further I would wish to say must hold until I am with you again . . . since the nature of it would indeed strain propriety's bounds were an accidental eye to come upon it. I shall merely ask you, my love, to recall a fine day when we walked down to the old place together . . . and for the rest, content myself with assuring you of my unfailing love and devotion.

Tears welling in her eyes, Kitty pressed the sheet to her full breasts, in a moment laughing as she looked down at her enormous belly. Roman would find it hard to hold her "close" were he to come home right this very day. But he would undoubtedly find a way, she thought, smiling still as she brushed her eyes dry and went back to attend their guest, anxious to hear all he could tell her of her husband.

And after supper they sat and talked before the fire, which was needed yet to relieve the chill of spring nights. Monsieur Malroux told her of their games of whist and modestly discounted Roman's account of his usually being the winner. "Perhaps a time or two . . ." He lifted his shoulders in an elaborate shrug, his mouth curving into a smile that caused his eyes to light and sparkle. "But once we journeyed, over the week's end, out to the countryside, where we did some shooting. And I tell you, madame, if France were filled with such marksmen as your husband . . . *mon Dieu!* We could conquer the world if we chose to! No wonder you won your revolution." He laughed heartily and took a sip from his mug of good strong corn liquor, which he seemed to have taken a liking to.

"You're sure he's well?" Kitty asked again.

"Indeed. His only complaint is that the board set at the Boar's Head is not the equal of what he gets here at his home. And after sitting at your table, I can well agree." He patted his full middle, and Kitty smiled her thanks.

"What brought you to America, Monsieur Malroux?" she inquired.

"I was aide to the Marquis de Lafayette," he replied, "and was at his side throughout the war."

"Then we are in your debt, as well as in the debt of the marquis."

"No," he said quickly. "For in coming here, I think that I have found my home, madame. In fact, after hearing your husband talk of his beloved Kentucky"—he pronounced it with three distinct syllables: *Ken-tuc-kee*—"I have come here to take up land in the county you have named for the marquis himself."

"Fayette . . ." Kitty smiled.

"*Oui*," he said.

"There is a lady waiting in Paris who has given her pledge to me." That charming grin broke over his face again. "And I intend before long to go there for our wedding and bring her back here."

"You will not miss France too much to stay?"

The smile faded and he shook his head, the dark eyes almost brooding. "No," he said, his voice definite. "There are dark currents that swirl there. I have made my choice, and my Claudette will gladly come to this beautiful land of yours . . . and, I hope, one day, ours.''

Hester came into the sitting room, a woolen blanket tucked under her arm. "Your room is ready whenever you've a mind for it," she told him. "I've but to take this extra cover upstairs. The wind is up, and 'twill be cold before morning.''

He would occupy what they called "the traveler's room" during his night with them. It was common enough now for a household to have one—situated, in this case, above the kitchen, with a narrow step to reach it and a door that could be locked on the outside in the upstairs hall. Since it was the custom to turn no traveler away without the offer of a bed, and the character of the visitor was oftentimes unknown, it seemed a wise precaution since it could assure the lack of intrusion on a man's family as they slept. But with the delightful little Frenchman so well known to Roman, both Kitty and Hester decided that precautions would be unnecessary.

He rose from his chair by the fire, drinking down the last of his whiskey. "With your kind permission, then," he said to Kitty, "I think I shall retire for the night. I have ridden far today . . . and must leave early in the morning.''

"Of course," Kitty said. But as Hester went ahead to take the blanket up, she stayed him for a moment. "There is something . . .''

He regarded her with those dark eyes. "A message, perhaps . . . to your husband?''

"I will write a letter yet tonight and give it to you in the morning. But I must ask you to keep my secret.''

"Secret?''

She faced him squarely. "Roman doesn't know that I am carrying a child.''

His eyes widened, mouth flying open in disbelief. "But, surely, madame—''

Kitty shook her head. "I knew before he left, but did not tell him because his attention has needed to be elsewhere. I wouldn't wish these months apart to be more difficult for him than they have been. He has needed to be about Kentucky's business. And you must promise me, Monsieur Malroux, that you will not tell him.''

Malroux studied her for a long moment, then he swept up her hand and kissed it to set her flushing with embarrassment. "You have my word, madame,'' he said. ''It is no wonder that your husband prizes you so greatly.''

Once Kitty had finished her letter to Roman and snuffed the candle before she climbed into bed, she lay awake for a while, giving in finally to a few tears as she accepted the fact that Roman would not be coming home as soon as she had expected him. But still, she comforted herself, he might surely yet arrive before the baby was born.

❋ 43 ❋

KITTY SAT IN THE DOGTROT TO CATCH THE BREEZE, EASY for the moment in the hickory chair that Tom Luttram had made for her. Polly and Hester had padded it with deerskin stuffed with goosefeathers and horsehair, and now that she was so ungainly, she preferred it to the hard bench out under the sycamore tree.

She was alone at the house—the others had all gone black-berry picking. The boys had brought in a bucketful that morning, surprising everyone with how early they were this year . . . and how big.

''Lord, we must pick all we can. I do purely love them,'' Hester had declared. And Earl Thomas and James had hitched one of the horses to the wagon and loaded up Polly and Hester and all of the children. Trace had looked back and waved at her as they pulled away, heading toward the far side of the woods that bordered the river road, where the berry bushes grew thick. She could almost see them from where she sat, would be able to were it not for the thick grove of cedars over that way that had taken on such a lovely muted shade of green, the afternoon sunlight somehow filtered through a hazy sky to cast a rosy glow over everything. As if it were meant to be a special day, she thought, flexing her legs and moving them apart a little as the pain came again, her huge belly hardening for a long moment and then easing.

She wasn't afraid to be alone. It would be a while before she needed anyone. And Tom Luttram was right down at the barn lot, working on a leather harness, if she should need to send him for the women.

She'd awakened with a restless energy that morning and had swept the floor of her room and dusted every piece of furniture throughout the house, then come into the kitchen to wash the dishes and scour the pots, until Hester insisted that she stop. She had come near to saying she'd go along with them to pick but had decided against it when she realized how hard it would be for her to get up and down from the wagon.

She caught sight of a robin, perched on a low limb of the sycamore, and waited for his throaty call. There were still not too many of them, but she loved it when she saw one. Way back, when she and the others had first come in, there had been no songbirds. The forests were too deep and dark, she remembered her father saying; not enough grain seed to attract them. But with the clearing of the land and the planting of crops, they'd finally started to appear over the last few years. She'd seen robins and finches and a bluebird or two. Even the jays had started to come in, though that raucous scolding could hardly be called a song. Still, they were beautiful, she acknowledged.

As the robin flew away, she thought of Roman, wondering what he was doing at that very instant, closing her eyes for a moment to bring his face up behind her lids. And for the first time the smallest doubt nagged at her certainty that she had done the right thing in keeping this from him. It seemed suddenly unfair that he had not the slightest notion that his child was coming into the world today . . . or tomorrow, if it took that long to get it here.

Still, she reminded herself, there was no way he could have known what day it was happening anyway. Not while he was so far away. And that might have made him worry all the more. No, it was best that she hadn't told him, she decided, putting the doubt aside. And she was positive that Henri Malroux had kept her secret for her.

A pain came again, and she put her head back and flowed with it. Lord, the early ones were easy, almost pleasurable in some strange way . . . knowing that you were at last into it, and soon, relatively soon, you would be able to give up the weight of the life you'd carried inside you for all the months and reclaim yourself. There were days when she'd longed not only for the baby to be here safe and sound, but, she smiled now, for a middle flat enough to allow her to get down on the pot and pee and get up again like a normal human being—something that you took for granted when you didn't have a stomach big as a hay bale to manage.

With the pain over, she got to her feet and went inside to see that there were plenty of rags and sheets, and that the baby's things were all ready. It was something to keep her occupied. She and Hester had gathered together what they would need several weeks ago, and they'd finished all the baby's clothing. It waited in the trunk in her bedroom.

She felt suddenly hungry, as if her body must gird up for what lay ahead, and went to the kitchen for a cornmeal muffin, left over from the noonday meal. A glass of cold sweet milk would be good with it, she thought. But the springhouse was too far away to walk there and back. She settled for some of the clabber that Hester had put aside in a stone jar.

She walked about the yard for a while, which made the pains come a little faster. But by the time the berry pickers had returned she was back in her chair, waving to them as the wagon pulled up and everyone climbed down. Michael was the first to come over to her, hurrying to show her a bucket brimming with berries that were fully ripe and as big as buckeyes.

"Look," he said, grinning. "And there are lots more over there. Hester says she'll make a cobbler for supper."

A contraction seized Kitty just then, harder than the others, to make her grasp at her stomach with both hands and grimace.

"It's time?" Michael said, the berries forgotten. "You're ready to have it?"

"Yes . . ." Kitty held herself a minute more, her breath coming out in a rush, and smiled at him then.

He put his hand out to rest it on her arm for a minute, seeming suddenly older than his almost ten years, that handsome face of his taking on an unnatural gravity. "It'll be all right," he said.

She nodded, putting her hand over his.

Hester came up, exclaiming over the wealth of berries, her voice trailing away as she peered at Kitty with sharp eyes. "You've started," she said, setting the big gourd she carried on the ground. "How long has it been?"

"Almost since you left," Kitty admitted.

Trace came racing up, his mouth purple with berry juice, and

Kitty admired the berries he'd picked and hugged him, drawing back in a moment as another pain started.

"Mercy, they're coming faster," she gasped, and Trace stood there, widened eyes seeking out her stomach, where he knew a baby grew.

"Does it hurt, Mama?" he asked, his face screwing up as if he might cry.

"Only a little," Kitty said, catching her breath and giving him a reassuring smile, though that one had been harder than any yet. "Why don't you and Michael help take some of the berries in the house. And then maybe James and Earl Thomas will take the rest down to their place. You could go along if you want to."

"Yes'm," Michael said. "Come on, Trace . . ."

Trace followed his brother reluctantly, looking back at Kitty, his face still screwed up.

Earl Thomas and James took the berries to the springhouse to keep them cool until Hester and Polly had time to see to them. Enough were kept at the house to make a huge cobbler later for supper, but now, Hester declared, it was time to get Kitty's bed readied. And while she did that, Polly helped Kitty out of her clothes and into one of her oldest and coolest nightshifts.

Kitty didn't want to get into bed until she had to, and she walked still, back and forth across the room, into the sitting room and back, stopping whenever a pain seized her.

As the afternoon waned, the shadows outside of her window lengthening, Hester cooked supper and Polly went to do the milking by herself, since Celie was minding the younger children.

Kitty tried to eat a little, but the pains were coming close now, and finally she pushed the plate away, sitting up and rocking in the bed as that swelling misery filled her. "Lord," she gasped, beads of sweat popping out on her face. "That one was hard."

" 'Bout time . . ." Polly grinned, and Hester nodded. They'd seen that everyone was fed, the kitchen cleared up, and everyone over to the Luttrams'. Now they could both give their full attention to Kitty. Polly, still grinning, pulled a small pair of scissors out of her apron pocket and held them up.

"My old Granny used to say that a pair of scissors or a sharp knife under the mattress would help to cut the pain," she said. "I don't know as I believe it, for sure. I've tried it with and without and own I couldn't tell much difference. Still, it don't hurt to put 'em under there.'' She wedged the scissors beneath the mattress, making sure that they were close enough to the bed frame that they didn't fall through to the floor.

"Help me get down on the pot,'' Kitty said. "I've got to pee.''

"I'll wager you don't,'' said Hester. "You just went a little while ago. More likely it's the pressure, but come on. . . .''

They helped her down, and she groaned as the downward weight pressed so hard that it seemed the baby must come out right then. But there was a long way yet, she knew. She was only able to pass a few drops of urine before she climbed back into bed, as uncomfortable as before. Hester had been right.

She gasped and moaned and sweated during the next few hours, rocking again and again, Hester bathing her face. "Mercy, it's worse than the others were. Or maybe I've forgotten,'' she conceded.

"Lord, you always *do* forget,'' said Polly.

This baby was bigger, Kitty thought, and she was older. She remembered the night that Rebecca had had Nathan. As another pain hit, she bore down instinctively, though Polly and Hester had not told her it was time to start that yet. Lord . . . God, it hurt! She cried out for the first time, and Hester was right there, wiping the sweat from her face and nodding her head.

"I think we're goin' to get to it now,'' she said.

It was close to midnight when Kitty, drenched with sweat and pale as a bedsheet, braced her back into the pillows propped behind her, digging her heels into the feather mattress and straining . . . face reddening now as the awful sounds, the ag-onized grunts and groans of labor, came from her.

"Keep on . . . keep on . . . there . . . a little more,'' Hester urged. And in another second Kitty screamed as the baby slith-ered halfway out, another push and a final shriek bringing it into Hester's waiting hands.

"A girl . . . Lord God, you've got yourself a girl!'' Polly cried out, and Kitty smiled, panting still, but easing back into the wet and bloody sheet beneath her, though she kept her head up as she tried to see.

"Oh, just look at her,'' Hester crooned as she lifted the bloody infant onto Kitty's stomach and began to clear the tiny nose and mouth of mucus.

And in a minute, as Kitty watched through tear-blurred eyes, such a wonder in her that she might never have experienced this before, her baby's arms flared out and back, the small face knotting. A healthy and outraged howl erupted . . . such a big sound from so small a source that Polly and Hester laughed, and Kitty smiled, reaching out to touch the shock of wet hair, which looked for all the world as if it must be almost as red as Trace's.

Suddenly she gasped and stiffened as a contraction, strong as the ones that had gone before, claimed her, and she arched and strained once more.

"There's another still to go," Hester said calmly, handing the first baby over to Polly now that the cord was cut.

"Oh, my God!" Kitty managed. Though Hester had insisted more than once that she was carrying twins, she had never considered it . . . not once.

It was only a few minutes before the next girl came, her lusty howls soon mingling with her sister's.

Hester and Polly set to work, laughing softly as they did what needed to be done for Kitty, then cleaned her and the bed, and the babies.

"My lands, they are as alike as two butter beans in a pod," Polly declared, chuckling as she finished drying one of the infants and then commenced to diaper it.

"Except this one has a birthmark on her shoulder," Hester said, holding that one close enough so that Kitty, who was too tired to do any more than lie and marvel at what she had produced, could see the tiny crescent shape that was very like the one she had between her breasts.

"I can't believe it," she said, looking from one to the other of her daughters.

"Well," Polly said, "you'll likely believe it soon enough when they commence to wakin' you up four or five times a night to tug at ye . . . which I think is just exactly what this one is a-wantin' right now. Look at that, will ye?" The baby had found her own fingers by accident and managed to suck the two middle ones into her mouth and was going at them as if she were starved.

"This one's smackin' her lips as well. Here now . . . ." Hester finished pulling the long nightgown down around the little legs and brought the child to Kitty just as Polly brought the other one to the far side of the bed.

Kitty untied the laces of her nightshift and, blissfully happy, took her babies into her arms and held them to her breasts, one on either side of her, giving a silent prayer of thanks . . . and thinking of Roman. Lord, what *would* he say when he found out? She had not only kept from him the knowledge that he was coming home to find a new baby in the house, but now when he arrived, he would find *two*!

She looked down at them as they mouthed at her breasts, screwing up their little faces. Like Trace . . . she laughed out loud. But soon they'd both gotten hold and began to suck away at the sore, tender nipples, the small shivers of pain seeming to tug at her emptied womb.

"They're strong," she said, smiling. "I do hope I'll have enough milk to keep both of them satisfied."

"Don't be a-worryin'," Polly comforted. " 'Tis about time my Jonnie was weaned, big as he is. And I've a Lord's plenty yet should you need me to help suckle 'em."

"One thing," Hester said, looking down at them with such pride on her face that they could have been her own, "we'll have to celebrate their birthdays different days."

Kitty looked up questioningly.

"I peeked into the sitting room to look at the clock as soon as the first was born," Hester explained. "It was right then two minutes to midnight."

"Then the last one . . ." Kitty's voice trailed off, and Hester nodded.

"Was born after midnight," she said.

"Which means that this'n right here in my arms is goin' to be a day older than her sister," Polly added, laughing.

The twin babies fast became the pets of the place, with Hester clucking and cooing over them constantly and Trace and Michael arguing over who was best at rocking their cradles—Tom Luttram had set to work at once to make a second one. And even Polly, with all her brood, stopped by often just to pat and fuss over them and declare that she never saw a healthier, or prettier, pair.

They *were* beautiful and, but for the birthmark, all but impossible to tell apart. Kitty's heart-shaped face was already evident in each of theirs, and the coppery hair, which they'd gotten from their father, was silky fine and curling.

When they were a month old and still Roman hadn't come home, Kitty declared that they must have names, and went ahead to record their births in the old Gentry bible: *Twins*, she wrote in her best hand. *Samantha, born May 10, 1788. Mariah, born May 11, 1788.* And she left room in case Roman wanted to give them a middle name. She hadn't gotten a letter since before they were born. But they kept her so busy, even with Hester's unfailing help, that she didn't have the time to worry quite as much as she would have otherwise.

But when yet another month had passed with no word, even the care of the twins could not prevent her unease. She knew that he would never go so long without writing, though the safe delivery of a letter over so long a way was understandably hit or miss, she reminded herself. Still, something could have happened. He could have started home, coming down the Ohio, and the boat waylaid by savages. . . . The very thought made her tremble.

One afternoon she took the twins outside with her, seeking out the shade of two big elms on the far side of the yard, settling them on a pallet where they could get the breeze from the river before she took up a basket of socks to be darned. After a while, Celie came around the corner of the house to coo at the babies and laugh at the faces they made.

"I left some greens in the kitchen. I couldn't find Mistress Hester," she said.

"She went off to see if that old goose that's setting in the long grass by the river has hatched out her goslings yet," Kitty told her. And as she thanked Celie for the greens, she caught the sound of Bear's baying far off down the creek and closer in the whinny of a horse from the direction of the barn.

"I 'spect that's Pa and Earl Thomas and James comin' back," Celie said. "They went down to the old place this mornin'. They're clearin' another patch fer corn."

Kitty nodded and went on with her darning. But in a moment she lifted her head, eyes narrowing. Just for a second she'd thought she heard Roman's voice.

"Kitty . . ." It came again, clear and strong, and with a trembling cry escaping her, she cast aside the basket and jumped to her feet, her legs suddenly atremble.

"Oh, Celie," she whispered, throwing the babies a quick look, "mind them for me a minute." She smiled, catching her lower lip between her teeth as Celie, grinning, said she would.

"Where is everybody?" Roman called again. Kitty caught up her skirts and ran around the side of the house, right into him—there in his worn old buckskins as if, she thought, he'd never been away, nor met in Philadelphia and again in New York with the most powerful men of the young union.

"Roman! Roman . . ." She laughed as he swung her up and about and then brought her face down to his to kiss her, and kiss her again . . . and again . . . her heart pounding so against her ribs that she was sure it must burst from her chest with happiness.

"Oh, my God . . . Kitty," he said, his blue eyes feasting on her, his face bronzed, white teeth flashing, "you cannot know, my love . . ."

"Oh, yes, I do," she whispered. "I have missed you so. . . ."

He set her on her feet, holding her arms out to look at her. "You're thinner," he declared.

"Am I?"

"I think so." He laughed, a sudden twinkle come to his eye. "Except for here . . ." He indicated her full breasts. "You always had a fine bosom for so small a mite."

She smiled, wondering what he would say when he found out why they were so well rounded.

"Did you get my letter that I was coming?" he asked.

"No. Nothing for two months now, and I have been worried," she admitted.

That crooked smile marked his face. "I'm sorry, my love. It could well be lying sodden at the bottom of the Ohio . . . or"—the grin broadened—"may yet come a week or month from now." He looked around, down toward the river, eyes sweeping on to the woods. "Where are the boys? I saw no one as I rode in."

"The boys went fishing down at the creek. It's low and safe enough for Trace," she added. "And Tom and his boys are down at the old place—" She broke off suddenly. "I have so much to tell you. . . ."

"And I, you. Let's go in."

He slipped an arm about her waist and had taken a step toward the dogtrot when Kitty's practiced ear picked up the fussy cry of one of the babies . . . a wail that grew quickly, as she'd known it would, into a full-fledged howl. It was time for them to nurse.

Roman cocked his head to one side as she met his questioning gaze with a certain degree of nervousness. "Is that a baby I hear?" he asked.

She nodded, and he drew her with him around the corner of the house, where Celie and the babies were in full sight there in the shade of the elms.

"Not two of them?" he whispered to Kitty, grinning in astonishment. " 'Twould seem Polly's outdone herself this time. And not a word of it in your letters."

He drew her along with him still, calling out a greeting to Celie. He had always been fond of babies, and as he hunkered down to see them better, Kitty watched him nervously. Lord, she had to tell him—was anxious to—but not here in front of Celie.

Samantha, red-faced, was kicking her little legs and howling still; she was always the one who demanded to be fed first. And Roman patted her. "Well . . . well," he said, smiling broadly, and she hiccuped and stopped crying, while Mariah merely waved her fists and pursed that tiny rosebud of a mouth, looking up at him solemnly.

"Well . . ." he said again, and Kitty's heart skipped a beat as she saw that sudden change in his face, a stillness, a bemusement come upon it as the red hair and the heart-shaped faces and the eyes that were so dark blue they were already holding a hint of violet took their effect upon him. "Oh, my God . . ." It was a husky whisper, and he turned his head to look up at her . . . the certainty all but there in his gaze.

Celie slyed her eyes at Roman and then toward Kitty, ducking her head to hide a grin and clearly anxious to be gone. "I'd . . . best get back," she stammered, and barely waited for Kitty's nod before she sped away.

Roman turned back to the babies, slowly reaching his hand out again, to each of them in turn . . . Samantha and then Mariah . . . as if he must make sure that they were really there. "God's blood . . . they're ours," he said in the voice of a man shaken to the roots.

And as Kitty nodded, he let out a great, gusty laugh. "Look at them! How could I not know at sight? And why," he demanded, "didn't you *tell* me?" He gave his head a shake. "Never mind. I shall have an explanation soon enough. Before anything I must hold my . . ." He looked to her and back to them.

"Daughters," she said softly, her eyes suddenly wet with the sharp sweetness of the moment and the tenderness on his face.

"Daughters," he repeated.

Samantha had begun to cry again, and, smiling, he picked her up and stood, cradling her in his arm and patting her bottom. "There now," he said, and there was something in the deep rumbling of his voice that seemed to soothe her.

"That is Samantha that you have," Kitty told him. "Mama had a sister by that name. And this"—she leaned to pick up the remaining twin—"is Mariah."

His eyes lit. "For my mother," he said, and she nodded. "Give her to me." He held out his other arm, and Kitty handed the baby over. "Lord save me"—he looked from one to the other of them—"I don't know how a man could be so blessed." And after a moment: "How old?"

"Two months."

"And are you all right?" His voice was anxious, his eyes searching her face.

She laughed and nodded.

They took the babies in the house, and once Kitty had let them nurse, she put them down, glutted and sleepy.

"You must have known before I left," he said.

"I did," she admitted.

"But why didn't you tell me?"

"Because"—she touched his cheek—"I did not want you distracted from the reasons that took you east—especially," she said, laughing, "since it was something that I would finally have to do without your help, my love."

"Still, you should have told me. If ever a man has a right to worry all he likes, it is surely at such a time."

They were in their bedroom, the babies on a quilt to catch the air from the window as they napped. Roman pulled her close to him, the smell of the twins nursing still about her, the long, long time they'd gone without each other firing them both. "Are you ready yet . . . I mean, is it all right?" he asked, his voice husky once he'd kissed her, his hands gentle on her breasts and throat and back, as if afraid to go too far until he knew.

"Yes," she whispered, guiding his hand to show him that she had no strip of linen between her legs.

They kissed and clung and would have fallen on the bed right then, except that Hester called out from the dogtrot, and in another moment the boys came racing in.

"Papa!" Trace allowed himself to be swung up high, forgetting for the moment that he'd informed everyone on his fifth birthday that he was now too big to be picked up any longer. "Oh, Papa," he said, blue eyes squeezing together with happiness, freckles shining, "I thought you were not ever, *ever* coming back. . . ."

"Don't be a dunce, Trace. Of course he was coming back." Michael grinned as Roman's arm came out to haul him into the three-way bear hug.

"Back to find my sons grown a head taller, I'd vow . . . Let me look at you." He set Trace on his feet and held the two of them at arm's length, shaking his head and grinning. "I've presents for you. . . . Go down to the barn and get my pack."

They sped away, stomping and whooping, Kitty scolding them not to wake the babies. And in a moment they were back, waiting anxiously as Roman searched in the oilskin-wrapped packet to bring up first a tortoise comb for Hester—which she must stop and put in her hair at once—and then an identical pair of carved bone-handled knives in leather sheaths.

"Oh, Roman," Kitty chided, "Trace is too young for it yet. He'll cut a finger off."

But Roman merely smiled. "He'll only use it when Michael and I are with him. We'll teach him, won't we?" Michael nodded.

Hester went off to make supper. And as Michael took Trace out to test their knives, promising that he would see his little brother did not hurt himself, it was Kitty's chance, at last, to hear what had finally happened in the East.

"The Congress did accept my petition and agree to Kentucky's becoming a state," he said, his face growing glum, "but then the news came that the legislature of New Hampshire had ratified the new constitution, the ninth state to do so and the number needed to make it the law of the union"—his mouth drew down wryly—"thereby dissolving the old Continental Congress. The members realized that they no longer had authority to act on Kentucky, and that the matter must be brought again before the newly elected Congress. Which means that once again we have missed the deadline set by Virginia."

It was clear that the turn of events had been difficult for him to bear, and Kitty reached out to touch his hand. "But Roman," she said, trying to cheer him, " 'tis surely only a formality."

"Perhaps," he said, sober still. "But I fear we'll have the devil's own time fending off those here at home who would have us take some rash course—whether from frustration or self-interest. As anxious as I was to get here, I stopped overnight at Isaac's house to tell him what had happened. And from what I learned from him, 'twould appear that Wilkinson has struck a bargain with the Spanish governor, Miro. 'Tis said his agents go through the countryside buying up every surplus of tobacco and cured pork, of tallow and butter and beef . . . anything to turn a tidy profit in the markets of New Orleans."

Kitty nodded. She had seen the general's advertisements in the *Gazette*.

"While other honest Kentuckians," Roman went on, "are denied the use of the Mississippi to send their goods to market, he seems to have free access to New Orleans. And, I would wager, not only fattens his purse, but schemes to make Kentucky at best a Spanish ally and at worst, by God, a subject of His Spanish Majesty." He jumped up to pace the room restlessly. "I shall do all in my power to see that does not happen."

When Hester had supper ready, Tom and Polly were sent for and told they must eat with them. Tom brought Roman up to date on all that had happened on the place in his absence, the two of them taking their pipes and their coffee laced with brandy in the sitting room while the women cleared up, Kitty seeing to the babies.

But when at last Kitty and Roman were together in their room and the house was quiet, he pulled a small leather pouch from his pocket and held it out to her.

She gasped as she drew out the strand of pearls, lustrous in the candlelight. "Oh, Roman . . ." Tears stung her eyes. "You shouldn't have . . . they must have cost so much!"

He shushed her, insisting that she put them on. "Someday," he said, "I shall build you a fine brick house, Kitty Gentry . . . perhaps in Lexington. Would you like that?"

"Roman . . . Roman," she whispered. "There is nothing that could make me happier than I am right now. . . ."

Her arms slipped up around his neck, and he picked her up and carried her to their bed.

* 44 *

As ROMAN HAD PREDICTED, WILKINSON AND OTHERS OF his political persuasion protested vigorously that Kentucky had shown patience enough with Virginia and, indeed, the Congress. It was time, they declared, that Kentucky pursued its own interests, and devil take the Union!

But Isaac Shelby and other men of reason rallied with Roman to stand squarely against such sentiments . . . reminding all who'd listen that with the British still entrenched to the north of them in Detroit, and the Spanish to the south, a Kentucky rash enough to declare its independence would be little more than a ripe plum waiting to be plucked. Roman mounted the podium at Danville to roar: "Spain does not seek to bestow favors for nothing! Would you trade your liberty for Spanish gold, by God?"

"Upon my soul," Isaac chuckled, cradling his cup of hot punch in his plump hands as he and his comrades gathered about the board at Grayson's Tavern, "for a man whose tongue was once ever hard to loose, 'twould seem we've found in Roman Kentucky's staunchest and most vocal champion!"

The struggle for Kentucky's future had barely begun, it seemed. And at those times when Roman paced the floor in anger over the ambitious and greedy men who would stand in the way of statehood, or despaired that the eastern block of states would forever put impediments in the way, it was Kitty who soothed him and packed his things when he had to go away again.

When the twins were two years old, he had consented to go to Richmond to argue over the terms of separation, but not before he'd taken Kitty into their bedroom and fixed her with those blue eyes of his. "You are *not* pregnant, are you?" he'd demanded sternly. To which she'd burst out laughing and assured him she was not.

She thought about it now and laughed again. And even as she packed Roman's things in his same old bag yet another time, she could take pleasure in the fact that the fight was all but over. Only last year Mr. Washington—elected the first president of the country—had recommended that the new Congress admit Kentucky into the Union, and they had voted to do so, setting a date for statehood that was less than two months away now— the first of June 1792. And come the morning, Roman would be off to Danville once again, the delegates' task this time to come to some agreement about the provisions of a constitution.

Lord help her, she guessed that she had made as many sacrifices as any woman for Kentucky's future. Ten conventions in eight years, and Roman had attended most of them . . . plus the months he had spent in the East. But it was worth it all. And she was proud indeed of her husband's part in it.

The throaty laughter of the twins drifted through the open window now, and Kitty put aside the linen shirt that she was folding and went to look out to the side yard, where Hester pushed them in the double swing that Roman had made for them—a pair of small, sturdy wooden seats braced together, with leather straps to hold the girls in securely. As she watched, Samantha laughed aloud, taking her small hands away from the ropes to clap them together in fearless delight, while Mariah held on tightly and smiled, the movement of the swing setting the wealth of coppery curls atumble about each of those enchanting faces. It did not seem possible that they would be four next month.

Kitty heard a step behind her as Roman, fresh from his efforts at writing his final draft for the new state constitution, came into the bedroom to slip an arm about her waist and gaze out at his daughters.

"Lord, when they are older, we can look for half the young men of the district to come flocking," he declared.

"Of the *state*," she reminded him.

He nodded, smiling. "Of the state. They do at times confound me, they are so different from the boys . . . such soft and pretty little things. 'Tis hard for me to deny them anything when confronted with their smiles or tears," he admitted.

"You spoil them," Kitty accused.

"I expect I do . . . and most likely because they remind me of you, my love." He kissed her lightly and ran a hand along her thigh, his eyes taking on a mischievous gleam as they lit on the bed.

"Roman . . ." she pushed his hand away, laughing softly. " 'Tis nearly time for supper. Don't you smell the stew cooking? Hester will be in shortly, and the boys any minute now."

"Tonight . . ." he said.

She nodded, smiling still as she watched him go back to his work, half sorry that they had not taken a chance on it. But in another minute she saw that Hester was lifting the girls out of their swings, the twins running ahead toward the dogtrot the moment they were down.

Oh, well . . . she sighed. She and Roman were not so young anymore that they couldn't wait a few hours. She had actually caught a hint of gray at Roman's temples the other day—which made him all the handsomer, if truth be known—and her reflection in the looking glass would not let her deny the lines about her eyes. Still, she was glad enough that bedtime wasn't *that* long away.

The boys trooped in soon, hungry as half-grown bear cubs and anxious for supper, breaking to their places at the table the

moment that it was ready. And Roman reminded them quietly
that gentlemen did not all but knock the chairs aside in their
haste to seat themselves.

"Yes, sir," said Michael, settling down at once. Close to
fourteen now, he was a good-size boy, gangly in his spurt to
manhood.

"Sorry," said Trace, spreading his napkin across his lap. He
was tall for his age, his hair as red as ever, his features beginning
to hold a hint of Roman's.

Hester had made a huge corn pone with a crusty bottom, and
cut it into wedges and passed it, well buttered, along with big
cups of cold buttermilk. The twins' chairs—made with longer
legs to bring them well up to the tabletop—were placed between
Kitty and Hester so that they could oversee their eating, and as
plates of hearty stew were passed, Samantha clutched her spoon
eagerly.

"I wike stew," she said, dimpling at the smiles which that
announcement brought.

"And what do you like, Mariah?" Kitty prompted.

She was the shyer of the two, but encouraged, Mariah's little
face broke into a grin. "Corn bwead," she said at once, and
Michael leaned to nod his head and smile at her.

"I do, too," he said.

Kitty's eyes met Roman's and then she looked around the table
at the children, knowing how lucky they were to have them. It
crossed her mind that she could yet have more. There had been
five years between Michael and Trace, and another five before
the girls were born. It could well be that this coming year would
be the one again. Mercy . . . maybe triplets this time. She lifted
a hand to her forehead at the thought, holding back a chuckle.

It had been a long time since Roman had seen such a throng of
people. The dusty streets of Lexington were crowded with riders
and wagons and citizens afoot. Surefooted old mountain men in
greasy buckskins shared a pull at the jug with leathery farmers,
who'd loaded up their worn-faced wives and scabby-kneed children and hauled them along to town for a day not to be missed.
Merchants sweated in their best frock coats, and bonneted ladies
clutched at their husbands' arms or kept a close watch on their
young ones, lest they get lost in the crowd. And all of them
come to see the new governor sworn into office.

At a nearby intersection a squad of militia drilled to the tune
of fife and drum. Samantha, whom Roman held up high so she

could see, grinned and called out to her sister—Levi Todd had swung Mariah up. And when finally the militia squad had turned and pranced and fired their rifles in the air, then marched on down the street to disappear into the press of people, the little girls were given back to Kitty. Michael and Trace were somewhere in the throng. But it was all right, Roman said. They knew how to get back to the Todds' house if they should become separated.

"It should not be much longer," Levi said, speaking above the rush of voices. They stood with the rest of the welcoming committee, ready to greet Isaac Shelby as he rode in on the Danville Road. John Bradford, that pugnacious lower lip softened for once, broke into laughter as he spoke to Ben Logan.

Roman looked over toward Kitty to smile. He suspected that, while she was happy for Isaac, she might still be a little disappointed that it was not he himself who would be sworn in as governor today. He wasn't. He had cast his vote for Isaac Shelby with every confidence in that honest, capable, and honorable man. Though he'd been right about the eastern bloc's disinclination to welcome another southern vote—they'd quickly pushed through Vermont's statehood to get it into the Union before Kentucky's date to enter—he'd seen Kentucky become the fifteenth state in the Union, and that accomplished, he was now content to go back to Otter Creek and see to his own affairs.

The thing that gave him as much pride as anything on this day of note was the constitution that he had had a part in writing. He was confident it would safeguard the true principles of liberty and free government—freedom of religion, speech, press, and assembly. It guaranteed representation by population, not by counties. And, unlike the other fourteen states, the new Kentucky constitution gave the right to vote and hold office to all free men, without any property or religious requirements whatever. And just in case they'd made mistakes that couldn't be foreseen as yet, the delegates had added provisions for the document to be revised, or rewritten, in five years, should the people decide that it was necessary.

The part that he was least satisfied with was the one that copied the federal Constitution, whereby the chief executive—as well as the state senate—was chosen by a group of electors who were decided by the ballot. He would have preferred a direct vote. But he had, in fact, been one of those elected by the people in his county to perform that task for them, and he was well pleased with the outcome. Kentucky would be in good hands with Isaac Shelby in control.

Michael edged through the crowd, Trace right behind him, their faces flushed with excitement.

"A man was walking on stilts down there by the bank," Michael said.

"He fell off," Trace added dryly.

There was a little tremor through the throng, a wash of sound.

"I think he must be coming," Levi said, and Roman nodded, turning his gaze down the Danville Road, which was lined with people fully two miles or more. His height giving him some advantage, he could make out riders coming in. And in another moment cheers echoed back and the militiamen stationed far out along the road fired off volley after volley as an old six-pounder roared.

The cheers grew more deafening as Isaac came closer, riding at the head of the procession come from Danville, the smiling new governor in typical frontier garb, stout breeches and linen shirt, powder horn and shot bag hanging at his waist, a rifle across his saddle, waving to the people who lined up on either side.

He reined up in front of the waiting committee, taking off his hat to reveal a head of hair that was well thinned out and streaked with gray at forty-two. Somewhere in the crowd a chant went up: "Old King's Mountain!" Though it had been a long time, they had not forgotten his distinguished part in that battle.

He held the hat up high and nodded his thanks, then climbed down from his horse to approach the official welcoming committee and shake each hand in turn. And when he came before Roman, his clasp was firm and long.

"Friend Roman," he said, eyes suddenly moist, "I doubt that I deserve this . . . but I shall do my best."

"And that best more than good enough," Roman returned. " 'Tis a good day for Kentucky, Isaac."

John Bradford read a welcoming speech, and after that a federal judge administered the oath of office. Isaac stood sweating slightly in the bright sunlight, his hand resting firmly on the big Bible held out for him. "I do solemnly swear . . . that I will be faithful and true to the Commonwealth of Kentucky . . . as long as I continue a citizen thereof . . . and I will faithfully execute to the best of my abilities . . . the office of governor . . . according to law."

Susannah Shelby, who had ridden in a coach toward the end

of the procession from Danville, had come to stand nearby, and now drew near her husband to squeeze his arm, happy tears brightening her eyes, as the town bells began to ring and volleys were fired off again.

Kitty tugged at Roman's coat sleeve, and he leaned down to hear her above the noise. "The girls are tired," she said, "and now that I've seen the swearing in, I think I'll go back to the Todds' and rest myself before the state dinner tonight."

"I'll take you. . . ."

"No, no . . ." She smiled up at him. "You stay for the speeches. Michael will drive us. Trace says he wants to stay with you."

Roman nodded. "We'll be back early," he said, chuckling as the twins waved their pretty little hands at him and puckered those adorable mouths to blow him good-bye kisses. Michael, considerably taller than his mother now, took them all in tow and headed toward the livery stable where Roman had left the buggy he had taken for their time in Lexington.

In a few minutes the participants in the ceremonies proceeded along the streets, accompanied by the beat of fife and drums, to regroup in front of the Sign of the Eagle Tavern at the corner of Main and Upper streets, where the new governor reviewed groups of militia, afoot and on horseback. And as the cheers continued and the bells clanged, Roman looked about the crowd to see if he could catch sight of some of his old friends. Surely Flanders Callaway must be there somewhere, and John Holder, and Simon Kenton . . .

It was sad to know that Daniel, who had done so much to open up this land for others, and paid such a high price for it—two sons and a brother—wasn't there for such a day. The prosperity that he had enjoyed for a time at Limestone had slipped through his fingers once again, claims against him piling up and judgments going against him.

It did seem, Roman thought, lost in memories for the moment, that ill luck had always plagued Daniel—some said of his own making. And there might be some small part of that true. But he had contributed so much to this land. Surely he deserved better. Roman didn't like to think that he was forgotten on this day . . . and he determined right then that at the state dinner that evening, he would offer a toast to Daniel Boone.

The roar of the old six-pounder, which signaled the end of the ceremonies, brought him abruptly out of his reverie. He realized that Trace was talking to him.

"Listen," Trace said. "They're counting off the states!"

And Roman clapped a hand on his son's shoulder, smiling along with the boy as the crowd yelled, "Twelve . . . thirteen . . . fourteen . . . *fifteeeeen!*"

And someone nearby shouted out: "We owe it to you as much as any, Roman Gentry!" And as his name was picked up by several others, Trace beamed up at his father.

But in a little while, when the new governor had gone off to the quarters that had been prepared for him, Roman said he guessed it was time they started back to the Todds' house.

"Can I go by the mercantile store for some chocolate?" Trace asked. "It was open a little while ago."

Roman nodded and pulled two coins from his pocket. "I'll meet you down in front of the new State House." He was anxious for another look at the handsome two-story brick structure, but recently completed, which would house the state government until a permanent capitol was chosen. He handed Trace the money. "Get enough for everyone," he said. "Your mother loves it."

"Yes, sir," said Trace, and sped away. He was tall for his age, Roman noted. Perhaps as tall as he had been when he was that age. It would be good to be with his children more . . . especially the boys. It wouldn't be long before he must think about their formal education, and he wanted every day with them that he could get before either of them had to go away to school.

The Todds had begged Kitty and Roman to stay over for a few days. "You must," Jane Todd insisted. "We don't have company that often, and the children get along so well."

Kitty said she'd like to and confided to Roman that she'd heard from Jane that there was actually a woman in town who'd set up a dressmaking business since she'd been left a widow. "I'll vow," she confessed, "the thought of paying someone else to make a dress for you does seem all but immoral. 'Twould likely set Ben to railing about the evils of sloth." They both laughed. Though Ben Tyler had mellowed over the years, as deacon of the Baptist church in Boonesborough he could work himself up to a righteous sermon still.

"But," she went on, "Jane said that the woman was widowed only a short time after coming here, and not only knows the latest fashions back in Virginia, but has had some fine fabrics shipped downriver to her from Philadelphia. She's willing to sell lengths of dress goods. Not," Kitty assured him, "that I would be extravagant. . . ."

They were in the privacy of their bedroom on the Todds' second floor, and Roman kissed her lightly. "Be extravagant if you like, my love."

There was a soft knock at the door, and Roman opened it to find their hostess standing there, smiling. "The governor is downstairs to see you," she said.

"Isaac?" Roman was clearly puzzled. "I should have thought that he would be busy over at the State House, with the legislature now in its first session."

"Aye. 'Tis Isaac," she said. "And he asked that you come down as well, Kitty."

"How nice of that dear man to call," said Kitty. "But that is like Isaac. He probably thinks we're going home tomorrow."

Roman nodded and they went down together, Shelby rising to greet them the moment they entered the sitting room.

"My dear Kitty"—he kissed her cheek—"I wanted you here to witness this." He shook Roman's hand, beaming. "I've come in my official capacity as governor, Roman. I've appointed myself messenger, because I find this such a pleasant task."

"What is it?" Roman asked.

There was a definite twinkle in Isaac's eye as he regarded his old friend. "The joint ballot of both houses of the legislature has just been returned and . . . you have been elected to represent Kentucky in the Senate of the United States."

As Roman stood there speechless, and Kitty found suddenly that she must sit down in the nearest chair, Isaac Shelby clasped Roman's shoulders, his heartfelt approval written on his face. "The choice was overwhelmingly in your favor. And I could not be more pleased, Senator Gentry."

Hester gaped at Kitty, coming around the dining room table to confront her. "Senator, did ye say? And we're all going *east*?"

"That's right," said Kitty, laughing at the look on Hester's face. She had come to find her the moment they arrived home.

"Well, when? How?" Hester demanded, clearly still flabbergasted.

"Isaac is sending a militia troop to escort us through to North Carolina, where we can take coaches the rest of the way. We leave in two weeks."

"Me? Go traipsin' over the mountains?" Hester threw up her

hands. "My lands, no! I'm too old for such. I'll stay here and keep the house while you're gone."

"No, you won't," Kitty said firmly. "The Luttrams can see to the place. You're going, Hester Worthington, because I couldn't do without you. None of us could." And though Hester harrumphed and grumbled, it was soon evident that she was as excited as any of them.

There were a great many things to be seen to before their departure, but Kitty went to visit with as many of her old friends as she could—Jemima and Fanny and Elizabeth Callaway. She must content herself with a letter to Rebecca, since the Boones were some distance away now. They had moved again, this time up near Point Pleasant on the Kanawha River.

But Faith and Ben loaded up the children and came to spend the day at Otter Creek. "I don't see why you have to go," Faith said as she hugged her sister good-bye, her nose reddening as her eyes welled up. "Seems like you could stay right here, and Roman could come back home between times."

Kitty shook her head. There'd never been a doubt that the family would go along. Roman had made that clear at once. "I've been too many times away from my family," he'd declared. "I'll not be without them again."

He sent word ahead to Philadelphia, where the Congress met now in the old State House. "I've asked Henri to lease a house for us," he said. Though Henri Malroux had carried out his aim of marrying his Parisian sweetheart and bringing her to the United States to live, his work had kept him in the East, his dream of coming to Kentucky one day still unfulfilled. "It should be ready by the time we arrive," Roman added.

There was a flurry of packing, and decisions to be made over what could go and what could not. It was still difficult to transport much over the mountains, and Roman had said that they must take as little as possible. They could get what they needed in the East.

The Luttrams agreed to look after Bear. Polly promised that the old dog—stiff with arthritis now, his muzzle and much of that great head gray—would have a place by her fire and all he could eat. But as if the animal knew what was ahead, he died quietly one night, beside Michael's bed where he'd always slept.

"He was a good old dog," said Hester, shaking her head.

Michael, who would let no one else do it, gathered Bear into his arms and, heavy as the dog was, carried him down to the woods himself. Roman and Trace went along. And Lonnie Luttram. They buried him near one of the great oaks, and Lonnie carefully blazed the trunk with his hatchet so that Michael would know where the grave was when he returned.

That same afternoon, Kitty and Hester sat together in the shade of the dogtrot, stringing beans for supper. The heat of summer—come upon them early this year—enveloped Kitty, something sweet and strangely sad about it. If she turned her head slightly, she could look down the hill and see Celie Luttram gathering up her brothers' breeches and shirts from the bushes where Polly had spread them to dry that morning. The sound of Roman's voice as he took the boys off to fish drifted to her, along with the honking of wild geese, flying in their perfect vee as they made their daily trip upriver.

A wasp caught her eye, and she spied the nest up under the log ceiling at the far end of the dogtrot. She'd tell Michael to get it down, she thought, before she remembered that it wouldn't matter. They'd be gone soon.

"Law, I feel for those boys," said Hester, snapping off a bean end and pulling the string along the length of it. "Seems like that dog was always Michael's, but don't forget that Trace never lived a day of his life without it."

"I know. I guess we'll all miss Bear."

Hester leaned to peer at her knowingly. "Is that what's grievin' you? Or is it something else?"

Under that steadfast gaze, the pain of leaving Otter Creek seemed to fill her. "Oh, Hester," she said softly, "there were those years in the fort . . . times when I thought I'd never get back here. And now to have to leave again . . . *Six years* . . . We'll be gone for six years . . ." She began to cry in spite of herself, searching through her pockets for a handkerchief that she couldn't seem to find.

"Oh, here now . . ." With a shake of her head, Hester put aside the beans and came up with her own handkerchief to press into Kitty's hand. "Ask yourself now, would ye have it any other way?"

Kitty caught her breath and wiped at her nose. "No," she said at last. "Of course I wouldn't. It's what Roman's worked for all these years. And none could do it better than he. I'm so proud of him."

"Well, of course you are," said Hester. "Don't you suppose I know that? Though one has naught to do with the other, it might ease you some to remember it. And this'll all be right here when we get back."

For a long moment Kitty looked into the face of the woman who'd been her closest friend for so long now, then, at risk of upsetting the bowl of beans, she threw her arms around Hester's neck. "Don't you dare tell Roman that I cried over going," she said. And Hester promised that she wouldn't, wiping a tear or two away herself, and reminding Kitty that it wasn't the first secret they'd kept from him.

On the day they were to leave, everyone was up early and ready when their escort arrived. The Luttrams had gathered to say good-bye, Tom assuring Roman once again that he and the boys would see to the place; Polly, red-eyed, pressing some of her best dried apple cobbler upon them for when they stopped to eat later in the day. Lonnie and his brothers helped Michael and Trace bring out the bundles and boxes that waited in the dogtrot, while Hester held the twins out of harm's way as the smiling militiamen maneuvered their horses, harnesses jingling.

"Oh, Roman," Kitty cried, "wait . . . there's one more thing!" She raced back into the house, going to the sitting room where she kept Ma and Pa's old Bible, letting her fingertips move over the worn leather cover beneath which the lives and deaths of the Gentrys were recorded. Her mother had carried it from Virginia to the Watauga . . . brought it all the way to Kentucky with them. And Kitty herself had taken it from the old cabin down on the creek, then to the fort at Boonesborough, and finally to this home she loved. She would not leave it behind now.

Outside again, she paused for a moment, her nose filled with the pungent smell of marigolds blooming near the house. Her gaze swept the woods in the distance, took in the growing corn-fields . . . and finally she looked toward the river, a rich, blue-green in the morning light, the mists rising now . . . She would come back, she knew. Hester was right. It was part of her. It would be here for her. Waiting.

She turned, smiling, the Gentry Bible in her arms, and walked toward Roman.

❋ AUTHOR'S NOTE ❋

WHEN A WRITER IS AS CONCERNED WITH HISTORY AS I am, there is always a conflict about which role to play in the course of a book—novelist or historian. I have tried to strike a balance in the writing of *Oh, Kentucky!* Where I have failed in that, my editors—praise to them—have came to my aid and made the cuts that I had neither the nerve, nor heart, to undertake.

I have attempted to make every detail as historically correct as possible. But there are times when the novelist must make arbitrary decisions. Were the first cabins at Boonesborough floored? I could find no definitive answer to that. Yet, if my characters were going to live in those cabins, I had to decide. There was certainly a case to be made that, with all their other immediate concerns, the men who first arrived at the fort site in the wilderness might well have considered floors unimportant. On the other hand, the first women came that fall—among them, Rebecca Boone and Elizabeth Callaway. After learning everything I could about the Boones and the Callaways, I was sure those women would insist on floors. My cabins have floors.

At other times, in the course of my story, I will admit to having taken small liberties with history. For instance, there is certainly no record that Rebecca Boone had any difficulty in delivering her last child, Nathan, nor that Elizabeth Callaway helped at that birth. However, Rebecca was in her forties by that time, at an age when problems during childbirth might occur with more frequency. And though their husbands had had a bitter falling out, the two women had been friends earlier. It is in the realm of possibility that the events that take place in the book, concerning the birth of Nathan Boone, *could* have hap-

595

pened. That "what if" thinking is surely one of the main differences between novelist and historian.

Still, I have made a diligent effort to present my historical characters as honestly as possible, fleshing them out with all the human qualities, but always in keeping with historical accounts. As for my fictional characters, I have sometimes borrowed for them the endeavors, the feats of heroism, the failures and accomplishments of people who really lived and whose deeds are recorded. But in the long writing of the Gentrys and the Claibornes, they have become as real to me, at least in my heart, as any noted in the pages of history.

Finally, I would like to express my undying respect and love for those who came into Kentucky in the early years. The hardships they faced were all but insurmountable, yet they stayed to plant their crops and raise their families . . . and to endure whatever came their way in the course of it.

They will forever be a part of me.

Betty Layman Receveur
Louisville, Kentucky

ABOUT THE AUTHOR

A seventh generation Kentuckian, Betty Layman Receveur has lived all her life in Louisville. She was raised by her grandparents, "wonderful storytellers," who told her many tales about the six generations of her family in Kentucky and filled her with "a mystical feeling for the people who came before us." Of her heroine in *Oh, Kentucky!* Betty says, "She is all my female ancestors."